Ancient and Medieval Worlds

Ancient and Medieval Worlds

HELEN HOWE
ROBERT T. HOWE

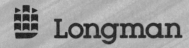 Longman

London; **430,** Pierpont Morgan Library, New York City; **435** *(right),* Royal Commission on Historical Monuments, England
Chapter 21   459, Alinari/Art Resource; **451, 454, 456, 460** *(left and right),* **461, 462,** Bettmann
Chapter 22   467, 468, 469, 472, 476 *(left and right),* **480, 481, 482,** Bettmann; **471,** Mansell
West Africa   485, 487, Frost; **490,** Newberry Libary, Chicago
Chapter 23   495, 499, 502, 504, 505, 506, Bettmann
Chapter 24   514, 522 *(right),* **523** *(top left),* **525** *(top right),* **527, 528** *(left),* **532** *(bottom),* Alinari/Art Resource; **526, 527, 529, 523** *(bottom left and top right),* **529** *(left and right),* **530, 532** *(top),* Bettmann; **523** *(bottom right),* Foto Enit Roma; **511, 533,** Giraudon/Art Resource; **512** *(right),* **513** *(left and right),* **521, 522,** *(left),* **528** *(right),* **531,** Mansell; **515,** Royal Library, Windsor Castle; **512** *(left),* Scala/Art Resource

COLOR PHOTOS
Cover photo: Throne of King Tut. **Lee Boltin,** Croton-on-Hudson, N.Y.

Art Resource. *1st color section:* Golden sarcophagus of King Tut (p. 2); Staircase reliefs at Persepolis (p. 3); Kamares ware (p. 5); Athenian vase design—Ajax and Achilles (p. 5); Athenian vase design—Helen and Priam (p. 5); Villa of Mysteries fresco (p. 7). *2nd color section:* Stained glass windows, Chartres Cathedral (p. 4); Facade of Bourges Cathedral (p. 5); Ghiberti's bronze doors (p. 6); Mona Lisa (p. 7); Russian icon (p. 7); Raphael's School of Athens (p. 8); Titian painting (p. 8).

British Museum. *1st color section:* Ram in thicket/photographer Michael Holford (p. 1); Assyrian hunting scene (p. 1); Funeral mound at Marathon (p. 4). *2nd color section:* Manuscript illustration from Lindisfarne (p. 1); Anglo-Saxon King and Council (p. 3).

C. M. Dixon, Canterbury, England. *1st color section:* Golden mask of an Aegean king (p. 5).

A. F. Kersting, London. *1st color section:* Ruins of Pathenon (p. 4).

Frederic Lewis, New York City. *1st color section:* Funeral mask of King Tut (p. 2); Ruins of palace at Persepolis (p. 3). *2nd color section:* Detail of Sistine Chapel ceiling (p. 7).

National Gallery of Art, Washington, D.C. *1st color insert:* Painting by Giovanni Paolo Pannini of Pantheon in Rome (p. 8).

Glossary

anthropology the study of mankind, usually through the examination and comparison of human cultures, institutions, customs, myths, etc.

anthropomorphic having human characteristics. An animal or god is described as *anthropomorphic* if people believe it has the appearance, emotions, or other traits of a human being.

archaeology the study of ancient peoples through excavation and analysis of artifacts and other physical evidence.

Arianism the doctrine that Jesus was a lesser divinity than God. Arianism was declared to be heretical by a council of bishops in 325.

autocracy a government in which one person or group of people has absolute, unlimited authority over others; despotism.

chivalry the code of honor for medieval knights. It included an obligation to be brave, to help the powerless, and to be courteous to women.

cynicism the attitude and beliefs of Diogenes (412–323 B.C.) and his followers; especially contempt for established values and social customs.

Dark Ages the Middle Ages; especially the period from the 5th through the 10th centuries.

diaspora the scattered settlements of the Jews after the Babylonian exile.

dynasty a succession of rulers from the same family.

Epicurianism the doctrine formulated by Epicurus (342–271 B.C.), emphasizing the achievement of pleasure and tranquillity through avoidance of pain.

feudalism the political and social system of early medieval Europe, in which peasants, or *serfs*, were bound to the land they worked and *vassals* received rights of tenancy in return for homage and allegiance to a lord.

fief the land granted by a lord to a vassal under the system of *feudalism*.

geocentric centering upon the earth. In a *geocentric* world scheme, the heavenly bodies are thought to revolve around the earth.

gnosticism the doctrine that knowledge of good and evil can be grasped through intuition.

Gothic the style of architecture first developed by Abbot Suger of Saint Denis in the 12th century. Characterized by the use of flying buttresses, tall, vaulted ceilings, and stained-glass windows.

guild an association of craftsmen practicing the same trade. Medieval guilds regulated the quality of crafted items and protected the interests of their members.

hegemony dominance or control. A nation is said to have *hegemony* over another if its leadership is unquestioned.

heliocentric centering upon the sun. In a *heliocentric* world scheme, the planetary bodies revolve around the sun.

heresy a religious belief which has been condemned by an established church as a possible danger to the well-being of the faithful.

hubris excessive pride or arrogance. The ancient Greeks believed that people displaying such an attitude were tempting Fate and would be punished for their presumption.

humanism the study of the arts and literature, with an emphasis on the works of man rather than religious subjects.

icon an image or picture of a sacred subject which is itself venerated as sacred.

indigenous native to or preexisting in a particular region.

manorialism the method of allotting farm lands under the feudal system. Tenant farmers received the right to work certain fields and in return gave a portion of the crops they harvested to the lord who owned the land.

matriarchal ruled by or dominated by women.

medieval pertaining to the Middle Ages. Originally, this term referred to the interim period between the Resurrection and the Last Judgment. During the Renaissance, it came to denote the interval from the Classical age to the 15th century.

monasticism the way of life of religious communities who cloister themselves in convents or monasteries.

monotheism doctrine that there is only one god.

necropolis a "city of the dead" or cemetery.

nemesis retribution or punishment. Also, the agent of such punishment.

oligarchy a government controlled by a small group of people.

parochial narrow or restricted. A *parochial* outlook or view is one of limited area or scope.

patriarchal ruled by or dominated by men.

proscription condemnation. In ancient Rome, the names of people to be killed or banished were publicly posted.

primogeniture the system by which the eldest son inherits his parents' estate.

satrap governor of a province or region (*satrapy*) of the Persian Empire.

scepticism the doctrine originated by Pyrrho of Elis (360–270 B.C.), who believed that nothing can be known with certainty.

schism the break or division of an organization due to a doctrinal dispute or other quarrel.

serf a peasant who is bound to the land he works and considered as property to be bought and sold.

simony the practice of buying or selling Church offices.

steppe a grassy plain with few trees. Applies to regions of eastern Europe and Asia.

Stoicism the doctrine originated by Zeno (335–261 B.C.), stating that man must learn to live in accordance with natural laws that govern the universe rather than relying upon his own laws and morals.

tell a mound representing the successive habitation of a site by several different communities.

theocracy a government ruled by a priest or priests who are considered to be the representative(s) of gods.

timocracy a government in which political power is directly related to the amount of property a person has.

tyranny In ancient Greece, the government of a ruler who has seized power by force. Also, a cruel or oppressive regime.

vassal a person or state subject to a higher authority. In the Middle Ages, a person who received protection and rights of land tenancy in return for homage and allegiance.

● *"History is bunk."*
HENRY FORD

Prologue

These three words of the American industrialist, Henry Ford, are perhaps the most popularly known definition of history. In fact, Henry Ford actually said, "History is more or less bunk." Is there a difference? Let us apply one of the techniques of the historian, and examine the context of the remark.

The statement was made in 1916, one year before the United States entered the first World War. Ford was giving an interview to a reporter from the Chicago *Tribune*, Charles Wheeler, to express his views on disarmament and pacifism. Ford was an ardent pacifist, and opposed the possible entrance of the United States into the war.

Wheeler had just given an example from history to demonstrate how Britain's military preparedness and the strength of its navy prevented Napoleon from crossing the English Channel and invading the British Isles. Henry Ford's response was:

● ● ● *What do I care about Napoleon. It means nothing to me. History is more or less bunk. We want to live in the present and the only history that is worth a tinker's damn is the history we make today. The men who are responsible for the present war in Europe*

knew all about history. Yet they brought on the worst war in the world's history.[1]

What other historiographical methods can we apply to Ford's statement? First, we might ask the question, "Is it true that all the major European leaders knew all about history?" There is no evidence for this in Ford's statement. This raises other questions: Was Ford an expert on history? Did the timing of the interview affect Ford's reply?

Given Henry Ford's pacifistic sentiments and commitment to disarmament, perhaps Wheeler's question received a response that was emotional rather than rational. The same question asked at another time might have evoked a different answer. In addition, Ford, one of the great captains of industry, lived in an era when there was great optimism about the future of the United States. Many Americans had little interest in looking backwards.

From his other actions, we know that Ford's attitude toward history was ambivalent. Years later he established a museum in

---

[1] John B. Rae, ed., *Henry Ford: Great Lives Observed* (Prentice-Hall, 1969), pp. 53-4.

Greenfield Village, near Dearborn, Michigan. It is a recreation of artifacts of American life from the 18th century through the early part of the 20th century. It contains a large collection of American tools, agricultural implements, decorative arts, transportation and communication artifacts.

When asked why he had invested so much money in the project, Ford replied that he "wanted to preserve what was the contribution of plain men who never got into history."[2] Ironically, it was the widespread use of the automobile, Ford's contribution to culture, that did much to change the earlier way of life that Ford now sought to preserve.

Moreover, Ford, in an area adjacent to Greenfield Village, set aside land for houses, workshops, and other structures that were significant in American history. At great cost, these were removed from their original locations and transported to Michigan. The area contains the courthouse where Abraham Lincoln practiced law as a circuit rider, the laboratories of Thomas Edison, and birthplaces or homes of such famous Americans as the Wright brothers, Robert Frost, and Noah Webster. So, in spite of his statement, Ford had some sense of the importance of history and the necessity of preserving the past.

WHAT IS HISTORY?

From the example of Henry Ford, it is clear that there is some confusion as to just what the discipline of history is and what its value is. Just what comes to mind when one asks, "What is history?" One of the clearest and simplest definitions of history is that by the American historian Carl Becker: "History is the memory of things said and done."

The historical memory is composed of many types of evidence. There are written records and artifacts that provide clues for the historian. By its nature this evidence is fragmentary. For some civilizations and periods, there is more evidence available than there is on others. Because it is impossible to know the complete picture at any given time in the past, much of history, particularly early history, is speculative.

Just imagine if the only evidence of modern American life were some scattered ruins of buildings. How could these be used to put together an explanation of American society? Yet this is the detective job necessary for historians who study early societies.

Written records would seem a better historical source than ruins or other archaeological evidence. However, these too can be misleading. If a historian of a thousand years from now had the full text of the United States Constitution, would it be possible to reconstruct what the American political system was like? The answer, of course, is no.

Even where there are extensive written materials available, the historian has a task of interpretation. For the names and dates of events are only the raw materials of history. It is the job of the historian to link together in a meaningful way what we know about the past. The historian's interpretations and re-creations, rather than the data, are what make up what we call history. Because of the historian's role as interpreter, history is an ever-changing field—for the same data will be viewed and evaluated differently by different people. Such factors as the selection of facts, the significance ascribed to them, and the climate of the times in which the historian is writing will affect his or her work.

This does not have to discourage us unduly. When we watch the most recent "history" on the television nightly news, we accept the fact that we are receiving only a minute fraction of the events that have happened that day. We are getting the "news" that seems important to whomever has prepared the news program. A description of every event that happened that day would

[2]Michael Kammen, ed., *The Past Before Us: Contemporary Historical Writing in the United States* (Ithaca: Cornell University Press, 1980), p. 24.

not only be impossibly long, but also not digestible. The same is true with history.

In order to make history intelligible, historians choose the items that they believe are significant from the data they have. No one could absorb history from the time of Sumerian civilization to the present if the material were not broken up into understandable periods. For European history, the traditional divisions of classical, medieval, and modern history are instructive for what they say about the study of history.

Obviously all history was originally experienced as contemporary events. No people actually thought of themselves as living in the classical period; they were living in their present. Labels such as these are given to the period by future generations. In addition they are not value-free labels. The implication of the term Classical Age, for example, is that the period was one of lasting achievement.

The term *medieval*, or *Middle Ages*, on the other hand, implies something that occurred between two periods of greater historical importance. During early modern times, when the medieval achievement was not clear to many, this term was used in a derogatory sense. People looked back with admiration to the Greeks and Romans, and felt that it was only with the period of the Renaissance (following the Middle Ages) that Europeans matched the achievements of their classical forebears. The Middle Ages was viewed merely as the long period in between. Today no historian would agree with that value judgment, but the name has stuck.

Moreover, out of the chaos of events, the historian must fashion order. To do this, he or she looks for patterns of continuity and discontinuity. For some periods of history, certain characteristics that fit the accepted pattern will be stressed; in other periods, alternate characteristics are emphasized.

Perhaps the most important influence on the shaping of history is that each historian by necessity brings to the study of the past the values and questions of his or her own time. This can be useful in that it enables the past to shed light on the present. Indeed many historians believe that this is the primary usefulness of the study of history. Henry T. Buckle, a 19th-century historian, claimed, "There will always be a connection between the way in which men contemplate the past and the way in which they contemplate the present."

However, other historians feel the past should be appreciated for itself. According to this view, the past should be captured as much as possible in its own terms, without attempting to impose modern viewpoints on it. Even if the relevance to the present is slight, there are benefits in understanding earlier societies and the experiences of the people who lived in them.

The degree of accuracy possible is also a topic of debate. Perhaps the Greek historian Herodotus spoke most honestly to this point: "My business is to record what people say. But I am by no means bound to believe it— and that may be taken to apply to this book as a whole."

INTERDISCIPLINARY APPROACHES

In recent years many historians have expanded the definition of history by using data and discoveries from other fields of knowledge. The social sciences—particularly anthropology, archaeology, and social psychology—have been utilized to draw historical conclusions. Psychoanalytic insights have been applied to important historical personages such as Martin Luther and Adolf Hitler. The field of social psychology has been used to explain the rise of totalitarianism, and also to explain the increase in warlike sentiments during certain periods.

The discoveries of modern archaeologists have revolutionized ancient history. New findings have forced historians to reconsider many of their previous descriptions of an-

The walls of Troy. Heinrich Schliemann never saw these city walls, for he excavated another part of the site. They were discovered by later teams of archaeologists.

cient societies. For example, until Heinrich Schliemann discovered the site of ancient Troy at Hissarlik in 1868, the *Iliad* of Homer was considered to be a work of considerable literary merit, but not an historical text. Later, the site was carefully analyzed by Carl Blegen and a team of archaeologists from the University of Cincinnati, who worked at Hissarlik from 1932 to 1938. They verified that the Troy described in the Homeric epic was at level VIIa.

There is convincing evidence that Troy VIIa was destroyed by human hand. The archaeologists found that the city was burned, and other findings suggest that few, if any, inhabitants survived this fire. Human bones have been found near houses and in doorways, and one skeleton was discovered outside the walls in a position that suggested that it was left to lie where it fell. Two bronze blades of late Mycenaean origin have been found lying in the streets. Between levels VIIa and VII there is a thin layer of dust, suggesting that the city was completely abandoned for several years after the attack.

These discoveries showed that Homer's work had historical accuracy. His descriptions of social customs, weapons, methods of fighting, and so forth, often conform more closely to the archaeological evidence than to the time when Homer was reputed to have lived. The verification of Homer's work led to a major overhaul of our historical understanding of pre-classical Greece.

The methods developed for the social sciences, such as the use of statistics and other types of analysis, have been useful to the historian. So have the findings of social sciences. Historians now draw on both the techniques and knowledge of many fields to study the past.

DIFFERING APPROACHES

It was only in the 19th century that history was established as an individual discipline and profession. Previously history was a branch of literature, whose practitioners might be propagandists or those who sacrificed accuracy for literary effect. There was no professional tradition of historical standards.

No country was more important in the birth of modern historical writing than Germany. It was there that history was tied to the growing studies in philology, the history of language. The man who was to become the leading figure in German historical studies was Leopold von Ranke. In his view, no one who could not read the language of the culture should write about it. He believed that only primary sources—evidence, written and otherwise, that dates from the time being studied—should be consulted by an historian, since things written afterwards could not be proved to be accurate.

Von Ranke's ideal was history that only conveyed "what actually happened." Today we know that this is an impossible goal. But von Ranke's recognition of the importance of primary sources has remained to this day as an important part of historical studies.

Another approach to history has been that of the great systematizers. These historians, such as Karl Marx and Arnold Toynbee, believed that they found laws of history that were relevant to all civilizations. Marx believed that the core element of history was the struggle between the various classes of society. Toynbee saw civilizations as following a cycle almost like that of an individual human. In Toynbee's view, each civilization had a developing period, a period of ripeness, and then a decay. A similar idea was expressed by Oswald Spengler, who posited that the West was in a period of decline. Spengler's thesis of the decline of the West was influenced by the disillusionment with western civilization that was an important intellectual current in the years following World War I.

Most historians no longer believe that there are any such grand unifying principles relevant to all civilizations. This mode of historical interpretation is definitely not in favor today.

The professionalization of history in the 19th century led to an increasing specialization among historians. Much of traditional history had primarily concerned itself with political, military, and diplomatic affairs. It made great use of official records and materials. With the specialization of the field, economic history, cultural history, and social history emerged as distinct areas of study and thought. The British historian George Trevelyan offered a definition of one of the new fields: "Social history might be defined negatively as the history of a people with the politics left out."

As historians have benefited from knowledge in other fields, new historical specializations have emerged. Demographics, or population studies, have provided a new way of looking at the past. Geography has been increasingly used in combination with history to find insights into the causes of historical currents. Cliometrics approaches history from the perspective of statistical evidence. (The term combines the name of the muse of history, Clio, with *metrics*, or measurement.) These are just a few of the new fields that are expected to yield new historical insights.

A much-discussed question for historical thinking is whether the historian should be partisan. Some feel that the historian should make every attempt to be a neutral observer. This was the position of von Ranke. But others have claimed that neutrality, or complete objectivity, is neither a realistic possibility nor the responsibility of the historian. In this view, the historian should be open about his or her position on particular issues. The question of integrity for the historian lies not with partisanship but rather in maintaining the integrity of sources and in attempting to get as full a picture as possible.

The question of whether people or events make history has been a point of controversy among historians. It is sometimes called the "great man vs. historical forces" dispute. In the 19th century, Thomas Carlyle was an important proponent of the "great man" theory. Today it is somewhat discredited, and there is more interest in the conditions that lead to change rather than just the biographies and influence of great historical figures.

One of the most exciting developments in today's new approaches to history is the increasing realization that many people have been left out of the history written in the past. Traditional histories stressed the powerful individuals and the great public events. This was natural, as there is more definite information available on political and military leaders. But today there is a realization that there was always more to history than what happened at the top of society.

Historians are now trying to reconstruct what was life for the ordinary people of the day. Their study begins with records of births and deaths, tax records, and other statistical information. These can give information on life expectancy and the effects of weather and climate on agriculture, as well as other facets of a civilization. Through these techniques it is hoped that more can be gleaned about overall conditions of an era. The historian today does not find it necessary to write in terms of individuals, but rather considers the way groups of people were influenced by long-term trends and economic conditions.

One aspect of this new approach explores the role of women and the position of the family in different societies and times. This emphasis was partly the result of the women's movement. There has been criticism that the only references to women in traditional histories concerned exceptional women who were rulers or able to excel in a man's world. Some people argue that women's role in the past has been a distinct one, separate from that of men, and that efforts to explore it will yield significant historical insights:

• • • *It is not surprising that most women feel that their sex does not have an interesting or significant past. However, like minority groups, women cannot afford to lack a consciousness of a collective identity, one which necessarily involves a shared awareness of the past. Without this, a social group suffers from a kind of collective amnesia, which makes it vulnerable to the impositions of dubious stereotypes, as well as limiting prejudices about what is right and proper for it to do or not to do.''*[3]

To get a truer picture of the recent past, many historians have made extensive use of the technique of recording oral histories. This allows the voices of ordinary people to be part of the record for historians of the future. Oral history has been used very effectively to document the civil rights movement, the Great Depression in the United States, and the experience of Holocaust survivors.

Moreover, historians today are willing to use literature and myths to deepen their understanding of a period or people. There is a feeling among today's historians that all information is grist for the historical mill. The search for undiscovered historical documents is a growth industry in the profession today. There is also a growing understanding that popular culture is a fertile field for study. Sports, amusements, and popular art forms all have a history, and they tell us something about the society in which they thrived. From this you can see the truth of the Carl Becker dictum: "Everyman is a historian." You already know some pieces of history even if it is only about the recent past.

WHY STUDY HISTORY?

The study of history is important for all citizens because knowledge about the past is essential for an understanding of the present. For our own history, a knowledge of how and why our political and social institutions were created deepens our understanding of how they work today and what they mean to the society in which we live.

Similarly, knowledge of European and world history deepens our understanding of our culture, and of the shrinking world in which we live. The achievements of classical Greece and Rome remain relevant today. More than 2300 years ago, Aristotle wrote, "Poverty is the parent of revolution and crime." Philosophers since then have not been able to improve on his observation. Thinkers of the past dealt with questions that people still ask, and we benefit from learning of the answers they found.

Much of the culture of the United States has antecedents in Europe. Thus the study of European history can lead to a greater appreciation of western art and music, which are surely some of the great joys of civilized people. Similarly, learning about European political institutions can increase our understanding of the American political system that sprang from them.

---

[3]Sheila R. Johansson, "Herstory as History: A New Field or Another Fad?", in Bernice A. Carroll, ed., *Liberating Women's History* (Illinois University Press, 1976), p. 427.

The study of history enables the student to see how the world came to be what it is today. Because we live in a world in which little-known nations suddenly take on a significant role—as the recent examples of Vietnam, Iran, Afghanistan, and Libya illustrate—it is important to understand the culture and history that have shaped the present. The importance of promoting a mutual understanding between the various peoples of the world has never been as important as it is today. The first step in understanding other people is in comprehending their history.

Furthermore, though history does not repeat itself, the study of past events teaches useful lessons because some characteristics of human nature remain the same. The study of history, if creatively used, can lead to a better understanding of interactions between people or the likely consequences of actions.

Knowing history enhances understanding of current events, because many problems have antecedents in the past. Being knowledgeable means that one can make more intelligent judgments about a situation. One is less likely to be swayed by people who oversimplify causes and solutions. Historical understanding makes it easier to form one's own opinions.

Looking at civilizations that are separated from ours by different cultural practices and time is also a refreshing intellectual experience. The history of different cultures is a vast reservoir of possibilities as to how things might be done. Knowledge of other cultures forces an intelligent person to confront his or her own ideas and see that perhaps there are other ways of life that might be as satisfactory as their own. The discovery of affinities with different times and places is a pleasurable and exciting intellectual experience. In addition, the discovery of alternatives helps one see more of the complexities in one's own situation.

Finally, studying history can be fun. Current movies and popular fiction—particularly in the broad genre called "science fiction"—often present imagined cultures. The popular movie sequence *Star Wars* begins with this message on the screen: "A long time ago, in a galaxy far, far away . . ." Substitute "place" for "galaxy," and you begin the study of history. The stories of real people in different times and places can be just as thrilling as any fiction.

Although the various cultures and times we study each has its own flavor, human nature is not so different wherever one looks. History is filled with figures who are villainous, outrageous, and infamous. Edward Gibbon, the English historian, described history as "little more than the crimes, follies and misfortunes of mankind." History is also filled with the good and the ordinary. The range of people we learn about runs the gamut of human experience and imagination.

The American historian Frederick Jackson Turner summarized the appeal of history this way:

● ● ● *History has been a romance and a tragedy. In it we read the brilliant annals of the few. The intrigues of courts, knightly valor, palaces and pyramids, the loves of ladies, the songs of minstrels, and the chants from cathedrals pass like a pageant, or linger like a strain of music as we turn the pages. But history has its tragedy as well, which tells of the degraded tillers of the soil, toiling that others might dream, the slavery that rendered possible the 'glory that was Greece,' the serfdom into which decayed the 'grandeur that was Rome'—these as well demanded their annals.*[4]

The study of history has the same joys as good literature. It is an attempt to capture the feeling of what is human, what endures. Discovering the past helps one to discover the present.

---

[4]Leften S. Stavrianos, ed., *Readings in World History* (Boston: Allyn and Bacon, 1964), pp. 784-5.

● *As we turned to leave, I noticed something lying on the ground partway up the slope. That's a bit of hominid arm, I said. We stood up and began to see other bits of bone on the slope: a couple of vertebrae, part of a pelvis—all of them hominid. . . . Could they be parts of a single, extremely primitive skeleton? No such skeleton had ever been found anywhere. In that 110 degree heat we began jumping up and down. . . .*
There was a tape recorder in the camp, and a tape of the Beatles song "Lucy in the Sky With Diamonds" went belting out into the night sky. . . . At some point during that unforgettable evening—I no longer remember when—the new fossil picked up the name of Lucy.

DONALD JOHANSON

Prehistory

The dramatic discovery of "Lucy" by Donald Johanson in 1974 is just one more piece in the unfinished mosaic of human prehistory. Prehistory is what happened before the beginning of recorded human history. The time-span of prehistory is much longer than that of the history of civilization.

In a universe which has an estimated age of 20 billion years, our little part of it, Earth, is barely 4.5 billion years old. Life on Earth began in the seas in the form of one-celled algae and bacteria about 3.5 billion years ago. For over three billion years, life was confined to the sea, and then, about 400 million years ago, some form of life crept onto the land. A long period of development ensued, during which reptiles—including dinosaurs—birds, insects, and mammals began to populate the earth.

Something like 60 million years ago, the first primate appeared. Primates are the order of mammals that include lemurs and bush babies, more developed forms such as monkeys and apes, and the most highly developed form of all: human beings.

You would not recognize that first primate, called a prosimian, as a close relative. Human-like primates did not appear until about 50-55 million years later, about 5-10 million years B.C.

The first creature that scientists classify in the genus *Homo*—true "human"—does not show up in the fossil record until about 2 million years ago. That was a creature called *Homo habilis*, distinguished from earlier creatures because of its larger brain, habit of walking upright, and ability to make tools.

Homo habilis' relatively large brain was not as large as yours. A creature with a larger brain, *Homo sapiens* (intelligent human), entered the world around 200,000 years ago. One type of *Homo sapiens*, called Neanderthal Man, who appeared in Europe about 100,000 years ago, hunted in groups, built fires, and had many of the characteristics of modern humans.

But scientists classify modern humans with an extra "sapiens" after their species name. By about 40,000 years ago, a type of creature had appeared, whose body and brain were the same as those of people today. These creatures made tools that were more highly developed than those of earlier human types; they made marks on bones that were apparently attempts to record the phases of the moon; and, as we shall see, they drew pictures on the walls of caves. This at last was *Homo sapiens sapiens*. Even then, *Homo sapiens sapiens* existed for at least 35,000 years before "history" began with the first real civilizations, some 5000 years ago. Thus, a time line showing the age of the earth would be 14 miles long if the era of civilized human beings were only one inch long.

Since the ancient ancestors of today's people left no written records, no tales or songs, how do we know anything at all about them, or about the creatures that lived even longer ago? The answer begins with fossils. Some fossils are the bones of ancient creatures which have turned to stone by reacting with the soil or lava in which they fell. A footprint of an animal left in soil that hardened is also a fossil record. So are the tiny impressions left in stone by shells, feathers, plants, or even by one-celled animals billions of years ago.

Fossils were noticed and speculated on by the ancient Greeks, and probably by earlier people. The Greeks recognized them as animal remains. From about the middle of the 16th century A.D., people have tried to use fossil remains to discover what ancient animals looked like. When it was discovered that some reconstructed fossils formed animals that no longer existed, people puzzled over why they had died out.

Two schools of thought developed. One group, called the diluvialists, relied on the story of the flood in the Biblical book of Genesis. According to diluvialists, the fossils were remains of animals who had somehow missed Noah's ark. Diluvialists held that God had created all species just as they were today, including his highest creation, human beings. Diluvialists were supported by the calculations of James Ussher, Archbishop of Armagh in the 17th century, who believed that the Creation took place in 4004 B.C. on the 23rd day of October at 9:00 a.m.

The other school, called the fluvialists, saw the physical world as part of an ongoing process set in motion by the Creator. They were quite willing to believe that some of God's creations had ceased to exist long ago,

and saw no conflict between their beliefs and the Book of Genesis.

In 1830, Charles Lyell published his *Principles of Geology*, in which he supplied strong proof that the world was much older than Ussher had thought. The diluvialists suffered another blow with the discovery of Windmill Cave along the English coast in 1858. This cave contained the bones of mammoths and other extinct animals. In another stratum of the cave, below the level of the bones of extinct animals, were found stone tools obviously made and used by human beings. In one of those unusual coincidences in history, the findings from Windmill Cave, proving that humans lived longer ago than some extinct animal forms, were read before the Royal Society in London the same year that Charles Darwin published his *On the Origin of Species*.

Darwin's work offered evidence that animals changed their form over a long period of time in an evolutionary process that he called "natural selection." What was most startling about Darwin's theory—alarming, to some—was the implication that human beings themselves had evolved from some other form of life. Immediately, the popular press distorted Darwin's work by spreading the idea that apes and monkeys—clearly similar in shape to humans—were, according to Darwin, human ancestors.

THE SEARCH FOR HUMAN ANCESTORS In 1856, the skull of what appeared to be a human was found in the Neander valley in Germany. Neanderthal Man (*Homo sapiens neanderthalensis*), as he was called, had a "brute-like" appearance which included a receding forehead, thick brow-ridges, a pronounced jaw, bowed legs, and arms that almost dangled to the ground. It is estimated that most Neanderthals lived in Europe and the Middle East between 100,000 and 40,000 years ago. In the popular consciousness, Neanderthals became the archetype of the primitive "cave men." During the 1950s, it was discovered that the original reconstruction of Neanderthal Man was based on a skeletal specimen that was distorted due to a bad case of arthritis. Considerable disagreement still exists as to how different Neanderthals looked from present-day people. Some argue that if a Neanderthal dressed in a three-piece suit sat down on a bus, he might draw only a few nervous glances.

The next important discovery in human prehistory came in 1868 in western France. Here, another kind of ancient skull was discovered. It was named "Cro-Magnon," after the rock shelter in which it was found. Cro-Magnon had a pronounced forehead and a small jaw, typical of modern-day humans. Today, scientists recognize Cro-Magnons as the first examples of *Homo sapiens sapiens*, the species we belong to, but at the time of its discovery the Cro-Magnon was only one more piece in a growing puzzle.

More pieces were found in other parts of the world. A Dutchman, Eugene Dubois, uncovered the cranium of a human ancestor in Java in 1891. He named his find *Pithecanthropus erectus* (erect-walking ape-man). Dubois' discovery became popularly known as Java Man. The scientific world did not take Dubois' work seriously. As a consequence, Dubois locked his fossilized bones in a safe and refused to allow anyone to see them for years. Now, we know that he had found evidence of a creature classified as *Homo erectus*.

The discovery of Peking Man (*Sinanthropus pekininsus*) in the mid-1920s is one of the more unusual stories of anthropological detective work. Dr. Davidson Black, on the staff of the Peking Union Medical College in China, came across some ancient human teeth in an apothecary shop. Dr. Black was told that the teeth originally were found in caves just above the small town of Choukoutien in northern China. At the bottom of a trench in one of the caves, Dr. Black uncovered the skullcap of a prehistoric ancestor of the modern-day Chinese. The site also yielded the first confirmation of primitive people's use of fire. More evidence was unearthed, suggesting that Peking Man may have practiced cannibalism.

The original fossilized bones of *Sinanthropus pekininsus* disappeared under bizarre circumstances in 1937. Because of China's war with Japan it was decided to move the fossils out of harm's way. They were entrusted to a contingent of American marines, who were to take them by train to the coast. While en route, the fossils disappeared, never to be seen since. However, from photographs and notes, scientists have identified them as another example of *Homo erectus*.

Until the middle of the 20th century, scientists were unable to clearly classify the types of humans and their ancestors. The belief that Darwin's theory implied a human descent from apes sent some on a search for the "missing link," a supposed connection between humans and apes. Others pointed out, correctly, that in Darwinian theory a superior characteristic (such as a larger brain) would give those individuals that possessed it a survival advantage over those that did not; thus, in a developing species, the superior individuals would gradually supplant those without the key characteristic. The most compelling proof that humans did not "descend" from apes is the fact that apes are still a thriving species.

However, the "missing link" idea gained currency with the discovery of a creature called Piltdown Man in 1912. The cranium was large enough to be human, but the jaw appeared ape-like. Found in southern England, Piltdown Man was long accepted as a legitimate part of the record of human fossil history. Only in the 1950s was it discovered that Piltdown Man was a hoax—the cranium was in fact that of a human, fitted together with the jaw of an orangutan, and passed off as the complete skull of one creature.

Because of the scientific community's preoccupation with Piltdown Man, it overlooked the significance of a discovery by Raymond Dart in a limestone cave in South Africa in 1925. Dart had found the skull of an infant "man-ape" which he called "Taung child." But later researchers would see Dart's discovery as the beginning of a new era in the search for the physical origins of the human race.

The person most responsible for redirecting the hunt for early humans by focusing on east Africa was Louis Leakey. Dr. Leakey was born in Kenya, where his mother and father served as missionaries. While still in his teens he went to England to attend Cambridge University. After suffering an injury while playing rugby, Leakey decided to recuperate by joining an expedition to Tanganyika (today Tanzania) sponsored by the British Museum. The purpose of the trip was to collect fossilized dinosaur bones. The training and experience acquired on this expedition initiated Leakey into his life's work—the search for human origins in the fossilized records of prehistoric Africa. After a brief return to England to complete his degree in anthropology, Leakey returned to Africa to start his search. That quest would continue to the end of his life in 1972, and his son Richard carries it on today.

Virtually no one in 1926 believed that human beings might have originated in Africa. Neanderthal, Cro-Magnon, and other examples of early human-like remains had been discovered in Europe and Asia. The only "find" in Africa was Raymond Dart's Taung child, and it was thought to be more ape than human.

Leakey devoted most of his efforts to surveying Olduvai gorge in present-day Tanzania. For the next 30 years, Leakey searched for the remains of early hominids, or human-like creatures, with very little to show for his efforts. Only his will and the conviction that he was right sustained him. Some very primitive tools were found, but nothing of the hands that made the tools. Mary Leakey, Louis' wife, shared in the excitement of the hunt as she became her husband's equal in field experience and knowledge.

It was Mary Leakey who found the first physical remains of a hominid in Olduvai gorge, on July 17, 1959. While working on her own, Mary Leakey spotted some bones protruding from the soil. Further investigation revealed that they were two large molar teeth. They clearly belonged to a hominid, but not one of the genus *Homo*. "Dear boy," as the Leakeys called their find, is estimated to be 1.75 million years old. It has since been categorized as *Australopithecus Boisei*. Other species of the *Australopithecus* genus (called australopithecines) had been found earlier in Africa, though the Leakeys' specimen was a larger creature.

Two years later the Leakeys uncovered a creature whose brain size led them to declare it was a member of the genus *Homo*. Because it was a tool-user, they gave it the species name *habilis*, meaning "skillful." Not all scientists agreed with this classification; some argue that the Leakeys' *Homo habilis* is another type of *Australopithecus*.

In 1976 at Laetoli, near Olduvai gorge, Mary Leakey discovered footprints of three hominids. Three and a half million years ago, these early hominids walked upright across a carpet of wet ash, leaving impressions that have been preserved to the present day.

These footprints may have been made by the same species of hominids discovered by Donald Johanson at Hadar. "Lucy" walked upright and had some other clearly human physical characteristics, and yet she had several australopithecine characteristics, including a smaller brain than true humans. What is unique about "Lucy" is that 40 percent of her skeleton was recovered, making her the most complete early hominid ever found. In 1975 Johanson unearthed at Hadar what has been named "the First Family," parts of approximately 13 individuals from about the same time period as "Lucy." This additional evidence suggests that "Lucy" and her kind are not another species of *Homo*, but rather other examples of *Australopithecus*.

If the Latin terminology in the foregoing discussion seems confusing to you, don't feel as if you are alone. Anthropologists themselves are hardly in agreement about what conclusions to draw from their discoveries. It is difficult to assign neat categories of genus and species from the fragmentary remains that are available. Furthermore, as indicated by the disagreement over the Leakeys' *Homo habilis*, it is not always possible to tell exactly what makes a human (the *Homo* genus). Three characteristics have been suggested as identifying factors: brain size, pelvic shape (indicating the ability to walk upright), and type of teeth (non-humans, in general, were plant eaters, while true humans widened their diet to include flesh).

Humans and apes may have shared a common ancestor. At some point, the line that led to human beings diverged from the line that led to apes. An ancient creature known as *Ramapithecus* is a possible candidate for the title of first hominid. Known only from a few teeth and jaw fragments, *Ramapithecus* is thought to have existed throughout Asia, Africa, and Europe between 14 million and 9 million years ago.

Around 3.5 million years ago the earliest forms of *Australopithecus* appeared in Africa. They share certain characteristics with both human and ape. Their brains are about the same size as those of apes, but smaller than those of humans. At least six species of *Australopithecus* have been identified. *Homo habilis*, the Leakeys' discovery, lived in Africa between two million and one million years ago. For a time, it coexisted with australopithecines in eastern Africa.

HUMAN EVOLUTION Examples of the first true human, *Homo erectus*, are found in Africa, China, and Indonesia. This creature appeared about 1.6 million years ago. It habitually walked upright, and made shelters and sophisticated tools. Its brain was larger than that of *Australopithecus*. It is probably in the direct line of human ancestors, evolving into the species *Homo sapiens* about 200,000 years ago.

The earliest form of *Homo sapiens* began to appear, possibly in Africa, about 200,000 years ago. The best known example is Neanderthal Man, which emerged around 125,000 years ago. The Neanderthalers were replaced by the Cro-Magnons who appeared in western Europe about 35,000 years ago. They are the first examples of *Homo sapiens sapiens*.

This accounting of human evolutionary history is far from complete. There are many gaps, differences of opinion, and possible reinterpretations as new information is unearthed. It is still a question as to what happened between eight million years ago and four million years later when the first australopithecines emerged. Richard Leakey and Donald Johanson disagree over the placement of "Lucy," "the First Family," and the hominids who made the footsteps at Laetoli. Did *Homo sapiens sapiens* evolve directly from Neanderthals, or were the Neanderthalers a dead end in evolutionary history? All of these and many other issues still need to be resolved.

HOW DID HUMANS DEVELOP?

The record of prehistory that scientists chip from the earth not only gives evidence of humans' physical development, but also provides clues as to the intellectual and cultural development of humankind. Somewhere in the sedimentary deposits of east Africa is evidence about the impact of the environment on human evolution. Although a few of those secrets have been brought to the surface, there are many more yet to be uncovered.

Twenty million years ago, the earth was warmer than it is now. In today's temperate zones it was blanketed with rain forests. Eurasia and Africa were joined, allowing many animals to move easily from one continent to another. Changes in environment encouraged the development of new species. These creatures lived primarily in trees, and probably had the ability to pick up objects and carry them. Long before, early primates had nails instead of claws and an opposable thumb that permitted them to close one hand on an object. They were probably herbivores, with a diet including plants, seeds, and nuts. Like monkeys today, they probably had the ability to stand for short periods of time, but the usual method of walking was on four legs. As the earth cooled, and the tropical forests receded, they came down from the trees and began to inhabit the open grasslands.

The first hominid habitually to walk on two legs appeared between nine million years and four million years ago. This creature known as *Australopithecus* was a biped, though it walked hunched over and low to the ground.

There are a number of theories explaining bipedalism. One advantage was that by standing up in the tall grasslands, a hominid increased the range of its vision. It could spot potential predators, or its own quarry. For *Australopithecus* had widened its diet from vegetable matter to small animals. It was the first hominid to hunt other animals for food.

Standing upright gave *Australopithecus* another advantage—it freed its front feet, now hands, for other activities. Among these activities was the making of tools. The earliest tools that appear to have been shaped by hominids date from 2.5 million years ago. Between the time when it developed the ability to walk on two legs and the time these tools were made, *Australopithecus* learned that a stick or a hand-sized rock could be used as an aid. Your imagination can supply the circumstances: to fend off an enemy, to stun or kill a small animal.

The ability to make tools coincides with the growth in brain size that eventually carried *Australopithecus* onto the next evolutionary step. Previously, the best survival tactics were the ability to run fast or to climb a tree or otherwise avoid a predator with sharper teeth and claws. Hesitating to "think" about the danger was not a good survival tactic. With the discovery and use of tools, the brain itself became a key to survival. The expansion of the brain found in *Australopithecus* was the result.

CHARACTERISTICS OF EARLY HOMINIDS

The new role of humans as hunters has been the subject of much speculation. Some argue that the aggressiveness and violent nature of modern human beings are a result of their hunter ancestry. Louis Leakey, when coming across the crushed bones of an early hominid, liked to theorize that what lay before him in the ground was the residue of an ancient murder or other form of violent death.

However, studies of contemporary primitive cultures, such as the San in southern Africa, suggest that these societies tend to be non-aggressive and rather timid. An argument can be made that the aggressive behavior of "civilized" people today is a product of the pressures of civilization rather than an instinct inherited from our primitive forebears.

Another characteristic of early hominids was their habit of sharing food. Many higher animals share their food with a family group, but of all the primates only the direct ancestors of humans seem to have been willing to portion out food to all members of the group—young and old, weak and strong. This too seems to have been a survival characteristic, for greater brain size meant that infant humans required a longer time of growth and development before they could fend for themselves.

Instead of finding the key to human survival in the male's aggressiveness and hunting skills, there are many anthropologists today who prefer to concentrate on the female's role in the food-gathering and sharing process. In this new interpretation, the female plays a more central role in the survival of the species. In contemporary hunter-gatherer societies, such as the Efe pygmies in the rain forests of Zaire, the women who forage for plants and small animals furnish at least 60 percent of the total diet of the group.

It is not necessary to view *Homo sapiens sapiens* as the victor in the race for "the survival of the fittest." It is just as reasonable to explain the success of early hominids in terms of cooperation and food-sharing, rather than in terms of competition and conquest over the environment and other species.

THE PALEO-LITHIC AGE With the exception of the occasional fossilized physical remains of humans themselves, things made of stone have been the most obvious and enduring evidence of human beings' residence on earth. Archaeologists thus traditionally have called the period of time between the first toolmaking hominids and the beginning of metalworking cultures the "Stone Age." This covers a period from about 2,000,000 years ago to 5000 B.C.

The Stone Age is further divided into three periods, the longest of which is the Paleolithic (the Old Stone Age). It lasted till around 10,000 B.C. Besides making tools and weapons, the early humans who lived in this period had many other important accomplishments. They learned to control and use fire; they made artificial shelters from branches; and they began to use needles to sew animal skins together. In addition, they held ritual burials of their dead; in these ancient graves, archaeologists have sometimes found the re-

mains of flowers. We may speculate that this is evidence of some form of belief in an afterlife. The oldest known written record dates from this period, between 30,000 and 40,000 years ago; it is a lunar calendar etched in bone, found in Europe.

Humans during the Paleolithic Era were nomadic, roaming in search of food. When their diet began to include meat, they hunted in groups. Organized hunts for elephants and mammoths took place in Europe. Recent archaeological work suggests that individuals in hunter-gatherer societies had a more varied diet than was previously thought.

DEVELOPMENT OF COMMUNICATION SKILLS

As *Homo sapiens* began to cluster into larger groups and share more activities, there developed a greater need for an organized form of communication. With the development of language, human activities could be coordinated more effectively. Plans could be laid out before the hunt, and inventions or new knowledge could be passed on to future generations. How and when humans developed the ability to communicate through symbolic means is mostly conjecture, although there are some interesting hypotheses.

An area in the frontal part of the brain, known as "Broca's area," coordinates tongue, throat, and mouth muscles, thus enabling us to speak. A barely discernible imprint of the brain left on the inside of a fossilized cranium helps us to determine the degree to which those sections of the brain associated with speech were developed in early hominids. Broca's area is identifiable in the australopithecines, and it becomes increasingly more distinct as *Homo erectus* evolves into *Homo sapiens*. This suggests the possibility that early hominids had already started to develop rudimentary communication skills.

Prehistoric stone tools are another source of information that could shed some light on the development of language. Until about 40,000 years ago, tools did not seem to have

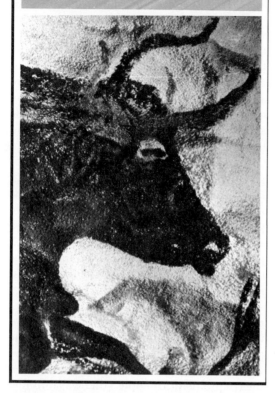
A detail of a bull painting from the caves of Lascaux in France. The Lascaux caves contain some of the most artistic works created by prehistoric man.

context, tonal level, and body movements. Maybe sounds within the context of "gestures" were a first step in the communication process of early humans. Clearly, the need for cooperation in the gathering and sharing of food, and the growing complexity of social relationships required a sophisticated form of communication.

Prehistoric art is another form of expression and communication used by early humans. The symbolism found in some examples of prehistoric art, such as zigzag markings and integrated color patterns, goes back as far as 250,000 years, and suggests that this form of expression could have been the end product of a fully developed language. There are two basic types of prehistoric art—"portable art" and "stationary art."

Portable art is art that can be readily picked up, easily moved, and looked at "in the round." Often it takes the shape of sculpted statuettes known as "Venuses." These are female figures, intentionally exaggerated and disproportionate in shape. Why they were carved in that way is not known, although it is assumed that it has some connection with prehistoric people's preoccupation with the concept of fertility. Another representative form of portable art is etching on tools and other personal items. Some examples of this art are quite old. An engraved ox-rib, discovered in France in 1969, is thought to be 300,000 years old.

The stationary art form includes the most impressive examples of prehistoric art. Paintings on the walls of caves became a form of expression about 30,000 years ago, and were created during the next 20,000 years.

In 1868, in northern Spain near a place called Altamira, a gentleman farmer, Don Marcellino de Sautola, learned that a hunter had discovered the entrance to a cave on his land. Being an amateur archaeologist, Don Marcellino explored the cave and found nothing but a few bones. It was not until 11 years later, in 1879, that Sautola's daughter,

any standardized form, although there were different types of implements serving a variety of functions. With the advent of *Homo sapiens sapiens*, standardization of tools within a culture becomes commonplace. This means that the maker of the tool has a preconceived idea of what the tool should look like, and could communicate his idea to others within his culture.

The "gesture" theory of language development suggests that there is more to symbolic communication than merely stringing a series of words together in some organized fashion. Meaning in a spoken language also requires an understanding of such things as

Maria, entered the cave and happened to look up at the ceiling to discover colored images of animals that appeared almost alive in the flickering light.

At Lascaux in southern France, in 1940, four teenagers decided to explore a hole left by an uprooted tree. As local rumor had it, at the bottom of the hole was a subterranean passage that led to a nearby castle. The four boys discovered a narrow entranceway at the bottom of the pit, but it did not lead to a medieval castle. Instead, they found themselves in the presence of a series of cave paintings of exquisite beauty. Other cave paintings have been discovered since, particularly in North Africa, but none have surpassed the beauty of those of Altamira and Lascaux.

Most of the depictions on the walls are of large meat-bearing animals—bison, mammoths, horses, cattle, and reindeer. The animals are painted only in profile, usually slightly distorted, and tending to be fat. There are few birds, no reptiles, and virtually no plants or scenery. Rarely—except on cave walls in North Africa—does one find any portrayals of humans, and when they do appear they are usually in the form of "stick-like" figures.

Most cave paintings were in a remarkable state of preservation when they were discovered because of the constant and cool temperatures. However, the thousands of people who have visited the underground chambers since have helped to dry and crack the paints, and contributed to the growth of bacteria and mold on the walls. Lascaux, in the last few years, has been closed to the public.

The tools and techniques used by prehistoric cave artists make their achievements all the more impressive. Most of the colors came from ground mineral oxides such as iron manganese and red ochre. The paints were mixed with water and some fatty substances, with a consistency of a heavy liquid or paste.

The artist applied the paint with a variety of instruments including fingers, wads of plant material, hair, shredded ends of sticks, or by blowing the powdered paint through a hollow tube onto a wetted surface. How difficult it must have been to paint on the uneven surface of a cave wall or ceiling, in cramped quarters, with the only illumination being the flickering light from an animal-grease candle. And yet the figures of the animals are so life-like that in a cave setting the shadowy outlines of 20,000-year-old buffaloes and bulls seem to be moving toward the person who has entered their sanctuary.

There have been a number of theories proposed over the years to attempt to explain the motives of prehistoric artists. The Abbé Breuil, for years the foremost authority on prehistoric art, believed the paintings to be a form of sympathetic magic. The artist would portray an exceptionally fat bison in the hope or belief that the hunters of the tribe would locate the living representation of the painting on their next hunt. One argument that raises doubts about Breuil's thesis is the minimal number of reindeer represented in the cave paintings. From archaeological sources we know that one of the most important staples in prehistoric people's diet was reindeer meat. Some scholars see the pictures as a memorial of a particularly successful hunt.

Other scientists see the caves at Altamira as a gathering point for various tribal groups who lived in the general area. Periodically, perhaps at the end of each season, they would meet to share ideas, swap stories, and possibly arrange marriages. The paintings are usually deep within the caves in hard-to-reach places. The lack of cultural debris and minimal evidence of food consumption indicate that these sites were not used for permanent habitations.

It is not necessary to accept only one motivation for the cave paintings, nor do the reasons have to be utilitarian. Art for art's sake should not be discounted as one possibility. Scholars now believe that prehistoric people had sufficient leisure time to pursue something as creative and demanding as art. Usually, the paintings are found in the most inaccessible part of the cave—on a ceiling, or in a corner area well 'above the floor. If the artists did not take some pride in their work, and if they were not concerned about the results of their efforts having some degree of permanence, they would have painted on the floors, and only on the flattest and most readily available surfaces. Whatever the reasons for this early and creative form of communication, it remains one of the most magnificent and impressive representations of prehistoric culture.

THE NEOLITHIC REVOLUTION

The last part of the Paleolithic Age coincided with what is called the last Ice Age. Earth's climate cooled noticeably, and glaciers formed, moving southward into what are today the northern temperate zones. With the freezing of a much greater part of the oceans, land bridges were formed between the continents. People who had moved into areas now threatened by cold, migrated into more southerly climates. But around 10,000 B.C., the climate of earth warmed up again.

During a brief transition period around 10,000 B.C. called the Mesolithic Era (Middle Stone Age), archaeologists find evidence of European people using a bow and arrow; in Japan the first pottery appears.

Then followed the remarkable Neolithic Era (New Stone Age). Though lasting a brief 5000 years, its developments in human skills gave rise to what can now be seen as the first real civilizations.

AGRICULTURE AND THE DOMESTICATION OF ANIMALS

The domestication of animals and the beginning of agriculture meant that people no longer needed to roam in search of food; organized agriculture produced a permanent surplus in food that allowed humans to turn their now fully-developed brains to other uses than merely providing bare subsistence. Tied to the crops they had planted, human beings began to settle in permanent locations. The first towns sprang up.

Archaeological evidence shows clearly what happened, and where. In the Middle East, people planted wheat and barley and tended these crops with the knowledge that they would reap the harvest at the end of the growing season. This took place around 8000 B.C. About 3000 to 4000 years later, agriculture was independently invented in other parts of the world—North China, Mexico (where corn, or maize, was the crop), and Peru (where it was potatoes). From these early centers, agriculture spread throughout the world.

Along with the planting of crops came the domestication of animals. Sheep, with their docile nature, were probably the first animals tended and bred by people for food. At around the same time, archaeologists find the bones of dogs appearing around human settlements. It seems possible that there was a connection, and that people first kept dogs for the same purposes as sheepherders do today. Not long afterward, around 6000 B.C., people began keeping cattle as well. The domestication of animals, along with the discovery of agriculture, make up what has been called the Neolithic Revolution.

Traditionally, it has been thought that the domestication of animals began less than 9000 years ago. New evidence, and old evidence looked at in different ways, suggests that our ancestors might have started domesticating animals as far back as 30,000 years ago. For instance, several cave paintings of horses have been found with a tell-tale line across the muzzle, indicating a harness. A stone-carved head of a horse, approximately 15,000 years old, was located recently in southern France. Carved across the head and the muzzle are

Ancient Civilizations

● *Many the wonders but nothing walks stranger than man.*
This thing crosses the sea in the winter's storm,
making his path through the roaring waves.
And she, the greatest of gods, the earth—
ageless she is, and unwearied—he wears her away
as the ploughs go up and down from year to year
and his mules turn up the soil....
He controls with his craft the beasts of the open air,
walkers on hills. The horse with his shaggy mane
he holds and harnesses, yoked about the neck,
and the strong bull of the mountains.

Language, and thought like the wind
and the feelings that make the town,
he has taught himself, and shelter against the cold,
refuge from rain. He can always help himself.
He faces no future helpless. There's only death
that he cannot find an escape from.

SOPHOCLES

● *Soldiers! Think that from the summit of these pyramids 40 centuries are looking down upon you.*

NAPOLEON

● *And it came to pass at the end of the 430 years, even the selfsame day it came to pass, that all*
the hosts of the Lord went out from the land of Egypt.
It is a night to be much observed unto the Lord for bringing them out from the land of Egypt:
this is that night of the Lord to be observed of all the children of Israel in their generations.
And the Lord said unto Moses and Aaron, This is the ordinance of the passover: There shall no
stranger eat thereof.

EXODUS 12:41

● *By the rivers of Babylon, there we sat down, yea, we wept, when we remembered Zion.*
We hanged our harps upon the willows in the midst thereof.
For there they that carried us away captive required of us a song; and they that wasted us
required of us mirth, saying, Sing us one of the songs of Zion.
How shall we sing the Lord's song in a strange land?
If I forget thee, O Jerusalem, let my right hand forget her cunning.

PSALM 137

were marched off into captivity. King Hezekiah was shut off "like a bird in a cage" in Jerusalem, the capital of Judah, surrounded by an overwhelming force of Assyrians. But he refused to surrender the city because the prophet Isaiah had assured him that the city could not be taken if the people would remain faithful to their god:

Thus says the Lord concerning the King
    of Assyria:
He shall not enter this city nor shoot an
    arrow there,
He shall not advance against it with shield
Nor cast up a siege ramp against it.
By the way on which he came he shall
    go back;
This city he shall not enter.
This is the very word of the Lord.
I will shield this city to deliver it.
For my own sake and for the sake of my
    servant David.[12]

Miraculously, Sennacherib abandoned his siege of Jerusalem and returned to Babylon. Scholars have not been able to explain this withdrawal of the Assyrian forces. Some suggest that an epidemic struck the soldiers, while others say that a rumor of revolt in Babylon forced Sennacherib to abandon his plans to take Jerusalem. Herodotus gave still another reason:

• • • [A] number of field mice, pouring in among their enemies, devoured their quivers and their bows, the handles of their shields; so that on the next day, when they fled bereft of their arms, many of them fell.[13]

In 681 B.C., Sennacherib was assassinated as the result of a palace conspiracy. When his son Esarhaddon came to the throne in Nineveh, he immediately made plans to avenge the murder of his father. The cruelty of Esarhaddon created great political unrest within Assyria and encouraged revolts throughout the empire. Nevertheless, he attempted to expand the empire by invading Egypt in 671 B.C.. He captured the city of Memphis and imprisoned the pharaoh, but found that Egypt was too large and too far from Nineveh to be controlled effectively. Within a short time the Egyptians rose up in arms and expelled the Assyrian invaders.

Among his peaceful accomplishments, Esarhaddon rebuilt the city of Babylon, which his father had destroyed. He voluntarily retired in 668 B.C., turning the throne over to his son, Assurbanipal.

During the 42 years of Assurbanipal's reign, the Assyrian empire reached its greatest extent, stretching from the Nile valley to the Caucasus Mountains.

Unlike most other Assyrian kings, Assurbanipal was known for peaceful accomplishments as well as conquests. He created a great library of ancient Mesopotamian texts, and here is shown helping to rebuild the city of Babylon.

---

[12] 2 Kings 19:32-34.
[13] Herodotus II, 141.

36

THE OLD BABYLONIAN, ASSYRIAN, AND CHALDEAN EMPIRES
Why was Assurbanipal's empire so much larger than those of Hammurabi and the Chaldeans?

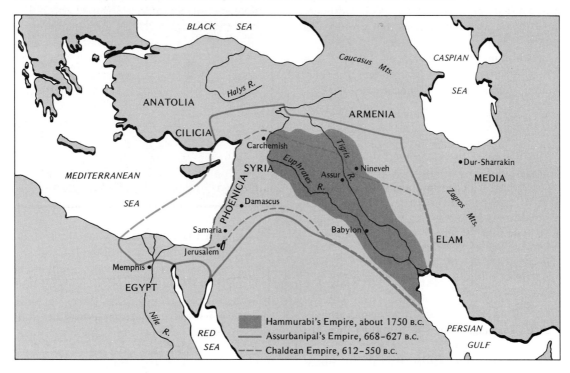

Hammurabi's Empire, about 1750 B.C.
Assurbanipal's Empire, 668–627 B.C.
Chaldean Empire, 612–550 B.C.

Using tribute collected from his vast empire, Assurbanipal made Nineveh the showplace of the ancient world. At his palace, he established a royal library where ancient manuscripts from Sumer and Akkad were collected and preserved. When the remains of this palace were excavated during the 19th century, archaeologists uncovered 22,000 clay tablets from the royal library, including hymns, dictionaries, grammars, treatises on astrology and medicine, lists of kings, chronicles of events, and myths about the creation of the world and a deluge that almost destroyed the world.

During the reign of Assurbanipal, the seeds of discord sprouted throughout the Assyrian empire. Nabopolassar, the governor of Babylon, encouraged other cities under Assyrian control to revolt. Unfortunately for Assyria, Assurbanipal's conquest of Elam had removed a buffer zone and had opened Assy-

ria's eastern borders to attack by the hostile Medes. In 612 B.C., the Chaldean people of Babylonia joined forces with the Medes of Persia to destroy Nineveh.

The prophet Nahum summed up the attitude of the victims of Assyria when he wrote:

Ah! blood stained city, steeped in deceit,
    full of pillage, never empty of prey!
Then all who see you shall shrink from
    you and say,
Where shall I look for anyone to
    comfort you? . . .
Your wounds cannot be assuaged, your
    injury is mortal;
all who have heard of your fate clap
    their hands in joy.
Are there any whom your ceaseless
    cruelty has not borne down?[14]

---

[14]Nahum 3:1, 7, 19.

37

To the present time, no nation has been so completely destroyed as was Assyria. Its three great cities, Dur-Sharrakin, Nineveh, and Assur, were burned to the ground and never rebuilt.

Although the downfall of Assyria was brought about by the Medes and the Persians, scholars have discovered that there were also events within Assyria that contributed to the invaders' success. Around 634 B.C., Assurbanipal had appointed one of his twin sons to be his successor. The other twin rebelled against his brother, and a bitter civil war ensued. The political divisions and economic disruptions caused by this war were probably an important factor in the Assyrians' defeat.

ARCHAEOLOGICAL FINDINGS

Prior to the 19th century, the Bible was the primary source of information about Assyria. The Biblical stories inspired several archaeologists to search for the ruins of Assyrian cities in Mesopotamia (present Iraq).

During the 19th century, Paul Emilie Botta, an agent in the French consulate at Mosul, Iraq, uncovered the ruins of the ancient city of Dur-Sharrakin and the palace that Sargon had built. The palace had 209 rooms and covered an area of 25 acres. Within the fortress-like walls were living quarters for the king and his servants, and treasuries and administrative offices. There were statues of awesome creatures, with human heads on bodies of winged lions or bulls, guarding the gates of the palace. The walls inside the palace were decorated with alabaster and limestone relief carvings depicting Sargon's military campaigns and royal lion hunts. The palace would certainly have impressed visitors with the power and majesty of the king of Assyria.

Another important discovery was made by Sir Henry Austen Layard in 1839. He excavated near present-day Mosul, and found the remains of ancient Nineveh. In particular, he found a 71-room palace built on a

A limestone relief found at Nineveh conveys the agony of a dying lioness. Assyrian palaces were decorated with many such artworks depicting the royal hunt.

terrace, and the remains of walls, with fortified gates, that once surrounded the palace. Layard estimated that these walls might have been eight miles in circumference and approximately 100 feet high. In 1852, Harmuz Rassam, a Turkish explorer, made additional excavations at Nineveh and uncovered the tablets of Assurbanipal's royal library, mentioned above, and sculptures of royal lion hunts. In these sculptures, the king was usually portrayed wearing the wings of an eagle, the horns of a bull, and the mane of a lion, symbolizing that he had the strength and ferocity of these wild animals.

THE ASSYRIAN CIVILIZATION

The Assyrians inherited many aspects of their civilization from earlier peoples and adapted ideas from their contemporaries, but they used this inheritance to create a very different type of society. Having learned from the Akkadians how to use cuneiform script to write their Semitic language, they used this valuable skill to administer their empire. The postal service that they created enabled the king to send written orders to the governors of his widespread empire and to receive information from them. The Assyrians also used writing to record the activities of the royal court: they were the first people to create a written chronicle of their kings.

From the Hittites, the Assyrians learned how to work with iron, and from the Mitanni tribes they learned how to breed and train horses. Their iron weapons and well-drilled cavalry and chariot troops made an important contribution to their war victories, for many of their opponents had only bronze weapons and infantry troops.

In government, too, the Assyrians made many important innovations in traditional practices. Although in theory the Assyrian kings ruled as representatives of the god Assur, in practice they did not derive their authority from this connection. Their monuments and palaces were not built in honor of the god, but for the use of the king. Religious leaders never became a political force in Assyria as they had in Sumer and Egypt.

One problem in the Assyrian system was that there were very likely to be disruptions and rebellions when a king died, since he was the source of all authority in government. To overcome this problem, each Assyrian king chose an *heir apparent* and made sure that this heir was recognized as such by the nobles and officials of the realm. Years later, the Persians and Romans adopted this and many other features of the Assyrians' imperial administration.

After the fall of Assyria in 612 B.C., the four most important powers in the Middle East were Egypt, Lydia, Chaldea, and Medea. The Egyptians, under the Saite dynasty (650-625 B.C.), enjoyed a period of prosperity and cultural renaissance. The Lydians, under King Croesus, were the chief power in Anatolia. The Chaldeans ruled Syria, Palestine, Phoenicia, and the Land between the Rivers, with Babylon, their capital, once again becoming the most important city in the Middle East. Farther east, the Medes took control of Persia in 550 B.C. Under the leadership of Cyrus the Great, they captured Babylon and established the *Persian Empire*, which dominated the Middle East for 200 years.

THE LAND BETWEEN THE RIVERS★

AKKAD	
2371-2316	*Sargon I*
2291-2255	*Naramsin*
2112-2004	**3RD DYNASTY OF UR**
2112-2094	*Ur-Nammu*
BABYLON	
1792-1750	*Hammurabi*
ASSYRIA	
884-859	*Assurnasirpal*
745-727	*Tiglathpilesar III*
722-705	*Sargon II*
705-681	*Sennacherib*
681-668	*Esarhaddon*
668-626	*Assurbanipal*
CHALDEA	
612-604	*Nabopolassar*
604-562	*Nebuchadnezzar*

★All dates are approximate years B.C.

CHALDEA Nabopolassar, who led the successful revolt against the Assyrians in 612 B.C., was proclaimed king of the Babylonians. The society he helped to build is called *Chaldea*, or *Neo-Babylonia*. He considered the kings of Syria and Phoenicia to be his vassals, and sent his son Nebuchadnezzar II to assert control over them. Meanwhile, Necho, pharaoh of Egypt, took advantage of the turmoil following the collapse of Assyria to become involved in Palestine and Syria. Necho marched northward into Syria and met Nebuchadnezzar at Carchemish, in 605 B.C. In the resulting battle, the Egyptians were defeated disastrously and retreated to Egypt.

When Nabopolassar died, in 604 B.C., Nebuchadnezzar returned to Babylon, claimed the throne, and became the most important ruler of the dynasty. The pharaoh again tried to stir up trouble by encouraging Jehoiakim, the king of Judah, to throw off the Chaldean yoke. In response to this threat, Nebuchadnezzar's army marched through Palestine and besieged Jerusalem in 597 B.C.. Jehoiakim was killed in battle, and his 18-year-old son, Jehoiachin, ascended the throne of Judah. Within three months the young king was forced to surrender, and Nebuchadnezzar confiscated the treasuries of both the palace and the temple. The king and his mother, together with almost 8000 Judeans, were marched off into captivity in Babylon.

A few years later, Egypt again stirred up revolt and again insisted that Judah join in the conspiracy against Chaldea. In 587 B.C., Nebuchadnezzar returned to Jerusalem and besieged the city. After 18 months, the starving people were forced to surrender. Zedekiah, whom Nebuchadnezzar had appointed as vassal king of Judah, was captured as he attempted to flee the city. His sons were executed before his eyes, and he was blinded and taken captive to Babylon. Thus the Jews began the "Babylonian Exile," which lasted until 538 B.C.

After the death of Nebuchadnezzar, in 562 B.C., several unpopular rulers came to the throne of Chaldea. One of these rulers, Nabonidus, antagonized the priests of Marduk, the god of justice, when he attempted to make the moon-god *Sin* the chief deity. While Nabonidus was absent from Babylon, in 539 B.C., his son Belshazzar governed the nation. The Book of Daniel tells the story of how the Chaldean monarchy was overthrown. As Belshazzar and his guests were feasting at a great banquet at the palace, Cyrus, the king of Persia, with help from the priests of Marduk, captured Babylon. Chaldea then became part of the vast Persian Empire.

ARCHAEOLOGICAL FINDINGS

While Nebuchadnezzar is best known today for destroying Jerusalem, he also made Babylon the most beautiful city in the ancient Middle East. In 1899, Robert Koldeway, a German archaeologist, excavated the site of Babylon and was eventually able to lay out the plan of the ancient city. The walls surrounding the city formed a square, and each wall was nine miles long. Outside the walls, there was a deep moat. For over 2000 years, scholars had assumed that Herodotus, writing in the 5th century B.C., had been exaggerating when he wrote the following description:

••• *on the top of the wall, at the edges, they built dwellings of one story, fronting each other, and they left a space between these dwellings sufficient for turning a chariot with four horses. In the circumference of the wall there were a hundred gates, all of brass. . . . This outer wall, then, is the chief defense, but another wall runs round within. . . .*[15]

Archaeologists now know that this wall was actually 300 feet high and 80 feet thick, with 250 watchtowers and 100 bronze gates.

Herodotus also described a bridge, 400 feet long and supported on seven boat-shaped

---

[15]Herodotus I, 180-1.

The Ishtar gate of ancient Babylon was constructed with glazed and molded bricks.

piers, that crossed the Euphrates River and formed a part of Babylon's Procession Street. This street passed through the outer walls and bisected the city. On both sides of the street were sidewalks paved with small red stone slabs, and along the edge of every stone were carved the words, "I am Nebuchadnezzar, king of Babylon, who made this." At the south end of Procession Street was a double gate covered with brilliant blue glazed bricks and bas relief animal sculptures, dedicated to the goddess Ishtar. This gate can be seen today in the German Museum in East Berlin.

• • • In the midst of this precinct is built a solid tower of one stade [517 feet] both in length and in breadth, and on this tower rose another, and another upon that, to the number of eight; and an ascent to these is outside, running spirally round all the towers. About the middle of the ascent there is a landing place and seats to rest on; . . . and in the uppermost tower stands a spacious temple, and in this temple is placed, handsomely furnished, a large couch, and by its side a table of gold. No statue has been erected within it, nor does any mortal pass the night there, except only a native woman, chosen by the gods out of the whole nation, as the Chaldeans, who are priests of this deity, say. These same priests assert, though I cannot credit what they say, that the god himself comes to the temple and reclines on the bed.[16]

The temple Herodotus described is now believed to have been the inspiration for the Biblical story of the Tower of Babel (Genesis 11:4-9).

Nebuchadnezzar's great palace in Babylon was, he declared, "the admiration of all who saw it." The walls were decorated with colorful friezes made up of blue and yellow enameled bricks, and the throne room opened onto a vast courtyard. A palace garden was built for the queen in the form of an artificial mountain, to remind her of her mountain

---

[16]Herodotus I, 181-2.

The hanging gardens of Babylon, built by Nebuchadnezzar for his queen, were one of the Seven Wonders of the World.

birthplace. This garden had several terraces supported by huge man-made vaults. Amid the ruins of these vaults, archaeologists found a well, with a pump designed to provide a continuous flow of water for the garden. The *hanging garden*, as it came to be called, was one of the legendary Seven Wonders of the World.

The construction of Babylon required many thousands of bricks, and it is probable that these bricks were molded and fired by captives. The story of Shadrach, Meschach, and Abednego, in the Book of Daniel, probably originated from this activity.

THE CHALDEAN CIVILIZATION

The Chaldean culture was essentially a continuation of the older cultures in the Land between the Rivers. The greatest contributions they made were related to their studies of the heavens and their observations of the movements of the sun, the moon, and the planets. Indeed, they may be considered to have been the first astronomers because they were able to forecast eclipses of the moon and identify the signs of the zodiac (12 constellations which are almost uniformly spaced around the celestial equator). Although the Babylonians continued to use a lunar calendar of 28-day months, Naburimannu, a priest, computed the length of a solar year. Kidinnu, another priest, determined the tilt of the axis of the earth and the precession of equinoxes.

The Chaldeans learned to distinguish the planets from the stars. They regarded the five planets closest to the earth (Venus, Mercury, Jupiter, Mars, and Saturn), together with the sun and the moon, to be manifestations of their major deities. Each of the deities was worshiped on a separate day, and this practice led to the concept of a seven-day week, which the Romans later adopted. The Chaldeans' work with lunar cycles strongly influenced Meton, a Greek astronomer of the 5th century B.C., who devised a workable calendar based on the Babylonian system. (In Meton's system, an extra month was added every few years to reconcile the lunar calendar with the solar year. His calendar was in error by only 5 days every 19 years.)

The Chaldeans developed the science of astronomy for a practical purpose: they believed that knowledge of celestial events would enable them to foretell the future. In addition to their work in astrology, the Babylonians became known in the ancient world for their expertise in several other forms of divination. They wrote detailed treatises, for instance, on the art of predicting the future through studying the liver of a sacrificial animal. Archaeologists have found models of livers which were probably used to train priests in this form of divination.

SUMMARY

The earliest major civilization developed in Sumer, which occupied the marshlands of the Tigris and Euphrates rivers. As early as 3500 B.C., under the leadership of their priest-kings, the Sumerians learned to work together to control the flooding of the two great rivers. Over the years, they invented cuneiform writing, a calendar, and a system of weights and measures. They also discovered the principles of metalworking and of the wheel and the arch.

The Sumerian civilization provided a foundation for the emerging cultures that overran the region in successive centuries. The Akkadians used the arts of the Sumerians to develop military skills, and adopted the Sumerian cuneiform to the writing of their own language. The Babylonians made a great contribution to legal philosophy in Hammurabi's code of laws. The Assyrians then conquered the land and established the greatest empire of the Western world up to that time. In the process, their name became synonymous with terror. The Chaldeans converted Babylon into a monumental city and contributed to human knowledge by observing the heavens and developing some principles of astronomy.

QUESTIONS

1 *How did geography affect the development of civilization in Sumer? Why did this civilization affect the development of all the peoples who invaded and conquered the Tigris-Euphrates Valley?*
2 *Explain the meaning of the phrase "codification of law." What is the significance of a law code? What would life be like if there were no codes of law?*
3 *What does the law code of Hammurabi tell us about the way people lived when he was king?*
4 *Compare the flood story in the Bible with that found in the "Epic of Gilgamesh."*
5 *What modern laws are similar to those described in Hammurabi's law code?*

BIBLIOGRAPHY

Which book would you use to learn more about the Behistun Rock?

CERAM, C. W. *Gods, Graves and Scholars.* New York: Knopf, 1967. *A popular book about the archeologists who have contributed to our understanding of the past; arranged by area rather than by chronology. Includes exciting human interest stories about the archeologists and emphasizes the significance of their findings.*

COTENAU, GEORGES. *Everyday Life in Babylonia and Assyria.* Chatham: Mackay, 1954. *Discusses the history of the Tigris-Euphrates Valley between the rise of Sargon II of Assyria and the conquest of the Babylonians (Chaldeans) by the Persians; reviews thousands of clay tablets, which revealed how the kings, nobles and common people thought and lived; includes stories, legends, religious rituals, hymns, and scientific and mathematical treatises.*

2 $\mathcal{Egypt}$

● *But concerning Egypt I will now speak at length, because nowhere are there so many marvelous things, nor in the whole world beside are there to be seen so many works of unspeakable greatness; therefore, I shall say the more concerning Egypt.*

HERODOTUS

The Nile valley was a second important cradle of civilization in the ancient world. Herodotus[1] described Egypt as a "gift of the Nile River," because in this almost rainless land, the Nile provides a ribbon of green bisecting hundreds of miles of scorched desert and barren hills.

Egypt has continued to fascinate travelers over the centuries. Visitors today can see the same river, the same desert, and the same ancient works that Herodotus described, varying from the towering Great Pyramid to the small treasures from the tomb of Tutankhamun.

THE NILE RIVER VALLEY The White Nile, which rises in Lake Victoria in equatorial Africa, and the Blue Nile, which has its origins in the highlands of Ethiopia, join at Khartoum, the capital of Sudan. Between the sites of present-day Khartoum and Aswan, six cataracts, or major "rapids," interfered with transportation on the river. (Some of these cataracts are now covered by Lake Nasser, created by the Aswan Dam in 1971.) From Aswan to Cairo, a distance of about 550 miles, the Nile is unobstructed and flows throughout the year. From a point north of Cairo to the Mediterranean Sea, the very large, fertile delta of the Nile provides many waterways and good agricultural land.

The distinctive landscape of Egypt provided the early Egyptians with natural defenses against invaders. The deserts to the east and west formed a vast ocean of sand, while the Mediterranean Sea formed a secure boundary to the north, and the cataracts discouraged Nubian raiders from the south. Because of this natural protection, the early Egyptians were undisturbed by invaders for many centuries and thus were able to develop a culture essentially free from outside influence.

The Nile River was a major factor in the development of the arts and sciences of civilization in Egypt. Since there was so little rainfall, the early people were forced to develop techniques for collecting and distributing waters from the annual flood. These techniques included the *shadoof*, a simple

---

[1]Herodotus was a Greek historian who traveled widely in the Middle East during the 5th century B.C. He is one of our most important sources of information concerning the cultures and events of the ancient world.

THE COURSE OF THE NILE
Look at a physical map of Africa to find the location of desert and mountains.

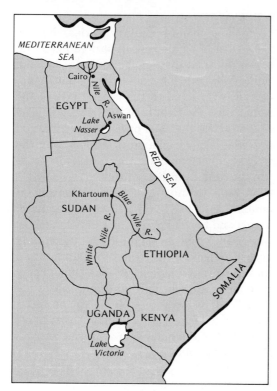

Nile. The stems of this plant could be pressed to make a form of paper, and the fibers could be twisted into rope. Copper and turquoise were available in the Sinai Peninsula, and gold was found in the desert to the east of Thebes. Limestone for many building purposes was available in Lower Egypt, and granite was quarried near the first cataract in Upper Egypt. Fine pottery clay was readily available; mixed with water and straw, this clay could be formed into bricks which were hardened by exposure to the sun.

When the Egyptians learned how to quarry and transport stone, this resource began to replace clay bricks as a building material for

The shadoof, a simple balance beam device, was invented by the ancient Egyptians to transport water to their fields. The device is still utilized today.

balanced beam with a bucket at one end, which was used for lifting water out of the river into irrigation ditches.

The need to relocate property lines inundated by the flooding led the Egyptians to develop the science of geometry: in fact, the Greek word *geometry* means "land measure." The long stretch of unobstructed river from the first cataract to the sea provided easy transportation, and thus promoted communication and trade between the towns along its banks.

NATURAL RESOURCES
The banks of the Nile, and the deserts and hills around them, provided a variety of resources which the Egyptian people learned to exploit. The papyrus plant grew profusely along the banks and northern marshes of the

some dwellings and houses. They used what is called a post-and-lintel construction.[2] By contrast, the people of Mesopotamia had no such rock, but discovered that they could build larger structures by adding supports and creating arches with clay bricks.

EARLY CULTURES

Campsites of Paleolithic people, dating from the 5th or 4th millenium B.C., have been discovered in gravel terraces along the Nile, and in places that are now in the desert. Judging from the well-made stone implements and the animal bones found in these camps, the people killed and ate wild cattle, antelope, and sometimes a hippopotamus. Fish must have been an important source of food because many hooks made of ivory, shell, or bone have been found. As the climate changed and the region turned into desert, the people of Egypt were forced to migrate to sites along the Nile.

PREDYNASTIC EGYPT

By the end of the 4th millenium B.C., many of the characteristic features of Egyptian society had been developed. Irrigation was practiced, a system of writing had been devised, and the basic religious beliefs of later generations were established. Wealthy people were buried in houselike tombs called *mastabas*, which are similar to the great tombs of later times. In the mastabas, archaeologists have found jewelry and vases wrought from gold and copper, and linen woven from flax. The mastabas also contained many slate cosmetic palettes, indicating that early Egyptian women were applying the makeup that became characteristic in later times. In the paintings of the mastabas, the artistic conventions of later times are also apparent: the torsos of human figures are seen in full frontal view, while the faces, legs, and arms are seen in profile.

GOVERNMENT

Over the course of many centuries, the various tribes of Egypt came to be organized into small political districts called *nomes*. Each nome was ruled by a leader called a *nomarch*, who lived in the capital city of the nome, near the temple of the tribal god. The nomarch was the chief priest of the tribal god and was also in charge of supervising the irrigation system, collecting taxes, and leading the nome's military force.

In time, the nomes came to be loosely organized into the two distinct kingdoms of Upper and Lower Egypt. The ruler of the most important nome in each kingdom gradually gained **hegemony** over the other nomes and took the title of *pharaoh* [FARE-oh]. *Upper Egypt* extended through the higher ground of the Nile River valley, from Nubia to the delta, and used the falcon as its symbol. *Lower Egypt* consisted of the delta area and was symbolized by the cobra.

RELIGION

From the earliest times, the Egyptians' most revered god was Re, or Ra, the god of the sun. Whereas certain other deities were worshiped only locally, in the towns that contained their temples, Re was worshiped by all Egyptians and became the state god during the dynastic period. The sun god had many different manifestations, since separate cults in honor of him had developed throughout Egypt. Re-Atum, whose temple was in Heliopolis, represented the declining sun and was associated with the wisdom of an aged man. The sky god Horus, originally represented as a falcon on the horizon, also came to have associations with the sun god.

One of the central legends of Egypt concerned the god Osiris, who was thought to have been a pharaoh in prehistoric times. Osiris was killed by the wicked god Seth and then brought back to life through the efforts

---

[2]In this system of construction, many upright *posts*, or columns, are used to support horizontal *lintels*, or beams. The maximum spacing between the columns is determined by the strength of the materials used.

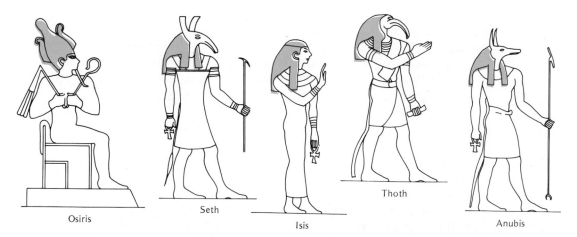

Osiris

Seth

Isis

Thoth

Anubis

of his wife, Isis. Osiris and Isis then conceived a son, Horus, who later took revenge upon Seth with the help of the benevolent god Thoth. The figures in this legend came to have important associations with the pharaohs of Egypt. Egyptians believed that their pharaoh, the son of Re, was also closely linked with the gods Osiris and Horus. In life, the pharaoh was associated with the living Horus, and in death he became joined to Osiris, the ancient pharaoh who had achieved life after death.

Most of the Egyptians' gods were *anthropomorphic* in character, even though they were frequently able to assume the strengths or capabilities of certain animals. In this respect they were very much like the gods of the Mesopotamians. However, several of the Egyptian gods were more animal than human in their conception. One of these animal gods was Anubis, the jackal who roamed the cemeteries and communicated with the dead. He was usually portrayed as a realistic-looking jackal, but occasionally was given the body of a man with a jackal's head.

Belief in a life after death remained fairly consistent throughout Egypt's history, although there were many contradictory ideas about the subject. From the earliest times, it was thought that dead people came to life again after they were buried, and for this reason their tombs were equipped with furniture, food, and other necessities of life. Later,

it was thought that the pharaoh, and perhaps certain nobles or members of his family, joined the sun god Re in his daily journey across the sky. To provide a vehicle for this solar journey, model boats were often included in the tomb furnishings. (There may have been some doubts about the solar journey, for the pharaohs' tombs continued to be furnished, as before, with the necessities of everyday life.)

During the period of the New Kingdom, the legend of Osiris provided the basis for an extremely imaginative conception of life after death. People began to think that Osiris' kingdom was beneath the western desert, and illustrated guides called Books of the Dead

The ancient Egyptians sometimes placed models of boats in tombs so that the souls of the deceased could travel. Two full-size boats were found near the pyramid of Cheops.

Egyptians of the New Kingdom period believed that, after death, a person's heart was weighed by the jackal-headed god Anubis against the feather of truth. If the scale balanced, the soul went to paradise.

were painted in tombs so that the deceased could find their way there. (Some guides showed both a land and a sea route to the underground kingdom.) Once the dead person had found the gates to the underworld, he confronted Osiris himself, who judged whether the person was worthy to enter. If the judgment was favorable and the person was admitted, people believed that life proceeded much as it had in the real world of Egypt. Many tombs contained small statues called *shabti* which the dead person could send out as substitutes if he or she were summoned to work in the fields.

THE DYNASTIES OF EGYPT

Around 3100 B.C., a political union of Upper and Lower Egypt was achieved under the leadership of Narmer, who was a ruler of Upper Egypt. To symbolize the unification of the two kingdoms, Narmer wore a crown that combined features of the orig-

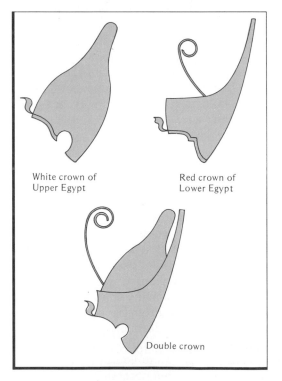

White crown of Upper Egypt

Red crown of Lower Egypt

Double crown

inal crowns of Upper Egypt (white, with a falcon symbol) and Lower Egypt (red, with a cobra symbol). Entwined stems of reed and papyrus plants were also used as a symbol of the combined kingdoms. To further symbolize the unification, Narmer built a new capital city, later called Memphis, at the meeting point of the Upper and Lower Kingdoms. The use of these symbols indicates how important the unification was to the people of the time, and it came to be equally important to succeeding generations. Later Egyptians considered the unification to be the beginning of their nation's history.

In 1898, archaeologists found the Slate Palette of Narmer, which became one of the most important sources of information about this early period. On one side of the palette, Narmer is shown walking in a procession while wearing the crown of Lower Egypt. On the other side, he is shown wearing the tall crown of Upper Egypt.

THE THREE KINGDOMS

According to Manetho, an Egyptian priest who lived in the 3rd century B.C., there had been 30 dynasties in the history of Egypt. Archaeologists have found a number of ancient inscriptions which support many of the listings in Manetho's chronology. In these inscriptions, years were often numbered in relation to an outstanding event in a pharaoh's reign, such as a major conquest, the erection of an important structure, or a tomb ritual. By comparing these inscriptions to the records left by the peoples of Mesopotamia, Syria-Palestine, Greece, and other areas, scholars have been able to establish many dates within reasonable limits. Modern Egyptologists now divide Manetho's dynasties into three major periods: the Old Kingdom, or Pyramid Age, covering the 3rd to 6th dynasties (2686-2160 B.C.); the Middle Kingdom, or Feudal Age, covering the 11th and 12th dynasties (2040-1786 B.C.); and the New Kingdom, or Empire, covering the 18th to 20th dynasties (1570-1075 B.C.).

Narmer's Slate Palette celebrates his victory over Lower Egypt, around 3100 B.C. This is the oldest surviving image of an historic person identified by name.

THE OLD KINGDOM

Nothing was more representative of the absolute power and imputed divinity of the pharaohs of the Old Kingdom than their pyramids. The inscriptions and statues in each pyramid complex tell us much of what we know about each pharaoh's reign. Zoser, in the third dynasty, was the first pharaoh to build a monumental structure to house his remains. The fact that he was able to marshall the immense work force needed to quarry and transport the stone for such a structure indicates that his administration was highly centralized and efficient.

Imhotep, Zoser's *vizier*, or chief official, is credited with being the architect and engineer of the Step Pyramid at Sakkara. The impressive stepped construction with its facade of limestone represented a great advance in the techniques of stoneworking and was considered a miraculous achievement at the time. Imhotep was regarded as a great philosopher and healer as well as an architect, and in time was even worshiped as a minor deity.

Because of his special relationship with the sun god Re, the pharaoh was believed to be immortal and to have the power to intervene with the gods on behalf of his people. His authority rested on *ma'at*, a concept that cannot be expressed in one English word. It related to continuity, eternity, harmony, goodness, and truth. As head of government, the pharaoh and his officials were in charge of administering the gods' law. In fact, there were no written laws, since the pharaoh and his appointed officials were considered to be in communication with the gods. Special altars were included within the complex of each pharaoh's tomb so that priests could pray to him for his continued guidance in the affairs of Egypt.

With the beginning of the fourth dynasty, around 2613 B.C., the building of great pyramids began in earnest. The biggest of these, located at Gizeh, is the Great Pyramid of Khufu. The name *Khufu* means "smasher of

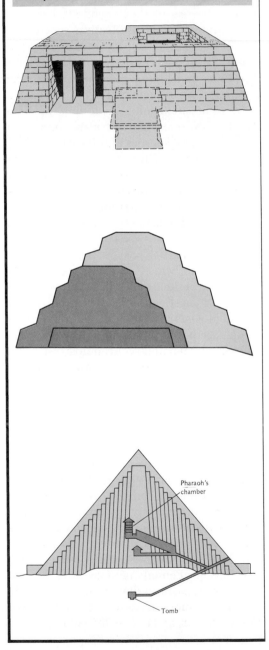

Top: *Mastabas of the predynastic period resembled houses. The entrance to the underground burial chamber was filled with stones after the funeral.* Center: *Zoser's Step Pyramid was redesigned during construction to add two additional stages.* Bottom: *Chambers and passageways were cut into the Great Pyramid of Cheops after the interior was constructed.*

Pharaoh's chamber

Tomb

A photograph taken in the 1920s shows the Nile in flood, with the great pyramids of Cheops at right and that of his son Khafre (Chephren) at center.

foreheads," and this pharaoh was known as a particularly autocratic and difficult ruler. The ancient Greeks referred to him as *Cheops* [KEY-ops], and most people use this name today.

The pyramids at Gizeh, and particularly that of Cheops, so impressed the people of later times that they devised various explanations of their purpose. Some early Christians believed that they were granaries erected by the Jewish patriarch Joseph. Other people suggested that they were treasuries, or the palaces of kings, or astronomical observatories. The Great Pyramid is indeed an awe-inspiring structure. Herodotus reported that Cheops' pyramid, as originally built, was 481 feet high, and each side was 755 feet long. The average block of stone weighs 5000 pounds, and some of the granite blocks that were quarried at Aswan and brought to the site by boat weigh 30 tons. Each block was measured and cut so precisely that even today a knife blade cannot be slipped between two adjacent blocks.

Khafre (or Chephren), the son of Cheops, continued the tradition of pyramid-building at Gizeh, and also added an enormous sphinx to the mortuary grounds. He had his own features inscribed on the face of the sphinx, and thus commemorated his reign in this statue as well as in his pyramid. Like his father, Khafre was known as a difficult king.

The sphinx erected by Khafre still guards the royal tombs at Gizeh.

51

THE THREE KINGDOMS OF EGYPT★

-3100	Predynastic Period
	OLD KINGDOM
2686-2613	3rd dynasty
	Zoser
2613-2494	4th dynasty
	Khufu (Cheops)
	Khafre (Chephren)
2494-2345	5th dynasty
2345-2160	6th dynasty
	Intermediate period
2160-2040	7th-10th dynasties
	MIDDLE KINGDOM
2040-1991	11th dynasty
2040-2010	Mentohotep II
1991-1786	12th dynasty
1991-1961	Amenemhet I
1961-1938	Sesostris I
	Intermediate Period
1786-1674	13th dynasty
1674-1570	Hyksos rule
	NEW KINGDOM
1570-1320	18th dynasty
1570-1546	Ahmose I
1504-1482	Hatshepsut/Thutmose III
1482-1450	Thutmose III
1417-1379	Amenhotep III
1379-1362	Akhenaton
1361-1352	Tutankhamun
1352-1348	Ay
1348-1320	Horemheb
1320-1200	19th dynasty
1320-1318	Ramses I
1318-1304	Seti I
1304-1237	Ramses II
1200-1075	20th dynasty
1198-1166	Ramses III

★All dates are approximate years B.C.

First Intermediate Period. Some of the Old Kingdom pharaohs became so preoccupied with the building of pyramids that they exhausted their treasuries and had to look to the nobles of the provincial districts for financial aid. In return for such aid, these nobles were given large tracts of land or important positions of authority in their districts, and eventually developed autonomous small kingdoms of their own. As the pharaoh's power declined, there was no longer any central authority to set irrigation policy or to administer justice. Periods of famine and social unrest began to occur, and many people enriched themselves at the expense of others. The following lament expresses the indignation of a person who had been used to a more stable social order:

● ● ● *The land spins like a potter's wheel;*
noble ladies are gleaners, and nobles are in
the workhouse, but he who never slept on so
much as a plank is now the owner of a bed;
he who never wove for himself is the owner
of fine linen.[3]

Since the pharaohs no longer had the means to deal with these issues, the nation again broke into two separate kingdoms.

THE MIDDLE KINGDOM

The 11th Dynasty. After a long period of turmoil, the reunification of Egypt was achieved under the leadership of Mentohotep II, who founded the 11th dynasty. A new capital was established at Thebes, where the ancient temple of Amun, a god associated with life-giving qualities, was located. This god became the new national god under the name Amun-Re.

Mentohotep II was one of the first pharaohs to build his tomb in the Valley of the Kings and Queens, a range of hills to the west of Thebes. His reign and that of his succes-

[3]"Lament of Ipuwer," quoted in *Temples, Tombs and Hieroglyphs*, revised ed., by Barbara Mertz (New York: Dodd, Mead & Co., 1978), p. 99.

sors was also marked by the opening of trade relations between Egypt and the peoples of Syria and Palestine.

The 12th Dynasty. About 1991 B.C., the grandson of Mentohotep II was succeeded as pharaoh by his vizier, Amenemhet, who founded the 12th dynasty. Under Amenemhet I and his successors, Egypt enjoyed one of the most stable and prosperous periods of its history. Late in his reign, Amenemhet initiated a new policy of appointing a co-ruler in order to assure an uneventful succession to the throne. Thus, his son Sesostris ruled with him for the last 10 years of his life and succeeded him when he died. This policy of co-regency was later adopted by the pharaohs of the New Kingdom.

Under the pharaohs of the 12th dynasty, a number of new projects were carried out. To facilitate trade with the countries around the Mediterranean Sea, the Egyptians learned to build ocean-going ships, using wood from the renowned "cedars of Lebanon." They also built a canal, the Wadi Tumilat, to allow boats to pass from the Red Sea to the Mediterranean Sea. In order to develop trade with the peoples to the south, the pharaohs cut a canal into the first cataract so that boats could proceed past the falls and into Nubia. The marshes of Fayum, an area about 50 miles southwest of Memphis, were drained so that the region could become an agricultural center. In addition, the monumental city of Heliopolis was built to the northeast of Memphis.

The prosperity of Egypt under the 12th dynasty attracted a group of Asiatic peoples called the *Hyksos* to the area. These people—sometimes known as the Shepherd Kings—migrated from Palestine, Syria, and Phoenicia, and found work in Egypt as artisans in various trades. Eventually, they established a small kingdom at Avaris, in the delta region. They assimilated many aspects of Egyptian life into their own culture.

Although we do not know exactly how the Hyksos went about conquering Egypt, we

ANCIENT EGYPT
Why did Herodotus call Egypt "the gift of the Nile River"?

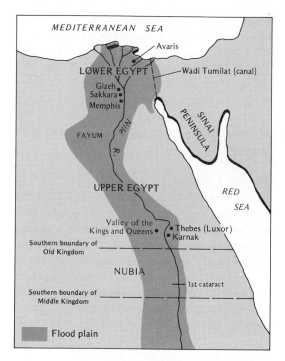

do know that their military equipment, including horse-driven chariots and a new, stronger type of bow, was superior to that of the Egyptians. In 1674 B.C., the Hyksos captured Memphis, and sometime after this date, a Hyksos ruler was crowned as pharaoh. An Egyptian pharaoh continued to rule at Thebes, under relaxed control of the Hyksos ruler. Although the Hyksos controlled Egypt, they did not interfere with the religion and customs of the Egyptians, but rather assimilated Egyptian customs into their own system.

After about a hundred years of fairly peaceful coexistence between the Egyptians and the Hyksos, quarrels began to break out between them. Because the Hyksos were allied with the Nubians to the south, the Egyptians felt that they were caught between two alien powers. The Egyptian pharaoh Kamose expressed his view of the situation:

. . . I sit associated with an Asiatic and a Negro. Each man has his slice of Egypt. . . . My wish is to smite the Asiatics.[4]

Kamose carried out his wish by launching a surprise attack on the Hyksos, using the military technology that they had introduced to Egypt. His campaign succeeded, but he was not able to drive the Hyksos out of their strongholds in the delta. Finally, his younger brother, Ahmose, succeeded in expelling the Hyksos, and became the founder of the 18th dynasty.

THE NEW KINGDOM

During the New Kingdom period (1570-1075 B.C.), Egypt developed into an imperial power and experienced one of the most glorious periods in its long existence. Whereas the pharaohs of the Middle Kingdom had fought only occasional battles in order to keep their trade routes open, the pharaohs of the 18th dynasty found it necessary to establish a permanent military presence in Syria and Palestine. The Egyptians' chief rivals for influence in the Middle East were the Hittites and the Mitanni, each of whom at times controlled the northern part of Mesopotamia and part of Syria. The Egyptians eventually used diplomacy as well as military campaigns to establish their sphere of influence in the area.

The 18th dynasty. When Ahmose I, the first pharaoh of the 18th dynasty, returned to Thebes after his successful campaign against the Hyksos, he brought with him a large army which had grown rich with the spoils of war. These troops became the nucleus of a permanent professional army. Under Ahmose and his immediate successors, the Egyptians annexed territory in Nubia and carried out a military campaign in Syria. They then realized that a literate bureaucracy was needed to administer the affairs of the expanding empire. To meet this need, they or-

dered the priests who ran temple scribal schools to train young prospective bureaucrats to read and write. The new emphasis on literacy eventually meant that many of the common people of Egypt had a chance to enter a career that had not been open to their parents.

The first rulers of the 18th dynasty made several other changes in the established order as well. To emphasize the separateness and divinity of the ruling family and to provide for a peaceful succession in the event there was no male heir, the pharaohs' daughters were each given the title "god's wife" in childhood. If a pharaoh had no male heirs, he could appoint a successor from outside the royal family; that person would then le-

SITES OF THE NEW KINGDOM PERIOD
Why did Egypt develop to the northeast rather than to the west, south, or east?

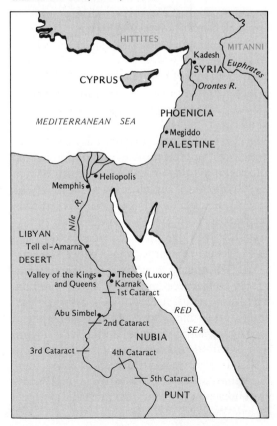

---

[4]J. B. Pritchard, *Ancient Near East Texts Relating to the Old Testament* (Princeton: Princeton University Press, 1955), pp. 232-4.

In this statue of Hatshepsut, the queen wears the regalia of a pharaoh but is definitely feminine in appearance. In other portraits, she sometimes wore a beard.

The funerary temple of Hatshepsut. The paintings within describe her peaceful accomplishments, such as the expedition to Punt and the construction of obelisks.

gitimize his claim to the throne in the eyes of the people by marrying a "god's wife."

In about 1504 B.C., the new succession procedure resulted in the reign of Hatshepsut, the first woman pharaoh. As a "god's wife," Hatshepsut had been married to the pharaoh Thutmose II. When he died, Hatshepsut's 10-year-old stepson, Thutmose III, became pharaoh in name. However, Hatshepsut seized the authority of the pharaoh and was herself crowned in a ceremony at Karnak. For the next 30 years, Hatshepsut was the dominant ruler, and Thutmose III served in a minor role.

Hatshepsut is known for several special achievements: she expanded the Egyptians' trade network to the south by organizing an expedition into the heart of Africa, to a re-gion known as Punt (possibly modern Somalia). From Punt, the Egyptians were able to obtain valuable exotic products such as leopard skins, feathers, hardwoods, and myrrh, a valuable resin used to make fragrant oils. Hatshepsut also carried out several monumental building projects, including an enormous funerary temple for herself in the Valley of the Kings and Queens and several great obelisks for the temple of Amun in Thebes. In most respects, Hatshepsut seems to have operated just as a male pharaoh would. She probably commanded the expedition to Punt, and, in some portraits and statues, she was portrayed as a man. In several of these, she even wore the decorative long, narrow beard that the male pharaohs sometimes taped to their chins.

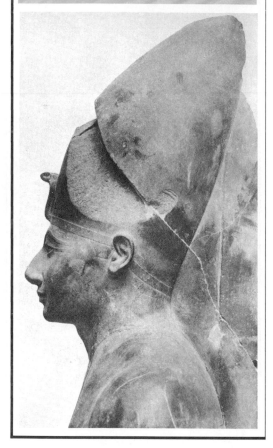

Thutmose III was one of the great military strategists of the ancient world. His conquests led to increased trade and commerce between Egypt and the rest of the Mediterranean world.

Babylonians, Assyrians, and Hittites all sent tribute to Egypt in recognition of Thutmose's conquests.

Thutmose waged a total of 17 military campaigns during his reign. At its peak, his empire extended from the fourth cataract of the Nile, in present-day Sudan, to the Euphrates River in modern Iraq. To administer his empire, Thutmose instituted a policy of bringing nobles from the conquered areas to Egypt, where they were educated and trained at the Egyptian court. Many of these people then returned to their homelands and governed them as loyal vassals of Egypt.

The tribute submitted by Thutmose's vassals greatly enriched the royal treasury and led to a period of great prosperity for Egypt. Trade with the peoples of Crete and the city-states around the Aegean Sea enabled the wealthy people of Egypt to import many new luxuries and to enjoy the art and culture of other civilizations.

The Amarna Period. The pattern of military conquest and domestic prosperity continued under Thutmose's successors, Amenhotep II, Thutmose IV, and Amenhotep III. Then, with the accession of Amen-

Statues of Amenhotep III, the father of Akhenaton, were called the Colossi of Memnon by Greek travelers. They were a very popular tourist attraction in the ancient world.

When Thutmose III ascended the throne after the death of Hatshepsut, he immediately faced a threat from the Mitanni tribes, who were gathering an army at Megiddo and possibly intended to march into Egypt. Thutmose quickly proceeded to Palestine with his army. As he drew near to the Mitanni forces, he decided to overrule his military commanders and make a very risky approach to Megiddo through a mountain pass. His tactics succeeded, and he was able to establish Egyptian domination over the entire area of Palestine and Syria. Although he was never able to subjugate the Mitanni completely, the

hotep IV, a strange interlude in the history of Egypt began to develop. Amenhotep IV had an eccentric personality and probably also suffered from a glandular disease which gave him an odd physical appearance. Egyptologists refer to his reign as the *Amarna* period, because the art and religious customs that he developed at Tell el-Amarna are quite different from those of any other pharaoh's reign.

Some of the origins of Amenhotep's radically "new" ideas were actually to be found in Egypt's ancient history. For many centuries, the priests of Heliopolis had been concerned about the adoption of Amun-Re as the state god. Whereas the pharaohs of the Old Kingdom had worshiped the sun god as Re-Atum, the pharaohs of the Middle and New Kingdoms worshiped him as Amun-Re. Although the two gods were almost identical, they were symbolized differently. The priests of Heliopolis believed that the true sun god could only be symbolized by the solar disk (the *aton*); the feathers and other insignia of Amun-Re were, they believed, a corruption. In the fifth year of his reign, Amenhotep IV became convinced that the priests of Heliopolis were correct. He then went a step further and proclaimed that the *only* true god was the Aton. To emphasize his proclamation, he built a new temple to Aton and suspended the worship of all other gods. In addition, he changed his name to Akhenaton [ak-NA-ton], meaning "the glory of Aton."

It is not known how much active opposition Akhenaton encountered in Thebes as he proceeded to carry out his ideas. Soon, however, he found it convenient to move to the site of present-day Tell el-Amarna, an area midway between Thebes and Memphis. Encouraged by his beautiful and influential wife Nefertiti, Akhenaton proceeded to build an open-air temple to Aton. Unlike the temples of Amun-Re and other gods, which had been filled with mysterious corridors and dark inner sanctuaries, the new temple of Aton

Akhenaton insisted that he be portrayed realistically. In some depictions, such as this one, Egyptian artists even emphasized his physical deformities.

was completely open to the light and air. Akhenaton encouraged his retainers and followers to share his uncomplicated life and religion, which he described as "living in truth." He commissioned artists to portray himself, Nefertiti, and their six daughters being blessed by the sun's rays and making offerings of flowers, and he insisted that the artists portray them as they really were, not in the stylized manner of previous times.

This bust of Nefertiti, Akhenaton's beautiful queen, is one of the best known works of Egyptian art.

While Akhenaton was busy introducing his new ideas, the political and business affairs of the empire were neglected. A library of tablets found at Tell el-Amarna includes a number of urgent messages to Akhenaton from his generals and vassals, all urging him to take one action or another. Very few of these messages were acted upon.

Return to Thebes. When Akhenaton died, his 10-year-old son-in-law, Tutankhaton, became pharaoh. Although Tutankhaton had been brought up in the Aton religion, pressure from the priests of Amun forced him to abandon these beliefs. He moved to Thebes and reinstated the worship of Amun-Re and other gods. He then changed his name from *Tut-ankh-aton* (meaning "living image of Aton") to *Tut-ankh-amun* (meaning "living image of Amun"). The real powers behind the throne during Tutankhamun's reign were his vizier and his chief general, whose names were Horenheb and Ay.

Tutankhamun, popularly known as "King Tut" since 1922, was not an important pharaoh in the history of Egypt: he died at the age of about 19, before he could make his character known. But he became world famous when his undisturbed tomb was discovered by Howard Carter, a British explorer, in the Valley of the Kings and Queens.

After many months of searching, Carter happened to discover the buried entrance to the tomb of King Tut. After forcing his way in, Carter found four successive burial chambers filled with priceless objects of gold, alabaster, lapis lazuli, and other precious materials. This discovery led to a great popular and scientific interest in Egyptology. During the late 1970s, Egypt exhibited 50 pieces from the tomb in museums around the world.

Tutankhamun was succeeded as pharaoh by his vizier, Ay, and then by his general, Horenheb. Both of these rulers justified their reigns by marrying into the family of the 18th dynasty. Despite Horenheb's military background, Egypt's campaigns in Syria-Palestine did not resume until the accession of the 19th dynasty.

The 19th Dynasty. The 19th dynasty was founded by Ramses I, a long-time military colleague of Horenheb. Ramses' reign was fairly uneventful, and was overshadowed by that of his grandson, Ramses II. During his 67 years as pharaoh, Ramses II established himself as the most important ruler of this dynasty.

Unlike his predecessor Thutmose III, who left an accurate and matter-of-fact account of his achievements, Ramses II tended to embroider his military feats. He also inscribed his name on many monuments that had been built by earlier pharaohs. Because of these embellishments, early scholars, seeing Ramses' name everywhere, referred to him as "Ramses the Great." When later scholars succeeded in distinguishing Ramses' real achievements from the false ones, they found that he nevertheless still deserved his original nickname.

When Ramses II came to the throne in 1304 B.C., the growing Hittite empire in northern Syria posed a possible threat to Egypt's interests. In the fifth year of his reign, Ramses decided to challenge the Hittite kingdom in Syria. He led his army northward as far as the Orontes River and approached the town of Kadesh. Reportedly, Hittite spies then infiltrated the army and spread the false information that the Hittite troops were far to the north. Ramses was not prepared for battle when the Hittite troops made a surprise attack, and the Egyptians were driven out of the area. Nevertheless, Ramses had inscriptions carved in the temples of Egypt stating that he had defeated the Hittites.

Sixteen years after the battle at Kadesh, Ramses again led his army through Palestine and Syria, with the intention of confronting the Hittites. This time, the Hittite king was preoccupied with other problems, so he negotiated a treaty with the Egyptians. This treaty has been called the first nonaggression treaty in history. In it, the two kings agree not to make any further attacks upon each other, and to come to each other's aid if attacked by a third party. The northern part of Syria was allocated to the Hittites, and the southern part, with Palestine, was allocated to the Egyptians.

The treaty with the Hittites meant that the Egyptians no longer had to mount frequent military campaigns in order to protect their interests in Syria-Palestine. Ramses was now free to embark on one of the most massive building programs in Egypt's history.

Ramses II made Thebes the first monumental capital city of history. The already large temples at Luxor and Karnak were further enlarged to reflect the vast wealth of the pharaoh. The temple of Amun-Re, at Karnak, grew to be 1200 feet in length, and a sacred lake was built adjacent to it to supply holy water for religious rituals. A *hypostyle* hall (meaning "resting on pillars") was built as part of this temple. The walls and columns were inscribed with hieroglyphics glorifying the pharaoh and his accomplishments, and clerestory windows permitted light to penetrate throughout the hall so that these inscriptions could be read.

In addition to expanding the temples at Karnak and Luxor, Ramses II built a magnificent mortuary temple for himself on the west bank of the Nile opposite Thebes, a temple to Ptah at Memphis, and a gigantic temple at Abu Simbel in Nubia.

In this scene from a mural painting, Ramses II is shown leading his troops to battle. He devoted the first years of his reign to military conquest and the last 45 years to large-scale building projects.

The temple of Amun-Re at Karnak, built by Seti I and his son Ramses II, contains a hippo-style hall. Columns are almost 43 feet tall.

One of the four colossal statues of Ramses II that once guarded his temple at Abu Simbel. The temple now lies under Lake Nasser.

The temple at Abu Simbel was built by removing an estimated 365,000 tons of rock from the cliff. It was oriented in such a way that on two mornings each year, about 30 days before the spring equinox and 30 days after the autumnal equinox, the sun's rays would penetrate 200 feet into the temple to illuminate the interior statues. When construction was begun on the Aswan High Dam in 1964, it was known that this temple would be flooded by the reservoir. The United Nations then sponsored a project to carve the original temple out of the cliff and re-erect the excavated blocks of stone above the highest level of the reservoir. Visitors to the site today can see the outline of the temple as Ramses II created it, but about 200 feet above the site Ramses selected, while deep-water divers today can find a huge cave where the temple existed for more than 3000 years.

The 20th Dynasty. When Ramses III ascended the throne of Egypt, around 1198 B.C., the nation was confronted by a new and formidable enemy called the Sea Peoples. These mysterious people, probably of Indo-European stock, had plundered the Hittite king-

dom and were attempting to find homes along the southeastern coastline of the Mediterranean Sea, from Syria through the Egyptian delta. Ramses III proved to be a very competent military commander, and succeeded in driving the Sea Peoples away from the area after fighting two great battles. These victories were commemorated in an Egyptian temple inscription:

● ● ● *Now the northern countries [people] which were in their islands were quivering in their bodies. They penetrated the channels of the river mouths [the Nile delta]. They struggle for breath, their nostrils cease. His majesty is gone out like a whirlwind against them fighting on the battlefield like a runner, the dread of him and the terror have entered their bodies, they are capsized and overwhelmed where they are. Their heart is taken away and their soul is flown away, their weapons are scattered upon the sea. His arrow pierces whom he wishes, and the fugitive is a drowned man.*[5]

Unfortunately, Ramses' defensive battles against the Sea Peoples did not enrich his people, as earlier campaigns had done. During his rule, the royal treasury became impoverished, and the common people began to express dissatisfaction with their lot. On several occasions, the workers in the royal necropolis were not paid their rations of food on time. As a result, they refused to go to work, and thus carried out the first recorded labor strike in history.

The Final Years. After the brilliance of the 18th and 19th dynasties, Egyptian civilization suffered a period of decline. Nubian and Libyan mercenaries of the army settled in the Delta under the weak successors to Ramses III. A group of powerful priests gained dominance over the pharaohs and passed regulations which exempted all temples from taxation. The enormous cost of operating the temples, which employed two percent of the population and controlled 15 percent of the arable land, ruined the economy.

The conservatism of Egypt's **theocracy** discouraged the development of new ideas, such as the use of iron in place of bronze for tools and weapons. Thus, the Egyptians were surpassed in technology by other powers of the Middle East, and their attempts to undermine the Assyrian and Babylonian empires in Syria-Palestine were unsuccessful. In 525 B.C., Egypt was conquered by the Persians; in 322 B.C. by the Greeks and Macedonians; and in 30 B.C. by the Romans. When Queen Cleopatra committed suicide to avoid surrendering with Anthony's Romans in 30 B.C., Egypt ceased to be an influence in the Western world.

WRITING Even before the beginning of the Old Kingdom period, the Egyptians had developed a system of writing. Like the Mesopotamians, the Egyptians began by creating a group of *ideograms*, small pictures that represented various ideas and objects. These pictographs were often straightforward drawings of the objects or ideas they represented, but sometimes a well-known legend could be used as the basis for devising them. The following passage explains how a legend was used to create symbols for fractions:

The wicked god Seth plucked out the eye of Horus and tore it into bits. But the wise god Thoth stuck it back together again —as if it were just a cracked grain of barley. And so each part of the eye became a hieroglyphic sign for a fraction used in measuring out bushels of grain: ⟨ *for ½; ○ for ¼;* ⌒ *for ⅛;* ▷ *for 1/16; ⟨ for 1/64. When the fraction symbols are put together, the marvelously restored "sound eye" looks like a composite of the symbols shown in this paragraph.*[6]

One of the disadvantages of the pictograph system is that the reader sometimes cannot tell exactly which word the writer had in mind, since some words have many synonyms. (For example, a hieroglyph might be devised for the concept of "area," but it would not be certain whether the writer meant to say "space," "distance," or "region.") To overcome this problem, symbols called *phonograms* were developed to indicate syllables or individual sounds. Since some phonograms were also ideograms, scribes indicated which meaning they intended by using a *determinative* symbol.

Even though the Egyptians very early developed an abbreviated, cursive script which could be written much more quickly than the pictorial symbols, they continued to use

---

[5]M. K. Sandars, *The Sea Peoples* (London: Thomas and Hudson, 1978), p. 124.

[6]*Ancient Egypt: Discovering Its Splendors*, ed. Jules B. Billard (Washington: The National Geographic Society, 1978), p. 155.

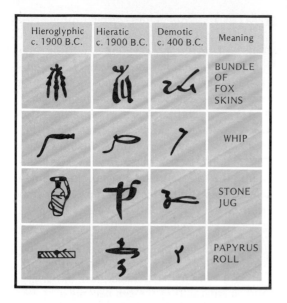

Hieroglyphic c. 1900 B.C.	Hieratic c. 1900 B.C.	Demotic c. 400 B.C.	Meaning
			BUNDLE OF FOX SKINS
			WHIP
			STONE JUG
			PAPYRUS ROLL

the original symbols for most of their formal writings. The old pictorial symbols were used for official inscriptions such as those carved on stelae or on temple walls. The cursive script, called *hieratic*, was used for less formal writings such as temple accounts, recipes, and poems. Around 700 B.C., an even more abbreviated script called *demotic* was developed. This was a type of shorthand and was often used by busy merchants and traders. Although the Phoenicians developed an alphabet around 1000 B.C., the Egyptians never adopted this more convenient system.

Many of the hieroglyphic inscriptions were chiseled on hard surfaces such as slate, granite, or limestone. However, the scribes also had the option of using paint brushes or sharpened reeds as writing implements, for the invention of papyrus paper occurred at least by 3000 B.C.[7]

When the Greeks first encountered the Egyptians' pictographs, they called them

"sacred writings" (*hieroglyphics*), because they assumed the inscriptions had a religious purpose. Many of the hieroglyphics did in fact communicate messages to the gods or describe religious ceremonies, and the scribal schools were sponsored by the temples. However, an accomplished scribe in ancient Egypt might find a variety of careers open to him aside from the priesthood. Because of the pictorial nature of the Egyptian writing system, many scribes went on to become artists after mastering the approximately 700 hieroglyphic characters. Others became accountants, writers, and poets. And during the period of the New Kingdom, as literacy became increasingly important in government, scribes had the additional option of entering the pharaoh's civil service.

For many centuries, the writings of the ancient Egyptians were a complete mystery and a subject of much conjecture. Then, in 1798, Napoleon invaded Egypt, bringing with him a number of scholars who were interested in Egypt's history. When one of Napoleon's engineers discovered a large, flat slab of basalt with three sets of inscriptions, the French scholars recognized its importance. The slab, which came to be known as the Rosetta stone, contained Greek, hieroglyphic, and demotic translations of the same message. When the finding became known, a number of scholars throughout the world set to work to decipher the hieroglyphics.

A British scholar, Thomas Young, realized that some hieroglyphics represent individual sounds, much like alphabet letters. Soon afterwards, a French scholar, Jean-François Champollion, decided that the *cartouches* (oval outlines) he had seen in many inscriptions contained the names of Egyptian rulers. Champollion deciphered the hieroglyphics in several cartouches, and then used the Greek letters on the Rosetta stone to enlarge his vocabulary of hieroglyphics. In 1828, he announced that he had deciphered the entire message of the Rosetta stone. The message proved to be a proclamation

---

[7]One of the oldest known papyrus documents dates to the Old Kingdom period, around 2500 B.C. It is a temple accounting, written in hieratic script. A blank role of papyrus from a tomb dated 3000 B.C. has also been found.

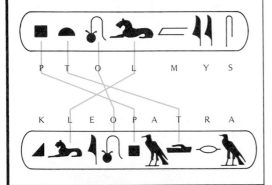

Jean-François Champollion realized that the cartouches he saw on obelisks and in tombs contained the names of rulers, and deciphered these letters.

P T O L M Y S

K L E O P A T R A

After deciphering several hieroglyphic signs through his work with cartouches, Champollion proceeded to translate the message of the Rosetta stone.

THE ROSETTA STONE

issued by Ptolemy V in 196 B.C., and with the basic vocabulary of signs that Champollion had deciphered, scholars were able to deduce the meanings of many more hiero-glyphics. Eventually they could read almost all of the innumerable symbols on the walls of ancient monuments.

SCIENCE One of the most surprising achievements of the ancient Egyptians was their discovery that the solar year has 365 days. Whereas the Mesopotamians and other ancient peoples based their calendars on the moon's cycle, the Egyptians had discovered the solar cycle as early as 4000 B.C. They accomplished this feat by noting that the highest flood levels of the Nile occurred on the same day that the star Sirius aligned with the rising sun. By counting the days between the annual floodings (and the alignment of Sirius), they realized that the lunar calendar of 28-day months did not correspond to the Nile's year.

The Egyptians' "Nile Year" was divided into twelve 30-day months, with an added 5-day festival period. The Romans later adopted this calendar, and it continued in use for many centuries. (Later, the need to add a quarter day each year—a "leap year" every four years—was recognized.)

By 3000 B.C., the Egyptians had learned to make papyrus paper by crosshatching the fibers of the plant, then pressing them together to allow the natural gums to bond the materials. The invention of paper undoubtedly encouraged the communication of ideas and the growth of literature and other arts.

One of the most famous papyrus scrolls is the so-called Edwin Smith papyrus, named after the person who once owned it. Although many other manuscripts illustrate the Egyptians' interest in surgery and medicine, the Edwin Smith work is unique in its methods and exposition. Rather than just describing a "cure" for each disease discussed, the papyrus sets forth a detailed description of 48 cases of clinical surgery. It describes how to make a diagnosis in each case, and what course of treatment to follow. In a case of severe head injury, for instance, the physician is instructed to pick out the fragments

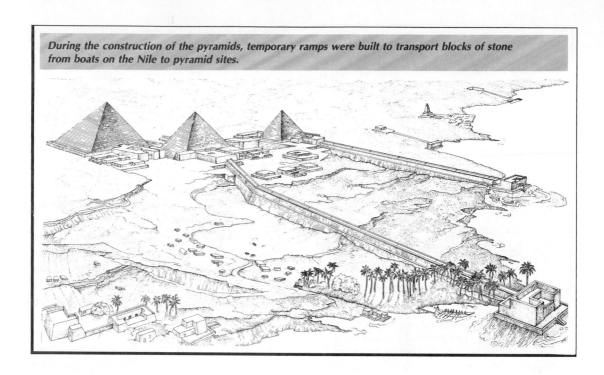

During the construction of the pyramids, temporary ramps were built to transport blocks of stone from boats on the Nile to pyramid sites.

of bone, feel the pulse, move the legs to check for paralysis, and watch for irregular movements in the face. The scholar J. H. Breasted believed that this papyrus was the work of Imhotep, the Old Kingdom vizier who built the first pyramid.

For many years, travelers and scholars speculated about the construction methods used to build the pyramids. Egyptologists now believe that the pyramids of the Old Kingdom were built by free peasants, paid by the pharaoh, and that most of the work was carried out during the months of the Nile's inundation—when the land was under water and could not be farmed. Large sledges were used to slide the gigantic blocks of stone over the wet ground to the site of a pyramid. To move the heavy blocks in a vertical direction, the Egyptian workers utilized a system of ramps and balanced levers. Of course, the construction of a pyramid also required careful measuring and an application of geometrical principles. The Egyptians had developed much knowledge in these areas through their measuring of the annual flood levels and surveying of property lines.

SUMMARY

Egypt is truly a marvelously mysterious land and culture. It has the world's longest continuous record of civilization, one that has been thoroughly researched by a great variety of scholars, and yet there are still many things we do not know about it.

Because the Egyptians' form of government was founded on their religious beliefs, the nation had a sense of purpose and a rare unanimity of opinion. Under a pharaoh who was just and capable, the people could achieve a high standard of living and enjoyed a sense of stability and continuity. However, the same system could lead to disaster if a pharaoh used his power for selfish purposes, or was too weak or indecisive to administer the nation effectively.

The Egyptians' art and culture exerted a fascination over many later peoples, and their concept of a life after death became very influential in the development of other civilizations.

While recent leaders of Egypt have worked hard to modernize life in this ancient land, Egyptians today practice some of the same ways of life that were developed during the 3000 years we have been discussing in this chapter.

QUESTIONS

1 Discuss the influence of geography and climate on the culture and history of Egypt.
2 Create pictographs to express several words or concepts.
3 Debate the issue: the need to control floods and to allocate irrigation waters to farmers led to the formation of centralized government in Egypt.
4 Look at some examples of Egyptian art. What are some of the principal artistic conventions? How do you explain the fact that Egyptian art changed so little over the centuries?
5 Most archaeological discoveries in Egypt and Mesopotamia reveal the way of life of the upper classes. Why? What should archaeologists look for in order to help us understand how the common people lived?
6 What did the Egyptians believe about their gods and their pharaoh? What changes did Akhenaton attempt to make? Why was his "revolution" a failure?

BIBLIOGRAPHY

Which books might tell when the tombs at Thebes were looted?

CASSON, LIONEL. *Ancient Egypt.* New York: Time, Inc., 1985. *A comprehensive, readable discussion of the ancient Egyptians by an eminent Egyptologist; includes a chronological chart of Egyptian technological developments and other events of interest to scholars; beautifully illustrated with color maps and photos.*

MERTZ, BARBARA. *Temples, Tombs, and Hieroglyphs: the Story of Egyptology.* New York: Coward-McCann, 1964. *Straightforward history of Egypt, from predynastic times to the New Kingdom; includes many inferences concerning the intellectual and cultural life of the Egyptians, based upon their inscriptions and artifacts.*

RUFFLE, JOHN. *The Egyptians: An Introduction to Egyptian Archaeology.* Cornell University Press, 1977. *A review of archaeological findings and what they reveal about the Egyptians' accomplishments in science, art, and writing.*

3

If we trace the Indo-European language back far enough, we arrive hypothetically (at any rate according to some authorities) at the stage where language consisted only of roots out of which subsequent words have grown. . . . The association of words with their meanings must have grown up by some natural process, though at present the nature of the process is unknown.

BERTRAND RUSSELL

The Arrival of the Indo-Europeans

About 2500 B.C., waves of migrating tribes swept into the known centers of civilization in the Middle East. One group, the *Semites*, moved northward from the desert peninsula of Arabia and settled in the Fertile Crescent. Their descendants became the Babylonians, whom we studied in Chapter 1, and the Phoenicians, Arameans, and Hebrews, whom we shall study in Chapter 4. Another group moved southward from the **steppe** lands, or grassy plains, which lie between the Danube and Volga rivers, to the north of the Black and Caspian seas. Because the descendants of these latter people eventually settled in many places over the vast area stretching from India to Europe, scholars have named them *Indo-Europeans.*

The Indo-Europeans were probably forced to migrate from their homelands with their flocks and herds because of famine, climatic changes, or pressure from other tribes. In their search for pasture lands, these tribes roamed far and wide, and tended to lose contact with each other. Some of them eventually settled in western Europe, where their descendants became known as the Celts. Others moved into Italy, the Aegean area, and Anatolia (modern Turkey), where their descendants became known, respectively, as the Italic tribes, the Greeks, and the Hittites. The Indo-Europeans who settled farthest to the east split into two groups: one group entered northwestern India and destroyed several cities of the Indus River Valley about 1500 B.C. The other settled in Persia and gave their tribal name (Aryan) to the area now known as Iran.

The term *Indo-European* is also used to designate the family of languages derived from the original language of these migrants. The intruders interacted with so many different native peoples that each migrant tribe eventually developed individual cultural and linguistic characteristics. The most remarkable aspect of this interaction was the fact that the migrating people retained so many words of their original language. Linguists have found many similar words in Sanskrit (the language of ancient India), Greek, Latin, German, and English.

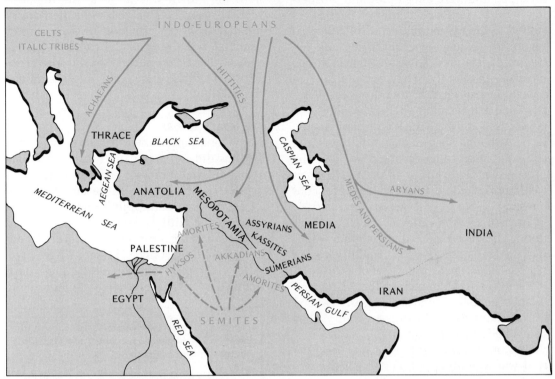

Greek	Latin	English	German	Sanskrit
treis	tres	three	drei	trayas
	vidua	widow	witwe	
		assemble	samm-eln	sam-adhi
bous	bos	bovid (cow)		
meli	mel	mellifluous	mil	
mater	mater	mother	mutter	matar

By studying the various Indo-European languages, linguists have been able to reconstruct, to some extent, the way of life of the people who spoke the original Indo-European language. The fact that no common root for *sea* or *ocean* has been found suggests that they may have lived far from large bodies of water. Because they had several words for *snow* and *ice*, they probably lived in a cold climate. They domesticated cattle, sheep, and horses, and probably stayed in one place long enough to plant and harvest wheat and barley. They worked with copper and bronze, and they were organized in a **patriarchal** society; that is, one ruled by men.

THE HITTITES The earliest known group of Indo-Europeans to migrate into Asia Minor arrived in Anatolia about 2500 B.C., and became the ancestors of the Hittites. These people established the third oldest civilization in the western regions of

Asia. While the civilizations of Egypt and of Mesopotamia were developing and prospering in broad, fertile river valleys, the Hittites settled in the rugged highlands of Anatolia, where the climate was difficult, with extremes of heat and cold, and fierce storms occurred frequently. They learned how to utilize the metals they found in the mountains and to farm in the sheltered valleys that are scattered through the high Anatolian plateau. Although they managed to develop a self-sufficient, well-organized society, the prosperous civilizations to the south eventually presented an attractive target for conquest.

In 2000 B.C., the valley of the Halys River (today known as the Kizil) and the surrounding highlands were settled by a little-known people called the Khatti. By about 1900 B.C., the Hittites had conquered the Khatti and established their capital at Hattusas, in a bend of the Halys River. Within a century, they controlled most of Anatolia.

The most powerful king of this early period was Mursilis I, who established a federation of 10 great city-states, each owing allegiance to him as the Great King. Around 1595 B.C., he led his army through the passes of the Taurus Mountains and conquered northern Syria. He then continued down the Euphrates River valley, captured Babylon, and, together with the Kassites from the mountains of western Persia, overthrew the kingdom that Hammurabi had built. After completing these conquests, he was called home to deal with a domestic crisis. Soon after his return to Hattusas, he was murdered as the result of a palace conspiracy.

At the royal court of the Hittites, the conspiracies and blood feuds that had led to Mursilis' death continued for almost a century, and the country fell into a state of anarchy. Finally, in about 1525 B.C., a noble named Telipinus seized the throne. He consolidated his authority by killing his rivals and married a princess of the royal family. He then published new, precise rules for the succession to the throne: if a king had no heir, the crown was to go to the noble of highest rank. This noble would then marry a daughter of the previous king in order to establish continuity of the royal line. Telipinus' rules accomplished the purpose of ensuring a fairly uneventful succession for several centuries.

THE HITTITE EMPIRE

For a long period after Telipinus' rule, the Hittites did not make any notable attempts to extend their borders. Then, in 1380 B.C., a period known as the Hittite empire began under the reign of Suppiluliumas. This Great King of the Hittites ruled for 40 years and proved to be the most capable military leader in the Middle East since Thutmose III of Egypt. After his military conquests had been achieved, Suppiluliumas took the trouble to

The Hittites built their chariots large enough to hold two or three men for added advantage in hand-to-hand combat.

Hittite warriors were renowned for their skill in battle. They carried iron-tipped lances, as shown here, swords, and battle axes.

set up a permanent administration for the new territories, and so was able to consolidate his rule over them.

By the 14th century B.C., the Hittites, like the Egyptians and the Mitanni, had adopted a new chariot design. The new chariot was lighter and faster than the old models, since it had two spoked wheels rather than four solid-wood wheels. The Hittites had also made another improvement: their chariots were built to hold three men, while the Egyptian chariots held only two. The extra man in the Hittite chariots provided a definite advantage in hand-to-hand combat, and the Hittite charioteers were renowned for their skill and discipline.

While Egypt was preoccupied with the religious revolution of Akhenaton, Suppiluliumas gradually brought his army south. In 1375 B.C., he crossed the Euphrates River and fought a battle with the Egyptian loyalists at Kadesh on the Orontes River. Due to this successful show of force, almost all of Syria fell to the Hittites. Suppiluliumas appointed two of his sons to govern the conquered territory, and he himself returned to Anatolia.

Late in Suppiluliumas' reign, an incident occurred which illustrated the new international status he had achieved through his conquests. The young widow of Tutankhamun, the late pharaoh of Egypt, sent him a letter requesting that he send one of his sons to Egypt to marry her and become pharaoh. Suppiluliumas sent one of his sons, but the young man was murdered as soon as he entered the country, perhaps at the order of the Egyptian general Horemheb, who shortly afterward seized the throne. (Suppiluliumas was not able to avenge this murder, for he died shortly afterwards.)

Under the rule of Suppiluliumas' successors, the Hittite empire was not seriously threatened. Although the towns of Syria occasionally revolted, the appearance of the Hittite charioteers was sufficient to restore order. Then, with the accession of Seti I and his son Ramses II of Egypt, the Egyptians once again became interested in regaining their former territory.

The Egyptians and the Hittites fought at Kadesh in 1300 B.C. While both sides claimed victory, only the personal courage and skill of Ramses prevented a disastrous defeat for the Egyptians. The battle at Kadesh was the first military engagement of which we have a detailed contemporary account, thanks to Ramses' commemoration of it on a temple wall in Egypt.

Sixteen years later, Ramses realized that he could not dislodge the Hittites from Syria. At the same time, Hattusilis III, the Hittite king, was fearful of the growing power of the Assyrians and did not want to waste his resources in fighting the Egyptians. The two rulers agreed to a treaty of peace. This treaty survives in two fragmentary copies; one on a silver tablet in the temple of Ramses at Thebes, and the other on a clay tablet which was found at Hattusas, the Hittite capital.

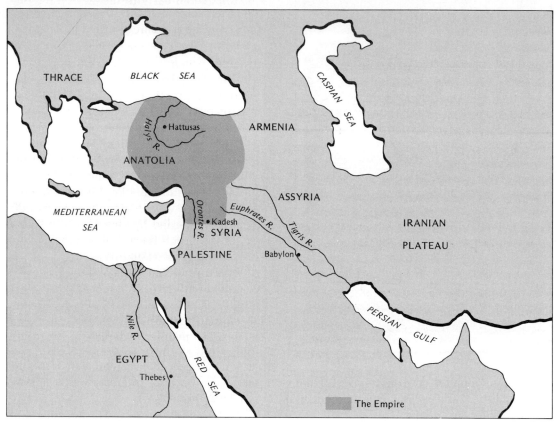

THRACE

BLACK SEA

CASPIAN SEA

Halys R.

• Hattusas

ARMENIA

ANATOLIA

MEDITERRANEAN SEA

Orontes R.

Euphrates R.

ASSYRIA

• Kadesh
SYRIA

Tigris R.

IRANIAN

PLATEAU

PALESTINE

Babylon •

Nile R.

EGYPT

RED SEA

PERSIAN GULF

Thebes •

The Empire

The following quotation has been translated from the Egyptian version, in which the Hittites were referred to as the *Kheta*.

• • • *There shall be no hostilities between them, forever. The great chief of the Kheta shall not pass over into the land of Egypt, forever, to take anything therefrom. Ramses-Meriamon, the great ruler of Egypt, shall not pass over into the land (of Kheta, to take anything) therefrom, forever. . . .*

If another enemy come against the land of Ramses II, the great ruler of Egypt, and he shall send to the great chief of Kheta, saying: "Come with me as a reinforcement against him," the great chief of Kheta shall come, and the great chief of Kheta shall slay his enemy. But if it is not to be the desire of the great chief of Kheta to come, he shall send

his infantry and his chariotry, and shall slay the enemy.

Or if Ramses, the great ruler of Egypt, be provoked against his delinquent subjects, when they have committed some other fault against him, and he come to slay them, then the great chief of Kheta shall act with the lord of Egypt.[1]

In the two versions, each king claimed to have yielded to a plea for peace from the other. The two kings swore an oath to maintain the peace, to provide mutual assistance in time of danger, and to exchange fugitives. Although there had been earlier treaties among the nations of the ancient world, this

[1]J. H. Breasted, *Ancient Records of Egypt*, Vol. 3 (Chicago: University of Chicago Press, 1906), p. 45.

treaty has been called the first *nonaggression* treaty in recorded history. The agreement between the two kings was strengthened by Ramses' marriage to a Hittite princess 13 years later.

Around 1200 B.C., the Hittites, like the other civilizations of the Middle East, were confronted by a mass migration of peoples from the west and north. At the same time that Egypt was threatened by the Sea Peoples, the Hittites were overwhelmed by tribes known as the Phrygians. Unlike the Egyptians, the Hittites did not succeed in driving off the invaders. The Hittite civilization was completely supplanted by that of the Phrygians. Except for a few Biblical references to a group of Hittites who had settled in Palestine,[2] there

---

[2]One notable Biblical mention is the account of how King David sent *Uriah the Hittite* into the front lines of battle so that he could marry Uriah's beautiful wife, Bathsheeba (2 Samuel 11). Another mention occurs in Genesis 23:10, where it is related that Abraham purchased a burial place for his wife from *Ephron the Hittite*.

was no historical record of them until a site was uncovered early in the 20th century.

ARCHAEOLOGICAL FINDINGS

In 1906-7, the German archaeologist Hugo Winckler began to excavate the site of Hattusas (modern Boghazköi in Turkey). He uncovered impressive sculptures and the remains of a massive fortress. This city was built about 1650 B.C., and surrounded by stone walls almost 25 feet thick. The walls were pierced every 100 feet by double-towered gates, the best known of which is strikingly similar to the famous *Lion Gate* at Mycenae in Greece. The entrance to the palace of the kings was guarded by stone lions. On each side of the porch there was a square tower, so archaeologists called this palace the *House of Two Towers*. The walls of the palace were decorated with large slabs of stone carved in relief. In these reliefs, the chiefs and priests are shown participating in religious ceremonies. The people are depicted as short and heavily built, with prominent cheekbones,

The Hittites fortified their capital city of Hattusas with a 4-mile-long stone wall. The lions at this gate were carved from massive blocks of stone.

sloping foreheads, and recessed chins. Soldiers are armed with swords, spears, and bows. Women are wearing long veils.

LANGUAGE

At Hattusas, archaeologists found thousands of clay tablets inscribed with hieroglyphic symbols. They deduced that the Hittites had developed their own system of hieroglyphics to write their language, and later adopted the Egyptians' practice of decorating their buildings with inscriptions. In 1915, Bedrich Hrozný, a Czechoslovakian linguist, was studying a Hittite writing when he suddenly:

. . . *took a deep breath and, conscious of the boldness of his own thesis, dared to think: "If I am right about the interpretation of this line, there is going to be a scientific storm." But the sentence he was reading seemed clear and unambiguous. He had only one choice: to say what it was he saw—even if it overturned the views of all specialists in ancient history.*

The text which led Hrozný to this resolve was the sentence: nu ninda-an ezzatteni vâdor-ma ekutteni.

In this sentence there was only a single known word: ninda. *It could be deduced from the Sumerian ideogram that this word meant "bread."*

Hrozný said to himself: "A sentence in which the word bread is used may very well (though it need not necessarily, of course) contain the word eat." Since at this point the indications that Hittite might be an Indo-European language were already becoming overwhelming, he drew up a list of various Indo-European words for "eat." Was it possible that he was dealing here with a Hittite cognate? English "eat" was in Latin edo, *in Old High German.... As soon as Hrozný wrote down the Old High German word he knew that he was on the right track.* Ezzan *certainly bore a strong resemblance to the Hittite* ezzatteni.[3]

---

[3]Kurt W. Marek, *The Secret of the Hittites*, trans. by Richard and Clara Winston (New York: Knopf, 1958), pp. 82-3.

After much further study, Hrozný concluded that the Hittite language was of Indo-European origin. He supported this conclusion by pointing out that many suffixes of nouns and verbs, as well as many root words, were similar to those of other languages of Indo-European origin. While much progress has been made in understanding the Hittite writings, several major problems remain. A few scholars have refused to accept Hrozný's theory at all, because they cannot believe that any Indo-European language could have been written in cuneiform.

GOVERNMENT

The Hittites had a form of feudal society, much like the Assyrian society as it evolved. A group of nobles held important offices and large tracts of land, and in return for these benefits, they supplied the king with weapons, soldiers, and chariots for his campaigns. In the early period of the Hittite settlements in Anatolia, the Hittite nobles assembled to hear and pass judgments on legal cases, and possibly also elected the king. However, after Telipinus' rules of succession were published, around 1525 B.C., the assembly of nobles lost much of its importance in national affairs. After this period, the king of the Hittites gained supreme authority, comparable to that of the Mesopotamian and Egyptian monarchs. In fact, the Hittite kings were often referred to as "the Sun," and were believed to have a special relationship with the gods.

The wives and mothers of Hittite kings had more authority than did the women of other royal families in the ancient Middle East. They frequently participated in affairs of state and sometimes cosigned the official documents of the king.

THE LEGAL SYSTEM

Clay tablets found at Hattusas reveal that the Hittites had a well-developed legal system. Capital punishment was seldom used, and most criminals were called upon to compensate their victims for the damages they had caused by paying a fine. In contrast to the "eye for an eye" philosophy of Hammurabi's code, the Hittites' code emphasized compensation to the victims of a crime, and recognized the difference between accidental injuries and those that were committed purposefully.

THE ECONOMY

Because of the cold winters in the Anatolian steppe lands, the Hittites were not able to harvest two or three crops per year, as the Egyptians and Mesopotamians did. However, they were able to grow good crops of barley and wheat in their fertile river valleys, and they cultivated grapes on the hillsides. Agriculture was the mainstay of their economy.

Another primary source of wealth for the Hittites was iron. Their lands contained the only extensive source of iron ore in the Middle East, and they were the first people to learn to extract iron from this ore. Earlier peoples had learned that copper and tin were both rather soft and melted at relatively low temperatures. They had also discovered that when the melts were mixed, they produced the much harder and stronger material called bronze. The Hittites learned that they could extract metal from iron ore by creating a still hotter fire and by mixing limestone with the ore. When the liquid iron was poured into molds, it produced a relatively weak material which we call *cast iron*. The Hittites discovered that they could reheat this iron, beat it, and then cool it, producing a much more useful material, which we call *wrought iron*. The Hittites jealously guarded the secrets of working with iron, and once suggested to an Egyptian pharaoh that he could purchase iron from them for an equal weight of gold.

RELIGION

The gods of the Hittites were *anthropomorphic* in character, and were believed to have the same needs and shortcomings as human beings. Priests gave them daily offerings of food and clothing, and were not surprised if the gods did not respond to their prayers. The most important deity of the Hittites was Teshub, the god of weather. He was often shown with a thunderbolt in one hand and an axe in the other, with a bull close behind him. The concept of a sun god was adopted from the Egyptians, but this god never became a real part of the Hittites' pantheon. Rather, a Hittite sun goddess was assigned the role of Teshub's wife. Another important deity was Ishtar, the goddess of fertility, who was adopted from the Babylonians.

Teshub, the weather god, was the most important deity in the Hittites' pantheon. In this relief, he holds a 3-pronged bolt of lightning and a battle ax. Above him is the solar disk, an Egyptian symbol of divinity.

The shrines of the Hittites' gods were located in the small towns throughout Anatolia. One of the main duties of the king was to visit each small town during festival times and serve as chief priest for the special services.

The Hittites probably introduced the worship of Ishtar to the Lydians, who developed an important civilization in Asia Minor during the 8th century B.C. The Lydians, in turn, introduced Ishtar to the Greeks, who renamed her *Cybele*, meaning the Great Mother. The Hittites used the Egyptian art forms of the winged sun disk, relief sculpture, and hieroglyphics to decorate their buildings, and passed these practices on to the Lydians. The Lydians, in turn, had great influence on the Greeks.

THE PERSIANS The descendants of the Aryans who settled on the Plateau of Iran came to be called the Medes and the Persians. These two tribes were first mentioned in the 9th century B.C. in the tribute lists of the Assyrian royal court. When Assyrian power began to disintegrate, the Medes, who were great warriors, were able to form a strong kingdom in northern Iran, with their capital at Ecbatana. They gradually extended their control over the Persians who lived in the southern part of Iran. In 612 B.C., the Medes, in alliance with the Babylonians, captured Nineveh and brought an end to the Assyrian empire.

The Persians originally migrated to the southwestern edge of the Iranian Plateau. This plateau, which extends from the eastern portion of Mesopotamia in the west to the Indus River valley in the east, and from the Caspian Sea in the north to the Arabian Sea in the south, is a high, bowl-shaped desert surrounded by mountain ranges. Although much of Iran is barren today, in ancient times herds could be pastured on the hillsides and bountiful crops of wheat, barley, grapes, and figs were grown in the valleys. The lower slopes of the mountains were then covered with for-

ests, and the land yielded such valuable minerals as iron, lead, turquoise, and lapis lazuli.

CYRUS THE GREAT

Cyrus II, known as Cyrus the Great, was the first important ruler of the *Achaemenid* dynasty, so called because the line was founded by a leader named Achaemenes.

In 559 B.C., Cyrus began to rule the Persians as a vassal of the Median empire. Although he married a daughter of the Median king, he soon began to organize a rebel coalition of Persians and other tribes, and eventually challenged the Medes in battle. By 550 B.C., the Median empire had fallen under the control of Cyrus and the Persians.

The sudden change of government between the Medes and Persians was a cause of concern for other countries in the area. Because Cyrus and the Babylonians were on friendly terms, Croesus, the fabulously wealthy king of Lydia, began to fear that he might be the next target of the new Persian empire-builder. Croesus consulted the oracle at Delphi, in Greece, for advice as to whether he should lead his army against Cyrus. According to Herodotus, the oracle told Croesus that if he attacked the Persians he would destroy a great empire. Croesus believed that this message supported his in-

Cyrus the Great was buried in a simple tomb at Pasargadae.

tentions, so he gathered his army for an attack. But in 546 B.C., Cyrus made a surprise move into Lydia, defeated Croesus, and captured Sardis, the capital city. Cyrus then annexed the Greek city-states of Ionia along the shores of the Aegean Sea.

In 540 B.C., Cyrus took advantage of an unpopular monarchy in Babylon to assert his presence there. The priests of Marduk (the Babylonian god of justice) and the captive Jews of Babylon were among the groups who welcomed his intervention. With hardly a struggle, Cyrus was recognized as king of the Babylonians and acquired all of the Chaldean empire, including the former Assyrian colonies of Syria, Phoenicia, and Palestine.

In 530 B.C., Cyrus was killed in battle while fighting Iranian tribes on the eastern boundary of his empire. He was buried at a simple tomb in Pasargadae. Alexander the Great found this tomb when he led his troops through the area 200 years later.

Cyrus had not only been a capable military leader, but he had shown excellent political skills as well. He courted the good will of potential subject peoples, and proved himself a wise and capable ruler once he had completed his conquests. Unlike the Assyrian and Babylonian conquerors, he spared the lives of his conquered enemies, and left their cities intact. He permitted the Jews, who had been enslaved in Babylon for 50 years, to return to Jerusalem and rebuild their temples. In just 20 years, he created a vast empire stretching from the Mediterranean Sea to the steppes of Asia, and from the Black and Caspian seas to the Arabian Sea.

Zoroastrianism. Traditionally, the Persians worshiped a pantheon of nature gods. They made animal sacrifices at altars on mountains and in other open-air sites, and believed that these sacrificial offerings could appease the gods who controlled the wind, sun, fire, and water. A special caste of people called *Magi* officiated at the ceremonies and were believed to have special powers to drive away evil spirits.

Around 600 B.C. or possibly earlier, a prophet named Zoroaster withdrew to a wilderness for a period of meditation, and then returned to society to teach a radically new religion. He denounced the practice of animal sacrifice and the worship of nature gods. Instead, he preached that there are just two forces in the world: the force of truth, goodness, and light, personified by the god Ahuramazda; and the force of evil, deceit, and darkness, personified by the evil god Ahriman. He stressed that each individual had to decide which power to serve, and that this decision would result in happiness or despair in the afterlife. Because the teachings of Zoroaster emphasized righteous *conduct* rather than religious rites or "magic," his theology is known as an *ethical* religion.

For Zoroaster, fire was the symbol of Ahuramazda and signified purification and truth. Thus, his followers built fire altars much as the traditional Magis had done. However, in the new religion, fire was used as a symbol and as a reminder of how people should conduct themselves; not to invoke magic or to show reverence for the forces of nature.

Zoroastrianism was opposed by the Magi and many other traditionalists in Persia, who maintained their old religion and supersti-

Although Zoroastrianism won many converts, the ancient gods of the Magi were not forgotten. One of these ancient gods was Mithras, who created the world by sacrificing a bull. He was still worshiped in Roman times.

tions for several centuries to come. However, the new religion was embraced by the Achaemenid dynasty and had a great impact upon all of the people they ruled. As one historian put it:

• • • *Zoroaster's teachings deeply affected the religious ideas, and tinctured the conduct of the Persians who ruled the civilized world. This fact alone sufficed to bring his ideas to the attention of the medley of peoples within the empire. Zoroastrianism was thus bound to influence other religious traditions, notably Judaism; and through Judaism it has played a far wider role in the world's history than would be suggested by the comparatively modest number of those who through subsequent ages have looked directly to Zoroaster as the founder of their faith.*[4]

Zoroastrianism had an important effect on later Judeo-Christian thinking because of its emphasis of a final judgment, immortality, and Satan.

Centuries later, when the Arabs invaded Iran in the 8th century A.D., many followers of Zoroastrianism took refuge in India, where their descendants came to be known as Parsis. It has been estimated that the Parsis who live today number about 100,000, and most of them reside in and around Bombay.

CAMBYSES

The death of Cyrus prompted civil unrest in Persia, perhaps due to a religious struggle between the Magi and the followers of Zoroaster. After ascending the throne, Cyrus' eldest son, Cambyses, killed his own brother, Smerdis, in order to prevent a possible threat to his rule. He then carried out his father's plan to conquer Egypt, and continued his campaign in Nubia.

In the seventh year of his reign, Cambyses was forced to abandon his military cam-

paigns after receiving news of a revolt in Persia. The revolt was led by a Magi who was impersonating the dead prince, Smerdis, and claiming to be the rightful king. Cambyses departed for Persia, but died enroute. The cause of his death remains a great mystery. Some historians believe that he died accidentally, others that he committed suicide.

DARIUS

By the late 6th century B.C., the support of the army had become critical to the success of any Persian monarch. The elite of the army were the 10,000 Mede and Persian troops, the so-called "Immortals," and thousands of additional troops were levied from the vast areas the Persians had conquered. In 522 B.C., Darius, a distant cousin of Cambyses, won the support of the army and was declared king. Because he had the loyalty of the troops, Darius was able to overcome the false Smerdis and consolidate his own reign within a year.

At the beginning of his reign, Darius took some time to establish administrative and judicial reforms throughout his empire. He divided his territories into 20 *satrapies* (administrative districts), each under the control of a *satrap* (governor) chosen from the royal family or from the nobility. The satrap collected taxes, administered justice, and raised levies for the army. Inspectors, the "eyes and ears" of the king, traveled throughout the realm and reported regularly to the king as to whether or not the satrapies were well-governed and prosperous. Laws were enforced uniformly throughout the empire by royal judges, whose personal conduct was closely watched. As long as the conquered people paid their tribute promptly, they were permitted a large degree of self-government and religious freedom.

Darius also enhanced the unity of his far-flung empire by improving transportation. He ordered that roads be built in order to promote trade throughout the empire and to enable his armies to move quickly in time of

[4]William H. McNeill, *The Rise of the West: A History of the Human Community* (Chicago: University of Chicago Press, 1963), p. 172.

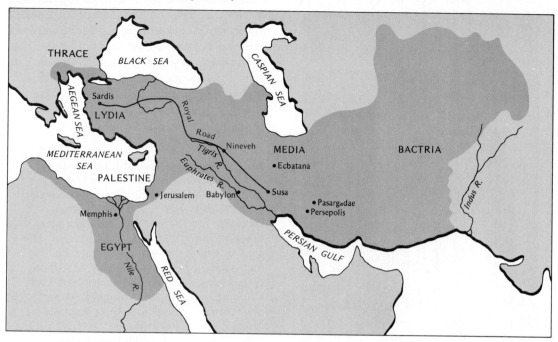

danger. The most famous of these roads was the *Royal Road* from Sardis, in Lydia, to Susa, in Persia, a distance of 1680 miles. Royal messengers, mounting fresh horses at stations spaced 14 miles apart along this road, could cover the distance in seven days, whereas ordinary travelers required almost three months to move the same distance. Military garrisons were stationed at strategic points throughout the empire so that the armies could respond quickly to threats of revolt or invasion.

Like the Sumerians before him, Darius established a standard system of weights and measures, and he issued gold coins (darics) which were accepted as the standard of exchange throughout the empire. He conscripted Greek, Phoenician, and Egyptian ships and sailors to form a navy, and sent an expedition to explore the possibility of a trade route from the mouth of the Indus River, in India, along the coast of the Arabian Sea and Red Sea to northern Egypt.

In 516 B.C., after Darius had consolidated his control over the Middle East, he crossed the Bosporus, the narrow waterway that connects the Black Sea and the Mediterranean and separates Europe from Asia at the site of present-day Istanbul. He conquered Thrace to gain access to its silver mines and to acquire a base from which to attack the Greeks, who controlled the trade routes from the Black Sea to the Aegean Sea.

In 490 B.C., Darius invaded Greece and was defeated by a united Greek army at the battle of Marathon. The Persians then spent several years making extensive preparations for another invasion of Greece, but these plans were interrupted by Darius' death in 486 B.C. (The wars which Darius and his son Xerxes fought against the Greeks are covered in detail in Chapter 6.)

Inscriptions. In the first year of his reign, Darius had had an inscription carved on a mountainside in Behistun, 500 feet above the road that connected Persia to Babylon. In it,

Darius' inscription on the face of a mountain at Behistun, Iran, contained a message translated into the Old Persian, Babylonian, and Elamite languages. It enabled scholars to decipher Babylonian cuneiform symbols.

Art and Architecture. Although the Persians made their own distinctive contribution to civilization in the areas of government and religion, most of their art and architecture was borrowed from other cultures. This *eclecticism*, or process of selecting elements from diverse sources and styles, is best illustrated in the remains of their great palaces at Susa and Persepolis. Darius himself described the palace at Susa as follows:

● ● ● *The decoration of this palace which I built at Susa was fetched from far away. . . . The bricks were molded and baked in the sun by the Babylonians. The cedar beams were brought from a mountain called Lebanon. . . . The wood called yaka was brought from Gandhara and Karmana. The gold was brought from Sardis and Bactria and wrought here. The magnificent stone called lapis lazuli and the cornelian were wrought here but were brought from Soghdiana. The precious turquoise was brought from Kharizmia and wrought on the spot. The silver and ebony were brought from Egypt. The decoration for the walls was brought from Ionia. The ivory wrought here, was transported from Kussa, Sind, and Arachosia. The stone columns, which were wrought here, were transported from Elam. The stone dressers were Ionians and Sards. The goldsmiths who wrought the gold were Medes and Egyptians. The men who worked the sun-baked bricks, they were Egyptians.*[5]

Darius selected *Persepolis* ("City of the Persians" to the Greeks) as the site for a new capital in 518 B.C. The palace at Persepolis was begun by Darius and completed by his successor, Xerxes, over several decades. The palace complex included royal apartments, rooms for the king's harem, treasuries, and an audience hall. It was constructed of sun-dried clay bricks, and erected on a man-made stone terrace which covered 33 acres. A monumental staircase was built from the natural ground level to the level of the palace.

he described how he had defeated the false Smerdis and restored law and order to his empire. In later inscriptions, he indicated that he was as proud of the fairness and efficiency of his rule as of his military exploits. Darius' effectiveness as a ruler was evident in the fact that he was able to administer an empire composed of many different people and cultures.

[5]*Ancient Civilizations*, ed. F. Clapham (New York: Warwick Press, 1978), p. 69.

SUMMARY

About 2500 B.C., waves of Indo-Europeans swept into the Middle East. Among their descendants were the Hittites, the first Western people to work with iron. Their introduction of iron, through trade and military conquest, to other peoples prior to 1200 B.C. led to the transition from what is known as the Bronze Age to the Iron Age. The Hittites also provided an important link between the civilization of the Middle East and that of the Aegean world.

The Persians created the first great Indo-European empire in history, and the people of the Middle East enjoyed 200 years of relative peace and prosperity under their rule. The religion founded by Zoroaster had great influence on Judaism and early Christianity, and survives even today among the small but influential community of Parsis in India. The Romans learned from the Persian example how to govern an empire of diverse peoples by granting certain rights to all citizens and creating an equitable system of justice.

QUESTIONS

1 How did the Hittites manage to establish and maintain hegemony over northern Syria-Palestine?

2 Why was the ability to make iron tools and weapons an important technological development?

3 Explain why Cyrus is referred to as "the Great."

4 What were the main features of the Zoroastrian religion, and in what ways might it have affected how the Persian kings ruled their empire?

5 Why is Darius considered to be one of the greatest administrators in history?

BIBLIOGRAPHY

Which book might describe the decoding of ancient languages?

LEHMANN, JOHANNES. *The Hittites: People of a Thousand Gods.* New York: Viking Press, 1977. *Presents the history of a vanished people whose power once rivaled that of the Egyptians and the Assyrians; provides illustrations of archaeological findings.*

PIOTROVSKY, BORIS. *The Ancient Civilization of Urartu.* New York: Cowles Book Co., 1969. *Author recounts his experiences on an archaeological "dig" in the 1930s; reconstructs the world of the Urartu, a major civilization which gave its name to Mount Ararat. Illustrated with splendid photographs of the sites and of museum artifacts.*

4

● *The Lord said to Abraham, "Leave your country, your kinsmen, and your father's house, and go to a country that I will show you. I will make you into a great nation, I will bless you and make your name so great that it shall be used in blessings: Those that bless you I will bless, those that curse you I will execrate. All the families of the earth will pray to be blessed as you are blessed."*

Genesis 12: 1-3

The Eastern Mediterranean

At the beginning of the 12th century B.C., widespread migrations throughout the ancient world created such chaotic conditions that several powerful empires were destroyed, and many people were forced to move from their homelands. The Hittite civilization was overrun by migrating peoples called the Phrygians, and the Egyptians defended their borders against tribes they called the Sea Peoples.

The political vacuum created by the decline of the Hittite and Egyptian empires meant that several small groups of people were able to establish independent nations in the area of Syria and Palestine. Between 1200 and 600 B.C., the fates of these small nations inversely reflected the fortunes of the stronger nations around them. When the surrounding powers were strong, the small nations were dominated by them. When the surrounding powers were weak, the small nations enjoyed independence.

The portion of the eastern Mediterranean world we shall study in this chapter is presently occupied by the states of Israel, Lebanon, Syria, and Jordan. For simplicity, we shall call it Syria-Palestine. Overall, this area covers approximately 400 miles from north to south, and 200 miles from east to west. It extends from the northeastern shore of the Mediterranean Sea to the Egyptian delta in the southwest, and includes the northern portion of the Euphrates River. While the terrain is predominantly a mixture of mountain and desert, the entire western branch of the Fertile Crescent has been a land of agriculture and a corridor of travel for thousands of years, and frequently a battleground for competing great powers.

For many centuries, the available recorded history of this area was limited to Biblical accounts. During the 20th century, however, a great deal of knowledge has been gained through excavations. In fact, archaeology is considered to be a national pastime in Israel today, and exciting new discoveries are made every year.

THE PHOENICIANS   In the northern part of Syria-Palestine, the snow-covered Lebanon Mountains are very close to the Mediterranean Sea, creating a narrow coastal strip which the Greeks called *Phoenicia*. The Phoenicians were related to the Canaanites, a mixture of Semitic and Hittite peoples who had given up nomadic ways

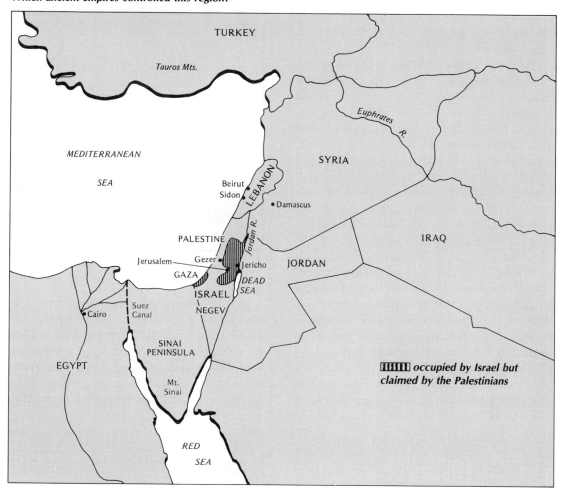

and adopted a blend of Egyptian and Babylonian cultures.

Much of our knowledge of the Phoenicians has come from the records of other people, which indicate that the Phoenician traders and sailors were known throughout the ancient world. In some of the Egyptian tombs there are paintings showing Phoenician ships, laden with cedar logs from Lebanon, tied up at Egyptian docks. These logs were used by the Egyptians to build masts for the boats they sailed on the Nile and on the Mediterranean. Temple inscriptions at Thebes-Karnak show Thutmose III boasting

of using Phoenician harbors as bases for military campaigns against the people of Syria-Palestine. The Phoenicians were listed as vassals on tribute lists of Sargon I of Akkad, and of Hammurabi of Babylon. The great Hebrew king, Solomon, obtained artisans and lumber from the Phoenician ruler of Tyre (1 Kings 5:6), and the Persians confiscated Phoenician ships and sailors to create a Persian navy.

Phoenicia was made up of four small city-states: Beirut, Byblos, Tyre, and Sidon. Tyre was the most defensible of these coastal cities—it was strategically located on a small offshore island, with an excellent harbor, and strong fortifications. Each Phoenician city-state was ruled by a king, but in times of danger the city-states joined together for mutual defense.

Between 1200 and 900 B.C., following the decline of the powerful Egyptian and Hittite empires, the prosperity and influence of the Phoenician city-states was far out of proportion to the small area they occupied. Their fertile land produced wheat, olives, and figs. The Lebanon Mountains were thickly forested with the famous "cedars of Lebanon." Along the Mediterranean coast there were beds of murex—shellfish from which the people extracted a purple-red dye which they used to color cloth. The Greek word for this dye was *phoinix*, and thus the people who produced it became known as the Phoenicians. (Because this dye was difficult to produce, the cloth that was colored by it was one of the Phoenicians' more expensive products. It is for this reason that purple became the color associated with royalty.)

The narrowness of the coastal plain was probably one of the factors that led the Phoenicians to turn to the sea for their livelihood. As Herodotus said:

• • • *they migrated from that which was called the Red Sea to the Mediterranean, and having settled in the country which they now inhabit, forthwith applied themselves to distant voyages.*[1]

The Phoenicians became the first great navigators of the Western world. They manufactured bronze weapons and armor, gold, silver, and glass vessels, wine, inlaid furniture, carved ivory, woolen and phoinix dyed cloth, and traded these goods for the products of other people throughout the Mediterranean world. They charted sea routes and were the first to use the *Polaris* (north star) for navigation at night. The Greeks came to call this star the "Phoenician star."

Phoenician merchant ships were a common sight in ports throughout the Mediterranean world.

In their never-ending search for new markets and natural resources, they sailed through the Strait of Gibraltar, perhaps as far as Britain in the north. According to Herodotus, they also circumnavigated Africa, many centuries before the Portuguese explorers. They established colonies, primarily as trading

Colored glass objects were one of the Phoenicians' most popular exports.

[1]Herodotus I, 1.

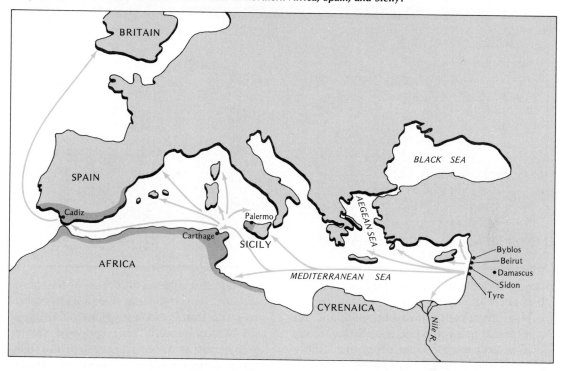

stations to exploit the raw materials of the local region, in various places along the shores of the Mediterranean. Many of these colonies developed into cities that still exist today, such as Cadiz in Spain and Palermo in Sicily.

Founded by merchants from Tyre in 814 B.C., Carthage, on the north coast of Africa in present Tunisia, was by far the most important of the Phoenician colonies. When the central power of Phoenicia waned during the 7th century B.C., Carthage was still powerful enough to hold the Mediterranean colonies in a strong maritime empire, stretching from Cyrenaica (on the north coast of Africa) on the east to Iberia (present Spain) in the west. During the 3rd century B.C., Carthage was the chief rival of Rome for control of the Mediterranean world.

In order to facilitate their trade, the Phoenicians abandoned the use of cuneiform writing on clay tablets, and developed a sim-ple alphabet of 22 symbols, representing consonants adopted from Egyptian hiero-glyphics. The Phoenician traders carried this concept of *alphabet* throughout their world of trade. The Greeks later modified the Phoenician alphabet by using as vowels those Phoenician consonants for which the Greeks had no equivalent sounds. A few centuries later, the Romans modified the alphabet of the Greeks and spread their version through-out the Western world.

Despite their innovations in navigation and trade, the Phoenicians did not have a dis-tinctive culture of their own. Their art imi-tated the art of other peoples. Their religion, borrowed from early settlers in Syria-Pales-tine, was centered on the worship of the forces of nature, and marked by cruel rituals and human sacrifices. They believed that each city-state was owned by a deity (*Baal*) who would aid his people if they asked for his

Early Phoenician	Early Hebrew	Later Phoenician	Early Greek	Early Etruscan	Roman
The Phoenicians introduced the concept of an alphabet to their many trading partners. Most civilizations of the ancient Middle East eventually adopted this system of writing.					
≮	≮	≮	⋀	A	A
9	9	9	8	8	B
1	1	1	1	⅂	C
◁	९	٩	◁	⋂	D
∃	∃	∃	∃	∃	E
Y	Y	4	⅃	⅃	F

help, but demanded no ethical behavior on the part of the worshipers.

The Phoenicians spread the peaceful arts of weaving, glass-making, metallurgy, naval science, and the alphabet, from the Middle East to points throughout the Western world. Their independence came to an end in 854 B.C. when they were conquered by the Assyrians. During the 8th century B.C., their trade and colonization were greatly diminished because of competition from the Greeks. In 612 B.C. Phoenicia was overrun by Chaldea, and in 540 by the Persians. In 333 B.C. the city of Tyre fell to Alexander the Great. By 64 B.C. the remains of the original four Phoenician city-states had become part of the Roman province of Syria.

THE ARAMEANS Like the Phoenicians, the Arameans were a Semitic people who gave up their nomadic ways to become farmers and traders. During the 12th century B.C. they gradually moved from the Arabian desert into Syria. They took over existing city-states and established new ones, the most important of which was Damascus, considered to be the oldest continuously inhabited city in the world today.

When the Hittite empire collapsed, about 1200 B.C., the Arameans were able to control the trade routes between Phoenicia, Egypt, and Mesopotamia. Their caravans carried ideas as well as wares. Their system of weights and measures came to be adopted throughout the Assyrian and Persian empires, and their Aramean language became the universal language of the Middle East. In Palestine, Aramaic replaced Hebrew as the spoken language, and was commonly used at the time of Jesus.

THE HEBREWS The Semitic people who established the strongest monarchy in Syria-Palestine, and whose religion exerted the greatest influence on Western civilization, were the Hebrews. In fact, most of what we know about them is derived from their scriptures, which Christians call the *Old Testament*. These scriptures include books of law (*Torah*), history, prophecy, poetry, and wisdom. Like the Arameans, the Hebrews may have been nomads in the Arabian desert as early as 2000 B.C. According to tradition, Abraham, the forefather of the Hebrews, had a vision in which God instructed him to:

PALESTINE AND PHOENICIA, 900 B.C.
In what ways were Israel and Judah different?

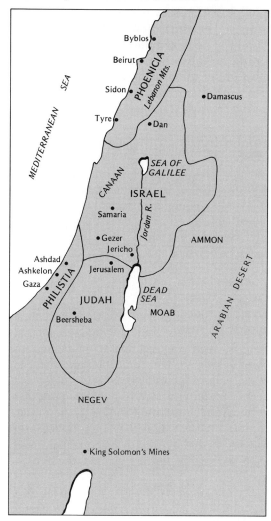

● ● ● *leave your own country, your kinsmen and your father's house, and go to a country that I will show you. I will make you into a great nation. I will bless you and make your name so great that it will be used as a blessing.*[2]

The Torah relates that Abraham and his family left Ur in Sumer and traveled along the Fertile Crescent into southern Palestine. This migration may have occurred during the

[2]Genesis 12: 1-2.

20th or 19th century B.C. Because of a famine, Abraham's grandson Jacob (who came to be known as Israel) led the Hebrews to the northern edge of the Egyptian delta. For a time they prospered, but later (perhaps at the end of the 18th century B.C.) they were enslaved and forced to build storehouses for the pharaoh. A leader named Moses followed the commands of his God and led the Hebrew captives out of Egypt, across the Red Sea, and into the desert of Sinai.

The Torah also relates that Moses went up on Mount Sinai to receive from God what came to be called the Ten Commandments. These commandments became the foundation for the social order of the Hebrews. Moses also received the following instructions:

● ● ● *Speak thus to the house of Jacob, and tell this to the sons of Israel: You have seen with your own eyes what I did to Egypt, and how I carried you on eagle's wings and brought you here to me. If only you will now listen to me and keep my covenant, then out of all the peoples you shall become my special possession; for the whole earth is mine. You shall be my kingdom of priests, my holy nation. These are the words you shall speak to the Israelites.*[3]

The covenant with Yahweh, or Jehovah, as their God came to be known, bound the Israelites to worship and obey him to the exclusion of all other possible objects of faith. The concept that obedience to Yahweh would bring blessings, while disobedience would bring adversities, became a basic concept of their faith. Throughout the centuries since the time of Moses, the affirmation of the Jews (as the Israelites came to be called) has been:

● ● ● *Hear, O Israel, the Lord is our God, one Lord, and you must love the Lord your God with all your heart and soul and strength.*[4]

The Jews thus became the first practitioners of *ethical monotheism,* the worship of one

[3]Exodus 19: 3-6.
[4]Deuteronomy 6:4.

god, based on love between god and man and between man and man.

After many years of wandering in the wilderness of Sinai, the Hebrews entered the promised land of Palestine. There they displaced the Canaanites, a mixture of Semitic and Hittite peoples who had long ago given up nomadic ways and adopted elements of Egyptian and Babylonian cultures.

The Philistines. Before the Hebrews could fully occupy the land promised to them by Yahweh, they were confronted by the Philistines, who were called "Sea People" by the Egyptians. One of the Biblical prophets states that the Philistines had come from *Caphtor*, which may have been present Crete or Cyprus. He also indicates that the Hebrews intended to expell them:

Because the day is upon them when Philistia
  will be despoiled,
And Tyre and Sidon to the last defender;
For the Lord will despoil the Philistines,
That remnant of the isle of Caphtor.[5]

Although the Philistines had failed in their attempts to invade Egypt, they had managed to gain control of the coastal area just north of Egypt's border by 1125 B.C. The region came to be known as Philistia, and it eventually contained five city-states: Ashkelon, Ashdad, Ekron, Gath, and Gaza. The Philistines' superior iron weapons and their well-disciplined military forces made it possible for them to keep the Hebrews well away from their coastal settlements.

The 12 Tribes. There were 12 tribes of Hebrews, each descended from, and named for, one of the sons of Jacob (who was also known as *Israel*). As they occupied the land of Palestine, they formed a confederacy, or religious league, in which the member tribes were bound together by the same religion, language, and laws. Each of 11 tribes was assigned a particular area of settlement, while the 12th tribe, the Levites, were named the

religious leaders of all the others. In times of crisis, the tribal elders chose a leader, called a judge, whom they believed had *charisma*, or special blessings from God. All tribes worshiped at the Ark of the Covenant, a portable shrine to Yahweh which the Hebrews had built under the direction of Moses and carried with them during their years of wandering through the Sinai.

THE KINGDOM OF ISRAEL

After many years of existence as a confederation of tribes, about 1000 B.C. the Hebrews united under the leadership of an outstanding young man named David to form the kingdom of Israel. Less than a century later, Israel split into two kingdoms: the northern one was called Israel and the southern one was called Judah.

DAVID

When the Israelites were unable to defeat the Philistines, their leaders demanded that Samuel, who was a judge at this time, appoint a king to lead them. Samuel tried to warn them of the evils that would befall the people under a monarch, but they persisted until Samuel appointed Saul to be their king, around 1020 B.C. Saul died in 1000 B.C. and was succeeded by David, who had achieved fame in several battles against the Philistines.

David's reign (1000-965 B.C.) soon became the model for all future rulers of the Israelites, for he confined the Philistines to the area known today as the Gaza Strip and united the 12 tribes into a single kingdom. Under his leadership, this new nation captured the Canaanite fortress at Jerusalem, converted it into a political capital, and made it the home of the Ark of the Covenant. Henceforth, the Jews referred to Jerusalem as *The City of David.*

SOLOMON

David was succeeded by his son Solomon (reigned 965-927 B.C.), who raised the nation

---

[5] Jeremiah 47:4.

Artists' reconstructions of the exterior (left) and interior of Solomon's Temple at Jerusalem. According to the account in the Book of Kings, Solomon conscripted 30,000 stonemasons and carpenters to build the Temple. The walls and floors as well as the altar were overlaid with gold.

to its pinnacle of prestige. Solomon acquired cedar logs and artisans from the Phoenician king of Tyre, and used them to build a great temple for Yahweh at Jerusalem and a palace for himself. He divided the kingdom into 12 administrative districts, each headed by a governor who was required to provide the court at Jerusalem with food for one month each year. He made trade alliances with the Egyptians and the Phoenicians, and sealed these by marrying princesses from each place.

Solomon built fortresses at strategic places throughout the realm. On the Red Sea, he constructed a fleet of ships which sailed to distant ports, including Ophir (which was probably in the vicinity of modern Yemen), to exchange copper, wheat, olive oil, and wool for products such as gold, silver, ivory, peacocks, and apes.

During the reign of Solomon, the Hebrews played their greatest role in the political and economic life of the Middle East. However, the oppressive taxes, conscripted labor, and loss of tribal independence led to dissension. When Solomon died, the 12 tribes split into two separate kingdoms.

Archaeological Findings. Yigael Yadin, the former director of the Institute of Archaeology at the Hebrew University in Jerusalem, was the major contributor to modern knowledge about ancient Palestine, and many of his excavations were of sites associated with King Solomon. The Bible mentions that Solomon conscripted forced labor to build a number of large constructions—a temple, a palace, the wall of Jerusalem, and the towns of Hazor, Megiddo, and Gezer—so Yadin decided to explore some of these sites.

Because the towns of Hazor, Megiddo, and Gezer had identical architectural features, Yadin decided that they had been built from the same set of plans. Each of the three towns was built on a *tell*, that is, a mound created by a sequence of towns built and destroyed on the same site over a period of many centuries. For example, Solomon's construction at Megiddo was on top of 18 earlier towns.

The outstanding engineering feat at both Hazor and Megiddo was the water supply system, an essential feature of every fortress designed to resist long sieges. In both cases, Solomon's new construction was between 50 and 100 feet above the original level of the ground; both had springs at the original ground level. In both cases, large square shafts were dug with flights of steps descending down to the level of the springs. From these points, tunnels were dug from the bottom of the steps toward the springs, and from the springs toward the bottom of the steps. These tunnels were high enough that women could walk through them carrying jars full of water on their heads. In his book describing the exploration of Hazor, Dr. Yadin writes:

● ● ● *In 732 B.C. Hazor fell to Tiglath-pilesar III and was destroyed. The Bible (2 Kings 15:29) describes this tragedy very laconically: "In the days of Pekah king of Israel, Tiglath-pilesar king of Assyria came and captured . . . Hazor; and he carried the people captive to Assyria." It is only through the archeological excavations that we now know the meaning of the words "came and captured." Tiglath-pilesar razed to the very ground the city of Hazor, once a key stronghold of the northern Kingdom of Israel. The sight we encountered in area B is worse than any I can remember in archeological excavations. The entire area was covered by a layer of ashes one metre thick and still black! Everything in sight was broken and scattered on the floors of the houses. We could visualize the Assyrian soldiers roaming about the houses, looting whatever they could and destroying the rest. The fire was so violent that even the stones were black, and numerous charred beams and pieces of burned plaster from the ceilings were strewn all over. The eastern side of the citadel, from which the fort had been attacked, was destroyed so thoroughly that in some places only the foundations below the floor level were visible. Here again we had visual evidence of the methods of destruction so vividly described by the Bible: "Rase it, rase it! Down to its foundations!" (Psalms 137:7.)[6]*

---

[6]Yigael Yadin, *Hazor* (New York: Random House, 1975), pp. 175-6.

THE TWO KINGDOMS

After Solomon's death, the 10 northern tribes asked Solomon's oldest son and legal successor, Rheoboam, to ease their burdens. When he refused to do so, these tribes, under the leadership of Jeroboam, another son of Solomon, established a separate kingdom which they called Israel, with a capital at Samaria. The two tribes in the south remained loyal to Rheoboam and formed the kingdom of Judah. The southern kingdom had few natural resources and its only large town was Jerusalem, the religious center for the entire 12 tribes. The people of the south remained true to the worship of Yahweh. The northern kingdom had several times as many people as the southern and was fertile and prosperous. The people of the north frequently forgot about Yahweh and turned to the worship of the Canaanite *Baal*.

After about 850 B.C., the fate of Israel and Judah was determined by the succession of nations that controlled the Land between the

After the Babylonian exile of the 6th century B.C., the torah served as a guide to faith for widely scattered Jewish communities.

Rivers. In 722 B.C., Samaria was captured by Assyria and many of the people were marched to that land. In 587 B.C., Jerusalem was destroyed by the Chaldeans and the people were marched off to Babylon. From this point on, the Hebrews were commonly referred to as Judeans or Jews. During the period of the exile, the bonds of kinship among the Jews were strengthened, and a community created which stressed tradition, law, and ritual. After Cyrus conquered Babylonia in 540 B.C., he permitted the Jews to return to their homeland. The Persians helped to finance the reconstruction of the temple at Jerusalem, and returned temple objects that had been taken by Nebuchadnezzar II.

The Prophets. Between the 8th and 6th centuries B.C., the religion of the Jews, which came to be called *Judaism*, was shaped by the teachings of a succession of prophets whom the Hebrews believed spoke for Yahweh. In their teachings, these prophets denounced the sins of the people and warned them repeatedly that they faced the punishment of God for their transgressions. But they also preached a message of hope—that Yahweh was just and merciful and ready to forgive those who repented.

Amos was the first of a group of prophets whose messages were put into written form. He spoke out against the social and economic injustices of his time, denouncing wealthy merchants who exploited the poor and the hypocrisy of self-righteous people. Amos rebuked his listeners by crying out that Yahweh had told him to say:

. . . *I hate, I spurn your pilgrim-feasts; I will not delight in your sacred ceremonies. When you present your sacrifices and offerings I will not accept them, nor look on the buffaloes of your shared offerings. Spare me the sound of your songs; I cannot endure the music of your lutes. Let justice roll down like a river and righteousness like an ever flowing stream.*[7]

[7]Amos 5: 21-24.

Several of the prophets taught that catastrophic events were a punishment for the people's sins. Jeremiah, in the 7th century, saw Assyria and Chaldea as the "rod of God's anger," used to chasten the sinful people. He preached that Yahweh would proclaim a new covenant with the Jews if each individual would make religion a matter of the heart and conscience. Jeremiah also proclaimed that the nation should be prepared to receive a *Messiah*, or God-appointed leader, who would save Israel from political bondage. Later, some people considered these and other teachings to have been predictions about Jesus.

Sacred Literature. The three most important items of sacred Jewish literature are the *Torah*, the *Mishnah*, and the *Talmud*. In 450 B.C., while the Persians still controlled Palestine, the scrolls of the Torah, or law, were written to systematize and preserve earlier writings and teachings. Several centuries later the Torah was incorporated into the Bible of the Christians as the first five books of the Old Testament.

Subsequent to 450 B.C., each generation of Jewish *rabbis*, or teachers, attempted to interpret these religious laws in ways relevant to their followers. Originally these interpretations, or *traditions of the elders*, as they came to be called, were passed along orally, but in time they became so extensive that memorization was very difficult. In 200 B.C., a group of very learned rabbis compiled the many interpretations into a scroll which they called the Mishnah (repetition). Many copies of the Mishnah were prepared and sent to Jewish communities everywhere to provide a uniform interpretation of the Torah and a common bond among the dispersed Jews.

About 500 A.D., all of the known laws and interpretations that evolved after preparation of the Mishnah were gathered together by another group of distinguished rabbis into the Talmud (instructions). Throughout the long centuries of *diaspora* (persecution and dispersion), the Torah and Talmud have provided Jews everywhere with a common bond.

SUMMARY

Between 1200 and 900 B.C. several small nations played important roles in the Middle East. The Phoenicians were a great seafaring people who carried the arts of civilization to all points on the coastlines of the Mediterranean Sea. The Arameans specialized in overland trade. Their language—Aramaic—and their system of weights and measures were used throughout the region for several centuries. The Hebrews had the most influence on other civilizations. Their concept of ethical monotheism had important consequences in the development of many other cultures.

QUESTIONS

1 In what ways have Biblical accounts of the Assyrians and Chaldeans been substantiated by archaeology and modern research?
2 How did the three small kingdoms of the Hebrews, Arameans, and Phoenicians manage to survive in the Fertile Crescent?
3 Research the circumstances under which the Dead Sea Scrolls were discovered. Why do modern Biblical scholars believe that this is one of the greatest archaeological discoveries ever made? In what ways has it changed our interpretation of the Bible?
4 Why are the ancient Phoenicians and Arameans called the "carriers of civilization"?
5 Explain the origin of the terms "Hebrew," "Israelite," and "Jew."
6 Jerusalem is a holy city to the Jews, Christians, and Moslems. How does this fact affect the political situation in Israel today?

BIBLIOGRAPHY

Which books might tell what event is celebrated during Passover?

KENYON, KATHLEEN. *Royal Cities of the Old Testament.* New York: Schocken Books, 1971. *The author, a renowned archaeologist, relates the evidence revealed by excavations to Biblical accounts of Solomon's royal cities: Jerusalem, Hazor, Megiddo, Gezer, and Samaria.*

MAGNUSSON, MAGNUS. *Archaeology of the Bible.* New York: Simon & Schuster, 1977. *Presents new interpretations of the religion, history, and literature of Biblical times, based on recent excavations in Israel, Jordan, Syria, and Iraq; illustrated with informative maps, drawings, and photographs.*

MOSCATI, SABATINO. *The World of the Phoenicians.* New York: Praeger, 1965. *Analyzes the civilization of the Phoenicians, emphasizing little known facts about the culture; traces the influence of the Phoenicians' culture through their Mediterranean settlements.*

SEIDMAN, HILLEL. *The Glory of the Jewish Holidays.* New York: Shengold Publishers, 1980. *Reveals the spirit of Judaism as it is reflected in the festivals and holy days; recalls the reasons for the establishment of these days and the laws and customs associated with them. Includes photographs of the art and literature associated with each festival.*

5

*One of the great islands of the world
in midsea, in the winedark sea, is Krete:
spacious and rich and populous, with ninety
cities and a mingling of tongues. . . .
Here lived King Minos whom Zeus received
every ninth year in private council. . . .*

HOMER

The Aegean Civilization

The *Iliad* and the *Odyssey* by the great Greek poet Homer inspired archaeologists to find out whether the people and places in these epics actually existed.[1] Excavations made since the middle of the 19th century have uncovered remains of a brilliant Bronze Age civilization which flourished around the Aegean Sea from about 2000 to 1100 B.C.

The three major centers of the Aegean civilization were: the *Trojan*, named for Troy, the most important ancient city on the western coast of Asia Minor; the *Minoan*, named for a legendary King Minos, who ruled Knossos on the island of Crete; and the *Mycenaean*, named for Mycenae, the largest settlement of the time on the mainland of Greece. This Aegean world was close enough to both Egypt and the Middle East to exchange goods, settlers, and ideas, but isolated enough to develop a distinctive culture of its own.

---

[1]The *Iliad* describes a war between the Greeks and the Trojans that may have taken place at the beginning of the 12th century B.C., four centuries before Homer's lifetime. The *Odyssey* relates the adventures of the Mycenaean leader Odysseus on his voyage home after the war.

THE ARCHAEOLOGISTS Because scholars have not yet deciphered the language of the Aegean world, most of our knowledge of this area has come from the material remains uncovered by archaeologists since the middle of the 19th century. The first important archaeologist to go into this area was Heinrich Schliemann (1822-1890). When he was a small boy in Germany, his father read to him the *Iliad* and the *Odyssey* of Homer. Fascinated by these tales, young Heinrich dreamed of searching for the places described in these poems. After he became a very successful businessman, he decided to use his wealth to fulfill his childhood dreams. In 1870, using the *Iliad* and the *Odyssey* as his guidebooks, Schliemann began to dig at a place currently named Hissarlik, in Turkey, because he believed that this site most closely resembled Homer's description of the location of Troy. He found the remains of not just one level of development, but of several levels. In the second oldest level he uncovered, Schliemann found a store of objects made of gold. He promptly called these objects *The Treasure of Priam*, because he assumed that they had belonged to Priam, the king of Troy dur-

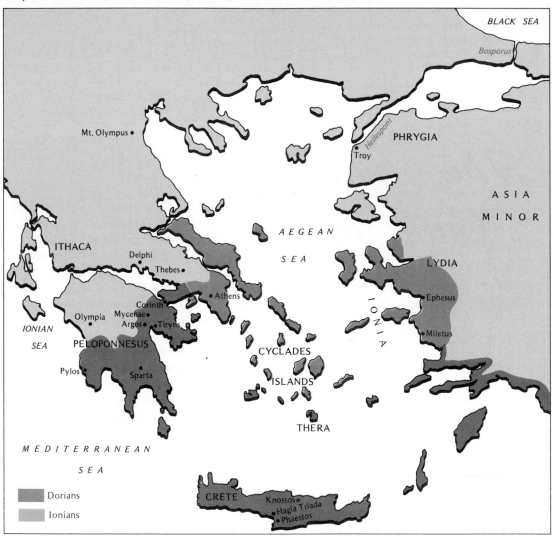

ing the Trojan War. Later, it was found that this level actually dated to about 2200 B.C., or about 1000 years before the date traditionally given for the Trojan War. Many later scholars concluded that the city described by Homer had been destroyed by fire and was to be found on a higher level.

After his successful explorations at Troy, Schliemann's search for his heroes led him to Mycenae, in the Peloponnesus, which Homer said was the city of Agamemnon, the leader of the Achaeans in their attack on Troy. Here Schliemann found gold ornaments and bronze weapons similar to those described by Homer. Still in pursuit of his childhood dreams, he bought land at Knossos, on the island of Crete, but died before he could begin to explore there.

Another 19th century archaeologist, Sir Arthur Evans, curator of the Ashmolean Museum at Oxford University in England, visited Greece in search of examples of early

Greek writing. In an antique shop in Athens he found two small stones inscribed with pictographs. Such stones were called "milk-stones" by the peasant women of Crete, who often wore them as charms to ensure that they could produce enough milk for their babies. Evans decided that these particular stones were inscribed with an early form of writing, and his search for the meaning of the pictographs led him to Knossos, where he spent the remainder of his life and his fortune excavating the sites of a civilization which he called *Minoan.*

THE MINOAN CIVILIZATION

Between 2000 and 1450 B.C., the island of Crete was the center of an advanced maritime civilization which dominated the islands of the Aegean Sea, the mainland of Greece, and the coastal areas of Asia Minor. We know little about the people who preceded this civilization, but there is evidence to suggest that the first inhabitants of Crete could have immigrated there from Anatolia between 4000 and 3000 B.C. It has also been suggested that the first Cretans might have been refugees from Libya, near the Egyptian delta. In either case, the earliest peoples had close ties with the Egyptians of the dynastic period (beginning about 3100 B.C.), for many Cretan artifacts have been found in Egyptian tombs of that era, and a number of Egyptian artifacts have been found in Crete.

Around 2000 B.C., mainland Greece was invaded by Indo-European tribes from the north. Although the islands were not directly affected by this invasion, archaeologists have noted that important changes were occurring in Crete at the same time. These developments included the construction of palaces, a wholly new style for pottery decoration, the use of the pottery wheel, and the invention of a method of writing. It is not known whether these changes in Crete occurred naturally or if they were introduced by new settlers. It is possible that some of the peoples of mainland Greece migrated to Crete to avoid the Indo-European invaders. Alternatively, new settlers may have arrived from Anatolia or Phoenicia.

One of the significant changes that occurred in Crete was the building of great palaces such as those at Knossos and Phaestos. In time, Knossos became the most important city in Crete, and, under the leadership of the legendary King Minos, it became the most important city in the Aegean world. Thucydides, a Greek historian of the 5th century B.C., used an ancient Greek tradition as his source in telling how King Minos made himself master of the seas.

. . . And the first person known to us by tradition as having established a navy is Minos. He made himself master of what is now called the Hellenic sea, and ruled over the Cyclades [a group of islands in the southern Aegean Sea], into most of which he sent his first colonies, . . . appointing his own sons as governors; and thus did his best to put down piracy in these waters, a necessary step to secure the revenues for his own use.[2]

---

[2]Thucydides I, 1, 4.

As Thucydides indicates, the Minoans developed an extensive fleet of ships to protect their trade routes. In fact, their navy was so powerful that their government came to be called a *thalassocracy*, or "rule by the sea."

The wealth and power of King Minos were evident in the ruins of the palace at Knossos which were uncovered by Evans. Construction of the palace, which covered about six acres, was begun about 2000 B.C., but additions were made over several centuries. It consisted of brick and limestone buildings arranged around an open courtyard, 200 feet long by 100 feet wide. Broad stairways from this central courtyard led to the upper stories, and a maze of corridors connected the royal apartments, reception halls, administrative offices, workshops, and storerooms. The roofs were supported by columns that were tapered at the bottom.

The walls of the palace were decorated with frescoes, an art form in which artists apply colors to plaster before it hardens. Many of the decorations incorporated stylized horns of bulls. An elaborate sanitary system included running water and flush toilets, and

A stone chair found in the palace at Knossos may have been the throne of the fabled King Minos.

Immense clay jars called pithoi *were used to store food for the large number of people who lived in King Minos' palace.*

lightwells permitted daylight to illuminate interior rooms. An audience chamber contained a simple stone chair which may have been the throne of King Minos; if so, this is the oldest throne thus far discovered in Europe. In the basement rooms, archaeologists found lead-lined chests, which probably held royal treasures, and storage spaces containing immense *pithoi*, or clay jars, which may have held olive oil, wine, or grain. An outdoor theater, made of stone steps rising on a moderate slope, could accommodate up to 500 seated spectators: here the Minoans probably watched a variety of performances, including dancing, wrestling, and boxing.

After uncovering the remains of this palace, Arthur Evans reconstructed several portions of it as he conceived it to have looked, based on the remnants found. Steel girders and concrete slabs were erected to protect portions of the original buildings. Evans even engaged artists to recreate some of the frescoes, and these can still be seen today. These frescoes show men with red-hued skin and women with white skin. The women appear to be participating with the men in festivals, dancing, and athletic events. In fact, all of the Minoan people are depicted as young, lively, and pleasure-loving. The discovery of a gaming board, similar to the kind used for backgammon, indicated that the Minoans also enjoyed less strenuous activities.

Homes of the common people, made of bricks and built on foundations of stone, surrounded the palace. These buildings were one or two stories high, had flat roofs, few windows, and were coated with stucco.

RELIGION

Since no temples or large cult statues have been found, scholars have determined that priests did not play as important a role in Minoan society as they did in Egypt or Mesopotamia. The Minoans believed that gods resided in trees, stones, and other natural objects. They worshiped these deities in sacred groves, in caves, and at shrines in their own homes. To avoid displeasing the gods when they were busy with other duties, they often placed *reverence statues* in the holy places to act as their representatives.

The most important Minoan deity seems to have been a Mother Goddess, similar to the fertility goddesses worshiped in many other places throughout the Middle East. She was usually depicted as holding a snake in each hand and with a bird perched on top of her head. The snake may have been a symbol of renewal, because snakes regularly slough off their old skins and promptly develop new ones. The dominance of the Mother Goddess in Cretan religion could have meant that women served as priestesses and held important positions in the society. Another important deity was a bull god, who may have symbolized male strength and creative energy.

The Greeks of the Classical period (5th and 4th centuries B.C.) believed that Zeus, their chief deity, often assumed the form of a bull and was born in a cave on Crete. Other

The Mother Goddess of Knossos holds a snake in each hand, perhaps symbolizing her powers of renewal.

crafted items. After 2000 B.C., they adopted the use of the potter's wheel and produced eggshell-thin pottery, called *Kamares* ware from the name of the cave in which it was first found.

In earliest times Cretan pottery had been decorated with simple geometric designs and painted in earth colors such as brown, rust, and black. After about 2000 B.C., the Kamares style pottery began to be decorated in a "light on dark" style, with white and other light colors applied over a dark background. The patterns of this later pottery were based on the shapes seen in plants, animals, and marine life, and were much more naturalistic than the earlier designs.

The Minoans also crafted fine gold and silver jewelry and made vases of soapstone, a soft, easily carved mineral, which they decorated with sculptures. Many of the objects that have been found have been quite small, even miniature, but all have been beautifully worked, and all of them were in great demand throughout the Aegean world.

The renowned skill of Minoan craftsmen can be seen in this pendant of embossed and fili-greed gold. At the top, two wasps are arranged around a honeycomb.

Greek gods also show the influence of Minoan nature worship. Athena, for instance, was usually represented with an owl, and Aphrodite with a dove.

ECONOMY

The island of Crete was, and is, very mountainous, but the pleasant climate and the fertile volcanic soil which fills the small valleys provided abundant harvests of cereals, vegetables, flax, olives, and grapes.

Since they were skilled in seafaring, the Minoans developed an extensive maritime trade in these agricultural products and in

Around 2000 B.C., the Minoans began to develop a system of writing. They kept accounts of their wide-ranging trading activities on clay tablets, thousands of which have been found on Crete. While the earliest inscriptions were hieroglyphic, these soon evolved into an essentially syllabic script; that is, the signs represented syllables rather than single letters. Examples of this latter script, called *Linear A*, have been found at Phaestos and at Hagia Triada, but it has not yet been deciphered satisfactorily.

About 1600 B.C., Knossos, Phaestos, and most other settlements of Crete were showered by debris from a volcanic eruption on nearby Thera. After this disaster, the Cretans seem to have had about 150 years of peace and prosperity. But around 1450 B.C., the Minoan civilization came to a sudden and unexpected end. Most of the small villages and farms and all of the major towns in Crete were looted and destroyed by fire. Many scholars believe that invaders from the mainland of Greece, probably the Mycenaeans, were responsible for this destruction.

LEGENDS

For many centuries, scholars assumed that the adventures of the heroes of ancient Greek legends were fictional. But after Schliemann's explorations had demonstrated that the epics of Homer dealt with real places and people, they began to analyze other myths for possible references to actual events.

According to one of these myths, King Minos kept a Minotaur, a monstrous creature which was half man and half bull, in a labyrinth beneath his palace at Knossos. No one who entered the labyrinth was able to escape from being killed by the creature. Minos demanded that the Greeks of Athens, on the mainland of Greece, pay tribute to him by sending seven maidens and seven young men to be sacrificed to the Minotaur once every nine years.

The legend continues by relating that Theseus, the son of Aegeus, a legendary king of Athens, volunteered to try to put an end to payment of this tribute. As Theseus set sail for Crete, along with six other youths and seven maidens, he told his father that he would change the black sails on his boat to white ones for the journey home if he succeeded in killing the Minotaur.

When Theseus reached Knossos, Ariadne, the daughter of Minos, fell in love with him and offered to help him escape from the labyrinth. She gave him a sword and a ball of thread, and instructed him to tie one end of the thread to the door at the entrance of the labyrinth, then unwind the rest as he moved through the labyrinth. Theseus did as she advised, killed the Minotaur with the sword, and then followed the thread back to the entrance.

While sailing back to Athens after his exploit, Theseus forgot the agreement with his father and did not change the sails from black to white. When Aegeus saw the ship approaching, he thought that his son had perished in his struggle with the Minotaur. In his grief, he hurled himself from a cliff into the sea, thus giving his name to the Aegean Sea.

Some scholars believe that this legend may reflect an actual situation in which the Athenian Greeks paid tribute to the Minoans, or were forced to send a group of young nobles to Crete as hostages. The triumph of Theseus over the Minotaur was celebrated as late as the Hellenistic period (323-30 B.C.), when children played a game based on a maze of lines marked on a pavement, which they called a *labyrinth*.

Homer related another myth about King Minos of Crete. According to tradition, he said, King Minos was the son of a Phoenician princess. The god Zeus, disguised as a bull, abducted her from her native land and swam

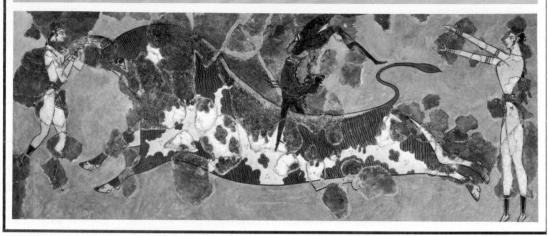

The Minoan sport of bull-vaulting required great daring and acrobatic skill. In this restored fresco, one acrobat somersaults over a bull's back while another grabs the bull's horns.

with her to his cave in Crete. There, Zeus fathered the child who later became known as King Minos. This myth raises the possibility that an actual Phoenician king could have journeyed to Crete and become the first King Minos.

Because there were so many colorful legends about King Minos, most scholars have concluded that the name *Minos* probably referred to a dynasty of kings, not to a single individual.

The Minoan sport of *bull vaulting* may also have had a mythic or religious basis. In this sport, acrobats (both men and women) would attempt to seize the horns of the charging beast and vault over its back in a somersault. The exact significance of this sport is not known.

THE MYCENAEANS About 2000 B.C. or earlier, an Indo-European tribe known as the Achaeans invaded the peninsula of Greece. In time, they were able to overcome the earlier settlers and established several fortified strongholds, the most important of which were Pylos, Tiryns, and Mycenae—all in the region called the Peloponnesus. By 1600 B.C., the *Achaeans*,

or *Mycenaeans*, as they are usually called, were sailing the Aegean Sea in their ships, first as pirates and later as traders. They became wealthy and powerful, and after Knossos was destroyed in 1450 B.C., the Mycenaeans became the most powerful group in the Aegean world.

The Mycenaeans adopted the art styles of the Minoans and took over the trading partnerships that the Minoans had developed throughout the ancient world, but their culture was very different. Whereas the Minoans' economy had been based on peaceful industries such as pottery-making, the Mycenaeans used their skills in warfare to gain and keep the territory they occupied. Archaeologists have found a vast array of bronze weapons in Mycenaean graves, which tend to support the portrait of Mycenaean warriors presented in the *Iliad* and the *Odyssey*. And while the Minoans had built their palaces without fortifications, secure in the protection of their navy and their good relations with their neighbors, the Mycenaeans built fortified citadels with walls so massive that the later Greeks believed that the stones had been put into place by a mythical race of giants called the *Cyclopes*.

A view of the citadel of Mycenae. The circle of shaft graves excavated by Sir Arthur Evans can be seen in the foreground, the plain of Argos in the background.

The Lion Gate is the principal entrance to the citadel of Mycenae, which was encircled with a massive Cyclopean wall. Unfortunately, the lions' heads have been lost.

GOVERNMENT

Archaeological findings and the writings of Homer indicate that the Mycenaeans retained many of their ancestral Indo-European customs. Tribal leaders established hereditary monarchies and ruled territories that were probably the size of city-states. Very often one king established his authority over a number of others, but none of the Mycenaean kings had the absolute powers of the Egyptian and Mesopotamian monarchs. Before making decisions, a king was expected to consult with an assembly of nobles. In the *Iliad*, Homer describes several of the assemblies that the Mycenaean king, Agamemnon, called in the course of the Trojan War. In these assemblies, Odysseus and other kings and nobles speak frankly to Agamemnon, and their advice is heeded. Although the position of the Mycenaean kings was hereditary, the continuation of their rule probably depended upon the quality of their leadership and the support of the nobles.

THE EPICS

In peacetime, the kings and nobles of Mycenaean Greece devoted much of their leisure time to athletic contests in order to keep themselves physically fit for battle. On cold evenings, they would gather around a glowing hearth in the great central hall of the king's palace to hear bards recite heroic tales about their exploits. These tales were passed down to succeeding generations over the course of several centuries. Around 750 B.C., according to tradition, the poet Homer recited the epic stories of the *Iliad* and the *Odyssey*, based upon an oral tradition at least four centuries old. Soon afterwards, the epics were finally written down.

Homer's epics reflect a society in which men are motivated to great deeds by the pursuit of honor. In the *Iliad*, Hector's speech to his infant son demonstrates a belief that courage and leadership in battle, not material possessions, will determine his son's place in society.

When he had kissed his child and swung him
high to dandle him, he said this prayer:
"O Zeus
and all immortals, may this child, my son,
    become like me a prince among the
    Trojans.
Let him be strong and brave and rule in
    power at Ilion [Troy]; then someday
    men will say
'This fellow is far better than his father!'
seeing him home from war, and in his arms
the bloodstained gear of some tall warrior
    slain—making his mother proud."[3]

The epics also depict other aspects of Mycenaean society. Families dutifully fulfill their obligations to the gods, and offer hospitality to all strangers, because it was believed that such guests might be gods in disguise.[4] In contrast to the cordiality shown to strangers,

however, there was no code of honor regarding enemies. While it was considered a sin to lie to a friend, it was admirable to deceive an enemy. In fact, craftiness and guile are the most outstanding characteristics of the hero Odysseus. Throughout the *Iliad* and the *Odyssey* he is spoken of admiringly as "wily Odysseus" and "Odysseus, master of stratagems."

Long after the Mycenaeans moved off the stage of history, their epics were recited for entertainment, for instruction in proper behavior, and as explanations of natural events. In the 4th century B.C., Plato complained that Homer's epics were still relied upon by the educators of his time.

ARCHAEOLOGICAL FINDINGS

Before 1500 B.C., the Mycenaeans buried their dead in what have come to be called "shaft graves." These graves were dug for family groups, and were arranged in a circle, perhaps 50 feet in diameter, with each grave marked by a sculptured limestone slab. Schliemann excavated one such circle containing the graves of a royal or noble family, and found a treasure of gold ornaments and bronze weapons inlaid with ivory and semiprecious stones. The faces of several of the skulls were covered by gold portrait masks, one of which Schliemann promptly decided was the *mask of Agamemnon*. Later scholars determined that the objects found by Schliemann were from a period almost 300 years before the dates traditionally given for the Trojan War (1194-1184 B.C.).

After 1500 B.C., the Mycenaeans built into hillsides large, circular, domed structures, up to 30 feet in diameter, called *tholoi* ("bee hive tombs"). The entrances were in the form of large trenches, with stone walls retaining the earth. Many artifacts which the wealthy might need in the afterlife were placed beside the bodies at the time of burial. The most famous *tholoi* at Mycenae are believed to be royal tombs. They are known as the Treasury of Atreus and the Tomb of Clytemnestra.

---

[3] *Iliad* VI, 474-87.
[4] The Greek word for "guest" (*Xenos*) is the same as the word for "stranger."

The chambers within the tholoi ("beehive tombs") at Mycenae had vaulted roofs.

THE TROJAN WAR

Troy was strategically located at the west end of the Hellespont, so that the rulers of Troy were able to control not only the water route from the Aegean to the Black Sea, but also the most direct land route between Europe and Asia. By the early 12th century B.C., the military and commercial ventures of the Mycenaeans had probably brought them into conflict with the Trojans.

Although the Trojan War was very likely fought for control of the Hellespont, the Mycenaeans and Greeks invented a much more romantic story of its origins. According to the *Iliad*, the cause of the conflict was the abduction of Helen, the wife of Menelaus, king of Sparta, and the most beautiful woman in the world. Paris, the son of the king of Troy, abducted Helen with the help of Aphrodite, the goddess of love. Aphrodite's action in helping Paris caused great dissension among the deities who resided on Mount Olympus. When the Mycenaeans went to war with Troy to rescue Helen, the gods quarreled among themselves about which side should be victorious, with many of the gods and goddesses intervening from time to time on behalf of their favorites.

The so-called Treasury of Atreus is the tomb of a Mycenaean royal family who lived about 1300 B.C. It is the largest of the tholoi at Mycenae and has an interior chamber nearly 50 feet high.

> *The Trojan War was one of the first wars fought in the ancient world in the region of the Hellespont, which today is called the Dardanelles. Subsequently, several other major battles were fought there, for the area had great strategic importance. In 495 B.C., the Persians seized the Hellespont in order to cut off the grain supplies that Athens received from the Black Sea area. Later in that century, the Spartans fought the Athenians on the shores of the Hellespont for the same reason: they wanted to stop the trade that Athens conducted with the Black Sea region. The area continued to be important throughout the centuries, for ships from the Black Sea must pass through the Dardanelles strait to reach the Mediterranean. During World War I, British Commonwealth troops fought a major battle at Gallipoli in an attempt to prevent the Germans from occupying this strategic area.*

The second great epic of Homer, the *Odyssey*, tells of the adventures of Odysseus, who fought with the Mycenaeans in the Trojan War, but then had many adventures and suffered many hardships on his journey home to Ithaca, in western Greece.

THE END OF MYCENAEAN RULE

At the end of the 13th century B.C., many Mycenaean cities and palaces in the Peloponnesus were overrun by invaders from the north and destroyed by fire. It is not known for certain whether these invaders were the Dorians, an Indo-European tribe who settled in Greece around 1100 B.C., or another group.

Around 1100 B.C., the Dorians conquered the citadels of Mycenae, Pylos, and Tiryns. The surrounding countryside was abandoned, and the Mycenaeans who could not escape were enslaved. Many Mycenaeans fled to the islands of the Aegean Sea, and others settled in Athens, which was such a small village that the Dorians had ignored it. Other refugees founded settlements on the eastern coast of the Aegean Sea (the western coast of Asia Minor), a region known as *Ionia*. There they preserved and enhanced their customs and culture, and by the 9th century B.C. a brilliant civilization had evolved (see Chapter 7). Much of what later came to be called Greek philosophy, literature, science, and architecture actually had origins in Ionia. Ionian merchants traveled far and wide, creating trading settlements around the Mediterranean Sea. One such settlement was made at Massilia (modern Marseilles) on the south coast of present France, and from this point they traveled up the Rhone River far enough to encounter people from Cornwall, in present England.

The Dorians continued to migrate into Greece for several centuries. In the confusion that they created, earlier skills of writing, technology, and trade declined. The economy regressed to simple farming and animal husbandry. This period of Greek history, from 1100 to 700 B.C., is sometimes called the *Greek Dark Ages* or the *Archaic Age*. It is also known as the *Iron Age*, because iron tools and weapons increasingly replaced the bronze implements of the Mycenaeans.

SUMMARY

A brilliant Bronze Age civilization flourished around the Aegean Sea between 2000 and 1100 B.C. Remains of this civilization have been discovered at three distinct places: at Knossos on Crete, at Mycenae in the Peloponnesus, and at Troy in modern Turkey. The people of these cities developed an important and distinctive culture which was passed on to succeeding generations through their myths and epics.

The Minoan civilization ended abruptly about 1450 B.C., and leadership of the Aegean world passed to the Mycenaeans, or Achaeans, as Homer called them. The Mycenaeans then fought with the Trojans for control of the passageway to the Black Sea. About 1100 B.C., the Mycenaean civilization collapsed when the Dorians overran the peninsula of Greece.

QUESTIONS

1 What changes occurred in Minoan society around 2000 B.C.? What factors could have accounted for such changes?

2 In what ways did the early civilization of the Aegean world differ from that of Egypt? From that of the Land between the Rivers?

3 Compare examples of Minoan art with tomb paintings found in Egypt. What do these paintings tell us about the two societies?

4 How would the Minoan culture have been affected if the Mycenaeans had never learned seafaring skills?

5 Greek mythology explains that the Trojan War was brought about by Paris' abduction of Helen. What are more likely to have been the causes of this conflict?

BIBLIOGRAPHY

Which references might discuss the origin of the Minoans?

BLEGEN, CARL W. *Troy and the Trojans.* New York: Praeger, 1963. *An archaeologist who excavated Homer's Troy describes the various levels of the site; explains how the royal stronghold was destroyed and rebuilt several times and finally abandoned. Includes drawings of the plans of the various towns.*

COTTERELL, ARTHUR. *The Minoan World.* New York: Scribner's Sons, 1979. *Provides a comprehensive outline of what is known about the Minoans and their world; explores the problems associated with various theories of the origin of the Minoans.*

FINLEY, M.I. *Early Greece: The Bronze and Archaic Ages,* 2d ed. New York: Norton, 1982. *Reconstructs the preliterary age of Greece through examination of recent archaeological findings; traces the development of Greek institutions, providing an excellent background for the study of Classical Greece.*

"Minoans and Mycenaeans, Sea Kings of the Aegean." *National Geographic* 153, 2 (1978): 142-84. *Beautifully illustrated account of the Bronze Age civilization that developed on Crete and on the mainland.*

INDIA

3000–500 B.C.

To the east of Mesopotamia, in what is today Pakistan, a great civilization developed in the fertile Indus River valley. Like the early civilizations of the Tigris-Euphrates valley and the Nile valley that flourished about the same time, Indus valley civilization was built by people who established farming and herding communities.

Flanked on the west and northwest by the Hindu Kush Mountains and on the northeast by the Himalaya Mountains, the Indus valley civilization extended the length of the river and included the delta adjoining the Arabian Sea. Archaeological evidence suggests that trade took place between the peoples of the Indus valley and those of both Egypt and Mesopotamia. Trade goods were brought by boat through the Red Sea or Persian Gulf.

INDUS VALLEY CIVILIZATION

The origin of Indus valley civilization is largely unknown. It reached its height about 2500 B.C., began to decline about 1700 B.C., and collapsed about 1500 B.C. Archaeologists have excavated its two chief urban centers—Harappa and Mohenjo-daro. The carefully planned layout and rigorously uniform building materials found at these sites suggest that a strong, central authority exerted control over the people. Buildings were made of bricks dried in kilns, but the unusual feature of these bricks was that they conformed to a standard size over many centuries.

Harappa and Mohenjo-daro had well-planned sanitation systems that were superior to those in western Europe almost 4000 years later. Most homes had wells for water and drainage systems. Houses were built along wide streets that were laid on a grid pattern. The most important streets were oriented north-south; secondary streets ran east-west. Each city had large public baths that archaeologists hypothesize were used for religious as well as hygienic purposes.

At their height, Harappa and Mohenjo-daro may have had as many as 35,000 inhabitants and extended over six or seven square miles. They were the centers of an essentially agricultural region almost twice the size of the Old Kingdom of Egypt and almost four times the extent of Sumer and Akkad.

Very little is known about the political, social, and economic life of the Indus valley civilization. The cities were probably ruled by priest-kings who had the power to enforce the strict building standards that remained in use for a thousand years. The people, who were later called Dravidians, were polytheistic, and archaeological evi-

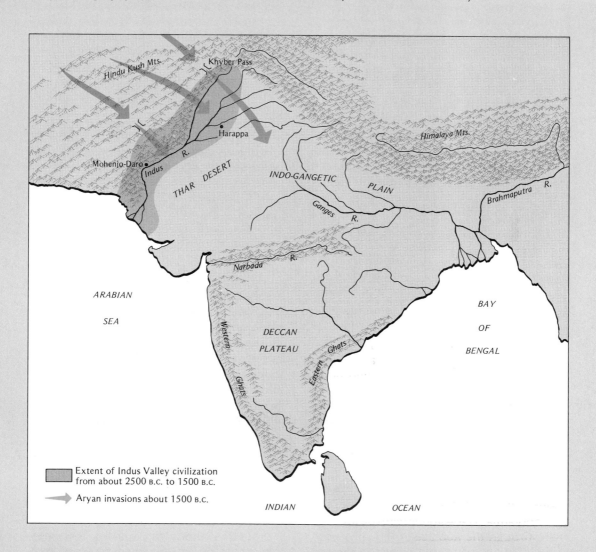

Extent of Indus Valley civilization from about 2500 B.C. to 1500 B.C.

Aryan invasions about 1500 B.C.

dence suggests that they worshiped a mother-goddess and a three-faced god. Stone seals with carved inscriptions indicate that the Dravidians had some kind of recordkeeping system, although these inscriptions have yet to be deciphered.

About 1700 B.C., the Indus valley civilization suffered a decline, as evidenced by lowered building standards and other indications. The exact reasons for this decline are unknown. Recent excavations have suggested that mud and silt accumulations may have led to floods that severely damaged Mohenjo-daro over several centuries and weakened its authority at a time when new groups of people with more advanced (iron) weapons and horsedrawn chariots swept into the region. By 1500 B.C. Indus valley civilization was replaced by a group of Indo-European invaders, known as the Aryans, who pushed through the Hindu Kush Mountains from what is today Iran.

Carved stone seals like this one were probably used by Mohenjo-daro merchants to stamp their possessions, and may also have had a religious meaning. On this seal, a bull stands near an incense burner.

ARYAN CONQUEST

Archaeologists believe that the Aryan conquest of India was part of a larger migration of Aryan people, some of whom pushed into Greece, Persia, and Italy. In India, the tall, light-skinned Aryans saw themselves as superior to the darker-skinned people they conquered, and they either enslaved the Dravidians or forced them to flee into other parts of India. Thus, unlike the early civilizations of Egypt and Sumer that greatly influenced later peoples, the Indus valley civilization was largely destroyed. It is only in the 20th century that archaeologists and historians have begun to explore its mysteries. They have slowly started to piece together evidence that this early Indian civilization did influence the Aryans, but the record is still incomplete.

The Aryans were only one of many invaders who pushed across the Hindu Kush Mountains into the northern plain in the course of India's long history. However, the Aryan influence on later Indian civilization was lasting and profound. The early Aryans were nomadic people loosely organized into tribes. After overwhelming the Indus valley civilization, they migrated eastward and eventually settled the entire region known as the Indo-Gangetic plain. During this period from about 1500 B.C. to 1000 B.C., their chief enemies were the Dravidians, probably survivors of the Indus valley civilization, who were forced to retreat into southern India. Between about 1000 B.C. and 700 B.C., various Aryan tribes led by *rajahs*, or elected chiefs, fought for control of the Indo-Gangetic plain. Gradually, individual rajahs carved out small kingdoms across the northern plain.

ORIGINS OF HINDUISM

Very little material exists to reconstruct the early history of the Aryans, for these tribes had no method of writing their language until they developed Sanskrit about 700 B.C. Most of our knowledge about the early Aryans comes from the carefully guarded oral traditions that were handed down by the priests.

The earliest of these religious traditions are the *Vedas* (meaning "knowledge"), a collection of poems, religious writings, and hymns composed between about 1500 B.C. and 1000 B.C. The original Vedas were the *Rig Veda*, the *Sama Veda*, *Yajur Veda*, and *Atharva Veda*, and like the hymns and prayers of ancient Egypt, they offer our principal source of information about the people, their beliefs, and their daily lives. The *Rig Veda*, which is the oldest, includes 1028 hymns to various gods. Later writings, the *Upanishads*, are commentaries on the ideas expressed in the Vedas.

Together, the Vedas and Upanishads became part of the sacred literature of Hinduism, the religion that grew out of the beliefs of the Aryans, and the period from 1500 B.C. to 700 B.C. has been called the Vedic Age. Because Hinduism evolved slowly, it is said to be a religion without a founder. Within Hinduism, many ideas and inconsistencies coexist. However, the diversity and adaptability of this religion ensured its survival, and it is the oldest of the world's major religions.

Hindus believe in *brahma*, a single unifying force, but they worship many gods, each

Shiva the destroyer is one of the most important Hindu gods. Like other gods in the Hindu pantheon, Shiva is considered to be a manifestation of the supreme god, Brahman.

The elephant-headed god Ganesha, son of Shiva, is possibly the most popular divinity in the Hindu pantheon. His fat belly represents the prosperity he brings to his worshipers.

of whom is seen as a different aspect of brahma. By acting in accord with *dharma*, or universal moral laws, Hindus believe that an individual can attain the ultimate goal of existence—the reunifying of the individual soul with *atman*, the universal soul. Hindus believe that most people cannot achieve this reunion with atman in a single lifetime, and therefore that most souls pass through a series of rebirths. In each reincarnation, or rebirth, an individual has the opportunity to move closer to the ultimate goal.

While the Vedas provide valuable evidence about the development of Aryan religious beliefs, another series of oral traditions tell about the wars among rival Aryan kingdoms between about 1000 B.C. and 700 B.C. Two epic poems, the *Mahabharata* and the *Ramayana*, recount the struggles of this time. Like the Homeric epics, the *Iliad* and the *Odyssey*, these narratives mix fact and fan-

tasy. The *Mahabharata*, the longest poem ever composed, consists of 90,000 stanzas and describes the actions of gods and mortals.

The *Ramayana* relates the wanderings of the hero, Rama, who has been banished from his home by his father while Rama's faithful wife, Sita, awaits his return. The epic does more than tell a story, however. It also focuses on the ideals and virtues expected of both men and women. The religious themes woven into these two Aryan epics account for their importance as sacred Hindu literature.

ARYAN SOCIAL STRUCTURE

During the Vedic Age, the Aryans evolved a social structure that would eventually develop into the caste system of today's India. Among the early Aryans, there were three social classes: warriors, priests, and com-

An 18th-century illustration of an episode from the ancient Hindu epic, the Ramayana. *The* Ramayana *is an action-packed tale of love, abduction, and heroic rescue.*

moners, and it was possible to rise in society. By the end of the Vedic Age, however, the class system had become more rigid. A person's status was determined by birth, and priests replaced warriors as the highest order. Thus the Aryans were differentiated into four *castes*, or social groups based on birth: (1) Brahmans—priests and scholars; (2) Kshatriyas—rulers and warriors; (3) Vaisyas—craftworkers, merchants, and farmers; and (4) Sudras—unskilled workers and peasants tied to the land. Outside the caste system were the untouchables, completely without status. They included the Dravidians and those who had intermarried with them.

Over the centuries, the caste system became more complex as the four major castes were further divided into numerous sub-

castes, and strict rules governed the behavior of people within each group. These rules applied to marriage, friendship, and work. The caste system became closely tied to Hindu concepts such as *karma*, the belief that all of a person's actions in this life determine his or her fate in the next life. By accepting this belief, Hindus acknowledged that their position in life was due to actions in their previous existence. They believed that they could acquire good karma only by obeying the social, religious, and moral laws of their caste.

RISE OF BUDDHISM

By the end of the Vedic Age, the Brahmans, or priestly caste, had acquired great power and influence in society because of their role as guardians of the sacred Hindu texts and their control of the rituals that enabled the soul to achieve oneness with atman. Their power did not go unchallenged, and various reformers sought to simplify the rituals by which the individual soul might achieve a higher level of understanding. Among the reformers was Siddhartha Gautama (563 B.C.– 483 B.C.), a member of the Kshatriya caste, who was born to wealth and power. As a young man, Gautama became haunted by the suffering that he saw all around him, so he gave up a life of comfort and pleasure to seek understanding. After wandering for six years and searching for answers, he finally achieved enlightenment and became known as the *Buddha*, or the Enlightened One.

The Buddha taught the Four Noble Truths: (1) all life is suffering; (2) the cause of suffering is desire; (3) the only way to escape suffering is to end desire; (4) the way to end desire is to follow the Noble Eightfold Path that includes right belief, right thoughts, right conduct, right speech, right living, right ambition, right pleasures, and right effort. The goal of existence, the Buddha taught, was the attainment of *Nirvana*, the condition of emptiness.

This stupa, or burial mound, in central India is one of many such memorials that were raised to commemorate the death of the Buddha.

The Buddha set out to reform Hinduism, and his teachings reflected many Hindu beliefs. However, he did reject the increasingly rigid rules of the caste system and the domination of the Brahmans. After his death, his disciples spread his teachings, and these came to form the basis of a new religion, Buddhism. In India, Buddhism flourished for several centuries and was then merged back into Hinduism. But in the Far East, the message carried by Buddhist missionaries took root in China, Korea, Japan, and Southeast Asia. The impact of Buddhism on Asia parallels that of Christianity on Europe in the centuries after the death of Christ. Buddhist missionaries brought not only a system of religious beliefs and ethical values but also art, architecture, and literature.

INTRODUCTION TO THE DOCUMENTS

During the Vedic Age, the beliefs of the early Aryan invaders were gradually formulated into religious doctrine and dogma. In early Aryan society, war, drinking, chariot racing, and gambling featured as prominent activities. The chief Aryan god was Indra, a great warrior. Over the centuries, as Hinduism emerged, it incorporated a variety of beliefs and became intertwined with the increasingly rigid social structure. The *Rig Veda* describes the origins of the four castes and emphasizes that people of the lowest caste are to serve the three higher castes.

Of significance at the end of the Vedic Age is the emergence of Buddhism and its appeal to many Hindus. The Buddha was a skilled teacher who initiated a call for change and won many converts to his beliefs. Emerging at a time of political chaos, Buddhism offered an alternative to Hindu ideas with their emphasis on the caste system and the correct performance of prescribed behaviors. By contrast, Buddhist teachings focused on noble thoughts as a means to salvation and suggested that individuals held control over their destinies.

The following documents provide sources for analysis and comparison of developing religious traditions within the context of Indian civilization.

DOCUMENT 1   THE HYMN OF CREATION

This is one of the many hymns and prayers that make up the sacred Hindu text, the
Rig Veda.

The Hymn of Creation

Then even nothingness was not, nor existence.
   There was no air then, nor the heavens beyond it.
What covered it? Where was it? In whose keeping?
   Was there then cosmic water, in depths unfathomed?

Then there were neither death nor immortality,
   nor was there then the torch of night and day.
The One breathed windlessly and self-sustaining.
   There was that One then, and there was no other.

At first there was only darkness wrapped in darkness.
   All this was only unillumined water.
That One which came to be, enclosed in nothing,
   arose at last, born of the power of heat.

In the beginning desire descended on it—
   that was the primal seed, born of the mind.
The sages who have searched their hearts with wisdom
   know that which is is kin to that which is not.

And they have stretched their cord across the void,
   and know what was above, and what below.
Seminal powers made fertile mighty forces.
   Below was strength, and over it was impulse.

But, after all, who knows, and who can say
   whence it all came, and how creation happened?
The gods themselves are later than creation,
   so who knows truly whence it has arisen?

Whence all creation had its origin,
   he, whether he fashioned it or whether he did not,
he, who surveys it all from highest heaven,
   he knows—or maybe even he does not know.

SOURCE: A. L. Basham, *The Wonder That Was India* (New York: Grove Press, 1954), pp. 247–48.

**What questions was the poet who composed this hymn trying to answer? What clues
to Hindu beliefs does this hymn provide?**

BHAGAVAD GITA

The "Bhagavad Gita" (meaning "Song of God") is among the most popular Hindu literature. Composed sometime between the 5th and 2nd centuries B.C., it is a religious poem in which Krishna, a god who has taken mortal form, and a prince named Arjuna engage in a long dialogue against the background of an impending battle.

At the beginning of the poem, Arjuna is reluctant to go into battle against friends and relatives, but the Lord Krishna instructs him to follow his duty.

ARJUNA: But, Krishna, if you consider knowledge of Brahman superior to any sort of action, why are you telling me to do these terrible deeds?

Your statements seem to contradict each other. They confuse my mind. Tell me one definite way of reaching the highest good.

KRISHNA: I have already told you that, in this world, aspirants may find enlightenment by two different paths. For the contemplative is the path of knowledge: for the active is the path of selfless action.

Freedom from activity is never achieved by abstaining from action. Nobody can become perfect by merely ceasing to act. In fact, nobody can ever rest from his activity even for a moment. All are helplessly forced to act. . . .

Activity is better than inertia. Act, but with self-control. If you are lazy, you cannot even sustain your own body.

The world is imprisoned in its own activity, except when actions are performed as worship of God. Therefore you must perform every action sacramentally, and be free from all attachments to results.

In the beginning
The Lord of beings
Created all men,
To each his duty.
"Do this," He said,
"And you shall prosper. . . ."

But when a man has found delight and satisfaction and peace in the Atman, then he is no longer obliged to perform any kind of action. He has nothing to gain in this world by action, and nothing to lose by refraining from action. He is independent of everybody and everything. Do your duty, always; but without attachment. That is how a man reaches the ultimate Truth; by working without anxiety about results.

SOURCE: *The Song of God: Bhagavad-Gita,* trans. Swami Prabhavananda and Christopher Isherwood (New York: New American Library, 1944), pp. 44–47.

What ethical values does Krishna seek to teach Arjuna in their dialog? How can these values help the young prince achieve his dharma?

As Buddhism spread, it split into two sects: the Theravada sect, which was carried to Ceylon and Southeast Asia; and the Mahayana sect, which was carried into China, Korea, Tibet, and Japan. Despite differences over doctrine, both schools accepted the fundamental teaching of Buddhism: the Four Noble Truths and the Noble Eightfold Path. These teachings are contained in the "Sermon of the Turning of the Wheel of the Law."

Thus I have heard. Once the Master was at Banaras, at the deer park called Isipatana. There the Master addressed the five monks:

"There are two ends not to be served by a wanderer. What are those two? The pursuit of desires and of the pleasure which springs from desires, which is base, common, leading to rebirth, ignoble and unprofitable; and the pursuit of pain and hardship, which is grievous, ignoble and unprofitable. The Middle Way of the Tathagata avoids both these ends; it is enlightened, it brings clear vision, it makes for wisdom, and leads to peace, insight, full wisdom and Nirvana. What is this Middle Way? . . . It is the Noble Eightfold Path—Right Views, Right Resolve, Right Speech, Right Conduct, Right Livelihood, Right Effort, Right Recollection and Right Meditation. This is the Middle Way. . . .

"And this is the Noble Truth of Sorrow. Birth is sorrow, age is sorrow, disease is sorrow, death is sorrow, contact with the unpleasant is sorrow, separation from the pleasant is sorrow, every wish unfulfilled is sorrow—in short all the five components of individuality are sorrow.

"And this is the Noble Truth of the Arising of Sorrow. [It arises from] thirst, which leads to rebirth, which brings delight and passion, and seeks pleasure now here, now there—the thirst for sensual pleasure, the thirst for continued life, the thirst for power.

"And this is the Noble Truth of the Stopping of Sorrow. It is the complete stopping of that thirst, so that no passion remains, leaving it, being emancipated from it, being released from it, giving no place to it.

"And this is the Noble Truth of the Way which Leads to the Stopping of Sorrow. It is the Noble Eightfold Path—Right Views, Right Resolve, Right Speech, Right Conduct, Right Livelihood, Right Effort, Right Recollection and Right Meditation."

SOURCE: A. L. Basham, *The Wonder That Was India* (New York: Grove Press, 1954), pp. 268–69.

Compare the teachings of the Buddha in this excerpt to those of Hinduism in the excerpts from the Bhagavad-Gita.

TIME LINE FOR INDIA AND THE WEST*

INDIA		THE WEST	
		3100	Narmer unites Upper and Lower Egypt; Sumerian city-states flourish in Mesopotamia
3000	Rise of Indus valley civilization		
		2600	Pyramid of Khufu built
2500	Height of Indus valley civilization; Harappa and Mohenjo-daro flourish	2350	Akkad flourishes
		2000	Minoan civilization established on Crete; Mycenaeans invade mainland Greece
		1750	Hammurabi's law code in effect
1700	Indus valley civilization declines		
1500	Aryan invaders destroy Indus valley civilization; Vedic Age begins— development of Hinduism	1480– 1450	Thutmose III of Egypt conquers Syria-Palestine; Knossos destroyed
1400	Rig Veda composed		
		1375	Hittite invasions of Syria-Palestine
		1200	Hittite civilization overrun
		1100	Dorians conquer Greece; Mycenaean civilization collapses
1000– 700	Mahabharata and Ramayana composed	1000	David rules the kingdom of Israel
		750	Homer recites the Iliad and the Odyssey(?); Iron-Age Greeks begin to colonize the Mediterranean; Assyrians conquer Syria-Palestine
700	Sanskrit developed		
550	Siddhartha Gautama (the Buddha) attempts to reform Hinduism	550	Cyrus the Great creates Persian Empire

* All dates are approximate years B.C.

Rise of Classical Civilizations

- The ideal state is that in which an injury done to the least of its citizens is an injury done to all.

  SOLON

- Our constitution...favors the many instead of the few; this is why it is called a democracy. If we look to the laws, they afford equal justice to all in their private differences....The freedom which we enjoy in our government extends also to our ordinary life. There, far from exercising a jealous surveillance over each other, we do not feel called upon to be angry with our neighbor for doing what he likes, or even to indulge in those injurious looks which cannot fail to be offensive, although they inflict no positive penalty. But all this ease in our private relations does not make us lawless as citizens.

  PERICLES

- Our Twelve Tables of law only carried the death penalty for a few crimes. Among these crimes was singing or composing a song that was derogatory to insulting to someone. This was a good law.

  CICERO

- Every man should be responsible to others, nor should any one be allowed to do just as he pleases; for where absolute freedom is allowed there is nothing to restrain the evil which is inherent in every man.

  ARISTOTLE

- If the people are sovereign in a state and the government is run according to their will, it is called liberty. But it is really license.

  CICERO

- The law speaks too softly to be heard amidst the din of arms.

  GAIUS MARIUS

● *Under this monument lies Aeschylus the Athenian,*
Euphorion's son, who died in the wheatlands of Gela.
The grove of Marathon with its glories can speak of his
valor in battle.
The long-haired Persian remembers and can speak of it too.
AESCHYLUS

The Greek City-States

Around 1100 B.C., the Mycenaean civilization collapsed as Dorian tribes from the north invaded Greece. In the resulting confusion, some displaced Mycenaeans, or *Achaeans*, sought refuge along the northern shore of the Peloponnesus; in time, that area came to be known as Achaea. Others sought refuge in Attica, where they mixed with the original inhabitants of the area and eventually developed the great city-state of Athens. Still others migrated across the Aegean Sea to Ionia on the coast of Asia Minor.

The Dorian invaders claimed the fertile valleys of the southern Peloponnesus for their main settlements. In the valley of Laconia, they eventually developed the distinctive society that we know as *Sparta*.

The earliest societies of the Dorians in Greece followed the Indo-European pattern, and their political system was quite similar to that developed by the Mycenaeans. By the 7th century B.C., however, Sparta, Athens, and other city-states throughout Greece had evolved a variety of different political systems. This chapter will deal with the development of the Greek city-states and the spread of their culture throughout the Mediterranean world prior to the 5th century B.C.

GEOGRAPHY AND NATURAL RESOURCES

The geography of Greece is very different from that of Egypt and the Fertile Crescent. Greece is a mountainous peninsula bordered on the west by the Ionian Sea, on the south by the Mediterranean Sea, and on the east by the Aegean Sea. The few rivers are short, swift, shallow, and mainly seasonal—they are, therefore, unsuitable as inland transportation routes. Since the plains and valleys in which the early people settled were isolated from each other by the mountains, political unification was not possible for many years.

The peninsula is separated into two parts by the Gulf of Corinth, but the land masses are linked by the Isthmus of Corinth. The portion south of the Isthmus has been called the *Peloponnesus* for at least 3000 years, for the Mycenaeans who inhabited the area believed that they were descended from a legendary king named *Pelops*.

The mountains of Greece were once more wooded than they are today, providing timber for constructing buildings and ships and fuel for smelting metals. Unfortunately, the forests were not protected or replanted, and the denuded hills were subject to severe ero-

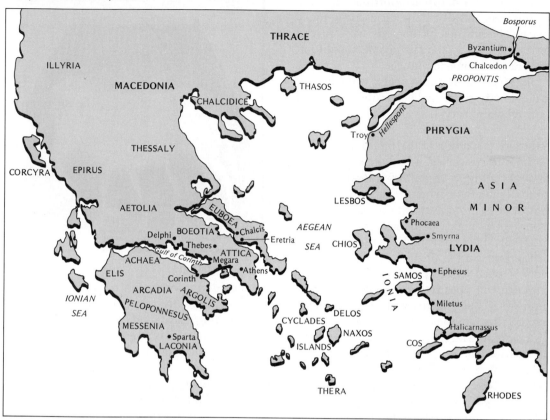

GREECE IN THE 8th CENTURY B.C.
Suggest a reason why Athens, Corinth, and Megara became more prosperous and influential than many other Greek city-states.

sion of the soil. Natural regrowth of the forests was prevented by the herds of goats which ate the tree shoots as they emerged.

The mountains contained few minerals, and those that were available were soon exhausted. While there was some copper, there was no tin available to make bronze, and the known deposits of gold, silver, and iron were small and widely scattered. The ancient people did have large deposits of clay suitable for making pottery. They also had marble and limestone in abundance for building and sculpture.

The moderate climate in the lowlands of Greece encouraged the Greeks to spend much of their leisure time outdoors. The steady summer winds, combined with the lack of inland transportation and the many offshore islands, encouraged them to become sailors. Through their seafaring ventures, they came into contact with the ancient civilizations of the Middle East.

In ancient times olives and grapes were very important crops, and they continue to be so today: unlike grain crops, grapes and olives can be grown successfully in hilly, rocky areas. The ancient people made wine from their grapes and pressed olive oil for use in cooking. Both of these products became important export items.

THE POLIS Because inland transportation was so difficult in Greece, the inhabitants of each valley tended to develop

117

small, independent communities. Each city-state or *polis* included an *agora* (market place), and an *acropolis* (fortified citadel), which was usually built on a high, rocky place. The shrines of the gods were placed on the acropolis, and the people sought refuge there in times of danger.

In Mycenaean times, each city-state or group of city-states had been ruled by a tribal king who also served as military commander in times of war. Gradually, these monarchies began to lose much of their authority. Some of the city-states began to elect kings rather than accepting a hereditary monarchy, and council members, who were also elected, began to have more authority in making decisions. An assembly of the people, which had originally been convened to hear the rulings of the king and council, began to have the right to participate in certain decisions.

Since the population of each polis was quite small, all male citizens were expected to participate in the defense and government of the community. This process became the foundation for the Greek democracies that evolved during the 5th and 4th centuries B.C. Nevertheless, a relatively small number of people usually controlled the polis at any given time, and the question of representation was the subject of much debate throughout the centuries.

THE IRON AGE The Greeks of the 8th century B.C. believed that they were living in a period of decline which they called the *Iron Age*. In the mythical past, they believed, there had been a Golden Age, in which men and women lived like gods without care or trouble; a Silver Age, when a weaker generation of men antagonized the gods and lost many of the blessings their ancestors had enjoyed; a Bronze Age, in which a fierce, warlike people with superhuman strength roamed the earth and ended by destroying each other; and finally the Heroic Age of the Mycenaean and Trojan heroes. The Iron Age was considered to be the least

An episode from Homer's Odyssey: *the hero escapes from his enemies by hiding under a ram.*

happy of the five ages; a time when men and women had fewer heroic qualities, and were beset by anxieties and pain.[1]

The *Iliad* and the *Odyssey* of Homer preserved memories of the Heroic Age in which the legendary heroes Odysseus, Agamemnon, Achilles, and Hector had demonstrated their physical strength and grandeur of character on the battlefield of Troy. These epics became an important part of the education of young people during the Iron Age and for centuries to come, for people believed that they provided moral instruction as well as entertainment.

Homer was a native of Ionia, according to tradition, and Greeks of the 5th century thought that he had lived in the 8th century B.C. Although his epics concerned events that took place at the beginning of the 12th century, his narrative blended the traditions and customs of his own age with those of the ancient Bronze Age Minoan-Mycenaean civilization. For example, Homer's stories depict the Greek gods and goddesses that he and his contemporaries worshiped rather than

---

[1]Hesiod, *Works and Days*, lines 109-184.

An episode added to Homer's Iliad *by a later writer: Achilles kills an Amazon warrior.*

the nature deities of the Minoans and Mycenaeans. On the other hand, he describes the Mycenaean warriors as carrying bronze weapons and wearing helmets topped with boar tusks, equipment that was long outdated by his own time. Today, Homer is considered one of the most important sources of information about the Iron Age of Greece (1100-700 B.C.) as well as for the civilization of the Mycenaeans. Hesiod, a poet who may have been a contemporary of Homer, is another important source of information about this period.

EARLY RELIGION: THE GREEK PANTHEON

Through the writings of Homer and Hesiod, we have a very clear idea about what the Greeks of the Iron Age believed about their gods. The Greeks believed that their gods resided on Mount Olympus in northern Greece. These gods had supernatural powers and yet often showed human failings: they could be envious, proud, or overly impetuous. In Homer's epic stories, the gods helped certain heroes who were deserving, giving them added strength or wisdom to carry out their appointed tasks. However, they were not always consistent in their support—a hero might find, for instance, that his patron god or goddess had shifted loyalties in the midst of a battle.

Zeus, the father of the gods and lord of the sky, was considered to be the most pow-

erful god, and yet, on some occasions, he was the victim of plots conceived by the other deities. Zeus and Hera, his wife, were considered to be the patrons of married couples. Apollo was associated with the sun and provided inspiration for music and poetry. Athena was the special protector of Athens, and was looked to for special aid in times of war. Aphrodite was worshiped as goddess of love and beauty. She was known for her constant involvement in match-making schemes, which usually led to disaster for the human beings who became involved in them. Poseidon, whose symbol was a trident, a long three-pronged fork, was associated with the

The Muses provided inspiration for artists, writers, and orators. They were associated with measure and grace.

sea and was thought to be responsible for earthquakes and tides. Hermes, who wore winged sandals, served as messenger of the gods. He was associated with eloquence of speech, but also with lies and deceit. Demeter was the goddess of agriculture, and was associated with the fertility of the earth.

In addition to their pantheon of gods, the early Greeks also believed in the *Muses*, the *Fates*, and the *Furies*. The *Muses* were associated with the god Apollo and were originally three in number; they provided inspiration to artists, writers, and musicians. Eventually nine muses were named, including Terpsichore, the muse of choral dance and song; Clio, the muse of history; and Euterpe, the muse of lyric poetry. The six other muses provided inspiration to writers of epics, hymns, comedies, tragedies, and poetry, and to astronomers.

In very early times, the Greeks believed that there were three female deities called *Fates* who supervised, but did not control, the destinies of human beings. Later, the Greeks portrayed the Fates as three old women who spun the destinies of human beings like threads, with one drawing out the thread of life, another measuring it, and the third cutting it.

The *Furies* were believed to have been born from the spilled blood of Uranus, an ancient god who had been slain by his son, Cronus. They were considered to be fearsome beings who barked like dogs and had writhing snakes for hair. Their principal role was to enforce family law, and they were noted for avenging the murders of people who were killed by family members.

The Greeks traditionally believed that the souls of the dead were transported across an underground river to Hades, a mysterious shadowy afterworld. In the *Odyssey*, Homer portrays the inhabitants of this afterworld as dispirited beings who miss the light of day. For example, when Odysseus visits Hades, he encounters the soul or "shade" of Achilles and politely congratulates him upon his lot in the afterworld. Achilles responds that life is much to be preferred to death:

> *Let me hear no smooth talk*
> *of death from you, Odysseus,*
>   *light of councils.*
> *Better, I say, to break sod as a farm hand*
> *for some poor country man, on iron rations,*
> *than lord it over all the exhausted dead.*[2]

ECONOMY AND SOCIAL STRUCTURE

Although Odysseus and the other kings and lords that Homer described usually had a few servants or slaves, they actively participated in the work of their estates. In the *Odyssey*, Odysseus describes how he built his own house, and boasts that he can drive a plow as straight as anyone. His father, the old king Laertes, tends his own vineyard, and his wife, Penelope, weaves her own cloth. Homer's great noble families have a great emotional attachment to their homes and estates, and do not aspire to live differently by seizing the wealth of others. Although Odysseus becomes rich through spoils of war, he longs for the day when he can put aside his weapons and return to his farm in Ithaca. These vignettes very likely give us a truer picture of Homer's own time than of the society of the Mycenaeans.

Hesiod also emphasizes that the gods intended men to work hard on their estates rather than achieving wealth by other means.

> *It is from work that men grow rich and own*
>   *flocks and herds;*
> *by work, too, they become much better*
>   *friends of the immortals. . . .*
> *If any man by force of hands wins him*
>   *a great fortune,*
> *or steals it by the cleverness of his*
>   *tongue. . .*
> *lightly the gods wipe out that man, and*
>   *diminish the household*
> *of such a one, and his wealth stays with*
>   *him for only a short time.*[3]

---

[2]*Odyssey* XI, 481-4.

[3]Hesiod, *Works and Days*, lines 308-9, 321-2, 325-6.

SITES OF GREEK COLONIZATION
Why did the Phoenicians and Greeks select these sites for their colonies?

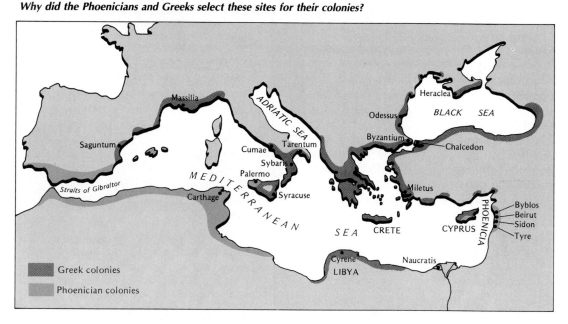

Greek colonies

Phoenician colonies

As indicated in the works of Homer and Hesiod, farming and raising livestock were the principal occupations of the Greeks during the Iron Age. The family-managed estates were almost totally self-sufficient, and were able to produce their own shoes and clothing as well as food and other necessities. The scholar H. D. F. Kitto speculated that there were only two specialized trades during this era in Greece: pottery-making and metal-work. He supported this theory with the observation that these were the only trades which had guardian deities to oversee them:

● ● ● *Of specialized trades we hear of only two, the trades of the smith and of the potter. . . . It is interesting to notice that these two are the only crafts which, in Greek, have divine exponents. . . . There is no god of shoemaking or farming or building. Obviously, these things everybody knows how to do, but it is very different with elaborate metal-work, or the making of an elegant piece of pottery.*[4]

[4]H. D. F. Kitto, *The Greeks*, revised ed. (New York: Penguin Books, 1957), pp. 40-41.

The family came to be the principal focus of the laws and traditions of Iron Age Greece, just as it was the basis of the economy. In Homer's world, family ties were sacred, and marital fidelity was considered to be highly important. The most admirable wife was one who conscientiously raised her children and ran an efficient household. Although a wife's status depended upon that of her husband, she was considered to be the social equal of her husband. In fact, women were held in much greater esteem during this era than in later periods of Greek history. Penelope, Odysseus' wife, is considered especially admirable because she remains faithful to Odysseus during his long absence and struggles to keep the family estate intact.

TRADING AND COLONIZATION
During the 8th century, many people found that their family farms could not support all of the people who depended upon them. As the population grew, trading and sea-faring increasingly became an attractive alternative to farming. Hesiod described the benefits of

this new livelihood, but emphasized the risks involved:

You will find it hard
   to escape coming to grief. Yet still
and even so, men in their shortsightedness
   do undertake it;
for acquisition means life to miserable
   mortals;
but it is an awful thing to die among the
   waves.[5]

There were undoubtedly those who shared the conservative attitudes of Hesiod, but many others discovered the benefits of earning their living through seafaring. The new products and ideas that these seafarers brought back made a permanent difference in the Greeks' culture and way of life. Through their contacts with the Phoenicians, they discovered that they could use an alphabet to write their language; thus, the art of writing, which had been lost since the Dorian invasion, was revived in the 8th century. They also found many areas throughout the Mediterranean world which could be colonized and which, in total, would provide thousands of acres of additional land for farming.

In searching for new lands for farming, the Greeks tended to select uninhabited coastal areas. The first settlements in Ionia had been possible because the Lydians and other inland peoples were not greatly interested in building ports or in farming the coastal plains. During the 8th century B.C., the Greeks found that a similar situation prevailed in a number of other areas along the southern coast of Europe, in southern Macedonia, around the Black Sea, and on the northern coast of Africa. Many of the colonies that the Greeks established in these areas became important cities.

A group of colonists from Megara, whose soil was so poor that it was said to "grow rocks," established the cities of Byzantium and Chalcedon on the two shores of the Bos-

Around 750 B.C., the Greeks learned from the Phoenicians how to use an alphabet. Prior to this, the Greek language had not been written since the Dorian invasion of about 1100 B.C.

Early Greek (8th cent. B.C.)	Classical Greek (5th cent. B.C.)	Modern names of letters
A	A	ALPHA
ᛒ	B	BETA
ᛌ	Γ	GAMMA
Δ	Δ	DELTA
Ⅎ	E	EPSILON
ᛅ		
I	Z	ZETA
ᛒ	H	ETA
⊗	θ	THETA
ᛎ	I	IOTA
ᚷ	K	KAPPA
ᛀ	Λ	LAMBDA
ᛗ	M	MU
ᛒ	N	NU
	Ξ	XI
O	0	OMICRON
ᚌ	Π	PI
ᚱ	P	RHO
ᛧ	Σ	SIGMA
X	T	TAU
	Y	UPSILON
	Φ	PHI
	X	CHI
	Ψ	PSI
	Ω	OMEGA

porus. Both cities grew prosperous by charging tolls for ships passing through the strait. Chalcidice was established on the northern shore of the Aegean Sea to provide homes for the land-poor farmers of Chalcis and Eretria in Euboea. Miletus, itself one of the first

---

[5]Hesiod, *Works and Days*, lines 684-6.

settlements of Ionia, participated in the colonization movement by establishing at least 80 settlements on the shores of the Black Sea. These settlements became so prosperous through the export of their wheat and fish that the Black Sea came to be known as the "hospitable sea" (*Euximus Pontus*). The people of Miletus also secured permission from the pharaoh of Egypt to establish a trading post in the delta, at Naukratis. At this trading center, Greek pottery, wine, and oil were exchanged for Egyptian wheat. Colonists from the island of Thera established a city called Cyrene on the northern coast of Libya. There, the coastal land was used to cultivate wheat, barley, and fruit, and to raise cattle and horses for export.

In Italy, the Greeks found that the Apennine Mountains on the eastern coast were a barrier to settlement. They were able to establish colonies on the western coast, however, because the Etruscan tribes had not yet begun to exert their influence in this area. Colonists from Euboea established the colony of Cumae on the western coast of Italy, and then set up a "new city" (Neapolis) just a few miles to the south. Today we know this second colony as Naples. Settlers from Achaea established Sybaris, which became so wealthy that its name became the source of our term *Sybarite*, meaning a person who lives in fantastic luxury. Sparta established one colony, named Tarentum, on the "instep" of the Italian peninsula. Altogether, so many Greek colonies were formed in southern Italy and Sicily that the region came to be called *Magna Graecia* (Great Greece).

When Corinth established its colony of Syracuse on the eastern coast of Sicily, the Phoenicians realized that this new city could become a threat to their own interests in the area. They therefore began to establish colonies on the western coast of Sicily, and did not allow the Greeks to settle near them. None of the Phoenician cities had a harbor as excellent as the one at Syracuse, however.

Massilia, the modern city of Marseilles, was founded by settlers from Phocaea, in Ionia. This colony became the center of Greek influence in ancient Gaul (present France). From Massilia, Greek traders moved up the Rhone valley far enough to meet traders from Cornwall, in England, who traveled down the Seine and Loire rivers. From these traders they were able to obtain rare commodities such as tin.

The colonizing movement produced important economic improvements in Greece. The settlements not only provided additional acreage for farming, but also opened up new markets and new sources of raw materials. A great colonizing city such as Corinth could provide unlimited job opportunities for ship builders, traders, and farmers in its home port and colonies. Even a city like Athens, which did not directly participate in the colonizing movement, benefited from the new opportunities opened up by trade. The Athenians developed several specialized industries to take advantage of the expanded markets. They were able to trade their pottery, textiles, and metalware for wheat and other foods which were difficult to cultivate in the rocky soil of Attica.

As they came into contact with other peoples and civilizations, the Greeks became more conscious of their own identity. They began to refer to themselves as Hellenes and to their native land as Hellas. They also began to use the descriptive term barbaroi ("jabberers") to describe certain foreign-language speakers. Thus, the term "barbarian" originally designated people whose language sounded inelegant or harsh to the Greeks. Within a few centuries, however, both the Greeks and the Romans used the term barbarian to deride any group of people who did not share their culture.

An artist's reconstruction of the Athenian harbor at Piraeus. The development of seafaring enabled the Athenians to import the grain they needed in exchange for such products as wine, olive oil, and pottery.

As manufacturing and trade grew in importance, the structure of Greek society began to reflect the changes brought about by these new ways of life. Land ownership continued to be the mark of nobility, but it was no longer the only measure of wealth and prestige. The influence of wealthy merchants and traders eventually led to important social and political changes. By the end of the Iron Age, the social structure of Greece was much less stable and predictable than it had been in Hesiod's time.

THE SPIRIT OF PANHELLENISM

The inhabitants of the Greek city-states referred to themselves as *Hellenes* and believed that they had descended from a common ancestor named *Hellen*, who was a grandson of Prometheus.[6] The spirit of pan-

An outstanding event of the Iron Age was the institution of athletic games at Olympia in the Peloponnesus. This is the athletes' entrance to the stadium.

---

[6]Prometheus was the ancient god who gave fire to mankind.

An Athenian relief shows athletes training for Olympic events: running, wrestling, and javelin throwing.

hellenism was reflected in a number of traditions and events. One of these was the institution of athletic competitions. The Panhellenic (all-Greek) Games were so important to the Greeks that a sacred truce was proclaimed in any war that might be underway at the time of a scheduled game, and all travelers to and from the games were given protection.

The most important of these games were the Olympic Games, which were held every four years at Olympia in honor of Zeus. Beginning in 776 B.C., the traditional date of the first Olympic Games, the Greeks dated all events by the *Olympiads*.

Only free Greek citizens could compete in these games, and each participant had to swear to abide by the rules. Later, some foreigners were granted citizenship so that they could participate. The athletes first competed in foot races. These were followed by the *Pentathlon*, a group of five contests involving discus throwing, spear throwing, running, jumping, and wrestling. The contestant who won three of these five events was declared the winner of the Pentathlon. Races of horse-drawn chariots were the next event, and the final event was boxing. The

prize awarded to winners, a crown made from olive leaves, was regarded as the greatest honor a man could achieve. The victors of the games were commemorated in the sculptures and poems of famous artists.

Another common bond that united the ancient Greeks was the tradition of seeking advice from *oracles* which were thought to transmit prophecies from the gods to mortals. The oracle of Apollo at Delphi was the most famous. A supplicant wrote a question on a piece of lead and put it into a clay jar. A priest then read the question and listened for the answer of Zeus, which was uttered through the rustling of leaves in an oak tree. Three priestesses, known as "doves," interpreted the rustling and reported the response of Zeus to the supplicant.

Twelve city-states banded together in a religious league called the *Delphic Amphictyony* to protect the oracle and temple at Delphi. The oracle was renowned throughout the Greek world, and acquired great political importance. It was consulted by Greek colonists who wanted to find the best sites for new settlements, and its advice was also sought by such distinguished visitors as Alexander the Great and King Croesus of Lydia.

Several members of the Delphic Amphictyony set up individual treasury buildings near the temple of Apollo. This is the treasury building of the Athenians.

EVOLUTION OF GOVERNMENT

In the Greek language, the word *polis* refers to "the people" or "the community" as well as the actual city in which the people live. In ancient Greece, it was expected that each citizen would perform certain civic duties as a member of this community, and the *polis*, in turn, was responsible for educating its citizens and for teaching them its laws. Even after many of the city-states had grown into large areas with many thousands of citizens, people still retained the ideal of citizens being directly involved in government, and of a government concerned with every aspect of the lives of its citizens.

During the 7th century B.C., the various city-states began to follow different lines of political development. The typical sequence of events found the monarchy replaced by an *aristocracy*, or a government by a few; then a *timocracy*, a government in which participation is based on wealth. At this point, a *tyrant* who acted as champion of the common people and foe of the aristocracy often seized control. Finally, the tyrant might be expelled and a *democracy*, or government by the people, established.

Of all the Greek city-states, we have the most information about Athens and Sparta. Since both of these city-states were much larger than the average polis, there were certain problems involved in creating a government in which all members of the community were included. The Athenians' struggle for political equality led to the democracy of the 5th century B.C., for which Athens has been renowned throughout history. By contrast, the Spartans resisted any changes in their form of government. The Spartan government regulated every aspects of its citizens' lives, and applied stern military control to prevent the political evolutions which ultimately brought democracy to many city-states.

ATHENIAN GOVERNMENT

In the earliest times, the government of Athens followed the pattern that had been established in Mycenaean societies prior to 1100 B.C. A hereditary monarch ruled the polis, and he was advised by a council of aristocrats who represented the most important tribes in the area. During the Iron Age, the civil, military, and religious duties of the monarch gradually came to be assumed by nine *archons*, who were chosen by an assembly of citizens from among the wealthiest and most influential families of Athens. By the 8th century B.C., the monarchy had disappeared completely, and its functions were taken over by the elected council of archons.

The nine archons were advised by a council of men who had formerly held office as archons. This group of advisers was called the Council of the *Areopagus* after the hill on which its meetings were held. The archons served in office for only one year, but then could continue to influence policy by joining the Council of the Areopagus.

During the 7th century, the outlying districts of Attica were incorporated into the polis of Athens, and the population of Athens itself became more diversified. While many Athenians had become wealthy through trading and colonization ventures, there was also a growing class of poorer citizens who came to resent the prosperity and expanding influence of the rich. Due to a combination of circumstances, these poorer people gradually lost their political rights, and Athenian society came to be polarized by social, economic, and political inequalities.

REPRESENTATION

Because the Assembly of Athens was responsible for electing the nine archons who ruled the polis, the question of who was entitled to belong to the Assembly was important. By 650 B.C., the Greeks had devised a new strategy of waging war, and this change came to have a bearing on the question of membership in the Assembly.

Because of the scarcity and high cost of horses, the use of chariots in battle became uneconomical. To replace the chariots, the Greeks adopted the *phalanx* method of fighting in which *hoplites*, or foot soldiers, equipped with spears, swords, and bronze armor, fought in close ranks. Thus, aristocratic heroes such as those Homer wrote about could no longer determine the outcome of a battle. Instead, those citizens who could afford to arm themselves in the new fashion became the mainstay of the army. These citizens continued to have the right to belong to the Assembly. However, the *thetes*, the class of poor, free farmers who could not afford weapons, were excluded from military service and consequently from the political process. The exclusion of the thetes meant that the government of Athens became a *timocracy* in which membership in the assembly depended upon property qualifications.

POLITICAL DEVELOPMENTS

Aristotle, the great Greek philosopher who lived during the 4th century B.C., is one of our most important sources of information concerning early political developments in Athens. Aristotle described 7th-century Athens as a city divided by bitter class antagonisms. The greed and political power of the oligarchs, or wealthy families, had led to this situation, he reported. Many of the small farmers and other common people of Attica had gradually fallen into debt to the oligarchs. Because they controlled the government of the polis, the oligarchs had been able to strengthen the rights of creditors. They had the right to seize the lands and property of the poor, and could even force debtors into slavery. As Aristotle concluded:

• • • *Thus the most grievous and bitter thing in the state of public affairs for the masses was their slavery; not but what they were discontented also about everything else, for they found themselves virtually without a share in anything.*[7]

The bronze helmets of hoplite soldiers protected the face as well as the head. A well-equipped hoplite also wore a bronze breastplate and leg shields (greaves).

[7]Aristotle, *The Constitution of Athens* II, 1.

127

The middle classes and the poor of Athens began to look to the government of the polis for a resolution of their grievances. Due to the efforts of several prominent Athenians, the government did succeed in averting a civil war and in asserting its authority against the interests of the powerful noble families. By the end of the 6th century B.C., the government was much more representative of all of the diverse groups who lived in the city and in the countryside of Attica.

Draco. In 621 B.C., the archons appointed an aristocrat named Draco to codify the laws of Athens. Only one of Draco's laws has been found, and it pertains to the case of involuntary homicide. From the content of his law, it is evident that his main concern was to put an end to private vendettas and blood feuds.

Draco's law stipulated that a court would convene to judge whether a murder had been committed intentionally or by accident. If the court decided that the murder was accidental, the family of the victim could agree to pardon the murderer. If the family did not agree with the court's verdict, however, the defendant would be banished from the area. Thus, the court played an important part in resolving a complex situation, while still allowing the victim's family a voice in deciding the affair.

It is not known for certain whether Draco concerned himself only with the subject of homicide, or if he also wrote other laws which were later destroyed. Later traditions, recorded several centuries after Draco's lifetime, indicated that Draco had written a complete code of laws. Reportedly, the laws were so severe that capital punishment was stipulated for even the most trivial offenses. Thus, Draco's name became the source of our adjective *draconian*, meaning "extremely severe or oppressive." Many modern scholars believe that these traditions concerning Draco may be inaccurate, for Solon did not mention such a state of affairs when he recounted his own achievements a few decades later.

Solon. Several years after Draco's term of office, Solon, a philosopher and poet who came from an aristocratic family, was appointed to deal with the problems of the Athenians. He was given unlimited authority to exact measures to benefit the polis, but it was understood that he would leave office once he had completed his task.

In poems written before he took office, Solon had expressed his deep distress over the divisions that had arisen among Athenians. He believed that the main cause of the trouble was the selfishness and greed of the wealthy and privileged classes. As he took office, around 594 B.C., he warned these people that their selfishness would, in the end, be self-destructive:

• • • *Confine your swelling thoughts within reasonable bounds. For we shall not comply with your present disposition, and you yourselves will not find it meet for your own interests.*[8]

Solon had no sympathy with the extremists who demanded redistribution of the land, and yet he clearly understood that reform was needed in order to alleviate the miserable plight of the masses. To correct the most pressing injustices, he proclaimed a policy of "shaking off the burdens," under which all debts of the small farmers were canceled. Enslavement for debt was forbidden, and those who had been enslaved were set free. Athenian citizens who had been sold abroad as slaves could, if they chose, return home to be set free.

Solon encouraged the development of industry and trade by several means. Since small, independent family farms were no longer practical in view of the cheap grain imported from the colonies, he encouraged farmers to find other trades or to use their land only for the crops that were best suited to it. To this end, he forbade the export of any farm product except olive oil. He re-

---

[8]Ibid., IV, 2.

quired each father to teach his sons a trade, and encouraged foreign artisans to come to Athens to teach new techniques and art forms. He granted citizenship to those skilled foreigners who promised to settle permanently in the city.

Solon instituted important political reforms to increase the number of citizens who could participate in government. He categorized citizens according to property qualifications, and set aside the special privileges of the nobility. The first of Solon's classes, the *pentecosiomediamni* ("500-bushel men") were those people who could produce the equivalent of 500 bushels of grain or an equal measure of wine or oil. The second and third classes were those people who were capable of producing 300 and 200 bushels, respectively. The fourth class, the thetes, were those who did not have property. Only men of the two highest classes were eligible to hold office as archons, but all citizens, including the thetes, could serve in the assembly. The shift from hereditary to property qualifications for the highest offices made it possible for those who had become wealthy through commerce and trade to participate more fully in the government. The inclusion of the poor people in the Assembly meant that their needs could no longer be ignored.

Solon's judicial reforms were also important. He codified the laws of the polis, except those dealing with homicide, to prevent favoritism and other abuses on the part of judges. (The laws pertaining to homicide, which had been codified by Draco, remained unchanged.) Law cases continued to be judged by the nine archons and by special courts of law. However, the most serious cases were judged by the assembly of all citizens. The Assembly became the court of final appeal for penalties of death, exile, or heavy fines which might be set by magistrates of the regular courts.

When Solon left office, he noted that his achievements had been made possible only because of the special authority he had been given. Without this authority, he said, the Athenians never would have reached a consensus on reform, for the privileged classes had a vested interest in keeping the lower classes enslaved.

● ● ● *These things I accomplished through arbitrary action, bringing force to the support of the dictates of justice, and I followed through to the end the course which I promised. . . . I drafted laws which show equal consideration for the upper and lower classes, and provide a fair administration of justice for every individual.*[9]

Solon realized that, if he had truly succeeded in being fair and impartial, no class within Athens would be entirely satisfied with the new state of affairs. He therefore left Athens to travel for a period of 10 years, and decreed that his laws should remain in effect for 100 years. His reforms made such a great contribution to the development of the Athenian democracy that he came to be regarded as one of the great sages of the ancient world.

THE TYRANTS

As the appointment of special administrators such as Draco and Solon suggests, there were times when the Athenians were not able to resolve their differences within the traditional government of the polis. During periods of crisis, many Athenians were willing to accept a strong central authority with the hope that order might be restored and their grievances resolved. During the 6th century B.C., this need led to the rise of *tyrants*,[10] men who were not elected by the people but had enough supporters that they were able to seize power.

Many of the tyrants who seized power in Athens and in other city-states were wise and able rulers who reduced the political

---

[9]Ibid., VII, 4.

[10]The word "tyrant" originally meant a person who seized political power illegally. Only later did it become a synonym for a cruel and oppressive ruler.

control of the aristocrats and paved the way for the institution of democracy. They often appeared to be champions of the poor and of the middle class, for by making economic concessions to these groups, the tyrants could count on their support to maintain their own political power. Successive tyrants fostered the development of art and literature, encouraged trade through the process of colonization, built temples, aqueducts, and harbors, and redistributed the lands of the aristocrats to the poor.

It is difficult to evaluate the period of tyranny in Greek history because later accounts were usually sympathetic to the aristocracy and disparaged the achievements of the tyrants. For example, in the 4th century B.C., Socrates expressed the opinion that the main goal of a tyrant was to remain in power:

• • • *At first, in the early days of his power, he is full of smiles, and he salutes every one whom he meets—he to be called a tyrant, who is making promises in public and also in private! liberating debtors, and distributing land to the people and his followers, and wanting to be so kind and good to every one! ...*

But when he has disposed of foreign enemies by conquest or treaty, and there is nothing to fear from them, then he is always stirring up some war or other, in order that the people may require a leader.[11]

Although Aristotle approved of certain individual tyrants, he felt that, in general, "the evil practices of the last and worst form of democracy are all found in tyrannies." He indicated that tyrants were able to retain their offices because it was so difficult to overthrow them, not because they ruled with the consent of the people. The basis of a tyrant's power, he said, was:

• • • *1. The humiliation of his subjects; he knows that a mean-spirited man will not conspire against anybody: 2. the creation of mistrust among them; for a tyrant is not overthrown until men begin to have confidence in one another; and this is the reason why tyrants are at war with the good [people]; they are under the idea that their power is endangered by them, not only because they will not be ruled despotically, but also because they are loyal to one another, and to other men, and do not inform against one another, or against other men: 3. the tyrant desires that his subjects shall be incapable of action, for no one attempts what is impossible, and they will not attempt to overthrow a tyranny, if they are powerless.*[12]

Pisistratus. Many Athenians were not satisfied with the reforms that Solon had made. The aristocrats, who had lost their exclusive rights, thought that Solon had gone too far in his reforms; the masses thought that he had not gone far enough. Although Solon had enacted important changes, he had not changed the basic form of government: there were still only nine archons, and this council was too small to represent all of the different interests in the city and the surrounding countryside. By 560 B.C., there was again great unrest in Athens as three groups struggled to control the government: the Plain party, consisting of the landed aristocracy; the Hill party, made up of the landless citizens and small farmers from the countryside outside of Athens; and the Shore party, representing the craftsmen and traders. In 546 B.C., Pisistratus, a leader of the Hill party, appeared in the marketplace, covered with blood, and asked for a bodyguard. Since he was a popular military hero, his request was granted. With the help of these guards, he seized the acropolis and established himself as a tyrant.

Pisistratus was an effective champion of the poor people of Athens. He exiled several important nobles, confiscated their estates, and divided the land among landless citizens. He used the revenues from a 10 percent tax imposed on the incomes of the wealthier

---

[11]Plato, *The Republic* VIII, 567.

[12]Aristotle, *Politics* V, 11.

classes to equip and stock these new farms. Public works projects were created to provide jobs for the unemployed. One such project was the construction of a large cistern near the headwaters of the Ilisus River and an aqueduct to convey the water to Athens.

New colonies were founded at strategic points along the important trade routes, including Segeum, on the coast of Asia Minor near the Hellespont, and Chersonesus, on the peninsula extending southwest from Thrace. New trading alliances were established with other Greek city-states, including Thessaly and Naxos. Pisistratus also developed a strong navy which came to be respected throughout the Aegean area.

In order to evoke civic pride among the Athenians, Pisistratus began the construction of the *Propylaea*, a monumental approach to the acropolis, and built or renovated several temples to the Olympian gods. He established the Panathenaic and Dionysiac Festivals to encourage the writing and public performance of epics and dramas, and consecrated the island of Delos as a religious center for all Greeks.

Aristotle evaluated Pisistratus' leadership in this way:

••• *But most important of all the qualities mentioned was his popular and kindly attitude. For in every respect it was his principle to regulate everything in accordance with the laws without claiming a special privilege for himself. . . . For the majority both of the nobles and of the common people were in his favor. The former he won over through his friendly relationship with them, the latter through the help which he gave them in their private affairs; and he always proved fair to both of them.*[13]

John V. A. Fine, a modern historian, credits Pisistratus with maintaining a state that was free from factional strife:

••• *One of Pisistratus' greatest services to Athens—if not the greatest—was that for a whole generation under his rule and that of his son Hippias, the country enjoyed almost complete freedom from factional strife. . . . As a tyrant he contributed greatly to the growth of a united state. . . . On the basis of the limited evidence, it seems clear that these were the ways in which he attempted to foster a spirit of unity among the Athenians: his conciliatory attitude to some prominent families and his suppression of those stubbornly resistant to his rule by exile or seizing their sons as hostages; his building program, which not only provided employment to many, but also must have increased the pride of Athenians in their city.*[14]

Pisistratus died in 527 B.C., and his son, Hippias, succeeded him as tyrant. Hippias' reign was an oppressive one, and he made a number of powerful enemies. He was overthrown by a faction of noble families aided by the Spartans.

THE 5TH-CENTURY DEMOCRACY

Once again the various factions struggled to gain control of the government, and in 508 B.C., Cleisthenes [KLICE-the-neez], a statesman with great popular support, came to power. He was determined to break down the sectional interests of the three major parties and to create a unified city-state in which all citizens could participate equally.

Cleisthenes. Cleisthenes recognized that the tribal and geographical factions that had developed among the Athenians would continue to prevent the creation of a unified state and an effective government for the polis. He therefore set up ten artificial "tribes," each including scattered precincts or *demes* from each of the three geographical areas: hill, shore, and plain. Each "tribe" thus contained a cross-section of interests and a mix-

---

[13]Aristotle, *The Constitution of Athens* XVI, 9.

[14]J. V. A. Fine, *The Ancient Greeks* (Harvard University Press, 1983), pp. 218-9.

ture of family loyalties. Since the territory of each tribe included a portion of Athens, the city became the focal point of the polis.

Every male of 18 years or older was required to register in the deme in which he lived. Membership in the deme became hereditary, and even if a person moved to another deme he retained his original registration. Although the Athenians would not accept Cleisthenes' suggestion that they change their surnames to the names of their demes, he did succeed in getting them to shift their basic allegiances from their clans or tribes to the polis.

The Boule. Cleisthenes made the Assembly of Athens the most important part of the government. To ensure that the Assembly could function effectively as a decision-making body, Cleisthenes created a committee called the *Boule* consisting of 50 men from each tribe. The Boule was responsible for preparing business for the assembly to vote upon, and its 500 members served for a term of one year. Within the Boule there were ten governing committees, each having 50 members, which rotated in office. Each committee had full-time responsibility for the Boule's business for one-tenth of the year, so that the Boule at any given time was represented by these 50 acting members.

The existence of the Boule ensured that the important business of the polis would be brought to the Assembly rather than to any other council. In order to prevent certain citizens from becoming too influential, the members of the Boule were chosen by lot rather than by election. Each day, an administrator was chosen, also by lot, from the members of the governing committee. This person was responsible for administering the government for that day.

The Assembly. All adult male Athenians over 18 years of age were eligible to vote in the Assembly. The members of this body discussed legislation submitted by the Boule, passed laws, voted on issues of war and peace, instituted taxes, and reviewed the accounts

Members of the Athenian Assembly wrote the names of those they wished to exile on these ostraka. Most of Athens' prominent citizens—including Miltiades and Themistocles, the historian Thucydides, and the philosopher Socrates—were impeached or exiled by the Assembly at some point in their careers.

of officials when their terms of office expired. In order to vote on any matter before the Assembly, a member had to be present from the beginning of the session and hear every speech dealing with the topic. A person could not speak before the Assembly if he was in debt to the state or if he had ever thrown his shield away during a battle.

Once a year, the Assembly met to discuss whether or not anyone posed a threat to the polis, and if so, whether that person should be exiled. To settle this question, each person qualified to vote picked up an *ostrokon*, a piece of broken pottery, from the ground and wrote the name of the person he thought should be *ostracized* (exiled). The votes were then carefully counted, and if a person received 6000 votes by this method, he was sent into exile for 10 years.

Courts of Law. The courts of law consisted of a committee of 6000 men chosen by

THE ASSEMBLY

Members:	All citizens of Athens. *Requirements for citizenship: Either* both parents Athenians, *or* awarded citizenship for distinguished service to state; 18 years of age or older; male.
Role:	Make all important decisions concerning foreign and domestic policy; appoint diplomats, *strategoi,* and other magistrates to carry out policy.

LAW COURT

Members:	6000 citizens chosen by lot from the Assembly to serve as jury pool. For important trials, several hundred citizens might serve on court.
Role:	Act as judge and jury for all major criminal and civil law cases of Athens and subject city-states.

THE BOULE

Members:	500 citizens, 50 men from each of the 10 tribes. Chosen by lot annually. Governing committee of 50 members serves in office for 1/10 year. Each day, an administrator for the committee is chosen by lot.
Role:	Prepare agenda for public discussion in the Assembly; prepare legislation to be debated by Assembly; administer policies enacted by the Assembly.

BOARD OF GENERALS

Members:	The 10 *strategoi,* or generals, are elected by the Assembly. In times of emergency, the office of supreme commander is rotated daily among the 10 *strategoi.*
Role:	Advise the Assembly on matters of war and peace; lead the army and navy on military campaigns.

lot from the Assembly. From these 6000, a jury was chosen by lot to hear each case.

Board of Generals. Each tribe was required to contribute a quota of men to the army, and to elect its own *strategos* (general). Unlike other magistrates, the generals could be re-elected for any number of terms. At first they served only as military leaders, but later, during times of crisis, they assumed control of finances and foreign affairs.

Cleisthenes' Legacy. Due to Cleisthenes' reforms, the opportunity to participate in the political process was open to all Athenian citizens. For the first time in history, common men had an opportunity to participate in the political process. They could speak in the Assembly, elect their leaders, and even hold public office. The reforms that Cleisthenes implemented eliminated the old tribal loyalties and instead people began to think of themselves as Athenians. By 500 B.C., Athens was the most powerful and influential city-state in Greece.

Beginning about 450 B.C., the important decrees and decisions of the Assembly were carved on stone tablets and set up in a public place so that everyone could see them. This measure ensured that no one could tamper with the laws that had been enacted by the Assembly and the courts.

SPARTA During the Iron Age, the Dorian invaders from the north established villages in Laconia, a fertile valley in the Peloponnesus. In the 8th century B.C., Sparta, one of the most powerful and centrally located of these villages, established hegemony over the others.

The Spartans kept themselves separate from the original inhabitants of Laconia and did not grant them the privilege of citizenship. Those who chose to stay remained free, but had no political rights. The largest group within Spartan society consisted of the *helots*, peoples whom the Spartans had conquered in war and enslaved. These people had no personal freedom or political rights.

The early government of Sparta consisted of a monarchy, a council of aristocrats, and an assembly of weapon-bearing citizens. It was much like the governments that evolved in other city-states throughout Greece during the Iron Age. The Spartan government, however, traditionally had *two* kings instead of one, possibly to prevent one king from seizing too much power.

During the 8th century B.C., as city-states throughout Greece were solving their problems of over-population by establishing colonies, the Spartans decided upon a different solution. They established one colony, Tarentum, but gained most of the extra land that they needed by invading Messenia, their neighbor to the west. The combined territories of Laconia and Messenia were called *Lacedaemon*, and they were governed by the polis of Sparta.

In 640 B.C., the Messenians revolted against Spartan rule and continued to revolt for about 20 years. Because the Spartans were a minority in the state they had created, they had a great deal of difficulty in putting down the rebellions and in enforcing their rule. In addition, the common people of Sparta, who served as hoplites (foot soldiers), began to demand political reforms in return for their services. They wanted a greater voice in the government of Sparta, a removal of class distinctions among Spartans, and a redistribution of land. The Spartan leaders turned to the Constitution of Lycurgus for a solution to their internal problems.

The Constitution of Lycurgus. It is not known whether Lycurgus was a real or mythical person. Later generations of Spartans believed that he had been a real king and that he had created all of the laws and institutions of Sparta. The laws attributed to Lycurgus probably retained many of the ancient traditions of Sparta and added several important innovations. They were considered to be sacred, and represented an entire way of life as well as a political system.

The system of Lycurgus emphasized the equal treatment of each citizen under the law. The officials of the polis sternly regulated every aspect of the citizens' lives, but the powers of the government were carefully bal-

According to tradition, Lycurgus established Sparta's unique laws and institutions. Plato and Aristotle later expressed admiration for many aspects of his constitution.

anced so that no one person could usurp too much power.

In addition to the traditional monarchy, the council of elders, and the assembly, the laws of Lycurgus added a fourth agency of government: a council of five *ephors*. Under the system of Lycurgus, the authority of the monarchy, as before, was shared by two kings. The *Council of Elders*, or Senate, consisted of 28 citizens over the age of 60. It advised the kings, discussed matters that might be presented to the Assembly, and served as a court of law. The *Assembly* included all citizens over the age of 30. It had the powers of declaring war or making peace, of approving the choices of kings, and of electing the council members and the five *ephors*. The ephors exercised great power in Sparta. By the 6th century B.C., they had the authority to arrest a king and could recommend to the Assembly that he be put on trial. They were present at council meetings, and probably helped to prepare business for the Assembly to consider. They supervised the military training of young citizens, and they were in charge of public morals and of foreign affairs.

Spartan citizens were expected to devote themselves to the interests of the state, and every aspect of their lives was controlled so that they would do so. New babies were inspected by the Council of Elders, and babies considered to be too frail were left on a mountaintop to die of exposure. At the age of seven all boys were placed under the care of the state. Xenophon, a writer of the 4th century B.C., reported that the smallest offense was punished by whipping, and that food was rationed so stringently that the boys were forced to steal additional food in order to sustain themselves. Xenophon also reported:

• • • *Instead of softening the boys' feet with sandals he [Lycurgus] required them to harden their feet by going without shoes. He believed that if this habit were cultivated it would enable them to climb hills more easily and descend steep inclines with less danger, and that a youth who had accustomed himself to go barefoot would leap and jump and run more nimbly than a boy in sandals.*[15]

The Spartan young people were thoroughly indoctrinated in the ideology of the state. Most of their time was spent in physical exercises to make the boys excellent soldiers, and the girls good mothers who could produce strong, healthy children for the state. Little emphasis was placed on reading or writing. All luxuries and frivolity were forbidden, but dancing was encouraged, because the Spartans believed that dancing taught physical coordination.

Spartan men were forbidden to have any other career besides that of soldier: all other occupations were filled by non-citizens. Plutarch, a Greek historian of the 1st century A.D., described the effect that this law had on the lives of Spartan men:

• • • *Their discipline continued still after they were full-grown men. No one was allowed to live after his own fancy; but the city was a sort of camp, in which every man had his share of provisions and business set out, and looked upon himself not so much born to serve his own ends as the interest of his country.*[16]

Spartan men were permitted to marry at age 20, but all had to enter military training at that time. Married or not, the men were required to live in communal barracks until they reached the age of 30.

All Spartans were forbidden to travel abroad, and foreigners were not welcomed within Sparta for fear that they would corrupt the citizenry. All of the land was the property of the state, and each citizen was allotted the use of only enough land to support his family. Helots performed all of the

---

[15]Xenophon, "The Lacedaemonians." In *Scripta Minora* II, 3.

[16]Plutarch, *Lives*, Modern Library ed., p. 68.

work on the land so that the citizens could be available for military service.

The Spartans were constantly on guard against the possibility that the helots would revolt. Special secret police spied on them constantly, and each year one day was set aside to "wage war on the helots." On this day, a Spartan citizen could put to death any helot whom he disliked. In wartime, the helots served the Spartan soldiers but did not actually fight in battle.

The Peloponnesian League. Throughout their history, the Spartans were reluctant to send troops outside of the Peloponnesus for fear of a helot uprising or an attack from nearby city-states. In an effort to control the threat posed by Tegea, Argos, and other neighboring city-states, the Spartans formed the Peloponnesian League around 540 B.C. The purpose of the league was to unite all of the important city-states in the Peloponnesus. Each state was bound to Sparta by a separate 100-year treaty, during which time Sparta would provide military leadership for the League while the other members furnished troops.

The creation of the Peloponnesian League reduced the Spartans' fears about attacks from their neighbors, and was very effective in discouraging potential enemies because of the international reputation of Spartan soldiers. Herodotus reported the following conversation, in which the Persian king Xerxes learned of Sparta's military prowess:

●●● *the Lacedaemonians [Spartans] in single combat are inferior to none, but together are the bravest of all men; for, though free, they are not absolutely free, for they have a master over them, the law, which they fear much more than your subjects do you. They do, accordingly, whatever it enjoins; and it ever enjoins the same thing, forbidding them to fly from battle before any number of men, but [commanding them] to remain in their ranks, and conquer or die.*[17]

[17]Herodotus VII, 104.

> *Several English words had their origins in Sparta: for example, Spartan, meaning "self-disciplined and austere"; laconic, meaning "extremely concise of speech"; and appellate, meaning "having the power to hear appeals."*

Relations with Athens. In 500 B.C., Sparta and Athens were scarcely in the same world philosophically, although they were separated by less than 100 miles geographically. Sparta was closed to new ideas and foreign people, and dedicated to military self-preservation under a communal form of government. Athens sought out new ideas and people, and eventually developed the most nearly pure form of democracy that has ever existed. Although there was little possibility that these two leading city-states would give up their independence in order to form a unified nation, they did learn how to cooperate with each other under the threat of a foreign invasion.

THE PERSIAN WARS During the 5th century B.C., the Greek city-states united to defend themselves against a series of attacks by the Persians. The Persians had an untold wealth of men and materials, and were united under one rule. The Greek army, in contrast, was made up of troops from a number of independent city-states, and its generals were accountable to these small states rather than to one central authority.

The Greeks first became involved with the Persian Empire when Cyrus the Great, king of Persia, conquered the kingdom of Lydia in Asia Minor. The Ionian city-states, although they had their own independent governments, were considered to be part of Lydia and were incorporated into the Persian Empire. Under Darius the Great, the Ionians and the Lydians were placed under the control of a satrap (governor) who resided in Sardis. The satrap encouraged the development of tyrannies in the Ionian city-states, and permitted these local governments to function independently as long as they paid their taxes and provided military levies when required by Persia.

In 499 B.C., Aristogoras, the ambitious tyrant of Miletus, the most prosperous and cultured of the Greek colonies of Ionia, led a revolt against the Persians. Athens aided this uprising by sending 20 shiploads of soldiers. Eretria, on the island of Euboea, sent 5 shiploads. Sparta refused to participate when Cleomenes, one of its two kings, learned that the Persian capital at Susa was three months' march from the nearest seaport.

The Ionians and their allies advanced to Sardis, the headquarters of the satrap, and burned the city. Athens and Eretria then withdrew their forces. The Ionians continued the struggle, but collapsed when their navy, consisting of 353 ships, was defeated by the Persian navy, of almost double the strength, off the coast of Miletus.

In retaliation for this revolt, the Persians sacked and burned Miletus in 495 B.C., and deported the inhabitants to the Tigris-Euphrates valley, about 1000 miles away. Herodotus, who lived during this era and is our most important source of information on the Persian Wars, wrote:

> • • • *the Athenians made it evident that they were excessively grieved at the capture of Miletus, both in many other ways, and more particularly when Phrynichus had composed a drama of the capture of Miletus, and presented it, the whole theater burst into tears, and fined him a thousand drachmas for renewing the memory of their domestic misfortunes; and they gave order that henceforth no one should act this drama.*[18]

In 492 B.C., Darius sent an army westward through Thrace and Macedonia to attack

---

[18]Ibid., VI, 21.

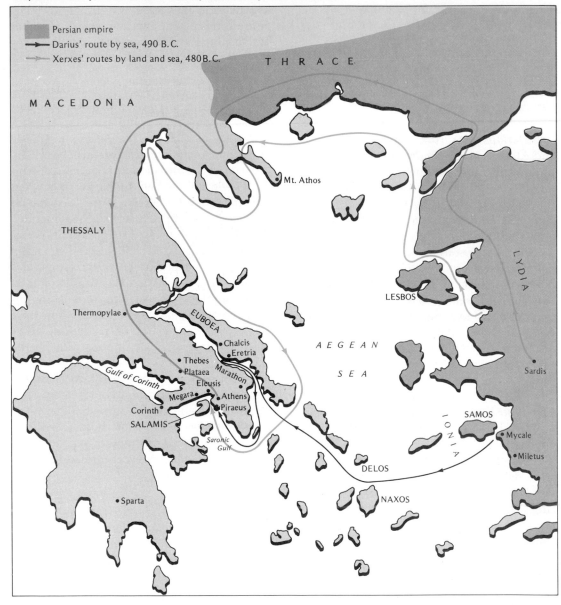

THE PERSIAN INVASIONS OF GREECE, 490 AND 480 B.C.
Why did Xerxes plan to advance both by land and by sea in 480 B.C.?

Persian empire
Darius' route by sea, 490 B.C.
Xerxes' routes by land and sea, 480 B.C.

THRACE

MACEDONIA

Mt. Athos

THESSALY

LYDIA

LESBOS

Thermopylae

EUBOEA

Chalcis

Eretria

Thebes

Plataea

Marathon

Eleusis

Gulf of Corinth

Megara

Athens

Corinth

Piraeus

SALAMIS

Saronic Gulf

AEGEAN SEA

Sardis

IONIA

SAMOS

Mycale

Miletus

DELOS

Sparta

NAXOS

Athens in retaliation for its support of the Ionians. As the troops marched along the coast, they were supplied by the Persian navy, but the fleet was wrecked in a storm off the promontory of Mount Athos. Because his army now lacked naval support and he did not wish to risk a battle, Darius sent envoys to various Greek city-states to demand tokens of submission in the form of earth and water. According to stories that were later told, the Athenians threw the Persian envoy into a pit and told him to dig his own earth; then the Spartans threw him into a well and told him to gather his own water. But although they were united in their determination to resist, Athens and Sparta could not agree upon a plan of action. Meanwhile, the Persians strengthened their control over the northern coast of the Aegean, and returned to their bases in Asia Minor.

In 490 B.C., Darius subdued the city-states of Euboea and landed on the plain of Marathon. From here, the Persians planned to lay seige to Athens and at the same time prevent the Spartans from coming to the city's aid. The Athenian *strategos* Miltiades, one of the greatest military geniuses of all time, had served as governor of Thrace and was familiar with Persian battle tactics. He understood what the Persians were attempting, and sent a message to the Spartans asking for aid. He then persuaded the Athenians and the Plataeans, who were allies, to seize the initiative immediately by marching 26 miles eastward to Marathon.

When the Greeks arrived at Marathon, the Persian cavalry troops were not present at the site; but neither were the Spartan allies,

for they had been delayed by a religious observance. Miltiades decided to take advantage of the cavalry's absence and attacked the Persian troops at dawn rather than waiting for the Spartans. Herodotus described the battle as follows:

● ● ●*The battle of Marathon lasted a long time; and in the middle of the line, where the Persians themselves and the Sacae [their allies] were arrayed, the barbarians were victorious; in this part, then, the barbarians conquered, and having broken the line, pursued to the interior; but in both wings the Athenians and the Plataeans were victorious; and having gained the victory, they allowed the defeated portion of the barbarians to flee; and having united both wings, they fought with those who had broken their center, and the Athenians were victorious. They followed the Persians in their flight, cutting them to pieces, till, reaching the shore, they called for fire and attacked the ships.*[19]

---

[19]Ibid., VI, 113.

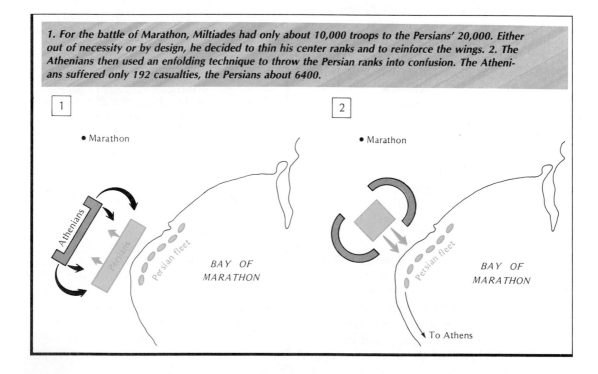

1. For the battle of Marathon, Miltiades had only about 10,000 troops to the Persians' 20,000. Either out of necessity or by design, he decided to thin his center ranks and to reinforce the wings. 2. The Athenians then used an enfolding technique to throw the Persian ranks into confusion. The Athenians suffered only 192 casualties, the Persians about 6400.

After the battle of Marathon, a runner was ordered to report the victory to the people of Athens. According to tradition, he ran the entire distance, managed to make his report, and then died from exhaustion. Today this athlete's feat is commemorated by marathon races in which runners compete over 26-mile-long routes.

According to Herodotus, the Persians had lost 6400 men in the battle of Marathon, and the Athenians only 192. In spite of the Persians' heavy losses, Miltiades suspected that they would attempt to attack Athens from the sea. He led his army swiftly back to Athens. When the Persians found the Athenians waiting for their next attack, they abandoned their plans and returned to Asia Minor. The small city-state of Athens had, almost single-handedly, defeated the Persian empire.

The Athenians' victory at Marathon was an astonishing achievement, and the participants were long remembered: the dead were given a state burial and the survivors were honored throughout their lives. People continued to be impressed by the Athenians' feat for many centuries. Two thousand years after the battle, Lord Byron, a supporter of Greek independence from the Ottoman (Turkish) Empire, was moved to write:

The mountains look on Marathon
And Marathon looks on the sea,
And musing there an hour alone
I dreamed that Greece might still be free;
For standing on the Persian's grave
I could not deem myself a slave.[20]

Xerxes, the son of Darius, came to the throne of the Persian Empire in 485 B.C. His desire for revenge against the Greeks led him to make elaborate preparations for war against them. He planned a joint attack by land and sea, and made careful preparations for both campaigns. Supply depots were established along the line of march, and two pontoon bridges were constructed to cross the Hellespont. A canal was dug across the peninsula of Mount Athos in order to prevent the possibility of another disaster while sailing around the dangerous cape.

When news of these elaborate invasion plans reached the Greeks, they were undecided about how to defend themselves. The leader of Athens at this time was Themistocles. He was greatly concerned about the Persian threat, and, when a rich mine of silver was discovered near Athens, he persuaded his fellow citizens to finance the building of a navy rather than distribute the new wealth as a dividend among themselves. He also advised the Athenians to build a new harbor at Piraeus, which would be easier to fortify than the existing harbor, and to build two long walls from Piraeus to Athens to provide a safe passageway between the city and its port.

Although the Athenians had defeated the Persian army at Marathon without help from the Spartans, most of the Greek city-states

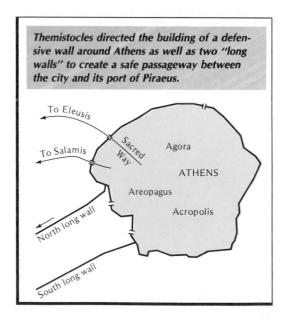

Themistocles directed the building of a defensive wall around Athens as well as two "long walls" to create a safe passageway between the city and its port of Piraeus.

[20]*Don Juan*, canto 3, stanza 83.

still regarded Sparta as the foremost military power in Greece. In 481 B.C., a league of Greek city-states was formed, and all members pledged to end their destructive quarrels for the duration of the Persian threat. Sparta was given command over the combined land forces and Athens command over the combined naval forces. After much discussion and with great reluctance, the two sets of leaders finally agreed to abandon a plan for making a major stand at Corinth, because this plan would have ceded all of northern and central Greece to the Persians. They decided instead to take their stand at Thermopylae, a pass on the Gulf of Euboea about 75 miles northwest of Athens.

In August of 480 B.C., the armies of Xerxes advanced across Asia Minor toward the Hellespont. Herodotus reported that the Persians had 2,641,610 men and 1207 warships, while the Athenians and their allies had 150,000 men and 700 to 800 vessels. Herodotus was probably exaggerating the Persian strength, but it was considerably greater than that of all the Greek allies combined. Herodotus also reported that when Xerxes reached the Hellespont, he had a pontoon bridge built to convey his troops across the water. The bridge was destroyed by a storm, and Xerxes, according to Herodotus, revealed his astonishing *hubris* (pride) by trying to punish nature for its insubordination:

• • • *When Xerxes heard of this [the destruction of the bridge], being exceedingly indignant, he commanded that the Hellespont should be stricken with 300 lashes of a scourge, and that a pair of fetters should be let down into the sea. I have moreover heard that with them he likewise sent branding instruments to brand the Hellespont. He certainly charged those who flogged the waters to utter these barbarous and impious words: "Thou bitter water! thy master inflicts this punishment upon thee, because thou hast injured him; and King Xerxes will cross over thee, whether thou wilt or not; it is with justice that no man*

sacrifices to thee, because thou art both a deceitful and briny river."[21]

Xerxes rebuilt his bridge and proceeded overland toward mainland Greece. As the Persians approached Thermopylae, a narrow mountain pass to the north of Delphi, King Leonidas of Sparta, with 300 of his own men and 6700 others, waited expectantly for reinforcements that had been promised as soon as the Olympic Games had ended. A Persian spy reported to Xerxes that the Spartans were exercising and combing their hair. Xerxes was puzzled by such behavior, and when he sought an explanation, he was told that:

• • • *These men have to fight with us for the pass, and are now preparing themselves to do so; for such is their custom, when they are going to hazard their lives, then they dress their heads; but be assured, if you conquer these men, and those that remain in Sparta, there is no other nation in the world that will dare to raise their hand against you, O king; for you are now to engage with the noblest kingdom and the city of all among the Greeks, and with the most valiant men.*[22]

About two weeks later, a Greek traitor agreed to lead a Persian force up a mountain path to a point behind the Greeks. Leonidas detected the movement of the Persians and called a council of war. It was agreed that some of the Greek troops should remain with Leonidas, while the remainder would move southward, perhaps to attack the Persians from the rear.

In the fierce fighting that ensued, Leonidas and many of his remaining troops were slain. Throughout history Thermopylae has been a symbol of heroic struggle against overwhelming odds. Herodotus described how these heroes were memorialized:

• • • *In honor of the slain, who were buried on the spot where they fell, and of those who*

---

[21]Herodotus VII, 35.
[22]Ibid., VI, 209.

died before they were dismissed by Leonidas and went away, the following inscription has been engraved over them: "Four thousand from Peloponnesus once fought on this spot with three hundred myriads [3,000,000 men]." This inscription was made for all; and for the Spartans in particular: "Stranger, go tell the Lacedaemonians that we lie here, obedient to their commands."[23]

Xerxes' army moved south through central Greece. The allies of Athens retreated to the Isthmus of Corinth, thereby abandoning all of northern Greece to the enemy. The Athenians sent messengers to the Delphic oracle to learn what course of action they should follow. The messengers were told:

• • • *wide-seeing Jupiter gives a wooden wall to the Triton-born goddess [Athena], to be alone impregnable, which shall preserve you and your children.*[24]

Some Athenians believed that the oracle was referring to a wall of wood on the Acropolis. But Themistocles persuaded the people that the oracle's use of the term "wooden walls" referred to the Athenian fleet. Hoping to defeat the Persians at sea, and thereby force them to leave Greece, he ordered the evacuation of all women and children to the nearby island of Salamis, and recruited all able-bodied men to take to the fighting ships. When Athens was abandoned, the Persians moved in and looted and burned the city.

The Greek city-states held a council of war, but argued among themselves. Corinth objected to the presence of Athenians at the council, arguing that they had no place there because their city had been destroyed. Most of the Greek allies wanted the combined navies to be close to where the armies were assembled near Corinth. But Themistocles urged that the fleet stay in the straits of Salamis, the narrow channel of water above the island of Salamis. He went so far as to threaten to withdraw the Athenian navy from the alliance if the others did not follow his recommendation. Realizing that there was no hope of victory without the Athenian navy, the others acquiesced.

Themistocles then secretly sent a slave to Xerxes with a false rumor that the Greeks were in disagreement and planned to withdraw without a fight. As Themistocles had anticipated, the Persians then decided to send a fleet to the straits of Salamis to cut off the escaping armies.

The heavy Persian sailing ships could not maneuver in the narrow straits, and the lighter Athenian ships, which could be easily rowed and turned, inflicted heavy damage on them.[25] The last major action of the war took place at Mycale, where the Greeks attacked what remained of the Persian fleet that had been routed at Salamis.

After the naval defeat in the straits of Salamis, Xerxes withdrew his armies to the north to prepare for a new campaign in the spring. Again the Greeks disagreed about how to prepare for this new threat. In the spring of 479 B.C., the Persians marched south and reoccupied Athens. The Spartans, under Pausanias, attacked and drove the Persians about 40 miles northwest to Plataea. The Persian commander was killed, and the Persians were forced to flee. The remnant of this once great army faced disease and starvation as it retreated through northern Greece, and only a few troops finally returned to Persia.

The outcome of these 20 years of fighting was remarkable when one realizes that the Spartans were the only well-trained soldiers in all of Greece, and that the leaders of the various Greek city-states seldom could agree on a course of action. This great victory over the power of Persia imbued the Greeks with a great sense of self-confidence, and marked

---

[23]Ibid., VII, 228.
[24]Ibid., VII, 141.

[25]Two thousand years later, Sir Francis Drake used this same strategy to defeat the Spanish Armada.

the beginning of the brilliant era of civilization known as the Classical period.

Although they had been defeated in Greece, the Persians still had a great empire which controlled the city-states of Ionia. In order to forestall the possibility of another attack by the Persians, in 478 B.C. the Athenians persuaded 350 of the Greek city-states to form a defensive alliance, which came to be known as the Delian League. To seal this pact, the allies threw a lump of iron into the sea and pledged to support each other until the lump should rise to the surface. The league was named for the island of Delos, where the treasury was established and where meetings of the representatives took place. Athens determined the contribution, or tribute, each member should make, and these "tribute lists" were carved into marble slabs and set up in the agora at Athens.

In 454 B.C., the league's treasury was moved to Athens. By 450, the Persians had been driven from the Aegean, and the Athenian fleet patrolled the sea with ships financed by the league. Thereafter, Athens dominated the league completely, and would not permit members to secede from it. In time, the Delian League was transformed into the Athenian Empire, thereby creating frictions which ultimately led to the Peloponnesian War. Meanwhile, the Athenians developed ideas of art, government, philosophy, and science which continue to influence the thinking of the Western world.

SUMMARY

During the Iron Age of Greece (1100-700 B.C.), the governments of the city-states of Greece began to evolve from the system that had prevailed in Mycenaean times: monarchies were gradually replaced by elected councils and public assemblies. At the same time, the economy of Greece came to be based upon small, independent family farms rather than military ventures abroad.

During the 8th century B.C., when family farms could no longer support the growing population, the Greeks undertook colonization and trading ventures. These activities greatly expanded the economy and led to a more diversified society.

In the next century, various city-states began to experiment with different forms of government. Sparta, for example, adopted the laws of Lycurgus and resisted any change in this system. Athens, on the other hand, evolved into a democracy.

During the 5th century B.C., many of the city-states put aside their differences and combined forces to ward off several attempted invasions by the Persians. This success gave the Greeks a new self-confidence which led them into the brilliant era of achievement known as the Classical period.

QUESTIONS

1 Why is the study of the Homeric epics so important to historians who are seeking to understand the values and beliefs of Iron Age Greece?

2 Describe the political, legal, and economic reforms brought about by Draco, Solon, Pisistratus, and Cleisthenes. What impact did each have on the development of democracy?

3 Compare Athens to Sparta in terms of values and distribution of political power.

4 Read Plutarch's Lives of Lycurgus and Pericles. What can you learn from Plutarch about the societies in which these men lived?

5 Compare the ancient Olympic Games with the modern ones.

6 Why has the battle of Marathon been regarded as one of the most important battles in history?

7 Research one of the lesser-known Greek city-states, such as Corinth or Syracuse, and compare its political development with that of Athens or Sparta.

BIBLIOGRAPHY

Which books might discuss the leadership of Athens' democracy?

FINLEY, M. I. *The Ancient Greeks.* New York: Viking Press, 1963. *Discusses the culture and politics of the ancient Greeks from the Archaic, or Iron Age, through the 4th century. Includes such topics as the amateurism of office-holders in Athens' direct democracy; popular attitudes and morals.*

HUXLEY, G. L. *The Early Ionians.* New York: Humanities Press, 1968. *A comprehensive, scholarly history of the Ionian Greeks; their intellectual achievements and political history.*

LISTER, R. P. *The Travels of Herodotus.* London and New York: Gordon and Cremonesi, 1979. *Describes Herodotus' travels throughout the ancient world as he investigated the origins of ancient Greek legends and the culture of other civilizations; provides the same kind of detailed observations that have endeared Herodotus to generations of readers.*

• *In short, I say that as a city we are the school of Hellas;*
while I doubt if the world can produce a man, who where he has
only himself to depend upon, is equal to so many emergencies,
and graced by so happy a versatility as the Athenian.

PERICLES

Classical Greece

IONIA During the 7th and 6th centuries B.C., Ionia in Asia Minor was a center of Greek intellectual achievement. The wealth of the cities encouraged the pursuit of creative activities, and the adoption of the Phoenician alphabet facilitated the exchange of ideas. Many of the forms of learning that we enjoy today, such as literature, history, philosophy, and science, were initiated or perfected by the Ionian Greeks.

Sappho. Sappho of Lesbos was the first woman to gain fame from her writings. Her poems were often read to the accompaniment of a lyre (a small harp), so that the style came to be called *lyric* poetry. Her keen observations of nature, her vivid imagination, and her melodic cadences inspired Plato to call her the "Tenth Muse." Her poem *The Young Bride* reflects these qualities:

A Young Bride
(i)
Like the sweet apple which reddens on the
topmost bough,
A-top on the topmost twig—which the
pluckers forgot somehow—
Forgot it not, nay, but got it not, for
none could get it till now.

(ii)
Like the wild hyacinth flower, which on
the hills is found,
Which the passing feet of the shepherds
for ever tear and wound,
Until the purple blossom is trodden into
the ground.[1]

Hecataeus. The Ionians also created other forms of literature. Hecataeus of Miletus wrote a book of geography which described the world as he observed it during his travels, with the Mediterranean Sea as the center. He also wrote *genealogies* which traced all of the identifiable ancestors of certain noble families, and then named heroes or gods as the more distant ancestors.

Herodotus. Herodotus of Halicarnassus (484-425 B.C.) was the first Western writer to use the word *historia* ("inquiry"). He traveled widely throughout the Greek world, Egypt, and Mesopotamia, investigating legends about Greek history and gathering information on other cultures which he later

---

[1]T. F. Higham and C. M. Bowra, eds. *Oxford Book of Greek Verse in Translation* (Oxford University Press, 1938), p. 209.

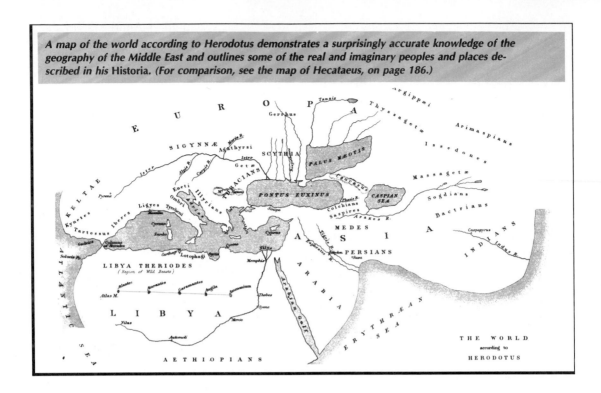

A map of the world according to Herodotus demonstrates a surprisingly accurate knowledge of the geography of the Middle East and outlines some of the real and imaginary peoples and places described in his Historia. (For comparison, see the map of Hecataeus, on page 186.)

consolidated into his great book. His writings are one of the most important sources of information that we have concerning the events and peoples of the ancient world.

In addition to his history of ancient times, Herodotus recounted the events of his own time, especially the ongoing conflict between the Greeks and the Persians. In the introduction to this important work, he said:

● ● ● This is a publication of the researches of Herodotus of Halicarnassus, in order that the actions of men may not be effaced by time, nor the great and wonderous deeds displayed by both Greeks and barbarians deprived of renown; and among the rest, for what cause they waged war upon each other.[2]

In the first four of his books on the Persian-Greek conflict, Herodotus discussed the backgrounds of the two nations, and then traced the progress of the war. The events of the war, he believed, were directed by the gods. For example, he wrote that the defeat of Xerxes was brought about by his overwhelming pride (hubris), which had aroused the envy of the gods and led them to plot his destruction (nemesis) at the hands of the Greeks.

Over the centuries, scholars have known that Herodotus' fondness for a good story often led him to accept unreliable information. But as investigations of those ancient cultures have expanded in recent years, scholars have found his descriptions of places and events to be an invaluable resource. The historian Edith Hamilton evaluated Herodotus in this way:

● ● ● Herodotus is a shining instance of the strong Greek bent to examine and prove or disprove. He had a passion for finding out. The task he set himself was nothing less than to find out all about everything in the world. He is always called the "father of history,"

---

[2]Herodotus I, 1.

but he was quite as much the father of geography, of archeology, of anthropology, of sociology, or whatever has to do with human beings and the places in which they live. The Greek contempt for foreigners—in Greek, barbarians—never touched him. He was passionately on Athens' side in her struggle against Persia, yet he admired and praised the Persians. He found them brave and chivalrous and truthful.[3]

THE EARLY PHILOSOPHERS

During the 6th century B.C., some Ionians were seeking to understand the world through introspection and analysis. Their investigations led them to be called *philosophers* ("lovers of wisdom"). They rejected the idea that the gods controlled the universe, and sought to discover instead the laws of *physis* (nature). Much of their philosophic thinking dealt with what we would call science. Today the science of energy and matter is known as *physics*.

Thales. The earliest known philosopher was Thales of Miletus (636-546 B.C.). After studying earlier Egyptian and Babylonian discoveries in astronomy and mathematics, he came to believe that the heavenly bodies were controlled by fixed laws. Like many later Greek philosophers, Thales believed that all things in nature derived from one basic element. He concluded that this element was water.

Thales was once ridiculed by his friends for his strange ideas. They taunted him, saying "If you are so smart, why aren't you rich?" Sometime later, his observations led him to believe that the olive crop would be exceptionally good that year, so he leased all of the oil presses he could find. Farmers with large olive crops were forced to come to him to have their crops processed, and he charged them very high fees for his services. He thus proved that he could become immensely

wealthy if he wanted to. Another story about him relates that he inadvertently fell into a well while gazing at a star.

Anaximenes and Anaximander. Thales' successor as the leading philosopher of the day was Anaximenes, who also lived in Miletus during the 6th century B.C. Anaximenes decided that the basic element of the universe was air, and that the rarefaction and condensation of air produced all forms in nature. One of his pupils, Anaximander (610-546 B.C.), concluded that the basic element was an undefined, formless, immortal substance, which he called "the Boundless." This substance contained elements of earth, air, fire, and water, and combined in different proportions to create everything in nature.

Heraclitus and Democritus. Heraclitus (540-475 B.C.) stated that the basic element of the universe was fire, and that all life went through a continual process of decay and regeneration. He is reported to have said, "Everything flows and nothing remains the same."

Democritus (460-370 B.C.) decided that the universe was made up of an infinite number of invisible and indivisible particles, which move about continuously and combine with other particles to create matter. His concept was close to modern ideas about the behavior of atoms.

Pythagoras. Pythagoras (582-500 B.C.) was born on the island of Samos. He believed that the underlying system of the universe could only be discovered by studying numbers, and that the sun, moon, and earth were round bodies which revolve around a central fire. He speculated that each celestial body produced a distinct tone. These tones were inaudible to the human ear, but corresponded to the notes of the musical scale. (This idea became the basis of the later concept of "the harmony of the spheres.")

The relationships between mathematics and music became an important part of the theories of Pythagoras and his followers. He analyzed the behavior of a lyre and discov-

---

[3]Hamilton, Edith, *The Greek Way* (New York & London: W. W. Norton, 1930), pp. 121-2.

ered that the vibrations of two strings, or wires, of the same material and diameter vary in inverse proportion to their lengths. The fact that harmonies in music—thirds, fifths, octaves, etc.—can be expressed in numbers reinforced Pythagoras' belief that numbers are the true expression of reality.

Hippocrates. Hippocrates (460-377 B.C.) founded a school of medicine on the island of Cos in 420 B.C. He rejected the belief that disease was caused by demons, and sought to find natural causes for various illnesses. He emphasized the value of careful observation and interpretation of patients' symptoms. He was the first to use such words as *crisis, acute,* and *chronic* to describe illnesses. His concept of "holistic healing," including hygiene, diet, and the curative powers of nature, is remarkably similar to the practices of many people today. The "Hippocratic Oath" he devised has served as an ethical guide for many generations of physicians.

The Ionian theorists were among the first people to pursue what is known as *disinterested* inquiry; that is, knowledge for its own sake rather than for a practical purpose; to understand nature, rather than to exploit it. While some of their ideas may seem fantastical, it must be remembered that their methods helped to create an atmosphere in which important discoveries could be made. Disregarding the evidence of their eyes, they theorized that the earth is round, not flat; and they searched for universal laws in nature rather than accepting its apparent diversity. Their work was later refined by Plato, Aristotle, and others, and became the foundation of modern science.

ATHENS After the Persian Wars ended, Athens emerged as the political and cultural center of the Greek world. The supremacy of Athens during the Classical period (479-323 B.C.) was largely due to the influence of Pericles, who was the most prominent politician in Athens between 461 and 429. Under his guidance, Athens' leadership of the Delian League became the basis for the creation of an empire. When Athens' hegemony over its empire was secure, Pericles encouraged his fellow citizens to use the tribute money they collected to underwrite the development of Greek culture. Due to his efforts, Athens became, in his words, the "school of Hellas." The Athenians' achievements in architecture, sculpture, drama, and philosophy are studied and emulated even today. Many scholars believe that the Classical period of Greece was the most fruitful period of development of thought in the history of the Western world.

PERICLES AND THE ATHENIAN EMPIRE

Pericles. Pericles' ancestry included two of the most distinguished families of Athens: his father was Xanthippus, the commander of the Athenian navy at Mycale in 479 B.C., and his mother was a niece of Cleisthenes, the statesman who reformed Athens' democracy. Like Solon, Pisistratus, and Cleisthenes, Pericles belonged to the aristocracy and yet encouraged the development of Athens' democracy.

Early in his political career, Pericles helped to strengthen the democratic system that Cleisthenes had instituted. To ensure that even the poorest citizens had an opportunity to serve in public office, Pericles initiated a policy of paying citizens for their time of service in the Boule and the law courts.

The Empire. In foreign affairs, Pericles became known as a strong advocate of Athens' supremacy in the Greek world. When the Persian Wars ended, in 479 B.C., Athens assumed the leadership of the Delian League, a confederation of Greek city-states (see Chapter 6). The purpose of the league was to avert any further threat of a Persian invasion, and the Athenian navy was the mainstay of the league's military force. Each member state contributed money (or ships) to the league, whose treasury was located on the island of Delos. Within a few years of its

Pericles—general, orator, and statesman of Athens—chose to be depicted with a war helmet in this portrait.

league: all major law cases had to be reviewed by the Athenian court, which consisted of a committee within the Assembly.

In 443 B.C., an Athenian *strategos* (general) who had disapproved of Athens' imperial policies was ostracized, and Pericles was elected in his place. Pericles continued to uphold a stern policy toward Athens' allies. Each time that one of the city-states within the empire threatened to secede, Pericles argued that Athens must enforce its hegemony by sending troops to the scene of the trouble. As a citizen of the Athenian democracy, he had no more power than any other citizen to promote his policies. But because of his immense popularity and powers of persuasion, he was almost always able to convince a majority of the Assembly to follow the course he recommended. The historian Thucydides, who was a contemporary of Pericles, evaluated his leadership in this manner:

● ● ● *Pericles indeed, by his rank, ability, and known integrity, was enabled to exercise an independent control over the multitude—in short, to lead them instead of being led by them; for as he never sought power by improper means, he was never compelled to flatter them, but, on the contrary, enjoyed so high an estimation that he could afford to anger them by contradiction. Whenever he saw them unseasonably and insolently elated, he would with a word reduce them to alarm; on the other hand, if they fell victims to a panic, he could at once restore them to confidence. In short, what was nominally a democracy became in his hands government by the first citizen.*[4]

The Athenians used the money that they gathered in tribute to make Athens the center of culture in the Greek world. In return, the Athenian navy policed the seas, enabling all of the Greek city-states to develop a thriving trade. To ensure the loyalties of the league's members, Athens actively encouraged the installation of democracies. This type of po-

founding, however, several members of the Delian League tried to secede from it. These actions caused great concern to Pericles and other prominent Athenians, who strongly believed that Athens needed to maintain the league in order to survive.

Beginning in 465 B.C., the Athenians made it clear that membership in the league was no longer voluntary. They forcibly put down several attempted revolts of the allies, and moved the league's treasury from Delos to Athens. Athens also showed its imperialistic intentions through two other measures. The Assembly decreed that all of the league's members must use Athens' coinage as well as its system of weights and measures. In addition, the Assembly itself became a final court of appeal for every citizen within the

---

[4]Thucydides II, 7, 65.

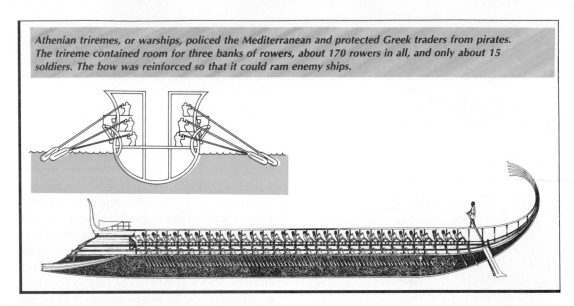

Athenian triremes, or warships, policed the Mediterranean and protected Greek traders from pirates. The trireme contained room for three banks of rowers, about 170 rowers in all, and only about 15 soldiers. The bow was reinforced so that it could ram enemy ships.

litical interference was the cause of most of the rebellions which broke out among the member city-states. For example, a revolt by the island of Samos, in 440 B.C., was led by wealthy oligarchs who did not want to see the spread of Athens' democracy.

The revenues from the empire enabled Pericles to administer the reconstruction of Athens, which had been destroyed by the Persians in 480 B.C. As architects rebuilt the public monuments of the city on an unprecedented scale, Athenian poets, philosophers, and artists also helped to make Athens the cultural and intellectual center of the Greek world. Within several decades, however, the firm imperialistic policies of Pericles led Athens into the devastating Peloponnesian War.

ARCHITECTURE

The most impressive remains in all of Greece are on the acropolis in Athens, the rocky citadel that rises approximately 200 feet above the plain on which most of the city is situated. Because the Persians had destroyed the earlier city, these magnificent buildings were entirely the product of the insight, vision, and persuasive powers of Pericles, who used the tribute money that Athens collected from members of the Delian League to make Athens a symbol of power and wealth.

The Parthenon. By far the most beautiful building on the acropolis was the Parthenon, dedicated to Athena Parthenos, the patron deity of Athens. It was begun in 447 and completed in 438 B.C. The sides of the temple had a width-length proportion of four to nine, which is considered, even today, to be the most perfect proportion for appearance. The temple held a 40-foot-high statue of Athena by the sculptor Phidias, which was carved from wood and ivory, and covered with gold plates. Pausanias, a Greek traveler and writer of the 2nd century A.D., described this statue as follows:

● ● ● *On the middle of her helmet is placed a likeness of a sphinx . . . and on either side of the helmet are griffins in relief. . . . Athena stands erect with a tunic reaching to her feet, and on her breast, the head of Medusa is worked in ivory. She holds a statue of victory about 4 cubits [6 feet] high and in the other hand a spear; at her feet lies a shield and near the shield a serpent.[5]*

---

[5]*The Horizon Book of Ancient Greece* (New York: American Heritage Publishing Co., 1965), p. 214.

An artist's reconstruction of the 5th-century Athenian acropolis. The large building at the top of the hill is the Parthenon, which suffered great damage during an 18th-century battle.

Our only knowledge of this statue is from contemporary accounts, such as that of Pausanias, and from coins which depict it. During the 1st century A.D., it was carried off to Byzantium as a spoil of war and later destroyed by fire.

Phidias is also believed to have designed and supervised the many sculptures which adorned the exterior of the Parthenon. Above the two porticos were triangular gables or *pediments* containing sculptured scenes related to the cult of Athena. The eastern pediment depicted an array of gods witnessing the birth of Athena from the head of Zeus. On the western pediment, the rivalry between Athena and the sea-god Poseidon for possession of the city was shown. In addition to the pediment sculptures, there was a frieze, or band containing sculptures, just below the roof. The sculptures in the 525-foot-

A detail of the Parthenon frieze (west side) depicts two horsemen taking part in the Panathenaic Festival procession.

long frieze depicted a procession in the Panathenaic Festival, a celebration held every four years in honor of Athena.

The roof of the northern porch of the Erechtheum is supported by six caryatids, or maidens. Like the Parthenon, the Erechtheum was constructed of fine white marble.

The statues in the Parthenon's frieze and pediments were badly damaged over the centuries. Early in the 19th century, Lord Elgin, the British ambassador to Constantinople, obtained permission to remove many of these statues and to take them to the British Museum in London. The Elgin Marbles, as they are called, can still be seen at that museum.

The Erechtheum. The Erechtheum, which was built several decades after the Parthenon, is unusually interesting for two reasons: it was built on several levels to fit the terrain on the brow of the acropolis, and the columns which form the south portico are figures of *caryatids* (maidens) who appear to support the pediment on their heads.

SCULPTURE

The art form which has survived in greatest quantity from the Classical period of Greece is stone sculpture. Early stone statues, from the 7th century B.C., were very similar in appearance to the cult statues of ancient Egypt. The human figures were shown in a rigid frontal stance with hands clenched against the body and the left foot slightly forward. The fixed smiles and wig-like treatment of hair also resemble Egyptian techniques. Later statues were quite different from these models. They were free-standing, and the arms were separated from the body except at the wrists. Almost all of the earliest Greek statues represent either a *kouros* (young man) or a *koure*

(young woman). They may have been used as grave markers or as votive offerings to the gods.

After about 500 B.C., Greek sculpture became naturalistic, with human bodies standing in a relaxed position so that the weight seems to rest on one leg. The eyes of these statues seem to engage the viewer in direct gaze, and the earlier stylized smiles were changed to thoughtful expressions. The clothing is delicately draped to suggest the form of the body beneath. Throughout the 5th century B.C., sculptors strove to emphasize the divine qualities of man. Ironically, the statues of human beings, with their serene expressions and perfectly porportioned features, appear to be divine, while statues representing the gods often have more irregular, individualistic features.

The 5th Century B.C. The most important sculptors of the 5th century were Phidias, Polyclitus, and Myron. In addition to the statue of Athena and the other sculptures of the Parthenon, Phidias created a 60-foot statue of Zeus for a temple in Olympia.

Both Polyclitus and Myron were famous for their bronze figures of athletes. None of their original works survive, but several of them are known through Roman copies. Myron's "Discus Thrower" portrayed an athlete at the very moment when his body is poised to hurl a discus. It is said that his statue of a heifer was so realistic that when it was placed in a pasture, it deceived the cows who were grazing there.

The 4th Century B.C. The outstanding sculptors of the 4th century were Praxiteles, Scopas, and Lysippus. Two of Praxiteles' best known works were "Aphrodite of Cnidus" and "Hermes and Dionysus." The statue from Cnidus is known only through copies, but that of Hermes, now in a museum in Olympia, may be an original.

The style of Scopas was very different from that of Praxiteles. His figures were characterized by their vigor and intensity, in contrast to the grace and ease of Praxiteles'

Praxiteles' statue of Aphrodite created a great sensation in the Greek world when it was first unveiled. This is one of many Roman copies of the original.

images. In Scopas' work, staring eyes, dilated nostrils, and taut muscles were characteristic features.

Lysippus may have been the first sculptor to use casts of living models in his studio. His statues were free-standing so that they

Praxiteles may have created this statue of Hermes and Dionysius about 360 B.C. With his right arm, now lost, Hermes dangled some grapes in front of the infant Dionysius.

The works of Scopas were known for their turbulence and emotion. This is a Roman copy of his portrait of Meleager, an angry young man who murdered his uncle and was in turn killed by his mother.

Lysippus was one of the most admired artists of his time. This sculpture shows an athlete scraping oil from his body with a tool known as a strigil.

could be viewed from any angle. One of his works, of a young athlete scraping oil from his arm, is known to us through a copy. He also created idealistic portraits of Socrates and of Alexander the Great.

DRAMA
Greek drama had its origins in an annual religious festival in honor of Dionysus, the god of wine and immortality. In the earliest festivals, a chorus of men dressed as *satyrs*

The plays of Sophocles, Aeschylus, and Euripides were performed in theaters like this one throughout the Greek world. This is the theatre of the city of Ephesus in Ionia.

would sing *tragedoi* ("goat songs") as they danced about the altar. During the 6th century B.C., the tyrant Pisistratus enlarged the festival of Dionysus. Under his sponsorship, the festival lasted for three days, and four or five plays, written especially for the occasion, were presented each day. According to contemporary accounts, most of these plays were tragedies which centered upon ancient historical events or myths. None of these early works have survived to the present day.

Aeschylus, Sophocles, and Euripides, the great dramatists of the 5th century B.C., also chose ancient myths and legends as the basis for most of their dramas and tragedies. In fact, only one drama concerning a contemporary event has come down to us—namely, Aeschylus' play *The Persians* about the Persian Wars. But although these playwrights rarely dealt with topical themes directly, they often chose subjects which had clear parallels to contemporary events.

Like the philosophers of Ionia, the dramatists of 5th-century Athens believed that, in spite of the diversity and inconsistencies that could be seen in everyday life, there were universal laws of order. These moral laws were a mystery to mankind and could only be known after they had been violated. Thus, the action of the plays often centered upon a tragic hero who violated one of the hidden laws and, inevitably, had to suffer dire consequences—even if the transgression had been committed unknowingly or for a just cause. Edith Hamilton wrote that the dramatist Aeschylus, for instance:

● ● ● *knew life as only the greatest poets can know it; he perceived the mystery of suffering. Mankind he saw fast bound to*

Aeschylus. Aeschylus, the "Father of Greek Tragedy," was born at Eleusis, in Attica, in 524 B.C. He fought in the battles of Marathon and Salamis during the Persian Wars, and died in Sicily in 456 B.C. He wrote more than 80 plays, but only 7 of them, including *The Persians*, have come down to us.

In his three plays known as the *Oresteian Trilogy*, Aeschylus addressed the conflict between tribal traditions of justice and the law of the Athenian state. The trilogy concerns the story of the legendary hero Agamemnon, who was murdered by his wife, Clytemnestra, when he returned home from the Trojan War. Aeschylus used the events and characters of this story to demonstrate how the early development of the Athenian polis contributed to justice and moral order.

In the play, Orestes, the son of Agamemnon, is encouraged by the god Apollo to avenge the murder of his father. This act was in accord with ancient tribal traditions, which dictated that a family must avenge the murder of one of its members. However, in kill-

calamity by the working of unknown powers committed to strange venture, companioned by disaster.[6]

The "unknown powers" responsible for mankind's tragedies were known as *Fate*, and were considered to be more powerful than any of the deities of the Greek pantheon. In the 5th-century dramas, the benevolent gods of Olympus often have the power to intervene in human affairs, but they, too, are subject to the laws of Fate.

Because the works of the Greek dramatists were concerned with Athenian traditions and values, performances were considered to be an important part of community life. Athenian citizens who could not afford the admission price were admitted as guests of the state.

[6]Hamilton, *The Greek Way*, p. 176.

This plate painting shows Clytemnestra killing the prophetess Cassandra, a scene from Aeschylus' Oresteian Trilogy.

A scene from Euripides' *Hecuba:* the soul of Achilles flies over a departing Greek ship, demanding that his death be avenged.

ing Clytemnestra, Orestes incurs the wrath of the Furies, the fierce female deities who enforce family law.

In the resolution of the play, the role of the emerging Athenian state becomes apparent. The goddess Athena convinces the Furies to put aside their anger and to abide by the decision of the court of Athens. Finally, even though the court's decision goes against them, the Furies are placated. They become known as the *Eumenides* ("The Kindly Ones"), and agree to uphold the authority of the state.

Sophocles. The second of the three great Greek tragedians was Sophocles (496-406 B.C.), who was born of noble parents and received the best education available. His friends included Pericles, Euripides (who will be considered next), and Herodotus. He served in public office on several occasions, and for 30 years received the first or second prize for the plays he wrote for the Festival of Dionysus. He wrote more than 100 plays, but only 7 are available to us today.

Sophocles believed that the inflexible moral laws of the universe made it impossible for a man to control his own destiny. But through the suffering which inevitably resulted from the imposition of these laws, man could gain wisdom and righteousness. His *Oedipus Rex* tells the story of a man who unknowingly murdered his father and married his mother. The more he struggled against his fate, the more enmeshed he became. At last, he recognized what he had done and blinded himself in remorse. A few years after the play was written, Aristotle referred to *Oedipus Rex* in creating his definition of a "perfect tragedy":

● ● ● *A perfect tragedy should . . . imitate actions which excite pity and fear. . . . The change of fortunes presented must not be the spectacle of a virtuous man brought from prosperity to adversity, for this moves neither pity nor fear; it merely shocks us. Nor, again, that of a bad man passing from adversity to prosperity: for nothing can be more alien to the spirit of tragedy. . . . There remains, then, the character between these two extremes—that of a man who is not eminently good and just, yet whose misfortune is brought about not by vice or depravity, but by some error or frailty. He must be one who is highly renowned and prosperous, a personage like Oedipus.*[7]

Euripides. The third of the great tragedians was Euripides (484-406 B.C.), who also wrote approximately 100 plays, only 19 of which have survived. Euripides' plays usually concern passionate characters who commit rash actions which they later regret. In the plays, irrational passions are seen to be an essential part of humanity; they are an uncontrollable force which inevitably lead to tragedy.

Euripides' tragedies are thought to reflect the disillusionment and uncertainty that many Athenians felt during the years of the Peloponnesian War. In the *Trojan Women,* for instance, Euripides depicted a military action of the Trojan War. In the play, the Mycenaeans inflict terrible atrocities upon their defeated enemies at Troy, then are themselves destroyed by a shipwreck at sea.

---

[7]Aristotle, *Poetics* (trans. George Howe and Gustave Harrer), lines 25-43.

Euripides may have intended *The Trojan Women* as a warning to the Athenians concerning their heartless destruction of the city-state of Melos, an action that was carried out while Euripides was writing the play (416 B.C.). If so, his prophesy came true a short time later, for a large Athenian force then suffered a devastating defeat in Sicily.

In the play *Medea*, Euripides expressed great sympathy for the tragic, legendary heroine who had helped her husband, Jason, acquire the Golden Fleece and was then abandoned by him. As she struggled between her love for her children and her hatred for her faithless husband, she became distraught and murdered her sons. When Jason learned that Medea had killed the children, he sought revenge, but Medea appeared out of his reach above the palace roof, in a chariot drawn by dragons. This unusual scene allowed Euripides to end the play without pronouncing a judgment upon his heroine.

A terracotta mask worn by an actor in Athenian comedy. Actors also wore costumes that were padded to produce a grotesque effect.

In the staging of Euripides' play Medea, *the god and chariot of the final act were raised to the top of the set by a crane. This device for ending a play therefore came to be known as* deus ex machina *("god from a machine"). For centuries to come, certain playwrights copied Euripides' strategy of introducing an extraneous character in the final scene of a play in order to resolve a complex situation.*

Euripides' plays won few prizes, but—perhaps because of their sensational content, and because the language was similar to everyday speech—they were immensely popular with audiences. His plays were staged more often than those of Aeschylus and Sophocles, and continued to be popular with later generations.

COMEDY

In contrast to the dramatists of the 5th century, the writers of comedies dealt almost exclusively with current events rather than with mythological themes. The greatest writer of comedies was Aristophanes (446-388 B.C.), who satirized well-known politicians, dramatists, and other public figures of Athens. Aristophanes was once impeached by the Assembly of Athens, but this experience did not temper his irreverent attitude.

Two of Aristophanes' favorite targets were Pericles and the demagogue Cleon, the politicians who promoted a warlike policy in the Assembly. He also satirized the endless litigation of court cases, and the beliefs and practices of the Sophists. He achieved comic effects through the use of grotesquely padded costumes, exaggerated facts, impossible situations, and coarse, but usually good natured humor. One of his most famous plays is *The Clouds*, in which he showed Socrates suspended in a basket in the heavens, dispensing his new philosophy.

PHILOSOPHY

The "new learning" that Aristophanes satirized in his comedies appeared in Athens during the last half of the 5th century. In Athens' democracy, a person had to be able to speak clearly and persuasively in order to achieve political power. Teachers who could offer such training gave exhibitions of their knowledge and skills, and offered to teach anyone willing to pay their fees. Young men from wealthy families enrolled in the classes of these *sophists* ("teachers of wisdom") to learn debating techniques and the art of *rhetoric* (public speaking).

The sophists were rather controversial figures because they demanded pay for their teachings, and this policy, as well as some of their teachings, conflicted with traditional concepts. In his comedy *The Clouds*, Aristophanes expressed the view that the sophists conveyed materialistic values to their students:

But so you'll enter me amongst your
  scholars,
And tutor me like them to bilk my
  creditors,
Name your own price, and by the gods I
  swear
I'll pay you my last drachma.[8]

Socrates. Socrates (469-399 B.C.) was one of a group of original thinkers who were wrongfully accused of being sophists. His method of thinking and teaching was actually quite different from that of the sophists: he did not claim to have answers, but instead asked questions of his students in order to explore their values and beliefs. Through his questions, he often forced his listeners to admit that their beliefs and opinions were not well-founded. The inscription "know thyself" in the temple of Apollo at Delphi was the theme of his teachings, for he believed that "the unexamined life is not

Socrates' teachings provided the foundation for Greek philosophy and inspired the schools of thought that came to be known as Scepticism, Stoicism, and Epicurianism.

worth living." He stressed that the conscience of an individual was a better guide to action than the laws of a government.

Socrates fulfilled his duties as an Athenian citizen according to his conscience and beliefs. He served as a soldier during a mil-

---

[8]Aristophanes, *The Clouds* (trans. Patric Dickinson), lines 248-51.

itary campaign in Thrace and later was remembered by his fellow soldiers for his heroism and his ability to withstand cold. In the Assembly, Socrates was known for his steadfast refusal to compromise. On one occasion, he became the leader of the government for a day when he was chosen by lot to serve as chairman of the Boule. The Assembly on that day was clamoring to impeach the ten *strategoi*, because the Athenian military forces had recently suffered a setback. Socrates, however, refused to present this business to the Assembly. Plato quoted his philosophy concerning his duty to himself and to the state as follows:

• • • *Doing wrong, and disobeying the person who is better than myself, be it man or god, that I know is base and wicked. Therefore, never for the sake of evils which I know to be such, will I fear or flee from what for all I know may be good.*[9]

Socrates worked as an artisan and refused to take money from his students. Although he had many rich and powerful friends, he lived in poverty all his life, and was often criticized for his appearance and behavior. In 399 B.C., Socrates was impeached by the Assembly on charges of "corrupting the young" and "undermining religious beliefs." These charges may have had something to do with his association with Alcibiades, a former pupil who had disregarded his ethical teachings and had become a traitor to Athens.

After a trial, the Assembly voted to give Socrates the death penalty. Under Athenian law, he had the right to make a counterproposal suggesting a less severe penalty. Instead of proposing a true compromise, however, Socrates suggested that he be given a small fine. The Assembly then reconfirmed the death penalty. Socrates' friends urged him to flee the city, and offered to help him do so.

Socrates refused, however, and when the time came, he calmly took a potion of hemlock and continued to converse with his friends until the poison had acted.

Socrates left no writings, but after his death Plato made a record of several dialogs that Socrates had conducted with other citizens of Athens. These dialogs convey a vivid portrait of the personalities involved as well as of the great philosopher's teachings and method.

Plato. Plato (427-347 B.C.) was born of wealthy parents and received an excellent education. He originally intended to enter politics, but eventually became disenchanted with Athens' form of government: he described *democracy* as a tyranny of the common people. Around the time of Socrates' trial, Plato left Athens for a period of several years. In 388 B.C., he returned to Athens and established a school called the *Academy*, where he taught philosophy and science until his death at 81 years of age.

Plato taught that perfect truth, beauty, and wisdom existed only as ideas, and that every object was an imperfect reflection of the idea underlying it. For example, no one can draw a perfect circle freehand, but the idea of a perfect circle can be easily accepted.

His most important work was *The Republic*, in which he described an ideal state. The objective of such a state would be to ensure the welfare of all citizens, and to utilize the special talents and abilities of each class. The good of all could be achieved only when every citizen adhered to the four basic virtues of truth, wisdom, courage, and moderation. Each person could best attain these virtues by fulfilling the function in society for which he was best suited.

Plato decided that an ideal state could be established in a community of about 5000 people, with each citizen examined in infancy and placed in one of three categories: to serve as a worker producing the necessities of life; to be a soldier to guard the state; or to become a philosopher-king to rule the

---

[9]Plato, *Apology* (trans. George Howe and Gustave Harrer), lines 25-29.

state. To ensure that only the most capable would rule, he proposed that children who displayed virtue at an early age should be educated to govern. Insulated from all pleasures and luxuries, these future rulers would devote themselves to the study of philosophy so that, when they achieved enlightenment, the government of the state might be placed in their hands.

Plato was given an opportunity to put his theory into practice when the tyrant of Syracuse, Dionysius II, invited him to supervise the education of a group of children selected to be philosopher-kings. Unfortunately, the experiment failed. Later, Plato's educational theories were again tested—and achieved notable results—when his disciple Aristotle served as tutor to Alexander of Macedonia.

After Plato's death, his Academy continued in existence for almost 1000 years until the Byzantine emperor Justinian ordered that all pagan (non-Christian) schools of philosophy be closed.

Aristotle. Plato's best known pupil was Aristotle (384-322 B.C.). Aristotle was born in Macedonia, where his father was physician at the court of the Macedonian king, Philip II. At the age of 17, Aristotle enrolled at Plato's Academy in Athens, and he remained a disciple of Plato until Plato's death 20 years later. In 343 B.C., Aristotle accepted an offer to tutor the young prince of Macedonia, who later became known as Alexander the Great.

In 335 B.C. Aristotle returned to Athens to establish his own school, the Lyceum. Because he usually strolled along with his students as he taught, his school became known as the *peripatetic* ("walking") school.

While Aristotle was interested in logic, ethics, rhetoric, and political science—the conventional topics of philosophy—he was primarily interested in what we call biology. He came to believe that all natural phenomena are awesome, and even suggested that a spider is as divine as a star. He also taught that all organisms evolved from simpler to more complex forms. He collected over 500 specimens of flora and fauna, noted distinctions between them, classified them according to these distinctions, and arrived at general conclusions about what he observed. His inductive system of investigation is still the basis of the modern science of biology.

Aristotle agreed with his teacher, Plato, that the city-state was the best setting for a good life, and that an ideal state would help its citizens achieve a good life rather than mere existence. To better understand the nature of government, he wrote a work entitled *Politics* in which he analyzed the constitutions of 158 places, including Athens. Like Plato, he disapproved of democracy as a form of government, and advocated rule by philosopher-kings. He believed that justice would prevail only if all people practiced moderation so that no one group would have either too much or too little.

Aristotle's death marked the end of the great age of Greek philosophy, but his ideas have influenced Western thought ever since. In medieval Europe, his theories were so revered that scholars would ignore their personal observations if these seemed to contradict what Aristotle had written. The modern world is indebted to him for the scientific method he introduced, for his emphasis on balance between liberty and authority, for his insistence on the value of public education, and for the concept that government should help to provide a good life for all citizens.

ECONOMY AND SOCIAL STRUCTURE

Most areas of Greece were dependent upon foreign supplies of grain and other foods. In Boeotia and in the Peloponnesus, the soil was fertile enough to produce sufficient food for the local populations, but in the rest of Greece, and especially in the large urban areas, people depended upon imported foods. In fact, the very existence of Athens depended upon her ability to secure grain from the Black Sea area.

Most of the land of Attica was planted in orchards and vineyards. The olive oil and wine produced there were traded for grain and dried fish from the Black Sea area, timber and hides from Thrace, dates from Phoenicia, papyrus from Egypt, wool from Asia Minor, tin from Britain, and metals from Cyprus and Thrace.

Many citizens considered agriculture to be the most desirable way of life, but the aristocrats who owned the land often were more interested in manufacturing and commerce. The factories and shops owned by these wealthy investors were operated by slaves, poor free men, and resident aliens. The factories were very small, each one employing only a few people. The manufacturing operations were divided among several workers. For instance, in a pottery factory, one person prepared the clay, another molded vases, another prepared handles, and still another applied decorations. Such factories were usually located to the rear of the small shops in which the products were sold.

Slaves and Resident Aliens. About one-third of the population of Athens consisted of slaves who were acquired in raids or as prisoners of war. Many worked as domestic servants and as artisans, teachers, doctors, or scribes. Those slaves who received wages for their efforts were permitted to keep a portion of their earnings and, in time, could purchase their freedom. After they acquired their freedom, however, they had the status of aliens and did not enjoy the full rights of Athenian citizens.

Pericles encouraged foreigners to live and work in Athens, but citizenship in the polis was limited to Athenian men whose parents were Athenians. Resident aliens could not own land, but were required to pay taxes and to perform military service. Citizenship in Athens, as in most Greek city-states, was highly valued, and was granted to aliens only for meritorious service to the state.

Taxation. The Athenians early developed a unique form of taxation by which wealthy citizens were expected to subsidize public

Athenian pottery factories were usually located behind the shops that sold their wares. Vase painters seldom signed their work, but scholars have developed descriptive names to identify several individuals.

works through payments called *liturgies*. Although these *liturgies* were financial burdens, wealthy citizens competed with each other to see who could produce the best-trained chorus for a play or the best-equipped warship.

Expenditures by the state included wages for soldiers and sailors, payment to citizens for service on the Boule and in the courts, and expenses related to religious festivals. During the period of Athens' Empire, Athenian citizens paid few taxes to cover these expenditures, for tribute payments from the allies had created a booming economy. After the Peloponnesian War, a property tax was levied to compensate for the loss of tribute payments.

Family Life. In Athenian society, wealthy men had complete freedom and found pleasure in endless discussions of politics, exercise at the gymnasia, in drinking bouts, and in athletic contests. Men met at the agora to discuss public issues, to conduct business, and to listen to orators. Three sides of the agora were lined by colonnades to provide convenient places for such meetings.

Women, by contrast, were subject to their fathers before marriage, and to their husbands after marriage. Women of the upper classes were secluded in their homes and never participated in the entertainment of their husbands' guests. They left their homes only to attend a tragic drama, a funeral, or a wedding. They were excluded from all political rights. Outside their homes, men usually enjoyed the companionship of unmarried women who were knowledgeable about music, poetry, and dancing. Pericles, in his Funeral Oration, summed up the attitude of Athenian men to women as follows:

● ● ● *Great will be your glory in not falling short of your natural character; and greatest will be hers who is least talked of among men whether for good or for bad.*[10]

Some scholars believe that the importance of female characters in Greek dramas may indicate that women actually enjoyed more freedom and esteem than other writings seem to indicate.

Education. The purpose of education in ancient Athens was to produce citizens capable of serving the state. While there was no system of public education, most boys learned the fundamentals of literary knowledge. Poor boys were apprenticed to craftsmen, while the sons of wealthy citizens were enrolled in private schools. When a wealthy boy was eight years old, a *pedagogos* (slave) would accompany him to school and tutor him at home. Such boys studied reading, writing, and arithmetic, and learned to play a seven-string lyre. They practiced gymnastics, because the Greeks believed that physical fitness was as important as mental stimulation. They were required to memorize selections from the *Iliad* and the *Odyssey* of Homer, and the poems of Hesiod. At 18 years of age, each young man became eligible to vote, and enrolled in his *deme*. He took the oath of citizenship, vowing that:

● ● ● *I will not disgrace the sacred arms, nor will I desert my comrade in the ranks. I, alone or with many others, will defend the sacred and holy places. My fatherland I will transmit in no worse state but greater and better than I found it. I will obey those in authority, and I will observe wholeheartedly the laws now in force and whatever others the people may pass. And if anyone seeks to annul the laws or refuses to obey them, I will not heed him; but, alone or with many others, I will defend them. And I will honor the religion of my fathers.*[11]

Each young man was then required to complete two years of military service, and afterward continued his education by informal methods. Girls were rarely educated in

[10]Thucydides II, 6, 45.

[11]"The Ephebic Oath" in *Greek Literature in Translation*, trans. George Howe and Gustave Harrer (New York & London: Harper & Row, 1924), p. 586.

The agora of Athens was lined with colonnades where men could meet to discuss private business and public issues. The plan of the agora with its large open square was later copied by the Romans in the design of their Forum.

schools, but were taught by their mothers to manage a household and care for children.

Houses. The citizens of Athens were far more concerned about beautifying their city with impressive public buildings than about adorning their own homes. Their houses were constructed of sun-dried bricks and covered with stucco. They were usually two stories high with flat, tiled roofs. The side of the house facing the street was blank except for the door. A passageway led from the door to a small courtyard, which was surrounded by several rooms. There were openings in the interior walls to allow passage and to admit light, but no doors or windows as we know them. A limited amount of light was provided by oil-burning lamps, and water was obtained from the nearest public well. The houses were furnished with chests, couches, chairs, and tables, and were heated with portable braziers. Because the climate was mild, people spent most of their free time outdoors, in the public areas of the city.

THE PELOPON- The glory of Athens came
NESIAN WAR to an end during the Peloponnesian War, which began in 431 and ended in 404 B.C. Due to the economic and psychological strains of the war, the moral and religious beliefs of the Classical Greeks were undermined, and social cohesiveness was lost. By the end of the war, all of the participants were so weakened that they became prey to a series of foreign invaders.

Thucydides. Our most important source of information for the events of the Peloponnesian War is the history written by Thucydides, an Athenian citizen who lived during this period and began his history of Greece at the point where Herodotus had left off.[12] In the first chapter of his book, Thucydides stated his belief that the Peloponnesian War

---

[12]Herodotus' history concluded with an account of the final battles against the Persians. His work was published in 430 B.C.

"would be a great war, and more worthy of relation than any that had preceded it."[13] To do honor to his subject, Thucydides took great care to evaluate the reliability of his sources and to let his readers know which statements were well founded and which could not be substantiated. He is known as the first *critical* historian.

Thucydides served as *strategos* in the battle of Amphipolis in 424 B.C. Due to the Athenians' defeat in that campaign, he was banished from Athens for a period of 20 years. He did not appeal this unjust sentence, but instead took the opportunity to travel and to gather information about the Peloponnesians' point of view in the struggle.

According to Thucydides' account, there were a number of incidents in the prewar years which caused tensions between the Peloponnesian League, led by Sparta, and the Delian League. Although each party honored the terms of a nonaggression treaty signed in 461 B.C., Athens committed a number of actions that violated the spirit of the agreement. In 435 B.C., Athens agreed to send military aid to the island of Corcyra, which was at war with Corinth. Since Corcyra did not belong to either the Peloponnesian League or the Delian League, this action did not violate the terms of the treaty. Nevertheless, the Corinthians deeply resented Athens' intervention in the war. At a meeting of the Peloponnesian League in 432 B.C., the Corinthians persuaded Sparta to prepare for a war against Athens.

Thucydides believed that although the immediate cause of the Peloponnesian War was the action of Corinth, the underlying cause was Sparta's fear of the growing power of Athens:

● ● ● *The real cause I consider to be the one which was formally most kept out of sight. The growth of the power of Athens, and the*

alarm which this inspired in Lacedaemon, made war inevitable. Still it is well to give the grounds alleged by either side, which led to the dissolution of the treaty and the breaking out of the war.[14]

In 431 B.C., the Spartans sent envoys to Athens with three separate ultimatums demanding that Athens avoid any interference in the affairs of the Peloponnesus. In the Assembly of Athens, Pericles argued that to give in to the Spartans' demands would only betray weakness and invite still more demands. He advised against any concessions, and urged his countrymen to prepare for war. He pointed out that the Spartans did not have any reserve of money with which to wage a war and did not have an experienced navy. Although the Spartan army was three times as strong as that of the Athenians, Pericles argued that internal divisions among the members of the Peloponnesian League would make their forces vulnerable.

The Peloponnesian War broke out in 431, when Spartan armies invaded Attica and plundered the countryside. Because Pericles thought it best to avoid a pitched battle, the Athenians gathered within the walls of the city while their navy engaged the enemy along the Peloponnesian coast.

During the second year of the war, in 430, a terrible plague swept over Athens, and one-third of the people within the walls died. Thucydides described the symptoms of the disease as follows:

● ● ● *There was no ostensible cause; but people in good health were all of a sudden attacked by violent heats in the head, and redness and inflammation in the eyes, the inward parts, such as the throat or tongue, becoming bloody and emitting an unnatural and fetid breath. These symptoms were followed by sneezing and hoarseness, after which the pain soon reached the chest, and produced a hard cough. When it fixed in the*

---

[13]Thucydides I, 1, 1.

[14]Ibid., I, 1, 24.

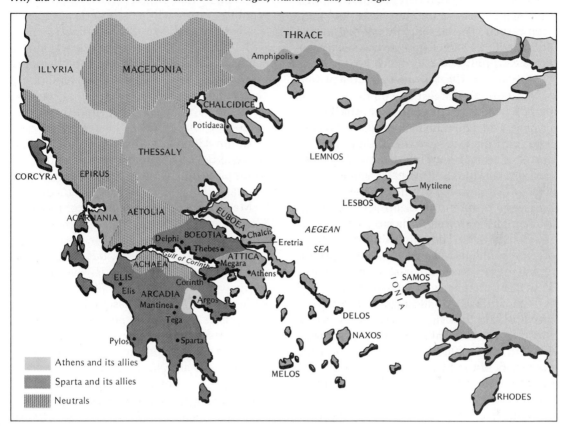

Athens and its allies

Sparta and its allies

Neutrals

stomach, it upset it; and discharges of bile of every kind named by physicians ensued, accompanied by very great distress.[15]

Pericles died during the plague epidemic. The leadership of Athens then fell to Cleon, a demagogue[16] whose policies were much more belligerent and uncompromising than those of Pericles.

Cleon. According to Aristophanes, Cleon had a voice "like a mountain torrent," and had been a tanner before he entered public life. Aristophanes often invented occupations and parentages for the targets of his satire, but it is known from other sources that Cleon was a very persuasive speaker and that he had made his fortune in the leather business. In his play *Knights*, written during the Peloponnesian War, Aristophanes included this caricature of Cleon:

Now at the beginning of last month,
He bought a new slave, a tanner,
Called Cle —, I mean Paphlageon —
The filthiest, most blatant, lowest-down
Liar of all time.[17]

---

[15]Ibid., II, 7, 49.

[16]The term *demagogue* in ancient Greece denoted a politician who rose to power as a leader of the common people. A demagogue often achieved his ends by playing upon the emotions of a crowd.

---

[17]Aristophanes, *Knights* (trans. Patric Dickinson), lines 43-45.

As early as 431 B.C., Cleon had criticized Pericles, arguing that Athens should enforce its hegemony over its allies with more severity than Pericles recommended. After Pericles died, in 429 B.C., there was no speaker in the Assembly who could effectively counter Cleon's arguments. The next year, the people of Mytilene, the largest city on the island of Lesbos, voted to withdraw from the Delian League. The Athenian fleet blockaded the island until the people were forced to surrender. Cleon then prevailed upon the Assembly to order the harshest possible sentence for Athens' former ally: all of the men of Mytilene were to be put to death, and all of the women and children enslaved. The Assembly dispatched a ship to Mytilene to carry out the sentence. The next day, the people of Athens repented the harsh and indiscriminate measure they had passed, and met again to reconsider their decision. Cleon argued that it would be a sign of weakness to show pity, but the Assembly, by a small margin, voted to send a second ship to countermand the orders of the first. Thus, the massacre of the citizens of Mytilene was narrowly avoided.

At this point in the war, Thucydides concluded that the spirit that had made Athens the foremost city among the Greeks had begun to deteriorate:

● ● ● *Reckless audacity came to be considered the courage of a loyal ally; prudent hesitation, specious cowardice; moderation was held to be a cloak for unmanliness; ability to see all sides of a question inaptness to act on any. Frantic violence became the attribute of manliness; cautious plotting, a justifiable means of self-defence. The advocate of extreme measures was always trustworthy; his opponent a man to be suspected. To succeed in a plot was to have a shrewd head, to divine a plot still shrewder.*[18]

---

[18]Thucydides III, 5, 82.

At the outset of the war, Pericles had recommended that Athens not attempt to expand its empire while the war lasted. Cleon, however, wished to pursue a more aggressive policy. In 425 B.C., Cleon persuaded the Assembly to open a new front in the Peloponnesus, and he was elected general for a campaign to seize the city of Pylos. Together with the capable general Demosthenes, he succeeded in capturing the city. The next year, the Athenians tried to capture the territory of Boeotia, where they hoped that the common people would join them against the Spartans. This time they were unsuccessful.

Meanwhile, the city of Amphipolis in Chalcidice rebelled against Athenian rule. Thucydides led an army to the area in order to put down the rebellion, but the Spartans came to the aid of Amphipolis. The Athenian troops were defeated, and Thucydides was exiled by the Athenian assembly. Two years later, in 422 B.C., Cleon attempted to recapture Amphipolis and was killed in battle.

The loss of Cleon meant that other politicians were able to develop their policies. In 422 B.C., a popular Athenian politician named Nicias negotiated a peace treaty with the Spartans. Under the terms of the treaty, Pylos was to be returned to Sparta, and Amphipolis was to be returned to Athens. The Peace of Nicias, as the cessation of war came to be known, was a fragile truce and was soon threatened by the rise of aggressive pro-war politicians in both Sparta and Athens.

Alcibiades. Alcibiades belonged to an ancient Athenian noble family and also had family ties to one of the royal families of Sparta. He was known for his intellectual brilliance, personal charm, and unprincipled character. In the *Symposium*, Alcibiades gives this evaluation of his own character and of his relationship with Socrates, his long time friend and teacher:

● ● ● *Socrates is the only man in the world that can make me feel ashamed. Because there's no getting away from it, I know I ought to do the things he tells me to, and yet the moment I'm out of his sight I don't care what I do to keep in with the mob. So I dash off like a runaway slave, and keep out of his way as long as I can, and then next time I meet him I remember all that I had to admit the time before, and naturally I feel ashamed.*[19]

Due to his family connections and political gifts, Alcibiades became a prominent politician during the war. In the Assembly, he advocated that Athens ignore the treaty with Sparta and develop a strategy to overthrow the power of Sparta. In 420 B.C., Alcibiades persuaded Argos, Elis, Mantinea, and Tega, four cities of the Peloponnesus, to form an alliance with Athens.

In 418 B.C., the Spartans tested the alliance that Alcibiades had engineered by attacking Mantinea. They soundly defeated the allies, who did not receive sufficient support from Athens. The allies were bitter about the lack of support, and Sparta was bitter about the intrigue.

Having been defeated in their strategy to divide the Peloponnesus, the Athenians turned to the city-states of the Aegean. In 416, they demanded that the island of Melos, which had been neutral in the war, pay tribute to Athens. The people of Melos refused, and an Athenian force was sent to subdue the island. When they had captured Melos, the Athenians executed all men who were old enough to fight and enslaved the women and children. Thus, the policy that Cleon had advocated and that the Assembly had rejected for Mytilene in 427 was carried out against the people of Melos 11 years later.

In 415 B.C., the people of Segesta, in Sicily, appealed to Athens for protection against Selinus, another colony in Sicily. Alcibiades saw this appeal as an opportunity to achieve a great military triumph and to add the island of Sicily to Athens' empire. The Assembly of Athens agreed to this campaign, and three generals were appointed to lead the Athenian forces: Alcibiades himself; Lamachus, a competent military man with little political influence; and Nicias, who was opposed to the plan from the beginning. A force which represented a substantial part of Athens' military capability was gathered. It included 140 ships, 5100 hoplites, and about 130 archers, slingers, and lightly armed troops.

Shortly before the force was to leave Athens, the Athenians discovered that the statues of Hermes that guarded temples and homes throughout the city had been defaced. Since this was regarded as a bad omen, there was a thorough investigation. The culprits could not be identified, but several citizens remembered that Alcibiades had, in the past, parodied sacred rituals. His opponents demanded that charges be brought against him, but the Athenian force left before the Assembly had acted.

Several days after the Athenian force had sailed, the Assembly formally brought charges against Alcibiades, and a ship was dispatched to bring him back to Athens. Alcibiades, realizing that he had little chance to prove his innocence in a trial, escaped his escort and fled to Sparta. There, he provided the Spartan kings with valuable information and advice. He told them how they could defeat the Athenian forces in Sicily, and advised them to place a garrison in northern Attica to blockade the city of Athens.

In Sicily, the arrest of Alcibiades was a severe blow to the morale of the Athenian force, and was later blamed for the disaster that occurred there. The Athenians began to besiege the city of Syracuse, but soon began to suffer heavy losses as Spartan and Corinthian forces came to the aid of the Syracusans. Lamachus was killed in battle, and Nicias sent to Athens for reinforcements. The reinforcements arrived the next spring, led by the general Demosthenes. After sizing up the situation, Demosthenes saw that the Ath-

---

[19]Plato, *Symposium* (trans. Michael Joyce), 216.

enians were in a hopeless situation and advised that they withdraw. However, an eclipse of the moon convinced Nicias that the Athenian troops should stay and engage the enemy. During the following week, the Spartans and Syracusans blockaded the harbor and bottled up the Athenian fleet. In attempting to break through the blockade, the Athenians lost their entire fleet. The roads leading inland were also blocked to them. Thucydides described the final hours of the Athenian forces as they struggled to march inland toward their allies:

● ● ● *[They fancied] that they should breathe more freely if once across the river, and driven on also by their exhaustion and craving for water. Once there they rushed in, and all order was at an end, each man wanting to cross first, and the attacks of the enemy making it difficult to cross at all; forced to huddle together, they fell against and trod down one another, some dying immediately upon the javelins, others getting entangled together and stumbling over the articles of baggage, without being able to rise again. Meanwhile the opposite bank, which was steep, was lined by the Syracusans, who showered missiles down upon the Athenians, most of them drinking greedily and heaped together in disorder in the hollow bed of the river. The Peloponnesians also came down and butchered them, especially those in the water, which was thus immediately spoiled, but which they went on drinking just the same, mud and all, bloody as it was, most even fighting to have it.*[20]

Most of the Athenian troops, including Nicias and Demosthenes, perished.

The failure of the Sicilian expedition left Athens with many severe problems: most of its fleet had been lost, the treasury was depleted, its prestige among the Greek city-states was shattered, and the remaining subject allies were in revolt. Because the Spartans had taken Alcibiades' advice to place a garrison in Attica, Athenian farmers could not cultivate their lands, and the silver mines could not be operated.

After their victory over the Athenian navy in Sicily, the Spartans commandeered additional ships from their allies, and soon gained control of the western Mediterranean and of the Hellespont. Nevertheless, the Spartans did not have enough resources to destroy the remaining Athenian fleet, and they therefore approached the Persians for financial help. Meanwhile, Alcibiades had been forced to leave Sparta after it was reported that he had made improper advances to the wife of a Spartan king. He fled to Asia Minor, and attached himself to Tisaphernes, the Persian satrap at Sardis, who agreed to protect him from his enemies. Plutarch described how Alcibiades ingratiated himself with the Persian:

● ● ● *This barbarian, not being himself sincere, but a lover of guile and wickedness, admired his address and wonderful subtlety. And, indeed, the charm of daily intercourse with him was more than any character could resist. . . . Even those who feared and envied him could not but take delight, and have a sort of kindness for him, when they saw him and were in his company.*[21]

Since both the Spartans and the Persians were in favor of oligarchic governments, it appeared that the Persians would give aid to the Spartans. But Alcibiades was also negotiating with the Persians, on behalf of Athens, and finally won a promise of aid. Thus, through his influence with the Persians, Alcibiades succeeded in regaining a role in Athenian politics. Although he was still in exile in Asia Minor, he was then given command of an Athenian fleet. He proceeded to win several important victories for Athens, and finally destroyed the Spartan fleet in the Hellespont. The Athenians thus recovered control over this important area, and were

---

[20]Thucydides VII, 23, 84.

[21]Plutarch, *Lives*, Modern Library ed., p. 250.

again able to import grain from the Black Sea region.

In 407 B.C., Alcibiades decided that it was safe to return to Athens, for his naval victories had won him many new supporters, and the charges against him had been dropped. Plutarch described his homecoming as follows:

• • • *As soon as he was landed, the multitude who came out to meet him scarcely seemed so much as to see any of the other captains, but came in throngs about Alcibiades, and saluted him with loud acclamations. . . . They made reflections, that they could not have so unfortunately miscarried in Sicily, or been defeated in any of their other expectations, if they had left the management of their affairs . . . to Alcibiades.*[22]

Alcibiades was elected supreme commander of all the Athenian forces, but within a few months he lost several ships during a minor skirmish with the Spartans. The Assembly then voted to dismiss him from his command, and he fled again to Asia Minor.

In 405 B.C., the Spartan navy made a surprise attack on a large fleet of Athenian ships anchored in the Hellespont. As Alcibiades watched from a castle overlooking the Hellespont, the Athenian ships were destroyed. Because Athens' trade route to the Black Sea was now closed by the Spartans, it was evident that Athens would have to surrender eventually. All of its allies, except for the island of Samos, capitulated.

During the following year, the Athenians were starved into submission. By the terms of the peace treaty negotiated with Sparta in 404 B.C., Athens became a member of the Peloponnesian League, relinquishing its empire and most of its navy; the walls defending the city were torn down; and a government of 30 oligarchs was instituted. Many of the democrats of Athens took refuge in Boeotia.

THE GREEK CITY-STATES: 404-323 B.C.

To the bitter surprise of everyone, the end of the 27-year Peloponnesian War did not bring peace to the Greek city-states; instead, the 4th century B.C. was marked by constant warfare between them. Sparta did not have enough resources or capable leaders to maintain its empire without Persian support. Athens and Thebes each managed to create short-lived empires, but were unable to achieve unity among the city-states for a sustained period. Finally, the growing empire of Macedonia put an end to Greek independence.

In Athens, the oligarchy that had been instituted by the Spartans soon became a reign of terror, as the 30 oligarchs removed the laws that had been displayed in the agora and murdered more than a thousand of their political opponents. The democrats of Athens secretly negotiated with Thebes for aid. With the help of the Thebans, they were able to overthrow the oligarchy only eight months after it had been imposed, in 404 B.C. Meanwhile, the Spartans installed oligarchies in most of the Aegean city-states, and tried to create enthusiasm for their rule by organizing an expedition against the Persians. But in 395 B.C., while the Spartans were fighting the Persian armies in Asia Minor, the city-states of Athens, Thebes, Corinth, and Argos banded together and began to threaten Sparta's hegemony in the Peloponnesus. Faced with this threat, the Spartans again turned to the Persians for aid. In 386 B.C., a treaty known as the "King's Peace" was finally concluded. By the terms of the peace, the Persian king claimed the Greek city-states of Ionia for his own empire and pledged to support Sparta's hegemony over mainland Greece.

The peace established by the Persians was soon threatened by capable leaders in Thebes and Athens, who were determined to overthrow Spartan hegemony in Greece. In Thebes, the leaders Pelopidas and Epaminondas quietly worked for eight years to create an alliance of Boeotian city-states and to

[22]Ibid., p. 257.

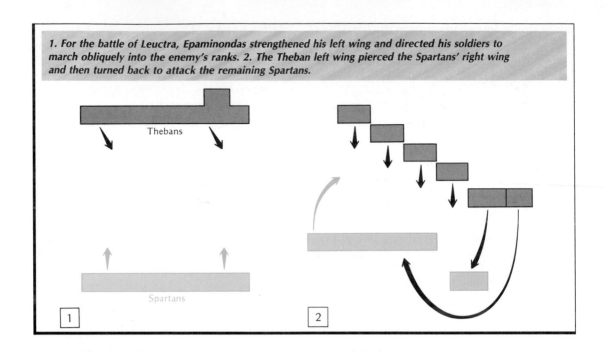

1. For the battle of Leuctra, Epaminondas strengthened his left wing and directed his soldiers to march obliquely into the enemy's ranks. 2. The Theban left wing pierced the Spartans' right wing and then turned back to attack the remaining Spartans.

Thebans

Spartans

1

2

modernize the Theban army. In 371 B.C., a Spartan army of 10,000 hoplites invaded Boeotia and was surprised by the Thebans at Leuctra. In defeating the Spartans, the Theban army, under the leadership of Epaminondas, used a new tactic called the "oblique phalanx" in which soldiers penetrated the enemy's ranks at an angle. With the victory at Leuctra, Thebes was recognized as the most powerful city-state in Greece. The Athenians also benefited, as city-states from the Peloponnesian League rushed to join the new Athenian Confederation. Under the leadership of Iphicrates, the Athenian army and navy were strengthened and began to assert Athens' influence throughout the Aegean.

The Theban army invaded the Peloponnesus and liberated the territory of Messenia, formerly subject to Sparta, in 369 B.C. The Thebans then challenged the Athenian naval power in the Aegean, and forced Thessaly and Macedonia to ally themselves with Thebes. Athens, however, was unwilling to submit to the domination of Thebes, and or-

ganized a new coalition of city-states to oppose the Thebans. In 362 B.C. the Theban army led by Epaminondas met the combined armies of Athens, Sparta, and northern Arcadia at Mantinea in the Peloponnesus. Just as it seemed that the Theban army was about to win the battle, Epaminondas was killed and the Thebans withdrew.

As he lay dying, Epaminondas urged the Thebans to make peace with their fellow Greeks. A treaty was concluded later and was effective for several years, but only because the city-states were too exhausted to fight another prolonged war. Athens continued its attempts to build and maintain an empire through force, and the Thebans engaged in various plots to undermine Athens' plans. Between 354 and 338 B.C., Philip II, king of Macedonia, took advantage of the chronic quarrels among the city-states to advance his own plans (Chapter 8). In 338, the Athenians and Thebans finally united to oppose him, but Philip defeated the Greek army at Chaeronea, and realized his ambition to impose Macedonian rule upon all of Greece.

SUMMARY

After its military successes in the Persian Wars, Athens became the center of influence in Greece. Under Pericles' leadership, the Athenians' achievements in art and architecture, philosophy, and government made Athens the "school of Hellas," and inspired many important developments in both Western and Eastern cultures.

Athens was not able to maintain its hegemony in the Greek world for a sustained period, however. Conflicts between Athens and Sparta led to the outbreak of the Peloponnesian War, which so weakened all of the Greek city-states that Philip of Macedonia was able to impose his rule over the area in 338 B.C.

QUESTIONS

1 What were the most important contributions of the early Greek scientists? Why did the Greeks consider science and philosophy to be one and the same discipline?

2 Choose one structure, artifact, or literary work and explain how it symbolizes the Athenians' concept of mankind in the 5th century.

3 Summarize briefly the plots of Aeschylus' Oresteia, Sophocles' Oedipus the King, and Euripides' Medea. Give reasons for the apparent timelessness of these plays.

4 Compare Herodotus and Thucydides in terms of their philosophies about history and their historiography. Why is Herodotus called the "father of history" and Thucydides the "first scientific historian"?

5 Describe the similarities and differences between a demagogue and a tyrant in ancient Athens. How did each one achieve and retain political power?

6 Read a sample of Socrates' dialog in the Phaedo, The Republic, Book 1, or another of Plato's works. Why do you think that Socrates had—in Alcibiades' words—an "extraordinary effect" upon his listeners?

BIBLIOGRAPHY

Which books might discuss the Spartans' foreign policies?

HAMILTON, CHARLES D. *Sparta's Bitter Victories: Politics and Diplomacy in the Corinthian War.* Ithaca: Cornell University Press, 1978. Covers the period of Spartan supremacy from the end of the Peloponnesian War in 404 B.C. to the King's Peace of 386; analyzes the political situation in each city-state and the impact of the war upon their economies and social structures.

H. D. F. KITTO. *The Greeks*, revised ed. New York: Penguin Books, 1957. A comprehensive, readable discourse on the ancient Greeks; their political systems, ways of life, and unique contributions to Western civilization.

YONAH, MICHAEL AVI and ISRAEL SHATZMAN. *Illustrated Encyclopedia of the Classical World.* New York: Harper & Row, 1975. A concise and reliable guide to every aspect of Greek and Roman life and thought; subjects include classical terms, institutions, literature, religion, and society. Beautifully illustrated.

There are three Alexanders; the legendary Alexander, the historical Alexander, and the real Alexander. The first was born in men's minds soon after the death of the last, and he still lives in the East as Iskander. He has been many things: a saint and a devil, a defender of civilization and a barbarian, a perfect knight and a worthless debauchee. The historical Alexander is dead, but he is frequently revived in the pages of histories and biographies that fashion him in the image that each particular age admires; in one age he may be "greater than Napoleon," and in another he may be the man who first dreamed of "one world." The real Alexander died in Babylon about the thirteenth of June, 323 B.C. We know little of what he was like. The real Alexander is gone forever.

TOM B. JONES

Alexander and the Hellenistic Era

The failure of the Greek city-states to create a unified nation led to the conquest of Greece by Philip of Macedonia in 338 B.C.. But Philip was assassinated two years later, just as he was about to realize his plan to lead a united Greek-Macedonian army into Persia. He was succeeded by his son, Alexander (356-323 B.C.), who, during his brief reign, established a kingdom which stretched from the Adriatic Sea to the Indus River.

Alexander's death in 323 B.C. ushered in the Hellenistic era. Greek ideas were spread throughout the ancient world and the Greeks, in turn, were affected by their contacts with Asia. Many new cities were established, and for more than a century, the Greeks enjoyed a period of cultural unity and of economic expansion and prosperity. After 200 B.C., however, the Hellenistic influence declined because of the expansion of the Roman Empire in the West and of the Parthian Empire in the East.

MACEDONIA Macedonia (also called Macedon) was a mountainous country extending from Thrace (present northeast Greece and European Turkey) on the east to Illyria on the west. The Greek states of Thessaly and Epirus bordered on the south. The Macedonians were known as rough, hardy peasants, accustomed to constant warfare with their Illyrian and Thracian neighbors. Their form of government was similar to that of the ancient Mycenaeans: a king was elected from a select group of noble families, and was advised by an assembly of weapon-bearing men who represented the various tribal factions in the mountains and countryside. Although the Macedonians were of the same ancestry as the Greeks, they spoke the Greek language with a dialect not easily understood by other Greek peoples, and were thus regarded as barbarians.

During the Peloponnesian War, the Greeks had considered Macedonia to be an important ally because of its valuable resources and strategic location. Although the countryside was poor, the king's forests contained valuable shipbuilding timber. The area was also on the overland route used to transport grain to Greek cities from the Black Sea region. The Macedonians had not shown a partiality for either Athens or Sparta during the war, and had supported both cities at different times. By the end of the 5th century, however, the Macedonian kings began to take a real interest in Greek affairs. Archelaus, who ruled from 413 to 399 B.C., created a new capital city at Pella and invited some of the leading artists of Athens, including Euripides, to live and work there.

PHILIP

Under the leadership of Philip, who ruled Macedonia from 359 to 336 B.C., the process of Hellenization was greatly expanded. And, at the same time that Greek culture was developed and emulated, Philip encouraged his countrymen to respect their own traditions and to unite under his leadership to accomplish certain goals. Under his influence, the Macedonians came to think of themselves as citizens of a nation rather than of the particular localities in which they lived. For this reason, Macedonia is considered to have been the first nation established in Europe.

As a teenager, Philip had spent three years as a hostage of the Thebans. During his stay in Thebes, he gained an appreciation of Greek culture, learned many valuable lessons in military tactics, and, most importantly, gained an understanding of the weaknesses of the Greeks. It was probably during this time that he developed the ambitions that he later tried to fulfill as king of Macedonia: to raise the cultural level of his people; to unite the Greek city-states under his rule; and to lead a united Macedonian-Greek army against the mighty Persian Empire.

In 359, at the age of 23, Philip was appointed by the Macedonian army council to serve as regent for his young nephew. Philip immediately embarked on a program to Hellenize his country and to develop a professional army. He built urban centers modeled after Greek cities, and encouraged rural Macedonians to settle in them. He improved the road system, and began to train Macedonian peasants to fight in regiments.

In 356 B.C., Philip's wife, Olympias, gave birth to a son, Alexander. Soon afterwards, Philip declared himself king. He then invaded Thrace and seized an important gold mine there. With an assured income of 1000 talents a year from the mine, he was able to recruit and train a large army, including two cavalry units. One of these units, called the "King's Companions," was composed of 2000 noblemen trained to charge at high speed into enemy ranks. The other, more lightly armed, was trained to pursue fleeing enemy forces. Infantrymen were equipped with spears 14 feet long, and were trained to fight in an improved version of the phalanx system developed by the Thebans. Philip also built a navy, and developed siege machinery, such as movable towers and torsion catapults, for use in attacking fortified towns.

During his first year as king, Philip subdued Thessaly, and seized the city of Amphipolis in order to gain access to the Aegean Sea. His early achievements in mobilizing his countrymen and providing them with the benefits of an advanced civilization were later summarized by his son, Alexander, when he addressed a group of mutinous soldiers in 324 B.C.

● ● ● *Philip took you over when you were helpless vagabonds, mostly clothed in skins, feeding a few animals on the mountains and engaged in their defence in unsuccessful fighting with the Illyrians, Triballians and the neighboring Thracians. He gave you cloaks to wear instead of skins, he brought you down from the mountains to the plains; he made you a match in battle for the barbarians on your borders, so that you no longer trusted your safety to the strength of your positions so much as to your natural* courage. He made you city dwellers and established the order that comes from good laws and customs. It was due to him that you became masters and not slaves and subjects of those very barbarians who used previously to plunder your possessions and carry off your persons. He annexed the greater part of Thrace to Macedonia and, by capturing the best placed positions by the sea, he opened up the country to trade. . . .[1]

Conquest of Greece. Soon after Philip's conquest of Thrace, a religious war among the city-states of Greece gave Philip an opportunity to intervene in Greek affairs. The war had started when the city-state of Phocis seized the treasury of the religious sanctuary at Delphi. The Thebans prepared to avenge this outrage, and Philip's army soon came to their aid. In 353, Philip led his army through Thessaly, which he had annexed, and appeared at Thermopylae.

Philip's presence at Thermopylae created an excited reaction among the city-states of Greece. In Athens, two opposing parties arose to debate Athenian policy in front of the Assembly. The pro-Macedonian party of orators argued that Athens should maintain the peace and develop its economic interests. The anti-Macedonian party was led by the great orator Demosthenes (not to be confused with the Athenian general killed during the Peloponnesian War), who believed that Philip's ambitions were a threat to Athens' independence. Demosthenes was not a military strategist, but he became active on every other possible front in his efforts to defeat Philip's plans.

In 353, the anti-Macedonian party within Athens prevailed. The Athenians, with help from the Spartans, raised a force of 10,000 men and sent it to aid the Phocians. The arrival of this force convinced Philip to postpone his plans for conquest, and he withdrew without giving battle.

The orator Demosthenes devoted his life to an unequal battle against Philip of Macedonia. The original of this statue once stood in the marketplace of Athens.

Philip next turned his attention to the Chalcidice region and the Hellespont. Demosthenes realized the danger that Philip posed to Athenian interests in this area and delivered the first of his series of "Philippics" (orations concerning Philip) in 351. Due to his efforts, the Athenians sent three expeditions to aid the city of Olynthus in the Chalcidice. Philip was able to overcome these forces, however, and by 348 he had incorporated the Chalcidice into his territory.

---

[1] Arrian, *Anabasis of Alexander* VII, 9, 2-3.

The defeat in the Chalcidice convinced the Athenians, even Demosthenes, that it was necessary to come to terms with Philip. Demosthenes and two leaders of the pro-Macedonian party traveled to Philip's court on a diplomatic mission. There, they hoped to negotiate an agreement that would recognize the status quo: Athens would accept the loss of Amphipolis and the Chalcidice if Philip would renounce any further conquests in Greece. While treating the diplomats with great courtesy and charm, Philip postponed the signing of such an agreement for several months. Meanwhile, he completed his conquest of Thrace and seized the sanctuary of Delphi from the Phocians. Finally, he agreed to sign a treaty with Athens.

Despite the treaty with Macedonia, and the dangers that any resistance to Philip now posed, Demosthenes continued his efforts to undermine Philip's plans. He delivered his third "Philippic" in 341 B.C., as Philip prepared to besiege the city of Byzantium. He urged the Assembly to aid Byzantium and to recognize that the treaty with Philip would never guarantee Athens' safety:

● ● ● *Neither the Greek nor the barbarian world is big enough for this fellow's ambition. And we Greeks see and hear all this, and yet we do not send embassies to one another, and express our indignation. We are in such a miserable position, we have so entrenched ourselves in our different cities, that to this very day we can do nothing that our interest or duty demands; we cannot combine, we cannot take any common pledge of help or friendship; but we idly watch the growing power of this man, each bent . . . on profiting by the interval afforded by another's ruin, taking not a thought, making not an effort for the salvation of Greece. For that Philip, like the recurrence or attack of a fever or some other disease, is threatening even those who think themselves out of reach, of that not one of you is ignorant.*[2]

---

[2]Demosthenes, *Third Philippic* 27, 29.

Demosthenes' arguments prevailed in the Assembly. To prepare for war against Philip, he personally supervised the modernization of Athens' naval forces and the creation of new treaties with the city-states of central Greece. As a result, Athenian forces successfully repelled Philip's attack of Byzantium. Almost immediately, however, Philip invaded the island of Euboea. He then sent envoys to Thebes in order to win the Thebans' assent to this invasion. Demosthenes realized what Philip was planning, and hurried to Thebes himself. There, he convinced the Thebans to stand with Athens against the Macedonians rather than signing a treaty with Philip.

The combined army of Thebes and Athens won two minor battles against Philip's forces in 339 B.C. In 338, however, Philip appeared with an even larger army and decisively defeated the allies at Chaeronea, in Boeotia. After Philip's victory, he garrisoned Thebes, but extended very favorable terms of peace to Athens because of his admiration for that city. Athens was forced to ally itself with Macedonia, but it was not garrisoned; its ports remained free, and it kept its navy.

The League of Corinth. After signing treaties with Thebes and Athens, Philip summoned all of the city-states of Greece to a convention at Corinth. In 337 B.C., the participating cities agreed to join a new general alliance, the League of Corinth. The member city-states were not required to pay tribute to Philip, and would remain independent. They agreed, however, to contribute troops to the league's army and navy and to accept Philip's direction of the league's affairs. The city-states also pledged that they would put aside their grievances against each other and renounce any further war against fellow Greeks. Thus, through the league, Philip succeeded in creating the framework for a unified Greek nation. Of all the city-states, only Sparta refused to participate.

The next year, Philip proposed to the League of Corinth that they undertake an expedition against the Persians, with the immediate goal of freeing the Ionic Greek cities from Persian rule. He sent a Macedonian army of 10,000 men to Asia Minor under the leadership of his capable general, Parmenio, and planned to join him with a Greek force soon after. But during the summer, as he was celebrating the wedding of his daughter, Philip was assassinated.

Philip's assassin was a Macedonian named Pausanias, but it is not known who, if anyone, encouraged him to commit the deed. The murder may have been planned by the Persians, who wanted to put an end to Philip's invasion of their territory. Alternatively, Philip's first wife, Olympias, may have been responsible. Because she was known to have a strong character and a fierce temper, some people believed that she had engineered the murder in order to assure the succession of her son, Alexander. The fact that she soon afterwards murdered Philip's second wife and infant son gave support to this belief.

Archaeological Findings. During the 1970s, Manolis Andronikas, a renowned Greek archaeologist, uncovered an ancient tomb at Vergina, in northern Greece. The tomb contained many treasures, and had been protected over the centuries by a large mound of earth which looked like a natural hill. One important finding was a pair of greaves (leg coverings), apparently fashioned for a man with one leg three centimeters shorter than the other. Andonikas also found a gold burial casket with a star engraved on the lid. Since, according to legend, one of Philip's legs was shorter than the other, and because stars were symbols of royalty in the ancient world, Andronikas decided that the remains within the casket were those of Philip of Macedonia.

ALEXANDER THE GREAT

Alexander, at the age of 20 years, succeeded his father, and became such a dramatic figure in the ancient world that he was called "Alexander the Great." For the details of Alexander's life and campaigns, our two most

At the age of 22, Alexander the Great set out to conquer the world at the head of a united Greek-Macedonian army. This portrait of Alexander may be based upon a contemporary statue by Lysippus.

important sources are Plutarch, who wrote essays on Alexander and other famous Greeks and Romans during the 1st century A.D., and Arrian, who wrote the *Anabasis* ("Campaign") *of Alexander* in the 2nd century A.D. Although no contemporary accounts of Alexander have come down to us, Plutarch and Arrian referred to eyewitness accounts that still existed during their lifetimes, including Alexander's own letters and the memoirs of two of his generals. Both Plutarch and Arrian describe the combination of shrewd calculation, reckless daring, and administrative skill which characterized Alexander's campaigns and enabled him to achieve his great victories.

Childhood. Alexander was born in Pella, Macedonia, in 356 B.C. Plutarch wrote that when Alexander was born, Philip received three messages:

. . . that Parmenio [his general] had overthrown the Illyrians in a great battle, that his race horse had won the course at the Olympic Games, and that his wife had given birth to Alexander; with which being naturally well pleased, as an addition to his satisfaction, he was assured by the diviners that a son, whose birth was accompanied with three such successes, could not fail of being invincible.[3]

When Alexander was 13 years old, Philip hired Aristotle, the Athenian philosopher, as tutor for his son. Aristotle instilled in his eager pupil a love for Greek art and poetry, and a lasting interest in Greek science and philosophy. Alexander is said to have remarked that he loved Aristotle more than his father, for while his father gave him life, Aristotle taught him how to live well. At other times, Alexander indicated that he wanted to be a man of action like his father. Plutarch reported that he once expressed anger after hearing about one of his father's conquests, remarking that his father would leave nothing for him to accomplish.

Campaign in Greece. Soon after he ascended the throne, Alexander traveled to Corinth to ensure that the League of Corinth would elect him commander-in-chief in place of his father. He then led his troops northward across the Danube River in order to subdue a revolt in Thrace (present Bulgaria and Rumania).

After subduing the Thracian revolt, Alexander marched west to deal with rebellious tribes in Illyria. While he was in Illyria, a group of Thebans circulated a rumor that he had been killed in battle, and the citizens of Thebes and Athens began to consider seceding from the League of Corinth. Alexander soon heard about this plot, and hurried to the scene, covering 300 miles in just two weeks. The Thebans refused to surrender to Alexander, and he proceeded to overrun the city. After conquering the city, Alexander massacred the Thebans who had resisted his troops and sold the rest into slavery. The city was then razed, except for the temples and the house that had belonged to the poet Pindar. By these actions, Alexander demonstrated that he respected Greek culture but would tolerate no rebellion.

The Aetolians and Athenians, horrified by the events at Thebes, hastened to ask Alexander's pardon for their part in the revolt and to congratulate him upon his safe return from Illyria. After some hesitation, Alexander granted them what they asked and proceeded to work with them to organize a campaign against the Persians. According to Plutarch, Alexander later regretted his retribution against Thebes and, for the rest of his life, freely granted any favor asked of him by a Theban.

Voyage to the East. Before leaving Greece, Alexander stopped at Delphi to receive the oracle's advice concerning his plans to invade Persia. Plutarch reported that he soon received the prophecy he had hoped for:

. . . [H]appening to come on one of the forbidden days, when it was esteemed improper to give any answers from the oracle, he sent messengers to desire the priestess to do her office; and when she refused, on the plea of a law to the contrary, he went up himself, and began to draw her by force into the temple, until tired and overcome with his importunity, "My son," she said, "thou art invincible."[4]

The priestess's words came true in his brief lifetime.

In 334 B.C., Alexander set out for Persia with an army of more than 30,000 infantry troops and 5000 cavalry, recruited from Macedonia and the League of Corinth. His father's trusted advisor Parmenio was second in

---

[3]Plutarch, *Lives*, Modern Library ed., p. 803.

[4]Ibid., p. 810.

THE EMPIRE OF ALEXANDER THE GREAT AND HIS SUCCESSORS
Why did Alexander's empire split into three separate kingdoms after his death?

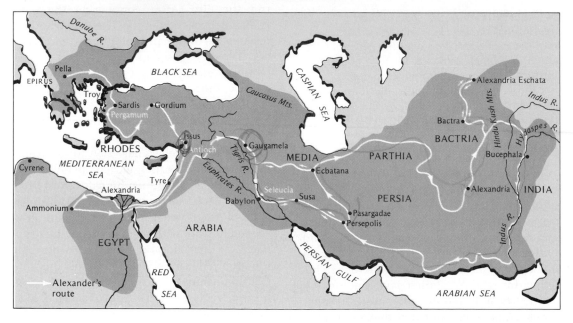

command, and another of his father's friends, Antipater, was left in charge of Macedonia and Greece. Traveling with the expedition were such practical specialists as engineers, carpenters, and seers—the former to build siege machinery and ships, and the latter to read the omens before each major battle. Alexander also took with him geographers, philosophers, and zoologists to record the strange new ideas and sights he expected to encounter on his travels.

Alexander's romantic ideas about his campaign were indicated by his choice of reading material: he carried with him a copy of the *Iliad*, personally annotated by Aristotle. And, upon arriving in Asia Minor, his first action was to visit the site of ancient Troy. There, he visited the tomb of his personal hero, Achilles, whom he looked upon as his ancestor, and offered sacrifices to Athena. According to Arrian's account, he then left his armor in Athena's temple and took in exchange a suit of armor which was said to date from the Trojan War period.

After a two-day march inland, Alexander and his troops reached the Granicus River, where they encountered the army of the Persian satrap for Asia Minor. In this first battle of the campaign, Alexander narrowly escaped death when a Persian commander struck him with a battle-axe. The axe split Alexander's helmet, but he survived the blow and his army routed the Persian soldiers. After the battle, Alexander honored the 25 Companions who had fallen in the first charge by having the famous sculptor Lysippus carve their statues. To honor the Greek forces, he sent battle trophies to Athens with the following inscription:

● ● ● *Alexander the son of Philip, and the Grecians, except the Lacedaemonians, won these from the barbarians who inhabit Asia.*[5]

After capturing Sardis, the most important Persian city in Asia Minor, Alexander

---

[5]Ibid., p. 812.

180

marched south along the coast, freeing Ephesus and the other Ionian Greek city-states from Persian rule. In each Greek city, he installed a government modeled on Athens' democracy in place of the oligarchies established by the Persians.

In 333 B.C. Alexander visited Gordium, the capital of the old Phrygian kingdom. On display in the city was the famous Gordian knot, securing a chariot said to belong to the legendary King Midas. According to legend, whoever could untie the intricate knot would be lord of all Asia. Alexander reportedly slashed the knot with his sword, thereby foreshadowing the fulfillment of the prophesy. Before moving on, he appointed one of his commanders as satrap of Phrygia.

Alexander then led his army southward through the Cilician Gates, a mountain pass so narrow that two loaded camels could not walk side by side, and moved into Syria. There, Alexander hoped to find Darius III, king of the Persians, and the main body of the Persian army. Darius, who was leading an army much larger than Alexander's, was also anxious for battle. Disregarding the advice of his generals, he advanced toward Cilicia rather than choosing a battle site and waiting for Alexander to appear. During the night, the two armies passed each other without realizing it. At the break of day, Alexander saw that Darius' army was scattered and disorganized as it negotiated the narrow mountain passes, so he arrayed his army and attacked the Persians near the town of Issus. The Persians, realizing that they were outmaneuvered and might be forced into the sea, beat a hasty retreat. Alexander actually captured Darius' family, but the king himself escaped.

After the battle of Issus, Alexander sent troops to Damascus to retrieve the baggage and treasures of the Persian army. He was greatly impressed by the vast wealth of articles his men brought back, but he kept for himself only a jeweled casket in which to carry his treasured copy of the *Iliad*. By this

A mosaic found in a Roman villa depicts the terrified Darius as he prepares to flee the battle at Issus.

act, Alexander perhaps intended to emphasize the contrast between himself and Darius, and to demonstrate his belief that a true king should be measured by his exploits, not by the luxuries he enjoyed.

Because Persia could not be truly conquered as long as its fleet continued to operate freely, Alexander's next goal was to seize the Phoenician ports where the Persian fleet was based. The towns of Sidon and Byblos surrendered without a battle and hailed Alexander as a liberator from Persian tyranny. The people of Tyre, however, decided to pursue a policy of neutrality, and announced that they would admit neither Persians nor Macedonians into their city. Arrian explained why the Tyrians could make this stand:

● ● ● *For the city was an island, protected on all sides by high walls, while any action at sea clearly favored the Tyrians in their present circumstances, because the Persians had command of the sea and the Tyrians themselves had numerous fleet. . . .*[6]

To overcome the city's advantages, Alexander's forces built a *mole*, or passageway of

---

[6]Arrian, *Anabasis of Alexander* II, 18, 2.

stones, through the water and constructed towers to defend the workers. When the mole was completed, Alexander's troops marched across it to storm the fortifications of Tyre, while supporting ships engaged the Tyrian navy. After seven months, Tyre surrendered, and the Persian fleet scattered because it no longer had a harbor.

During the siege of Tyre, Darius sent a messenger to Alexander with an offer of peace: Darius would yield all of the land west of the Euphrates River, 10,000 talents in gold, and his daughter in marriage. Parmenio urged the young king to accept, but Alexander refused the offer.

Alexander's army moved south along the Mediterranean coast, capturing Philistia (the present Gaza strip), and entering Egypt in 332 B.C. The Egyptians, who had been under Persian domination since 525 B.C., welcomed Alexander as a successor to their pharaohs. The city of Memphis, where the Persian satrap lived, surrendered without a battle. Alexander then founded the city of Alexandria, on the north end of the Nile delta. This city became the commercial and intellectual center of the Hellenistic world, and even today is one of the busiest ports in the Mediterranean region.

From his new city, Alexander made a perilous journey across the Libyan Desert to consult the oracle of Ammon. Plutarch observed that Alexander was well rewarded for his troubles when the high priest of Ammon addressed him:

• • • the priest, desirous as a piece of courtesy to address him in Greek, "O Paidion" [My Son], by a slip in pronunciation ended with the **s** instead of the **n**, and said "O Paidios" [Son of Zeus], which mistake Alexander was well enough pleased with. . . .[7]

Before leaving Egypt, Alexander appointed an Egyptian governor in place of the Persian satrap, and left troops to guard the country.

Campaign in the East. Alexander then led his army through the Fertile Crescent in pursuit of the Persians. In 331 B.C., at Gaugamela, he met the army of Darius. For this important battle, Darius had chosen a large, level field in order to obtain maximum advantage for his chariot troops. The chariots themselves were equipped with scythes on the wheels to cut through the Macedonian phalanx. Soon after the start of battle:

• • • the enemy launched their scythe-chariots in the direction of Alexander himself in order to disrupt his phalanx. But in this they failed badly, for as soon as they approached . . . they were met with a volley of javelins. They [Alexander's advance troops] also caught hold of the reins, pulled down the drivers, and surrounded the horses and cut them down. Some of the chariots did get through the ranks, but these [ranks] parted, as they had been told to do, where the chariots attacked, and the result was that the chariots were undamaged and those whom they attacked were unhurt.[8]

Soon afterwards, Darius gave up the battle and fled, pursued by Alexander and his Companions. But the Persian cavalry, not realizing that Darius had left, charged the left wing of Alexander's army. Alexander wheeled back to help his army, and encountered some retreating Persian troops. At this point, Arrian related, the fiercest fighting of all occurred, for the trapped Persian troops were now struggling for their lives. Sixty of the Companions fell, but Alexander's forces were finally victorious.

Darius fled on horseback across the mountains into Media. Alexander, meanwhile, proceeded to Babylon, where he was hailed as king. He permitted his weary troops to rest and celebrate for a month, and then marched toward Susa, the administrative capital of

---

[7]Plutarch, *Lives*, Modern Library ed., p. 821.

[8]Arrian, *Anabasis of Alexander* III, 13, 5-6.

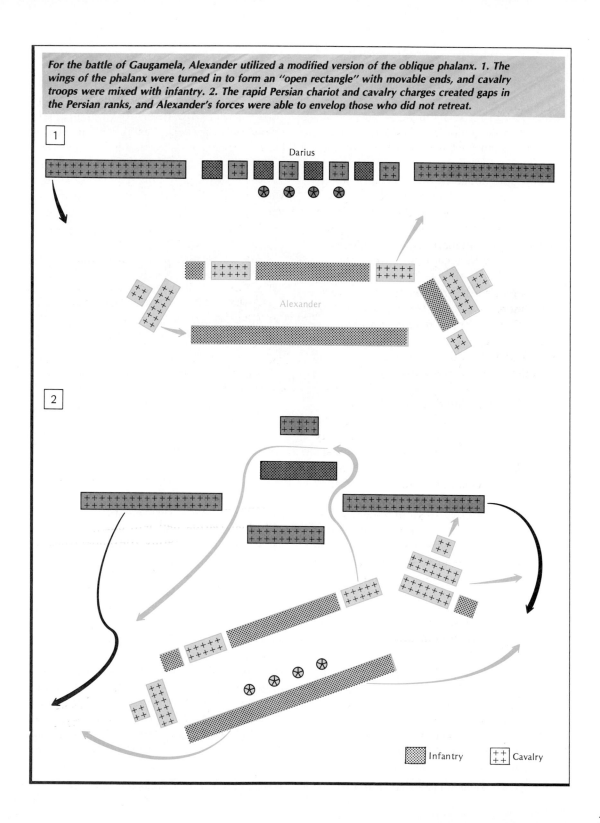

For the battle of Gaugamela, Alexander utilized a modified version of the oblique phalanx. 1. The wings of the phalanx were turned in to form an "open rectangle" with movable ends, and cavalry troops were mixed with infantry. 2. The rapid Persian chariot and cavalry charges created gaps in the Persian ranks, and Alexander's forces were able to envelop those who did not retreat.

1

Darius

Alexander

2

Infantry   Cavalry

After the battle of Gaugamela, Alexander triumphantly entered Babylon. He later revisited the city to celebrate his victories in the Far East.

the Persian Empire. The people of Susa opened their gates to Alexander and handed over the city's treasury, which, Arrian reported, included 50,000 silver talents and several valuable bronze statues that Xerxes had taken from Athens in 480 B.C.

At this point in his campaign, Alexander began to take steps to unify and reconcile the peoples of his empire. He began to wear a modified Persian costume, and further demonstrated his respect for Persian culture by freeing Darius' mother and sisters, who had been his prisoners since the battle of Issus. Because the people of Susa had surrendered voluntarily, he appointed a Persian governor for the city.

Alexander and his army next proceeded to the Persian holy city of Persepolis where,

Plutarch reported, the Persian treasure they seized was "as much as ten thousand pair of mules and five thousand camels could well carry away."[9] An immense banquet was arranged and, after the participants had drunk a great deal, Alexander and his fellow celebrants set fire to the palace that Xerxes had lived in. Plutarch believed that Alexander regretted setting the fire almost immediately, and made an effort to put out the flames. Arrian, in contrast, stated that the fire was set deliberately, to avenge Xerxes' destruction of Athens.

At Pasargadae, Alexander stopped to meditate at the simple tomb of Cyrus the Great

---

[9]Plutarch, *Lives*, Modern Library ed., p. 828.

and to read that king's message to the world:

. . . O man, whosoever thou art . . . I am Cyrus, the founder of the Persian empire; do not grudge me this little earth which covers my body.[10]

Darius had now fled to Bactria, and Alexander pursued him, following the trail that later became part of the Silk Route between China and Arabia. But before Alexander could reach him, Darius was killed by Bessus, the satrap of Bactria. Plutarch described Alexander's reaction to finding Darius dead:

. . . [H]e showed manifest tokens of sorrow, and taking off his own cloak, threw it upon the body to cover it. . . . Darius' body was laid in state and sent to his mother with pomp suitable to his quality.[11]

Arrian reported that, some years later, Alexander ordered that Bessus be punished according to Persian tradition:

. . . He then gave orders that his nose and the tips of his ears should be cut off, and that thus mutilated he should be taken to Ecbatana to suffer public execution before his own countrymen, the Medes and the Persians.[12]

With Darius dead, the Persians considered Alexander to be the legitimate successor to the Persian throne. According to their customs and beliefs, the king was a living god, and they worshiped Alexander accordingly. Alexander did not discourage the cult that grew up around him. In 327 B.C., he married Roxane, the beautiful daughter of a Bactrian prince, an act which also indicated his intent to create a true union of Greek and Asian peoples under his rule.

Alexander's appointment of Persians to important positions in the army and government, his adoption of Persian manners and dress, and his claim of being a living god caused great resentment among his Macedonian and Greek troops. Eventually, the loyalty and steadfastness of the Macedonians began to disintegrate. Philotas, a friend of Alexander's since childhood, was found guilty of treason and was executed. His father, Parmenio, who probably had no part in the conspiracy, was also killed on Alexander's orders, for he was widely respected and could have posed a grave danger to Alexander if he had tried to avenge his son's death.

Two years after Philotas' treason had been revealed, Alexander again found himself in conflict with one of his oldest friends. Clitus, a chief officer of the Companions, was the victim of this second tragedy. One evening, after a long drinking bout, Clitus began to taunt a group of Companions who were flattering Alexander. When rebuked by Alexander, Clitus reminded him that he had saved his life at the battle of the Granicus River. Alexander's guards separated the two angry men by removing Clitus from the room, but he soon reappeared at the doorway, still yelling taunts:

. . . Upon this, at last, Alexander, snatching a spear from one of the soldiers, met Clitus as he was coming forward . . . and ran him through the body. He fell at once with a cry and a groan. Upon which the king's anger immediately vanishing, he came perfectly to himself, and when he saw his friends about him all in a profound silence, he pulled the spear out of the dead body, and would have thrust it into his own throat, if the guards had not held his hands, and by main force carried him away into his chamber, where all that night and the next day he wept bitterly, till being quite spent with lamenting and exclaiming, he lay . . . speechless.[13]

Expedition in India. In 326 B.C., Alexander set out to conquer India with a force of

---

[10]Ibid., p. 849.

[11]Ibid., p. 833.

[12]Arrian, *Anabasis of Alexander* IV, 7, 3.

---

[13]Plutarch, *Lives*, Modern Library ed., p. 838.

135,000 men. Before setting out, Alexander noticed that his soldiers were loaded down with a vast amount of booty, which would slow the army's progress. He set fire to his own superfluous baggage, and ordered his troops to do the same. The men enthusiastically complied with this order, Plutarch reported.

Alexander's army crossed the Hindu Kush ("Killer") Mountains, and then followed the Kabul River downstream to the Indus River, where a bridge of boats was built for the army to cross. He then continued eastward to the Hydaspes River, another tributary of the Indus, where he was confronted by Porus, the King of Punjab. Although Porus' war elephants made it necessary to revise his battle plan, Alexander and his troops were finally able to overcome the Indian forces. In recognition of Porus' valor, Alexander left him as governor of his own kingdom and of several other conquered cities. He also founded several cities in strategic locations and settled his veterans in them. Most of these cities were called *Alexandria*, but one was named after Alexander's beloved horse *Bucephalus*, who had died in India.

Alexander wanted to press further into India, to the limits of the known world, but his weary and homesick men threatened to mutiny. A spokesman presented their reasoning to Alexander:

. . . *Under your leadership, supported by those who set out with you from home, we have achieved very many great successes. But all the more because of that, I think it is right to set a limit to the tasks we undertake and the risks we run. You yourself see how many Macedonians and Greeks set out with you, and how few are left . . . but even they are not as vigorous as they were, and they are still more broken in spirit. All these long to see their parents, . . . to see their wives and children, to see their homeland, which they are eager to revisit, especially since they will be going back as great and rich men*

Hecataeus' view of the world. Prior to Alexander's trip to India, many people thought that the Indus River was the source of the Nile.

instead of insignificant and poor, with the treasures which they have gained for you.[14]

Return to Persia. Alexander sulked in his tent for three days, and then ordered his carpenters to build a fleet on the Indus River for the return to Persia. In following this river to a point near its mouth, he discovered that the Indus flowed into the sea and was not, as had been believed, the source of the Nile River. He then divided his men into three groups, assigning each a different route back to Susa. One army, led by Craterus, was to take a northern overland route; a second group, under the command of Nearchus, was to sail, via the Arabian Sea, to the Persian Gulf; and the third group, under Alexander's command, would march west across the Sind desert.

The route that Alexander himself took was so incredibly difficult that three-quarters of his troops perished. Nevertheless, the army overcame despair and struggled on through the desert sands, finally meeting the naval

---

[14]Arrian, *Anabasis of Alexander* V, 27, 5.

force led by Nearchus. Arrian described how the army dealt with one of the most difficult hardships, the lack of water:

● ● ● *Some of the light infantry, who had gone off from the rest of the army in search of water, found a meager little trickle collected in a shallow gulley. They collected it up with difficulty and hurried to Alexander as if they were taking him a great gift. When they approached they poured the water into a helmet and offered it to the king. He accepted it and thanked those who brought it. But when he received it he poured it out on the ground for all to see. The whole army was so heartened by this act that you would have thought that the water which Alexander had poured away had provided a drink for every man.*[15]

Nearchus, traveling the sea in improvised river boats, managed to collect many specimens of plants and animals from the desert coastland, which he eventually carried back to Greece for Aristotle to study. He also charted the sea route to India, making it possible for future sailors to open a trade route from West to East.

When Alexander heard about Nearchus' adventures, he immediately thought of making a voyage himself, planning to sail around the coasts of Arabia and Africa, then enter the Mediterranean through the Pillars of Hercules (Strait of Gibraltar). He was forced to postpone these plans, however, for a number of problems had arisen in his absence. Alexander spent several months straightening out these administrative problems and re-establishing his control over Persia and the Greek world.

Early in 324 B.C., Alexander presided over an extraordinary ceremony to celebrate the reunion of his three armies at Susa and to symbolize the union of the western and eastern halves of his empire. A mass wedding was performed, uniting 80 of Alexander's of-

ficers with Persian women. Alexander himself took Barsine, the daughter of Darius, as his second wife. In addition, nearly 10,000 Macedonians who had previously married Persian women were invited to the banquet with their wives and were rewarded with generous gifts.

Soon after the wedding ceremonies, Alexander made arrangements to release those veterans of his army who were too old or disabled for active service and to replace them with 30,000 young Persians, who would be trained to fight in the Macedonian phalanx system. This action caused great resentment among the Macedonian and Greek troops, and spokesmen from the army announced that all of the troops, as a gesture of pride, intended to join the disabled veterans in returning home. Alexander then addressed an eloquent speech to his troops, reminding them of all that he and Philip had achieved for them, and promising them that the returning veterans would be richly rewarded for their service. Finally, the troops relented and agreed to accept Alexander's decisions and the enhanced role of the Persians.

Last Days. Alexander traveled to Babylon to supervise the building of a Babylonian temple and to make plans to explore the Caspian Sea. There, at the age of 33, he was suddenly stricken by a fever and soon became too weak to leave his bed. Arrian described the events of his last hours:

● ● ● *The soldiers were anxious to see him, some wanting to see him while he was still alive, others hearing a rumor that he was already dead and, I suppose, suspecting that his death was being concealed by his bodyguards. But most pushed their way in to see Alexander in grief and longing for their king. They say that he could not speak as the army filed past, but that he raised his hand, and with an effort raised his head and had a sign of recognition in the eyes for each man.*[16]

---

[15]Ibid., VI, 26, 3.

[16]Ibid., VII, 12, 1.

THE HELLENISTIC ERA

Alexander's place in world history is based on far more than his military victories. He mapped previously uncharted territories, opened new trade routes, and stimulated the exchange of ideas between the West and the East. He promoted the fusion of two peoples, the Greeks and the Persians, by his own marriages and the marriages he encouraged his men to make. He founded at least 20 cities in the territories he had conquered, thereby supplying an opportunity for thousands of Greek colonists to settle in the East.

When Alexander's friends asked him, on his deathbed, to name a successor, he reportedly replied "To the strongest!" But no one person was capable of seizing and ruling the vast empire he had created. For 25 years, Alexander's generals battled among themselves for control of the empire. Finally, the empire split into three regional kingdoms, each ruled by one of Alexander's associates. Despite these destructive power struggles, Alexander's conquests produced an enduring legacy. One historian described his achievement in this way:

● ● ● *The body of Alexander's empire had disintegrated, but its soul survived, vigorous and as though arrayed in a new youthfulness. There was something touching, almost miraculous, about its resurgence. To what was this due? . . . To the fact that during the dark night which had descended upon the East, during all those years of rivalry and turmoil, the cities which Alexander had founded never ceased to shine like stars. Notwithstanding the breakdown of political ties, they had succeeded in preserving this inestimable benefit: the memory of their attachment to a common civilization.*[17]

PTOLEMY

Egypt, the richest and most powerful of Alexander's kingdoms, was seized by Ptolemy, whom Alexander had named governor of Egypt in 323 B.C. Ptolemy captured the embalmed body of Alexander, and then fought a fierce battle with three leading generals of Alexander's army to retain his possession. Ptolemy emerged victorious from this struggle, and by 305 B.C. he had eliminated all other claimants to the throne of Egypt. With Alexandria as his capital, he eventually assembled an empire which included Cyrenaica and Cyprus as well as the Syria-Palestine territory claimed by earlier Egyptian pharaohs. He and his descendants ruled Egypt until Cleopatra, the last of the Ptolemaic dynasty, committed suicide in 30 B.C. and Egypt became a Roman province.

Ptolemy and his successors encouraged Greeks to migrate to Egypt by granting them special privileges and appointing them to important positions in the government. Naukratis, Ptolemais, and the capital city of Alexandria soon became important centers of Greek culture.

Alexander's successors minted coinage in his name to encourage trade and commerce throughout his empire. On this coin, he is depicted with ram horns, a symbol of divinity.

[17]Jacques Benoist-Mechin, *Alexander the Great* (New York: Hawthorne Books, 1966), pp. 229-30.

Seleucus became governor of Babylon after Alexander's death, and eventually controlled most of the former empire of the Persians, a vast territory inhabited by many diverse peoples. In 303 B.C., he lost the easternmost provinces to an Indian emperor, Chandragupta Maurya, who established the Mauryan dynasty in India (322-232 B.C.).

In an attempt to unify the remaining peoples of his empire, Seleucus and his descendants (the *Seleucids*) encouraged the Persian tradition of emperor-worship. Seleucus himself was deified after his death, and his descendants were treated as gods during their lifetimes. As another strategy of unification, the Seleucids promoted the spread of Hellenistic culture by encouraging Greek colonists to settle in his territories and by sponsoring Greek theater and festivals. Like the Persians, the Seleucids appointed many native satraps to administer local areas, but also established two capital cities for their own administration—Seleucia, on the Tigris River, and Antioch, in Syria.

In spite of all of their efforts, the Seleucids were unable to control their vast empire. The Iranian peoples in the East— especially those who lived in rural areas— retained their own language and religion, and were not influenced by Greek culture. The Parthians gradually gained control of Media, Bactria, and Persia; most of the region east of the Tigris River. In Asia Minor, an independent kingdom arose around the city of Pergamum, which was considered to be one of the most beautiful cities in the world. Pergamum extended its control over all the Seleucid territory north of the Taurus Mountains, and remained independent until its childless king, Attalus III, bequeathed the kingdom to Rome in 133 B.C. By that time, the Seleucid kingdom consisted of little more than Syria.

ANTIGONUS

Antigonus had served Alexander as governor of Phyrgia in Asia Minor. After Alexander's death, he seized control of a vast territory in Asia and competed for control of Greece and Macedonia. In 315 B.C., he declared the Greek city-states to be autonomous and independent, and helped to establish a federation of island city-states.

At one point, Antigonus appeared to be in a position to control all of Alexander's empire, but he was defeated by Seleucus in 301 B.C. After his death, his descendants ruled Macedonia, and his eastern territories were incorporated into the Seleucid empire.

The Greek Federations. In keeping with their political traditions, most of the Greek city-states struggled to maintain their independence during the wars between Alexander's associates. After several decades, however, a number of them combined to form leagues for mutual defense.

The Achaean League, made up of 12 city-states in the northern Peloponnesus, was established in 280 B.C. It was governed by two bodies: an assembly in which the number of delegates from each city was based on population, and a federal council composed of one representative from each city-state. The council met twice a year to determine the general policies of the league. The assembly met annually to vote on questions of war and peace and to elect administrators.

Several city-states of central Greece formed the Aetolian League. This league was ruled by a popular assembly made up of all citizens of the member city-states. The assembly, which met biennially, proved to be too large to be effective. There was also a federal council in which the number of representatives from each city-state was based on the size of the military force that it furnished to the league. The member city-states remained independent in their internal affairs, but yielded control of external affairs to the league.

The Greek leagues were important historically because they represented the earliest instances of *federal* government, in which independent local governments yielded specific powers to a federation. Unfortunately, the leagues had limited effectiveness because Athens and Sparta, the two strongest city-states, refused to participate. Nevertheless, the concept of federalism was studied by the founders of the United States of America and influenced the framing of the Constitution.

THE HELLENISTIC ECONOMY

The Hellenistic era (323-30 B.C.) was a period of great economic prosperity in the Mediterranean world and the Middle East. In the interest of encouraging trade between the countries of Alexander's empire, the vast stores of gold and silver which the Persian kings had accumulated were minted into a standard coinage. Uniform systems of weights and measures were adopted, standard banking practices were established, and harbors and roads were improved.

Political barriers to trade were reduced, and a wide variety of products began to move freely between various lands. Sailors explored new routes and began to travel across open seas, navigating by the stars rather than staying within sight of land. The Hellenistic world obtained silver from Spain, tin from Britain, cattle and wine from Italy, ivory from the Sudan, and wheat and dried fish from southern Russia.

The Ptolemies improved the agriculture of Egypt by expanding the irrigation systems and by reclaiming marshlands in the Nile delta. Egyptians were encouraged to introduce new species of plants and to use iron tools. Farmers began to use fertilizer, to practice crop rotation, and to breed livestock selectively.

The Ptolemies also introduced a new system for collecting taxes: they contracted various individuals to collect taxes in exchange for a percentage of the money they collected. This system became the model for the "tax farming" which the Romans later practiced.

The Seleucid governments encouraged and protected overland trade, for this was the most important source of wealth for the region. Caravan routes connected Mesopotamia with Iran, Bactria, and India, and even extended to China after the 2nd century B.C. From ports in Asia Minor, ships carried parchment, silk, agricultural products, and manufactured goods throughout the Mediterranean region.

CITIES

Each of the cities Alexander established had a council and assembly similar to those traditional in Greek city-states, but each was administered by a royal governor. Each city was laid out on the Greek model with a market place, a gymnasium, a theater, a race track, and one or more temples and government buildings. Royal parks and gardens were adorned with statues and fountains.

Most Hellenistic cities had three levels of society, not including the population of slaves. Greek colonists formed the privileged class and served as officers in the army and officials in the government. The middle class was made up of tradesmen, bankers, craftsmen, physicians, and teachers.

The third class of free people was made up of the native peoples in the countryside who did not participate in the Hellenistic movement, but instead retained their own language, religion, and traditional way of life. They did not share in the growing prosperity, and the widening gap between the Hellenized middle classes and the poor led to social unrest. Many farmers did not own the land they tilled, and were forced to compete in marketing their crops against large estates worked by slaves. Impoverished farmers sometimes sought sanctuary in the temples while their elected leaders attempted to negotiate with the landowners. Artisans in the cities formed *collegia*, or trade associations, as a remedy against exploitation. They chose their own deities and looked after their mutual welfare.

The large population of slaves in the Hellenistic era had few recourses against unjust treatment. The Stoics taught that there was no such thing as a "natural" slave, and certain Hellenistic dramatists and artists portrayed the human suffering caused by slavery. But the Hellenistic economy was dependent upon slave labor, and most middle class people opposed any movement to free slaves or to improve their living conditions. Beginning in 135 B.C., large slave uprisings began to occur in Sicily, Athens, and elsewhere. These rebellions caused a great deal of panic and fear among the free peoples of the Hellenistic world until they were finally suppressed by Roman armies.

Alexandria. Alexandria, the capital of the Ptolemaic Empire, was the most important city of the Hellenistic world. It was located on a narrow strip of land on the Nile delta. The two major cross-streets, each 100 feet wide, were paved with squares of granite and illuminated at night by blazing torches. Alexandria had a waterway connection to the Red Sea, and was thus an important transshipment point for goods moving from the Mediterranean area to the East.

The lighthouse at Alexandria was considered to be one of the Seven Wonders of the World. Located on the island of Pharos, it could be reached by land via a mile-long causeway. The light generated by a fire was intensified with reflectors so that it could be seen 20 miles away. A *Museum* ("Temple of the Muses") established by the Ptolemies was the first institute to be founded and subsidized by a Western government for purposes of research and learning. Today we could call such an institution a university. About a hundred scholars were paid generous salaries to study botany, zoology, astronomy, and the graphic arts. Not everyone appreciated such learning, as demonstrated by this satiric verse:

Egypt had its mad recluses
Book bewildered anchorites,
In the hen coop of the Muses,
Keeping up their endless fights.[18]

The most important library of the ancient Western world was established at Alexandria by Ptolemy I. Modern scholars believe that the library held 700,000 papyrus scrolls by the 1st century B.C. At this library, scribes translated manuscripts into *koine*, a dialect of Greek which became the international language of the Hellenistic world. The librarians sought to preserve literary works by copying and translating them. Zenodotus, the chief librarian in 284 B.C., studied the extant manuscripts of the *Iliad* and the *Odyssey*, and prepared a standard version of the two epics. Callimachus, Zenodotus' successor, prepared the first catalog of the most important manuscripts in the library. This great library was destroyed in the 4th century A.D. (see Chapter 14).

The lighthouse that guided ships to the port of Alexandria was one of the Seven Wonders of the World.

---

[18]Tom B. Jones, *Ancient Civilizations* (Chicago: Rand McNally, 1960), p. 310.

Alexandria became a major center of Judaism. To meet the religious needs of those Jews who did not speak the Hebrew language, a group of scholars translated the Holy Books, which are known to Christians as the Old Testament, from Hebrew into *koine*. Today this translation is referred to as the *Septuagint* Bible because there were 70 translators.

Pergamum. The kingdom of Pergamum in Asia Minor prospered from its silver mines, its agriculture, and its textile and parchment industries. The capital city was renowned above all for its library of more than 200,000 volumes. A competition developed between the Ptolemies of Egypt and the Attalid dynasty of Pergamum to see who could develop the finest library. To prevent the Attalids from adding volumes to their library, the Ptolemies banned the export of papyrus to Pergamum. In response to this ban, the people of Pergamum began to process skins of sheep and goats to produce a writing material called *carta pergama*, which came to be known as parchment. This material had the advantage that both sides could be written on, and it was widely used for manuscripts until a process for making paper was invented during the Middle Ages.

Antioch. Seleucus named his second capital city after his father, a Macedonian named Antiochus. Antioch was located on the Orontes River, in Syria, and served as administrative center for the western portion of the Seleucid empire. The city prospered from manufacture of luxury goods and from the caravan trade, and continued to be important after the fall of the Seleucid dynasty. In 64 B.C., it was occupied by the Romans and became the capital of their province of Syria.

Rhodes. The island of Rhodes was situated near the southern coast of Asia Minor, and its capital city became the busiest commercial port in the Mediterranean. Its trading partners, which included Sicily, Egypt, and the countries of the Black Sea region and Asia Minor, helped to establish Rhodes as an international banking center. The city also became renowned as a cultural center and for its school of philosophy. The "Colossus of Rhodes," a statue of the sun god, was one of the Seven Wonders of the World. This bronze statue, over 100 feet high, stood in Rhodes' harbor until it was destroyed by an earthquake in 227 A.D.

LITERATURE

During the Hellenistic era, more men and women could read and write than at any earlier time. The availability of papyrus and parchment for the manufacture of scrolls, and the fact that literary works were written in *koine* created great demand for written material. The potential patronage of monarchs and wealthy citizens encouraged would-be authors to settle in the major cities. But, for the most part, these authors tended to be critics and commentators on earlier writings rather than creators of new literature. Those who did create original works placed a great deal of emphasis on style and form. Many of their writings provided ideas for later Roman writers, who, in turn, influenced European writers many centuries afterwards.

Theocritus. One of the most famous poets of the 3rd century was Theocritus of Syracuse (315-250 B.C.) He wrote *idylls*, or short poems celebrating the joys of rural life, which appealed to the sophisticated urban readers of the Hellenistic world. His vivid descriptions and sincere expressions of feeling had great influence on later Roman poets.

Callimachus. Callimachus (310-240 B.C.), the librarian of Alexandria, disliked long epic poems, and advocated an *epigrammatic* style. He became known for short, carefully written poems that convey an emotional impact in very few words. One well-known example is *Heraclitus*, an epitaph he wrote in tribute to an old friend. In the first line, the poet concisely conveys his surprise and grief at hearing of his friend's death: *"They told me, Heraclitus, they told me you were dead."*

This figure of a ram in a thicket was found in the Royal Cemetery of Ur. It is wrought of gold and lapis lazuli.

A tomb painting of the New Kingdom period depicts a scene of everyday family life in Egypt: waterfowling in the marshes of the Nile.

An Assyrian king hunting onagers. Most Assyrian art centered on the military skills of the king.

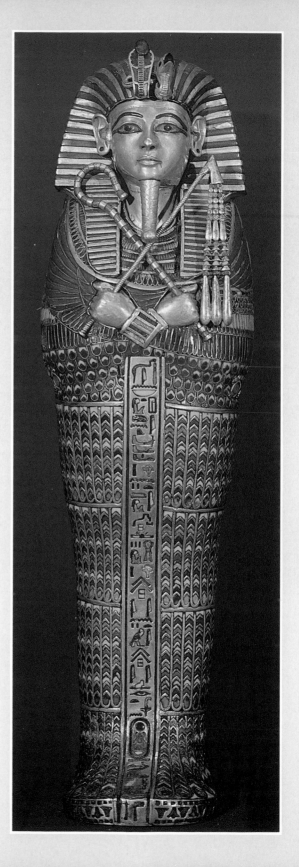

Below: *The golden funeral mask of Tutankhamun. On the top of the mask are a falcon and a cobra, symbols of the two kingdoms the young king had ruled. Right: The internal organs of King Tut were enclosed in four separate coffins of pure gold. On this one, he is depicted as Osiris.*

The ruins of the great palace at Persepolis, built by Darius and his son Xerxes. Persepolis became the capital of the Persian Empire in the 6th century B.C.

The reliefs adorning the grand staircase at Persepolis depict a procession of Mede and Persian nobles.

The Greek heroes who died fighting the Persians in 490 B.C. were memorialized by this funeral mound on the plain of Marathon.

The ruins of the Parthenon. This temple was once the centerpiece of Pericles' acropolis and the symbol of Athens' supremacy in the Greek world.

The portrait mask discovered by Heinrich Schliemann at Mycenae is still known as the "Mask of Agamemnon."

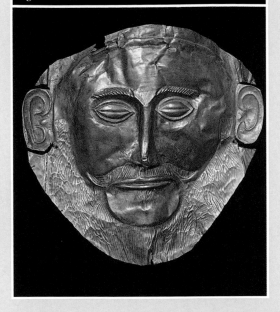

The Kamares pottery of the Minoans was characterized by light-on-dark decoration and often featured designs inspired by the sea.

The distinctive pottery of Athenian artists was known throughout the Greek world. Shown are two designs based on Homer's epics. Right: Ajax and Achilles play a boardgame while waiting for a battle to begin. Below: Helen of Troy, whose affair with Paris inspired the Trojan War, converses with Priam, king of Troy.

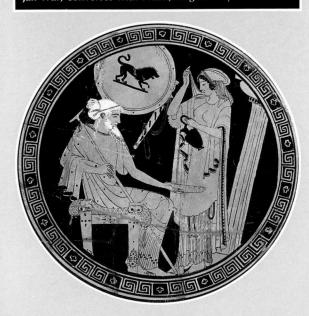

Trajan's column, erected in celebration of a victory over the Parthians. The reliefs show the emperor addressing Roman soldiers as they build defensive walls, besiege a city, and carry out other military activities.

One of the many treasures uncovered at Pompeii is the so-called "Villa of Mysteries," the country house of a wealthy Roman family. The mural that gives the house its name shows a religious initiation, the exact nature of which is unknown. At left, a woman carries an olive branch and a silver platter containing food offerings. At right, a priestess is seated at a table.

An 18th-century view of the Pantheon in Rome. This magnificent temple, constructed by the emperor Hadrian, can still be visited today.

Callimachus carried on a lifelong feud with the poet Apollonius, who wrote in the epic mode. To contrast his own style with that of Apollonius, Callimachus wrote the *Hecale*, describing a single episode in the life of Theseus. Only a few lines of this poem are known to us.

Apollonius of Rhodes. Callimachus' great rival originally lived in Alexandria, but moved to Rhodes as a result of his feud with Callimachus. Apollonius is best known for his *Argonautica*, a lengthy epic poem based on the story of Jason's search for the Golden Fleece.

Polybius. One of the most important historians of the Hellenistic era was Polybius (201-120 B.C.), whose father was president of the Achaean League. After the war between Rome and Macedonia (171-167), Polybius was taken to Rome as a hostage and became acquainted with many prominent Romans. After his return to Greece, in 150, he wrote a history of Rome to explain the successes of the Romans to his countrymen. His history, based on written sources, interviews with Roman leaders, and personal experiences, was a comprehensive account of the period from the second Punic War to the destruction of Corinth in 146 B.C. Unfortunately, only 5 volumes remain of Polybius' 40-volume work.

Menander. The most popular form of comedy during the Hellenistic era was that which originated in Athens. Menander (342-291 B.C.) was the outstanding writer of comedies for the Athenian stage. He amused his audiences by putting stock characters—lovelorn young men, bullying fathers, and clever slaves—in stock situations, frequently involving mistaken identities. In contrast to the "Old Comedy" of Aristophanes, the "New Comedy" of Menander dealt with family and social issues rather than political themes. Although many people did not share his irreverent view of authority figures and traditional beliefs, Menander's plays were staged—in modified form—throughout the Roman Empire.

ART

Artists, like writers, were drawn to the prosperous cities of the Hellenistic era, where monarchs commissioned public buildings and monuments, and wealthy merchants spent lavishly to adorn their homes. In contrast to the artists of the Classical age, Hellenistic artists tended to strive for realistic and dramatic effects in their sculpture and painting.

One important example of Hellenistic sculpture is the "Great Altar of Zeus" in Pergamum, which was completed in 180 B.C. to commemorate the victories of Attalus I over the Celtic Gauls. This altar was an open structure with colonnades on three sides and a grand staircase on the fourth side. A frieze on the base depicted the victory of the gods of Olympus over the giants, perhaps symbolizing the triumph of civilization over barbarism.

During the 3rd and 2nd centuries B.C., the kings of Pergamum erected a number of monuments to memorialize their victories over the invading Gauls. In the sculptures that are known to us, the Gauls are depicted as courageous and dignified opponents. "The Dying Warrior" shows a wounded Gaul who is supporting himself on one arm while his strength

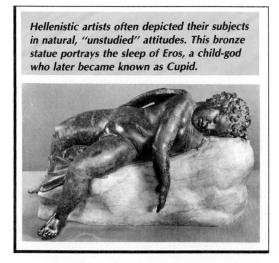

Hellenistic artists often depicted their subjects in natural, "unstudied" attitudes. This bronze statue portrays the sleep of Eros, a child-god who later became known as Cupid.

"The Gallic Chieftain." A brave Gaul kills himself and his wife to avoid surrendering to his enemies.

The statue known as the "Winged Victory of Samothrace" was erected about 190 B.C. to celebrate a Greek victory over Syria.

slowly ebbs away. "The Gallic Chieftain" depicts an officer who supports his dying wife while preparing to plunge his sword into his own chest.

Another world-renowned piece of sculpture from this era is the "Venus de Milo," whose appearance of serene dignity is suggestive of Praxiteles' work, but whose heavy drapery is typically Hellenistic in style. An equally fine work was the "Winged Victory of Samothrace," which depicted the goddess of victory alighting from the prow of a ship. Her clinging garment conveys a sense of the motion of wind and waves.

The "Old Market Woman" also exemplifies the realism and dramatic qualities of Hellenistic art. The strained facial expression and bent back of the old woman still evoke sympathy from the viewer.

PHILOSOPHY

During the Hellenistic era, uncertainties about existing political and social systems led to a renewal of interest in philosophy. As a result, the beliefs of Socrates, Plato, and Aristotle concerning the "good life" and the nature of truth were reevaluated and redefined, and four major schools of thought emerged. Each advocated a new way to achieve tranquillity and peace of mind.

Skepticism. The founder of skepticism was said to be Pyrrho of Elis, who lived from about 360 to 270 B.C. He denied the possibility of finding truth, arguing that everything is discerned through the senses, which are totally unreliable. In keeping with his belief that nothing can be stated with certainty, Pyrrho left no writings.

Cynicism. Diogenes taught that happiness

The artist who created "Old Market Woman" realistically portrayed the age and suffering of his subject. This approach is in marked contrast to the art of the Classical age, in which artists strove to present an ideal, dreamlike image of human beings.

that when Alexander the Great passed through Corinth, he sought out Diogenes and asked him, "What would you like me to do for you?" Diogenes, who was basking in the sun, had just one simple request: "Move aside. You're blocking my sun."

Diogenes mistrusted all social conventions and traditions, believing that they inspired falsehood and self-deception. He reportedly once walked through the streets of Corinth with a lighted lamp, seeking an honest man—or perhaps demonstrating that it would be difficult to find one.

Although Diogenes preferred to live without physical comforts himself, he deplored the existence of poverty, for he believed it produced a love of money. His followers continued his practice of criticizing the existing social order, and also imitated Di-

The "Laocoon" is one of the most famous Hellenistic sculptures. It portrays a mythical event of the Trojan War: Apollo has sent snakes to punish Laocoon, the priest of Troy, for warning his fellow citizens about the Trojan horse.

results from becoming self-sufficient, and that this state is achieved by limiting one's desires and needs. He actually attempted to live like a dog, using rags and a wooden barrel for clothing and shelter, and carrying on his private life in public view. In fact, the term cynicism was derived from the Greek word kyon, meaning "dog." Stories about Diogenes emphasized his efforts to live in the most "natural" state possible. For example, it was said that he once rolled in the snow clasping a marble statue in order to inure himself to the cold. Another story related

ogenes' direct speech and rude manners. As a result, the term *cynic* came to refer to a person who has a contemptuous and critical attitude toward accepted beliefs and ways of life.

Epicureanism. One of the most popular schools of philosophy was founded by Epicurus (342-271 B.C.), who established a school in Athens in 306 B.C. He decided that pleasure is derived from the satisfaction of wants, and that pain results from the inability to satisfy them. Therefore, wise people will live in such a way that they have no wants that cannot be satisfied. The greatest obstacle to tranquillity of soul, he thought, was the fear of the gods and of death. Epicurus devised reassurances for people troubled by each of these fears. Humans have no reason to fear the gods, he said, because the latter have no interest in human affairs. And there is no reason to fear death, he maintained, because the soul would not survive the disintegration of the body's atoms.

Later followers of Epicurus corrupted his teachings to the point that today we refer to a person who is devoted to the pursuit of pleasure—especially the enjoyment of fancy foods—as an "epicure."

Stoicism. Zeno, the founder of Stoicism, was born on Cyprus in 335 B.C. Like Diogenes and Epicurus, he was greatly influenced by the teachings of Socrates and Plato, and used them as a starting point for his own thinking. Because Zeno taught in a building called the *Stoa Poikile* ("Painted Porch"), his teachings came to be called *stoicism*. He believed that the universe is governed by laws that guide all events to good, and that these laws are superior to the laws and customs of any human society. He taught that a wise person lives in harmony with these laws and recognizes that, since pain and misfortune are inescapable, all events should be borne with calm acceptance.

Zeno's followers later developed a theory that fire was the supreme power of the universe, that a spark of such fire resides in every individual, and that, because each person has a spark of divinity, all people are related as equals to all other human beings. The philosophy developed by the Stoics became very popular among Roman intellectuals during the period of the Roman Empire, and the concept of accepting all of the events of life as divine will later found its way into the theology of Christianity.

SCIENCE

During the 3rd century B.C., the observations that Babylonian astronomers had made over the course of several centuries were translated into Greek, and Greek scholars also became aware of the work of Egyptian and Babylonian mathematicians. The exchange of ideas between these cultures, as well as a widespread interest in new learning, led to great achievements in various fields of science during the Hellenistic era.

The Greeks used their knowledge of astronomy and mathematics to create incredibly accurate theories concerning the solar system and the laws of nature. They realized, for instance, that the earth is round, and that the planets revolve about the sun. However, the great theorists of the ancient world seldom put their discoveries to practical use. Because slave labor was cheap and plentiful, there was little incentive to invent labor saving tools. And the scientists tended to feel that practical applications were vulgar or demeaning. Even Archimedes, who became famous for his ingenious devices, was reportedly reluctant to allow his experimental machines to be utilized, for he did not want to be looked upon as a mere engineer.

Euclid. The most famous mathematician of the age was Euclid (365-300 B.C.), who is still known as the "father of scientific geometry." During the reign of Ptolemy I, Euclid opened a school in Egypt where he taught the theorems of plane and solid geometry. He blended original ideas with long established concepts in a book called *Elements of Geometry*, which remained a standard textbook until the 20th century. Ptolemy reportedly voiced the thoughts of many students by asking Euclid whether geometry might not be made easier to learn. Euclid replied, "There is no royal road."

Archimedes. One of the greatest scientists of ancient times was Archimedes (287-212 B.C.), who was born in Syracuse, Sicily, and studied at Alexandria. He developed new methods for measuring the surface area and volume of objects—the field now known as solid geometry—and was the first to compute the value of "pi," the ratio of the circumference of a circle to its diameter. He accidently discovered the concept of "specific gravity" when he observed the displacement of water as he entered a bath. Legend has it that he became so excited about this discovery that he ran naked through the streets shouting "Eureka!" ("I have found it.").

Archimedes was interested in both theoretical and applied mechanics. He invented a planetarium to demonstrate the movements of heavenly bodies and to explain the phenomenon of eclipses. He studied the ratio of force and weight involved in moving heavy bodies with the assistance of pulleys and levers, and his knowledge of this subject led him to claim that he could move the earth if he had a long enough lever.

While living in Alexandria, Archimedes invented a water screw to raise water from the Nile River to irrigate the fields. The "Archimedian screw," as it came to be called, could also be used to pump water out of mines and from the holds of ships. When Rome besieged Syracuse in 215-212 B.C., the war machines designed by Archimedes helped to defend the city. One of the most famous of his "engines of war" was a group of concave mirrors arranged so as to focus the energy of the sun onto a very small spot. This device was used to set Roman ships afire before they could enter the harbor of Syracuse. One day, after Syracuse had fallen to the Romans, Archimedes told a Roman soldier not to interrupt him while he worked on a mathematical problem. The soldier took offense at this and killed him.

Aristarchus. Aristarchus of Samos (310-230 B.C.) proposed the heliocentric theory of the universe; that is, that the earth and other planets revolve around the sun. His theory was rejected by other prominent astronomers of the Hellenistic age, but it was finally confirmed many centuries later by Copernicus and Galileo.

Eratosthenes. Eratosthenes (276-195 B.C.), the chief librarian at Alexandria, was one of the most versatile thinkers of his age. He wrote manuscripts on mathematics, philosophy, grammar, and literary criticism, but is best known today for his contribution to geography. He was the first person to use grid lines to represent latitude and longitude on a map. He then used measurements of the sun's altitude on the horizon to calculate the circumference of the earth. Realizing that the sun would be directly overhead the city of Syrene in Egypt on the day of the summer solstice (June 21), Eratosthenes measured the angle of a shadow that the sun cast on the same day in Alexandria. Using an estimate of the distance between the two cities, he then used geometry to arrive at a surprisingly accurate calculation of the circumference of the earth.

Hipparchus. Hipparchus (165-125 B.C.) rejected the heliocentric theory of the planets, but used his knowledge of geometry and astronomy to develop many accurate observations. He refined the concept of latitude and longitude developed by Eratosthenes, and created the 360 divisions that are still used by cartographers today. He described the precession of equinoxes, and compiled a catalog of 1000 stars. His geocentric theory of the universe was supported by Ptolemy, who published a treatise on mathematical astronomy in the 2nd century A.D. The *Ptolemaic system* was universally accepted until the 16th century, when Copernicus proved, at least to his own satisfaction, that the sun is the center of our planetary system.

SUMMARY

During the 4th century B.C., the resources of the Greek city-states proved to be no match for the permanent, professional army and capable leadership of Philip II of Macedonia. Although Demosthenes, in Athens, succeeded in mobilizing the Greek city-states to fight the Macedonians, the fragile, temporary coalitions he created could not prevent Philip from conquering Greece. Philip succeeded in creating a united Macedonian-Greek empire, but was assassinated before he could fulfill his dream of conquering the Persian Empire.

Philip's dream of further conquests was realized by his son, Alexander, who came to be called "the Great." Alexander's empire became the basis for a vast colonization movement as thousands of Greeks and Macedonians settled in the cities that Alexander and his successors founded. The cultural exchanges and economic prosperity of the era following Alexander's death contributed to the artistic, literary, and scientific achievements of the Hellenistic era.

QUESTIONS

1 What effects did Philip II, Alexander the Great, and their successors achieve by developing cities? How did this policy of urbanization help them to promote Hellenistic civilization?

2 Why did Alexander become a model of the hero for many generations after his lifetime? How do you think his untimely death might have contributed to the mystique about him?

3 How was Alexander's conquest different from previous conquests? How might the world have been different if Alexander had lived longer?

4 How did the advocates of Cynicism, Stoicism, and Epicurianism define the good life?

5 What relation do you see between the government of the Aetolian and Achaean Leagues and that of the United States?

BIBLIOGRAPHY

Which reference might discuss Alexander's battle strategies?

FOX, ROBIN LANE. *The Search for Alexander. New York: Little, Brown, 1980. Traces the career of Alexander and evaluates the probable content of the memoirs written by Ptolemy and Nearchus, Alexander's boyhood friends and fellow adventurers. Lavishly illustrated with color photographs of the sites, landscapes, and artifacts associated with Alexander.*

"In the Footsteps of Alexander the Great." *National Geographic* 133, 1 (1968): 1-65. *The authors traveled 25,000 miles by jeep, by foot, and on horseback to trace the route of Alexander. They provide well-informed descriptions of the difficulties of the terrain and the physical hardships that Alexander and his men faced; excellent illustrations of the territories as they look today.*

9

Rome:
City-State to Empire

The peninsula of Italy was invaded by Indo-European peoples about 2000 B.C. One of these tribes, the Latins, founded a settlement on the Tiber River which came to be called Rome. At the beginning of the 7th century B.C., a second wave of invaders descended into the area. These invaders were the Etruscans, a people whose culture and language still hold many mysteries for modern scholars. Within a century, the Etruscans established control over much of northern Italy and imposed their own government on the Romans.

In the year 509 B.C., according to tradition, the Romans threw off the yoke of their Etruscan overlords and established a republic. During the following years, the Romans refined the institutions of their republic in response to the need for a strong military establishment and to the demands of the common people. By 287 B.C., Rome had gained control of all of Italy, and had developed an effective system of governing conquered areas.

GEOGRAPHY AND NATURAL RESOURCES The best-known feature of the geography of Italy is its resemblance to a boot. The ranges of latitude and longitude are very nearly equal to those of California, but the area is only about two-thirds that of the state. Both Italy and California are quite mountainous, the Apennines forming a spine down the peninsula similar to the Sierra Nevada spine of California. The broad valley of the Po River, across the northern end of Italy, is a rich agricultural area, as is the Central Valley of California.

The best natural harbors on the Italian coasts were occupied by the Greeks by about 600 B.C. The Romans, therefore, tended to expand overland. To facilitate transportation inland, the Romans periodically dredged the seabed near the city of Ostia, at the mouth of the Tiber River, so that boats could pass from the Tyrrhenian Sea to Rome.

The minerals of Italy were an important resource in ancient times and continue to be utilized in the modern world. Italian marble, which is still used throughout the world for impressive structures, enabled emperors of the 1st century to create the monuments that symbolized Rome's imperial period. Tufa, an easily cut volcanic rock, was also utilized for building construction in Italy. Another important resource was clay, which was widely used for making bricks and pottery.

The climate and soil of Italy compared favorably to those of Greece. In ancient times, Italy had many forests and an abundance of wild animals, which the early inhabitants utilized for shipbuilding timber and food. When the forests were cleared, the fertile volcanic soil and mild climate proved to be highly suitable for growing grain as well as for cultivating grapevines and olive trees. The ancient Italians thus had two important resources—timber and grain—which were in short supply on the Greek peninsula.

THE ROMANS Historians have difficulty when they try to reconstruct the early history of Rome. The Greek colonists who settled in Magna Graecia (Chapter 6) did not consider the Romans to be worth writing about, and most of the physical facilities of the earliest city were destroyed by the Gauls in 390 B.C. Later Roman historians utilized oral traditions and written inscriptions that existed in their time to reconstruct the first few centuries of the city's history.

ORIGINS

The historians Livy and Dionysius, who lived in the 1st century B.C., are our most important sources of information concerning Rome's earliest history. Livy, who lived and worked in Rome, emphasized the dignity and virtue of the earliest Romans in his work *Ab Urbe Condita* ("From the Founding of the City"). Dionysius of Halicarnassus, a Greek writer, described the development of Roman civilization for the benefit of Greek readers. His *Roman Antiquities* draws many parallels between Greek and Roman civilization, and even suggests that the Romans' ancestors were Greek and Trojan heroes.

According to one ancient tradition, Rome was first founded by Aeneas, a hero of the Trojan War, and his followers, who conquered the native Latin tribes of the area and eventually intermarried with them. A second tradition recounted the founding of Rome

The story of Romulus and Remus was one of the central legends of Rome's early history. This statue of a wolf dates from the 5th century B.C.; the figures of the twins were added during the Renaissance.

as a city of Latins during the 8th century B.C. According to this story, Romulus and Remus, twins of royal birth, were nursed by a wolf and raised by a shepherd after their uncle abandoned them in the wilderness. Later, they discovered the secret of their royal birth and resolved to create a new city near the cottage where they had grown up. They fought a battle to decide who would be king of the new city, and Romulus finally emerged as the victor.

Archaeological Findings. Livy noted that the legends concerning Rome's beginnings could not be confirmed or denied by researchers of his own generation:

• • • *Events before Rome was born or thought of have come to us in old tales with more of the charm of poetry than of a sound historical record, and such traditions I propose neither to affirm nor refute.*[1]

Modern archaeologists, however, have found limited evidence for both legends of Rome's founding. They have discovered scattered traces of Bronze-Age navigators in Italy, making it possible to believe that Mycenaean adventurers explored and colonized the area. Also, post holes carved in the tufa rock of

[1]Livy I, Preface, 6.

the Palatine Hill in Rome have supplied important clues about the civilization that existed there in the 8th century B.C. Using the post holes as a guide, archaeologists have built round huts of wattle and mud to reconstruct the settlement that existed in Romulus' time.

RELIGION

The earliest Romans believed that there were spirits everywhere: in fire, water, stones, and trees; in the planting of seeds and the baking of bread. These spirits had no names and no specific shape, but people believed that they could help or hurt them. The spirits were at first worshiped by families in their own homes. Respect for the spirit of fire, for instance, was demonstrated by throwing salt into the hearth at mealtimes, and the spirit of the doorway was appeased by a special ceremony when a stranger entered. In time, these rituals became more public, and priests were appointed to build temples for the deities. As they established community cults,

After Jupiter, Mars was the most revered deity of the early Romans. In this portrait, the self-assured god poses on a war chariot.

Janus was one of the household spirits worshiped by the earliest Romans. With his two faces, he watchfully guarded all doorways and gates.

the priests assigned names to the ancient household spirits. The spirit of fire, for instance, became known as Vesta; the spirit of the doorway was named Janus; and the spirits that guarded cupboards were called the Penates. Other early deities were adopted from the Etruscans and Greeks, including Jupiter, the sky-god; Mars, the god of war; and Minerva, the goddess who protected cities.

According to tradition, Numa Pompilius, who succeeded Romulus as king of Rome, was responsible for creating the religious institutions of Rome. He reportedly appointed the first *Vestal Virgins*, the priestesses who maintained a temple of Vesta, and the *fla-mines*, or priests, who supervised the wor-

> *Several months in our modern calendar preserve the names of gods worshiped by the ancient Romans. January (Januarius) was sacred to Janus, the god of entrances and beginnings. March (Martius) was dedicated to a festival in honor of Mars, the god of war and agriculture. Juno, the wife of Jupiter, gave her name to June (Junius), the month considered most propitious for marriage.*

ship of Mars and Jupiter. Numa was also credited with reforming the Roman calendar so that special religious holidays could be named by date and observed by all.[2]

THE ETRUSCANS

Rome began as a small village in a world not yet dominated by the Greek culture we have just studied. The village was, however, adjacent to the remarkable civilization of the Etruscans. We know much about the politics, philosophy, religion, and arts of the ancient Greeks, but very little about the Etruscans.

Ancient sources indicate that scattered groups of Etruscans had been present in Italy since prehistoric times. The first sizable group of Etruscans settled on the western coast of Italy about 700 B.C.. The territory they inhabited came to be known to the Latins as Etruria; today it is called Tuscany.

The Etruscans were accomplished metalworkers: they knew how to use the copper and tin that they found locally, and they refined iron ore obtained from the nearby island of Elba. They traded objects made from these metals with merchants from Egypt, Greece, Magna Graecia, and the Middle East for glass objects, textiles, and other items. In this process, they came in contact with the Greek and Phoenician civilizations.

[2]The reformed calendar had 12 months and corresponded to the solar year; the earlier calendar had been based on the moon's cycle of 10 months.

LANGUAGE

Because later Romans were not greatly interested in the Etruscans, their literary works were not translated or preserved. Most of the Etruscan writings that have come down to us are very short tomb inscriptions. The longest known Etruscan text, about 1300 words, was found on a linen cloth used to wrap a mummy in Egypt. Scholars have had little difficulty in deciphering these inscriptions, for the Etruscans used a 27-letter alphabet based on the Greek alphabet. But because the writings are limited in content and are quite brief, little can be discovered concerning the grammar and syntax of the language.

ORIGINS

Dionysius reported that there were two theories concerning the origin of the Etruscans: one theory was that they had migrated to Italy from Lydia, an ancient kingdom of Asia Minor; the other that they were **indigenous**, or native, to Italy. These two theories are still debated today.

Herodotus, who lived 400 years before Dionysius, reported that the Etruscans, or Tyrrhenians, as he called them, came from Lydia. Dionysius himself believed that the Etruscans were indigenous to Italy, arguing that their language was quite unlike that of the Lydians. Modern scholars tend to support Herodotus' opinion. Linguists studying the Etruscan and Lydian languages have found some similarities between the two. And in 1885, archaeologists discovered two funerary stelae with similar inscriptions; one on the island of Lemnos in the Aegean Sea, and the other in Tuscany. Many scholars now believe that the stelae were carved by the ancient Etruscans, indicating that the Etruscans used Lemnos as a supply point as they traveled from Lydia to Italy.

CULTURE

Like the Egyptians and Sumerians, the Etruscans spent much time and care in their preparation for life after death. Most of our

The tombs of this Etruscan necropolis are arranged like houses on a narrow street.

chaeologists have found sculptures, shields, pottery, and jewelry. Some of the tombs also contain frescoes that show fascinating glimpses of the everyday lives of these people, including scenes of chariot races, bull fights, dancing, and fishing. The pictures indicate that Etruscan women enjoyed equality and freedom, advantages enjoyed by few other women in ancient societies.

Between 650 and 600 B.C., a federation of Etruscan city-states moved south and conquered the plain of Latium, including the village of Rome. During the reign of the Etruscan monarchy in Rome (616-509 B.C.), the Etruscans made a lasting contribution to the city's institutions and government. Such distinctive features of later Roman life as gladitorial contests, chariot races, and symbols of *imperium*, or absolute authority, were inherited from the Etruscans. Through the Etruscans, the Romans also learned about certain aspects of Greek culture, including the use of an alphabet and the worship of anthropomorphic gods.

knowledge of the Etruscans has been derived from their *necropoleis* ("cities of the dead"), in which tombs were arranged like houses on small streets. Within these tombs, ar-

A gayly painted fresco in a 5th-century B.C. Etruscan tomb shows musicians marching to a banquet hall.

This painted statue of Apollo dates from the 6th century B.C. Apollo was one of many gods whom the Etruscans adopted from the Greeks.

THE FIRST KINGS OF ROME

Modern scholars have found evidence to support some of the ancient legends concerning the early kings of Rome, but they also have determined that these stories contain certain inaccuracies and exaggerations. For instance, all of the early Roman historians reported that the Etruscans were expelled from Rome in 509 B.C. Other evidence indicates, however, that the Etruscans actually ruled Rome for several years after this date. The Romans may have set the earlier date because they did not wish to credit the Etruscans with several large building projects completed after 509 B.C. But in spite of doubts concerning certain dates and details, modern scholars believe that the Roman historians were correct in stating that the central institutions and customs of later Rome were developed during the 140-year reign of Romulus and his three Latin-Sabine successors.

In ancient Rome, as in Greece, the basic unit of society was the tribe, a group of families who had a common ancestor. The Latin term for these related families was *gens*.

Romulus. According to tradition, Romulus organized the *gentes*[3] of Rome into larger groups called *curiae*. He established a total of 30 *curiae*, and decreed that they would meet in an assembly called the *Comitia Curiata*. Romulus is also credited with establishing the Senate, or "Council of Elders." This assembly consisted of 100 *patricians*, or nobles, who were summoned by the king to give their advice. Excluded from the *Comitia Curiata* and the Senate were the *plebeians* or *plebs*, a group of people who could not prove that they belonged to one of the recognized *gentes*. The plebs were also excluded from military duties, since army levies were contributed by the *curiae*.

In the system established by Romulus, the king served as war chief, high priest, and

---

[3]*Gentes* is the plural form of *gens*.

supreme judge. He had absolute powers while he lived, but could not designate his successor. The *Comitia Curiata* nominated a new king, and the Senate, after consulting soothsayers, confirmed or denied the nomination.

In addition to founding Rome as a city of Latins and establishing its laws and institutions, Romulus is credited with two other achievements. He reportedly united his own people with the Sabines, a neighboring tribe, by forcibly seizing the young women of the tribe and marrying them to his soldiers. He also established Rome's military domination over the surrounding countryside.

Numa Pompilius. The second of the legendary kings of Rome was known as a highly religious king. Later Romans believed that he established the religious institutions of Rome and revised the calendar (as mentioned above), assigning specific dates for religious festivals.

Tullus Hostilius. The third legendary king of Rome reportedly increased the population of his city through conquest. After destroying the nearby city of Alba Longa, he forced its citizens to move to Rome.

Ancus Martius. The last of the Latin-Sabine kings was credited with two peaceful achievements. He was reportedly the first king to think of dredging a harbor near Ostia, at the mouth of the Tiber River, and to build fortifications to protect commercial traffic on the river.

ETRUSCAN RULE

It is not known exactly how the Etruscans seized control of Rome. One tradition related that Tarquinius Priscus, the first Etruscan king, entered Rome in a cart to show his peaceful intentions. Little by little, he then gathered enough supporters to seize the throne.

The Etruscan monarchs of Rome, known as the Tarquins, introduced several innovations in the monarchy of Rome. To symbolize the absolute power of the king, an official called a *lictor* stood in front of the king, holding a *fasces*. The *fasces* consisted of a bundle of elmwood rods bound together around an axe, signifying the power of the king to scourge or behead his subjects. The Etruscans were also responsible for at least two important construction projects: under their rule, the *Cloaca Maxima* ("great sewer") was built to drain the site of the Roman Forum, and a wall was built around the seven hills of Rome. The Etruscans probably also constructed the *Capitoline Jupiter*, a magnificent temple to Jupiter on the Capitoline Hill.

THE REFORMS OF SERVIUS TULLIUS

According to tradition, Servius Tullius, a Roman plebeian, married the daughter of Tarquinius Priscus, and ultimately succeeded his father-in-law as king of Rome. He was credited with making important and lasting reforms in the army and government of early Rome. Some modern scholars believe that Roman historians may have invented the figure of Servius Tullius so that they could attribute certain important developments to a Latin king rather than to the Etruscans. Others believe that Servius was an historical character, arguing that an invented king would have been given a patrician name rather than a plebeian one.

The basis of the reforms attributed to Servius was the need for a larger army. Because of changes in military tactics throughout the Mediterranean world, *hoplites*, heavily armed footsoldiers, came to be considered the most important part of the army. An effective phalanx of infantry therefore became necessary for Rome's security, but the *curiae* were unable to supply sufficient troops.

Servius' first reform was to expand the number of *curiae* so that plebeians and resident foreigners could be included. For this purpose, he took a census of all of the inhabitants of Rome, enumerating the property holdings of each person. He then created 4 new tribes in the city of Rome, and 16 tribes in the surrounding countryside.

Comitia Curiata. The enlarged *Comitia Curiata* continued to function as it had under the monarchy. It was organized by tribes, and its voting procedures were fairly democratic. In private meetings held by each *curia*, the *gentes* were polled by their leaders to determine the majority opinion of the *curia* on any given issue. Each member had an equal vote in this preliminary poll, and the *curia* then delivered its majority opinion in public meetings of the *Comitia Curiata*.

Comitia Centuriata. To determine how the burden of military service should be apportioned, Servius used the results of his census to divide the people of Rome into five classes. The first class consisted of men who could afford to supply a full set of armor and weapons for hoplite fighting: helmet, bronze body armor, shield, sword, and spear. The second class comprised those who could not afford bronze armor; and the third and fourth classes those who lacked other pieces of the equipment. The fifth, and last, class included men who were armed only with slingshots. In addition to the five hoplite classes, the census also defined a class of *equites*, or knights, men who could afford to maintain a horse for the service of the state; and a class of *proletarii*, men who were not armed at all, but acted as servants to the armed men.

Because fully armed men were the most valuable to the state, Servius inducted more wealthy citizens than poorer ones into the army. Altogether, there were 80 *centuries*, or groups of 100 men, in the first two hoplite classes, and 18 *centuries* in the *equite* class. In times of danger, the *Comitia Centuriata*, an assembly of all of the *centuries*, was summoned to the Campus Martius ("Field of Mars"). Each *century* voted as a block, and was called upon to vote in order of rank. Because the wealthier, well equipped *centuries* outnumbered the poorer ones, they were able to decide an issue if they voted as a block. The votes of the poorer citizens of Rome therefore had less weight in the military assembly of the *Comitia Centuriata* than in the *Comitia Curiata*.

In time, the *Comitia Centuriata* took over many of the responsibilities of the *Comitia Curiata*. Servius' reforms thus led to the development of a modified **timocracy**. Many more people were included in the political process, but the poorest people had less influence than the wealthier ones.

RETURN TO ETRUSCAN RULE

According to Roman tradition, Servius Tullius was succeeded by an Etruscan named Tarquinius Superbus (Tarquin the Proud), who became the most repressive king Rome had ever known. In 509 B.C., it was said, the outraged Romans overthrew the Etruscan monarchy and established a republic.

ORGANIZATION OF THE COMITIA CENTURIATA	
Equites (Cavalry)	*18 centuries*
Hoplites - 1st class	*80 centuries*
- 2nd class	*20 centuries*
- 3rd class	*20 centuries*
- 4th class	*20 centuries*
- 5th class	*30 centuries*
Proletarians (support)	*5 centuries*
Total	*193 centuries*

THE ROMAN REPUBLIC

After the downfall of the Etruscan monarchy, the word rex (king) became a detested symbol of excessive power, and it remained so throughout the long history of Rome. The expulsion of the Etruscans was later celebrated as the foundation of Roman liberty.

DUAL CONSULSHIP

In place of the monarchy, the Romans instituted a system in which two *consuls* were elected by the *Comitia Curiata* for a one-year term. The consuls had *imperium*, or absolute power, during their term of office, and on formal occasions they were preceded by a dozen *lictors* who carried the *fasces*. But although each consul could issue edicts which had the force of law, the other consul could nullify such an edict by exclaiming *Veto!* ("I forbid."). During times of peace, the two consuls alternated in office each month, and during times of war they alternated each day. When a crisis occurred, the Senate and consuls together could appoint a *dictator* who would exercise absolute power for a period of six months. The legend of Cincinnatus relates how one citizen reluctantly agreed to serve Rome as dictator, then happily returned to his farm when the emergency was over.

THE ASSEMBLIES

Under the republican system, the *Comitia Curiata* and the *Comitia Centuriata* continued to play an important part in public affairs. They elected the consuls and other public officials, and also served as a court of appeal for citizens convicted of a capital offense. In day-to-day affairs, however, the Senate had a greater role than the assemblies.

THE SENATE

Because the senators served for life and represented the oldest and most prestigious families of Rome, a consul could not easily disregard their advice. They represented continuity and authority, and, as long as they upheld high standards of conduct, their opinions had the force of law in Rome's republic. In times of war, the Senate influenced the appointment of military commanders and determined how troops would be levied. In times of peace, it controlled the state treasury and collected taxes. The Senate also had an important role in foreign affairs: it received foreign ambassadors, and ratified treaties and alliances with other nations. As Rome acquired more territory, the senators no longer performed all administrative duties themselves, but they appointed many of the officials who governed the provinces.

During the early years of the republic, only *patricians* were eligible to belong to the Senate. In time, however, membership was open to all people who had served in public office, except those excluded for bad conduct. Thus, as plebeians won the right to hold public offices, they also gained representation in the Senate.

CONCILIUM PLEBIS

The plebeians of Rome were soon dissatisfied with the constitution of the republic. In 494 B.C., according to tradition, plebeian soldiers went on strike, stating that they would form an independent city unless they were granted important political rights. Realizing that Rome would be greatly weakened without the plebeians' military services, the Senate granted them the right to form a political assembly of their own. The plebeian assembly became known as the *Concilium Plebis*.

The *Concilium Plebis*, like the *Comitia Curiata*, was organized by tribes into *curiae*. It had the authority to pass *plebecita* ("peoples' decrees"), but these were binding only on plebeians. Thus, Rome had, in effect, one government for the patricians and one for the plebeians.

The Tribunes. The leaders of the plebeians did not have *imperium*, but they were

GOVERNMENT OF THE ROMAN REPUBLIC

CONSULSHIP

Members: Two consuls elected by the *Comitia Centuriata* annually.

Role: Issue laws and decrees—usually, but not necessarily, after submitting decisions to the Senate for a vote. Each consul has the authority to veto a decision of the other.

SENATE

Members: In the early days of the Republic, 100 senators were chosen from the most prominent patrician families of Rome. Later, all who have served in public office are eligible to belong.

Role: Administer the laws and decrees enacted by the consuls; issue resolutions on important matters; receive foreign ambassadors; ratify treaties and alliances with foreign powers.

ASSEMBLIES:

Comitia Curiata

Members: The recognized *curiae* of Rome. (Each *curia* consists of several related *gentes*, or tribes.)

Role: Formally confer *imperium* on newly elected consuls and *praetors*; approve family documents, as for adoptions and wills; vote on legislation presented by the magistrates of Rome.

Comitia Centuriata

Members: The army of Rome, organized into *centuries*, or groups of 100.

Role: Elect *consuls, praetors,* and *censors;* serve as court of appeal for major law court cases; vote on legislation presented by the magistrates of Rome. After 287 B.C., this assembly could enact legislation of its own.

Concilium Plebis

Members: Plebeian *curiae*.

Role: Enact *plebecites,* or people's decrees, which are binding upon all plebeians; elect 10 *tribunes* to defend and represent plebeians in the government of Rome. After 287 B.C., plebecites of the *Concilium Plebis* were binding upon all Romans.

Comitia Tributa Populi

Members: All free citizens of Rome, organized by *curiae*.

Role: Elect *quaestors;* propose legislation; serve as court of appeal for minor law court cases. In 287 B.C., this assembly received the right to enact legislation.

---

accorded several important privileges and powers. In their role as protectors of the plebeians, they were recognized as sacrosanct: anyone who injured a tribune was declared an outlaw, and the house of a tribune was considered an inviolable sanctuary. Thus, a tribune could shield plebeians who had been declared criminals by the consuls or other magistrates. Within a few years, the tribunes also won the right to veto any official act passed by the consuls or the Senate. By 449 B.C., there were 10 tribunes to represent the plebeians.

The power of veto gave the tribunes great importance in the government of Rome, but they had only a negative role: they could prevent the Senate from passing a law, but did not have the authority to substitute laws of their own. During the next century, the plebeians struggled to gain public offices and to make the decisions of their assembly binding upon all Romans. They eventually achieved representation in the highest government offices: a plebeian first achieved office as *quaestor* in 409 B.C.; as consul in 366; as dictator in 356; and as *censor* in 351. (See the descriptions of *quaestor* and *censor* below.) Finally, in 287 B.C., a plebeian dictator passed the *Hortensian law*, making plebiscites of the *Concilium Plebis* binding upon all citizens.

COMITIA TRIBUTA POPULI

Due to the initiative of the plebeians, a public assembly called the *Comitia Tributa Populi* was formed in 447 B.C. This assembly included all free citizens of Rome, and provided a means by which the "will of the people" could be ascertained.

The creation of the Comitia Tributa Populi meant that there were four public assemblies in Rome. None of the three earlier assemblies was abolished, but instead the four assemblies functioned independently, with overlapping functions and membership. In 287 B.C., the *Comitia Tributa*, like the *Concilium Plebis*, received the right to enact laws.

OTHER MAGISTRATES OF THE REPUBLIC

Early in the republic, a number of offices were created to administer the decisions of the consuls and the Senate, and to assist the tribunes. As Rome acquired additional territories, the number of *consuls, tribunes,* and *censors* remained constant, but additional offices of *quaestor, praetor,* and *aedile* were created to handle the increasing burden of administration.

Quaestor. The first consuls of the republic appointed officials known as *quaestors* to serve as their assistants. The *quaestors* were responsible for investigating murder cases and for financial administration. In 447 B.C., as a concession to the plebeians, *quaestors* were elected by the *Comitia Tributa* rather than being appointed by the consuls.

Praetor. In 366 B.C., the office of *praetor* was created. This official assisted the consuls by acting as a judge and had the power of *imperium*, but to a lesser degree than the consuls. He could take charge of the city if the consuls were absent, and could, in an emergency, assume command of the army.

Aedile. The tribunes originally appointed two *aediles* to assist them in administrative matters. In time, two patrician *aediles* were also elected, and the four officers then met as a committee to arrange public games and to supervise the grain supply.

Censor. The important office of *censor* was created in 433. The two censors were responsible for assessing the property holdings of all citizens and assigning them to their *gentes, curiae,* and *centuries.* They also acted as enforcers of public morality. They had the authority to appoint new senators, and to expel from the Senate those whom they considered unworthy to hold office. Although the *censors* did not have *imperium,* their authority to appoint and remove senators gave them great influence. The *censors* were elected by the *Comitia Centuriata* for a term of five years, but they were expected to complete their work within 18 months.

EARLY DEVELOPMENT OF THE CONSTITUTION

Law of the 12 Tablets. Even after the establishment of the *Concilium Plebis* and the guarantee of the tribunes' authority, the plebeians of Rome felt that they needed further protection against the judicial powers of senators and other magistrates. The second major victory won by the plebeians—after the establishment of the Concilium Plebis—was the right of all Roman citizens to be judged equally under the law. In 449 B.C., the traditional laws of Rome were written on 12 wooden tablets which were set up in the Forum for all to see. The Law of the 12 Tab-

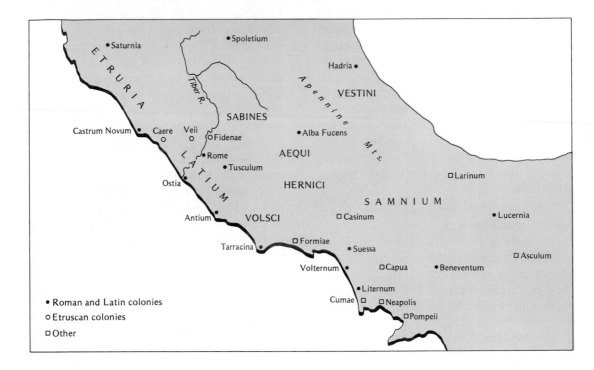

lets, as the code came to be knòwn, was considered to be the source of all civil and criminal law. Every Roman citizen was expected to memorize the laws contained on the tablets.

Canuleian Law. Several years later, in 445 B.C., the plebeians gained another concession: the Canuleian Law, named after Canuleius, the tribune who proposed it, permitted marriages between patricians and plebeians.

EXPANSION IN CENTRAL ITALY

In 493 B.C., Rome and several other Latin city-states created a confederation known as the *Concilium Latinorum*, or Latin League. During the 5th century, the members of the league agreed upon a common foreign policy and, in times of war, elected a dictator to lead their combined armies. The league's forces successfully repelled invasions of the Sabines, the Aequi, the Volsci, and other mountain tribes who were attempting to move into the plain of Latium.

Eventually, the Romans demonstrated that they had enough military power to act independently of the league. In 426, Rome resolved a long-standing dispute with the Etruscans over inland trade routes by conquering the Etruscan city of Fidenae. And in 405, the Romans began to besiege the powerful Etruscan city of Veii. In 395, after a 10-year siege, Veii finally fell to the Romans.

INVASION OF THE GAULS

Shortly after Rome's conquest of Veii, the Gauls, or Celts, warlike Indo-European tribes from the north, began to invade Italy. Because the Etruscan cities to the north had been weakened by their long struggle with Rome, they were unable to stem the force of the invasion, and the members of the Latin

League failed to organize a military force. As a result, Rome was struck particularly hard by the Gauls. In 390 B.C., the Gauls defeated the Roman army and entered Rome. As the Gauls besieged and sacked Rome, many Romans found refuge in the nearby Etruscan city of Veii. For a short time, they even considered relocating to Veii. But they decided that Rome must be rebuilt on its original site because the ground had been blessed by the gods when the city was founded. According to tradition, the Romans paid the Gauls 1000 pounds in gold to leave Rome. The Gauls then withdrew to northern Italy and settled in the area that came to be known as *Cisalpine* ("This side of the Alps") Gaul.

The Romans built aqueducts to bring fresh water to their city from the earliest times. In 272 B.C., an 40-mile-long aqueduct was built between Rome and a spring in the Sabine hills.

One benefit that Rome provided to the members of its confederation was good roads. This is a section of the Appian Way, built in 312 B.C. between Rome and Capua. Eventually, the road extended all the way to Brundisium on the east coast.

THE ROMAN CONFEDERATION

After the Gauls had withdrawn to northern Italy, the Romans gradually rebuilt their city and their army. Most importantly, they began to solve the internal political and economic problems that had arisen by making fundamental changes in their constitution (see page 212). Once their internal affairs were in order, the Romans began a program of territorial expansion. Taking advantage of the disorder that prevailed among the other city-states of Latium, Roman legions swiftly conquered several nearby city-states. The Roman Senate then concluded friendly alliances with the remaining members of the Latin League. By means of treaties and victories in battle, the Romans soon established hegemony throughout central Italy. The Latin League was dissolved, and a new confederation created in which each member was bound by an alliance to Rome.

In dealing with their former allies of the Latin League and other conquered city-states, the Romans created alliances which granted varying degrees of privileges. City-states which had close ties to Rome and had accepted

Rome's domination were granted full Roman citizenship and privileges. Their citizens could vote in Rome's public assemblies and even run for public office in Rome. A second type of alliance governed city-states who were not considered ready to share the responsibilities of Roman citizenship. City-states of this second class were allowed to keep their own independent governments and public assemblies, but were overseen by a Roman praetor, or governor, who encouraged them to follow Roman law and to worship Roman gods. A third class of city-states included those located in outlying areas of Rome's territory. These city-states agreed to defend the borders of Rome's territory against attack by foreign invaders or hostile tribes, and in return were promised Roman aid in the event of such an attack.

The confederation of city-states that Rome created through its alliances was quite different from those that the Greek states had formed. The members of the new Roman confederation were bound only to Rome through alliances; not to each other. Thus, the members could not easily form a coalition against Rome, and Rome was able to arbitrate disputes that arose among the members. The general condition of peace enforced by Roman governors and Roman legions was one of the most important benefits gained by the members of the confederation. Secondly, by holding out the promise of Roman citizenship and by granting trading privileges, the Romans gained the goodwill and cooperation of most of their allies. City-states who were granted Roman citizenship were eligible to share in any spoils that Rome gained through its conquests, and all benefited from the roads that the Romans built to facilitate trade throughout central Italy. Finally, in contrast to the policy of Athens toward members of the Delian League, the Romans did not demand tribute payments to maintain its army. Instead, the troops levied from member city-states were maintained by Roman taxpayers. By 340 B.C., Rome was the recognized leader of central Italy.

REVISION OF THE CONSTITUTION

In the decades following the Gallic invasion of 390 B.C., the Romans faced a severe economic crisis. The greatest losses were suffered by the plebeians, especially those who owned small farms in the countryside surrounding Rome. In order to finance the rebuilding of their farms, many of these small landholders became deeply indebted to wealthy patricians. Under the laws of the 12 Tablets, debtors were subject to imprisonment or even slavery if they failed to pay back their creditors. Thus a situation arose in which the men who had formed the bulk of Rome's army during the Gallic invasion were forced, by economic conditions, into a position of dependence or even slavery.

In the political struggle that followed, the plebeians pressed for both economic and political reforms, and were eventually accommodated. In 357 B.C., indebted farmers were given some relief by a new regulation that limited the amount of interest a creditor could charge. In addition, small landholders were given the right to colonize territory that Rome had conquered in Italy. These colonies eventually enabled many farmers to free themselves from debt, and at the same time established a Roman presence throughout the conquered areas.

The wealthy plebeians of Rome were more interested in political representation than in economic measures, and they, too, won important concessions. In 367, after a 10-year political struggle, they succeeded in breaking the patrician monopoly of high offices with the enactment of the Licinian law. This law stipulated that one of the two consuls must be a plebeian, and a plebeian was elected as consul the following year.

During Rome's wars against the Samnites (see below), the plebeians demanded and gained additional concessions from the patricians. In 306, a law was enacted which prohibited the imprisonment or enslavement of debtors. And in 287, the Hortensian law made plebescites of the Concilium Plebis binding upon all Romans. This latter law was of great importance, for it meant that Rome at last had a unified government in place of the "state within a state" that had existed since the founding of the Concilium Plebis.

EXPANSION TO THE SOUTH

As Rome expanded its influence in central Italy, it developed several friendly alliances with the Greek city-states of Magna Graecia. Through these alliances, Rome was drawn into a long series of wars against the Samnites, a fierce, well-armed people who inhabited the foothills of the Apennines. The Roman army suffered several devastating defeats at the hands of these tribes, but finally won a decisive victory over them in 306 B.C. A few years after this victory, the Samnites regrouped and united with the Etruscans and Gauls in a final attempt to check the growing power of Rome. The Romans defeated this coalition in 295, and were then recognized as the dominant power in Italy.

THE PYRRHIC WARS

In 281 B.C., Rome became involved in a dispute with Tarentum, the most powerful of the Greek colonies on the southern coast of Italy. The people of Tarentum apparently resented the influence that the Romans wielded in Magna Graecia, and provoked a fight with Rome over the issue of harbor rights. A military force from Tarentum attacked and sank several Roman ships docked in their harbor, and the Tarentines then insulted the Roman ambassador when he arrived to make inquiries. Knowing that the Romans would soon respond to these unprovoked attacks, the people of Tarentum appealed to Pyrrhus, the ruler of Epirus, for military aid.

Pyrrhus, the king of Epirus in Greece, hoped to build an empire by conquering Rome. In their wars with Pyrrhus, the Romans learned how to cope with such tactical elements as charging elephants and the Macedonian phalanx.

Pyrrhus, the ambitious king of Epirus, came to the aid of Tarentum with a force of 25,000 soldiers and 20 elephants. He met the Roman legions at Heraclea. Using the phalanx tactics of Alexander the Great, Pyrrhus managed to defeat the Romans. His victory was so costly, however, that the phrase "Pyrrhic victory" came to mean a victory that is offset by staggering losses. Pyrrhus then moved north, hoping to gain the support of Italian city-states subject to Rome. These cities, however, remained loyal to Rome, and the Roman Senate refused to negotiate peace terms as long as Pyrrhus remained in Italy.

Roman legions again met Pyrrhus' forces in battle at Asculum in 279. Again, Pyrrhus narrowly won victory but left Italy soon afterwards to fight the Carthaginians in Sicily. In 275 Pyrrhus returned, hoping to conquer all of Italy in a final battle with the Romans. The Romans, however, defeated Pyrrhus in this battle. Rome then incorporated many of the cities of Magna Graecia into its confederation through a new series of alliances.

When Pyrrhus left Italy to return to his home in Epirus, he is said to have remarked, "How fair a battlefield I am leaving to the Romans and Carthaginians!" His remark proved to be prophetic. By 265 B.C., Rome was the recognized leader of Italy, and was soon to be drawn into a prolonged war with Carthage, the other great military power of the Mediterranean world.

THE PUNIC WARS It was inevitable that Rome's conquest of southern Italy should bring her into conflict with Carthage, a city founded by the Phoenicians during the 9th century B.C. While Phoenicia itself was successively conquered by Assyria, Egypt, and Persia during the following centuries, Carthage became the center of a rich and powerful maritime empire.

Prior to the Pyrrhic wars, Rome had remained an agricultural society and had not been involved in trade and commerce with the rest of the Mediterranean world. However, Mediterranean trade was of vital concern to the city-states of Magna Graecia who had been incorporated into Rome's confederation after the withdrawal of Pyrrhus. Thus, to maintain its position as the leader of Italy, Rome had to become involved in the ancient struggle between Carthage and the Greek colonies for control of the Mediterranean.

The immediate cause of the conflict between Carthage and Rome was the interest of each in controlling trade with Sicily. In 288 B.C., the Mamertines, a group of Italian mercenary soldiers, had seized the town of Messina in Sicily and established a base for piracy there. In 265 B.C., Hiero II, the king of Syracuse, tried to evict the Mamertines from Sicily. Both Carthage and Rome sent troops to assist the Mamertines, but these two great powers were soon fighting each other. The series of wars that followed came to be known as the Punic Wars from the Latin word *Punicus*, meaning "Phoenician." The Punic Wars lasted for more than a century, and were bitterly fought throughout the western Mediterranean; in Sicily, Italy, Spain, and Africa.

FIRST PUNIC WAR (264-241 B.C.)

In 262 B.C., the Romans captured Agrigentum, but could not take the Carthaginian fortresses on the west side of Sicily, for these strongholds were constantly supplied by the Carthaginian fleet. Realizing that they would have to achieve mastery of the seas in order to defeat Carthage, the Romans captured a Carthaginian ship and used it as a model to build their own fleet of 120 ships. In 260 B.C., the Roman fleet won its first victory over a Carthaginian fleet near Mylae, on the northern coast of Sicily. Following this victory, the Romans seized the island of Corsica, but they still could not manage to expel the Carthaginians from Sicily.

In 256 B.C., the sphere of war shifted to Africa, where the Romans managed to establish a base at Clypea. The next year, however, the Carthaginians turned over the command of their army to a capable Spartan general named Xanthippus. Xanthippus defeated the Roman armies in Africa and forced them to return to Italy.

The Romans next renewed their attacks upon Sicily and achieved some successes there. In 250, the Romans lured a Carthaginian army into battle near the city of Panormus. After capturing Panormus, the Romans besieged the Carthaginian stronghold of Lilybaeum both by land and by sea. This battle ended in a stalemate, for the Romans lost their entire fleet in a storm, while the Carthaginians had to withdraw many of their troops in order to deal with an uprising in Africa.

During the next few years, private Roman citizens made great sacrifices in order to finance and build a new fleet of 200 ships. But due to the brilliant leadership of the Carthaginian general Hamilcar Barca, who had taken charge of operations in Sicily, Roman military forces still could not manage to dislodge the Carthaginians from their strongholds there. Nevertheless, the Roman fleet won a major naval victory over the Carthaginians near the coast of Africa, and in 241 Carthage finally sued for peace. Under the terms of the treaty, Carthage agreed to leave Sicily and the surrounding small islands and to pay an indemnity of 3200 talents.

Although Rome gained control of Sicily, the first Punic War was in fact a "Pyrrhic victory." The cost of the war to Rome is estimated to have been seven times the amount of the indemnity that the Carthaginians paid. And the cost in human life was enormous: the Romans lost about 30,000 of their own citizens as well as 20,000 allied soldiers.

Sicily. In dealing with their new domain of Sicily, the Romans adopted a different policy than the one they had used after earlier conquests. Because the city-states of Sicily did not have a direct interest in Rome's military activities, they were not required to supply troops to Rome. Instead, the farmers of Sicily were asked to pay an annual *tithe,* or 10 percent of their annual harvest, to Rome. A Roman praetor was sent to Sicily to supervise the collection of this tax and to administer the judicial system of the island. Because the Sicilians had been accustomed to paying tribute to Carthage, they made no objection to this system. In this way, Rome established a new type of provincial government; one that would later be utilized to govern vast areas of conquered territory.

SECOND PUNIC WAR (218-201 B.C.)

After the conclusion of the first Punic War, Hamilcar Barca devoted himself to developing and enlarging Carthage's empire in Spain. After his death in 228, his son Hannibal and son-in-law Hasdrubal continued his work. The Romans became concerned about this increasingly powerful Spanish empire, and encouraged the town of Saguntum to resist the Carthaginians. Hannibal complained to Rome about this interference in his affairs, but received no reply. He captured and destroyed Saguntum. After this episode, Rome decided that it had no choice but to declare war on Carthage.

When the second Punic War began, the strategy of the Romans was to hold Hannibal in Spain with their fleet of warships and at the same time mount an attack against Carthage itself. But Hannibal had his own plan for the war. Since he was blockaded by sea, he decided to advance by land into Italy itself. He marched across the Pyrenees Mountains into Gaul with a force of 40,000 soldiers, 37 elephants, and 8000 horses. Five months later, he reached the Alps. The steep descent of the Alps on the Italian side meant dreadful suffering for both men and animals. Livy wrote:

• • • *Then came a terrible struggle on the slippery surface, for it afforded them no foothold, while the downward slope made their feet the more quickly slide from under them; so that whether they tried to pull themselves up with their hands, or used their knees, these supports themselves would slip, and down they would come again! Neither were there any stems or roots about, by which a man could pull himself up with foot or hand—only smooth ice and thawing snow, on which they were continually rolling.*[3]

The difficult terrain and hostile Alpine tribes took a great toll on Hannibal's army; only one-half of his men and a few elephants survived the trip. Nevertheless, Hannibal easily won his first major battle with the Romans, which took place in 218 near the town

[4]Livy XXI, 36.

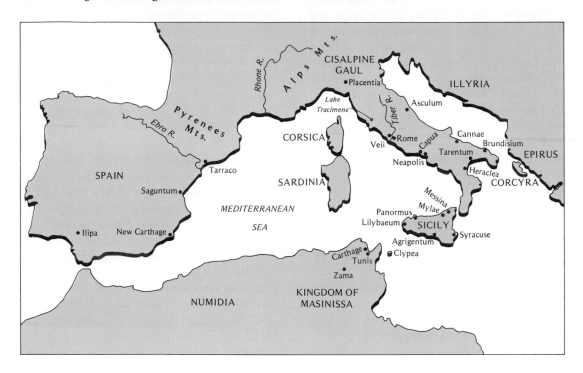

of Placentia in northern Italy. In this battle, Hannibal's superior tactics and well-trained cavalry troops were largely responsible for his overwhelming victory, in which two-thirds of the Roman force was destroyed.

After their defeat in northern Italy, the Romans elected to concentrate upon the defense of central Italy. Two Roman armies, under the commands of the consuls Flaminius and Servilius, took the field to guard the main routes that Hannibal might take to cross the Apennines in the spring. Their plan was to intercept Hannibal close to his point of entry, then unite their armies to fight him. But in May of 217, Hannibal crossed the Apennines and lured Flaminius into following him to Lake Trasimene. There, Hannibal's troops, who had stationed themselves in the hills surrounding the lake, ambushed and killed the consul and two of his legions. Shortly after this disaster, Hannibal's cavalry encountered and defeated Servilius' advance troops.

The way to Rome now seemed to be open to Hannibal, but before attacking this well-fortified city, he counted on enlisting the support of the Etruscan city-states along the route. Surprisingly, not a single one of these cities opened its gates to him.

In Rome, the *Comitia Centuriata* responded to the emergency by electing a dictator to lead the army against Hannibal. Their choice was Q. Fabius Maximus, a cautious and experienced general. During the next year, Fabius followed a policy of avoiding open battle with Hannibal, using his troops instead to harass the Carthaginians and prevent them from establishing a permanent camp. Although Fabius' delaying tactics successfully avoided any new military disasters, the Roman people became impatient with the situation. When the dictator's term of office expired in 216, they elected in his place two aggressive consuls, Paullus and Varro.

Battle of Cannae. Knowing that the newly elected Roman consuls were eager to give battle, Hannibal carefully chose an advantageous site. He camped near the Roman post at Cannae, in a large, level field where his cavalry troops would be able to maneuver easily. The Roman army led by Paullus and Varro soon arrived.

The Roman army of about 50,000 men far outnumbered Hannibal's army, but Hannibal found a way to turn the Romans' superior strength against them. Before the battle, Hannibal, like the Roman commanders, posted his infantry troops in the center ranks and his cavalry in the wings. But he formed his troops in a crescent rather than a straight line. He then allowed the strong Roman infantry to push back his center ranks, while his cavalry troops engaged the Roman cavalry in the wings. Then, just as the Roman infantry was about to break through his center, Hannibal directed his cavalry troops to turn back and surround the Romans' center and rear. In this way, the Roman advantage in numbers became a liability: massed together and unable to move, the Roman legions were completely encircled by Hannibal's army. The result was an overwhelming defeat: the Romans lost about 25,000 troops, while Hannibal lost only 5700.

The defeat at Cannae was the most devastating that the Romans had ever suffered, and a great effort of will was required even to continue the struggle. The various classes of Rome united as they never had before to contribute to the war effort. Incredibly, they not only managed to raise new forces to defend Italy, but also sent armies to attack the Carthaginians in Spain, Sardinia, Sicily, Africa, and Greece. Although Hannibal continued to make inroads in Italy and established a strong base in the south, the task of meeting the Romans on additional fronts throughout the Mediterranean world prevented him from gathering the strength he needed to besiege the city of Rome.

Spain. Two capable Roman generals, the brothers Publius and Gnaeus Scipio, won the Senate's permission to take a small army and navy to Spain in 218. Because Carthage controlled important bases and valuable silver mines in Spain, the Scipios believed that their attacks would divert Carthaginian troops from the war in Italy.

Soon after his arrival in Spain, Gnaeus captured the important base of Tarraco. He then led his army and navy to the mouth of the Ebro River, where he defeated a much larger Carthaginian fleet. As a result of this battle, the Romans not only gained control of the river, but also asserted Rome's mastery of the sea. This victory provided an important morale boost to Rome and its allies, and helped to offset the loss at Cannae.

In 212, Publius Scipio captured Saguntum, forcing the Carthaginians to divert troops to Spain which had been intended for Hannibal in Italy. But in 211, the reinforced Carthaginian army defeated both Roman armies in Spain. Although the Scipio brothers were killed and their small armies destroyed, they had achieved several important objectives: they had carried the war into the enemy's territory, diverting Carthaginian resources from Hannibal; they had won some allies for Rome north of the Ebro; and they had destroyed Carthage's ability to challenge Rome's navy.

In 210, the Roman Senate yielded to popular demand and placed Publius Scipio's son, also named Publius, in command of a second expedition to Spain. After several years of hard fighting, young Scipio managed to complete the work that his father and uncle had begun. He conquered the important base of New Carthage, and then won an overwhelming victory over the Carthaginians at Ilipa. In 206, Scipio drove the Carthaginians out of Spain entirely.

Sardinia and Sicily. As the agricultural

lands of Italy were destroyed by Hannibal's army, the Romans and their allies increasingly depended upon imports of food from Sicily and Sardinia. Realizing this dependence, the Carthaginians attempted to seize Sardinia in 215. They failed in this effort, but another crisis soon arose in Sicily, the other major supplier of grain to Italy.

In 215, King Hiero II of Syracuse died, and his successors broke the alliance that Hiero had made with Rome. Revolt against Rome then spread to other towns in Sicily, and the Carthaginians gained control of the southern coast of the island. A Roman army and fleet were sent to besiege Syracuse, but for two years they were defeated by the ingenious war machines devised by the mathematician Archimedes (see Chapter 8). Finally, in 212, the Roman general Marcellus succeeded in taking the town. After another year of fighting, the Romans regained all of Sicily.

Greece. The action in Greece did not have a major impact on the outcome of the second Punic War, but it eventually involved Rome in the intricate politics of the Greek peninsula.

After the battle of Cannae, Philip V, the king of Macedonia, allied himself with the Carthaginians. In making this alliance, Philip hoped that Hannibal would help him to seize Illyria and Corcyra, where Rome had recently established bases. Philip attacked Illyria in 214, expecting that he would soon be aided by a Carthaginian fleet. The Carthaginians never appeared, however, and the Roman praetor Laevinus was able to force Philip's departure from the area.

Although Laevinus had successfully dealt with the first emergency, he feared that the Carthaginians might yet come to Philip's aid. He then devised an ingenious solution to the problem: an alliance was arranged between Rome and the Aetolians, stipulating that Rome would enforce the Aetolians' rights over any territory they seized from Philip. Through this alliance, Laevinus managed to enroll the Greeks in the fight against Philip, and conserved the resources that Rome desperately needed to fight Hannibal.

Philip continued to threaten Rome's bases in the eastern Adriatic, but he never received the support of the Carthaginians. In 206, the Aetolians concluded a peace treaty with Philip, for they had not received enough help from Rome to prevent his attacks upon their territory. The next year, Rome, too, made peace with Philip in order to prevent any further distractions in the Aegean area.

Africa. After his successful exploit in Spain, Publius Scipio tried to convince the Senate to let him take the war to Carthage. Although Scipio was recognized as Rome's most capable general, the senators were at first reluctant to send an army to Africa while Hannibal was still in Italy. Finally, however, they yielded to Scipio's enthusiasm. Scipio recruited and trained an army in Sicily and departed for Africa in 204.

Soon after his arrival, Scipio achieved several great victories in Africa. When he captured Tunis, only 15 miles away from Carthage, the Carthaginians began to discuss peace terms and, at the same time, recalled Hannibal to Africa. The conditions of peace could not be resolved, and in 202, Scipio met Hannibal's army at Zama, about 50 miles south of Carthage. The two armies were about equal in strength, each with about 35,000 men, but Scipio had a stronger cavalry division.

From the details that are known of the battle between the two great strategists, Scipio apparently intended to use the enveloping techniques that Hannibal had demonstrated at Cannae. During the battle, however, one of Hannibal's lines remained stationary, and Scipio realized that his plan would not succeed. He then took the unusual step of stopping the battle in midcourse, allowing each commander to regroup his troops. During this interval, Scipio's cavalry troops, who had pursued enemy troops off the field, were given time to rejoin the battle. In the end, Scipio managed to destroy Hannibal's army, while Hannibal himself escaped.

Terms of Peace. The peace treaty that ended the second Punic War allowed the Carthaginians to keep their original territory in Africa, but forbade them from waging any war without Rome's permission. Spain was ceded to Rome, and the Carthaginians also agreed to pay an indemnity of 10,000 talents. Thus, Carthage's term as ruler of a great Mediterranean empire was put to an end, and Rome assumed the responsibility of governing its former possessions.

THIRD PUNIC WAR (149-146 B.C.)

In the years following the second Punic War, Carthage quickly recovered from the devastations it had suffered. Under the able leadership of Hannibal, the Carthaginians enacted measures to help their poorest citizens, revived their agriculture, and developed a thriving international trade. Hannibal's efforts in these areas made him enemies both at home and abroad. His success in creating a more equitable political system inspired the wrath of the powerful oligarchs of Carthage, while the prosperity of Carthage's economy aroused the jealousy of Roman merchants.

In 195, the anti-Carthaginian faction in Rome combined with the oligarchs of Carthage to demand Hannibal's surrender. Hannibal fled to Syria, where he became an adviser to the Seleucid king, Antiochus III. Rome continued to pursue him, and in 183 he took his own life rather than surrender to the Roman delegates sent to extradite him. The Greek historian Polybius paid this tribute to Hannibal's career:

● ● ● *Who can help admiring this man's skillful generalship, his courage, his ability, if he will consider the span of time during which he displayed these qualities? . . . For sixteen years on end he maintained the war with Rome in Italy without once releasing his army from service in the field; he kept vast numbers under control like a good pilot, without any sign of dissatisfaction towards himself or friction amongst themselves. And the troops under his command, so far from being of the same tribe, were of many diverse races who had neither laws nor customs nor language in common.*[4]

Even after Hannibal's death, the anti-Carthaginian party within Rome continued to press the Senate to take additional action against Carthage. One of the most notable leaders of this faction was Cato the Censor, who concluded every speech he made in the Senate—no matter what the subject of the speech happened to be—with the phrase *Carthago delenda est.* ("Carthage must be destroyed.") Scipio, who had become known as Scipio Africanus after his victory over Hannibal, was one of those who argued that Rome should not take any further reprisals against Carthage.

For 50 years, the Carthaginians carefully obeyed every provision of the treaty they had made with Rome, careful to offer no pretext for their enemies to seize upon. Finally, however, a longstanding territorial dispute between Carthage and Masinissa, the ruler of a large Numidian kingdom, gave Cato and his followers the excuse they needed to declare war against Carthage.

As a young man, Masinissa had provided valuable military aid to Scipio Africanus in the battle at Zama. As a result, the Roman Senate overlooked his repeated aggressions against Carthaginian territory in the decades following the second Punic War. Finally, the Carthaginians became exasperated with the situation and declared war on Masinissa. Because this action was a direct violation of the treaty with Rome, Cato and his followers had the pretext they needed to intervene. In 150,

---

[5]Polybius (trans. Moses Hadas), XI, 19.

a Roman delegation traveled to Carthage and demanded that the Carthaginians surrender all of their arms as well as 30 hostages to them. The Carthaginians complied, only to be told that they must evacuate their city. Realizing that the Romans intended to destroy their city, the Carthaginians then shut themselves within the city walls and began to manufacture weapons with the materials at hand.

The Romans' first efforts to storm the city of Carthage were unsuccessful. In 146, however, the grandson of Scipio Africanus—who became known as Africanus Minor—came to Carthage and set up an effective blockade of the city. When the starving Carthaginians had surrendered, the Romans burned the city to the ground and plowed salt into the soil. Reportedly, Scipio wept as he viewed the burning city, and recited Homer's lines concerning the end of Troy. In fact, the episode marked a new era in Rome's history. To those who had taken pride in Rome's early policy of fairness towards its defeated enemies, the destruction of Carthage was a shameful event. But to others, who foresaw the benefits that Rome could derive from the downfall of Carthage, it signified a new beginning.

EXPANSION TO THE EAST As we have seen, the Romans did not set out to conquer the world, but gained a Mediterranean empire as the result of a series of defensive wars against Pyrrhus and Hannibal. This pattern of unplanned expansion was to continue. In the years following the second Punic War, Rome was called upon to mediate disputes within the Greek world and to check the growing power of Antiochus III in Syria. As a result of these interventions, Rome acquired the responsibility of administering vast territories in the East.

GREECE AND MACEDONIA
In 205, Rome concluded its first war with Philip of Macedonia and withdrew its troops from Greece. But three years later, Greek independence was again threatened when Philip invaded Samos, the Cyclades Islands, and Attica. Athens and Rhodes then appealed to the Romans for aid against the Macedonians. Although Roman law prohibited the Senate from declaring war except in defense or on behalf of a close ally, the majority of senators decided that Philip's recent alliance with Antiochus of Syria made him a real danger to Rome. Thus, the Roman people were drawn into a new foreign conflict only four years after the second Punic War had ended.

The Romans declared war on Philip in 200. During the next four years, the Roman army and navy forced Philip to retreat from nearly all of the territory he had conquered in Greece. In 196, after suffering a major defeat, Philip· signed a peace treaty with T. Quinctius Flamininus, the Roman commander who had defeated him. In the treaty, the Romans announced that they intended to restore the full independence of Greece, and would soon withdraw all of their troops from the peninsula. Philip agreed to renounce his claim to the territories he had conquered in Greece and Asia, but was allowed to keep his Macedonian kingdom. The generous terms of Flamininus' treaty outraged the Aetolians, who wanted to invade Macedonia. But the agreement provided several important advantages to Rome. By leaving Philip with enough resources to defend Macedonia, Rome ensured that this strategic region would continue to be an effective buffer zone rather than the object of further conquests by Antiochus or the Gauls. In addition, the lenient terms of peace secured for Rome the friendship of Philip, which would prevent him from aiding Antiochus. In 194, the Roman Senate kept its promise and withdrew all Roman legions from Greece.

ASIA MINOR
As Roman armies were fighting Philip in Greece and Macedonia, Antiochus was completing a wide circle of conquest in Asia Mi-

nor. After following the trail that Alexander the Great had taken to India, Antiochus traveled up the Mediterranean coast, conquering the Ionian Greek city-states along his route. In 196, as Rome was concluding its peace treaty with Philip, Antiochus invaded Thrace. He then proposed an alliance with Rome, suggesting that if Rome accepted the status quo, he would not intervene any further in the affairs of the Mediterranean world. But because Antiochus was giving sanctuary to Hannibal, the Roman Senate refused to consider such an alliance. Antiochus proceeded to conquer Thessaly and central Greece, and in 192 the Senate declared war.

The Romans met Antiochus near Thermopylae in central Greece, at the same site where Leonidas and his Spartan army had fought the Persians three centuries earlier (Chapter 6). There, the Romans defeated Antiochus' army and forced him to leave Greece. The Senate then resolved that Antiochus must be pursued to his home territory, for otherwise he might gather another army and conquer Greece again. Accordingly, a Roman army passed through Philip's kingdom and entered Asia in 189. Antiochus gathered an army of 70,000 troops, about two times the strength of the invading Roman army, and met the Romans in Magnesia. In spite of his overwhelming advantage in numbers, Antiochus was defeated and forced to surrender.

Under the terms of the peace treaty negotiated with Rome, Antiochus surrendered all of his conquests and agreed to remain in Syria. Much of the territory he had controlled was given to Rhodes and Pergamum.

ROME'S POLICY IN THE EAST

After its victories in Greece and Asia, Rome did not annex the territories it had conquered, but withdrew its legions as soon as peace had been established. Within a few years, however, Roman policy began to change. Partly in response to continuing disturbances in these areas, Rome began to exert a stern, direct rule in both areas.

Macedonia. When Philip's son Perseus took up arms against Rome and was defeated, the Romans deposed him and divided Macedonia into four independent republics. But many Macedonians longed for the return of their traditional form of government, and by 148 a movement to reinstitute a monarchy had gained momentum. In response, Roman legions landed in Macedonia and quickly defeated the would-be king and his army. Macedonia, Illyria, and Epirus were then declared to be Roman provinces, and a praetor was sent to govern them.

Greece. Even after Rome became the informal protector of Greece, the Achaean League in Greece continued to pursue an aggressive foreign policy for several decades. Among other activities, the league fomented a bitter war against Sparta, and physically attacked Roman senators who had been sent to mediate the dispute. In 146, the same year that Carthage was burned to the ground, the Romans responded to these provocations by dissolving the Achaean League. Then they destroyed Corinth, its leading city. This action demonstrated that Rome was resolved to establish order in Greece at any cost, and marked the end of Greek independence.

Asia. Following the defeat of Antiochus in 189, the Seleucids regained much of their former power and prosperity. Dynastic disputes in Egypt emboldened the Seleucid king Antiochus IV to seize Egyptian territory in Syria-Palestine, and in 168 he invaded Egypt itself. The Roman Senate then sent an ambassador to him, demanding that he immediately evacuate his troops from Egypt and Cyprus. When Antiochus asked for time to consider the request, the ambassador drew a circle around him in the sand and told him that he must give his answer before he stepped out of it. Antiochus then complied with the Senate's request and returned to Syria. Within a few years, the power of the Seleucids was so weakened by their struggle with Egypt and by internal disorders that they no longer presented any cause of concern to Rome.

SUMMARY

Between 750 and 150 B.C., Rome developed from a small village to the capital of an empire. At first, Rome was controlled by a small group of patrician families who claimed a sacred right to govern the city. Eventually, however, military necessity and other factors led to the participation of the plebeians in all aspects of government.

At the same time as Rome's political institutions were being formed, the city was also developing a coherent policy to deal with its neighbors in Italy. Rome's comparatively stable government, respected judicial system, and wise alliances eventually made the city the acknowledged leader of the peninsula.

Beginning in 264 B.C., Rome fought a long series of wars with Carthage. At the end of the Punic Wars, the character of Roman civilization began to change. When Rome inherited Carthage's Mediterranean empire and became the protector of Greece and Asia Minor, it became necessary to create permanent military and bureaucratic establishments to govern these territories. As a result, the progress toward a democratic form of government in Rome was halted, and power was instead monopolized by a small group of ambitious men. In the next chapter, we will examine the effects of these changes.

QUESTIONS

1 According to Roman tradition, what influence did the Etruscan monarchy have upon the development of the Roman republic?

2 Compare the institutions of the early Roman republic to those of Athens' democracy in the 5th century B.C. Which government was probably more efficient? Which allowed a greater degree of participation to poor people?

3 What changes were made in Rome's laws and institutions in response to the demands of the plebeians? What bargaining power did the plebeians have?

4 Compare Athens' leadership of the Delian League and Rome's leadership of its confederation in Italy. How were Rome's policies toward its allies different from those of Athens? What privileges and benefits did Rome's allies receive?

5 What effect did the Punic Wars have on Rome's development? Debate the question: Would Rome have developed a Mediterranean empire if Scipio had fought Hannibal in Italy rather than mounting an expedition to Africa?

BIBLIOGRAPHY

Which books might discuss the influence of the Etruscans on Rome?

BLOCK, RAYMOND. *Ancient Civilization of the Etruscans.* New York: Cowles Book Co., 1969. *A discussion of the archaeological discoveries that have contributed to our understanding of the Etruscans. Conveys the sense of mystery and excitement involved in efforts to reconstruct their society.*

BRADFORD, ERNLE. *Hannibal.* New York: McGraw-Hill, 1981. *A biography of one of the world's most brilliant military strategists. Explores the flexible tactics that led to his incredible victories, and the diplomatic abilities with which he inspired the loyalty and cooperation of troops from many different cultures.*

The Horizon Book of Ancient Rome. Edited by William Harlan Hale. New York: American Heritage Publishing Co. *Follows the progress of Roman civilization from its beginning to the fall of its last outpost, the city of Constantinople. Includes vivid anecdotes of the outstanding personalities involved; beautifully illustrated.*

10

The End of the Republic

In the four centuries that followed the founding of its republic, Rome developed, as we have seen, from a city-state to the ruler of a large empire. At the same time, the character of Roman society was also transformed. In the first days of the republic, a small group of wealthy patrician families had controlled the economy and government of Rome. But during the 4th and 3rd centuries B.C., the plebeians, who formed the bulk of the Roman Army, won the right to hold public office and to colonize the *ager publicus*, or public lands, that Rome won through its conquests.

In 287, the struggle of the orders seemingly ended with the enactment of the Hortensian law, which made resolutions of the plebeian assembly binding upon all Romans. Surprisingly, however, this measure did not have the predicted result. The masses of poorer citizens did not participate in political decisions, nor did they benefit from the newly conquered territories. Instead, the government again came to be dominated by a small group of powerful men. Although the republic continued in existence for more than a century, its laws and institutions were gradually undermined. Finally, the republic

was replaced by a new form of government which came to be known as the *principate*.

IMPERIAL ROME   Although the constitution of the republic provided a way for its citizens to achieve political and economic equality, the vast majority of plebeians were not able to realize these benefits in the years following the Punic Wars. To a large extent, this failure can be attributed to the changing role of Rome in the Mediterranean world. The development of Rome from city-state to empire had far-reaching consequences in the political and economic affairs of its citizens.

POLITICAL CONSEQUENCES OF THE EMPIRE

During the long years of the Punic Wars, the Senate played the leading role in organizing and directing Rome's military forces. The Senate's success in this endeavor greatly increased its prestige and authority, and demonstrated that it had the qualities necessary to lead the nation in a time of crisis.

As Rome began to consolidate its control over its new empire, the members of the Senate—all of whom were public officials experienced in administration—again took a leading role. The public assemblies did not attempt to challenge the Senate's role in these matters, for most Romans were not interested in the complex problems and day-to-day business of the empire. Thus, by general agreement, the role of administering the Roman Empire fell to the Senate rather than to the public assemblies.

Since public officials received no salary for their service to the state, the administrative offices of the empire tended to be monopolized by a relatively small group of wealthy men. Thus, while the distinctions between patricians and plebeians had been eliminated, new divisions arose within Roman society. Those who served in public office came to be known as the *nobiles* or *Optimates*, and the remainder of Roman citizens, the nonsenatorial class, were known as the *Populares*.

ECONOMIC CONSEQUENCES OF THE EMPIRE

During the second Punic War, small farmers throughout Italy were forced to abandon their homesteads in order to join the fight against Hannibal. After years of service in the army, these men and their families returned home to rebuild their farms. They soon found, however, that their farms would no longer provide a livelihood: due to the new economic conditions that prevailed after the war, small farming had become an impractical venture.

The impoverishment of small landowners throughout Italy had a variety of causes. During the Punic Wars, Sicily and Sardinia had come under the administration of Rome, and continued to pay tribute to the empire in the form of grain after the war ended. The influx of this grain was of benefit to the Roman economy, but also established a market price that small farmers could not match. Moreover, the wars of conquest had brought an abundant supply of slaves to Italy, so that large landowners, by exploiting this free labor, could produce a variety of farm products

much more cheaply than independent farmers. Many small farmers flocked to the cities, but there, too, the easy availability of slave labor made it difficult to find work. As a result, the cities came to be crowded with a large group of unemployed, impoverished people.

THE GRACCHUS BROTHERS Tiberius Gracchus was a grandson of Scipio Africanus, and thus belonged to one of the most prominent *nobiles* families of Rome. As a young man, he distinguished himself during a military campaign in Spain, and earned the gratitude of his fellow soldiers by negotiating a treaty which saved the lives of 20,000 troops. According to the account of his younger brother, it was during his service in the army that he first developed his ideas for agricultural reform.

Traveling through the Italian countryside on his way to Spain, Tiberius noticed that almost no independent farmers remained there—the land was instead being farmed by large gangs of imported slaves. During his service in the army, Tiberius realized that this situation was also having an effect on Rome's military capabilities: the army was desperately short of soldiers, for farmers were no longer eligible to belong to the *Comitia Centuriata* once they had lost their property. Tiberius decided that the solution to this problem was to reinstate the farmers as independent landowners; to help them to again become responsible citizens and soldiers. Instead, Roman officials increasingly overlooked the property qualifications of the *Comitia Centuriata* and began to draft poor citizens into the army. Tiberius spoke about the injustice of this situation:

• • • *The savage beasts in Italy have their particular dens, they have their places of repose and refuge; but the men who bear arms, and expose their lives for the safety of their country . . . [have] no houses or settlements of their own, [and] are constrained to wander from place to place with their wives and children. . . . They fought indeed and were slain, but it was to maintain the luxury and the wealth of other men. They were styled the masters of the world, but had not one foot of ground which they could call their own.*[1]

To achieve his plan of distributing land to the poor, Tiberius intended to rely upon an ancient law that limited the amount of land one family could own to 300 acres. This law had been widely disregarded since its enactment in 367 B.C., so that enforcing the legal limit would bring many thousands of acres of land into the public domain. However, a political problem was caused by the fact that many of the most prominent violators of the law were senators. In fact, the Senate was composed almost exclusively of large landowners, for senators were prohibited from engaging in commercial activities.

Although there were many senators who supported Tiberius' ideas in spite of the personal losses they would suffer, Tiberius decided to present his proposal to the *Concilium Plebis*. In taking this step, he ignored the traditional jurisdiction of the Senate over such matters and alienated many of the senators who had supported him.

In 133 B.C., Tiberius was elected tribune, and soon afterwards presented his reform in the plebeian assembly. But the measure was vetoed by Octavius, a tribune who was acting on behalf of the Senate. Angered by this action, Tiberius persuaded the plebeians to depose Octavius from office and to pass his reform.

After his reform had been enacted, Tiberius formed a commission to administer the new law. The commission received little cooperation at first, but Tiberius soon found a way to obtain the funds he needed from the Senate. When Attalus, the ruler of Pergamum in Asia, bequeathed his kingdom to Rome, Tiberius suggested that some of Attalus'

wealth might be used to help Roman settlers colonize the new lands granted to them. The Senate, fearing that Tiberius might become involved in foreign affairs, then gave the commission the funds it needed to operate.

The next year, Tiberius decided to run for a second consecutive term as tribune. Because no tribune had run for reelection in more than 200 years, Tiberius' action was seen by his enemies as an attempt to establish a tyranny. On the day of the elections, a mob of conservative senators attacked and killed Tiberius and 300 of his followers.

After Tiberius' death, a year of civil disturbances and recriminations followed. The Senate established its own court of inquiry, and executed or banished many Gracchus supporters. The Populares were unable to organize an effective opposition to these repressions. Nevertheless, the land reform that Tiberius had initiated continued to be carried out. And when Tiberius' younger brother, Gaius, came of age, he helped to carry forward the program that his brother had begun.

THE REFORMS OF GAIUS GRACCHUS

Following Tiberius' death, the enactment of his reform continued, and thousands of Romans were given grants of land on which to establish farms. Within a few years, however, the lands under direct Roman control had all been distributed, while there remained a sizable group of poor Roman citizens who had not received allotments. The commission then began to apply the rule of 300 acres to the territories of nearby Italian city-states. The Latins and other allies began to protest the grant of their land to Roman citizens, and one Latin colony even rebelled against Rome. The resentment of the allies toward the land distribution program was to become one of the major problems facing Gaius Gracchus as he continued his brother's work.

Gaius Gracchus was known as one of Rome's greatest orators, and soon demonstrated that he was able to organize the Pop-

---

[1]Plutarch, *Lives*, Modern Library ed., p. 999.

ulares into an effective coalition. In 123 B.C., ten years after the death of his brother, he was elected tribune. Gaius then began to challenge the power of the Senate on several fronts. With the support of the public assemblies, he enacted a law that prevented the Senate from setting up its own court of justice, such as the one that had condemned many of Tiberius' followers. He also promoted the interests of the *equites*, the group of wealthy, nonsenatorial families who made their livelihood through trade rather than by owning land, and had been excluded from public office. In one law enacted by Gaius, the equites were assigned the important function of tax collection in the rich province of Asia. A second law provided for equites to serve on the juries in cases where provincial governors were accused of extortion. Through these measures, Gaius greatly reduced the opportunities for senators to abuse their privileges and enabled many members of the equite class to hold important offices in government.

During his two terms as tribune, Gaius took several important measures to alleviate the lot of the poor. He established two colonies in Italy and one near the site of Carthage to provide new opportunities for Roman citizens. He also set up a system whereby the government would buy large quantities of grain and sell it to poor citizens for slightly less than the market price. This system stabilized the price of grain and prevented profiteers from exploiting the poor, but also had an unexpected result: in later years, many people believed that the government had a responsibility to supply grain doles to the poor, and this issue became central to Roman politics.

During his second term as tribune, Gaius tried to solve some of the problems that the land redistribution program had caused for the Rome's allies in Italy. He proposed that all Latin city-states be granted Roman citizenship, and that other Italians be given the modified rights that Latins had held. This proposal cost Gaius much of his support among the Populares, for most Romans were not willing to share the benefits of colonization with other Italians. In 121 B.C., Gaius lost his office as tribune, and his enemies in the Senate moved to cancel his reforms. The Senate declared a state of martial law, and received the full support of the equites. Gaius and his supporters armed themselves to resist the cancellation of their reforms, but they were overpowered and killed. Soon afterwards, 3000 of Gracchus' supporters were arrested and executed without trial.

The Gracchus brothers had devoted their lives to enacting reforms that they believed would benefit their countrymen. After their deaths, many people considered them to be martyrs, for the motive of their actions had been unselfish, while their murderers had acted solely to protect their own interests. In sanctioning political murders and other unscrupulous actions against the Gracchi, the Senate had disregarded the laws and institutions of the republic and permanently destroyed its own reputation for integrity and patriotism. Although the Senate, by these means, triumphed over the coalitions that had challenged its authority, this gain was shortlived. In the long run, the Gracchi affair was to precipitate the end of the republic.

THE JUGURTHIAN WAR

After the destruction of Carthage in 146 B.C., much of North Africa was incorporated into the Roman Empire. Because the king of Numidia had helped Scipio Africanus to defeat Hannibal, however, the kingdom of Numidia retained some independence and was regarded as a vassal or client of Rome. In 118 B.C., trouble flared in the area when the king of Numidia died and divided his kingdom among his two sons and his nephew, Jugurtha. Despite the desperate appeals of the royal brothers for Roman support, Jugurtha murdered both of them and seized the entire kingdom for himself.

In Rome, rumors soon began to circulate

that Jugurtha had bribed a number of Roman senators, and that this was the reason the Senate had taken no action against him. The public assemblies of Rome demanded that action be taken against Jugurtha, but the Senate continued to delay, even after Jugurtha's troops killed several hundred Italian merchants in Africa. Finally, the plebeian assembly demanded that Jugurtha be summoned to Rome and forced to disclose the names of the senators and other officials that he had bribed. Jugurtha arrived in Rome in 111 B.C., but apparently bribed a tribune to let the matter drop. He then took the opportunity to murder a relative of his in Italy who had been seen as a possible successor. As he left Rome, Jugurtha was said to have remarked, "Everything in Rome is for sale."

There were several reasons—aside from the possible corruption of its members—for the Senate to avoid a war in Numidia. Little could be gained by such a war except to end the nuisance posed by Jugurtha, and Germanic tribes to the north, meanwhile, might take the opportunity to invade Spain or Gaul. The Roman people, however, refused to consider the legitimacy of such reasons. The Senate's behavior during the Gracchi affair had left a legacy of suspicion and mistrust that could not be overcome.

In 109 B.C., the Senate yielded to pressure from the public assemblies and sent one of its members, Q. Caecilius Metellus, to Africa to wage war against Jugurtha. Metellus belonged to an ancient patrician family, and was regarded as an honest, upright man both in the Senate and in the public assemblies. For the next two years, Metellus commanded the Roman armies in Africa, and achieved some successes. He was unable to capture Jugurtha, however, and so it seemed that the Roman army might be mired in the vast deserts of North Africa indefinitely.

GAIUS MARIUS Gaius Marius was known in Rome as a "new man" because he was the first in his family to be counted among the *nobiles*: none of his ancestors had held public office. Marius married into the ancient noble family of the Caesars, and rose to a high position in the army under Metellus. But Metellus refused to advance his career further, and Marius then returned to Rome to seek higher office on his own. In a speech to the Populares, Marius presented himself as a man who represented the ancient Roman virtues, and complained that the patricians of Rome refused to accept him as an equal:

● ● ● *Compare me, the "new man," my fellow citizens, with those proud nobles. . . . They despise me for an upstart, I despise their worthlessness. . . . My own belief is that men are born equal and alike: nobility is achieved by bravery. . . . If they are right to despise me they should despise their ancestors whose nobility began, like mine, with achievement.*[2]

Marius' political techniques met with success. In 107 B.C., the public assemblies cancelled Metellus' command and appointed Marius as consul in his place. To improve his chances of winning the African war, Marius recruited a large army of impoverished Romans, disregarding the rules that allowed only propertied men to be drafted. He and his quaestor, the patrician Cornelius Sulla, then departed for Africa.

In 105 B.C., after two years of fighting, Marius and Sulla captured Jugurtha and brought the war in Africa to an end. But in the same year, Celtic and Germanic tribes invaded southern Gaul and defeated a Roman army of 60,000 men. In the face of this new disaster, the Roman people again turned to Marius for leadership. He was elected consul in 104, and again the next year, and used these two years to reorganize the Roman army. In 102 and 101, Marius led a campaign against the Germans in Gaul and Spain and finally defeated them.

---

[2]Sallust, *Jugurtha* (trans. Moses Hadas), 85.

POLITICAL CHANGES

The career of Gaius Marius established a number of precedents that caused lasting changes in the Roman political system. One of these changes was brought about by the methods he used to establish his career. The fact that Marius successfully appealed to the public assemblies for his appointment as general meant that the traditional control of the Senate over such matters of state was overthrown. Later, such leaders as Pompey and Caesar followed the example that Marius had set: rather than advancing their careers in the customary way, these men appealed to the people to let them defend the state against a particular danger. Once they had successfully completed the stated task, they then had the popular and military support they needed to achieve prominence in political life.

REFORM OF THE ARMY

Many of the reforms that Marius introduced concerned the army. By recruiting soldiers from the nonpropertied classes, Marius created an army of professional soldiers—men who did not have homes or farms of their own to return to. Since these men did not have resources of their own, they expected their commander to reward them for the sacrifices they made. Eventually, it became commonplace for military commanders to recruit their own armies and to provide pensions for the veterans. As a result, the primary loyalty of the army was to its commander rather than to the Senate or the state.

During the two years that he was preparing to fight the Germans, Marius introduced several reforms which permanently altered the organization and tactics of the army. Long before the start of battle, he employed soldiers in construction tasks that would facilitate the movement of the army. In addition, Marius had each soldier carry equipment that was used in such construction, so that the army became less dependent upon its baggage train. (As a result, the army became known as "Marius' mules," but this innovation became a permanent feature of Roman military life.) To improve the tactical capabilities of his legions, Marius divided each one into six *cohorts* of six centuries (600 men) each. The army still depended upon the rigid discipline of the legion, but the cohorts allowed the commander more flexibility. Each legion was given its own silver standard, and each cohort, too, carried a flag to serve as a rallying point in battle.

MARIUS AS STATESMAN

In 101 B.C., Marius returned to Rome and received a magnificent triumphal procession in recognition of his defeat of the barbarians. In 100, he was elected to his sixth term as consul. But while Marius enjoyed the popular support needed for a productive career in political life, he proved to be less successful as a statesman than as a general. Instead of using his prestige and authority to reconcile the different political factions of Rome, Marius wavered between one side and the other. In the end, his failures led to the devastating Social War, so-called because the Latin word for allies is "socii."

The most pressing problem facing the republic in 100 B.C. was the need to award benefits to the Roman and Italian troops who had fought under Marius in Africa and in Gaul. To solve this problem, Marius gave his support to two popular leaders, Saturninus and Glaucia, who proposed measures very similar to those the Gracchi brothers had advocated: cheaper grain, colonization projects, and the granting of citizenship to Italians. As in the Gracchi's day, these reforms aroused much opposition—both from Roman plebeians, who did not want to share benefits with other Italians, and from the Senate. In 99, the Senate declared a state of emergency and demanded that Marius abandon his support of Saturninus and Glaucia. Marius complied, and his former allies were killed by an angry mob.

After his betrayal of Saturninus and Glau-

As a result of Marius' reforms, Roman soldiers were employed in a variety of tasks during military campaigns. In this tableau, Roman soldiers are shown destroying a German camp.

cia, Marius lost the support of many members of the Populares faction, and still was not accepted as an equal by the Optimates. Under these circumstances, he departed for Asia for an extended visit as a private citizen.

THE SOCIAL WAR

The failure of the Romans to recognize the contributions of their Italian allies in the Jugurthian and Germanic wars led to a revolt of the allies in 90 B.C. The Social War was waged in central Italy, where the Samnites and other tribes declared independence from Rome and invited other Italian city-states to join them. During the next two years, Roman armies of as many as 60,000 men, commanded by Marius, Sulla, and other generals, descended upon the rebel city-states. Many thousands of Romans and Italians were

killed before the two sides were finally reconciled in 88. In the end, the Romans extended privileges of citizenship to all of their allies in Italy, including the tribes that had rebelled.

MITHRIDATIC WAR AND CIVIL WARS

While the Romans were occupied with the Social War in Italy, a new threat to the Roman Empire arose in the East. Mithridates, the ruler of Pontus in the Black Sea region, began to incite the peoples of Bithyria, Cappadocia, and Ionia to revolt against Roman rule. In 88, Mithridates invaded Asia Minor, and was hailed as a liberator by many of the Ionian Greek city-states. In order to rid the area of Roman presence, Mithridates devised a drastic and terrible solution: he ordered that all Roman and Italian citizens be massacred on a given day. Accordingly, 80,000 civilians—Roman and Italian businessmen and their families —were overtaken and killed.

The Rival Generals. In Italy, Mithridates' massacre of innocent civilians caused a great public outcry, and the leading generals of Rome contended with each other for the honor of leading troops to the East. Cornelius Sulla, a patrician who had served under Marius in the Jugurthian War and had also led a successful campaign during the Social War, emerged as the leading candidate. He was elected consul in 88, and assigned the command of the Asian province.

While Sulla was away from Rome, gathering troops for the coming campaign, Marius illegally transferred the command of Asia to himself. In response, Sulla took an unexpected and unprecedented action: he brought his army to Rome and occupied the city. Marius escaped to Africa, but Sulla took his revenge upon many of his followers.

After asserting his control over Rome, Sulla departed for Greece to fight Mithridates. In his absence, Marius returned to Rome and occupied the city with an army that had been organized for him by Sulla's enemies. He and his followers brutally murdered the patricians who had supported Sulla, then began to kill indiscriminately:

• • • *In a word, so insatiable a passion for bloodshed seized Marius that, when he had killed most of his enemies and because of excitement could remember no one else he wished to destroy, he passed the word to his soldiers to slay every passer-by, one after another, unless he extended his hand to him. . . . Naturally in the great crowd and confusion . . . many whose deaths he did not in the least desire died needlessly.*[3]

Marius and his ally, the consul Cinna, then outlawed Sulla and his surviving supporters. Their reign of terror was shortlived, however, for Marius died in 86, and Cinna was killed by mutinous soldiers the following year. Meanwhile, Sulla continued his successful campaign against Mithridates.

VICTORY OVER MITHRIDATES

Sulla landed in Greece in 87 B.C., and began to besiege Athens, which had joined Mithridates' revolt. The city fell to the Romans within a year, and Sulla then met the great army of Mithridates at Chaeronea. Although Mithridates commanded a force that was three times as large as that of the Romans, Sulla overcame this advantage and won the battle. The next year, Sulla was able to arrange a truce with Mithridates. Because of his political problems in Rome, he extended relatively easy terms to the king—Mithridates was allowed to retain his kingdom of Pontus, and was assessed only a moderate indemnity. The cities who had supported the revolt, however, were brought under direct Roman rule and forced to pay ruinous taxes.

CIVIL WAR

In 82 B.C., Sulla returned to Italy with his victorious army and quickly overcame the forces that opposed him. He was elected dictator—an office that had not been held for more than a century—and began a systematic program of terror. Hundreds of people identified as his enemies were killed, and their property distributed to the veterans of his army. In the midst of these reprisals, Plutarch reported, a courageous nobleman asked Sulla to publish a list of his enemies before they were murdered. "We do not ask you," he said, "to pardon any whom you have resolved to destroy, but to free from doubt those whom you are pleased to save."[4] In reply, Sulla began to publish daily lists which came to be known as *proscriptions*. Those on the list were immediately killed and their property was seized. Moreover, the descendants

---

[3]Dio Cassio 30, 102.10.

[4]Plutarch, *Lives*, Modern Library ed., p. 569.

of a proscribed person also forfeited their property and civil rights, and anyone who sheltered a proscribed person was condemned to death. Plutarch described the spread of this process throughout Italy:

... Nor did the proscription prevail only at Rome, but throughout all the cities of Italy the effusion of blood was such, that neither sanctuary of the gods, nor hearth of hospitality, nor ancestral home escaped.... Those who perished through public animosity or private enmity were nothing in comparison of the numbers of those who suffered for their riches. Even the murderers began to say, that "his fine house killed this man; a garden that; a third, his hot baths."[5]

GOVERNMENTAL REFORMS OF SULLA

In reforming the institutions of the republic, Sulla's intention was to increase the authority of the Senate and to reduce the role of the public assemblies. Paradoxically, he also acted to prevent others from perpetuating the same abuses that had marked his own career.

In the second year of his dictatorship, Sulla appointed several hundred new senators to replace those that he and Marius had killed. Then, to prevent the public assemblies from enacting legislation of their own, he rescinded the traditional powers of the tribunes. The Senate, rather than the tribunes, became responsible for presenting legislation to the *Concilium Plebis*. Finally, to prevent others from following the example of his career, Sulla decreed that a century-old law concerning the *cursus honorum*, or progression of offices, be respected. Under this system, a young, inexperienced man could not attain high office, for he was required to be elected as quaestor and as praetor before becoming eligible for the consulship. Moreover, the minimum age of a quaestor was 30, and that of a praetor 39. Sulla also decreed that it was a crime, punishable by death, for

[5]Ibid., p. 570.

a commander to lead his troops outside the province to which he was assigned or to declare war without the approval of the Senate.

To the surprise of everyone, Sulla retired voluntarily in 79 B.C., and did not again intervene in public affairs. He died of natural causes a year later.

POMPEY AND CRASSUS

Sulla's work in reforming the institutions of the republic was soon undone, and two of his former lieutenants, Pompey and Crassus, played a prominent part in this process. Like Sulla himself and Marius before him, these two young men rose to the head of government by resolving the military crises that faced the empire.

THE CAREER OF POMPEY

In 78 B.C., civil war again broke out in Rome when Lepidus, a popular leader, was elected consul and began to repeal many of the measures that Sulla had enacted. He reinstituted the sale of cheap grain, which Sulla had cancelled, and proposed that the property of proscribed men be given to their survivors. The next year, Lepidus took control of Gaul and prepared to march upon Rome to enforce his demands for additional reforms. Sulla's followers in Rome chose Pompey to lead an army against Lepidus, even though Pompey met none of the criteria of the *cursus honorum*. Pompey defeated Lepidus within a year, and then forced the surrender of his supporters after a five-year campaign in Spain.

In 73 B.C., Pompey received another chance for military glory when a gladiator named Spartacus organized an army of 70,000 runaway slaves. By the time Pompey returned from Spain, in 72, Spartacus had defeated two Roman armies and had overrun central Italy. Although Crassus was commander-in-chief of the campaign against Spartacus, Pompey was able to capture some retreating slaves and later took much of the credit for suppressing the revolt.

POMPEY AND CRASSUS

In 70 B.C., Pompey and Crassus came to a private agreement that each would help the other to be elected as consul. Crassus was one of the wealthiest men in Rome, had served as praetor, and was qualified by age to run for the office. Pompey, on the other hand, was not qualified either by age or experience for the office. To gain public support for their candidacies, Pompey and Crassus promised to restore the powers of the tribunes, and they fulfilled this promise once they were elected. The support of the tribunes later helped both men to achieve the political prominence they craved, and effectively put an end to the *cursus honorum*.

The Pirates. With the support of the tribunes and the plebeian assembly, Pompey received a special commission to clear the Mediterranean of pirates in 67 B.C.. This task was considered so important to the welfare of Rome that Pompey was given an authority superior to that of any other general. Plutarch explained how the pirates had thrived during the years of civil war in Rome:

● ● ● *Whilst the Romans were embroiled in their civil wars . . . the seas lay waste and unguarded, and by degrees enticed and drew them [the pirates] on not only to seize upon the merchants and ships upon the seas, but also to lay waste the islands and seaport towns. . . . Nor was it merely their being thus formidable that excited indignation; they were even more odious for their ostentation than they were feared for their force. Their ships had gilded masts at their stems; the sails woven of purple, and the oars plated with silver, as if their delight were to glory in their iniquity.*[6]

Pompey cleared the Mediterranean of these audacious pirates in only three months, but his special authority lasted for three years. He then took his armies to the East and

[6]Ibid., p. 755-6.

Pompey first won fame by clearing the Mediterranean of pirates, and later reorganized the eastern provinces of the empire.

achieved several resounding victories there. By 62 B.C., he had defeated Mithridates and created an eastern province which extended from the upper Euphrates River to the Arabian Desert, excluding Parthia and Egypt.

JULIUS CAESAR

Caesar was an Optimate by birth, but like Pompey and Crassus, he achieved political power by appealing to the Populares and by winning the loyalty of an army. From the beginning of his career, Caesar emphasized his support for popular causes by subsidizing public works and entertainments. When he had exhausted his own resources, he borrowed vast sums from Crassus to continue this practice. Plutarch described how his methods succeeded:

• • • When he was made surveyor of the Appian Way, he disbursed, besides the public money, a great sum out of his private purse; and when he was aedile, he provided such a number of gladiators, that he entertained the people with 321 single combats, and by his great liberality and magnificence in theatrical shows, in processions, and public feastings, he threw into the shade all the attempts that had been made before him, and gained so much upon the people, that everyone was eager to find out new offices and new honors for him in return for his munificence.[7]

THE FIRST TRIUMVIRATE

In 60 B.C., Caesar returned to Rome after serving as praetor in Spain. Like Crassus and Pompey, Caesar had not received the cooperation he wanted from the Senate, and the three men decided to form an alliance of their own. This coalition, in which each member pledged to support the ambitions of the others, came to be known as the First Triumvirate, and was cemented by Pompey's marriage to Caesar's daughter, Julia.

In joining the triumvirate, Pompey's goal was to achieve ratification of his political arrangements in the East and land settlements for his veterans; Crassus wanted to command a military campaign in Parthia; and Caesar chose a five-year command in Gaul. To accomplish their ends, the triumvirs engineered the election of Caesar as consul in 59 B.C. As consul, Caesar was so effective in helping his friends—and his co-consul, a man named Bibulus, was so ineffective—that the consulship came to be known as that of "Julius and Caesar."

In 58 B.C., Caesar received a five-year appointment as commander of the armies in Gaul. Within a few years, he had brought a large part of Gaul under Roman rule, an achievement which rivaled the conquests of Pompey. In 55, Caesar met with Crassus and

Julius Caesar in military dress. In addition to his feats as conquerer, administrator, and politician, Caesar became one of the greatest writers of the Latin language.

Pompey in northern Italy to plan the future course of the triumvirate. They agreed that Caesar's command in Gaul would be extended another five years; Crassus would lead a campaign in Parthia; and Pompey would take charge of the armies of Spain and Africa. Within two years, however, the triumvirate collapsed. Crassus' campaign in Parthia ended in disaster, and he himself was killed by the

---

[7]Ibid., p. 857.

Parthians. The death of Julia in 54 dissolved the personal ties between Caesar and Pompey, and their alliance ended soon afterwards.

Cicero. One of the outstanding personalities of the late Roman republic was Marcus Tullius Cicero (106-43 B.C.), a prominent lawyer, orator, and statesman. Like Demosthenes of Athens, Cicero was known as a patriot who tried to uphold the ancient ideals of his country during a period of upheaval

The orator Cicero. At a time when Caesar, Pompey, and Mark Anthony wielded absolute power in Rome, Cicero advocated a return to republican principles.

and transition. But although he was devoted to the republic, he accommodated himself to the reality of the First Triumvirate. At various times, he was allied to Pompey, Crassus, and Caesar, and defended their interests in Rome while they were away on foreign campaigns.

Many of Cicero's letters and speeches have survived, and provide an invaluable portrait of the personalities and events of the late republic. In Cicero's private letters to his friends, for example, he expressed the hatred that he sometimes felt toward Caesar, and recorded the generous terms of friendship that Caesar always extended to him. During the civil war of 49 B.C. (see below), Cicero chose to ally himself with Pompey despite Caesar's pleas that he stay neutral. After Caesar won the war, one of his first acts was to extend a pardon to Cicero.

In 63 B.C., Cicero was elected consul. One of the most famous incidents of his career took place soon afterwards, when Catiline, a nobleman who had lost the election, plotted to seize the government by force. Catiline had attracted several thousand supporters by promising to cancel all private debts, and was gathering an army in Etruria. Cicero, meanwhile, had heard of these developments, but could not convince the Senate that his information was reliable. Then one evening, the conspirators tried and failed to kill Cicero. Soon after, Catiline appeared at the Senate as if nothing had happened, and Cicero—without any documentary evidence to prove his allegations—had to convince the Senate that Catiline had sponsored the assassination attempt.

● ● ● *Review with me then, that night before last; soon you will realize that I am far more keenly on the alert for the safety of the Republic than you are for its ruin. I say that you on that night came to the street of the scythmakers. . . . that in that same place many companions of your mad crime had come together. Do you dare to deny it? Why are you silent? I shall prove it, if you deny it, for I see here in the Senate certain men who were there together with you. O ye immortal gods! Where in the world are we? In what kind of city do we live, what sort of Republic do we have? Here, here in our number, Senators, in this most sacred and most important council in the world, are those who plot the death of us all, who plot the ruin of this city and even of the whole world!*[8]

The Senate declared a state of emergency, and, in a poll of its members, voted to execute five of the ringleaders. (Catiline himself had escaped to Etruria.) Without waiting for a court of law to convene, Cicero then carried out the Senate's decision. Most Romans applauded this illegal action, for they believed that it had averted a civil war. Several years later, however, Cicero's political enemies used the incident against him, and he was exiled from the city.[9]

CIVIL WAR In 50 B.C., as Caesar's second term of command in Gaul was about to end, Pompey began to prepare for a confrontation with his former ally. In an attempt to avert a civil war, the Senate passed a resolution asking both Caesar and Pompey to disarm their legions. Caesar indicated that he would comply, but Pompey refused. Instead, Pompey demanded that Caesar disband his army and return to Rome alone. Knowing that he would be at the mercy of his enemies if he did so, Caesar led his army across the Rubicon River, a small stream that marked the boundary between Cisalpine Gaul and Italy.

---

[8]*Greek and Roman Classics in Translation*, compiled by Charles T. Murphy, Kevin Guinagh, and William Jennings Oates (New York: Longmans, Green and Co., 1947), p. 792.

[9]Cicero remained in exile one year. Then, in 57 B.C., Pompey arranged his triumphant return to Rome.

Pompey's Italian legions were no match for the loyal, disciplined legions that Caesar was bringing back from Gaul, and Pompey withdrew to Greece to organize his campaign. Caesar pursued him there, and in 48 B.C., defeated Pompey's army in Thessaly. Pompey then fled to Egypt, but was assassinated when he arrived in that country.

Caesar spent a year in Egypt, consolidating Roman control over the area, and establishing Cleopatra on the throne in place of her younger brother. When he returned to Rome, in 46, Caesar generously extended a pardon to many of those who had supported Pompey's cause, including Cicero. He was elected dictator for a term of ten years, and celebrated elaborate triumphs for his victories in Gaul and over Pompey's forces in Egypt, Africa, and Pontus. Then he departed for Spain, where Pompey's sons had inspired a major revolt.

Caesar's Reforms. After quelling the revolt in Spain, Caesar spent 18 months in Rome administering the economic and political affairs of the empire. With the advice of Greek astronomers in Alexandria, he introduced a new calendar in which the system of months was reconciled with the solar year. The *Julian* calendar, which has only been slightly modified to the present day, had 365 days per year and an extra day every fourth year. Caesar took measures to reduce the debt obligations of poor citizens, and undertook public works such as the building of a new Forum and of roads throughout Italy. He began to draft legislation that would require high qualifications for Roman magistrates, and standardize the system of tax collection throughout the empire.

The Ides of March. Caesar's control of Rome was so absolute that many people feared he would declare himself a king. There was no solid evidence that Caesar actually intended such a step, but several events gave rise to rumors and speculation. In one of these, Caesar's friend, Mark Antony, playfully

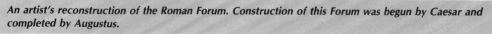

An artist's reconstruction of the Roman Forum. Construction of this Forum was begun by Caesar and completed by Augustus.

placed a crown upon Caesar's head during a public ceremony. Although Caesar brushed the crown aside, it was said he showed no great displeasure.

In reaction to such incidents, a group of 60 conspirators decided that the only way to save the republic was to assassinate Caesar. The leaders of the plot were Cassius, a praetor, and Brutus, an idealistic young man who had been Caesar's friend. Caesar's murder took place on the Ides (15th day) of March in 44 B.C., as Caesar was attending a meeting of the Senate. Plutarch reported that all of the conspirators participated in the murder:

● ● ● *Those who came prepared for the business enclosed him on every side, with their naked daggers in their hands. Which way soever he turned he met with blows, and saw their swords levelled at his face and eyes, and was encompassed like a wild beast in the toils on every side. For it had been agreed they should each of them make a thrust at him. . . . Some say he fought and resisted all the rest, but that when he saw Brutus's sword drawn, he covered his face with his robe and submitted, letting himself fall.*[10]

ANTONY AND OCTAVIAN

After Caesar's death, a struggle for power developed between the two men who had the best claims to be Caesar's heirs: Mark Antony, who had served as consul with Caesar in 44 B.C., and Octavian, Caesar's 18-year-old adopted son. Antony, the older and more experienced commander, assumed control of the city and arranged a public funeral for Caesar. Plutarch reported that, prior to the funeral, the Romans had listened without emotion as Brutus explained his motives and urged them to rejoice in their liberty. During the funeral, however, the crowd suddenly found a voice when it heard the terms of Caesar's will:

[10]Plutarch, *Lives*, Modern Library ed., p. 892-3.

. . . But when Caesar's will was opened, and it was discovered that he had left a considerable legacy to each Roman citizen, and when the people saw his body, all disfigured with wounds, being carried through the Forum, they broke through all bounds of discipline and order. They made a great pile of benches, railings and tables from the Forum, and placing his body upon this, burned it there. Then, carrying blazing brands, they ran to set fire to the houses of the murderers.[11]

Soon afterwards, Octavian, who had gathered together an army of Caesar's veterans, marched into the city and demanded that he be named a consul. Antony began to make plans to oppose him with his own army, but his soldiers refused to fight a civil war against their comrades in Octavian's army. Antony and Octavian, together with Lepidus, a proconsul of Spain, then reached an agreement to share control of Italy and to divide the remainder of the empire between them: Antony would command Gaul; Lepidus the province of Spain; and Octavian the provinces of Sicily and Africa. The eastern provinces of the empire were not included in the agreement, for Brutus and Cassius had seized control of them. In 43 B.C., an election was called, and the Second Triumvirate—as the alliance between the three was called—officially won the authority to reorganize the republic.

The following year, Octavian and Antony led an army of 20 legions to Philippi, in northern Greece, to meet the Republican forces led by Brutus and Cassius. They defeated the Republicans in two battles, and Brutus and Cassius committed suicide: Cassius, it was reported, killed himself with the same sword he had used to kill Caesar. Upon their return to Italy, the Triumvirs proscribed their personal enemies and used the property they seized to pay their armies. Ci-

The profile on this coin is probably one of the most realistic portraits of Octavian, who was to become the emperor Augustus. In most later portraits, his features are idealized.

cero, who had often opposed Antony in the Senate, was among the first to die.

As a gesture of unity, Antony married Octavia, the sister of Octavian, and the two triumvirs then combined forces to defeat Lepidus. The empire was divided into two parts, with Octavian controlling the West, and Antony the East. While Octavian began to consolidate his control over the western provinces, Antony retired to Egypt to pursue his celebrated love affair with the Egyptian queen, Cleopatra. In 37 B.C., he divorced Octavia and married Cleopatra.

Antony's action in divorcing Octavian's sister dissolved the alliance between the two triumvirs, and his long stay in Egypt made it appear that he wished to live as an Egyptian pharaoh rather than as a Roman commander. In 32 B.C., Octavian produced confirmation of the damaging rumors that had been circulating about Antony. Antony's will, which he had deposited with the Vestal Virgins in Rome, bequeathed the eastern provinces of the Roman Empire to Cleopatra and her children. When Octavian read this will to the Senate, Antony's supporters in Rome

[11]Ibid., pp. 893-4.

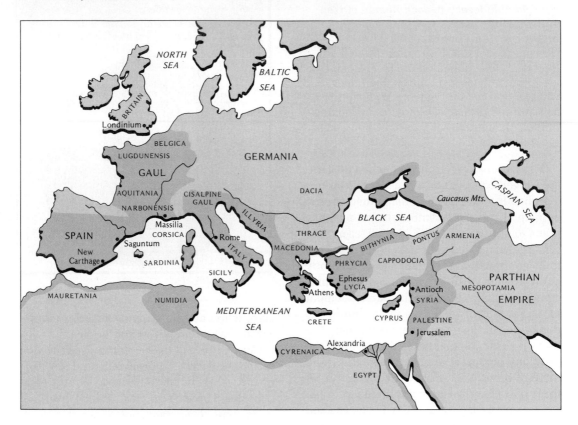

could no longer defend his conduct. There was a great public outcry, and Rome declared war on Cleopatra.

In 31 B.C., Octavian defeated the combined navies of Antony and Cleopatra near Actium, on the coast of western Greece. Antony and Cleopatra then returned to Egypt, and, to avoid being captured by Octavian, committed suicide. Plutarch described how Cleopatra died, shortly after receiving a basket of figs:

... *The messengers came at full speed, and found the guards apprehensive of nothing; but on opening the doors they [her guards] saw her stone-dead, lying upon a bed of gold, set out in all her royal ornaments. . . . Some relate that an asp was brought in amongst the figs and covered with the leaves and that Cleopatra had arranged that it might settle on her before she knew, but when she took away some of the figs and saw it, she said "So here it is," and held out her bare arm to be bitten.*[12]

PAX ROMANA After defeating Antony and Cleopatra, Octavian returned to Rome, where he received a magnificent triumph and was hailed as the savior of the republic. In a public ceremony, he closed the doors of the temple of Janus, an act which symbolized the end of the civil wars and peace between Rome and the rest of the world. Later, the grateful citizens of Italy bestowed upon him the title *Augustus*

[12]Ibid., pp. 1151-2.

("Highest one"), and he has been known by this name ever since.

Mindful of what had happened to Caesar when he assumed imperial powers, Augustus was careful to avoid the appearance of supreme authority. He accepted many of the offices and titles granted to him by the Senate, but was careful to put aside certain high offices after a few years. During his long reign, he served as consul, as tribune, as proconsul of his own provinces, and as censor. In each case, the Senate modified the rules of office so that Augustus would not be subjected to the same restrictions as other public officials. When he served as proconsul, for instance, the Senate made his *imperium*, or authority, superior to that of any other proconsul so that Augustus could, if he wished, intervene in the affairs of other provinces. Similarly, when he served as tribune, he was given precedence over others in his power to convene the Senate. Thus, while the rules and institutions of the republic were carefully preserved, Augustus in practice had unlimited authority to carry out his programs.

ORGANIZATION OF THE EMPIRE

In assigning control of the provinces, Augustus carefully arranged the distribution of power so that neither the Senate nor an ambitious general could challenge his authority. The government of stable, settled provinces was assigned to the Senate, while newer territories—those in which Roman legions were stationed—were controlled by Augustus. This arrangement allowed him to retain command of the armies and to prevent other generals from gaining the loyalty of the troops. In border regions, client kings such as King Herod of Judea were allowed to retain their thrones, but were expected to maintain the peace and prevent hostile tribes from invading Roman territory.

Augustus brought about many needed reforms in the administration of the empire. He established a more uniform system of taxation throughout the provinces, and set up an efficient bureaucracy to carry out various functions of government. The provinces under his control were governed by civil servants—often chosen from the equite

In the monuments he built, Augustus emphasized themes such as peace, religion, and family life rather than military exploits. This detail of his Arc of Peace shows members of the imperial family and Roman priests.

class—who were directly responsible to him. Augustus established defensible frontiers wherever possible, and buffer states—usually controlled by client kings—where there were no defensible frontiers. In his old age, Augustus tried to extend the boundary of the empire beyond the Elbe River in Germany, but in 9 A.D., a large Roman army under the command of his protege, Varus, was annihilated by the Germans in the Teutoburg Forest. After this experience, it was reported that Augustus often awakened at night and cried out, "Varus, Varus, bring me back my legions." As a result, Augustus changed his mind about the need for further expansion, and advised his successor to keep the borders as they were.

SOCIAL REFORMS

In the long term, Augustus believed, the success of the Roman Empire depended upon the image that Roman citizens projected to those they ruled. Augustus advocated a return to the simple, basic virtues that had characterized the earliest Romans. To this end, he forbade the use of ostentatious luxuries, and encouraged Romans to devote themselves instead to their family and religious duties. Childless couples were assessed a special tax as a penalty for not producing children, and Augustus often appeared in public in company with his family to illustrate the joys of parenthood. Religious piety was linked to the development of close family ties and also to the success of the an-

Although Augustus did not claim to be a god in Rome, he encouraged the development of an imperial cult in the provinces. This is his temple at Vienne, near Lyons.

Virgil with two muses. His epic poem the Aenead described the heroic origins of Rome.

cient Romans in building their civilization in Italy. To promote a return to traditional religious values, Augustus built and renovated many temples to the ancient gods, and led the observance of religious festivals. In some provinces, Roman subjects were encouraged to worship Augustus himself, in addition to the established pantheon of Roman gods, as an additional measure to promote respect for Roman government and civilization.

Virgil and Livy. As part of his program to encourage patriotism and reverence for the past, Augustus encouraged writers to record the history of Roman civilization. In 29 B.C., Augustus requested that Virgil, a writer known for his poems about rural life, compose an epic poem describing the rise of Roman civilization. The result was the *Aeneid*, a poem which traced the origins of Rome to the Trojan hero, Aeneas. Although Virgil did not live to finish his epic, it was immediately celebrated as a great work of literature and is still so regarded.

Livy devoted his career to the writing of a prose work which traced the history of Rome from its beginnings to his own time (Chapter 9). Although less than a third of Livy's history survives, it has been an invaluable source of information to later historians, for it drew upon many traditions and sources that can no longer be traced. Like Virgil, Livy hoped that his work would inspire Romans with pride in their origins and demonstrate the role of destiny in their achievements.

THE PRINCIPATE

The government that Augustus established blended the institutions of a monarchy with those of the republic. Because he was given the title of *princeps*, many people refer to his government as the *principate*. By the time Augustus died, in 14 A.D., Rome had achieved a level of peace and prosperity unparalleled in her history. To the Romans, it seemed that a golden age had dawned. Today we call the period of history from the beginning of Augustus' reign (29 B.C.) to the death of Marcus Aurelius in 180 A.D. the *Pax Romana*.

241

SUMMARY

During the span of history we have discussed, the institutions of the Roman Republic were undermined by a series of conflicts between the various factions of Roman society. Instead of trying to solve the underlying social and economic problems of the republic, the Roman Senate attempted to maintain its authority by forcibly suppressing its opponents.

After it sanctioned the murders of the Gracchi brothers and other reformers, the Senate lost much of the prestige and authority that had enabled it to govern. Many people came to regard the Senate as a group of men more concerned with their own interests than with the welfare of the republic, and began to question even its decisions about foreign policy. The public assemblies were not able to organize an effective resistance to the Senate, but they did promote the rise of military commanders who achieved dictatorial powers. The civil wars inspired by rivalries among these commanders brought an end to the republic and paved the way for the modified dictatorship of Augustus.

QUESTIONS

1 What pressing problems faced the republic in 133 B.C.? What specific reforms did the Gracchi brothers propose?

2 To what extent did the reforms of the Gracchi brothers succeed or fail? Why did their actions mark the beginning of the end for the republic?

3 Trace the rise to power of Caesar, Pompey, and Crassus. What common bonds between them led to the formation of the First Triumvirate? Why and when was the triumvirate dissolved?

4 Compare Caesar's treatment of his political enemies to the methods that Marius and Sulla used. Which method would be more likely to prolong a civil war?

5 What major problems faced Octavian when he returned to Rome in 29 B.C. What means did he use to restore order and consolidate control over Rome and its empire?

BIBLIOGRAPHY

Which books might discuss the government established by Augustus?

EARL, DONALD. *The Age of Augustus*. New York: Exeter Books, 1980. *Describes the personality and achievements of the man who established lasting peace and political stability in the Roman world during his long reign as emperor. Outstanding illustrations of the mosaics, architecture, and pottery of the imperial period.*

GRANT, MICHAEL. *The World of Rome*. Cleveland: World Publishing Co., 1968. *A survey of Roman civilization from 133 B.C. to 217 A.D., with emphasis on the commerce, architecture, and military activities of this period. Introduces the writings of Cicero, Tacitus, Seneca, and others, and emphasizes our heritage from ancient Rome.*

HUZAR, ELEANOR GOLTZ. *Mark Antony, a Biography*. University of Minnesota Press, 1978. *Recounts the events of Mark Antony's career, and describes the nature of Roman politics in his time; the alliances, feuds, and ambitions of rival generals. The author concludes that the empire required a dictatorship, but that Antony would have introduced this form of government in a more deliberate, less revolutionary way than did Octavian.*

11

● *While stands the Colosseum, Rome shall stand;*
  When falls the Colosseum, Rome shall fall;
  And when Rome falls — the world.

                                              BYRON

Rome: Pax Romana and Decline

During his long reign, Augustus respected the Senate and the forms of government established under the republic. Nevertheless, he had more authority than any other leader in Rome's history because of his personal prestige and his skillful diplomacy. Thus, while the institutions of the republic remained in place and were outwardly respected, the government had become dependent upon the strong, centralized leadership of the *princeps*.

During Augustus' reign, the division of authority between the *princeps*, the Senate, and the public assemblies became unclear and confused. There was no thought of reestablishing the republic, however. Although Augustus did not openly proclaim a successor, he copied Caesar's policy of private adoption to designate his intended heir. In the course of his 43-year reign, he adopted as his sons six members of his own or his wife's family, training each to assume the responsibility of public office.

The lack of a clear-cut succession policy and the unsuitability of some candidates were to pose serious problems throughout the period of the empire. At the end of each dynasty's rule, civil wars broke out over the question of succession. The support of the army became the critical factor in determining which candidate would prevail, and emperors were often chosen on the basis of the *donativum*, or gift of money, that they offered to the troops.

JULIO-CLAUDIAN EMPERORS

The four emperors who followed Augustus were known as the Julio-Claudian emperors because each was related by blood or marriage to Augustus, who was the grandnephew and adopted son of Caesar.

TIBERIUS (14-37 A.D.)

Tiberius, a step-son of Augustus, had served as general during several successful campaigns in Germany and was highly regarded by the army. He was described as having a reserved, aloof personality, in marked contrast to the easy manner of Augustus. During his first 10 years as emperor, Tiberius closely followed the policies of Augustus and governed wisely. As Tacitus explained:

● ● ● *Public business and the most important private matters were managed by the Senate:*

the leading men were allowed freedom of discussion, and when they stooped to flattery, the emperor himself checked them. . . . The consul and the praetor retained their prestige; inferior magistrates exercised their authority; the laws too, with the single exception of cases of treason, were properly enforced.[1]

Tiberius demonstrated his respect for the Senate in his administrative reforms. He gave the Senate the task of nominating candidates for public office, and even instructed the senators to nominate only one candidate for each office. Thus, the public assemblies, which had played a real role in nominating and electing public officials under Augustus, were left with only the ceremonial task of ratifying the Senate's choices.

In 23 A.D., Drusus, the only son of Tiberius, died suddenly. Tiberius was deeply affected by this event, and grew increasingly suspicious of those around him. In time, he began to conduct treason trials to prosecute those whom he believed were plotting to kill him. Suetonius, a gossipy biographer who lived two centuries later, gave this account:

. . . Not a day, however holy, passed without an execution, he even desecrated New Year's Day. Many of his men victims were accused and punished with their children—some actually by their children—and the relatives forbidden to go into mourning. Special awards were voted to the informers who had denounced them and, in certain circumstances, to the witness too. An informer's word was always believed. Every crime became a capital one, even the utterance of a few careless words.[2]

Suetonius' account, although probably exaggerated, points up a feature of the Roman judicial system that was to cause problems throughout the period of the empire: because there was no public prosecutor,

courts depended upon private citizens for their information about crimes. And, as Suetonius suggests, the court made little effort to investigate the motives of witnesses in cases involving the emperor. Tiberius executed at least 60 people on the basis of witnesses' accounts.

During the last years of his reign, Tiberius entrusted many of his administrative responsibilities to Sejanus, a trusted friend, and he himself retired to the Isle of Capri. In the year 31, Tiberius arranged Sejanus' election to the post of consul. Soon after attaining this high position, Sejanus began to plot to seize the throne for himself. But just as he was about to carry out his plot, Tiberius learned that Sejanus had murdered his son, Drusus, eight years earlier. In a dramatic message to the Senate, Tiberius accused Sejanus of treason. The senators then condemned him, and he was killed in prison.

The events of Tiberius' last years overshadowed his earlier achievements in the minds of his subjects. The common people of Rome disliked him because he managed finances carefully and refused to sponsor lavish gladitorial games. Many senators mistrusted him because of his participation in treason trials. Suetonius wrote the following account of his death:

. . . The first news of his death caused such joy at Rome that people ran about yelling: "To the Tiber with Tiberius!" and others offered prayers to Mother Earth and the Infernal Gods to give him no home below except among the damned.[3]

CALIGULA (37-41)
Tiberius was succeeded by his popular grandnephew, Gaius. As a child, Gaius had been nicknamed *Caligula* (Little Boots) by soldiers who served under his father. He is still best known by this name.

---

[1]Tacitus, *Annals* VI, 6.

[2]Suetonius, *The Twelve Caesars* III, 61.

[3]Ibid., III, 75.

Caligula's rule began with promise: he pardoned political offenders, abolished certain taxes, and put an end to treason trials. Then, shortly after recovering from a serious illness, he suddenly became mentally unbalanced. He began to use the treasury that Tiberius had accumulated to carry out lavish building projects which had little or no practical purpose. More seriously, he abused his powers and insulted public officials: on one occasion he demonstrated his contempt for the elected consuls by breaking their *fasces*. Many stories about his outrageous behavior were circulated. Suetonius reported one of the most famous anecdotes:

● ● ● *To prevent Incitatus, his favorite horse, from being disturbed he always picketed the neighborhood with troops on the day before the races, ordering them to enforce absolute silence. Incitatus owned a marble stable, an ivory stall, purple blankets, and a jewelled collar; also a house, a team of slaves, and furniture—to provide suitable entertainment for guests whom Gaius invited in his name. It is even said that he planned to award Incitatus a consulship.*[4]

When Caligula had exhausted the treasury, he revived the practice of conducting treason trials in order to force wealthy families to give him their money.

In the fourth year of his reign, Caligula was assassinated by members of the Praetorian Guard. While the Senate was pondering the question of succession, some soldiers of the Praetorian Guard discovered Caligula's uncle, Claudius, hiding behind a curtain in the emperor's palace. Claudius, not knowing whether he was to be murdered or made emperor, promised each member of the Guard a *donativum*, or reward, if he became emperor. With the Senate's agreement, Claudius was then proclaimed as Caligula's successor.

---

[4]Ibid., IV, 55.

CLAUDIUS (41-54)

Claudius had several physical handicaps; he walked with a tottering gait, slobbered, and spoke in a manner that was difficult to understand. Probably because of these eccentricities, Augustus and Tiberius had kept him in the background, and had not appointed him to public office. For most of his life, Claudius had occupied himself in writing about Roman history, with special emphasis on the careers of Julius Caesar and Augustus. After his accession, many of his reforms reflected his admiration of these two men.

Claudius proved to be an able and energetic ruler. He respected the Senate and dealt with it on easy terms, but, like Augustus, he served a term as censor so that he could expel senators he believed to be unworthy. Following Caesar's example, he began to finance and construct major public works, including two aqueducts, three new roads, and an improvement of the harbor at Ostia. In the second year of his reign, he personally participated in the conquest of Britain, thus completing a campaign that Caesar had begun in 54 B.C.

One of Claudius' major concerns was the issue of granting Roman citizenship to provincial peoples. He granted full citizenship to several "Romanized" provinces, those which had lived under Roman rule for a long time and had adopted Roman culture and values. He also insisted upon the right of Gallic chieftains to be seated in the Senate. In a speech to the Senate concerning these issues, he remarked that one of the sources of Rome's greatness had been its ability to absorb foreign peoples into its citizen body.

In the second half of his reign, Claudius increasingly fell under the influence of his wives and close associates. Late in his life, he married Caligula's sister, Agrippina, who persuaded him to name her son, Nero, as his successor. Once the succession was established, Agrippina determined to murder Claudius. Tacitus related how this deed was accomplished:

... *The poison was infused into some mushrooms, a favorite delicacy, and its effect not at the instant perceived, from the emperor's lethargic, or intoxicated, condition. . . . Agrippina was thoroughly dismayed. Fearing the worst, and defying the immediate obloquy [bad repute] of the deed, she availed herself of the complicity of the physician. . . . Under pretence of helping the emperor's efforts to vomit, this man, it is supposed, introduced into his throat a feather smeared with some rapid poison; for he knew that the greatest crimes are perilous in their inception, but well rewarded for their consummation.[5]*

Although Claudius' last years were marred by his willingness to promote the selfish interests of his friends and family, the many achievements of his early reign were not forgotten. After his death, the Senate conducted a ceremony of deification, an honor that had not been accorded to an emperor since the death of Augustus.

NERO (54-68)

Agrippina probably expected to act as the power behind the throne, for Nero was only 16 years old when he became emperor. The new emperor, however, turned to other advisers. Under the guidance of his tutor, the philosopher Seneca, Nero administered the empire well during his first few years in office. He prosecuted governors who extorted money from their subjects, forbade gladiatorial fights to the death, and refused to engage in wars except for defense.

In the second year of his reign, Nero became increasingly resentful of his mother's attempts to dominate him, and began to plot her death. To develop a justification for this act, he first sent several officials to her house to accuse her of treason. Agrippina, however, persuasively argued her innocence, and the officials could not think of any way to prove her guilty. Nero then arranged for her to take

[5]Tacitus, *Annals* XII, 67.

These three coins show Nero as a teenager, as a young man in his 20s, and shortly before his death at 30. In the first coin, he is pictured with his mother, Agrippina, who wished to be considered co-emperor.

a journey in a collapsible boat. But although the boat sank as planned, Agrippina managed to swim ashore. Finally, in desperation, Nero hired some sailors to kill her, without any court sanction.

After his mother's death, Nero showed no restraint in pursuing his desires. He murdered his wife so that he could marry his mistress, neglected the daily business of the empire, and devoted himself to music and poetry. Suetonius reported that he forced people to attend concerts in which he played the harp, sang, or recited his own poetry.

● ● ● *No one was allowed to leave the theater during his recitals, however pressing the reasons. We read of women in the audience giving birth, and of men being so bored with listening and applauding that they furtively dropped down from the wall at the rear, since the gates were kept barred, or shammed dead and were carried away for burial.*[6]

The beginning of the end for Nero came in 64, when a devastating fire ravaged the city of Rome. The fire rendered thousands of Romans destitute and homeless, and destroyed several sacred buildings associated with the legendary kings of early Rome. Rumors immediately began to circulate that Nero had set the fire, even though he probably had been in Antium, about 50 miles away, at the time. Suetonius recorded the colorful account of Nero's actions which was current a few years later. Nero, he said, had set the blaze for his own entertainment:

● ● ● *Nero watched the conflagration from the Tower of Maecenas, enraptured by what he called "the beauty of the flames;" then put on his tragedian's costume and sang "the fall of Ilium" from beginning to end. He offered to remove corpses and rubble free of charge, but allowed nobody to search among the ruins even of his own mansion; he wanted to collect as much loot as possible himself.*

Then he opened a Fire Relief Fund and insisted on contributions, which bled the provincials white and practically beggared all private citizens.[7]

To deflect criticism from himself, Nero blamed the Christians for the fire, and carried out the first recorded persecution of this sect (see Chapter 12). Many hundreds of Christians—including, reportedly, the apostles Peter and Paul—lost their lives.

The next year, many of the most prominent citizens of Rome took part in a conspiracy to murder Nero and replace him with another emperor. Nero discovered the plot, and ruthlessly crushed anyone whom he suspected of having taken part in it. Many citizens, including Seneca, were killed or forced to commit suicide during this period. Tacitus reported the last speech of one of the conspirators:

● ● ● *Questioned by Nero as to the motives which had led him on to forget his oath of allegiance, "I hated you," he replied; "yet not a soldier was more loyal to you while you deserved to be loved. I began to hate you when you became the murderer of your mother and your wife, a charioteer, an actor, and an incendiary."*[8]

Throughout the empire, rebellions broke out in response to Nero's administrative actions. In Germany, Roman soldiers became rebellious after Nero murdered their commanders. The citizens of Palestine revolted when the emperor demanded that they worship him in the Temple at Jerusalem. Roman army commanders in Spain, Gaul, and Africa began to make preparations to seize control of the government. Faced by these mounting insurrections, Nero fled from Rome and was condemned to death by the Senate in his absence. As he took his own life, he reportedly exclaimed, "Oh what a great artist the world is losing."[9]

---

[6]Suetonius, *The Twelve Caesars* VI, 23.

[7]Ibid., VI, 38.

[8]Tacitus, *Annals* XV, 67.

[9]Suetonius, *The Twelve Caesars* VI, 49.

FLAVIAN EMPERORS (69-96)

The death of Nero marked the end of the Julio-Claudian dynasty. After a year of civil war in which four military commanders claimed the title of emperor, Flavian Vespasian won the upper hand. In December of 69, he arrived in Rome with his legions to begin his principate. Although he was not related to the Julio-Claudians, Vespasian assumed the title of "Caesar" when he entered office.

Vespasian had a successful record in military service, and commanded 15 legions, or about half of the Roman armed force, at the time of his accession. Like Claudius, he made a practice of extending citizenship to the Romanized colonies, but exerted stern control over newly conquered and rebellious territories. He suppressed revolts in Gaul, and ordered his son Titus to put down a revolt in Judea (see Chapter 12). There, Roman forces sacked Jerusalem, destroyed the Temple, and forced most inhabitants to flee.

TITUS (79-81)

Titus succeeded his father as emperor and followed his father's practice of treating the Senate with respect while retaining the power of government firmly in his own hands. His rule, which lasted only two years, spanned a plague, another great fire in Rome, and the major eruption of Mount Vesuvius which buried the cities of Pompeii and Herculaneum in 79.

Pompeii was buried under 30 feet of volcanic ash which perfectly preserved the conditions that existed at the moment the volcano erupted. When the city was excavated during the 18th century, mosaics, paintings, furniture, food items, and other artifacts of everyday life were found— just as the inhabitants had left them.

DOMITIAN (81-96)

Domitian was the least popular ruler of the Flavian dynasty. He made little attempt to cooperate with the Senate, and insisted that he be called "Master and Lord." His ineffective military leadership led to defeats and to the payment of large bribes to rebellious tribes. These and other expenses led to tremendous financial deficits. Domitian made Christians and Jews the scapegoats for his empire's problems, and severely persecuted them. In 96, Domitian was murdered by palace conspirators, and the Flavian dynasty came to an end.

THE GOOD EMPERORS (96-180)

After Domitian's death, the Senate prevailed upon the Praetorian Guard and the army to establish one of its members as emperor. Nerva, an elderly senator, served as emperor for only two years, but managed to accomplish a great deal. He restored power to the Senate, adopted a frugal budget, and distributed land to the poor. Most importantly, he selected and trained a competent successor, just as Augustus had done after establishing the principate. The four emperors who succeeded Nerva also followed this important precedent, for none of them had sons of their own: they each chose a well-qualified successor and adopted him as a son.

TRAJAN (98-117)

Nerva chose Trajan, a Spaniard who had served as military commander in Germany, as his successor. Trajan was the first Roman emperor who was not of Italian origin.

As emperor, Trajan immediately became popular with the army because of his extensive military campaigns. He was also well-liked by the senators, for he sent them reports of his campaigns and waited for their approval before concluding any treaties.

In order to divide and weaken the hostile Germanic tribes who presented a constant

Trajan was the first Roman emperor of provincial birth. His military conquests extended the Roman Empire to the western boundary of Parthia.

HADRIAN (117-138)

In view of the revolts that threatened Rome upon his accession, Hadrian decided to reverse Trajan's policy of conquest. He renounced the annexation of Mesopotamia by withdrawing Roman troops from that region. In other parts of the empire, too, he elected to establish defensible borders rather than conquering new territory. He built a wall 73 miles in length across Britain to protect Roman settlements from the Picts and other fierce tribes of Scotland, and another wall in Gaul to protect the Rhine frontier from invading Germanic tribes.

During his term as emperor, Hadrian spent much of his time traveling in the provinces. His primary goal was to make sure that the army remained in a state of readiness, but he also took the opportunity to study and correct any other problems he noticed. He improved Roman administration in Italy and the provinces by ordering a complete modernization of the code of laws, which came to be known as the Permanent Edict.

threat to the western portion of the empire, Trajan led his armies across the Danube into Dacia (present Rumania). After conquering this territory, he relocated thousands of Dacians to areas south of the Danube, while colonists from eastern provinces were moved into Dacia. To reduce the threat posed by the Parthians in the East, Trajan annexed Armenia and northern Mesopotamia.

During Trajan's reign, the boundaries of the empire reached their greatest territorial extent, reaching from the Atlantic Ocean to the Caspian Sea, and from Britain to Egypt. But although these conquests brought many benefits, the lengthening of the frontiers was to cause severe problems for his successors. Trajan died in the East while on a campaign to suppress major revolts in Asia Minor, Mesopotamia, Cyprus, and Egypt. On his deathbed, Trajan chose Hadrian, another native of Spain, to be his successor.

The emperor Hadrian. During his 20-year reign, Hadrian concentrated upon the defense of the empire and supervised the construction of large-scale building projects.

THE ROMAN EMPIRE AT ITS GREATEST EXTENT, 117 A.D.
Why did Hadrian decide to pull back from some of the boundaries that Trajan had established?

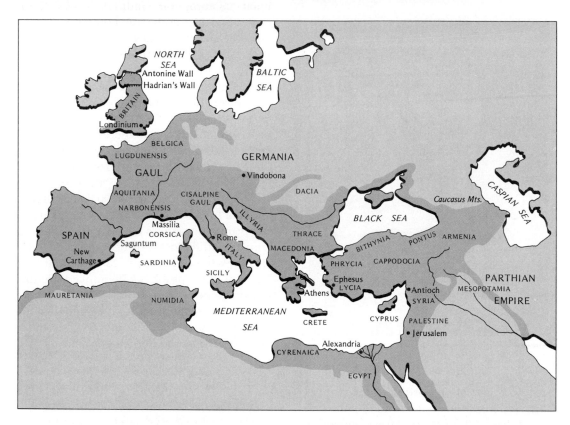

Hadrian's particular interest in Greek culture led him to spend six months in Athens, where he completed the temple of Olympian Zeus and built a magnificent library. Hadrian also planned the rebuilding of the Pantheon in Rome, and designed a beautiful villa, called Tivoli, in a suburb of the city. His tomb, on the bank of the Tiber River in Rome, was so large that it was used as a fortress during the Middle Ages. It is known today as the Castel Sant' Angelo.

Although no major military campaigns were conducted during Hadrian's rule, his decision to build a new city on the site of Jerusalem—which had been destroyed by civil disturbances at the end of Trajan's reign—precipitated a revolt of Judea. After three years, Hadrian's forces crushed the re-

One of Hadrian's most notable boundary fortifications was the 73-mile wall that protected the Roman province of Britain from the fierce tribes of Scotland.

volt and forbade the Jews to worship in their sacred city.

ANTONINUS PIUS (138-161)

Hadrian chose as his successor a wealthy senator from Gaul named Antoninus Pius. Antoninus' reign marked the climax of the era known as the Pax Romana.

Antoninus maintained excellent relations with the Senate, and presided over the great festivities that celebrated the 900th anniversary of Rome's founding. Although there were rebellions in all parts of the empire, Antoninus remained in Rome and did not mount any military campaigns. On his coins, he used such terms as "peace," "tranquillity," and "happiness" to describe his reign.

MARCUS AURELIUS (161-180)

Marcus Aurelius, whom Hadrian had designated an emperor candidate in childhood, succeeded Antoninus. A scholar and Stoic philosopher, Aurelius would have preferred a quiet life of contemplation and study. But his *Meditations*, written while he was engaged in a military campaign, indicate his determination to be a good emperor.

Unfortunately, Aurelius' immediate duties upon becoming emperor included the waging of difficult wars both in Dacia and Parthia. And while Roman troops were gathered in the East, German tribes began to threaten the western borders. In 166, a plague that had started among soldiers fighting in Parthia swept across the empire, killing at

One of the greatest architectural monuments of Hadrian's reign is the Pantheon in Rome, a temple in honor of the ancient Roman gods.

	Julio-Claudian Emperors
27 B.C.-14	Augustus
14-37	Tiberius
37-41	Caligula
41-54	Claudius
54-68	Nero
68-69	Civil Wars
	Flavian Emperors
69-79	Vespasian
79-81	Titus
81-96	Domitian
	"Good Emperors"
96-98	Nerva
98-117	Trajan
117-138	Hadrian
138-161	Antonius Pius
161-180	Marcus Aurelius
180-192	Commodus
192-193	Civil Wars

Marcus Aurelius was the last of the "good" emperors. A Stoic philosopher by vocation, he spent most of his reign on campaign.

least one-fourth of the population. This loss of life made it difficult to recruit soldiers for the army, to collect taxes to maintain the government, or to grow crops to feed the population. Aurelius himself was stricken by the plague while campaigning in Vindobona (present-day Vienna) and died there.

THE CHAOTIC THIRD CENTURY Marcus Aurelius did not follow the custom of adopting a qualified successor. Instead, he chose his son Commodus to succeed him, perhaps fearing that a civil war would result if he made another choice. Like Nero and Domitian before him, Commodus came to be so detested that his reign brought about the fall of his dynasty.

COMMODUS (180-192)

Soon after his accession, Commodus began to show signs of mental instability. He developed the characteristics of a megalomaniac, and demanded that the Senate recognize him as a reincarnation of the hero Hercules as well as emperor. He devoted most of his time to chariot races, lion baiting, and persecution of his political enemies. In 192, he was assassinated, and the Senate marked the ignominious end of his dynasty by expunging all mentions of his reign from its records.

THE SEVERI After Commodus' death, a civil war broke out over the question of succession, and three emperors were proclaimed within a few months. The second of these emperors, a wealthy ex-consul, actually bought the imperial office from the Praetorian guard, who had offered it to the highest bidder. Meanwhile, the armies of Syria, Britain, and the Danube each attempted to proclaim their leaders as emperor. Septimius Severus, the commander of the army of the Danube, finally prevailed.

SEPTIMIUS SEVERUS (193-211)

Severus' reign was a military **autocracy** based on the power and interests of his troops. He

Commodus was not satisfied merely to be honored as emperor, but demanded to be recognized as a reincarnation of Hercules.

inces, where he used Greek phalanx tactics to fight the enemy. He also issued an important decree which continued the work of his father: in Caracalla's decree, Roman citizenship was extended to all of the various peoples of the Roman Empire.

CARACALLA'S SUCCESSORS

Caracalla was murdered by one of his chosen officials. His two successors, Elagabulus and Alexander, were unable to provide the leadership so desperately needed to stem the invasions and revolutions that then threatened the empire. After the death of Alexander Severus, in 235, there followed 50 years of chaos in which 26 emperors were proclaimed, only one of whom died a natural death.

Taking advantage of the weakness of Rome, the Goths and Vandals from the eastern German provinces marched south and threatened the provinces of Greece and the Black Sea. In 267, they plundered Athens.

During this period, Rome was threatened by an internal weakening of its economy as

rarely consulted the Senate, and once advised his sons to "enrich soldiers and scorn all other men." An African by birth, Severus also made a policy of promoting the interests of provincials at the expense of Italians. He opened membership in the Praetorian Guard to men from the provinces, and dismissed the Italian guards. He accepted tribesmen from outlying territories into the army, and even enabled them to rise to the highest offices in the government. Finally, he withdrew the special tax exemptions that Augustus had granted to Italians, making them liable to the same taxes as provincials.

CARACALLA (211-217)

Severus named his eldest son, Caracalla, as his successor, and appointed his younger son, Geta, assistant emperor. Soon after Severus died, Caracalla murdered his younger brother and became sole emperor.

Caracalla fancied himself to be another Alexander the Great, and devoted most of his short reign to expensive wars in the prov-

Caracalla devoted his short reign to military campaigns, and extended Roman citizenship to all peoples of the empire.

well as by external factors. Pirates preyed upon shipping in the Mediterranean and disrupted the import of food to Italy. Inflation spiraled to the point where people stopped using Roman coinage and instead bartered goods and services. Still another plague struck Rome, and the deaths of 5000 people every day created further havoc in the economy. By the year 300, prices were 200 times greater than they had been a century before.

The chaos of the third century brought an end to the powers of the Senate, just as the civil wars of the first century put an end to the republic. After 300, the emperor ruled Rome as a despot.

DIOCLETIAN AND CONSTANTINE

The total collapse of the empire was delayed through the efforts of two strong rulers, Diocletian and Constantine. Both of these leaders believed that the only way to save the empire was to impose harsh controls over every aspect of their subjects' lives.

DIOCLETIAN (285-305)

Diocletian was born in Illyria into a poor family. But due to the measures enacted by Septimius Severus at the beginning of the century, Diocletian's provincial origins could not prevent him from rising to the highest offices in the Roman army and government.

In 285, at a time when many areas of the empire were in revolt, Diocletian's troops declared him to be emperor. He immediately assumed all powers of government without seeking the advice or consent of the Senate. By adopting the robes and court etiquette of Oriental kings, he made it clear that he intended his rule to be an autocracy.

As emperor, Diocletian led a successful campaign against the Franks and Burgundians, who were leading raids across the Rhine, but was unable to suppress revolts in Britain and Gaul. In 293, he decided that the empire had become too extensive to be ruled by one man, so he divided it into two parts.

He assigned the title of *Augustus* to himself as ruler of the eastern provinces and also to Maximian, whom he assigned to rule the western provinces. He then assigned the lesser title of *Caesar* to Galerius, whom he chose to be his assistant in the East, and to Constantius, whom Maximian chose as his assistant in the West. Diocletian announced that he and Maximian (the *Augusti*) would reign for 20 years, and would then step down in favor of the Caesars. All laws were to be issued jointly in the names of the Augusti and Caesars, and were to be uniformly enforced throughout the empire.

Diocletian decided that small units of government would be easier to administer than large ones, and would prevent lesser officials from gathering too much power. Therefore, he divided each of the four *prefectures* into 12 *dioceses* and appointed a ruler (*vicarius*) for each. Diocletian ruled the entire eastern area from his capital in Nicodemia, in Asia Minor, while Maximian ruled the western area from Milan, in Italy. Thus, Rome ceased to be the capital of the empire, and the Senate became the equivalent of a city council for the city of Rome.

Events soon demonstrated the wisdom of Diocletian's new administration in the military sphere. Constantius managed to reconquer Britain, as Diocletian had not been able to do as sole ruler. Maximian suppressed an uprising in the African provinces, while Diocletian himself overcame a pretender in Egypt, and Galerius defended Armenia from the Persians.

In civil matters, Diocletian's administration was not as successful. One of his most notable policies was the attempt to unify the empire by imposing one religion upon all of its peoples. To this end, he issued regulations which forced Christians to worship the gods of the state upon pain of death (see Chapter 12). The martyrdom of thousands of Christians did not have the effect of promoting Roman religion, however, nor did Diocletian's Caesars enforce the edicts uni-

After ruling the eastern half of the Roman Empire for 20 years, Diocletian retired to Split. This is a temple that he built in that city.

formly. In other edicts, he attempted to impose uniform taxes and to prevent merchants from "profiteering," but these regulations could not be effectively enforced.

In 305, Diocletian and Maximian abdicated their positions as Augusti, just as they had promised they would 20 years before. Diocletian retired to an estate in Split, in modern Yugoslavia, which was close to medicinal sulphur springs where he could receive treatment for the ailments of old age.

CONSTANTINE (312-37)

Constantius and Galerius advanced to the positions of Augusti, and selected two new men to serve as Caesars. When Constantius died shortly after his promotion, in 306, the armies of Britain and Gaul acclaimed his son, Constantine, as his successor. Constantine then became involved in a civil war as he struggled to assert his claim against six other candidates. In 312, he brought his army to Italy, and emerged as the victor of a great battle fought at the Milvian Bridge near Rome. Constantine then reached an agreement with Licinius, who had been appointed an Augustus, to share control of the empire.

After becoming Augustus, Constantine announced his conversion to Christianity. In 313, he and Licinius issued the Edict of Milan. This edict annulled the anti-Christian measures enacted by Diocletian and extended toleration to all religions—especially Christianity. When Licinius later renounced the decree and began to persecute Christians, Constantine defeated him in battle and became sole emperor.

In 330, Constantine built a new eastern capital on the site of Byzantium, in present-day Turkey, and renamed the town Constan-

255

tinople. This city eventually became the capital of the eastern portion of the empire and the center of the Byzantine Christian civilization (Chapter 13).

CONSTANTINE'S SUCCESSORS

After Constantine's death, his empire was divided among his sons, Constantine II, Constantius, and Constans. The three emperors soon began to fight each other, and in 340, Constantine II was killed and the empire redivided between the surviving two brothers. Ten years later, the great armies of Gaul and the Danube were nearly destroyed in a battle between Constantius and a usurper. In this and later dynastic struggles, the military resources of the empire were strained to their limit, and few troops could be spared to defend the borders. Taking advantage of this weakness, the Sassanian Persians in the East and the Goths in the West began to conduct frequent raids in Roman territory.

Julian, the army commander who succeeded Constantius as emperor, tried to unify the empire by instituting paganism in place of Christianity as the state religion. This program did not receive great popular support, however, and Julian lost his life while trying to defend the eastern borders of the empire against the Persians. All of the emperors who succeeded him, both in the eastern and western portions of the empire, were Christians.

THE 5TH-CENTURY INVASIONS

While the Roman emperors were preoccupied with dynastic struggles and religious controversies, the Huns, a fierce nomadic people from Asia, began to invade western Europe. Because they fought on horseback, the Huns were easily able to overcome the German tribes they encountered. In 376, the Romans allowed a large group of Visigoths (western Germans) to seek refuge from the Huns in Thrace, within the borders of the Roman empire. Within a short time, however, the Visigoths began to voice bitter complaints about the way that Roman bureaucratic

The conquest of Rome by the Visigoths, in 410, was one of the dramatic episodes that marked the fall of Rome. In 455, the city was again sacked by the Vandals.

officials were treating them. When no action was taken in response, the Goths rose up in arms. In 378, they defeated an imperial army led by the emperor Valens at Adrianople.

The battle between the Romans and Visigoths at Adrianople was followed by a century of invasions that finally brought an end to the Roman Empire in the West. In 406, the Vandals, a primitive Germanic tribe, invaded Gaul and Spain, then proceeded to northern Africa, where they set up a powerful seafaring kingdom. From their base in Africa, they were able to disrupt the supply of grain to Rome and prevent communications between the eastern and western portions of the empire. Britain fell to the Angles and Saxons, and the Franks and Alemanni moved into Gaul. In 410, the Visigoths entered and sacked Rome.

The sack of Rome by the Visigoths effectively marked the end of the Roman Empire in the West. Although emperors continued to be proclaimed in Rome, they were, in effect, the puppets of powerful Germanic leaders who were struggling for control of Europe. In 476, the German chieftain Odoacer deposed Romulus Augustulus, the last Roman emperor in the West, and proclaimed himself king. The eastern portion of the Roman Empire survived as what we call the Byzantine Empire until 1453.

DECLINE AND FALL OF ROME Ever since the capture of Rome by the Visigoths in 410, people have debated the causes of the empire's collapse. The early Christians were particularly troubled by this question, for they had believed that the period between Jesus' resurrection and the Last Judgment would be marked by an orderly progress of civilization. In response to their concerns, Saint Augustine, one of the early Church fathers (see Chapter 12), wrote the first major analysis of Rome's fall in *The City of God*. In this work, he argued that the decline of Rome was due to the character of the Romans themselves, not to the fact that the last emperors had promoted Christianity as the religion of the empire.

Since Augustine, many other writers have identified reasons to explain Rome's decline. It is now generally recognized that no one issue can be singled out as the most important; rather, a great number of different, often overlapping, causes were involved.

ECONOMIC AND SOCIAL CONDITIONS

During the 2nd and 3rd centuries, many regions of the empire suffered a prolonged economic crisis. This economic stagnation has been identified as a major factor in the decline of the empire, for it affected the emperors' ability to pay for the soldiers needed to defend Roman borders. The citizens of the empire, in turn, afflicted both by ruinous taxation and by the threat of foreign invasions, began to perceive that the emperors could no longer provide the conditions of peace and prosperity that had once justified their autocratic powers.

One major cause of economic instability throughout the Roman world was the institution of slavery. The Romans' widespread use of slave labor discouraged the invention and use of new technology which would have led to the development of more varied and sophisticated products. Instead, pottery, textiles, and other products tended to be manufactured in as simple and uniform a manner as possible, especially in the western portion of the empire. As a result, there was little variety in the goods produced in different provinces, and little incentive for trade and commerce. Although wealthy people continued to import finely crafted luxury goods from the East, there was no corresponding demand for western products. Frequent civil wars and repeated attacks by the barbarians accelerated the breakdown of trade and communication. By the middle of the 3rd century, the great trade route that had once linked London and Byzantium was nearly impassable.

Between 250 and 270, a plague decimated the population of Europe, causing further economic decline. In order to find the resources necessary to maintain the empire, successive emperors resorted to increasingly severe methods of taxation. The emperor Diocletian (285-305) was so desperate for funds that he imposed strict control upon all aspects of the economy: middle-class families were heavily taxed, and sons were obligated to follow the same trades as their fathers so that they could continue to pay at the same rate. In the long run, such measures bankrupted and alienated many citizens. In addition, the autocratic form of government imposed by Diocletian allowed little scope for the senatorial class to participate in the affairs of the empire. Rather than entering political life, many prominent families withdrew to the countryside and concentrated upon developing self-sufficient manor farms.

SUCCESSION PROBLEMS

The civil wars that accompanied each disputed succession played a major role in weakening the empire. These wars not only consumed valuable troops and resources in themselves, but often gave an opportunity for the Persians, Germans, and other hostile tribes to invade and plunder Roman territory.

Although disputed successions had been a problem throughout the period of the empire, the choice of Trajan, a professional soldier from Spain, as emperor (98-117) further complicated the question. Once it was established that emperors no longer had to be of Roman or Italian extraction, the number of possible candidates was greatly increased. As a result of the heightened competition, Rome gained some of the best rulers in its history, and citizens of outlying provinces gained a sense of citizenship in the empire. But it also meant that many more people became involved in disputes over succession. Armies in such faraway provinces as Syria, Africa, and Britain began to advance their generals as emperor candidates, and the resulting civil wars were fought on battlefields throughout the Roman world.

In an attempt to put an end to such internal struggles, Diocletian established a system whereby the emperor, or *Augustus*, chose a successor based on merit rather than blood relationship. The designated heir was then appointed to the office of *Caesar* so that he became known to the public well ahead of time, and at the same time gained valuable administrative experience before his accession. Even during Diocletian's lifetime, however, Roman armies continued to demonstrate their loyalty to certain leaders by honoring their sons or other relatives. In 306, for instance, the armies of Britain and Gaul acclaimed Constantine, the son of an Augustus, as his father's heir rather than accepting the designated ruler.

THE BARBARIANS AND THE PERSIANS

Although the invasions of the Germanic tribes were the immediate cause of Rome's downfall, there were also, as we have seen, internal economic and political problems within the empire which contributed to the success of the invaders. Another factor in Rome's inability to defend its western borders was the threat of invasion from the East.

From the time of Crassus' disastrous campaign in Parthia in 53 B.C., the Parthian Empire had occupied the attention of the Romans. The Parthians, an Iranian people, controlled much of the ancient Persian Empire, and their territories extended to the Euphrates River, the eastern boundary of Roman Syria. Although they were not strong enough to conquer the Roman Empire, they did pose a constant threat to Rome's rule of its eastern territories.

Trajan attempted to weaken the Parthians by conquering Armenia and Mesopotamia, thereby preventing them from using the resources of these territories. But Hadrian, his successor, decided that direct Roman rule over these territories was impractical. He reverted instead to the policy of creating a buffer zone, and installed vassal kings in Mesopotamia and Armenia. During the reigns of Marcus Aurelius and Septimius Severus, the Romans successfully repelled Parthian attempts to invade these kingdoms. But in 241, the threat from the East was unexpectedly revived when a new dynasty, the Sassanians, replaced the Parthians as rulers of Iran and Persia. Following the example of Cyrus the Great, the Sassanian rulers improved the political administration of their territories, and extended religious freedom to Jews, Christians, and other sects. They thus won the sympathy of peoples who had been persecuted under the Romans, and achieved several victories over Roman troops in Syria-Palestine, Cappodocia, and Mesopotamia.

SUMMARY

During his long reign, Augustus had carefully preserved the forms of the republic while at the same time creating an imperial administration in which he was the ultimate authority. The trend toward centralization continued under his successors until, in the third century, the emperor was recognized as a dictator.

Many of the emperors who succeeded Augustus were guilty of scandalous behavior, extravagant spending, and mismanagement of governmental affairs. But the administrative bureaucracy and judicial system of the empire continued to function effectively, and the necessity of the imperial office was never questioned. About the year 200, the emperor Septimius Severus made the government a military autocracy. But two centuries later, Rome had become so weak that its army could not defend it from civil uprisings and invasions. While the emperors Diocletian and Constantine stabilized the situation for a few years, the empire ultimately broke into two independent kingdoms. Within a century, the western portion had fallen to the Germans, but the eastern portion survived as the Byzantine Empire until 1453.

QUESTIONS

1 What were the major strengths and weaknesses of the system of government established by Augustus?

2 How did the office of the principate change under Augustus' successors?

3 The reign of Marcus Aurelius is sometimes considered to have marked the beginning of Rome's decline and fall. What special problems did this emperor have to deal with?

4 What measures did Diocletian take to meet the crises that the Roman Empire faced? Was it realistic to believe that his system could continue to function after his retirement?

5 What is a scapegoat? How were the Christians and Jews used as scapegoats during the period of the empire? What were the effects of their persecution and martyrdom?

6 Analyze the causes that have been given for the decline of the Roman Empire. Which do you think were most significant? Could the fall of the empire have been avoided, or was it inevitable?

BIBLIOGRAPHY

Which book might discuss the decline and fall of Rome?

KAHLER, HEINZ. *The Art of Rome and Her Empire.* New York: Greystone Press, 1965. *A survey of Roman art and culture, from the time of Romulus to the fall of Rome. The author stresses the unique quality and character of the Romans' art as seen in their architecture, reliefs, and murals.*

STARK, FREYA. *Rome on the Euphrates.* New York: Harcourt, Brace, 1966. *A discussion of the Roman Empire, ranging from such topics as Hannibal's personality to the character of Roman rule under each group of emperors. Describes how Rome defeated the Seleucids, Parthians, and other peoples and was in turn defeated by the Sassanians.*

STRINGFELLOW, BARR. *The Mask of Jove.* Philadelphia: Lippincott, 1966. *This narrative discussion deals with the character and reputation of the Romans, describing how the culture first defined itself, then learned to convey a positive self-image to others and mask any deficiencies.*

CHINA

3000 B.C.–220 A.D.

At the height of the Roman Empire, richly laden caravans traveled to markets in the Middle East, bearing exotic goods from the East. Fine silks from China were among the luxuries for which wealthy Romans were willing to pay dearly. By the 1st century A.D., however, when these contacts between China and the West were taking place, China already had a long history stretching back over 3000 years.

In China, as in Mesopotamia and Egypt, the earliest civilization grew up in a fertile river valley—the Huang Ho, or Yellow River, valley of northern China. Other rivers of importance to the early development of ancient China were the Yangtze, the Huai, and the Si rivers. Each river provided the fertile soil and the annual flooding that was crucial to the success of ancient agricultural societies. But the flooding of the Huang Ho was not regular and predictable as was that of the Nile River in Egypt. Instead, it often caused great devastation, and because of this the river became known as "China's Sorrow."

According to Chinese legend, the first cities were founded along the Huang Ho by the Hsia dynasty about 3000 B.C., but as yet, little evidence has been found to verify the existence of this ancient dynasty. China emerges onto the stage of history with the Shang dynasty (c. 1766–1027 B.C.). Archaeologists have found the remains of *Anyang*, the oldest known Chinese city and a Shang capital that dates to about 1300 B.C. The Anyang archaeological finds indicate that the Shang Chinese used wheeled chariots; had developed sophisticated methods of working with bronze; planted wheat, millet, and rice; and domesticated fowls, pigs, dogs, and elephants.

In addition, artifacts from the Shang period include oracle bones with pictographic writing, which were used by Shang priests to foretell the future. The pictograms that they carved on bones posed certain questions to the gods or to their ancestors, whom the Chinese revered. The bones were heated and the resulting cracks were interpreted as the answers to the questions. Although this pictogram writing developed later in China than in Mesopotamia or Egypt, it endured far longer. The 2000 or more Shang characters became the basis for the Chinese language that has survived, with modifications, to the present day.

CHOU DYNASTY

About 1027 B.C., the Shang capital of Anyang fell to rebels who founded the Chou dynasty

flooding was severe, famine occurred, invasions threatened, or the dynasty was unable to maintain law and order.

During the Chou dynasty, China moved ahead on many fronts. Metal coins were used as a money economy developed. Iron was introduced and was used in the making of tools and weapons. New farming methods, such as the ox-drawn plow, helped peasants increase food production. Work on major irrigation and transportation systems including the Grand Canal was begun, and Chinese scholars made great achievements in astronomy.

During the early Chou period, Chinese rulers expanded the boundaries of the kingdom both westward and southward to include the Yangtze River basin. As a result, the kingdom was four to five times larger than it had been under the Shang. To govern this large territory, the Chou rulers instituted a feudal system. That is, powerful nobles were given fiefs, or land to administer in return for their loyalty and obedience to the emperor. In addition to maintaining law and order in their fiefs, these local lords pledged to protect and fight for the em-

(1027–221 B.C.). The Chou justified their seizure of power by claiming that they had been granted the Mandate of Heaven—the approval or legitimation of Heaven. This concept became a central premise of Chinese government. According to the mandate, as long as a ruler governed well he enjoyed the approval or legitimation of Heaven. Conversely, a ruler lost the mandate when he governed badly, and Heaven transferred the mandate to other ruling families based upon their performance. The Chinese saw their rulers as humans but believed that they had been chosen by Heaven to carry out its divine purpose. Historically, Chinese dynasties were said to have "lost" the Mandate of Heaven when irrigation systems failed,

What political events facilitated the development of trade between China and the West in the first two centuries A.D.?

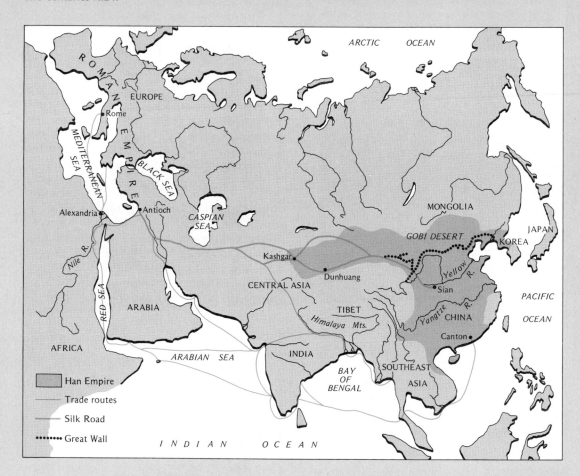

peror. In so doing, they became vassals of the emperor. In time, many local lords became powerful enough to challenge the authority of the emperor and also fought each other. Eventually, as the Chou dynasty disintegrated, it lost control over its vassals, and China endured a prolonged period of feudal warfare lasting from about 771 to 221 B.C.

During this period of instability and uncertainty, people looked around for reasons to explain the collapse of the social order. Many philosophers offered advice to rulers. Among the schools of philosophy that emerged in this period were three that had a profound impact on China: Taoism, Confucianism, and Legalism.

Unlike the religions of Hinduism and Buddhism that focused on the ultimate goal of freeing the individual soul from the cycle of rebirth, these traditional Chinese philosophies were concerned with the practicalities of everyday life—getting along with family, friends, acquaintances, and leaders. They were not concerned with sacred texts or revelations from a deity or supernatural being. They taught no "holy" commandments or rituals that must be observed. Instead, these Chinese philosophies were concerned with relationships—the establishment of harmonious social and political interactions.

Taoism. Lao-tse (born about 604 B.C.), the

"Old Philosopher," is traditionally considered the founder of Taoism. The earliest Taoist teachings are contained in the *Tao Te Ching*, or *The Way of Virtue*. Lao-tse believed that, whatever their basic nature was, people were corrupted by civilization. He urged people to follow the *tao*, or the way, which could only be felt and could not be explained. Taoists tended to shun the world and retire as hermits to a contemplative life. They looked on government as an unavoidable evil but believed the least government was the best.

In time, Taoism became both a religion and a philosophy. Taoist priests used charms and magical prayers to influence the spirits that they believed inhabited the world. From their studies of nature and the planets, Taoists are also credited with making advances in science and astronomy.

Confucianism. The great Chinese philosopher and teacher Confucius (551–479 B.C.) was descended from the Shang kings. To his students, he was known as Kung Tzu, or the Master Kung. When the first Christian missionaries reached China, they Latinized this name to Confucius. It is interesting to note that Confucius lived at a time of intellectual ferment around the world. In Persia, the teachings of Zoroaster were taking root; in Greece, the age of Socrates was dawning; and in India, the Buddha was trying to reform and revitalize the Hindu religion.

Confucius believed that people were by nature good, and he was concerned with ways to organize a stable and just society. He emphasized the virtues of loyalty, respect for elders, and hard work. Confucius propounded a code of ethical conduct that he believed would ensure a return to the peaceful order that had existed in the past. He set out five basic relationships that defined an individual's place in society. These were the relationships between ruler and subject; parent and child; husband and wife; older brother and younger brother; and friend and friend. In each relationship, individuals had duties and responsibilities toward each other. Only when people accepted these responsibilities, Confucius said, would an orderly society be possible.

Confucius, the great Chinese teacher, attracted many followers. The philosophy constructed from his sayings has influenced Chinese thought even to the present.

The teachings of Confucius were collected by his followers in a work known as the *Analects*. Besides defining the role of the individual in society, Confucius also emphasized the importance of education and *filial piety*, respect for one's elders. He believed the best government officials were those who

263

were well educated, and urged the rulers of China's warring feudal states to turn to such men. Although in his lifetime Confucius was unable to find any ruler who would accept his philosophy, his teachings had profound impact on later Chinese civilization.

Legalism. A third school of thought to develop in the late Chou period was Legalism. Among its chief proponents was Han Fei Tzu (died 233 B.C.), who rejected the Confucian emphasis on ethical conduct in favor of an authoritarian view of society. Legalists thought that people by nature were dishonest and lazy, and insisted that only strict laws and harsh punishments would ensure an orderly society.

CH'IN EMPIRE

In the 3rd century B.C., at the same time as Rome was expanding its power in Italy, the Chou dynasty collapsed after a prolonged period of civil war. Out of the chaos, a local feudal lord, the ruler of the Ch'in kingdom, led a successful attempt to unite and unify China. In so doing, he established the short-lived Ch'in dynasty (221–206 B.C.). Some scholars think that it is from the Ch'in dynasty that China derives its name. After subduing the other powerful feudal lords, the Ch'in ruler also successfully defended northern China from attacks by the Huns.

After crushing all opposition, the Ch'in ruler took the title Shih Huang-ti, meaning the "First Emperor," and he permitted his new subjects to call him the "Son of Heaven." Shih Huang-ti was determined to destroy the power of the feudal lords, and his reign was marked by cruelty and harshness. To destroy feudalism, he reclaimed all the land of China in the name of the emperor, confiscated and melted down the weapons of his enemies, and issued orders that only his own soldiers could possess weapons. To ensure obedience to his commands, the emperor maintained a strong, fully trained army. He improved existing roads and built new ones in order to facilitate the movement of his armies throughout the empire.

Further, Shih Huang-ti began the vast task of unifying, joining, and improving the scat-

These terracotta soldiers and horses guarded the tomb of Shih Huang-ti, founder of the Ch'in dynasty. The discovery of the tomb in 1974 focused much attention on this era of China's history.

tered earth walls that various local lords had built to keep out invaders from Central Asia. Using forced labor, the rebuilding process, completed under the succeeding Han dynasty, resulted in the construction of the massive Great Wall of China, which is 22 feet high, 20 feet wide, and approximately 1400 miles long. The emperor reorganized the government and adopted the Legalist philosophy. He divided China into 36 regions, appointing officials responsible to him to rule in each region. With rigid rules and harsh punishment, he sought to impose unity on all China.

Unlike the chaotic years of the late Chou dynasty, when intellectual freedom was permitted and encouraged, the Ch'in ruler decreed that all books, writings, and literature related to non-Legalist philosophies were to be confiscated and burned. However, as part of his plan to unify the empire, Shih Huang-ti also decreed that there should be a single form of writing throughout the empire, and he commanded his officials to institute such a system. By standardizing the writing of Chinese characters, people from different parts of China could communicate with each other through written documents even though they spoke different dialects. In addition to the standardization of the written language, Shih Huang-ti set up a uniform system of weights and measures, including a standard gauge for all wheel axles.

Although the Ch'in Empire collapsed a few years after the death of its founder in 210 B.C., the "First Emperor" had laid the foundations for a unified state. Two hundred years before the Roman emperor Augustus, Shih Huang-ti had issued coins that were used throughout his empire and had built an efficient road system, with lines radiating from his capital at Changan to the furthest outposts of the empire.

HAN EMPIRE

Out of the chaos that followed the collapse of the Ch'in dynasty, a peasant leader named Liu Pang rose to power at the head of a powerful army. In 202 B.C., Liu Pang became emperor by right of conquest and founded the Han dynasty (202 B.C.–220 A.D.). Under this dynasty, China enjoyed a golden age similar to that of the early Roman Empire. The first Han emperor restored peace and instituted programs to erase the harsh measures of Shih Huang-ti. In place of Legalist principles, he adopted Confucian ideas of government, and he restored intellectual freedom to writers and artists.

The Han dynasty reached its peak under the emperor Wu Ti (141–87 B.C.). Continuing the Han tradition of implementing Confucian ideas, Wu Ti created a system of civil service examination to find the best qualified individuals to administer the government. As a result, literacy became the means for government advancement. Confucian ideals were stressed, since the examinations were based on the Confucian classics as well as on knowledge of the law. This examination system provided China with some of its most gifted government officials and contributed to stability and order even when dynasties fell. In fact, this civil service system continued in China until 1912—nearly 2000 years.

A pottery model of a house unearthed from a tomb of the Han era. The 400 years of the Han dynasty were marked by many artistic and technological advances.

Wu Ti incorporated Korea and Southeast Asia into the Chinese empire and extended part of the western boundary to the Caspian Sea. In the process of expansion, he established commercial contact with Rome, India, and Southwest Asia. In creating the largest and wealthiest empire of that time, Wu Ti is also credited with establishing the *Pax Sinica* ("Chinese Peace")—a period of commercial and social stability that lasted for almost 200 years.

Commercial contact with Rome, Greece, and the Middle East necessitated the creation, maintenance, and protection of a trade route through the western territories of the empire. Along this route, camel caravans carried silk, jade, and lacquerware westward to exchange for glass, amber, asbestos, and

Silk, an important commodity in the East-West trade that began in the 1st century, was usually manufactured by Chinese women. In this painting, women are shown pounding the newly woven fabric to tighten its weave.

linen. Because silk was the mainstay of this trade, the route became known as the Silk Road. Although silk was commonplace in China (where it was issued as pay to the soldiers), it was a marvel to the people of the Mediterranean world.

During the Han dynasty, the Chinese made many technological and scientific advances. By the 2nd century B.C. the Chinese were using the foot stirrup, a thousand years before it reached the West. About 100 A.D., the Chinese invented paper. They developed other practical devices such as the wheelbarrow, water mill, and harness. In science, Chinese scholars emphasized observation, as the Greeks had done, and used their observations to discover natural laws of the universe. In addition, the Chinese invented the sundial and water clock, and developed a highly accurate calendar.

Increased trade and contact with the West brought new products and ideas to China.

During the Han dynasty, Buddhist missionaries made their way into China. At first, the Chinese found little appeal in the new religion, although they saw elements of Taoism in its rejection of worldly pursuits. As the Han dynasty weakened, however, Buddhism gained in popularity, offering hope to those who felt that life was full of suffering and sorrow.

By the 3rd century A.D., the Han dynasty was unable to defend itself from internal and external threats. Like the Roman Empire in the West, weak Han rulers were unable to maintain their power. China's traditional enemies, the Huns, again threatened in the north. In 220 A.D. the Han dynasty collapsed, and contacts between China and the Mediterranean world declined. In the next centuries, China experienced a period of anarchy with a succession of ruling houses attempting to restore order. It was during this "Period of Six Dynasties" (220 A.D.–589 A.D.) that

Buddhism took root in China and adapted itself to the traditional Chinese philosophies of Confucianism and Taoism.

INTRODUCTION TO THE DOCUMENTS

The teachings of Confucius pointed the way to happiness through correct behavior. A skillful teacher, much like the Buddha, Confucius considered himself not an innovator but a transmitter of the values that had ensured harmony in the past. Central to Confucian thought is the idea of *jen*—perfect virtue—which brings to society the cooperative behavior of individuals, and to the individual a sense of moral right.

Basic to Confucianism is the belief that individuals are innately good. Taoism, in contrast, accepts people the way they are with no moral judgment made about their innate character. According to legend, Lao-tse could never understand why Confucius worried so much about changing people and ordering their lives. He is said to have confronted Confucius, criticizing his attempt to change people with the comment that "the swan is white without a daily bath, and the raven is black without daily coloring itself." Lao-tse believed that people should not desire anything, not even goodness. For Lao-tse, hatred, greed, pride, and ambition were all a waste of time. Instead, he directed peo-ple to copy nature, saying that a tree does not want things or struggle to control other trees, it just grows. Taoism encouraged people to lead simple lives, while proclaiming love of nature and harmony with nature as goals for living.

Taoism is a philosophy based on harmony rather than on assertiveness. It views humankind as an integral part of nature rather than as a controller of nature. To attain harmony with nature and with all the forces of the universe, Taoists believed that people must utilize the principles of *yin* and *yang*. According to Chinese philosophy, the yin and the yang are the two primary principles, or forces, of the universe. These forces are said to be eternally interacting, and eternally opposed to one another.

The yin principle is equated with brightness, heat, activity, masculinity, Heaven, sun, south, above, roundness, and odd numbers, while the yang principle is equated with darkness, cold, inactivity, femininity, Earth, moon, north, below, squareness, and even numbers. The yin and the yang are said to work in conjunction with five elements: wood, fire, earth, metal, and water. According to Taoist philosophy, a person should not strive for the dominance of one set of principles over another. Instead, the goal of life is the attainment of harmony—the perfect balance between opposing principles.

DOCUMENT 1 *CONFUCIUS ON FILIAL PIETY*

The master [Confucius] said: "filial piety is the force that continues the purposes and completes the affairs of our forefathers. . . . To gather in the same place where they earlier have gathered; to perform the same ceremonies which they earlier have performed; to play the same music which they earlier did; to pay respect to those whom they honored; to love those who were dear to them; in fact, to serve those now dead as if they were living, and those now departed as if they were with us still. This is the highest achievement of filial piety."

SOURCE: Confucius, *Chung Yung*, Chapter XIX, as found in *The Sacred Books of Confucius and other Confucian Classics*, pp. 11–12.

How does the Confucian ideal of filial piety ensure social order?

DOCUMENT 2 CONFUCIUS ON GOOD GOVERNMENT

245.   The Master said: "One who governs by virtue is comparable to the polar star, which remains in its place while all the stars turn towards it."

246.   The Master said: "Govern the people by laws and regulate them by penalties, and the people will try to do no wrong, but they will lose the sense of shame. Govern the people by virtue and restrain them by rules of propriety, and the people will have a sense of shame and be reformed of themselves."

247.   Duke Ai asked: "What should I do to secure the submission of the people?" "Promote the upright and banish the crooked," said the Master; "then the people will be submissive. Promote the crooked and banish the upright; then the people will not be submissive."

248.   Chi Kang Tzu asked: "What should be done to make the people respectful and be encouraged to cultivate virtues?" "Approach the people with dignity," said the Master, "and they will be respectful. Show filial piety and kindness, and they will be loyal. Promote those who are worthy, and train those who are incompetent; and they will be encouraged to cultivate virtues."

255.   Tzu Kung asked about good government, and the Master said: "The essentials [of good government] are sufficient food, sufficient arms, and the confidence of the people." "But," asked Tzu Kung, "if you have to part with one of the three, which would you give up?" "Arms," said the Master. "But suppose," said Tzu Kung, "one of the remaining two has to be relinquished, which would it be?" "Food," said the Master. "From time immemorial death has been the lot of all men, but a people without confidence is lost indeed."

270.   The Master said: "If a prince has rendered himself upright, he will have no difficulty in governing the people. But if he cannot rectify himself, how can he hope to rectify the people?"

SOURCE: Confucius, *The Confucian Analects*, Lu Version, as found in *The Sacred Books of Confucius and other Confucian Classics.*

What does Confucius think is the best way of maintaining order? Why do you think the rulers with whom he tried to share his ideas rejected these teachings?

DOCUMENT 3

Although Lao-Tse, the supposed founder of Taoism, may only be a figure of legend, a number of works are credited to him. Typically, Taoists speak in paradoxes that often are seemingly contradictory and emphasize harmony with nature.

As the soft yield of water cleaves obstinate stone,
So to yield with life solves the insoluble:
To yield, I have learned, is to come back again.
But this unworded lesson,
This easy example,
Is lost upon men.

SOURCE: Arthur Cottrell and David Morgan, *China's Civilization* (New York: Praeger Publishers, 1975), p. 35.

Banish wisdom, discard knowledge,
And the people will be benefited a hundredfold.
Banish human kindness, discard morality,
And the people will be dutiful and compassionate.
Banish skill, discard profit,
And thieves and robbers will disappear. . . .
The more prohibitions there are, the more ritual
   avoidances,
The poorer the people will be.
The more "sharp weapons" there are,
The more pernicious contrivances will be invented.
The more laws are promulgated,
The more thieves and bandits there will be.
Therefore a sage has said:
So long as I "do nothing" the people will of themselves
   be transformed.
So long as I love quietude, the people will of
   themselves go straight.
So long as I act only by inactivity the people will of
   themselves become prosperous.
So long as I have no wants the people will of
   themselves return to the "state of the Uncarved
   Block."

SOURCE: Arthur Waley (ed.), *The Way and Its Power, A Study of the Tao Te Ching and Its Place in Chinese Thought* (Boston: Houghton Mifflin, 1935).

Compare Taoist ideas of government as reflected in these sayings to those of Confucius in Document 2.

Legalist principles were adopted during the brief Ch'in dynasty. All succeeding dynasties enthroned Confucian ideas over the harsh measures proposed by Han Fei Tzu. The selection below summarizes the beliefs of the Legalists.

When the sage rules the state, he does not count on people doing good of themselves, but employs such measures as will keep them from doing any evil. If he counts on people doing good of themselves, there will not be enough such people to be numbered by the tens in the whole country. But if he employs such measures as will keep them from doing evil, then the entire state can be brought up to a uniform standard. . . .

. . .when the Confucianists of the present day counsel the rulers they do not discuss the way to bring about order now, but exalt the achievement of good order in the past. They neither study affairs pertaining to law and government nor observe the realities of vice and wickedness, but all exalt the reputed glories of remote antiquity and the achievements of the ancient kings. . . . The intelligent ruler upholds solid facts and discards useless frills. He does not speak about deeds of humanity and righteousness, and he does not listen to the words of learned men.

Those who are ignorant about government insistently say: "Win the hearts of the people." . . . For all that the ruler would need to do would be just to listen to the people. Actually, the intelligence of the people is not to be relied upon any more than the mind of a baby. . . .

Now, the sovereign urges the tillage of land and the cultivation of pastures for the purpose of increasing production for the people, but they think the sovereign is cruel. The sovereign regulates penalties and increases punishments for the purpose of repressing the wicked, but the people think the sovereign is severe. Again, he levies taxes in cash and in grain to fill up the granaries and treasuries in order to relieve famine and provide for the army, but they think the sovereign is greedy. Finally, he insists upon universal military training without personal favoritism, and urges his forces to fight hard in order to take the enemy captive, but the people think the sovereign is violent. These four measures are methods for attaining order and maintaining peace, but the people are too ignorant to appreciate them.

SOURCE: Wm. Theodore de Bary, Wing-tsit Chan, and Burton Watson, *Sources of Chinese Tradition* (New York: Columbia University Press, 1964), Vol. I.

Why did Legalists reject the Confucian view of good government?

TIME LINE FOR CHINA AND THE WEST

CHINA		THE WEST	
		3100 B.C.	Narmer unites Upper and Lower Egypt; Sumerian city-states flourish in Mesopotamia
3000 B.C.	Legendary Hsia dynasty rules villages of Huang Ho valley		
		2600 B.C.	Pyramid of Khufu built
1766 B.C.	Shang dynasty; development of pictographic writing		
		1100 B.C.	Mycenaean civilization collapses
1027 B.C.	Chou dynasty wins Mandate of Heaven; begins to expand China's borders		
771– 221 B.C.	Stability of Chou government undermined by feudal warfare	750 B.C.	Assyrians conquer Syria-Palestine
		600 B.C.	Zoroaster founds new religion in Persia
551– 479 B.C.	Lifetime of Confucius	509 B.C.	Roman Republic founded
		500 B.C.	Cleisthenes reforms Athens' democracy
		479 B.C.	Persian Wars end; Pericles assumes leadership of Athens
		469– 399 B.C.	Lifetime of Socrates
221 B.C.	Ch'in dynasty overthrows Chou government; imposes unity on China	246 B.C.	Punic Wars begin
206 B.C.	Han dynasty; era of prosperity and expansion		
141 B.C.	Reign of Wu Ti; era of Pax Sinica	146 B.C.	Punic Wars end; Rome rules Carthaginian empire
		27 B.C.– 180 A.D.	Pax Romana; trade and commerce established between China and the West
220 A.D.	Collapse of Han Empire; period of Six Dynasties begins		
		476 A.D.	Collapse of Roman Empire in the West
589 A.D.	Buddhism takes hold in China		

Forces for Change

● If all the trees on earth were pens, and if there were
seven oceans full of ink, they would not suffice to
describe the wonders of the Almighty.

MOHAMMED

● If ye have faith as a grain of mustard seed, ye shall say
unto this mountain, Remove hence to yonder place; and
it shall remove; and nothing shall be impossible unto you.

JESUS

● It was given as the chief and most necessary sign of his coming on those who had believed,
that every one of them spoke in the tongues of all nations; thus signifying that the unity of the
Catholic Church would embrace all nations and would in like manner speak in all tongues.

AUGUSTINE

● Nature is nothing else but God and the divine Reason that pervades the whole universe. You
may, if you wish, address this creator of the world by different names, such as Jupiter Best
and Greatest, the Thunderer, or the Stayer. This last title does not derive from the tale told
by historians about the Roman battle-line being stayed from flight in answer to prayers. It
simply means that all things are upheld by his benefits....You may also call him Fate; that
would be no mistake. For since Fate is only a connected chain of causes, he is the first of
the causes on which all succeeding ones depend. Any name that you choose to apply
to him will be appropriate if it connotes a power that operates in heaven. His titles
are as countless as his benefits.

SENECA

12

● *Jesus was a little known Jewish carpenter who was born in a stable, died at the age of thirty-three as a criminal rather than a hero, never travelled more than ninety miles from his birthplace, owned nothing, attended no college, marshalled no army, and instead of producing books did his only writing in the sand. Nevertheless, his birthday is kept across the world and his deathday sets a gallows against every sky. Who, then, was he?*

GEORGE BUTTRICK

Christianity

During the reign of the emperor Augustus, an event occurred in an obscure town in Palestine, an eastern province of the Roman Empire, that would later transform the Roman world. That event was the birth of Jesus of Nazareth. One historian summarized the life of Jesus in the quotation above. The answer to who Jesus was—and how his teachings became the basis for a popular and powerful religion, Christianity—will be explored in this chapter.

At the time of Jesus' birth, many different religions flourished within the Roman Empire. Under the peaceful conditions of the early empire, a number of new religions were carried to Rome from the lands its legions had conquered in the East. The cult of Isis, an Egyptian goddess, and the worship of Mithras, a Persian god, gained followers among the Romans. Along with these great religions were many minor ones. All of them tried to explain the mysteries of the universe. Many spoke of sin and called for fasting and other rituals of purification. Their beliefs included faith in a god who had died and risen again and whose life and death were associated with the spring planting season and the winter season when nothing grew.

As Christianity grew, it gained a foothold amid these countless religious cults, but it drew on a different tradition, the ethical monotheism of the ancient Hebrews.

THE SETTING FOR CHRISTIANITY

In Chapter 4, you learned that the ancient Hebrews believed that God had made a covenant with Abraham and that they were God's chosen people. As part of that covenant, the Hebrews accepted the belief in one God. Unlike the other peoples of the Middle East, they held firmly to their monotheism.

The religion of the Jews was closely tied to their history. Palestine was conquered many times by the different strong empires that rose in the Middle East. In 536 B.C., the Persian emperor, Cyrus, allowed many Jews who had been taken into exile in Babylon to return to Jerusalem. The Jews rebuilt their Temple at Jerusalem and set up their own state, which enjoyed a measure of independence under its Persian overlord.

In the 4th century B.C., Alexander the Great conquered Palestine, and after his death in 323 B.C., it was ruled first by the Ptolemies and later by the Seleucid kings. Hellenistic culture came to influence the Jews, many of whom began to use the Greek language rather than Hebrew. Around 200 B.C., Hebrew scholars decided to translate their holy writings, or *scriptures*, into Greek. This work came to be known as the *Septuagint* because it was completed by 70 scholars.

During the 2nd century B.C., the Seleucid king Antiochus IV (175–163 B.C.) tried to force the Jews to accept Hellenistic forms of worship. He forbade them to observe their Sabbath or practice the rite of circumcision. He confiscated the wealth of the Temple at Jerusalem and set up a statue of Jupiter within the inner sanctum. Jews were outraged at the violation of their holy place. In 168 B.C., they revolted against the Syrians. Judas Maccabeus became the leader of this revolt and in 165 B.C. succeeded in driving the Syrian army out of Jerusalem. The Jews turned at once to the task of purifying the Temple and rededicating it to Yahweh, or God. This event is still celebrated by Jews each December as the "Feast of Dedication," or *Hanukkah*. Although Judas Maccabeus was killed in 161 B.C., his brothers continued the struggle, and the Maccabeans eventually set up an independent kingdom that lasted until a Roman army under Ptolemy the Great conquered Palestine in 63 B.C.

RIVAL JEWISH SECTS

During the 2nd and 1st centuries B.C., the Jews were divided into many factions. All Jews believed in the one God, but they differed over how to interpret God's law and therefore over how to conduct certain religious practices. The three main sects were the Sadducees, Pharisees, and Essenes. The Sadducees were wealthy, well-educated people—priests, landowners, and merchants—who controlled the Sanhedrin, the religious council that dealt with civil and criminal cases as well as with violations of Jewish religious laws. The Sadducees had little influence with the common people. While they believed that the Torah was the only source of authority for the Jews, they embraced the Hellenistic culture and were willing to compromise with the Roman rulers of Palestine.

The Pharisees, or "Separated Ones," were scholarly middle-class people who followed very closely the rituals of worship and living which set Jews apart from other people. They put great emphasis on living in accord with God's laws as set forth in the Torah and enforced by centuries of tradition. They believed that if they devoted themselves to the study of the scriptures and strictly observed the Mosaic laws, they would experience life after death.

The Essenes were a group of pious Jews who devoted themselves to the study of the scriptures, prayer, and fasting in preparation for the end of the world, which they believed was imminent. They looked for a Messiah, the "anointed one," to be sent by God to save his people. The Jewish historian Flavius Josephus described the Essenes in these words:

• • • *These last are Jews by birth, and seem to have greater affection for one another than the other sects have. These Essenes reject pleasure as an evil, but esteem continence [self-restraint], and the conquest over our passions, to be virtue . . . These men are despisers of riches, and so very communicative, as raises our admiration. Nor is there any one to be found among them who hath more than another; for it is a law among them, that those who come to them must let what they have be common to the whole order—insomuch that among them there is no appearance of poverty, or excess of riches, but everyone's possessions are mingled with every other's possessions; and so there is, as it were, one patrimony [heritage] among all the brethren.*[1]

Little was known about the Essenes, beyond what Josephus wrote, until 1947. That year, a Bedouin boy was searching for a stray goat when he saw a small, cave-like opening

---

[1]Josephus, *Wars of the Jews* II, 8, 2.

The Dead Sea Scrolls have provided much information about the culture of the Essenes.

senes were popularly known as "Followers of the Way," and they lived by a strict discipline laid out in their "Manual of Discipline." The Essenes believed that a new prophet would appear to help the Jews defeat their enemies and bring in a new age. They valued Jewish law and observed many rites, including a sacred meal of bread and wine.

Scholars have debated the influence of the Essenes on early Christianity. Some have suggested that John the Baptist and some early followers of Jesus were once members of the Essene community.

ZEALOTS

A fourth group of Jews, known as the Zealots, or people of action, came mostly from the Pharisees. The Zealots interpreted various prophetic writings concerning the coming of a Messiah as forecasting a great military leader who would restore the Jews to the political status they had enjoyed under King David. The success of the Maccabean uprising of 168 B.C. led them to organize local groups, which met in the hills of northern Palestine and plotted to throw off Roman control. They became interested in Jesus' ability to motivate large numbers of people, but when Jesus finally convinced them that his mission was not of a political nature, they ignored him.

LIFE OF JESUS Virtually no contemporary sources make any mention of Jesus and his teachings. Flavius Josephus, who was born about the time that Jesus died, mentions him in this description:

• • • *Now there was about this time Jesus, a wise man, if it be lawful to call him a man; for he was a doer of wonderful works, a teacher of such men as receive the truth with pleasure. He drew over to him many of the Jews and many of the Gentiles. He was [the] Christ.*[2]

in a hill near the Dead Sea. He threw some stones into the cave, but became frightened and ran away when it sounded as though one of the stones had smashed against something in the cave. Later, he returned to the site with a friend. Together, they worked their way into the opening, where they found several clay jars filled with scrolls.

At first, the scholars who examined these "Dead Sea scrolls" declared them to be worthless. But in 1951, a team of archaeologists explored the vicinity of Qumran, on the Dead Sea, more carefully and discovered the foundations of a building that they thought was an Essene monastery. They also found fragments of other scrolls dating from the three centuries preceding the birth of Jesus.

Other Essene scrolls referred to a "Teacher of Righteousness," whom the Essenes honored, but scholars have been unable to identify who this may have been. They estimate that the Essene group may have had 4000 members at the time of Jesus' birth. The Es-

---

[2]Josephus, *Antiquities of the Jews* XVIII, 3, 3.

THE GOSPELS

Historians and religious scholars have to rely on the New Testament to learn about the life of Jesus. The first four books of the New Testament—Matthew, Mark, Luke, and John—are believed to have been written shortly after the death of Jesus by his disciples, or followers. These books, often called the *Gospels,* or "good news," include many sayings of Jesus. But the Gospels themselves are the subject of heated debate because there were no scribes to record Jesus' words as he spoke, and the original manuscripts of the Gospels have been lost. In addition, the reports of the four disciples often differ and even contradict each other. The first three of these—Matthew, Mark, and Luke—are often referred to as the "synoptic gospels"[3] because they present similar, but by no means identical, information. The fourth gospel, John, says very little about the life of Jesus, but reports many things that he said. It was probably written about 70 years after the death of Jesus.

Despite the lack of contemporary sources, we can determine the outlines of Jesus' life. According to modern scholarship, Jesus was born in 4 B.C..

The name Jesus is a Greek version of the Hebrew name *Joshua.* Jesus was born to a Jewish family, was educated as a Jew, and taught in Jewish centers of worship. While some Jews accepted his teachings, the vast majority rejected them because they differed from orthodox Jewish teachings. Those who accepted his teachings found their lives so changed that they went through the Hellenistic world proclaiming that they had seen the Messiah.

At the time of Jesus' birth, Palestine was ruled by Herod, who had been put on the throne by the Romans. Herod adopted Jewish practices, married the daughter of the last Maccabean king, and put money into rebuilding the Temple. But he remained un-

[3]Synoptic means "same viewpoint."

In 525 A.D. a Christian abbot and astronomer, Dionysius Exiguus, made calculations that indicated that Jesus had been born 753 years after the founding of Rome. Pope Gregory XIII established a new calendar for dating Church events in 1382, based on the calculations of Exiguus. The new calendar, called the Gregorian calendar, divided time into the years before the birth of Christ (B.C.) and those after the birth of Jesus, anno domini or A.D., meaning "in the year of our Lord." In 1752 A.D., England and its American colonies adopted this Gregorian calendar; today most nations use it. Recent research into the exact year of Jesus' birth has found that the calculations of Exiguus were off by about four years.

popular with most Jewish leaders and the common people; in part because he promoted Hellenistic culture, and in part because he was seen as a puppet of Rome. About the time of Jesus' birth, he ordered the massacre of thousands of Jewish infants—which the Gospels connect to his hearing rumors that a Messiah had been born.

The Gospels reveal very little about Jesus' early life except that his family lived in the town of Nazareth in Galilee, the northern portion of Palestine, and that he was admitted to the Jewish faith in the Temple at Jerusalem at the age of 12. All four of the Gospels report that at the age of about 30 years (26 A.D.) Jesus appeared at the Jordan River, to be baptized by his cousin, a preacher named John the Baptist.

JOHN THE BAPTIST

John preached against sin and introduced the rite of baptism as an act of purification. This description of John in the Bible has led some scholars to suggest that he was a member of the Essene monastery at Qumran: "John's clothing was a rough coat of camel's hair, with a leather belt round his waist, and his food was locusts and wild honey." (Matthew 3:4). People from all over Palestine came to hear John preach and cry out, "Repent, for the kingdom of heaven is upon you!" (Matthew 3:1.) Many believed him and submitted to being baptized by immersion into the waters of the Jordan River, an act that symbolically washed away their sins. Because John's preaching attracted the attention of the authorities, who feared his success, he was arrested and executed.

THE TEACHINGS OF JESUS

According to the Gospels, after Jesus was baptized, he had a vision in which the holy spirit spoke to him, and soon after he began to preach. He traveled about Palestine teaching and healing people who came to him with a wide variety of illnesses. Wherever he went in public, he attracted large crowds. He preached a simple message that included these ideas. Because all people are the children of God, they should help one another. People should love God, repent their sins, and accept God's forgiveness. Forgiveness of others and concern for the poor also featured prominently in Jesus' message.

Central to this message was the idea that a new age—the kingdom of heaven—was at hand and that it would be ushered in by a Messiah, the son of God. The meaning of Jesus' teaching on this score has been much debated, especially the question of whether Jesus saw himself as the Messiah. As Richard Cavendish has explained it:

● ● ● *Jesus himself was not a philosopher or theologian and he was not given to precise utterance. His sayings are frequently mysterious and sometimes mutually contradictory. His followers found him both fascinating and puzzling, and what he thought about himself is a mystery. Nowhere is he quoted making a plain and*

This early Christian mosaic shows Jesus with two of his apostles.

unambiguous statement that he was divine. The sayings which seem most clearly to imply it—"I and the Father are one," for instance, and "I am the way, the truth and the life"—come from the latest of the gospels, John, and may represent later Christian beliefs rather than Jesus' own belief.[4]

The growing popularity of Jesus and his teachings along with his willingness to associate with persons despised by the Jewish leaders, including Gentiles (non-Jews), tax collectors, and prostitutes, made him increasingly unpopular with the various Jewish sects. The Sadducees feared him because his teachings about the Messiah and a new kingdom could disrupt their good relations with Rome. Moreover, they resented his criticism of the way they operated the Temple at Jerusalem: he said that they were "making it a robber's cave" (Matthew 21:13). The Pharisees despised him because he taught that God was more concerned with love and forgiveness than with the fine points of Jewish law.

---

[4]Richard Cavendish, *The Great Religions* (New York: Arco Publishing Co., 1980), p. 176.

Soon after Jesus started preaching, he chose 12 assistants known as the *apostles*. The Gospels relate how Jesus and his apostles traveled to Jerusalem to observe Passover, the celebration that commemorated the deliverance of the Jews from slavery in ancient Egypt. The city and Temple were crowded with Jews, for this was a most important religious event. When Jesus was hailed by the crowds as king or Messiah, the Temple authorities grew frightened that the Romans would interpret this outburst as a sign of revolt. So they arrested Jesus and turned him over to Pontius Pilate, the Roman procurator of the region. Pilate ordered Jesus' death by crucifixion, a traditional Roman form of execution. The date of this event was probably 30 A.D.

THE SPREAD OF CHRISTIANITY

During the next days and weeks, various followers of Jesus reported seeing him, talking to him, and even touching him. Moreover, they announced that Jesus was the long-awaited Messiah of the Jews and that he would soon return to establish the kingdom of heaven. The Temple authorities once more stepped in to prevent possible disturbances. They arrested some disciples and forced others to flee to neighboring cities, where they continued to preach the gospel and spread the teachings of Jesus.

After the death of Jesus, Peter, one of the 12 apostles, became the leader of the *Nazarenes*, as their enemies called them. (They called themselves the *Followers of the Way*.) At first, Jesus' followers continued to worship as Jews in the synagogues and the Temple in Jerusalem and to follow Jewish customs. But they often met together in private homes to pray, read the scriptures, and discuss their memories of Jesus and his teachings. They began to share a simple meal, similar to the one Jesus had shared with the apostles the night before his arrest. At that meal, he had given his followers bread and wine, saying that they were his body and blood. From these simple beginnings, Christianity would spread into a great world religion.

PAUL

A key figure in the spread of Christianity was Paul of Tarsus. Tarsus was a Greek city on the southeast coast of Asia Minor. Paul's Hebrew name was Saul. He was a brilliant young man who was educated as a rabbi and once boasted: "My brothers, I am a Pharisee, a Pharisee born and bred" (Acts 23:6). As a Pharisee, Saul despised the followers of Jesus and approved the stoning of one of them, a young man named Stephen. Saul never met Jesus, but a short time after the death of Stephen, Saul was traveling along the road to Damascus when he was confronted by a vision of Jesus asking him, "Saul, Saul, why do you persecute me?" (Acts 9:4). The experience so moved Saul that he changed his name to Paul and dedicated his life to carrying Jesus' message throughout the eastern Mediterranean world.

After his conversion, Paul moved to Antioch, the capital of the Roman province of Syria. There, the followers of Jesus took the name *Christians*, or followers of Christ (the Greek equivalent of Messiah). Paul was a tireless worker who preached the gospel to Jews and Gentiles. From Antioch, he carried the word of Christ throughout the cities of Asia Minor to Greece and eventually to Rome. As Paul moved from place to place, he established small groups of people who accepted Christian teachings. Groups would meet in the home of one of their members to pray and share in the breaking of bread and the cup of wine to commemorate Jesus' last supper. By setting up churches along the great routes of the Roman Empire, Paul laid the foundations for the powerful church organization that would emerge in later centuries.

Since Paul could not be everywhere at the same time and since the Christian groups that he helped to organize came from diverse

The apostles Paul and John made the city of Ephesus in Asia Minor a major center of Christianity. Ephesus was first settled by Greek colonists in the 10th century B.C.

religious backgrounds, many questions arose about Christian beliefs and forms of worship. To answer these questions, Paul wrote a series of letters interpreting Jesus' teachings and resolving disputes. These letters, which Paul wrote in response to Christians in Corinth, Colossi, Ephesus, Galatia, Philippi, Rome, and Thessalonica, were saved by the recipients and became the basis for several books of the New Testament.

A recurring question facing the early followers of Jesus was how to deal with Gentiles who wanted to embrace the teachings of Jesus. Would they have to accept Judaism first? Paul met with Jesus' disciples in Jerusalem and urged them to allow Gentiles to be baptized into the Christian faith without first adopting Judaism. By adopting this policy, the disciples were able to win many more converts than before.

In 58 A.D., Paul returned to Jerusalem, where he was arrested by the Roman authorities as a troublemaker. He exercised his right as a Roman citizen to appeal his case to the emperor. When he arrived in Rome, he was placed under arrest pending a trial. Tradition holds that he was executed in Rome at about the time when the emperor Nero launched a brutal persecution of Christians. Like Paul, the apostle Peter carried the gospel across the Mediterranean world and to Rome, where he was arrested and executed —probably at the same time as Paul.

PERSECUTIONS
The spread of Christianity created problems for Roman officials ranging from Pontius Pilate, who ordered the execution of Jesus, to the emperors themselves. From the first, Christians were suspect to Roman officials

because they worshiped Jesus, who had been crucified as a rebel. When Christians refused to serve in the Roman army or worship the emperor as a god, they ran into more trouble with the authorities. As a result of the persecutions, Christians met in secret, but this led to persistent rumors that they practiced immoral rites. They were accused of being cannibals (eaters of human flesh) because of their ritual of the bread and wine, which they said represented the body and blood of Jesus.

In 64 A.D., while Nero was emperor, a fire broke out in Rome. It raged for six days, causing tremendous destruction. When a rumor began to circulate that Nero himself had set the fire, the emperor tried to shift the blame onto the Christians. As Tacitus explained, this led to fearful persecutions.

• • • *Nero fastened the guilt and inflicted the most exquisite tortures on a class hated for their abominations, called Christians. . . . Accordingly, an arrest was first made of all who pleaded guilty; then, upon their information, an immense multitude was convicted, not so much of the crime of firing the city, as of hatred against mankind. Mockery of every sort was added to their deaths. Covered with the skins of beasts, they were torn by dogs and perished, or were nailed to crosses, or were doomed to the flames and burnt, to serve as a nightly illumination. . . . Hence, even for criminals who deserved extreme and exemplary punishment, there arose a feeling of compassion; for it was not, as it seemed, for the public good, but to glut one man's cruelty, that they were being destroyed.*[5]

The Jewish Revolt. During this same period, the Jews of Palestine suffered as severely as the Christians. In 66 A.D. the Jews rose up in a widespread revolt against Rome. The revolt was finally put down in 70 A.D. by Titus, who captured Jerusalem, looted the Temple, and destroyed the entire city. Only the foundation of the western wall of the

Temple remained intact. Once each year on the anniversary of the destruction of the city, Jews were permitted access to this foundation to offer prayers. Over the centuries, this remnant became known as the "Wailing Wall."

Jews who survived the destruction of the city fled in all directions—some went south into the Arabian desert, some escaped east to Babylon, and some crossed the Mediterranean Sea into Europe and North Africa. Wherever they went in this new diaspora, they established synagogues and schools to maintain their covenant with Yahweh.

A group of Zealots who escaped from Jerusalem fled to Masada, a hilltop fortress overlooking the Dead Sea. There, they resisted the Romans for three more years. When they saw that the Romans were about to overwhelm them, they made a pact with each other, which Josephus described as follows:

• • • *Let us die before we become slaves under our enemies, and let us go out of the world, together with our children and our wives, in a state of freedom . . . God himself hath brought this necessity upon us; while the Romans desire the contrary, and are afraid lest any of us die before we are taken. Let . . . us leave them an example which shall at once cause their astonishment at our death, and their admiration of our hardiness therein.*[6]

When the Romans took the fortress, they found few survivors.

Laws against Christians. By the time of the Jewish revolt, Christianity had taken its separate path from Judaism. As you have read, Paul made it possible for Gentiles to embrace the new faith, and during his missionary work, he won large numbers of Gentile converts. As the number of Christians increased, however, they were seen as a greater threat and so were subjected to intermittent persecutions. By tradition, Rome was tolerant of the

---

[5]Tacitus, *Annals* XV, 44.

[6]Josephus, *Wars of the Jews* VII, 8, 6.

This detail from the arch of Titus shows Roman soldiers looting the Temple of Jerusalem. After the Temple was destroyed, the citizens of Judah were forced to support the temple of Jupiter in Rome.

diverse religions practiced within its borders. However, Christians (and Jews) posed a special problem because they refused to worship any but their own God.

Even though there were some laws against Christians, Roman governors often overlooked them and tolerated Christians in their provinces. Nonbelievers, however, frequently blamed Christians for such natural disasters as earthquakes and floods and demanded that they be punished.

The dilemma of Roman officials who had to decide between toleration and persecution was evident in the letter Pliny the Younger, governor of Bithynia in Asia Minor, addressed to the emperor Trajan. In it, he asked for advice on how to deal with the Christians. Trajan responded:

••• *You have taken the right line, my dear Pliny, in examining the cases of those denounced to you as Christians, for no hard and fast rule can be laid down, of universal application. They are not to be sought out; if they are informed against, and the charge is proved, they are to be punished, with this reservation—that if any one denies that he is a Christian, and actually proves it, that is by worshipping our gods, he shall be pardoned as a result of his incantation, however suspect he may have been with respect to the past. Pamphlets published anonymously should carry no weight in any charge whatsoever. They constitute a very bad precedent, and are also out of keeping with this age.[7]*

During the next hundred years, the Christians were alternately tolerated and oppressed, but by 245, as the stability of the Roman government declined, persecution increased. The emperor Decius (245–251) made the worship of *Caesar* (the title of the emperor) compulsory for everyone living in the empire except the Jews. On a certain day,

---

[7]Trajan to Pliny, *Pliny's Epistles*, X, xcvii, in Henry Bettenson, ed., *Documents of the Christian Church*, 2nd Ed. (London: Oxford University Press, 1963), p. 6.

all people were required to enter the temple of Caesar in their community, burn incense before the emperor's statue in the temple, and proclaim, "Caesar is my Lord." Those who obeyed this decree were given certificates saying that they were loyal citizens of the empire. Anyone who ignored the decree was to be executed. Thousands of Christians died for their faith, but in the end the Roman government was unable to enforce its decree. Moreover, the persecution began to create sympathy for Christians. As one Christian writer pointed out, "the blood of the martyrs was the seed of the church."

The last and bloodiest persecution took place during the reign of the emperor Diocletian (284-305), but it failed to crush Christianity and within a few years an edict was issued granting toleration to all religions in the empire.

OFFICIAL RECOGNITION

The edict of toleration came from the emperor Constantine, who gained control of the Roman Empire in 312. He credited his success against rivals to the imperial throne to a vision of Christ. The following year he issued the Edict of Milan, which said, in part:

• • • *We therefore announce that, notwithstanding any provisions concerning the Christians in our former instructions, all who choose that religion are to be permitted*

The Western or "Wailing" Wall is all that remains of the Temple of Jerusalem.

to continue therein, without any let or hindrance, and are not to be in any way troubled or molested. . . . Note that at the same time all others are to be allowed the free and unrestricted practice of their religions; for it accords with the good order of the realm and the peacefulness of our times that each should have freedom to worship God after his own choice; and we do not intend to detract from the honour due to any religion or its followers.[8]

Sometime after this edict, Constantine's mother, Helena, went to Palestine, which Christians now called the Holy Land. On this trip, she attempted to find the places where the important events in Jesus' life had occurred. According to tradition, she even found the cross on which Jesus had died. Constantine then financed the construction of churches on several sites she identified, including the Church of the Nativity in Bethlehem and the Church of the Holy Sepulcher in Jerusalem.

Although Constantine took several other steps to promote Christianity, including the convening of the Council of Nicaea, he did not accept baptism into the faith until shortly before his death in 337. Some historians suggest that he was motivated to support Christianity out of a desire for unity in the empire rather than out of personal conviction. Whatever his motivation, he greatly enhanced the position of Christians in the empire.

In 381, the emperor Theodosius decreed that Christianity would be the official religion of the empire. He closed all non-Christian places of worship and discontinued the Olympic Games, which were seen as a form of "pagan" worship. (*Paganus* in Latin means "country fellow," and pagan came to mean any non-Christian.)

THE APPEAL OF CHRISTIANITY

Within 400 years of its founding, Christianity had grown from an obscure and persecuted sect in Palestine into the principal religion of the Roman Empire. How did it achieve this success? At first, Christianity appealed strongly to the poor and oppressed because of its promises of immortality and a better life in the world hereafter, and its teaching of the equality of all believers in the sight of God. Its founder, Jesus, was an actual person whose life, teachings, and martyrdom were easily understood. In time, Christianity won converts among the educated classes who accepted its ideas of discipline and moderation, which were reminiscent of the Greek philosophies.

In its early days, the new faith accepted women on a nearly equal basis with men. Christian missionaries worked with enormous dedication, and their work was helped by the *Pax Romana*, the good means of transportation throughout the empire, and a common language. While the persecutions resulted in many deaths, the faith and courage of the Christian martyrs often gained sympathy for a faith that inspired such loyalty. Then, too, as Christianity spread, it developed a strong organization that was modeled in part on that of the Roman Empire. Once recognized as the official religion of the empire, this church organization joined forces—though not always in harmony—with the political institutions of Rome to ensure religious unity.

THE EARLY CHURCH

The apostles and other early followers of Jesus expected him to reappear within a short time. When this did not happen and the number of Christians continued to grow, they realized the need to set down their beliefs in an orderly fashion and establish some sort of church organization. In the 1st century A.D., the earliest writings of the New Testament were collected. They included the letters that Paul wrote to the various Christian communities in which he dealt with disputes among members and clarified ques-

---

[8]Constantine, "Edict of Milan," in *Documents of the Christian Church*, ed. Henry Bettenson, p. 22.

284

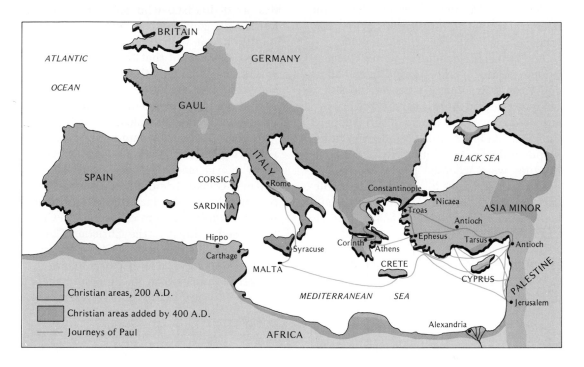

tions of belief. The four Gospels were also written down between about 50 A.D. and 70 A.D. Later, other books were added to and accepted as part of the New Testament.

As you have read, the first Christians met together in small groups in private houses. There was no distinction in rank between the teacher of a local group and the members. In fact, some early groups were led by women although Paul disapproved of the practice. These groups followed ceremonies that were similar to those held in the synagogues, including readings from the scriptures, prayers, and the singing of Psalms. Christians soon added two of their own rites—baptism for all new converts and the ceremony of eating bread and drinking wine to commemorate Jesus' last supper with the apostles.

As the new faith grew, however, many questions of belief and practice were raised. To answer these questions and to meet the other challenges confronting them, Chris-

tians developed a standard organization. A Christian community came to include a "bishop," from the Greek word *episkopos* which means "overseer;" a board of elders, called "presbyters" and eventually "priests;" and several assistants, called "deacons." The bishop was the highest authority on questions of faith and practice. He was helped in religious matters by the priests and in administrative matters by the deacons. By the end of the 1st century A.D., these Church leaders came to be known as the *clergy*, and the distinction grew between the clergy and the laity, or members of the congregation.

By the 2nd century A.D., the government of the Church had evolved a hierarchy with levels of administration that closely paralleled those of the Roman Empire. Each presbyter, or priest, led a local group, known as a *parish*. A bishop supervised a *diocese*, a region containing several parishes. By about 200 A.D., each city usually had a single bishop and a number of priests. At the next level was a region containing several dioceses, which became known as a *province*, and the bishop of the largest diocese within the province became known as an *archbishop*.

For a time, the bishops of Rome, Constantinople, Antioch, and Alexandria had about equal status. Eventually, however, the Bishop of Rome assumed the title of *pope* and claimed supremacy over the others. The bishops of Constantinople, Antioch, and Alexandria disputed the supreme authority of the pope, but they were accorded the lesser status of *patriarchs*. Struggles for power and jurisdictional disputes within the hierarchy would be only one of the problems facing the early Church.

CHURCH CONTROVERSIES

Jesus did not establish an organization to carry on his work. Nor did he put his teachings into writing. As long as the apostles lived, they could tell others about Jesus and his teachings, but even before they died, questions arose that Jesus had not discussed directly in his teachings. As the Church evolved, however, the clergy not only took charge of conducting services of worship and administering the Church but also became responsible for clarifying questions of Christian dogma, or doctrine.

Early Church leaders were faced with a large number of controversies. As conflicting points of view emerged, Church leaders attempted to resolve the controversies by meeting together in councils to establish *orthodox* (from the Greek meaning "right in opinion") answers. If Christians disregarded the decision of a Church council, they were guilty of heresy, and a heretic risked punishment such as *excommunication*—being cut off from membership in the Church. In the 2nd and 3rd centuries A.D., a variety of controversies arose. At issue were the nature of Christ, the role of the Church, and the means by which Christians could achieve salvation.

GNOSTICISM

The people who came to be known as *Gnostics* were dualists, who believed that two forces—of good and of evil—were constantly at war with each other in the universe. They taught that the physical world was evil and that only the world of the spirit was ideal and good. They believed that the God of the Old Testament was an evil force that had created the physical world. To them, Jesus was a messenger sent by the good, all-perfect God to reveal the knowledge (the Greek word *gnosis* means "knowledge") of good and evil. Gnostics denied that Jesus was fully human and emphasized the mystical and miracle-working nature of Jesus. The Gnostics posed a threat to the Christian Church by denying the humanity of Christ and leaning toward a mystical faith, closer to the older mystery religions than to Christian beliefs.

ARIANISM

A major controversy erupted over the teachings of a priest named Arius (256-336 A.D.) of Alexandria. It centered on the nature of Christ. Arius taught that God existed before Jesus; consequently, Jesus could not have been eternal or equal to God. Other Church leaders, led by Athanasius, the bishop of Alexandria, declared that Jesus was "true God" and even "of the same substance with God." Within a short time, the Arian controversy swept across the Christian world. Not only the clergy but also ordinary citizens debated the various points in the argument. In 325 A.D., the emperor Constantine called for a council of bishops to meet at Nicaea (present-day Iznik), in Asia Minor. After much deliberation, the Council of Nicaea condemned *Arianism* as heresy. The bishops also composed the "Nicene Creed" as a statement of orthodox belief.

● ● ● *We believe in one God the Father Almighty, Maker of heaven and earth, and of all things visible and invisible; and in one Lord Jesus Christ, the only-begotten Son of*

God, begotten of the Father before all worlds,
God of God, Light of Light . . . being of one
substance with the Father by whom all
things were made; who for us men, and for
our salvation, came down from heaven, and
was incarnate by the Holy Spirit of the
Virgin Mary, and was made man, and was
crucified also for us under Pontius Pilate. . . .
And we believe in the Holy Spirit, the Lord
and Giver of Life, who proceedeth from the
Father and the Son, who with the Father and
the Son together is worshipped and glorified,
who spoke by the prophets. And we believe
in one holy catholic and apostolic Church.
We acknowledge one baptism for the
remission of sins. And we look for the
resurrection of the dead, and the life of the
world to come. Amen.[9]

Constantine decreed that the writings of Arius should be burned and that Arius should be sent into exile. But Arianism was not so easily destroyed. Ulfilas, a priest who agreed with Arius, became a missionary to the Visigoths, Germanic tribes living north of the Danube River. He converted them to the Arian form of Christianity. The Visigoths spread Arianism to the Ostrogoths and later to the Vandals, who in turn carried Arianism into western Europe. As you will read (Chapter 15), at the end of the 5th century, the Church found a champion in Clovis, the king of the Franks, who successfully defended orthodox Christian teachings in western Europe against the heresy of Arianism.

Throughout the early centuries of Christianity, the bishops of the largest provinces met in councils to define matters of faith. Along with the beliefs expressed in the Nicene Creed, the Church adopted the concept of "apostolic succession," saying that Jesus had directed his apostles to carry his message throughout the world and that the apostles had in turn passed this authority on to the bishops. Because the chief apostle Peter

had gone to Rome, and had been martyred there, the bishops of Rome claimed that Jesus had chosen Rome as the site of his church and claimed authority over the other bishops and patriarchs.

To fight heresy and ensure orthodoxy, the Church also decided to establish an official body of Christian literature. Over a period of years, Church leaders examined all the existing writings about Jesus and the early spread of Christianity and decided which to accept and which to reject. The accepted writings were combined into the 27 books of the New Testament, while the Jewish writings of the Septuagint were defined as the Old Testament. Together, the New and Old Testaments became the Christian Bible.

THE CHURCH FATHERS During the 4th and 5th centuries, several prominent individuals helped formulate Christian doctrine. Among them were Saint Ambrose, a superb preacher, and Saint Jerome, who translated the Old and New Testaments into everyday Latin. These Christian thinkers became known as the Church fathers because they worked to develop a universal or "catholic" set of principles for the Church.

The most important of the early Church fathers was Saint Augustine (354-430), who was born in North Africa to a devoutly Christian mother and a pagan father. Augustine studied in Carthage to become a professor of rhetoric. There, he lived a decadent life and eventually became interested in Manicheanism, a Christian heresy similar to Gnosticism. Later, he received an appointment to teach rhetoric in Milan, where he heard Saint Ambrose, who was then the bishop of that city, preach about Jesus, human sinfulness, and divine forgiveness. Augustine was overcome by a sense of remorse for his past life and abandoned his old ways.

In his autobiography, *Confessions*, Augustine relates how he was meditating in a garden when he heard the voice of a child

---

[9]*Book of Confessions*, paragraphs 1.1-.3.

say, "Take up and read!" He picked up the Bible that he had carried into the garden, opened it at random and read "Let Jesus Christ himself be the armor that you wear; give no thought to satisfying the bodily appetites" (Romans 13:13-14). He decided that he must accept Jesus as his spiritual leader. Bishop Ambrose baptized him into the Church, and Augustine returned to North Africa. In 391, he was ordained as a priest, and four years later was named bishop of Hippo.

In this position, Augustine combated many heresies. When the Visigoths sacked Rome in 410, some people charged that Christianity was responsible for the "fall of Rome." This accusation inspired Augustine to write *The City of God*. In it, he set out a Christian philosophy of history that saw all human history as the unfolding of God's will. God, he said, had allowed the Romans to acquire their empire, but the only really worthwhile goal was to achieve the City of God. He compared the two cities—the earthly and the heavenly—in these words:

• • • *Two cities have been formed by two loves: the earthly by the love of self, even to the contempt of God; the heavenly by the love of God, even to the contempt of self. The former, in a word, glories in itself, the latter in the Lord. For the one seeks glory from men; but the greatest glory of the other is God, the witness of conscience. The one lifts up its head in its own glory; the other says to its God, "Thou art my glory, and the lifter up of my head." In the one, the princes and the nations it subdues are ruled by the love of ruling; in the other, the princes and the subjects serve one another in love, the latter obeying, while the former take thought for all. The one delights in its own strength, represented in the persons of its rulers; the other says to its God, "I will love Thee, O Lord, my strength."*[10]

Augustine elaborated other beliefs, including the concept of original sin—that as a result of the disobedience of Adam and Eve all humans are sinners from birth and that they are destined to eternal punishment. No one could escape from this fate except through the grace of God, but God only granted salvation to a select few. In this belief, he formulated the doctrine of predestination.

Not every Church leader agreed with Augustine. Pelagius, a British monk who arrived in Rome in 385, disagreed strongly with the concept of original sin. Moreover, he believed in a person's free will—that each individual has the ability to choose whether his or her life will be dedicated to good or evil, and that God bestows love and forgiveness on all who repent of evil deeds. Pelagius challenged Augustine's concept of original sin in these words:

• • • *Everything good and everything evil, in respect of which we are either worthy of praise or of blame, is done by us, not born in us. We are not born in our full development, but with a capacity for good or evil; we are begotten as well without virtue as without vice, and before the activity of our own personal will there is nothing in man but what God has stored for him.*[11]

Although Pelagius had many followers, Augustine fought his ideas and eventually triumphed. Pelagius was declared a heretic by the Church and condemned to exile.

Augustine died in 430, a year before the Vandals sacked Hippo. A few decades later in 476, Rome itself "fell" to invading Germanic tribes. With the collapse of the Roman Empire, the only central authority that survived in western Europe was the Church. Christians looked to the Church for leadership and security in a time of uncertainty and despair. From Rome, the pope began to exert authority not only over religious but also increasingly over secular affairs.

---

[10]Augustine, *The City of God* (trans. Marcus Dods, 1881) xiv, 28.

[11]Pelagius, "Concerning Original Sin," quoted in *Documents of the Christian Church*, ed. Bettenson, p. 75.

SUMMARY

Jesus was born into a Jewish family in a remote part of the Roman world. During his lifetime, he won a few devoted followers. After his death, his apostles and other missionaries persevered in spreading his teachings, winning converts first in the cities of the eastern Mediterranean and later in the western parts of the Roman Empire. By 200 A.D., a well organized Church had emerged. The early Christian Church faced persecutions from outside and controversies from within, but it continued to grow in size and strength until it succeeded in making Christianity the official religion of the Roman Empire. When Rome fell in 476, Christians throughout western Europe looked to the Church for guidance in political as well as spiritual matters.

QUESTIONS

1 What divisions existed within Judaism in the 1st century B.C.? How were the beliefs and practices of the Essenes similar to those of the early Christians?
2 How has archaeology thrown new light on the origins of Christianity?
3 Compare Christian teachings and beliefs to those of other religions within the Roman Empire.
4 How did the organization of the early Church meet its needs? Why did it use the organization of the Roman Empire as its model?
5 What issues were at the heart of the early Christian heresies? Why was the Church so concerned with proclaiming and defending orthodox beliefs?
6 What are the major similarities and differences between Church teachings and organization in the 1st century A.D. and today?

BIBLIOGRAPHY

Which book might describe the early Christian heresies?

MANSCHRECK, CLYDE. *A History of Christianity in the World.* Englewood Cliffs, N.J.: Prentice-Hall, 1974. *A chronological history of the development of Christianity with an emphasis on the forces that shaped current Christian beliefs and trends. Stresses recent developments in Christianity; places current problems in relation to political, social and economic issues; and offers a balanced view of these problems.*

PRITCHARD, JAMES B., ed. *Everyday Life in Bible Times.* Washington, D.C.: National Geographic Society, 1967. *A well-illustrated volume that traces the footsteps of Old and New Testament figures such as Abraham, Moses, David, Solomon, Jesus, and Paul. Increases understanding of the Bible by recreating the world of Biblical times.*

WHITNEY, JOHN R. and SUSAN W. HOWE. *Religious Literature of the West.* Minneapolis, Minnesota: Augsburg Publishing House, 1971. *A survey of the major themes of the three great religions of the West—Judaism, Christianity, and Islam—with selected readings from the Hebrew Bible, the rabbinic writings, the New Testament, and the Koran.*

13

● *O what a splendid city, how stately, how fair, how many monasteries therein, how many palaces raised by sheer labor in its broadways and streets, how many works of art, marvelous to behold; it would be weariness to tell of the abundance of all good things; of gold and of silver, garments of manifold fashion, and such sacred relics. Ships are at all times putting in at this port, so that there is nothing that men want that is not brought hither.*

FULK OF CHARTRES

The Byzantine Empire

The description above, which was written by an 11th-century visitor from western Europe, refers to Constantinople, the bustling capital of the Byzantine Empire. As the Roman Empire declined in the West, a new civilization emerged in the East and lasted for a thousand years. In 330, the emperor Constantine chose the small Greek trading town of Byzantium as his new capital. This "New Rome" was later called Constantinople, but it gave its ancient name to the Byzantine civilization.

The Byzantine Empire was heir to the Roman Empire; it was also heir to the learning, culture, and traditions of ancient Greece and the Middle East. Byzantine emperors claimed to be the successors of Augustus, but by the 7th century, Greek, and not Latin, was the language of the empire. The Byzantine emperors ruled over a vast territory stretching from the Balkans through Asia Minor, Syria, Egypt, and North Africa. They constantly had to defend their lands from determined invaders—first from the German tribes that overran western Europe, then from the Huns, the Persians, and the Arabs, each of whom seized parts of the empire for a time. Even when they lost territory to invaders, they held

firmly to Constantinople, an almost impregnable city which long sustained its reputation as the most marvelous city in the world.

CONSTANTINOPLE When Constantine decided to move his capital in 330, he selected Byzantium, which had been founded about 650 B.C. by Greek colonists under the leadership of Byzas.

Byzantium was closer than Rome to the prosperous provinces of the Eastern Roman Empire and to the centers of Christendom at

> The same natural advantages that drew Constantine to the site had influenced Byzas to select it originally. Byzas had been instructed by the oracle at Delphi to establish his colony "opposite the blind." He had been unable to interpret this directive, but later he realized that the Greeks who had settled earlier at Chalcedon, on the Asiatic side of the Bosporus, must have been blind to have overlooked the much more favorable site on the European side.

A stout wall three miles long protected the landward boundary of Constantinople. The city's defenses withstood invaders for more than 10 centuries.

This colossal head of Constantine once stood in the basilica that the emperor built in Rome.

Jerusalem, Antioch, and Alexandria. It was also at the crossroads of the busy trade routes between Europe and Asia and commanded access to the Black and Mediterranean seas.

Just as important, the city could be easily defended because it was bordered by water on three sides: the Sea of Marmara on the south, the landlocked harbor of the Golden Horn on the north, and the Bosporus on the east. During the reign of Theodosius II (408-450), three parallel walls, each 25 feet wide and 3 miles long, were erected across the western, and only landward approach to the city. The walls were built to protect it from the Germanic tribes who were penetrating across the Danube River. Other walls were also built along the Sea of Marmara, and a huge iron chain was forged to stretch across the Golden Horn to protect the harbor against seaborne invasions.

Like Rome, Constantinople was situated on seven low hills, and Constantine set out to make his new capital as beautiful as Rome. He built a forum, several temples, and a magnificent palace. He enlarged the Hippodrome (stadium), which had been built by Septimius Severus in the 3rd century. In time, Constantinople became the commercial and intellectual center of the Mediterranean world, as well as the administrative center of the Eastern Roman Empire.

JUSTINIAN In the 4th century, the emperor Theodosius divided the Roman Empire between his two sons, with one ruling the western provinces, the other controlling the eastern provinces. During the 5th century, you will recall, the Roman Empire in the West collapsed under the pressure of successive invasions. In the East, emperors managed to resist attacks from outside and ruled over a prosperous economy.

In 527, Justinian succeeded to the imperial throne and ruled until 565. He was an energetic and ambitious ruler who dreamed of restoring the unity of the Roman Empire. During his long reign, he fought many wars to expand the empire, but this policy of re-conquering the West aroused much controversy. So, too, did his marriage to Theodora, an actress and a courtesan. In time, however, Theodora became Justinian's most trusted adviser and proved to be a person of keen political insight and great personal courage.

THE NIKA REVOLT

Theodora showed her strong determination during an uprising just five years after Justinian took office. In Constantinople, chariot racing was such a popular pastime that it aroused great excitement and fury among the spectators. The two rival teams, the Blues and the Greens, were each supported by a different class. Wealthy aristocrats favored the Blues, while the common people backed the Greens. During the races in 532, fights between factions in the audience exploded into a violent uprising that was soon directed against the emperor who had imposed heavy taxes on the people to pay for his grand schemes for imperial expansion.

During the Nika Revolt—so called because the rallying cry of the people was "Nika!" ("Let us conquer!")—much of Constantinople was burned. At one point, as the mob gathered in the Hippodrome to proclaim a new emperor, Justinian reportedly wanted to flee. But Theodora persuaded him to remain by saying:

> ● ● ● My opinion then is that the present time, above all others, is inopportune for flight, even though it bring safety. For while it is impossible for a man who has seen the light not also to die, for one who has been an emperor it is unendurable to be a fugitive. May I never be separated from this purple, and may I not live that day on which those who meet me shall not address me as mistress. If now, it is your wish to save yourself, O Emperor, there is no difficulty. For we have much money, and there is the sea, here the boats. However, consider whether it will not come about after you have been saved that you would gladly exchange that safety for death. As for myself,

> I approve a certain ancient saying that royalty is a good burial-shroud.[1]

Emboldened by these words, the emperor held firm, and with the help of his general Belisarius, the rebellion was crushed. About 30,000 people died in this revolt, many of them massacred in the Hippodrome by the army.

CAMPAIGN IN THE WEST

By the 6th century, the lands once ruled by Rome in the West had been overrun by various Germanic tribes: the Visigoths occupied Spain, the Ostrogoths controlled Italy, and the Vandals held much of North Africa. Justinian longed to restore the power of the Roman Empire in these regions. Before embarking on this venture, however, he attempted to secure his eastern boundary by entering into a treaty with the Sassanids, the rulers of Persia.

Justinian then directed two of his generals, Belisarius and Narses, to lead a large expedition to the western Mediterranean. In 533, Belisarius defeated the Vandals in northern Africa, Corsica, Sardinia, and the Balearic Islands. Three years later, his army recaptured Rome and later Ravenna, from the Ostrogoths. The people of Rome welcomed Justinian's armies because they were unhappy about living under the Arian form of Christianity practiced by the Ostrogoths. Justinian's armies also pushed into southern Spain, overcoming the Visigoths.

During Justinian's reign, the Byzantine Empire reached its greatest territorial extent, and Justinian could claim to rule much of the ancient Roman Empire. But the reconquest of the West drained the empire's resources. Seeing this, the Persians soon renewed their attacks on its eastern borders. Soon after Justinian's death, the empire was besieged on all sides: the Slavs, Avars, and

---

[1]Procopius, *History of the Wars* I, 24.

The empress Theodora was an influential advisor to her husband. She is shown here with the members of her court.

Bulgars threatened from the north; the Lombards pushed into northern Italy; and the Persians moved in from the east.

JUSTINIAN'S ACHIEVEMENTS Despite his short-lived military triumphs, Justinian did make changes of lasting significance. Even before launching his campaign in the West, he drew up plans for building a beautiful new cathedral. *Hagia Sophia* (Holy Wisdom), as the cathedral was called, was an architectural triumph that still ranks as one of the world's most impressive buildings. Its relatively shallow dome is 108 feet in diameter and rises to a height of 184 feet. The dome is supported on a complex arrangement of arches and piers.

Originally, the interior of Hagia Sophia was lavishly decorated with mosaics and colored marble. When the cathedral was dedicated in 537, Justinian compared it with the Temple at Jerusalem, as described in the Old Testament, and he is reported to have proclaimed, "O Solomon, I have outdone thee!"

After the capture of Constantinople by the Ottoman Turks in 1453, Hagia Sophia was converted into a mosque. The mosaics of Christian scenes were covered with whitewash, and four towering minarets were added to the exterior. When the nation of Turkey was established in 1922, the whitewash was removed from the mosaics, and the building was made into a museum.

Perhaps the most outstanding achievement of Justinian's reign was his codification of Roman law. In 528, he appointed a commission to compile a new code of law for the empire. The commissioners were instructed

The Hagia Sophia is the greatest monument of Byzantine architecture. The many windows are made possible by the arches in the walls, which carry the weight of the dome.

to collect all laws from the existing law codes and eliminate any laws that were obsolete or contradictory. The results of this monumental work came to be known as the *Corpus Juris Civilis* (Body of Civil Law). The code consisted of three parts: the *Institutes*, a textbook of legal principles; the *Digest*, a summary of legal opinions; and the *Code*, a list of laws from the time of Hadrian to the reign of Justinian. The *Corpus Juris Civilis* preserved Roman legal traditions in the Byzantine Empire and later became the foundation of the legal systems of most European nations. Among the principles embodied in the code were rules of evidence such as the requirement that the accuser must prove that a charge is true.

After the fall of Rome, knowledge of Roman law was poorly preserved in western Europe. By the 12th century, however, some scholars in the West began to study Justin-

ian's *Corpus Juris Civilis* and thereby reintroduced these ancient principles. During the 14th and 15th centuries, some European monarchs surrounded themselves with advisers who understood and could apply the code because it stressed the concept that the ruler was the source of all law and that judges were the representatives of the ruler in administering the law.

CHURCH AND STATE

Justinian's motto, "One empire, one church, one law," summed up his major goals. Achieving religious unity, however, proved to be difficult. Justinian made membership in the Church a requirement for citizenship. He ordered the university at Athens to close because it was considered a center of pagan teachings. Yet he was unsuccessful in combating *monophysitism*, a heretical movement that claimed Jesus had only a divine nature, rather than a combination of human and divine natures. The problem was complicated by the fact that the empress Theodora was a monophysite. In the end, the emperor himself accepted the heretical teaching, which caused strained relations with the pope.

During his reign, Justinian moved the Byzantine Church along a different path from that taken by the Roman Catholic Church in

BYZANTINE EMPIRE	
305-337	Constantine I
408-450	Theodosius II
518-527	Justin
527-565	Justinian
610-711	Dynasty of Heraclius
610-641	Heraclius
717-741	Leo III
780-797	Constantine VI
797-802	Irene
867-1025	Macedonian Dynasty
976-1025	Basil II

the West. The emperor himself acted as head not only of the State but also of the Church. He controlled the election of the patriarch and administered Church affairs. This combining of secular and religious roles is sometimes called *Caesaropapism*. For Justinian, the Church was a rallying point and a symbol of unity, but in the years ahead, Byzantine emperors would become deeply involved in divisive religious controversies, as you will read later in this chapter.

DYNASTY OF HERACLIUS   In 610, Heraclius, the military governor of Carthage, seized power and established a new Byzantine dynasty. By this time, the empire that Justinian had expanded was threatened on all sides. The Lombards had conquered much of Italy, leaving the Byzantine Empire in control only of Sicily, southern Italy, and the areas around Venice and Ravenna. However, Heraclius and his successors had no time for Italy; instead, they were forced to concentrate their energies on threats to the empire's eastern provinces.

Early in his reign, Heraclius suffered a series of defeats as Chroeses II, the ambitious ruler of Persia, conquered Syria and Palestine, destroying many Christian churches in Jerusalem. The Persians carried back to their capital many Christian relics, including pieces of wood that supposedly came from the True Cross on which Jesus was crucified. They also invaded Egypt, capturing the fields and storage facilities which provided grain to the empire. Other Persian armies marched through Asia Minor and besieged Constantinople itself.

Heraclius rallied his forces to fight back. With funds confiscated from various churches and provincial treasuries, he bought off the Slavs and the Avars, who were threatening the empire in the north. He also abandoned the Roman system of provincial governments, in which civil power was separated from military power. In its place, he appointed a *strategos* to govern each province.

The *strategos*, who was directly responsible to the emperor, served as both military and civilian governor of the region.

In 627, Heraclius went on the offensive against the Persians. He led his army through Asia Minor into Persia, where he won a decisive victory over the Persians near the site of ancient Nineveh. When Chroeses II was murdered a short time later, Heraclius dictated the terms of a peace treaty to his successor. The Byzantine emperor regained Syria, Palestine, and Egypt and recovered the relics of the True Cross, which he personally returned to Jerusalem.

These long and devastating wars exhausted both Persia and the Byzantine Empire, so that both were ill-prepared to face a new threat—the invasion of the Arab armies who were inspired by the teachings of a new religion, Islam. As you will read in Chapter 14, the teachings of the prophet Mohammed formed the basis for the religion of Islam. Within 20 years of Mohammed's death in 632, Moslem armies had overrun the richest provinces of the Byzantine Empire from North Africa and Egypt to Palestine, Syria, and parts of Asia Minor. In 655, a Moslem fleet inflicted heavy losses on the Byzantine navy in the eastern Mediterranean; between 673 and 678, Constantinople itself was blockaded, and the trade of the empire was crippled. The Moslems were finally repulsed when the Byzantines began to use a powerful new weapon, called "Greek fire." Today, this weapon would be called a "flamethrower." A mixture of naphtha, sulfur, and saltpeter was put into a tube that was closed at one end. When water was added through the open end of the tube, these chemicals underwent combustion and the resulting fire was propelled at enemy ships, causing some damage and much fear.

By the end of the 7th century, the Byzantine Empire faced renewed attacks from the north. Slavs infiltrated the Balkan Peninsula, and Bulgars crossed the Danube in 679, defeating the Byzantine army and demanding tribute to maintain peace. By 700, the empire

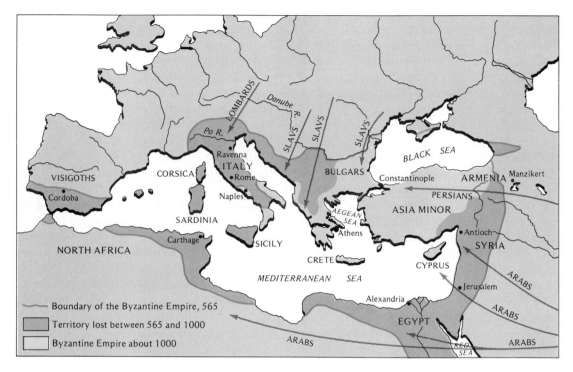

Boundary of the Byzantine Empire, 565

Territory lost between 565 and 1000

Byzantine Empire about 1000

consisted of little more than Asia Minor, the Balkans, southern Italy, and Sicily.

REIGN OF LEO III

In 718, Leo III, a powerful general from Asia Minor, gained the crown and set about restoring order in the empire. He reorganized its administration, dividing larger districts into smaller ones and making the local commanders responsible for civil and military matters in their own districts. At the same time, he strengthened his authority over them. Leo successfully directed the defense of Constantinople against a renewed Moslem blockade and finally drove the Moslems from Asia Minor. His policies succeeded in freeing the Byzantine Empire from attacks for a few years and restored a stability that enabled it to survive the political and religious controversies of the next few hundred years.

In 780, a 10-year-old boy, Constantine VI, ascended the throne. His mother, the empress Irene, ruled in his name until he reached maturity. With the support of the army, Constantine seized power in his own name in 790 and exiled his mother. After seven years of conspiring to regain the throne, Irene succeeded in overthrowing her son. She then had him blinded and imprisoned. A few years later, after Constantine's death, Irene assumed the title of emperor and ruled for five years (797-802). Her autocratic rule, mismanagement of finances, and unpopular positions on theological issues, which you will read about later in this chapter, created so much controversy that her reign was ended through palace intrigue, and she was again sent into exile.

Irene's rule led to strained relations with Pope Leo III in Rome. The pope declared that the throne of the Byzantine Empire was vacant because a woman was incapable of ruling an empire. He then bestowed the title of "Emperor of the Romans" on Charlemagne, the king of the Franks (see Chapter 14) in the hope that Charlemagne would help him exert control over the Church in the East. The Byzantines, who regarded themselves as the sole heirs to Roman power, greatly resented this interference. Their resentment grew in the years ahead as other controversies erupted, deepening the division between the eastern and western branches of Christendom.

MACEDONIAN DYNASTY Under the Macedonian dynasty, which lasted from 867 to 1025, the Byzantine Empire enjoyed a new period of expansion and prosperity. Well-equipped and highly trained Byzantine armies recovered Syria, Armenia, Cyprus, and Crete from the Moslems. Finances were handled wisely. The protecting walls of Constantinople were rebuilt, and that city enjoyed a cultural renaissance. The most outstanding emperor of this period was Basil II (976-1025), who earned the title "Slayer of the Bulgars" by crushing the Bulgars in 1004 and annexing their territory to the empire. Basil II maintained friendly relations with Vladimir, the ruler of Kiev in southern Russia, and helped bring about his conversion to Christianity. As a result, Byzantine Christianity and culture were carried into Russia.

DECLINE OF THE EMPIRE During the 11th century, the empire again went into a decline, which lasted for 400 years. Emperors faced both internal and external difficulties. In Asia Minor, noble landowners raised their own armies and rebelled against the central government. Faced with this threat, emperors were forced to increase taxes so that they could hire mercenary soldiers. Although Constantinople remained the richest trading city in the Mediterranean region, it faced competition from other centers, especially from Venice, whose merchants were actively trading with the Moslems. The growing economic rivalry between Venice and Constantinople would have disastrous consequences.

Another threat to the Byzantine Empire came from the advancing armies of the Seljuk Turks, who had converted to Islam and were invading both Arab and Christian lands. In 1071, a Byzantine army under the emperor Romanus IV was defeated at Manzikert in Syria by the Seljuk Turks, and the wealthy eastern provinces fell to the Moslem Turks.

LATIN EMPIRE

When various Byzantine emperors asked the pope for help against the Turks, the pope finally responded with a call for a *crusade*, or holy war against the "infidel," as Christians called all Moslems. Although the early Crusades were directed toward reconquering the Holy Land (see Chapter 16), the Fourth Crusade (1202-1204) proved costly for the Byzantine Empire. Urged on by Venetian merchants who wanted to eliminate their chief commercial rival, Constantinople, the Crusaders attacked Constantinople. For three days, Crusaders looted and burned the great city. Thousands of citizens were massacred, and much of the treasure of the city was carried to Venice and other parts of Europe.

The Crusaders established a Latin Empire over Constantinople and parts of Greece. It lasted for 60 years until the Byzantine emperor regained Constantinople. However, the city never fully recovered from the devastation caused by the Crusaders. Although the Byzantine Empire survived for almost 200 years more, its rulers presided over only a fragment of its former lands.

FALL OF CONSTANTINOPLE

In 1451, Mohammed II became ruler of the Ottoman Turks, who had migrated out of Central Asia and conquered the lands held by the Seljuk Turks. Two years later, Mohammed II decided to capture Constantinople. He hired a Hungarian military engineer to design huge cannons, which could project

In 1453, Constantinople was conquered by the Turks, who blockaded the city with a large fleet of ships and besieged its walls.

cannonballs weighing 1200 pounds each, to destroy the walls of the city. Mohammed II lay siege to the city with 100,000 soldiers and blockaded its harbor with a large fleet. For seven weeks, the city's defenders fought by day and repaired their walls by night. When the emperor Constantine XI appealed to Pope Nicholas V at Rome for help, the pope responded that help would be sent if the Church at Constantinople would accept the pope as its head. The division in Christendom was so deep by then that one Byzantine official replied, "It is better to see in this city the power of the Turkish turban than that of the Latin tiara." On May 29, 1453, Constantinople fell to the Moslem Turks. The last Byzantine emperor was killed valiantly fighting on the walls of his capital. Mo-

hammed II then made the city the capital of the new Ottoman Empire and changed its name to Istanbul.

THEOLOGICAL CONTROVERSIES

By 1453, the Byzantine Empire had endured for more than a thousand years. It enjoyed periods of prosperity and stability along with times of revolt and turmoil. Its rulers established an autocratic and centralized government and were supported by an efficient bureaucracy. The emperor controlled the Church, and the Church in turn was a unifying force. Yet despite the loyalty of the people to the Church, the Byzantine Empire was frequently torn by bitter theological disputes.

One controversy centered around the question of the nature of Christ. Monophysites, as you have read, maintained a belief that Jesus had only a single, divine nature. This belief was held by many Christians in Egypt, Syria, and parts of Asia Minor. However, it ran counter to orthodox Church teachings that Jesus was one person with two natures, human and divine. When the Church tried to fight the heretical belief, disputes arose throughout the East. Eventually, Christians in Egypt renounced the authority of the patriarch and developed their own Coptic Church.

ICONOCLASTIC CONTROVERSY

Another controversy arose in the 8th century over the use of **icons**, or sacred images. Many common people came to see icons as images to be worshiped rather than as representations of holy scenes or people. They burned incense, lit candles, and prayed to icons. Some Church leaders, and even some Byzantine emperors, claimed that this reverence for icons amounted to idolatry, or the worship of graven images, which was forbidden in the Bible.

In 725, the emperor Leo III issued an edict forbidding reverence for icons and ordering the removal of all religious paintings and

The Byzantines developed the distinctive iconographic style of art. Sacred figures are represented in a one-dimensional manner, and usually look directly at the viewer.

statues from churches and public places. This edict led to widespread rioting not only in Constantinople, but elsewhere in Greece and in other Byzantine provinces between *iconoclasts* ("image-breakers"), as those who opposed the use of icons were called, and people who felt that reverence for icons was a legitimate form of worship. During the riots, many icons were destroyed.

The pope soon took a stand on this controversy that was dividing the Byzantines. He decreed that icons could be used (though not worshiped) to help the masses of illiterate Christians to understand their faith, and he denounced the iconoclasts as heretics.

The iconoclastic controversy raged on into the 9th century with some emperors supporting the use of icons and others banning them. It soured relations between the Byzantine Empire and the pope. Although the quarrel was eventually resolved and icons were restored in the eastern Church, it contributed to the strains between eastern and western Christendom.

THE FINAL BREAK

Other antagonisms developed between the Byzantine Church and the Roman Catholic Church. Since early in the Christian era, leaders in the eastern and western Churches had been rivals for power and prestige. During the 9th century, several popes felt that they were not getting enough help from the Byzantine emperor in the struggles against the Lombards and Moslems in the West. At the same time, a rivalry developed between Latin- and Greek-speaking missionaries who were trying to convert the Slavs of eastern Europe to Christianity.

Old quarrels between the eastern and western Churches were revived and contributed to the growing split. One involved the Nicene Creed, which a Church council had issued in 325. The Church in Rome and the eastern Church had long disagreed over the wording of the creed. In the 11th century, this disagreement coupled with conflicting claims of the pope and patriarch to rule over the Church in southern Italy led to the final break. In 1054, the pope sent representatives to Constantinople to meet with the patriarch. The meeting quickly led to bitter denunciations, after which the patriarch and the papal representatives excommunicated each other. This event marked the *schism*, or division, between the eastern and western Church.

The Church in the West, which was headed by the pope and used Latin, came to be known as the Roman Catholic Church; the Church in the East, which was headed by the patriarch and used Greek, came to be known as the Orthodox (or sometimes the Eastern Orthodox) Church.

CONTINUING DIFFERENCES

The Orthodox Church and the Roman Catholic Church had grown apart over the centuries so that the schism in 1054 marked the final break in the unity of Christendom. Today, these differences still remain. For example, the Orthodox Church does not accept two doctrines of the Roman Catholic Church: the infallibility of the pope and the Immaculate Conception of Mary, the mother of Jesus. Roman Catholic priests must take a vow of celibacy, while Orthodox priests are permitted to marry, although a candidate for the office of bishop may not be married. Until 1964, all Roman Catholic services were conducted in Latin, while services in the Orthodox Church were conducted in the language of the people, thereby giving rise to what are known as the Russian, Greek, Serbian, and other Orthodox churches.

In 1964, Pope Paul VI met with Athenagoras, patriarch of Constantinople, at Jerusalem. Each leader rescinded the longstanding excommunication of the leader of the other church. While the churches of the East and West have had more cordial relations since that meeting, they remain widely separated in doctrine and administration.

BYZANTINE CIVILIZATION

Despite the theological controversies that erupted frequently, the Byzantine emperors presided over a brilliant civilization. At a time when western Europe was in a state of political, social, and economic decline following the invasions of the Germanic tribes, the people of the Byzantine Empire enjoyed the benefits of a stable and diverse economy.

COMMERCE AND AGRICULTURE

Constantinople was not only the political capital but also the commercial and intellectual center of the empire. With a population of about a half million people from all over the Middle East, it was a beautiful city, with splendid palaces, gardens, and fountains. It had hospitals for the sick, orphanages, and homes for the elderly; and it boasted great public works, including a municipal water-supply system and a sewer system.

Constantinople was the center of Byzantine commerce, with ships and caravans bringing spices, tapestries, leather goods, metalwork, and grain from all parts of the empire. The movement of all these goods was closely monitored by officials appointed by the emperor. Manufacturing was also closely regulated. Craftsmen and merchants were organized into guilds, associations formed for mutual aid and protection by people in the same trade or industry. Guilds were under strict government supervision. For example, sons of guild members were required to follow their fathers' occupations, and any infringement of a guild rule was punishable by expulsion from the guild. The government fixed wages and prices, and also controlled working conditions as well as weights and measures.

Byzantine emperors actively encouraged trade and commerce. Constantine introduced the bezant, a gold coin that remained the most stable unit of exchange in the Mediterranean world for 700 years. Justinian encouraged several monks who had lived in China to smuggle some silkworms to Constantinople. The smuggled silkworms became the basis for a flourishing silk industry that was made into a profitable government monopoly. Procopius, Justinian's official historian, gives the following account of the beginnings of the silk industry:

● ● ● While it is impossible to convey the worms thither alive, it was still practical and altogether easy to convey their offspring. Now the offspring of these worms, they said, consisted of innumerable eggs from each one. And men bury these eggs, long after the time when they are produced, in dung, and, after thus heating them for a sufficient time, they bring forth the living creatures. After they had spoken thus, the emperor promised to reward them with large gifts and urged them *to confirm their account in action. They then once more went to Serinda and brought back the eggs to Byzantium, and in the manner described caused them to be transformed into worms, which they fed on the leaves of the mulberry; and thus they made possible from that time forth the production of silk in the land of the Romans (i.e., the Eastern Empire).*[2]

The cities of the empire depended on the stable agricultural system. In the early days of the empire, Egypt provided the grain, as it had during the Roman Empire. After the Moslem conquest of Egypt, most food came from Asia Minor. *Serfs*, or peasants tied to the land, worked on huge estates owned by nobles or the Church. Their labor supported the landowners who lived in luxury in the cities.

LEARNING

Byzantine scholars studied and preserved the heritage of ancient Greece and Rome. They carefully copied the great works of ancient Greek literature. Scholars produced numerous digests of classical Greek works and wrote commentaries on them. During the Byzantine period, manuscripts began to appear in book form rather than as scrolls as they had in the past. These manuscripts became an invaluable source of information for later scholars.

In the early empire, literacy was widespread among people in the upper class. Sons of wealthy parents were educated either by tutors or in private schools. They learned to read the Bible and the writings of classical Greek authors, such as Homer, Sophocles, and Plato. Some boys were educated in monasteries. Wealthier young men often continued their studies in philosophy and rhetoric at the great centers of learning in Athens, Alexandria, and Beirut until the latter two cities fell to the Moslems in the 7th century.

---

[2]Procopius, *History of the Wars* VIII, 17.

Young girls were trained in the household arts by their mothers, while some from wealthy families were tutored in academic subjects as well. A few learned to read and write in convents.

ARCHITECTURE AND ART

Byzantine architecture and art forms reflected the several traditions that came together in the empire: Greco-Roman, oriental, and Christian. Since most palaces and government buildings were destroyed over the centuries, what remains of Byzantine architecture are the beautiful domed churches with their magnificent, ornate interiors and unadorned exteriors.

From the 9th to 11th centuries, Byzantine architects designed churches using the shape of the Greek cross, which has four arms of equal length. Frequently, they added a narthex (entry space) on one arm and an apse (rounded projection) on the opposite arm for balance. The most striking feature was a large dome arching over the center of the church. The Byzantine style of architecture was adopted by the Venetians when they built St. Mark's Cathedral and by the Russians, who modified the Byzantine dome into the onion-shaped domes seen on churches in Moscow and Kiev.

All forms of art flourished in Constantinople, whose wealthy families supported the finest artists and artisans. Byzantine artists portrayed human forms in a stylized manner: torsos were elongated, and people were almost always depicted in flat, frontal view, with relatively small, almond-shaped faces dominated by large eyes, peering out from under arched eyebrows. The mouths were small, and the noses were long and narrow.

Much art was devoted to portraying holy figures. The apostles and numerous saints were rendered everywhere in frescoes or mosaics. In the churches, these religious figures were always placed in prescribed relationships to one another to show the relative importance of each person. The figure of Jesus, for example, was always in the center of the main dome, with angels arranged in order of importance below him. Major events in the life, death, and resurrection of Jesus were shown below the angels. Representations of the apostles, prophets, and saints were placed at the lowest level.

Byzantine artists also fashioned exquisite secular works of art, such as ivory plaques, intricate gold jewelry set with semiprecious stones, beautifully decorated manuscripts, and small boxes called *reliquaries* that were designed to hold sacred relics. Artists decorated objects using the cloisonné process, in which colorful enamel is laid down between thin wires of gold. Brocade, velvet, and silk fabrics embroidered with gold and silver threads were shipped to all parts of the empire.

LASTING INFLUENCE

The Byzantine Empire was heir to the civilizations of ancient Greece and Rome. Although it developed its own civilization, its greatest legacy was the preservation of the learning of the ancient world. Through Justinian's code, it preserved the Roman concepts of law. By copying the manuscripts of the ancient Greeks, Byzantine scholars preserved the classical heritage of Greece.

Byzantine emperors developed an efficient bureaucracy that was able to maintain order even during times of dynastic turmoil. For many centuries, the Byzantine Empire fought off determined invaders from the East. In this way, it served as a buffer, absorbing the brunt of invasions that might otherwise have overwhelmed the kingdoms that were emerging in western Europe.

Byzantine monks and missionaries transmitted the ideas and inventions of the Greek and Roman worlds to the Slavic peoples, whom they converted to Christianity. In the 9th century, Saint Cyril and Saint Methodius, who had been educated in Constantinople, were sent as missionaries to the Slavs in Bohemia and Moravia. They created the *Cyrillic alphabet* from Greek letters modified to represent Slavic sounds, and they translated the Bible as well as hymns and rituals of the Christian Church into the Slavic languages. The Cyrillic alphabet is still used in several eastern European countries and in the Soviet Union.

When the split developed between the eastern and western branches of Christendom, the Poles, Bohemians, and Hungarians chose to follow the leadership of the pope at Rome, while the people of the present-day Balkan nations and Russia accepted the leadership of the patriarch at Constantinople. Byzantine culture and traditions profoundly influenced the princes of Kiev and Moscow. When the Ottoman Turks captured Constantinople in 1453, Ivan IV, ruler of an emerging Russian nation, claimed to be the successor of the Byzantine emperors. Russian rulers took the title *czar* meaning "Caesar." Moscow became the seat of the Orthodox Church, and the czars called their city the "third Rome" because it succeeded ancient Rome and Constantinople. They adopted the double-headed eagle, symbol of the Byzantine emperor. In political matters, too, they adopted Byzantine practices by maintaining absolute rule and asserting their authority over the Church.

SUMMARY

While Western Europe was plunged into chaos after the fall of Rome, a powerful new civilization emerged in the eastern provinces of the Roman Empire. The foundations of the Byzantine Empire were laid when the emperor Constantine built his new capital at Byzantium, a strategically located site on the Bosporus. In the 6th century, Justinian expanded the empire, regaining much of the lands lost in the West. In the centuries after Justinian's death, the empire experienced periods of strength as well as periods of decline.

In its long history, the Byzantine Empire developed a remarkable civilization that preserved the learning of the classical world, and this learning was eventually passed on to the West. Rivalry between the eastern and western branches of Christianity led to a schism and the emergence of two separate Christian churches. At its height, the Byzantine Empire with its splendid capital at Constantinople was the envy of the Western world. However, the riches of Constantinople and its rivalry with Venice led to its devastation during the Fourth Crusade. Although the empire recovered from that blow, it was not strong enough to withstand the onslaught of the Ottoman Turks, who captured Constantinople in 1453.

QUESTIONS

1 How did geography shape the development of Constantinople? Of the Byzantine Empire?

2 Describe Justinian's major goals. In what areas did he have the most success? Why? In what areas did he have the least success? Why?

3 Why was the Roman Empire in the East able to survive for a thousand years after the collapse of the Roman Empire in the West? Explain why this survival was so critical to the future of western Europe.

4 What differences developed between the Christian Church in the East and West? What were the causes of the schism? Analyze the immediate and longterm effects of the schism on both the Byzantine Empire and western Europe.

5 What evidence of Byzantine influence can you find in both eastern and western Europe?

BIBLIOGRAPHY

Which book might discuss Byzantine influence on the West?

HEAD, CONSTANCE. *Justinian II of Byzantium.* University of Wisconsin Press, 1972. *A thoroughly researched biography of a colorful Byzantine emperor who ruled from 685-695, was deposed by a usurper, wandered alone for about 10 years among the barbarian tribes before gathering an army of Bulgarian mercenaries and returning in victory to Constantinople. His career spanned a critical time within the Byzantine Empire.*

MANGO, CYRIL. *Byzantium, Empire of New Rome.* New York: Scribner's, 1980. *A study of life in Byzantium from the perspective of its language, society, economy, and religion; based on the point of view of the "average" Byzantine citizen.*

RICE, TAMARA TALBOT. *Everyday Life in Byzantium.* London: B. T. Batsford, 1967. *A discussion of the influence of the Byzantine Empire on Europe through its architecture and religion that examines both the way of life of the common people of Byzantium as well as the rituals of the imperial court and the Church.*

14

● *Say: Allah is One, the Eternal God. He begot none, nor was He begotten. None is equal to Him.*

MOHAMMED

The Islamic World

Islam, the youngest of the major religions of the world, developed in Arabia early in the 7th century. Its followers, who are called Moslems, worship Allah, the same, all-powerful deity worshiped by Jews and Christians. Moslems believe that Allah made his final revelations to his prophet, Mohammed. These revelations were later compiled into the *Koran*, the holy book of Islam. The Arabic word *Islam* means "submit," as Mohammed called on Arabs to submit to the will of Allah, while *Moslem* means "one who submits."[1]

Within ten years of receiving his first revelation, Mohammed had gathered a body of followers dedicated to spreading the message of Allah throughout the world. Within a century of Mohammed's death in 632, Moslem armies had conquered a region stretching from the Atlantic Ocean in the west to the Indus River in the east. Within the vast Islamic Empire, which rivaled that of the Byzantines and Persians, Moslem scholars developed a brilliant civilization incorporating knowledge from the Mediterranean world and eastern Asia.

After the 11th century, a series of invasions fragmented the Islamic Empire, but the religion of Islam continued to unite the various cultural and ethnic groups that had accepted it. As a result, Islam has continued to play an important role in the world to the present day.

ARABIA BEFORE ISLAM While the Middle East, especially the Fertile Crescent, has been mentioned earlier in this book, there has been little reference to the vast Arabian peninsula, which forms the southwest corner of the continent of Asia. The inhabitants of this desert region call their land *Jazirat al 'Arab*, "the island of Arabia," because it is a huge peninsula—approximately one-third the size of the continental United States—with the Red Sea to the west, the Mediterranean Sea to the north, the Persian Gulf along most of the east, and the Arabian Sea to the south. Much of the land in the south is called the "Vacant Quarter" because there is no water and few people. In other regions, there are oases which provide water for the sheep, goats, and camels of the Bedouins ("desert dwellers").

---

[1]Mohammed may also be spelled as *Muhammed*, Koran as *Quran*, and Moslem as *Muslim*.

Yemen, which occupies the southwest corner of the peninsula, was called *Felix Arabia* ("pleasant Arabia") by the Romans because it was a source of spices and of aromatic gums, myrrh, and frankincense. Because of its strategic location, Yemen was an important commercial center for caravans carrying goods from India, China, and Africa to the Roman world. With wealth from trade, the people built great cities and beautiful buildings. Many Jews who had fled from Palestine in the 1st and 2nd centuries settled among the Arabs in Yemen.

By 600, Arabs were divided into two groups, Bedouins and city dwellers. The Bedouins were nomads who moved with their herds from oasis to oasis. They were divided into tribes, each headed by a *sheik*, or chief, who was advised by the heads of leading families in the tribe. Each tribe also had its own set of customs, called *sunna*, which served as its code of laws. Strength, courage in battle, and tribal loyalty were the virtues they prized most highly. As in many other primitive societies, sickly infants and unwanted female children were abandoned to die. In the harsh conditions of the desert life, widows and orphans had no protection and were frequently forced to beg for alms to survive. Fighting was the accepted way of resolving disputes, and blood feuds were carried on for generations. Booty from raids on caravans supplemented the meager existence of many Bedouins.

The Bedouins worshiped a variety of nature gods, and each tribe had its own god, often associated with a sacred stone. Poetry was the chief artistic outlet for the Bedouins, and their poems often spoke of the forces of nature that shaped their lives.

City dwellers lived in the busy commercial centers along the eastern shore of the Red Sea. From there, merchants operated caravans that carried goods from Yemen across the desert to cities in Syria and Egypt. The main road ran a few miles inland, where the heat was less intense than along the coast.

Even before Mohammed's lifetime, the Kaaba at Mecca had been a holy shrine. Mohammed removed from it all holy objects except the Black Stone.

Important caravan stops grew up at strategic oases; two of these were Mecca and Yathrib, renamed Medina in the 7th century.

Mecca was the chief Arab city because it housed the *Kaaba* (Arabic for "cube"), a small building erected around a large black stone —probably a meteorite. Arabs believed that the stone had been sent to them from heaven, and they looked on the Kaaba as the holiest of places. Pilgrims flocked to Mecca to worship at this shrine, adding greatly to the prosperity of the city. The powerful Quraysh tribe served as guardians of the Kaaba, which in addition to the Black Stone housed the images of 360 gods and goddesses. The members of this tribe maintained a monopoly on the supply of food and water to the pilgrims who visited the shrine, and they controlled the government and commerce of Mecca.

Yathrib, about 200 miles north of Mecca, had a middle class that included a number of Jews. Although most Arabs remained loyal to their many gods, Judaism won some converts. In addition, the Arabs tended to worship one god—Allah—above the others. Thus, the seeds of monotheism were already planted before the 7th century.

LIFE OF MOHAMMED

Mohammed (Arabic for "highly praised") was born in 570 in Mecca. Although he was born into the powerful Quraysh tribe, his father died before his birth, and his mother died six years later. He was raised by poor relatives and had few advantages. At an early age, he worked as a camel driver and then led caravans to cities of Syria and Palestine. On these journeys, he probably came into contact with Jews and Christians and learned about their beliefs.

At about the age of 20, Mohammed was hired by Khadija, a wealthy widow 15 years his senior, to manage her caravans. Five years later, they were married. The marriage was a happy one, and his wife's wealth provided Mohammed with the leisure to wander into the desert to meditate on religion.

According to tradition, the angel Gabriel appeared to Mohammed as he was meditating in a cave one day. "O Mohammed," the angel reportedly said, "you are the messenger of Allah." At first, Mohammed told only close relatives of this vision.

Later, inspired by continuing visions which urged him to spread the message of Allah, Mohammed began to preach in public. The two fundamental themes of his teaching were summed up in the Moslem call to prayer: "There is no God but Allah, and Mohammed is his Prophet." Time and again, Mohammed called on people to renounce their faith in other gods and submit to the will of Allah.

FLIGHT TO MEDINA

At first, Mohammed won few followers. Instead, his preaching angered the powerful Quraysh leaders who saw in his monotheistic teachings a threat to the profitable business of the pilgrimages to the Kaaba. They ridiculed and then persecuted Mohammed and his followers. However, among Mohammed's early converts were several influential men of Mecca, including Abu Bakr, a successful merchant, and Ali, Mohammed's

According to Islamic tradition, Mohammed was guided by the angel Gabriel through seven heavens, where he met Adam, Moses, Jesus, and finally Allah.

cousin, who later married Fatima, a daughter of the prophet. As you will read, these men would play important roles in the development of Islam.

According to Islamic tradition, during this difficult period the angel Gabriel miraculously transported Mohammed from Jerusalem to heaven on a winged steed. Moslems celebrate this event as the "Night of Power," and because of it, they consider Jerusalem to be a holy city.

Mohammed's teachings were better received by pilgrims from Yathrib than by the people of Mecca. In 622, some leading citizens of Yathrib invited Mohammed to their city to settle a feud between two local tribes. Continued persecution convinced Mohammed to move from Mecca to Yathrib. Later, Yathrib was renamed Medinat-al-Nabi—"City of the Prophet"—which was shortened to Medina. Mohammed's escape from Mecca to Medina became known as the *Hegira*, or "flight," and the first year of the Moslems' calendar is dated from the year of the Hegira. This means that the year 2000 A.D. of the Christian calendar will be the year 1378 A.H. (after the Hegira) of the Islamic calendar.

Mohammed soon became both the political and the spiritual leader of Medina. He built the first *mosque*, or Moslem place of worship, appointed the first *muezzin* to call the faithful to prayer, and decided that all worshipers should face toward the Kaaba when they prayed or worshiped. He established Friday as the day for Moslems to worship together in a mosque. He also decreed that the faithful should give alms regularly to provide help for the poor and support the work of the mosques.

RETURN TO MECCA

Mohammed granted his followers in Medina permission to attack caravans originating or terminating in Mecca, and let them keep a portion of the booty. With these raids, he put pressure on the people of Mecca to convert, and at the same time he raised money for Islam.

When a few hundred followers of Mohammed routed a much larger army of Meccans, many Arabs became convinced that Mohammed was truly the prophet of Allah. These early battles in the desert gave rise to the concept of the *jihad*, or "holy war," which held that Moslems who died fighting the infidel, as unbelievers were called, would be immediately transported to heaven. This concept was similar to the Christian idea of a crusade, or holy war against unbelievers.

In 630, Mohammed led an army of converts against Mecca, and the city surrendered without a struggle. Mohammed then destroyed all the idols in the Kaaba except the

The mosque that Mohammed built at Medina had four basic features: a fountain at which the faithful could wash before entering, minarets for the muezzin to summon worshipers, a marker to indicate the direction of Mecca, and a pulpit from which the Koran could be read aloud.

Black Stone. After cleansing the Kaaba, he dedicated it to the worship of Allah. The Kaaba thus became the center of Islam and the holiest site for pilgrims to visit. Mohammed dealt leniently with those who had opposed him, granting them pardons. In the next two years, he sent out missionaries to convert the Bedouin tribes in the desert, and by the time of his death in 632, most of Arabia had accepted the teachings of Islam.

TEACHINGS OF ISLAM

Within a hundred years of Mohammed's death, Islam had spread from the Arabian peninsula across much of the world. By 750, it had won converts from Spain to India. One reason for the spectacular success of the new faith was its simple, straightforward message.

THE FIVE PILLARS OF FAITH

Every Moslem is called on to accept five basic duties. First, and foremost, is the reciting of the creed that is the central focus of Islam. The simple but powerful statement of the Moslem faith recalls that "There is no God but Allah, and Mohammed is his Prophet." A person may become a Moslem merely by making this statement. It is whispered into the ears of newborn babies, repeated frequently throughout life, and will, if possible, be the last words spoken before death.

The creed affirms the strict monotheism of Islam. To Mohammed, the Christian belief in the Trinity was equivalent to the worship of three gods and thus amounted to polytheism. To Moslems, the one God is absolute and all powerful, as these words convey:

Praise be to Allah, the Lord of Creation,
The Compassionate, the Merciful,
King of the last Judgement!
You alone we worship and to you alone we
    pray for help.[2]

---

[2]"Light," in Koran, trans. N.J. Dawood (Baltimore: Penguin Books, 1959), p. 15.

Although Mohammed rejected the Christian doctrine of the Trinity, he respected the monotheism of the Jews. He acknowledged that the prophets of the Old Testament and even Jesus were bearers of the word of God, but he saw himself as the final prophet.

The second duty of Moslems is to pray five times each day: at sunrise, noon, mid-afternoon, sunset, and nightfall. Each mosque has at least one minaret from which a muezzin calls the faithful to prayer. In preparation for prayer, worshipers wash head, hands, and feet (at least in symbolic fashion), lay out their prayer mats so that they will be facing toward Mecca, and then bend, kneel, and prostrate themselves in a prescribed way. A believer may pray alone or with others, at home, at work, or in a mosque.

The third duty of Moslems is to give alms, or charity to the poor. Devout Moslems often set aside a portion of their income to help those in need. In modern times, the governments of several Islamic nations have established the Red Crescent, an organization similar to the Red Cross that provides help in emergencies.

The fourth duty of Moslems is to observe a fast during the hours of sunlight in the holy month of Ramadan. Ramadan is the ninth month of the Moslem year and was the time when Mohammed received his first revelation. During Ramadan, devout Moslems spend much time in contemplation of the blessings of Allah. They are permitted to eat only after sundown and until the moment at dawn when "one can discern a white thread from a black thread." At the end of Ramadan, a three-day celebration commemorating Mohammed's "Night of Power" is observed with feasting and exchanging gifts.

The fifth duty of Moslems is to make a pilgrimage to Mecca (hajj) at least once in their lives. If physically or financially unable to make such a pilgrimage, a believer is expected to contribute to the pilgrimage of another. Over the centuries, this duty has helped to unite Moslems from all parts of the world.

No unbeliever may enter Mecca during the 12th month of the Moslem year when these pilgrimages are made.

In Mecca, all pilgrims wear simple, seamless, white garments to indicate equality within the brotherhood of Islam. Pilgrims may not shave, have their hair or nails trimmed, or engage in sexual relations. They are led to the Kaaba, and move around it three times rapidly and four times slowly, stopping each time to kiss or touch the sacred Black Stone.

On the ninth day of their pilgrimage, the faithful are conducted to the Plain of Arafat, nine miles southeast of Mecca, to worship on the spot where Mohammed delivered his last message. There, they stand in prayer from noon to sundown. On the following day, the pilgrims throw pebbles at three stone pillars to recall how the patriarch Abraham frightened Satan away by throwing stones at him. They then return to Mecca for three days of feasting before walking once more around the Kaaba. Moslems who participate in the pilgrimage, whether in person or by assisting someone else to do so, are referred to respectfully as *hajii*, and believe that they will enter paradise when they die.

THE KORAN

Like Judaism and Christianity, Islam has a sacred book, the *Koran*, that contains its basic teachings. To Moslems, the Koran is the sacred word of God as it was revealed to Mohammed through the angel Gabriel. It is considered God's final word on every subject, and because it was given to Mohammed in Arabic, Moslems believe that it can be studied only in that language. Since translation into another language might introduce errors, devout Moslems everywhere learn Arabic and memorize parts or all of the 78,000 words of their holy book. This widespread use of Arabic has helped to unite the many different peoples in the Islamic lands.

The Koran consists of 114 messages conveyed to Mohammed by the angel Gabriel. No one knows in what order these messages

A passage from the Koran, written about 1300. Moslem artists developed a highly decorative calligraphy to embellish their sacred literature.

were given, but as Mohammed passed them on to his followers, they were memorized or sometimes written down on paper, stone, dried palm leaves, and even on large bones. About 20 years after Mohammed's death, the sayings were collected in their present form and arranged so that the longest (consisting of several thousand words) would be first and the shortest (consisting of fewer than fifty words) would be last.

THE SUNNA

As Islam expanded, Moslems found that the Koran did not provide a guide to meet all the new situations that arose. Sometimes, too, passages in the Koran contradicted each other. Early on, Moslem leaders who had been closely associated with Mohammed tried to resolve these difficulties by recalling the Prophet's actions or words on specific occasions. Gradually, a code of detailed rules was put together to deal with situations that were not covered either by the Koran or by traditions associated with Mohammed. These rules came in part from the customs (sunna) that each tribe had developed and that served as their law codes. In time, the *Sunna* were collected and were used along with the Koran as the final authority on all questions. Since Moslems believe that the will of Allah embraces all aspects of life, including political activities, the devout look to the Koran and the Sunna for guidance in all their decisions.

MORAL AND SOCIAL CODE

Islam set up a strict moral code for Moslems to follow. It called on the faithful to be honest and just in all their dealings. It prohibited blood feuds, which had caused frequent warfare among the Arabs. The drinking of intoxicants and gambling were forbidden. Also, certain foods were considered unclean. For example, one passage in the Koran says:

• • • Eat of the good and lawful things which Allah has bestowed on you and give thanks for His favours if you truly serve Him. He has forbidden you the flesh of beasts that die a natural death, blood, and pig's meat; also any flesh consecrated in the name of any but Allah. But whoever is constrained to eat of it without intending to be a rebel or transgressor, will find Allah forgiving and merciful.[3]

Infanticide was prohibited, and new inheritance laws were proclaimed to protect the rights of widows and orphans. Although polygamy was permitted, a man could not have more than four wives, and each was to be treated equally. Moreover, a man could not divorce a wife on a mere whim.

• • • If a man accuses his wife but has no witnesses except himself, he shall swear four times by Allah that his charge is true, calling down upon himself the curse of Allah if he be lying. But if his wife swears four times by Allah that his charge is false and calls down His curse upon herself if it be true, she shall receive no punishment.[4]

The Koran accepted the practice of slavery, but it required that slaves be treated humanely. Slaves were permitted to marry, and could purchase their freedom.

• • • As for those of your slaves who wish to buy their liberty, free them if you find in them any promise and bestow on them a part of the riches which Allah has given you.[5]

Mohammed taught that there would be a Judgment Day on which Allah would judge all people by the acts they had performed while on earth. For those who obeyed Allah, he promised a joyful afterlife in paradise:

• • • They shall recline on jewelled couches face to face, and there shall wait on them immortal youths with bowls and ewers and cups of purest wine (that will neither pain their heads nor take away their reason); with fruits of their own choice and flesh of fowls that they relish.[6]

To unbelievers and those who disobeyed, Mohammed described the tortures of hell: "For the unbelievers We have prepared fetters and chains, and a blazing Fire."[7]

MULLAHS AND IMAMS

There is no priesthood in Islam, and Mohammed did not establish a clergy. Early on, however, the *mullahs*, who taught Islamic law, gained a respected position in Islam similar to that of the clergy in Christian lands. In addition, the religious services in the mosques came to be conducted by an *imam*, who led the prayers and delivered a sermon from an elevated place.

EXPANSION OF ISLAM

When Mohammed died in 632, he had named no successor, so a council of his closest associates met to decide who would lead the Moslem community. They

---

[3]"The Bee," *Koran*, p. 303. Hebrew Scriptures also forbid the eating of pork (Leviticus 11:7-8).
[4]"Light," *Koran*, p. 208.

[5]"Light," *Koran*, p. 210.
[6]"That Which Is Coming," *Koran*, p. 108.
[7]"Man," *Koran*, p. 18.

soon chose Abu Bakr, an early convert, trusted friend, and father-in-law of Mohammed. Abu Bakr assumed the title of *caliph* (from *khalifa* meaning "successor"). As caliph, he had absolute power.

THE FIRST FOUR CALIPHS
Between 632 and 661, four caliphs were elected: Abu Bakr (632-634), Omar (634-644), Othman (644-656), and Ali (656-661).

Abu Bakr. On assuming the caliphate, Abu Bakr immediately faced a serious problem. Several Arab tribes refused to acknowledge his leadership, claiming that they had pledged allegiance to Mohammed as a person, and not to Islam. Abu Bakr sent troops to put down this rebellion, reportedly saying:

● ● ●*Mohammed is no more than an apostle, and apostles before him have passed away. If then he dies or is killed, will you turn back upon your heels?*[8]

Although Abu Bakr died after serving only two years as caliph, he succeeded in bringing all of Arabia back under the control of Islam. Before his death, Abu Bakr named Omar, one of Mohammed's most trusted advisers, to be the second caliph.

Omar. The Islamic Empire was established under the caliphate of Omar. In 635, an Islamic army under the leadership of Khalid ibn-al-Walid (often referred to as "The Sword of Allah") defeated a much larger Byzantine army in Syria. The victorious army then laid siege to Damascus, which surrendered after six months. In 637, Jerusalem fell to the Moslems. A second army marched against Persia, and by 644, the Persian Empire of the Sassanids had crumbled. At the same time, the Arabs were moving into North Africa. In 639-40, they captured Alexandria and the rest of Egypt.

---

[8]Quoted in *Islam and the Arab World*, ed. Bernard Lewis (New York: American Heritage Publishing Co., 1976), p. 12.

> *For many centuries the Arabs were accused of having destroyed the great library at Alexandria by burning the books to heat the public baths. It is now known that Julius Caesar's soldiers destroyed it in 48 B.C.; that it was rebuilt into a great library; and was then destroyed again by the emperor Theodosius in 389 A.D.*

Othman. After Omar was murdered by a Christian slave in 644, Othman was named the third caliph. During Othman's caliphate, the first official Koran was compiled. However, Othman was unpopular, in part because of his appointment of relatives and friends to important positions. Like his predecessors, Othman tried to consolidate power in the hands of the caliph. This policy outraged many Arabs who were not accustomed to a strong central authority. Also, many Moslems felt that only a member of Mohammed's family should hold the position of caliph. Ultimately, hostility toward Othman resulted in his murder in 656.

Ali. Ali, Mohammed's cousin and the husband of the Prophet's daughter Fatima, was chosen to succeed Othman. The election of Ali sparked an immediate dispute. Muawiya, the governor of Syria and a member of Othman's family, challenged Ali's right to be caliph. Ali's refusal to apprehend and punish the murderers of Othman further added to his difficulties. In 661, Ali was assassinated, ending this early period of the first four caliphs.

REASONS FOR ISLAM'S EARLY SUCCESS
During these early years, the Arabs won a string of smashing victories and conquered most of the Middle East and much of North Africa. The Islamic armies achieved many great military victories in part because they were led by outstanding commanders like Khalid ibn-al-Walid. Arab commanders

THE EXPANSION OF ISLAM
Which areas shown on the map are still Moslem lands today?

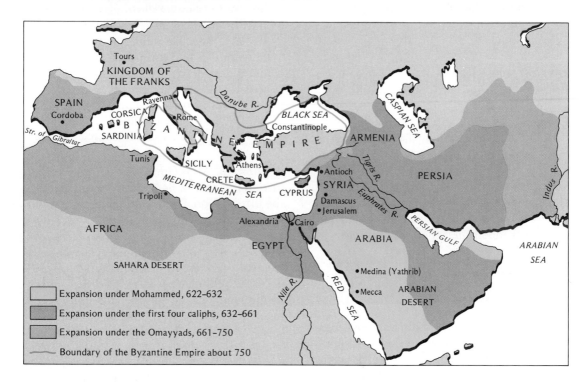

Expansion under Mohammed, 622–632

Expansion under the first four caliphs, 632–661

Expansion under the Omayyads, 661–750

—— Boundary of the Byzantine Empire about 750

launched attacks with speed and surprise, overwhelming their more numerous enemies. A second reason for the early success of Islam was the disaffection of people in parts of the Byzantine Empire. In Syria and North Africa, people looked on Byzantine officials as alien rulers. In the 7th century, their discontent with Byzantine rule found an outlet in their acceptance of Islam. The new converts soon swelled the armies of Islam and helped them on to new triumphs.

Third, both the Byzantine and Persian empires had exhausted themselves in recent wars against each other (Chapter 13). Fourth, Moslems fought for their cause with enormous zeal. The Koran commanded, "Believers, if you help Allah, Allah will help you and make you strong."[9]

---

[9]"Mohammed," *Koran*, p. 121.

The early caliphs established guidelines for dealing with the conquered peoples. Because the Arabs were relatively few in number, they usually left the existing political structure in place. Moslem soldiers garrisoned the towns, and churches were converted into mosques. In those lands where the people willingly accepted Islam, they were permitted to keep their property as long as they paid tribute. Those people who fought against the Moslems were forced to surrender all of their goods, with one-fifth going to Islam and four-fifths being divided among the Moslem soldiers.

Toward Jews and Christians, Moslems were tolerant. Moslems regarded the Old and New Testaments as the sacred word of God revealed before God's final messenger, Mohammed, had brought them the Koran. Moslems thus called Jews and Christians "the people of the Book" because they accepted God's word in the Bible. Therefore, Jews and Christians were accorded protection in theory, although this did not always happen in practice. Some Jews and Christians chose to convert, however, and thereby avoid the additional taxes paid by non-Moslems.

DIVISIONS WITHIN ISLAM

The murder of Ali in 661 brought to the forefront political and religious divisions that had existed in Islam since Mohammed's death. Even before Ali's death, Muawiya had called himself caliph. Muawiya began the Omayyad Dynasty (661-750), which you will read about shortly. His action split Islam into two groups: the Shiites and Sunnites.

The Shiites. The Shiites (from the Arabic *shi'i* meaning "follower") were loyal partisans of the murdered Ali. They believed that the caliph should be descended from the family of Mohammed—from Fatima and Ali—and thus they supported Ali's son, Husayn, as caliph. When Husayn was killed in a battle against the followers of Muawiya in 680, the Shiites grew even more adamant in their opposition to the Omayyads. They made the anniversary of Husayn's death a day of mourning that is still observed today.

The Shiites differed from their opponents on another issue. They insisted that the Koran was the only source of guidance for Islam. They rejected the body of traditions that were being accepted as part of the faith.

Shiites believe that there were 12 divinely appointed leaders of the faith (imams), the last of whom disappeared in 878 A.D. Even today, they await his return to earth as the Mahdi, or "Guided One," who will fill the world with justice.

The Sunnites. The followers of Muawiya and the Omayyad Dynasty were called Sunnites, or traditionalists. They believed that any spiritually qualified man could be elected caliph, not only descendants of Mohammed. The Sunnites accepted both the Koran and commentaries based on the customs, or *Sunna*, as valid parts of the faith.

The Sunnites were always far more numerous than the Shiites. They claimed to represent the orthodox, or correct, beliefs, and most Moslems accepted their point of view. The Shiites split into several sects that have survived until today. Many Moslems in Iran, Iraq, and Pakistan hold to the Shiite tradition.

OMAYYAD DYNASTY

The Omayyad Dynasty consolidated power in the hands of the Sunnites. To better deal with the growing Islamic Empire, Muawiya moved his capital from Mecca to the more centrally located city of Damascus in Syria. He appointed Syrian and Egyptian officials who had experience in the administration of the Byzantine Empire to positions of authority. He decreed that Arabic would be the official language of the Islamic Empire, and he minted new coins containing quotations from the Koran to replace the Persian and Byzantine coins which had been the money of the Middle East. He set up a postal system modeled on that of the ancient Persians and undertook an extensive program of building, improving transportation, and constructing several beautiful mosques.

During the Omayyad Dynasty, Islamic armies again moved westward, conquering all of North Africa. The Berbers, who lived along the route of the Islamic expansion, resisted strongly. After the Berbers were finally defeated, however, they adopted the teachings of Islam and the Arabic language. Because they were such strong warriors, they were soon recruited into the Islamic army.

In 711, Tarik, the Moslem governor of

North Africa, launched an attack against Spain. As this largely Berber army sailed across the strait separating Africa from Europe, Tarik challenged his men with these words: "The sea is behind you, the enemy is before you: by Allah, there is no escape for you save valor and determination."[10] Tarik landed near the great rock hill that has since borne his name—*Gebel Tarik* ("the hill of Tarik"), or Gibraltar. He defeated a much larger Visigothic army and proceeded to march through Spain.

By 721, the Moslems had won control of most of Spain. Spain yielded easily to the Moslems. The reasons were not hard to find. The harsh rule of the Visigoth rulers, who had conquered Spain in the 5th century, caused some people to look upon the Moslems as liberators. Also, the Goths had tried forcibly to convert the Jews of Spain to Christianity. As a result, the Jews along with many others welcomed the Moslem invaders.

In 732, the Moslem army crossed the Pyrenees Mountains and threatened the kingdom of the Franks. The Moslem advance was stopped, however, by a Frankish army under Charles Martel (see Chapter 15). The year 732 was the centennial of Mohammed's death. By that date, Islam had won a large empire not only in the West but also in the East.

Under the early Omayyads, an Islamic army crossed the Oxus River, the traditional border between the Persians and the Turks, and made Islam the dominant power in Central Asia. In 712, another army reached the Indus River and converted much of northwestern India—the region known today as Pakistan—to Islam.

In 673, a Moslem army had marched through Asia Minor to the eastern shore of the Bosporus, where it threatened Constantinople, the capital of the Byzantine Empire. As you have read, the Moslems continued to attack the city for six years until they were finally forced to retreat by the Byzantines. In 716, the Moslems again reached the Bosporus and prepared to attack Constantinople. The Byzantine emperor Leo III (Chapter 13) ordered the forging of a huge iron-link chain to place across the mouth of the Golden Horn, the harbor of Constantinople. The chain was meant to keep Moslem ships from entering this vital body of water. The plan worked, and the city remained in Christian hands.

THE ABBASID CALIPHATE

Under the Omayyad rulers, the Arabs received preferential treatment. Non-Arab Moslems were discontent with the policies that required them to pay heavy taxes while the Arabs paid none. Among the dissident groups were Persians, Egyptians, and Syrians, whose cultures were far more advanced than that of the Arabs.

The discontents were attracted to the Shiite sect that had opposed the Omayyads from the outset. They found a leader in Abu'l Abbas, who was not a Shiite but still claimed to be descended from the family of Mohammed. In 750, the rebels, led by Abbas, overthrew the Omayyad caliph and murdered 90 members of his family. Only one member escaped. He fled to Spain, where his descendants established the Omayyad caliphate at Cordoba.

Abbas established the Abbasid caliphate (750-1057). In 762, the Abbasids moved their capital from Damascus to Baghdad, a great new city on the west bank of the Tigris River. The Abbasids ruled with absolute power and established a centralized bureaucracy similar to that of the Byzantine Empire. The caliph was assisted in his work by his vizier, who often exercised as much power as the caliph.

Under the Abbasids, Moslems paid no head tax but did pay a small tax to support Islam. Non-Moslems, however, paid many heavy taxes that were used to support the empire. During the Abbasid caliphate, scholars from the Middle East—and from India—made

[10]Quoted in *Early Islam* by Desmond Stewart et al. (New York: Time, Inc. 1967), p. 62.

> *Harun was a contemporary of Charlemagne, the ruler of much of western Europe (see Chapter 15). These two great leaders corresponded with each other in an effort to create an alliance: Harun wanted Charlemagne to help him against the Omayyads, who controlled Spain, and Charlemagne needed Harun's help against the Byzantines.*

Baghdad one of the world's great centers of learning. The reigns of Harun al-Rashid (786-809) and his successor, al-Mamum (813-833), marked the golden age of the Abbasids because of the great advances made in mathematics, science, literature, and the arts.

In spite of the cultural achievements made under the Abbasids, the Islamic Empire entered into a political decline after the reign of al-Mamum. In the 9th and 10th centuries, its territory was fragmented. Separate Moslem kingdoms were established in North Africa, Arabia, and India. In Spain, a descendant of the last Omayyad assumed the title of caliph in 929, thus setting himself up as a rival to the Abbasid caliph in Baghdad. In Egypt, Shiite leaders created the Fatimid caliphate, named after Mohammed's daughter, Fatima. In 969, they established their new capital at *al Qahirai*, which we know today as Cairo. There, they built a university that rivaled Baghdad as a center of Islamic learning.

In the 11th century, the Seljuk Turks from Central Asia invaded the Middle East. They captured Baghdad in 1055 and turned the Abbasid caliphs into puppet rulers. The Seljuks then pushed into Syria and Egypt, where they overthrew the Fatimid caliphate in 1171. As you will read in Chapter 16, it was the conquest of Palestine by the Seljuk Turks that sparked the Crusades, in which the Christian knights of Europe invaded the Holy Land.

The 13th century saw the Mongols sweep out of Central Asia into the Middle East. The Mongols captured and destroyed Baghdad in 1258, killing the last Abbasid ruler.

Later, other rulers assumed the title of caliph, but they were no longer seen as the true successors of Mohammed. Despite the disintegration of the Abbasid empire, Islam remained a unifying force. The brilliant achievements of Moslem culture and loyalty to Islam served to bind peoples from all corners of the Moslem world.

ISLAMIC CIVILIZATION

From the 8th to the 12th centuries, the Moslem world was a thriving center of scholarship and scientific learning. Islamic civilization reached its zenith under the early Abbasid rulers. During this period, many non-Arabic peoples were merged into the empire, and Islamic civilization synthesized the best elements of all these cultures.

COMMERCE AND INDUSTRY

The achievements of Islamic civilization were due in part to the prosperous economic conditions that existed throughout much of the empire. Geographically, the Moslems commanded the trade routes of three continents—Asia, Africa, and Europe. Goods from China, India, Russia, Spain, and all parts of Africa passed through the markets of the Middle East. Greek, Jewish, and Armenian traders were allowed access to these markets, from which they carried the luxury goods of the East into western Europe.

In the great cities of Baghdad, Cairo, and Cordoba, industry and commerce thrived. Unlike the towns of western Europe which at this time were small and parochial, the cities of the Moslem world were bustling, cosmopolitan centers, where merchants and artisans enjoyed the benefits of a money economy. The wealth and splendor of Baghdad gave rise to legends such as the stories in the *Arabian Nights*, which you will read about shortly.

The textile industry was especially profitable as traders carried muslins, silks, and cottons across the empire. Crafts such as ironworking and ceramics were also economically vital. Along with commerce and industry, agriculture supported the empire. The fertile soils of Mesopotamia—the ancient Fertile Crescent—as well as the Nile Valley were carefully irrigated and farmed to produce a variety of crops, including wheat, cotton, and citrus fruits.

The movement of people and goods across the Islamic world brought together learning and knowledge from many cultures. The economic prosperity supported an intellectual class with the wealth and leisure to pursue this knowledge. In Baghdad, the caliph al-Mamum established a *House of Wisdom*, or center of learning, in which Greek and Persian works as well as Sanskrit writings from India were translated into Arabic. Under the supervision of Hunayn ibn Ishaq (809-873), a group of 90 scholars worked on these translations. Mamum is reported to have paid Hunayn and his assistants an amount in gold equal in weight to the manuscripts they translated. At first, Moslem scholars used the translations to produce commentaries and encyclopedias, but by the 10th century, they were expanding upon the wisdom of the ancient world to produce new works in the fields of medicine, mathematics, astronomy, and other sciences.

MEDICINE

Moslem scholars made outstanding advances in the study of anatomy, human illnesses, and other aspects of medicine. Two influential practitioners in this field were the Persian scientists al-Razi (c. 860-925) and ibn Sina (980-1037), better known to the Western world as Rhazes and Avicenna, respectively. Rhazes wrote more than 200 works on many subjects and compiled a huge encyclopedia of medicine that included both his own opinions on a variety of diseases, and Greek, Syrian, Persian, and Indian knowledge on each subject. Translations of Rhazes' mon-

This illustration from an Arabic text shows a pharmacist mixing a medicine. The Arabs learned much of their medicine from the ancient Greeks and also conducted their own experiments.

umental work later reached western Europe, where they influenced medical practice for many centuries.

Rhazes also published a treatise on smallpox and measles, describing their symptoms in careful detail:

● ● ● *The eruption of Small-Pox is preceded by a continued fever, pain in the back, itching of the nose, and terrors in sleep . . . pain and heaviness of the head; inquietude, distress of mind, nausea, and anxiety; (with this difference, that the inquietude, nausea, and anxiety are more frequent in the Measles than in the Small-Pox; while, on the other hand, the pain in the back is more peculiar to the Small-Pox than to the Measles).*[11]

---

[11]Philip Hitti, *Islam and the West* (New York: Robert E. Krieger Publishing Co., 1979), pp. 118-119.

Rhazes is believed by some to have been the first physician to suture wounds with thread made from animal gut and the first to immobilize fractured limbs using plaster casts. Like many Moslem scholars, Rhazes wrote on a variety of subjects, including mathematics, astronomy, and physics. When he was asked to select a site for a hospital to be built in Baghdad, he hung pieces of raw meat in various places throughout the city and examined the condition of each at regular intervals. He recommended that the hospital be built in the neighborhood in which the meat sample putrified most slowly.

Avicenna, too, was a man of many talents: philosopher, poet, astronomer, and physician, and like Rhazes, he compiled a medical encyclopedia, *Canon of Medicine*. It included descriptions of lockjaw and pleurisy, recommendations for proper diet, and "tender, loving care" in the treatment of disease. He correctly diagnosed tuberculosis as a contagious disease and decided that contaminated soil and water caused a number of illnesses. Avicenna wrote that cancer could be cured if diagnosed early and if the diseased tissue could be completely removed by surgery. He discussed various psychological illnesses, including "love sickness."

Physicians and pharmacists were regulated by the government. Before a physician could practice surgery, he had to pass an examination on his knowledge of anatomy and of the writings of the ancient Greek physician Galen. The dispensing of pharmaceuticals was closely supervised, and there were severe penalties for drug abuse.

Moslem physicians were very skilled surgeons despite the ban—for religious reasons—on dissecting cadavers to learn about human anatomy. Surgeons performed complex cranial and vascular surgery, amputated damaged or diseased limbs, removed soft cataracts from eyes, and inserted drainage tubes into the body to promote recovery from abdominal incisions.

Caliph Harun al-Rashid established the first hospital in Baghdad not only for the care of the ill, but also for the training of physicians. Later, other hospitals were built throughout the Islamic Empire. Each had separate wards for men and women as well as sections for the treatment of eye disease, fractured bones, and mental illness. Outpatient clinics were operated for the treatment of minor injuries. Each hospital had a pharmacy, and medications were prepared from plants, animals, or chemicals. For example, camphor was used in liniments, and copper sulphate was used to speed the healing of wounds.

MATHEMATICS

Moslem scholars also made important advances in mathematics. As in medicine, they synthesized the learning of the ancient Greeks and Persians and carried it many steps further. Most important, they learned from the Hindus of India to use the nine symbols, or numbers, that we call "Arabic numerals" but which in fact originated in India.

While many mathematical principles were known to the ancient Egyptians, Babylonians, and Greeks, the number systems that they used were not convenient for calculations. The Babylonians devised a very useful system based on the number 60 which is still used in the measurement of time and angles. The Romans used a system (*Roman numerals*) that was convenient for counting, but awkward for calculations. Hindu mathematicians in India devised a system based on the number 10 (*decimal*), which included the concept of zero. By adopting this system of calculation, they made possible advances into higher mathematics.

The mathematician al Khwarizmi (died about 850) wrote the first Arabic treatise on mathematics in which he used the word *al-Jabr*, meaning "bringing together separate parts," from which our word *algebra* is derived. Al Khwarizmi's treatise was later translated into Latin and became the standard textbook in mathematics in European universities until the 16th century.

Another mathematician, Omar Khayyam (d. 1123), is better known today as a poet. However, he devised an accurate calendar and made advances in algebra that led to the development of *analytic geometry*, the branch of mathematics that unites algebra and geometry and underlies calculus.

The Greek mathematicians, especially Euclid and Pythagoras, provided Moslem scholars with the foundations on which to build, but the Greeks had been primarily interested in the philosophy of mathematics. By contrast, the Moslems used mathematics to solve many practical problems and to make important astronomical observations.

ASTRONOMY AND GEOGRAPHY

As with the ancient religions of the Middle East, the requirements of religious observa-

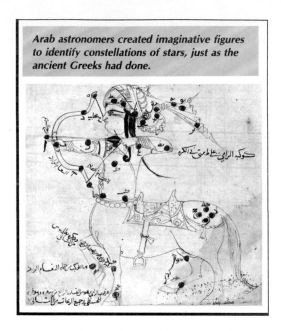

Arab astronomers created imaginative figures to identify constellations of stars, just as the ancient Greeks had done.

The astrolabe, an intrument invented by the ancient Greeks, enabled Arab astronomers to chart the positions of heavenly bodies.

tions in Islam stimulated the study of astronomy. The five calls to daily prayer required precise knowledge of the time of sunrise, noon, and sunset on each day and in each region of the Islamic world. The need to face toward Mecca while praying required knowledge of astronomical orientation. Prediction of the date of the new moon that marked the beginning of the holy month of Ramadan required knowledge of celestial movements.

In 771, a visitor from India brought a copy of a Hindu treatise on astronomy, *Siddhanta*, to Baghdad. After this work was translated into Arabic, Moslem astronomers used it as the basis for further studies. Harun al-Rashid also ordered that the astronomical works of Ptolemy be translated into Arabic. The Greek astrolabe was adopted to measure the angle of a heavenly body above the horizon. Ptolemy's calculations of the circumference of the earth were then checked and improved to within about one-half mile of the presently accepted value.

Improvements in astronomy allowed Moslem geographers to draw more accurate maps. In addition, the far-reaching scope of Moslem trading ventures gave them an extensive, firsthand knowledge of many regions of the world. Moslem geographers studied climates and developed tables of latitude and longitude. The outstanding Moslem geographer al-Idrisi (1099-1154) was born in Spain but worked in Palermo under the patronage of the Christian king of Sicily. In a landmark volume, he summarized the information submitted to him by assistants whom he had sent to explore the limits of the known world. Al-Idrisi was the first to create maps on spheres representing the shape of the earth. He engraved one such map on silver and presented it to his patron.

PHYSICS AND CHEMISTRY

Arab investigators made significant contributions to the world's knowledge of physics and chemistry. Al Hasan (965-1039), known to the Western world as Alhazen, is sometimes referred to as "the father of optics" because of his studies on light and vision. Alhazen wrote about the principles of convex and concave mirrors and the refraction of light. Most people of his day believed— like the ancient Greeks—that they could see an object because their eyes sent rays out to an object within their vision, but Alhazen proved that light traveling from an object affected the eye. Alhazen's successor, Kalam ad-Din al-Farisi, was able to explain the optical principles involved in seeing a rainbow.

Moslem scientists made progress in other areas. Like people in many parts of the world, they were interested in finding the *philosophers' stone*, a material that they believed would change common metals, such as iron, tin, or copper, into precious metals such as gold or silver. This notion came to be called *alchemy*, an Arabic word. An outstanding Moslem alchemist was Jabir (b. 721). Like Aristotle, he speculated that all objects were created from combinations of air, fire, earth, and water. However, Jabir experimented with these and other materials. He explored the processes now known as oxidation, crystallization, and filtration, and carefully recorded the steps he took, the equipment he used, and the results he obtained, thereby laying the foundation for the science of chemistry.

One of Jabir's students was the physician Rhazes, who wrote a book on alchemy titled *The Book of the Secret of Secrets*. This book classified all matter as animal, vegetable, or mineral and gave detailed descriptions of the preparation of the known pharmaceuticals of the day. Rhazes also described beakers, vials, distillation dishes, and other laboratory equipment that was used by alchemists and would be essential to the science of chemistry.

LITERATURE AND HISTORY

Poetry had played a role in pre-Islamic times, and its importance continued to be felt despite Mohammed's disapproval of the pagan poems of the Bedouins. In this early Arabic literature, poets praised their leaders, described the awesome beauties of nature, or extolled their life in the desert. Love was a favorite subject of Moslem poets, and this love poetry came to influence the troubadours of western Europe (Chapter 18).

The best known Moslem poet was the Persian mathematician Omar Khayyam. He wrote in the popular style of quatrains—four-line stanzas, called *rubaiyat* in Arabic. The *Rubaiyat* of Omar Khayyam contains elegant and haunting images, such as the one in this well-known stanza:

The Moving Finger writes; and having writ,
Moves on: nor all thy Piety nor Wit
Shall lure it back to cancel half a Line,
Nor all thy Tears wash out a Word of it.[12]

To Moslems, the most important prose work is the Koran, which they consider the

[12]Omar Khayyam, "Rubaiyat" (trans. Edward Fitzgerald), Stanza 71.

sacred word of God. Its language is rich in imagery, and certain passages seem as rhythmical as poetry.

To Westerners, the best known prose work is the *Arabian Nights* (also known as *One Thousand and One Nights*). It is a collection of love stories, tales of travel, and fables that came originally from many sources—Persian, Indian, Jewish, Greek, and Egyptian. In the *Arabian Nights* itself, the stories are told by a clever young woman named Scheherazade to outwit the Sultan Schahriar. After several years of blissful marriage, the sultan discovered that his favorite wife was unfaithful to him so he had her executed. As the story continues,

● ● ● *The blow was so heavy that his mind almost gave way, and he declared that he was quite sure that all women were as wicked as the sultana, if you could only find them out. So every evening he married a fresh wife and had her strangled the next morning before the grand vizir, whose duty it was to provide these unhappy brides for the sultan. . . .*

The grand vizir himself was the father of two daughters, of whom the elder was called Scheherazade . . . (who told her father) . . . "I am determined to stop this barbarous practice of the sultan's and to deliver the girls and mothers from the truly awful fate that hangs over them."[13]

Scheherazade marries the sultan but spends her first night with him telling a story that she refuses to finish until the next night. Left in suspense as to the outcome of the story, the sultan did not have her killed. The following night Scheherazade resumes the story but leaves off in the middle of a new one. After 1001 nights, the sultan decides to keep her as his favorite wife.

History was another area of Moslem scholarship. Among the great historians was ibn Khaldun, who compiled a seven-volume *Universal History*. In it, he wrote not only about history and politics but also about economics, climate, crafts, and other aspects of life in different parts of the world. He developed a comprehensive philosophy of history and made scientific observations of people living in groups, concluding that:

● ● ● *This science then, like all other sciences, whether based on authority or on reasoning, appears to be independent and has its own subject, viz. human society, and its own problems, viz. the social phenomena and the transformations that succeed each other in the nature of society.*[14]

Ibn Khaldun believed that the power of a state was determined by the depth of loyalty of its citizens, and he characterized an ideal ruler as follows:

● ● ● *Know then, that the use of the ruler to his subjects lies not in his person, his fine figure or features, his wide knowledge, his excellent penmanship or the sharpness of his intellect, but solely in his relationship to them.*[15]

ART AND ARCHITECTURE

Islamic architecture and art represented a blend of many traditions—Byzantine, Persian, and even Chinese. However, the overriding influence in this field was the Islamic prohibition against the representation of natural objects or people in a place of worship. As you have read, Mohammed destroyed the idols in the Kaaba and forbade the worship of any but the one God. To him, representations of the human form or natural objects were the equivalent of idols. As a result of this strict prohibition, Moslem artists developed stylized geometric designs to decorate

[13]*Arabian Nights*, collected and edited by Andrew Lang (New York: David McKay Co., 1960), pp. 2-3.

[14]*An Arab Philosophy of History: Selections from the Prolegomena of Ibn Khaldun of Tunis (1332-1406)*, trans. Charles Issawi (London: John Murray, 1950), p. 36.

[15]*An Arab Philosophy of History*, trans. Charles Issawi, pp. 128-129.

mosques. They also enhanced the art of *calligraphy*, or beautiful handwriting, by inscribing the sacred teachings of the Koran in graceful and elegant Arabic script.

In the design of Moslem cities, the mosque was the dominant structure. All mosques have certain features in common: an open courtyard with a large fountain, a covered area with a special niche, and minarets. From the Byzantines, the Moslems learned to use the dome, arch, and columns that feature so prominently in mosques. From the Persians, they adapted many of their decorative patterns. The prohibition against idols came from the Jews, whose scriptures were full of stories of God's anger when people disobeyed this command.

The oldest Islamic building outside of Arabia is the *Dome of the Rock* mosque in Jerusalem. This octagonal structure, with its high domed roof covered in gold leaf, was completed in 691 and still dominates the skyline of Jerusalem. It was built on Mount Moriah, the site of Solomon's Temple: according to Moslem tradition, it was on Mount Moriah that Mohammed had experienced his "Night of Power."

According to Jewish tradition, Mount Moriah was the place where Abraham had prepared to sacrifice his only son, Isaac, to God (Genesis 22:1:19), and it was also the site of the ancient Temple of Solomon. Christians, too, looked to Jerusalem for inspiration because it was the site of so many events in the life of Jesus. Some scholars have suggested that Omar selected this site either to demonstrate the superiority of Islam over Christianity and Judaism, or to encourage Moslem pilgrims to visit Jerusalem as well as Mecca.

One of the great monuments of the Omayyad dynasty is the Dome of the Rock mosque in Jerusalem. Its octagonal plan was adapted from the design of Byzantine churches.

Another well known example of Islamic architecture is the great Omayyad Mosque in Damascus, built on a site originally occupied by a temple to Jupiter and later by a Christian church. The Moslems razed all elements of these earlier structures except the exterior walls and the Roman watchtowers, which were converted into minarets.

Caliphs often built fortified palaces that were used as administrative centers in remote regions. These palaces with their many rooms and lavish decorations displayed to all the wealth and power of the caliph. Early in the 20th century, archaeologists working in Palestine found the remains of a great palace at Khirbet al Mafjar (Arabic for "place where the water flows"). It had been built by the Omayyad caliph Hisham (724-743) in the valley of the Jordan River east of Jericho. The huge palace was destroyed by an earthquake in 748 and was never rebuilt.

Two more lasting examples of Islamic architecture are the Alhambra Palace in Spain and the Taj Mahal in India. The former is a tribute to grace and beauty. The slender columns, multi-colored, horseshoe arches, and beautiful ceilings are all decorated with intricate calligraphy and fine *arabesque* designs showing acanthus vines interwoven in

The Alhambra palace in Granada was the headquarters of the caliphate in Spain. It was completed in 1391.

The Taj Mahal, built in 1648, was influenced by Persian, Byzantine, and Moslem architectural traditions. The impression of weightlessness that it conveys was achieved, in part, through the use of arches, a reflecting pool, and graceful minarets.

intricate patterns. The Taj Mahal was built by the shah Jahan as a monument to his beloved wife who died while she was still very young. Its design and decorations strongly reflect Persian influences as well as Byzantine and Arabic traditions.

Between 1000 and 1500, Moslem artists excelled in many areas: the making of pottery, glass, ceramic tiles, mosaics, and textiles, including carpets. Potters developed the technique of making lusterware, in which ordinary fired clay was glazed with various metallic oxides to produce metal-like finishes. Glassmakers revived the old Roman art of embedding threads of various colored glass into molten glass to produce intricate designs. Glasscutters produced beautiful bas-relief designs on the surfaces of glass objects. Metalworkers made objects of bronze or brass that were inlaid with designs of gold and silver. Lush fabrics of damask, muslin, and satin and richly-colored "oriental" rugs later became popular among the wealthy people of western Europe.

Despite the limitations on the representation of human forms and natural objects, Moslem painters created magnificent miniatures, or tiny, stylized pictures, which they used to decorate secular manuscripts. Moslem artists also used gold, silver, and other brilliant colors to *illuminate* manuscripts in a highly decorative style.

ISLAMIC SPAIN Aside from Baghdad, one of the greatest centers of Islamic civilization was found in Cordoba, Spain. As you have read, Moslem armies invaded Spain in the 7th and 8th centuries, and they laid the foundations for a civilization that flourished for more than 700 years. In 756, the only surviving member of the Omayyad family, Abd-al-Rahman, reached Spain, where his descendants established an independent caliphate at Cordoba.

Rahman wanted to ensure the survival and economic advancement of his family. He succeeded in winning control of the land and then devoted his attention to peaceful pursuits. He introduced the cultivation of silkworms and the manufacture of paper to Spain. He encouraged the production of fine leather goods and the fashioning of objects made of steel inlaid with gold and silver. He repaired long-neglected Roman walls and aqueducts and developed water power to drive mills. He encouraged the introduction of many edible plants from the Middle East, including citrus fruits, bananas, peaches, rice, sugar cane, almonds, and figs.

From the 9th through the 13th centuries, Cordoba flourished. It was a beautiful city adorned with luxurious palaces, impressive mosques, and attractive gardens and fountains. By the 10th century, it could boast of paved and lighted streets—conditions that were unknown in other parts of western Europe until 700 years later. During these centuries, Cordoba was famous as a center of learning on a par with Constantinople and Baghdad. Among the outstanding scholars of Cordoba was the philosopher, astronomer, and physician, ibn-Rushd (1126-1198), known in western Europe as Averroes. He studied the works of Aristotle and insisted on submitting all truths to the light of reason. Through the use of Aristotelian logic, Averroes sought to reconcile faith and reason. When his writings were introduced into western Europe, they had tremendous impact on Christian scholars.

A contemporary of Averroes, who was also born in Cordoba, was the brilliant Jewish philosopher and physician, Maimonides (1135-1204). Maimonides' family later settled in Cairo, but the work of this great scholar influenced Jewish, Moslem, and Christian thought. Maimonides tried to reconcile religion and science and championed the cause of scientific thought.

The writings of these and other scholars of the Moslem world slowly made their way from Spain across the Pyrenees into western Europe. In English, there are many words that provide evidence of the influence of Ar-

The great mosque at Cordoba, Spain was constructed by the Omayyads and enlarged over a period of several centuries. The columns are oriented in the direction of Mecca.

abic learning. Musical instruments such as the *lute, tambourine,* and *guitar* all entered Europe from Moslem lands. Terms such as *zenith* or *nadir* in astronomy, *cipher* (zero) in mathematics, or *syrup* and *soda* in medicine all have Arabic origins. When Christian Europe finally recovered enough from centuries of invasions to pursue higher scholarship and learning, it found a vast storehouse of knowledge in the Moslem lands beyond its borders.

SUMMARY

In the 7th century, a new religion, Islam, burst out of Arabia and swept across much of the world. Inspired by the Koran and the prophet Mohammed, Moslem armies won stunning victories. By the 8th century, Islam was the dominant religion of an area reaching from Spain to India. The primary article of the faith was belief in the one God, Allah. This belief along with the five basic duties of all Moslems helped bind together people from many different cultures.

Caliphs ruled over the Islamic Empire and presided over a brilliant civilization that reached its height during the 9th to 11th centuries. Baghdad and Cordoba were the two greatest centers of Moslem learning and culture. In these and other cities, Moslem scholars made important advances in many fields. Like the Byzantines, they helped to preserve the learning of the ancient world and passed it on to the peoples of western Europe.

QUESTIONS

1 How did the traditions and beliefs of pre-Islamic Arabs shape Mohammed's ideas?
2 Make a chart comparing the basic teachings and church organization of Judaism, Christianity, and Islam.
3 Why did Islam spread so rapidly after the death of Mohammed? Do you think the Arabs could have achieved these victories if Mohammed had never lived? What conclusions can you draw about the role of great individuals in history?
4 Explain the divisions that developed within Islam after Mohammed's death. Find out how the split between Shiites and Sunnites affects nations in the Middle East today.
5 Why did Islamic civilization flourish from the 8th to 12th centuries? How did Islamic civilization help to shape developments in western Europe?

BIBLIOGRAPHY

Which books might compare Judaism, Christianity, and Islam?

GLUBB, SIR JOHN BAGOT. *The Life and Times of Muhammed.* New York: Stein and Day, 1970. *A classic biography of the founder of the Moslem religion written by an eminent scholar who spent half his life among Moslems. It presents a balanced view of the Prophet's life and teachings and recreates the Arab world in the 7th century.*

LEWIS, BERNARD, ed. *Islam and the Arab World.* New York: Alfred A. Knopf and Co., 1976. *A collection of essays by 13 scholars on subjects ranging from the origins, history, and meaning of Islam, to the achievements of Moslem artists and architects. It explores the splendor of Islamic art; the originality and influence of its science and philosophy; and the range of its political and cultural history. Excellent illustrations.*

LIPPMAN, THOMAS W. *Understanding Islam: An Introduction to the Moslem World.* New York: New American Library, 1982. *A brief account of the founding and growth of Islam, Moslem beliefs, law and government, and the different groups within Islam today. It provides a framework for understanding conflicts within the Islamic world today.*

SEVERY, MERLE. *Great Religions of the World.* Washington, D.C.: National Geographic Society, 1971. *A comparative study of the five major world religions: Hinduism, Buddhism, Judaism, Christianity, and Islam; with fine illustrations and an emphasis on the historical background and rituals of each.*

JAPAN

500–1500 A.D.

Unlike the civilizations of Egypt, Mesopotamia, India, and China, early Japanese civilization is not associated with a river valley. Instead, the ocean played a dominant role in shaping Japanese civilization. The sea that separates the Japanese *archipelago*, or chain of islands, from the northeast coast of Asia has served many purposes. Besides providing an abundant source of food, it has protected Japan from invaders and enabled the Japanese to develop their own distinct culture. Prior to 1945, Japan was never subjected to military conquest and domination. Rather, as Japanese culture emerged, it blended local traditions and values with those it consciously borrowed and adapted from its powerful neighbor, China.

EARLY HISTORY AND RELIGION

The Japanese trace their earliest history back to a legendary first emperor, Jimmu Tenno, who is said to have ruled in the 7th century B.C. Later Japanese emperors traced their ancestry back to this first emperor. Unlike the nations of Europe, where warring nobles fought to establish their claims to the throne, the Japanese have maintained a single ruling dynasty in an unbroken line to Emperor Hirohito, the 124th ruler in the imperial line.

Also, unlike China, where the emperors were believed to enjoy the Mandate of Heaven as long as the kingdom was ruled with relative peace and justice, the Japanese believed that their emperor had divine origins and was descended from the sun goddess Amartersu.

During this early period, Japanese religious beliefs took shape into a religion that was later called *Shinto*, or the way of the gods. The original Shinto religion glorified nature and focused on the appreciation and awe of nature as a creative, destructive, and renewing force. The Japanese worshiped *kami*, the spirits or elements of nature. For the most part, they looked on these kami as benign.

Shinto was a religion based on ceremony, ritual, and custom, and not on a code of ethics or a concept of sin. Early Shinto beliefs did not contain any ideas about good or evil; instead, its rituals were associated with purification and cleanliness. Furthermore, the worship was individual and not congregational. The worshiper stood outside the shrine to offer prayer and make petition to the kami.

In the early Japanese society, people were organized into *clans*, groups of families who claim descent from a common ancestor. Clans

One of the oldest holy places of the Shinto religion is the Itsukushima shrine. The gateway shown in the background separates the outside world from the sacred precinct.

age in which China enjoyed great prosperity and a high level of cultural achievement. The extraordinary vitality of this period in Chinese history served as an inspiration for the Yamato rulers in Japan as they set about organizing their own government and military system.

Introduction of Buddhism. In the mid-6th century, Buddhism reached Japan by way of China and Korea. Around 552, the Yamato emperor eagerly questioned Chinese Buddhist missionaries and learned from them about the achievements of Chinese civilization. Buddhist missionaries of this era have sometimes been compared to the early Christian missionaries: the former transmitted the traditions and cultural heritage of China to Japan and other parts of Asia, just as the latter helped spread the achievements of Greco-Roman civilization to the peoples of western Europe.

At the time of its introduction into Japan, Buddhism was not a monolithic religion. Although the essence of Buddhism was the Four Noble Truths and the Noble Eightfold

in different regions had their own clan and regional gods as well as their own rituals. Also each clan chief had religious as well as secular duties. In the 5th century A.D., the Yamato clan began to extend its control over the large island of Honshu, and eventually it conquered the other Japanese islands. By claiming descent from the first emperor, the chief of the yamato clan won support for his rule, and the present-day emperor of Japan is descended from this clan.

INFLUENCE OF CHINA

The Yamato clan consolidated its power in Japan at the time of the Sui and T'ang dynasties in China. The Sui dynasty (589–618) was the first ruling house to reunite China after the collapse of the Han empire in 220. During the chaotic centuries between the end of the Han dynasty and the rise of the Sui, Buddhism took root in China. In reunifying China, the Sui and their successors, the T'ang emperors (618–907), revived the glory of the Han period, particularly in the arts and philosophy, and ushered in a golden

The Great Buddha at Kamakura, built in 1252, is Japan's second largest image of the Buddha. Buddhism was introduced into Japan in the mid-6th century.

JAPAN
What role did geography play in the development of Japan?

By the time Buddhism reached Japan, it had absorbed many Confucian ideas, including the emphasis on filial piety. These ideas came to have great influence on Japanese society. The introduction of Buddhism opened the door for further cultural borrowing from China. Early on, the Japanese adapted the Chinese form of writing to their own language, a step that made the Japanese interested in having many classical Chinese texts translated into their own language.

The Taika Reforms. Early in the 7th century, Prince Shotoku, a member of the Yamato family, encouraged carefully selected young men to visit China and bring back the best of its offerings. He inaugurated a period of massive cultural borrowing not only in government and military organization but also in philosophy, history, the arts, and literature. In so doing, the Yamato rulers hoped to recreate and surpass the culture of China. They created schools and universities in Japan and encouraged Chinese scholars to settle in Japan. They modeled their court on Chinese lines, dressed in Chinese fashions, and built their new capital at Nara using Chinese styles of art and architecture. In fact, Nara was modeled on the splendid T'ang capital of Changan. It included the Great Buddha Hall, the largest wooden building in the world.

Not everything that the Japanese tried to introduce suited their own traditions, however. For example, they tried to set up a civil service system similar to that in China. But the Japanese were accustomed to the idea of hereditary positions and could not accept the notion of selecting officials based on merit.

Taken together, the changes introduced from China became known as the *Taika Reforms*. The purpose of the reform was to strengthen the power of the central government of Japan by reducing the influence of the various clan leaders. Because of opposition to the civil service system and because of the need to give the nobles vast grants of land to gain their support, the reform movement failed in its primary purpose. It did produce a vital period of cultural activity, however, in which Chinese ideas were incorporated into Japanese traditions.

Path, it had a variety of sects. Belief in the ideas or rituals of one sect, however, did not preclude worshipers from sharing in the beliefs or rituals of another sect. As a result, in India, Hinduism and Buddhism coexisted and eventually merged; in China, Confucianism and related philosophies were adapted to Buddhist beliefs; and in Japan, Shintoism and Buddhism coexisted and blended. The blend suited the emperor, who continued to be seen as a divine being and the chief priest of Shinto, while at the same time adapting many Buddhist beliefs. The style of Buddhism that was introduced to Japan was Mahayana Buddhism. Zen Buddhism did not develop until a later time, and in fact, Zen is based on a blend of Buddhist and Taoist ideas.

The Heian period. In 794, the capital again moved to Heian, present-day Kyoto, and the period from 794 to 1185 became known as the Heian period. During this time, the T'ang dynasty declined in China, and contacts between China and Japan were infrequent. Although the Japanese court had adapted an elegant and refined pattern of life based on the Chinese model, it was burdened by endless power struggles. By the 9th century, the emperor was reduced to little more than a figurehead while the powerful Fujiwara family controlled the court and the government. Because of the emperor's semi-divine status, he continued to be treated with respect even though he had become a mere puppet in the hands of others.

JAPAN'S FEUDAL PERIOD

While powerful families vied for power at court, a new force emerged in the rural areas to threaten the leadership of the Heian court. It was made up of tough warrior-knights, called *samurai*. Many of the samurai were young members of the imperial family or of the lower aristocracy who had not been given the high-ranking positions they felt they deserved. During the 10th century, they began to seize control of territories in the provinces, and developed standing armies to protect their lands. The constant warfare that marked their reigns desolated the provinces and seriously weakened the prestige of the emperor. By the late 12th century, a samurai leader named Minamoto Yoritomo had put

This castle, built by the first Tokugawa shogun in 1603, symbolizes the samurai life of Japan's feudal period.

The tea ceremony, one of the most characteristic aspects of Japanese tradition, was introduced from China. The presentation of the tea is guided by well-defined rituals.

together a strong enough army to seize power and take the title *shogun*, or military governor. Yoritomo founded the first of three military dynasties that ruled Japan for almost 700 years from 1185 to 1868.

During this long period, feudalism became a way of life in Japan much as it did in Europe during the Middle Ages. Japan's feudal period was marked by frequent warfare as strong lords fought for power. At the head of feudal society was the emperor, who performed important religious functions but otherwise had no political power. The absolute ruler of Japan was the shogun. Below him were the great local lords, called *daimyo*. Like the great feudal lords in western Europe, the daimyo divided their lands among their vassals, the samurai, who were linked to them by ties of loyalty. The daimyo thus controlled private armies made up of their samurai vassals, and they used these armies to challenge one another and the shogun. As in medieval Europe (Chapter 16), towns began to grow up around the castles of feudal lords. As travel became safer and the money economy grew, merchants and artisans gathered in the towns and contributed to their development. Guilds were formed to protect the interests of the artisans, often under the direct control of the daimyo. In time, the leading merchants and tradesmen of the towns threw off the control of the

daimyo and began to take responsibility for the government of their municipalities. When the Europeans made their first appearance in Japan during the 16th century, they found that the free cities of Japan were much like those that had evolved throughout Europe.

Bushido. During the feudal period, the samurai developed a code of conduct called *bushido*, or the way of the warrior. Bushido was similar in some ways to the code of chivalry that developed in medieval Europe. Bushido glorified courage and honor and put obedience to one's lord above all else. A samurai who violated bushido was thought to have brought dishonor not only to himself but also to his family. Unlike the code of chivalry, however, which put noble women on a pedestal and encouraged respect for them, bushido required that the wives of samurai endure whatever hardships they faced meekly and without complaint.

Patterns of culture. During the feudal period, Buddhism gained ground in Japan. Trade with China and Korea kept up a steady flow of new ideas that were adapted to Japanese needs. Although tea was introduced to Japan as early as the 8th century, it did not become widespread for several centuries. By the 15th century, however, tea drinking had become transformed into the graceful and elegant ceremony that was closely associated with Zen Buddhism and its respect for the simple beauty and peaceful ways of nature. Like many other Japanese traditions, the tea ceremony originated in China, but once established in Japan it evolved its own patterns. Like the tea ceremony, *ikebana*, or flower arrangement, was another import from China and reflected Zen influences with its stress on physical and mental discipline as well as a love of nature.

The feudal period saw other cultural developments such as the Noh plays that taught Zen concepts through a combination of poetry and dance. Haiku poetry, a 3-line poem of 5, 7, and 5 syllables respectively, also became popular. Many haiku are about the beauty or simple virtues of nature. In this art form as in many other aspects of Japanese culture, the ancient Shinto respect for nature was combined with Zen ideals to create works of extraordinary and subtle beauty.

At temples of the Zen sect of Buddhism, it is common to encounter scenes of quiet meditation.

Despite its relatively isolated location on the rim of Asia, Japan has been the heir to both physical and cultural migrations from the mainland.

Between the 6th and 9th centuries A.D., the Japanese eagerly sought out and adopted major elements of Chinese culture. For example, the Taika reforms of the 7th century and the development of Buddhist philosophies were inspired by Prince Shotoku's admiration for Chinese culture. This importation of Chinese culture did not replace Japanese traditions, however. Rather, the new ideas were tested against the old; those that fit were kept while those that did not were cast aside. In the end, the cultural borrowing enabled the Japanese to make their own distinct contributions, especially after they evolved their own system of writing in the 10th century.

In the documents that follow, you will see how the Japanese adapted and transformed what they had borrowed from China in these early centuries.

DOCUMENT 1   *MAHAYANA BUDDHISM*

This excerpt is from the **Vimalakirti Sutra.** *(A sutra is a Buddhist dialogue or sermon.) It is an example of Mahayana Buddhism, also referred to as the "Greater Vehicle," one of the two principal divisions of Buddhism. In contrast to Hinayana Buddhism, or the "Lesser Vehicle," Mahayana Buddhists not only look on Buddha as a god but also believe that all living beings can attain Buddhahood. Implicit in this school of Buddhism is the messianic mission of helping others achieve salvation.*

At that time, there dwelt in the great city of Vaishali a wealthy householder named Vimalakirti. Having done homage to countless Buddhas of the past, doing many good works, attaining to acquiescence in the Eternal Law, he was a man of wonderful eloquence,

Exercising supernatural powers, obtaining all magic formulas, arriving at the state of fearlessness,

Repressing all evil enmities, reaching the gate of profound truth, walking in the way of wisdom. . . .

Residing in Vaishali only for the sake of the necessary means for saving creatures, abundantly rich, ever careful of the poor, pure in self-discipline, obedient to all precepts,

Removing all anger by the practice of patience, removing all sloth by the practice of diligence, removing all distraction of mind by intent meditation, removing all ignorance by fullness of wisdom;

Though he is but a simple layman, yet observing the pure monastic discipline;

Though living at home, yet never desirous of anything;

Though possessing a wife and children, always exercising pure virtues;

Though surrounded by his family, holding aloof from worldly pleasures;

Though using the jewel ornaments of the world, yet adorned with spiritual splendor;

Though eating and drinking, yet enjoying the flavor of the rapture of the meditation;

Though frequenting the gambling house, yet leading the gamblers into the right path;

Though coming into contact with heresy, yet never letting his true faith be impaired;

Though having a profound knowledge of worldly learning yet ever finding pleasure in things of the spirit as thought by Buddha. . . .

Teaching [nobles] patience when among them as the most honorable of their kind;

Removing arrogance when among [priests] as the most honorable of their kind;

Teaching justice to great ministers when among them as the most honorable of their kind;

Teaching loyalty and filial piety to the princes when among them as the most honorable of their kind;

Teaching honesty to the ladies of the court when among them as the most honorable of their kind;

Persuading the masses to cherish the virtue of merits when among them as the most honorable of their kind. . . .

—Thus by such countless means Vimalakirti, the wealthy householder, rendered benefit to all beings.

SOURCE: Tsunoda, Ryusaku, W. T. De Bary, and Donald Keene, eds., *Sources of Japanese Tradition*, Vol. 1, pp. 100–103.

What ethical guidelines does this sutra establish for members of the court? How do these guidelines reflect both Buddhist and Confucian thought?

DOCUMENT 2 PRINCE SHOTOKU TEACHES CONFUCIANISM

Setting an example for the court, Prince Shotoku learned to read and write Chinese and carefully studied Chinese literature, especially Confucian philosophy. Shotoku encouraged the Japanese to adopt Confucianism as the source of political and familial ethics as these excerpts from his writings indicate.

I.   Harmony should be valued and quarrels should be avoided. Everyone has his biases, and few men are far sighted. Therefore some disobey their lords and fathers and keep up feuds with their neighbors. But when the superiors are in harmony with each other and inferiors are friendly, then affairs are discussed quietly and the right view of matters prevails. Then there is nothing that cannot be accomplished!

III.   Do not fail to obey the commands of your Sovereign. He is like Heaven, which is above the Earth, and the vassal is like the Earth, which bears up Heaven. When Heaven and Earth are properly in place, the four seasons follow their course and all is well in Nature. But if the Earth attempts to take the place of Heaven, Heaven would simply fall in ruin.

IV.   The Ministers and officials of the state should make proper behavior their first principle, for if the superiors do not behave properly, the inferiors are disorderly; if the inferiors behave improperly, offenses will naturally result. . . .

V.   Deal impartially with the legal complaints which are submitted to you. If the man who is to decide suits at law makes gain his motive, and hears cases with a view to receiving bribes, then the suits of the rich man will be like a stone flung into water, meeting no resistance, while the complaints of the poor will be like water thrown upon a stone. In these circumstances the poor man will not know where to go, nor will he behave as he should.

VI.   Punish the evil and reward the good. This was the excellent rule of antiquity. Therefore do not hide the good qualities of others or fail to correct what is wrong when you see it. . . .

XV.   To subordinate private interests to the public good—that is the path of a vassal. Now if a man is influenced by private motives, he will be resentful, and if he is influenced by resentment he will fail to act harmoniously with others. If he fails to act harmoniously with others, the public interest will suffer. Resentment interferes with order and is subversive to law. . . .

SOURCE: Hyman Kublan, *Japan: Selected Readings* (New York: Houghton Mifflin, 1968), pp. 30–34.

What Confucian values did Prince Shotoku seek to introduce to Japan?

DOCUMENT 3 EMBASSY TO SHIRAGI

The Manyoshu (One Thousand Poems) *is one of the earliest anthologies of Japanese poetry. Written in 736, after the introduction of Chinese literature as well as Buddhism, these poems reflect Japanese culture during the 7th and 8th centuries. The poem below recalls the sorrow that a Japanese family feels when a loved one leaves on an embassy to China.*

Embassy to Shiragi

When I am parted from you, my dearest,
Who fold me as with wings,
As a water bird its chick on Muko Bay
On the sand-bar of the inlet—
O I shall die of yearning after you.

Could my great ship take you in,
I would keep you, beloved,
Folding you as with wings!

When mist rises on the seashore
Where you put in,
Consider it the breathing
Of my sighs at home.

When autumn comes we shall meet again;
Then how would you raise such sighs
That they would mist the shore!

Wear yourself not out
With yearning after me,
In the month when the autumn wind blows
We shall meet again.

For you, who journey to Shiragi,
I will, in purification, wait,
Longing to see your eyes again,
To-day or to-morrow.

Unaware that the ships must wait
For high tide,
I have parted, to my grief,
From my love so soon.

SOURCE: The Manyoshu, Translation of "One Thousand Poems" by The Nippon Gakujutsu Shinkokai (New York: Columbia University Press, 1965), pp. 242–243.

Why might a young Japanese in the 8th century have chosen to go to China despite the loneliness of leaving family and friends?

About 1000, at the height of the Heian period, several great ladies at court chronicled the events of the day. These women did not write in Chinese as the men of the court did; instead, they used the symbols that the Japanese had adapted from the Chinese to fit their own language. Among the best known works of this period are The Pillow Book *by Sei Shonagon and* The Tale of Genji *by Lady Murasaki. The latter, which has been called the world's first novel, recounts in leisurely fashion the adventures of Prince Genji, a son of the emperor. Through Murasaki's descriptions, we gain insight into the ceremonies and rituals of court life.*

Though it seemed a shame to put so lovely a child into man's dress, he was now twelve years old and the time for his Initiation was come. The emperor directed the preparations with tireless zeal and insisted upon a magnificence beyond what was prescribed.... The ceremony took place in the eastern wing of the Emperor's own apartments, and the Throne was placed facing towards the east, with the seats of the Initiate-to-be and his Sponsor (the Minister of the Left) in front.

Genji arrived at the hour of the Monkey [3 P.M.]. He looked very handsome with his long childish locks, and the Sponsor, whose duty it had just been to bind them with the purple fillet, was sorry to think that all this would soon be changed and even the Clerk of the Treasury seemed reluctant to sever those lovely tresses with the ritual knife. The Emperor, as he watched, remembered for a moment what pride the mother would have taken in the ceremony, but soon drove the weak thought from his mind.

Duly crowned, Genji went to his chamber and changing into man's dress went down into the courtyard and performed the Dance of Homage, which he did with such grace that tears stood in every eye. And now the Emperor, whose grief had of late grown somewhat less insistent, was again overwhelmed by memories of the past.

It had been feared that his delicate features would show to less advantage when he had put aside his childish dress; but on the contrary he looked handsomer than ever.

His sponsor, the Minister of the Left, had an only daughter whose beauty the Heir Apparent had noticed. But now the father began to think he would not encourage that match, but would offer her to Genji. He sounded the Emperor upon this, and found that he would be very glad to obtain for the boy the advantage of so powerful a connection.

SOURCE: Lady Murasaki, *The Tale of Genji*, trans. Arthur Waley (New York: Modern Library, 1960), pp. 18–20.

How can a novel such as The Tale of Genji **serve as a historical document? What are its limitations as a document?**

TIME LINE FOR JAPAN AND THE WEST

JAPAN

400	Yamato clan begins to extend military control over Honshu, neighboring Japanese islands, and parts of Korea
552	Buddhism introduced into Japan
604– 629	Prince Shotoku establishes a constitutional monarchy; opens relations with Sui dynasty in China
645	Taika reforms instituted—power of central government strengthened; tax-collecting system improved
794– 1185	Heian period begins. Capital moved to Heian (Kyoto); contacts with China become infrequent; power of emperor declines
1000	World's first novel—Tale of Genji—written by Lady Murasaki
1185– 1868	Feudal period. Shogun dynasties rule Japan; emperor becomes merely a ceremonial figure
1926	Emperor Hirohito begins his rule

THE WEST

476	Collapse of the Roman Empire in the West; Germanic invasions
528– 565	Justinian briefly reconquers western territories of Roman Empire
622	Beginning of expansion of Islam to North Africa and western Europe
732	Charles Martel stops Moslem advance at Tours
800	Charlemagne crowned Holy Roman emperor
840	Carolingian empire declines; feudalism emerges throughout western Europe as Viking, Magyar, and Moslem invasions begin
1096– 1099	First Crusade
1385	Canterbury Tales written by Geoffrey Chaucer
1453	Constantinople falls to Turks; end of Byzantine Empire

Life in the Middle Ages

● *The universal Church cannot err, since she is governed by the Holy Ghost Who is the Spirit of truth.*

AQUINAS

● *It is impossible for the Christian and true church to subsist without the shedding of blood, for her adversary, the devil, is a liar and a murderer. The church grows and increases through blood; she is sprinkled with blood; she is spoiled and bereaved of her blood.*

LUTHER

● *In form, then, of a white rose displayed itself to me that sacred soldiery which in his blood Christ made his spouse....*

They had their faces all of living flame, and wings of gold, and the rest so white that never snow reacheth such limit.

When they descended into the flower, from rank to rank they proffered of the peace and of the ardor which they acquired as they fanned their sides,

nor did the interposing of so great a flying multitude, betwixt the flower and that which was above, impede the vision nor the splendor;

for the divine light so penetrateth through the universe, in measure of its worthiness, that naught hath power to oppose it.

DANTE

Europe Under Pressure

The 10 centuries that followed the fall of Rome were once called the Dark Ages because people thought that during those years the "light" of knowledge had been extinguished until it was relit in the Renaissance in the 15th century. Today, however, the idea of the "Dark Ages" has long been discredited. Instead, we refer to these centuries as the Middle Ages, or the medieval period, the age between ancient and modern civilizations.

During the early Middle Ages—the period from the late 4th century to the 10th century—Europe was buffeted by a succession of invasions. The first invaders were Germanic tribes, who were pushing into the western portion of the Roman Empire as they sought refuge from ferocious attacks by the Huns on their eastern settlements. Moving west and south across the old Roman boundary of the Rhine and Danube rivers, the Germanic tribes won control of provinces in western Europe, and, by 450, had established their own kingdoms.

The rulers of these Germanic kingdoms did not destroy what they found; rather, they built on Roman traditions and shaped them to their own ends. When Roman officials abandoned their posts to the invaders, priests, bishops, and monks often stayed with their parishes or monasteries and even assumed control of the local government. The Germanic leaders usually realized that they needed the skills and knowledge of the Christians whom they conquered. The Christians, on the other hand, had no choice but to accept and accommodate themselves to their conquerors.

Late in the 8th century, one of these Germanic rulers—Charlemagne—sought to reunite the fragments of the Roman Empire in the West. Although he briefly succeeded in creating a large empire, it crumbled soon after his death when Europe faced new onslaughts from Moslem, Viking, and Magyar invaders. Ironically, during this time of hardship for the peoples of western Europe, the Byzantine and Islamic empires (Chapters 13 and 14) enjoyed their golden ages.

GERMANIC MIGRATIONS The unity and order of the Roman Empire were broken by the influx of successive waves of Germanic tribes, who included the Vandals, Lombards, Alamanni, Goths, Burgundians, Franks, and others. As mentioned above, the Huns, Asiatic nomads from the steppes of Russia, had invaded the territories of these tribes, forcing them to migrate westward across the Danube–Rhine border into the empire.

In 376, the *Visigoths* (western Goths), fleeing the Huns, asked and received permission from the emperor Valens to cross the Danube and settle inside the empire. After they were admitted, they were exploited by local officials who charged them exorbitant prices for food and other supplies. When the newcomers protested, Valens ordered them to leave the empire. Instead of leaving, the Visigoths took up arms against the emperor, whom they defeated and killed at Adrianople in 378. Later, they moved westward to occupy more land. In 410, under the leadership of Alaric, they captured and sacked Rome. Jerome, one of the early Church Fathers (Chapter 12), was stunned by the Visigoth attack on Rome: "Who could believe that Rome, built on the conquest of the whole world, would fall to the ground? that the mother herself would become the tomb of her peoples?"[1]

At about the same time that the Visigoths were attacking Rome, the Vandals crossed the Rhine and moved through Gaul and Spain into North Africa, where they established a kingdom on the site that was once occupied by Carthage. From this base, the Vandals attacked Rome and other parts of the empire by sea. (So terrifying were their raids that to this day one who plunders and destroys is called a *vandal*.)

Meanwhile, the Asiatic Huns continued their push westward. By 450, they were invading northern Italy and Gaul under the leadership of Attila, whom the Romans called the "Scourge of God." The Germanic tribes who had previously settled in Gaul united with the remnants of the Roman army in the region and defeated the Huns at the battle of

The octagonal church of San Vitale is is an enduring monument of Theodoric's rule at Ravenna. Theodoric planned the church during the last year of his life, and construction was completed by the Byzantines.

Chalons in 451. The next year, Attila invaded Italy, but Pope Leo, later called "Leo the Great," managed to persuade him not to attack Rome. After Attila's death in 453, the threat of the Huns dwindled.

After the collapse of the Hun threat, the *Ostrogoths* (eastern Goths) moved into Italy, where their leader Odoacer overthrew the last of the Roman emperors in the West. Odoacer's successor was Theodoric, an Ostrogoth who had been educated in Constantinople and had great respect for Greco-Roman civilization. Theodoric established his capital at Ravenna, and during his long reign (489-526), he maintained an uneasy relationship with the Byzantine Empire in the East.

After the death of Theodoric, the Byzantine emperor Justinian sought to reunite the old Roman Empire, and brought most of Italy under his control. As you have read, however, Justinian's success was short-lived. Within a few years of his death, Italy was again invaded. This time, a Germanic tribe known as the Lombards entered Italy, setting up a kingdom in the north—in a region that still bears their name, Lombardy—and conquering other parts of central and southern Italy. The Byzantine Empire held onto Rav-

---

[1] J. H. Robinson, ed., *Readings in European History*, Vol. 1 (New York: Ginn, 1904), p. 45.

enna and some surrounding lands, but Italy was no longer united.

The old Roman province of Gaul suffered a fate similar to that of Italy. The Burgundians gained control of eastern Gaul, while the Alamanni moved into the region to the west of the Burgundians. A short time later, the Franks displaced the Alamanni and eventually gained control of much of what is today France.

THE MEROVINGIANS   During the 4th and 5th centuries, Frankish tribes migrated from their homeland along the Rhine River into present-day Belgium and France. In 481, Clovis became the king of the *Salian* ("salty") Franks, a small tribe that lived near the North Sea. He was descended from Merovech, a warrior who reputedly had helped the Romans defeat the Huns at Chalons in 451. Clovis, who ruled until his death in 511, was the founder of the Merovingian dynasty (named after Merovech) and the conqueror of an empire that stretched from the Pyrenees to central Europe.

CLOVIS

As the young king of the Salian Franks, Clovis forced the general Syagrius, the last Roman commander in central Gaul, to withdraw his troops from Gaul in 486. He then strengthened his army and gained control of the other Frankish tribes of northern France.

In 493, Clovis married a Burgundian princess, Clothilde, who had converted to Christianity. The marriage was significant because it brought Clovis into the Roman Catholic Church. According to Christian sources, on the eve of a battle with the Alamanni, Clovis looked up to the sky and said, "If you give me this victory . . . I will believe . . . and will be baptized." Clovis defeated the Alamanni in 496, and, a short time later, triumphed over the Visigoths at Tours. After these victories, Clovis and 3000 of his warriors were baptized into the Roman Catholic Church. This baptism was important to Clovis and to the development of Europe. Clovis became a Roman Catholic at a time when the other Germanic rulers belonged to a rival Christian sect called Arians (see Chapter 12). Through his conversion, he won the support of the Roman Church. His action strengthened Catholicism and gave the Church a powerful ally against the Arians.

The Church soon made use of its alliance with Clovis by persuading him to attack the Visigoths, who were Arians and thus considered heretics. In 507, Clovis defeated Alaric II, the king of the Visigoths, at Poitiers and extended his control over southern France. The defeated Visigoths then withdrew into Spain. Clovis now ruled much of present-day France. He tried to establish a uniform system of government for the various peoples he ruled by codifying the *Salian Laws*, which were based on the customs of the Germanic tribes, and by encouraging his subjects to adopt Catholicism.

MAYORS OF THE PALACE

When Clovis died in 511, his kingdom was divided among his four sons, as Frankish custom demanded. This division of power was a basic weakness and prevented a single ruler from establishing effective control. Also, Clovis' sons were weak and frequently quar-

FRANKISH KINGS	
Merovingian Rulers	
481-511	Clovis
Carolingian Rulers	
714-741	Charles Martel
741-768	Pepin
768-814	Charlemagne
814-840	Louis the Pious
840-855	Lothair
840-876	Louis the German (east)
840-877	Charles the Bald (west)
899-911	Louis the Child

GERMANIC KINGDOMS IN THE WEST

Compare this map to the map on page 296. Which Germanic kingdoms did Justinian conquer in the 6th century?

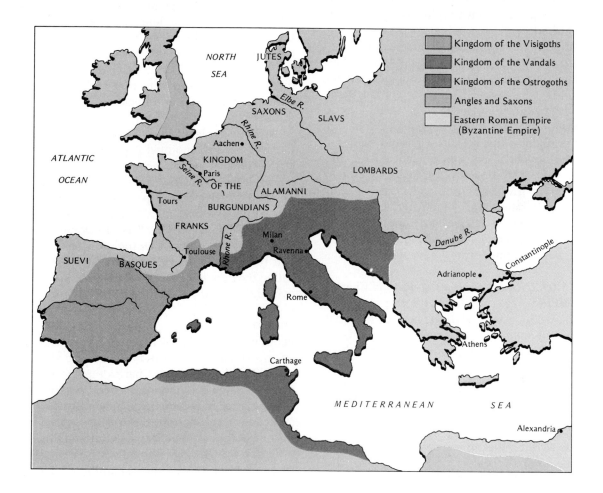

reled among themselves, while their heirs were incompetent. As a result, the rulers who followed Clovis came to be called the "do-nothing kings."

Under the do-nothing kings, local rulers gained control over their own lands and often ignored the commands of their overlord. During the 7th and 8th centuries, the weak Merovingian rulers turned over more and more of their power to officials called the "mayors of the palace." As Einhard, an 8th century chronicler, observed:

● ● ● Nothing was left to the king. He had to content himself with his royal title, his flowing locks, and long beard. Seated in a chair of state, he was wont to display an appearance of power by receiving foreign ambassadors on their arrival, and on their departure, giving them, as if on his own authority, those answers which he had been taught or commanded to give.[2]

---

[2]Einhard, "Life of the Emperor Charles," in *Readings in European History*, ed. Robinson, p. 120.

341

In time, the mayor of the palace became the power behind the throne. By the 8th century, one family had made this position hereditary. They were known as the *Carolingians* (from *Carolus*, the Latin form of Charles). The Carolingians passed the position of mayor from father to son, but always left a Merovingian king on the throne. The most important of these Carolingian mayors of the palace was Charles Martel ("the Hammer") who ruled from 714 to 741. While he exercised all of the powers of a king, he did not assume the title. His greatest achievement was organizing an efficient and reliable cavalry. With this cavalry, Charles was able to defeat the Moslem invaders at Tours in 732 (Chapter 14). Although the Moslems continued to attack western Europe, this battle is often considered a landmark because it marked their furthest advance.

CAROLINGIAN EMPIRE

After the death of Charles Martel, his heirs ventured along a new course that helped shape the subsequent history of Europe. First, his son, Pepin, gained the title of king; then, Pepin's son, Charlemagne, expanded the Frankish kingdom into an empire that stretched across much of Europe.

PEPIN

In 741, after his father's death, Pepin became mayor of the palace of King Childeric III. Pepin felt that Childeric was incompetent to serve as king and plotted to gain the title for himself. About 751, he asked the abbot of Saint Denis, a monastery near Paris, to go to Rome and ask for the pope's support.

● ● ● *Pope Zacharias, therefore, in virtue of apostolic authority, told the ambassadors that he judged it better and more advantageous that he should be king and be called king who had the power rather than he who was falsely called king.*

The said pontiff accordingly enjoined the king and the people of the Franks that Pippin [Pepin], who already exercised the regal power, should be called king and raised to the throne.[3]

The pope's willingness to endorse Pepin's claim was due in large measure to his need for an ally against the Lombards, who were threatening papal lands in Italy. In 752, with the Church to back up his claim, Pepin persuaded the Frankish nobles to name him as their king. Bishop Boniface then anointed Pepin with holy oil and declared him king of the Franks.

A few years later, Pope Stephen traveled to Paris and also anointed Pepin king. In exchange, Pepin led his army into Italy and defeated the Lombards. He then forced the Lombards to give up a strip of territory across central Italy, which he in turn presented to the pope. This gift, known as the *Donation of Pepin*, gave the pope temporal as well as spiritual power over the lands that were later called the *Papal States*. The pope would rule over these lands until the 19th century.

CHARLEMAGNE

Pepin was succeeded by his son Charles, who so impressed his contemporaries that he was called Charlemagne, or "Charles the Great." During a reign of almost half a century (768-814), Charlemagne conquered an empire that stretched from Spain in the west to central Europe in the east. According to Einhard, his personal friend and biographer, Charlemagne looked like the general and king that he was:

● ● ● *Charles was large and robust, of commanding stature and excellent proportions, for it appears that he measured in height seven times the length of his own foot. The top of his head was round, his eyes large and animated, his nose somewhat long. He had a fine head of gray hair, and his face was bright and pleasant; so that, whether standing or sitting, he showed great presence and dignity. Although his neck was thick*

---

[3]"The Lesser Annals of Lorsch," in *Readings in European History*, ed. Robinson, p. 121.

This bronze statuette may be a contemporary portrait of the emperor Charlemagne.

and rather short, and his belly too prominent, still the good proportions of his limbs concealed these defects. His walk was firm and the whole carriage of his body was manly. His voice was clear, but not so strong as his frame would have led one to expect.[4]

Conquests. Charlemagne's goal was to unite all the Germanic tribes into a single Christian kingdom. In pursuit of this goal, he conducted more than 50 military campaigns. In 774, when the Lombards renounced the treaty that they had made with Pepin and renewed their attacks on the papal territory, Charlemagne marched into Italy, defeated the Lombards, and declared himself their king. Then crossing the Pyrenees Mountains, he fought both the Moslems and the Basques, a native tribe, for control of northern Spain. He then carved out for himself a border kingdom called the Spanish March.[5]

After many campaigns against the Saxon tribes who lived between the Rhine and the Elbe rivers, Charlemagne subdued them and forced them to convert to Christianity. He then moved into Bavaria and drove the Slavs and Avars from the upper reaches of the Danube River. By the time he died, Charlemagne controlled the area of present-day France, Belgium, the Netherlands, West Germany, Austria, Switzerland, and northern Italy.

Government. Like his father, Charlemagne allied himself closely with the Church. In 799, when Pope Leo III was driven from the papal throne by a Roman mob and was almost killed in the street, he fled to Charlemagne's court. Charlemagne promptly went to Rome and restored the pope to his office. In gratitude, on Christmas Day in 800, Pope Leo crowned Charlemagne "Emperor of the Romans" and hailed him as *Augustus*, the ancient Roman title.

Charlemagne may have looked on this event as a mixed blessing. Although the Frankish king now carried the title of a Roman emperor and had the prestige of the Church behind him, the coronation implied that the pope had the power to crown (and perhaps remove the crown) of the ruler. When Charlemagne named his son as his successor, he was careful to preside over the ceremony himself without turning to the pope. Yet Charlemagne's coronation that Christmas Day showed that the tradition of a single, united Christian empire—like the one created by the ancient Romans—lingered in the minds of many people.

---

[4]Einhard, "Life of the Emperor Charles," in *Readings in European History*, ed. Robinson, p. 126.

[5]It was during Charlemagne's campaign in Spain that his rear guard was trapped at the pass of Roncesvalles in the Pyrenees Mountains. The heroic last stand of a Frankish noble named Roland later gave rise to the popular medieval epic, *The Song of Roland* (*Le Chanson de Roland*).

On Christmas day of 800, Pope Leo III crowned Charlemagne emperor in Rome. This ceremony pronounced Charlemagne as heir of the Roman emperors, but also implied that the pope had the right to consecrate kings. Charlemagne therefore took care to crown his own successor in Aachen.

Charlemagne proved to be an able administrator as well as a successful military leader. He chose capable people to help him; he delegated authority to them; and he insisted that they carry out his wishes. He divided his empire into 300 districts, or counties. In each, a count administered secular business, a duke directed military matters, and a bishop managed religious affairs. In the counties on the frontier, called *marches*, that were threatened by invaders, he appointed special commanders to administer civil and military affairs. A contemporary chronicler praised the quality of Charlemagne's appointments:

• • • *The most serene and most holy Christian lord emperor Charles has chosen from his nobles the wisest and most prudent men, archbishops and some of the other bishops also, together with venerable abbots and pious laymen, and has sent them throughout his whole kingdom.*[6]

Charlemagne sent out messengers who acted as royal inspectors, supervising the administrators and punishing those who misbehaved. These inspectors were changed frequently and rotated to different districts to prevent them from cheating the emperor. Each administrator, each inspector, and, indeed, each citizen was required to take an oath of allegiance to Charlemagne.

Charlemagne issued laws based on the

---

[6]The general capitulary for the *missi*, in *Readings in European History*, ed. Robinson, p. 139.

THE CAROLINGIAN EMPIRE
What modern countries include territories that were once part of Lothair's kingdom?

Kingdom of the Franks, 768
Conquests of Charlemagne, 768–814

principles of Germanic tribal laws. However, these laws were influenced by Christianity in that they condemned pagan practices and promoted Christian practices. Laws dealt with both secular and religious matters. One ordinance, for example, specified in great detail how royal farms should be operated. Each farm manager was required to submit an annual report of assets—such as size of fields, forests, mills, ships, and bridges—under his control. The report was also to include production statistics about everything from "hay, firewood, torches, planks, and other kinds of lumber," to "mulberry wine, coked wine, mead, vinegar, beer, and wine, new and old," and even including "iron, lead, or other substances."

CAROLINGIAN RENAISSANCE

Charlemagne was concerned not only with creating a strong and efficient government but also with improving learning throughout the empire. He was horrified at the lack of education among the clergy, many of whom did not know Latin or Greek. To improve this sorry state of affairs, he decreed that each cathedral establish a school for the training of the clergy. He even set up a palace school for his own family. Although he himself knew Latin and some Greek, he never mastered the art of reading and writing.

••• *Charles also tried to learn to write, and used to keep his tablets and writing book under the pillow of his couch, that when he had leisure he might practice his hand in forming letters; but he made little progress in this task, too long deferred and begun too late in life.*[7]

Charlemagne's establishment of learning centers throughout his empire stimulated a rebirth of learning and scholarship that later historians called the *Carolingian Renaissance.* (Renaissance is a French word meaning "rebirth".)

To advance learning, Charlemagne invited to his court at Aachen (or Aix-la-Chapelle) the most renowned scholars of the day, including the famous Anglo-Saxon scholar, Alcuin of York, who set up the palace school for Charlemagne's sons and daughters and for the children of the nobles at court. Charlemagne also encouraged monasteries to establish schools for able boys of all social classes, and he visited these schools to check on the progress of the students.

Charlemagne founded abbeys for the purpose of encouraging monks to make copies

The chapel of Charlemagne at his capital city of Aachen. This design of this church was influenced by two Byzantine monuments that Charlemagne had visited: Constantine's basilica in Rome, and the church of San Vitale at Ravenna.

of the works of Greek and Roman authors, of Jerome's Latin translation of the Old and New Testaments (the *Vulgate*), and of the writings of other early Church leaders. The scribes who did this work often illuminated the first letter of each paragraph with colorful and intricate designs and painted scenes in the margins of events described in the text. These scribes also developed a form of writing in which lower-case letters were used alongside the upper-case, or capital, letters inherited from the Romans.

As Charlemagne's health began to fail, he tried to teach his only surviving son, Louis, the methods that he had used to govern his vast empire. But Charlemagne's gifts as a ruler

---

[7]Einhard, "the Life of Emperor Charles," in *Readings in European History*, ed. Robinson, p. 128.

r sedpericulosapraesumptio iudicaredecese

uam ecanescentem iammundum adinitiaret

eruseuimhmanusuolumen adsumpserit eeas

could not easily be conveyed to another person. When he died in 814, an unknown monk was moved to write:

Dire sufferings has France endured,
Yet never grief like unto this,
Woe is me for misery;
Now Charles, voice of majesty and power,
To Aachen's soil she has given,
Woe is me for misery.[8]

These words were prophetic in many ways because Charlemagne's brilliant achievements did not survive him for long.

LOUIS THE PIOUS

Charlemagne's son Louis the Pious (814-840) inherited his father's vast empire, but as his name implies, Louis was more interested in religion than in governing the empire. Within a few years after assuming the throne, Louis lost the support of the clergy and nobles. When these powerful groups recognized his weakness as a ruler, they took more power themselves.

Louis' last years were spent watching the bitter battles among his sons over the spoils of his empire. As provided by German custom, Louis planned to divide the empire among his three sons. He proposed that Lothair, the eldest, succeed to the throne as emperor and supervise the regions inherited

by two other brothers: Louis, called "the German," and Charles, called "the Bald." But the three sons rebelled against their father, and after his death in 840, they quarreled with one another.

DIVISION OF THE EMPIRE

The empire, which had begun to disintegrate on Charlemagne's death, further declined under his grandsons. In 842, Louis the German and Charles the Bald met at Strasbourg, where they signed the *Strasbourg Oath*, in which they agreed to work together against their brother, Lothair. The oath was significant because it was written in two languages: one was the language of Charles' kingdom (west of the Rhine River), which was similar to Latin and would eventually become French; the other was the Germanic language of Louis' kingdom (east of the Rhine). Standing before their followers, each brother swore to the alliance in the language of the other. Their oath symbolized the growing split in the Carolingian Empire between the western and eastern lands of the Franks.

In 843, faced with the coalition of his two brothers, Lothair met with them at Verdun and accepted the terms of a treaty that divided Charlemagne's empire into three kingdoms. The western kingdom, which became present-day France, remained with Charles, and the eastern kingdom, which became present-day Germany, with Louis. A middle kingdom consisting of a long strip of land stretching from the North Sea into central Italy went to Lothair. This narrow corridor, known successively as Lotharii Regnum, Lotharginia, and Lorraine, was fought over by the Germans and French for a thousand years. Much reduced in size, Lorraine was taken by the Germans in the 19th century but was reclaimed by the French in 1919.

After the empire was divided, Lothair's central kingdom was soon fragmented. Descendants of Charlemagne ruled the eastern kingdom until 911, when the last Carolingian king died. In the western kingdom, Car-

---

[8]Quoted in E. S. Duckett, *Carolingian Portraits, A Study of the Ninth Century* (Ann Arbor: University of Michigan Press, 1962), p. 19.

The emperor Lothair inherited the central part of Charlemagne's kingdom, while his brothers ruled the eastern and western portions.

olingian rule came to an end in 987 when the French nobles elected Hugh Capet, count of Paris, as their king. The Capetians then ruled France for more than 300 years (Chapter 21).

The collapse of Charlemagne's empire was due only in part to the quarrels among his grandsons. At the same time as these internal wars were taking place, the empire was attacked on all sides by new waves of invaders. In the 9th century, the Vikings raided much of northern Europe; Moslems captured Sicily and launched raids on other parts of Italy; and the Magyars swept out of central Asia to terrorize eastern Europe.

THE VIKINGS Scholars are uncertain about the origin of the word *Viking*, which is used to designate the raiders who suddenly appeared from the sea to attack the coast of Britain and northern France shortly before the year 800. Some suggest that it may be derived from the Scandinavian word *vik*, meaning inlet or fjord, where boats could be sheltered; others believe that it may be derived from *vig*, meaning battle. The Vikings came to be known by other names—such as the Northmen or the Norse; their descendants in France were called Normans. Wherever Viking raiders struck, they inspired people to offer the prayer: *A furore Normanorum libera nos, domine.* (From the fury of the Northmen, O Lord deliver us.)

The Vikings were Scandinavians from the region of present-day Denmark, Sweden, and Norway. They were related to the Germanic tribes who moved into Europe during the 4th and 5th centuries. Scholars do not know why the Vikings launched their fearful raids on western Europe in the 9th and 10th centuries. Some theorize that climatic changes lay behind the Viking expansion. Others believe that overpopulation or else the practice of **primogeniture**, in which the eldest son inherited his father's estate, left younger sons without any other means of earning a living.

Because of the geography of Scandinavia, the sea was important to the Viking way of life. By the 9th century, the Vikings had developed technologically advanced sailing ships which carried them on their raids across the seas. Viking ships were propelled by sails and long oars, and could achieve a maximum speed of about ten knots.[9] The largest of these ships could hold up to 100 men, and yet could be maneuvered on the open sea by as few as 15. Since they required a depth of only about three feet, Viking ships could be used on rivers to travel far inland. These remarkable vessels were strong enough to withstand

[9]A speed of one knot is equal to one nautical mile (6080.2 feet) per hour.

The remains of several Viking ships have been discovered. Two ships, the Gokstad and the Oseberg, are on exhibit in the Viking Ship Hall in Oslo, Norway. Both were used for royal burials: the Gokstad for a chieftain and the Oseberg for a queen. The Gokstad, which was discovered in 1880, was an 80-foot-long warship with 16 pairs of oars. In 1893, an exact replica of this ship was built and sailed from Norway to New-foundland in 28 days. The Oseberg, which was found in 1904, contained the skeletons of a queen, a slave girl, 12 horses, several dogs, and a peacock with feathers. It also contained beautifully carved furniture and a cart, all of which was meant to make life comfortable for the deceased in the afterlife.

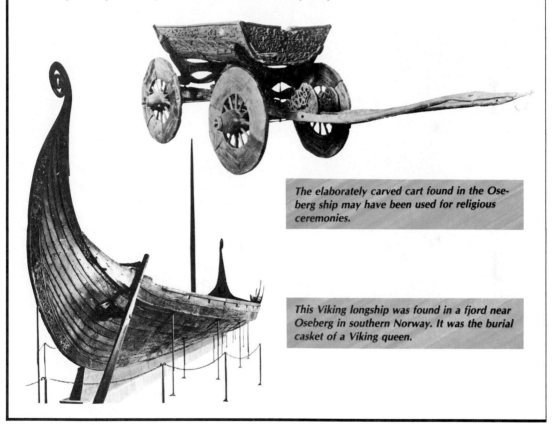

The elaborately carved cart found in the Oseberg ship may have been used for religious ceremonies.

This Viking longship was found in a fjord near Oseberg in southern Norway. It was the burial casket of a Viking queen.

the buffeting of the sea but light enough to be carried around waterfalls, rapids, or fortified bridges.

ATTACKS ON WESTERN EUROPE

Late in the 8th century, Vikings from Norway occupied islands to the north and west of Scotland. Others created settlements on the coast of Ireland, occupying the ports of Dublin, Waterford, and Limerick. In 793, they attacked the monastery of Lindisfarne, a thriving center of Irish Christian civilization. The Anglo-Saxon scholar, Alcuin, was moved to write about this event.

• • • *Lo, it is some 350 years that we and our forefathers have inhabited this most lovely land, and never before has such a terror*

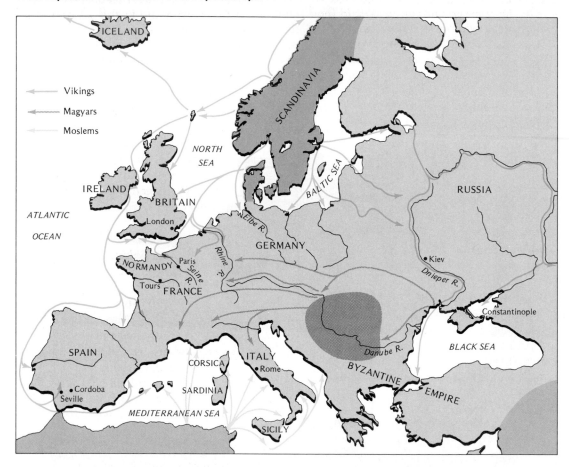

appeared in Britain as we have now suffered from a pagan race, nor was it thought possible that such an inroad from the sea could be made.[10]

In the 9th century, Vikings—whom the English called the Danes—began attacking the northern and eastern coasts of England. In 886, Alfred the Great, the Anglo-Saxon king of Wessex, made a treaty with Guthrum, king of the Danes, by which the Danes gained control of northeastern England. This region

then became known as the *Danelaw*. For the next century, there was almost continuous warfare between Alfred's successors and the Danes. In the 11th century, new waves of Danes attacked England. In 1016, the Danish king, Canute, became king of England, and in 1066, a descendant of the Vikings, William of Normandy, seized the English throne (Chapter 20)

While the Danes were attacking England, other Vikings were raiding the coast of France. Late in 885, a Viking fleet of 700 ships sailed up the Seine River and laid siege to Paris. Under the leadership of Count Odo, the city withstood the siege for several months but was becoming desperate for help when:

---

[10]Alcuin, *Anglo-Saxon Chronicles*, quoted in *Viking, Hammer of the North* by Magnus Magnusson (New York: Galahad Books, 1976), p. 22.

. . . Odo . . . went forth secretly to seek aid from the nobles of the kingdom, and to send word to the emperor that the city would soon be lost unless help came. When Odo returned to Paris he found the people lamenting his absence. Nor did he reenter the city without a remarkable incident. The Northmen had learned that he was coming back, and they blocked his way to the gate. But Odo, though his horse was killed, struck down his enemies right and left, forced his way into the city, and brought joy to the anxious people.[11]

Although the siege was eventually lifted, the fear of Viking attacks remained very real. From their base on the lower Seine River, the Vikings raided, looted, and burned rich monasteries, convents, and the few towns that still existed in France. In 911, the Frankish king Charles the Simple, a descendant of Charlemagne, ceded a region on the north coast of France to the Viking leader Rollo, on the condition that Rollo be baptized as a Christian and defend the region against other raiders. This region, the land of the "Northmen," soon became known as Normandy.

MIGRATIONS INTO RUSSIA

Vikings from Sweden sailed across the Baltic Sea and the Gulf of Finland into present-day Russia. They found their way by water courses and short portages to the headwaters of the Volga River. Following the Volga, they reached the Caspian Sea. They also moved southward from present-day Leningrad to the Dnieper River, which led them to the Black Sea and Constantinople. In 862, they dominated the Slavic peoples along the river valleys and set up their own Viking kingdom centered at Kiev. In time the region came to be known as *Ruotsi*, which was later corrupted to *Russia*.[12]

From Kiev, the Vikings, or *Varangians* as they were called in the east, launched attacks against Constantinople in the 9th and 10th centuries. The Byzantine emperors were impressed with the reckless courage of the attackers. After fending them off, the emperors agreed to use them as an elite corps in the Byzantine army. The Volga and Dnieper rivers became arteries of commerce between the Viking and Byzantine civilizations. Blonde slaves, who were in great demand among the Byzantines, and furs, honey, and amber were carried southward to Constantinople while silk and other luxury goods were carried into Russia and northern Europe.

OTHER VIKING SETTLEMENTS

In the mid-9th century, Viking warships sailed into the Mediterranean Sea, and Norse raiders attacked settlements along the Iberian coast, invaded North Africa, and possibly roamed as far east as Alexandria, Egypt. Meanwhile, other Vikings sailed westward from Norway and discovered Iceland, where they built settlements. About 980, Eric the Red led settlers from Iceland to the island of Greenland, which he had discovered. The Viking settlements on Greenland lasted until about 1500, by which time, some scholars theorize, the climate of Greenland had become too harsh to support settlers.

Late in the 10th century, Vikings from Greenland explored the seas further to the west. About 1001, Leif Ericson reached the coast of North America, where he established a settlement called *Vinland*, or "Land of the grapes." Archaeologists believe that Vinland was probably on the northern tip of Newfoundland where they have found remains of a Viking longhouse, weapons, and tools. The Vikings fought with the native population, whom they called *Skraelings*, but

---

[11]From the *Annals of St. Vaast*, quoted in *Readings in European History*, ed. Robinson, p. 162-3.

[12]The origin of the word *Russian* is not actually known. The Finns called the Vikings *ruotsi*, mean-

ing "seafarers." By 900, the most powerful branch of the eastern Slavs was known as the *Rus*, and the Vikings may have accepted this designation for themselves.

whom we would probably call *Eskimos*. Within a few years, however, the Vikings abandoned Vinland and returned to Greenland or Iceland.

VIKING CULTURE

In most contemporary accounts, the Vikings were portrayed as savage pirates intent on loot and destruction. These accounts were written by the people who suffered at the hands of the Vikings. Yet there was another side to these fearless seafaring raiders. They developed their own literature—long narrative poems, called *sagas*, that have been found in Iceland. Like the epic poems of Homer, the Icelandic sagas mix facts with fancy and were sung to audiences by wandering bards. These sagas were not written down until the 13th or 14th centuries, but they memorialize events of several centuries earlier. In fact, our information about the deeds of Eric the Red and his son, Leif, come from these sagas.

The Vikings had a written script known as *runic*, and runic inscriptions on rock and metal have been found in places stretching from North America to the Caspian Sea. The fact that the names of women often appear in the runic inscriptions seems to indicate that women played an important role in Viking society. We know, for example, that women could own property, had the right to consent to their marriages, and could initiate divorces.

In their homelands, the economy of the Vikings was based on agriculture, herding, hunting, and fishing. As you have read, they made the excellent sailing ships that took them on long and dangerous voyages. Artists carved the prow of each ship to resemble a fanciful creature. They also decorated weapons and jewelry with intricate abstract designs and heads of fanciful horses, serpents, and dragons.

The Vikings worshiped a pantheon of gods. Thor, whose symbol was a hammer, was the most important. He was the guardian of humans and the other gods. Odin was the god of wisdom and of war, and Frey was the goddess of fertility. Sacrifices were made to these gods to ensure their protection at home and in battle. Warriors who were slain in battle were called *val*, and they were carried to heaven (*Valhalla*) by handmaidens of the gods (*Valkyries*). Valhalla was a place where heroic battles were fought and celebrations were held with feasts of pork and mead (honeyed ale).

Whenever possible, a Viking chieftain was buried in a ship, with everything he would need in the afterlife: slaves, weapons, armor, food, and furniture. Such a burial is described in the Anglo-Saxon saga *Beowulf*:

There at the quay, stood a ring-prowed ship—
The radiant and eager ship of the lord.
They laid down the beloved lord,
The giver of rings, in the bosom of the ship,
The lord lay by the mast. They brought from afar
Many great treasures and costly trappings.
I never heard of a ship so richly furnished as this,
With weapons of war, armour of battle,
Swords and corselets. Many treasures lay
Piled on his breast.[13]

By 1000, the Vikings had settled in many parts of Europe. In France, England, and elsewhere, they converted to Christianity and their culture blended into that of Christian Europe. After the 11th century, their raiding forays ended, but the bold spirit of the Vikings continued in the Norman knights who conquered England in 1066, seized Sicily from the Moslems, and embarked on the Crusades (Chapter 16).

THE MOSLEMS While the Viking raids on northern Europe were the most widespread and destructive of the great invasions of the 9th and 10th centuries, the

[13]Quoted in *The Vikings and Their Origins*, by David M. Wilson (New York: McGraw-Hill, 1970), p. 66.

Moslem attacks were equally terrifying to the Christian communities of southern Europe. As you have read, Arab armies conquered the Middle East, the coast of North Africa, and much of Spain in the century after Mohammed's death in 632. By 732, they had crossed the Pyrenees and were turned back by Charles Martel at Tours.

During this same period, the Moslems gradually gained control of the islands in the western Mediterranean, including Sicily, Corsica, and Sardinia. In 827, they virtually completed their conquest of Sicily and soon afterward made Palermo their capital.

ATTACKS ON SOUTHERN EUROPE

From their strongholds in Sicily and Spain, the Moslems launched frequent raids on Italy and the coast of southern France. Europeans called these invaders *Saracens*, from *sarakenos*, a Byzantine Greek word meaning "easterners." Although Christians in Europe were terrified of the Saracens, they were not above appealing to them on occasion for help in their own quarrels. This was the case in Italy when rivalry among the Lombards and the Byzantine emperor led Naples to ask for Moslem assistance in 838. The Moslems took the opportunity to make new conquests along both the western and eastern coasts of Italy.

They attacked and destroyed the famous monastery founded by Saint Benedict at Monte Cassino and even besieged Rome in 846. Although they did not capture the city, they did plunder the cathedrals of St. Peter and St. Paul outside the walls. A Christian eyewitness described this event:

• • • *At this same time, as no one can mention or hear without great sadness, the mother of all churches, the basilica of the apostle Peter, was taken and plundered by the Moors, or Saracens, who had already occupied the region of Beneventum. The Saracens, moreover, slaughtered all the Christians whom they found outside the walls of Rome, whether within or without this church. They also carried men and women away prisoners. They tore down, among many others, the altar of the blessed Peter, and their crimes from day to day bring sorrow to Christians.*[14]

The Moslems extended their raids into other parts of Europe. They built forts along the south coast of France, which they used as bases to attack merchants carrying goods across the Alps.

In 972, the Moslems captured the abbot of Cluny from a famous monastery in southern France and held him for ransom. Because the abbot was an influential Church leader, French nobles put aside their personal differences to secure his release. Late in the 9th century, Christians began to dislodge the Moslems from their bases on the Italian mainland. However, the Moslems held onto Sicily until the mid-11th century.

CHRISTIAN-ISLAMIC CULTURE OF SICILY

In Sicily, the Moslems imposed their own culture on the local population. Palermo grew into a thriving commercial center and became a leading Moslem city like Cordoba in Spain or Cairo in Egypt. The impact of the Moslem occupation of Sicily would remain long after the island had been recaptured by Christian Europeans.

The conquest of Sicily was carried out by the Normans between about 1060 and 1091. By the 11th century, these descendants of Viking raiders who had settled in France were looking for new lands to conquer. They were soon expanding their power and influence into the Mediterranean, where they fought and often defeated not only the Moslems but also the Byzantines.

In 1071, the Normans captured Palermo and by 1091 had ended Moslem control of Sicily. The Norman count Roger who then ruled Sicily left much of the Moslem culture in place, and the next two centuries saw Christian and Islamic traditions blended into

[14]From the *Annals of Xanten*, quoted in *Readings in European History*, ed. Robinson, p. 160.

a flourishing culture. Roger appointed Moslems to high positions in government and respected the advanced learning of Moslem physicians and philosophers. His son, Roger II, established a brilliant court in which the Moslem geographer al-Idrisi (Chapter 14) wrote his great works based on reports from travelers to distant lands. In the 13th century, Roger's grandson, Frederick II continued the official patronage of Islamic learning. Through trade with the Islamic world as well as his support of Moslem scholars at court, Frederick helped to introduce the more advanced culture of the East into western Europe.

THE MAGYARS The third group of invaders to devastate Europe in the 9th and 10th centuries were the Magyars. These ruthless invaders probably came from the region of the Ural Mountains and the Volga River. From there, they migrated southwestward into the steppes of southern Russia. In the 9th century, they descended on the Slavic and Germanic settlements of eastern Europe with unmatched ferocity.

The Magyar warriors were brilliant horsemen. They had learned to use the stirrup—an invention that scholars believe was slowly making its way to the west from its place of origin in India or perhaps China. With the stirrup, an armed rider could stand upright while on horseback and shoot arrows in any direction.

In the 10th century, the Magyars, who had already pushed into present-day Poland and Romania, swept into lands at the base of the Alps. They left a path of destruction across northern Italy, eastern France, and southern Germany. They kept up their devastating raids until 955, when Otto the Great (see Chapter 19) met them at Lechfeld in southern Germany. There, he soundly defeated them. Contemporaries thought Otto's victory at Lechfeld as significant as the victory of Charles Martel at Tours. Certainly, it ended the Magyar threat, for the surviving Magyars escaped eastward, where they settled along the Danube River in the area that we know today as Hungary.

There are at least two theories about how the land of the Magyars came to be called Hungary. One theory claims that it comes from the Magyar word *onogur*, meaning "ten arrows," which symbolized the confederation of ten tribes that invaded Europe. Another theory says that the destruction of the Magyars reminded people of the Hun invasion of the 5th century, and so they called the new invaders Hungarians.

RESULTS OF THE INVASIONS The invasions of the Vikings, Moslems, and Magyars completed the course of destruction that had started several centuries earlier when the Germanic migrations across Europe contributed to the collapse of the Roman Empire in the West. The centuries of invasions transformed western Europe into a land made up of many small kingdoms. The constant warfare had cut off trade. As a result, many towns and cities of Roman times had disappeared; others were much reduced in size.

These and other effects of the invasions will be discussed further in later chapters. Faced with the need to repel invaders, local leaders developed new means to raise armed and mounted horsemen. As early as the 8th century, Charles Martel had seen the importance of having *knights*, or mounted warriors, to resist the Moslem invaders. The upkeep of a horse, the making of armor, and the training of knights required money and time, which the Merovingian mayor of the palace did not have. Instead, he used the one commodity he did have—giving knights the right to certain lands in exchange for military service. The land provided a knight with a means of support. This practice, which was first developed in France, spread to the rest of Europe and became the basis of a new order, called feudalism, which you will study in Chapter 17.

SUMMARY

For more than 500 years—from the 5th to the 10th centuries—Europe experienced a succession of invasions. First, the Germanic tribes poured across the borders of the Roman Empire, contributing to its collapse. In the former Roman provinces, German leaders set up small, warring kingdoms.

For a brief time, Charlemagne succeeded in reuniting many of the lands once ruled by Rome. During his rule, a revival of learning known as the Carolingian Renaissance brought new life to the fading cultural traditions of the ancient world and helped lay the foundations for medieval civilization. On Charlemagne's death, however, his empire collapsed as his heirs quarreled and divided up his land.

The collapse of the Carolingian Empire was hastened by three new waves of invasions: the Vikings from the north, the Moslems from the south, and the Magyars from the east. By the time these threats had ended late in the 10th century, western Europe was devastated and a new way of life based on the need to resist invaders had developed.

QUESTIONS

1 What impact did the Germanic migrations of the early Middle Ages have on the Roman Empire in the West?
2 Describe the origins, organization, and decline of the Carolingian Empire. How did Charlemagne reflect both ancient and medieval traditions?
3 How does the Carolingian Renaissance refute the old notion that the period between the fall of Rome and the Renaissance was the "Dark Ages"?
4 Why do you think the Viking invasions were so widespread?
5 On a map of Europe, trace the invasions of the Vikings, Moslems, and Magyars in the 9th and 10th centuries. In what part of Europe would you have chosen to live at that time?
6 Describe how the invasions of the 9th and 10th centuries completed the process of destruction begun in the 5th and 6th centuries.

BIBLIOGRAPHY

Which books might discuss the Carolingian Renaissance?

CABANISS, ALLEN. *The Son of Charlemagne.* Syracuse: Syracuse University Press, 1961. *A reappraisal of Louis the Pious, demonstrating how his achievements have been largely overlooked by historians.*

GORDON, C. D. *The Age of Attila.* Ann Arbor: University of Michigan Press, 1960. *A description of the collapse of classical civilization in the 5th century and the ensuing turmoil that engulfed Europe. Includes contemporary accounts of events such as the siege of Rome by Alaric and the Visigoths.*

HEER, FRIEDRICH. *Charlemagne and His World.* New York: Macmillan, 1975. *An illustrated biography of the great Frankish warrior-king. Examines the social, economic, and cultural developments of Charlemagne's reign along with his political and military successes.*

MAGNUSSON, MAGNUS. *The Vikings!* New York: E. P. Dutton, 1980. *A highly readable, illustrated account of the history, mythology, and society of the Vikings.*

RICE, DAVID TALBOTT, ed. *The Dawn of European Civilization.* New York: McGraw-Hill, Inc., 1965. *A careful reconstruction of Western civilization in the early Middle Ages, focusing on four areas: the Islamic world, the Byzantine Empire, the Germanic kingdoms in the West, and the Carolingian Empire.*

● *No king can reign rightly unless he devoutly serves Christ's vicar. The priesthood is the sun, and monarchy the moon. Kings rule over their respective kingdoms, but . . . the Lord gave Peter rule not only over the universal church, but also over the whole world.*

POPE INNOCENT III

The Church in the Middle Ages

The Middle Ages has often been called the Age of Faith because Christianity as a religion shaped the minds of medieval people and the Church as an institution occupied a dominating position in medieval life. At the height of its power in the 13th century, Pope Innocent III could proclaim that the Church was supreme on earth (see quote above). Medieval men and women were deeply concerned with salvation, and the Church alone held the key to salvation. As a result, the Church had enormous power over the minds of individuals. It also ruled their lives, performing the ceremonies that marked their births, marriages, and deaths; and presiding over other services, feasts, and holy days throughout the year.

In the early Middle Ages, the Church was on the defensive. It inherited the mantle of Roman authority at a time when Europe was battered by invasions. Yet it did not falter in its drive to win the invaders over to Christianity. By the 10th century, it had largely succeeded in its missionary goals, converting the "heathen" peoples of the north to Christianity. As the Church consolidated its power and influence, it set off on a new course, one that would put it in conflict with the Is-

lamic world. This chapter focuses on the central role played by the Christian Church in western Europe during the Middle Ages.

CIVIL ROLE OF THE CHURCH

When the Roman Empire collapsed, the people of western Europe were forced to look to new leaders for security and guidance. The Church and the leaders of the local Germanic kingdoms took control of the land, but there was no longer a single, central civil authority to whom everyone was responsible. With the disappearance of Roman officials and administrative structure, the Church authorities assumed civil responsibilities along with their spiritual leadership. Thus, the Church operated the only schools, hospitals, and orphanages in Europe. Churches and monasteries became *sanctuaries*, or places of refuge where people could find at least temporary protection from a violent world.

The Church also gradually became the largest landowner in western Europe as the secular rulers gave it vast tracts of land as acts of charity or repentance. These land grants enabled the Church to fulfill its spiritual and temporal duties, and they also made it rich and powerful. In the Middle Ages, both wealth and power were based on land ownership. Thus, bishops and abbots were often more powerful than secular nobles or even rulers, and they were frequently in conflict with these secular rulers. The Church has always been a primarily spiritual institution, but in the Middle Ages it was also the most powerful political organization in Europe.

SACRAMENTS The basis of the Church's spiritual role was its claim, accepted by all Christians during the Middle Ages, to be the sole channel through which people could approach God. Divine worship took the form of prayer, attendance at services, and participation in sacred rituals, called *sacraments*, that only priests could perform. The seven sacraments were related to the most important aspects of life from birth to death, and are still fundamental to the Catholic Church. They are baptism, confirmation, matrimony, penance, extreme unction, Holy Orders, and the *Holy Eucharist* (also known as "Holy Communion"), a commemoration of the last supper that Jesus had with his 12 apostles.

Medieval people believed that all people were sinners by nature and that only through the sacraments could they achieve salvation in the next life. Those who were denied the sacraments by the Church were shunned in this life and condemned to eternal damnation in the next. People could be denied the sacraments by the clergy for wickedness or for disobeying Church law. The threat of *excommunication*, of being put outside the sacramental life of the Church, was a powerful weapon in the hands of the Church leadership. Fear of excommunication undoubtedly helped maintain social order and public morality. However, the threat of excommunication was also used by the Church in its political struggles. For centuries, powerful lords and even monarchs were forced to yield to the Church when faced with the penalty of excommunication or of the *interdict*, which

meant that no one living in their territory could participate in the sacraments. Almost invariably, this latter threat forced a lord to yield to the Church.

Through its hierarchical organization, the Church reached all levels of medieval society. At the lowest level were the parishes. Local parish priests were the people on whom medieval Christians depended, for it was the priest who officiated over the sacraments so necessary to salvation. Most ordinary people knew little of the bishops and archbishops who held the higher offices in the Church.

CANON LAW In addition to administering the sacred rituals, the Church fulfilled many functions of a secular state. Among the most important were the functions performed by Church courts. The Church courts tried both civil and criminal cases involving the clergy, and made their decisions based on canon law. *Canon law* was a mixture of Roman law and of the regulations that had been issued over the years by Church authorities and councils.

Decisions of Church courts related to many subjects including marriage, divorce, and wills. On these matters, Church decisions were accepted as having the force of law by Christian rulers and were enforced by public officials. In other areas, however, secular rulers claimed a jurisdiction that the Church fiercely resisted. One of the most disputed issues was whether secular or Church courts could try members of the clergy who were charged with criminal offenses. In some places, this issue created bitter struggles between Church and state which were not resolved until the end of the Middle Ages.

In the first centuries after the fall of Rome, when the states of western Europe were weak and much of Roman law had been forgotten, canon law and the Church courts had no rivals in most of Europe. However, civil law and civil courts eventually developed as secular power grew in the later Middle Ages. Inevitably, there arose conflicts of jurisdiction between civil and Church courts, especially since the fines levied by the courts provided a substantial income.

MONASTICISM   During the early years of Christianity, some Christians chose to isolate themselves from society and devote their lives to the contemplation of God and the salvation of their souls. Some lived in solitude and were called *hermits* (from the Greek *eremos*, meaning "desolate"). Others lived together in religious communities called *monasteries*. Both men and women entered into this monastic movement, which spread from Egypt, where it began, across the Mediterranean into Europe. Early leaders of these monasteries established rules by which *monks* (from the Greek *monos*, meaning "alone") lived. Late in the 4th century, a Greek monk named Saint Basil (329-379) drew up a rule, or code of behavior, that was adopted by monasteries in the Byzantine world. Later, another monk, Saint Benedict (480-547), wrote a rule that was adopted by monasteries in the West.

THE BENEDICTINES

Benedict was born into a patrician family in Rome after the city had fallen to the Goths. When he reached maturity, Benedict decided to remove himself from the moral decadence of Rome, and went to live in a cave near the ruins of Nero's palace. After three years in solitude, he came to the realization that it would be more useful to live with a group of devout men who could pray and work together. In 529, he established a monastery at Monte Cassino, midway between Rome and Naples. There, he put into practice the code of conduct that he had prepared and that became known as the *Benedictine Rule*.

Each man who applied for admission to

The monastic movement founded by Benedict at Monte Cassino had great influence on the subsequent history of the Church. Through the efforts of Pope Gregory, Saint Augustine, and other reformers, Benedict's rules became the accepted standard of conduct for Church officials as well as for monks.

Monte Cassino underwent a period of training called a *novitiate*. If he was then approved for membership in the Benedictine Order, he was required to take a vow that he would live a life of poverty, chastity, and obedience to the Benedictine Rule. The rule governed every activity of a monk's daily life. Each day was spent in specified periods of prayer, manual labor, study, and rest.

The monastery was a self-governing body, led by an abbot who was elected to the position for life by the monks and was thereafter answerable only to the pope. It served as a hospice for travelers, the ill, and the lonely. Some monks worked as scribes, copying ancient manuscripts in Greek and Latin; others recorded current events. These records now provide us with valuable information about the life of the times. The monastery was economically self-sufficient and pioneered in a variety of farming techniques. Monte Cassino wine, for example, has been on the world market for centuries.

CONTRIBUTIONS OF MONASTERIES

Many Benedictine monasteries were established throughout Europe, and the Benedictine Rule became the model for other orders of monks. The monasteries played several important roles. First, they collected and copied valuable manuscripts at a time when the scholarship of the ancient world was being lost. By doing so, they made monasteries into centers of learning. To ensure that monks would be able to read and write Greek and Latin, monasteries operated schools.

Besides protecting learning and promoting education, monasteries were frequently the training ground for missionaries who dedicated their lives to converting the pagan peoples of northern and eastern Europe. Many Benedictines as well as monks from other orders went out to distant places—including Ireland, Scotland, and Germany. Among the most renowned missionaries were Columban and Boniface. Like Saint Benedict, they were later canonized by the Church.

AUGUSTINE'S MISSION TO ENGLAND

One of the most influential popes of the medieval period, Gregory the Great (pope from 590-604), began his religious life as a Benedictine monk. In 599, Gregory sent Augustine and several other monks as missionaries to England, where Christianity had been largely wiped out by the Germanic invasions of the 5th and 6th centuries. The Venerable Bede (672-735), an English Benedictine monk and chronicler, reported on the mission of Augustine and his companions. Soon after setting out:

> ● ● ● *they were seized with sudden fear and began to think of returning home, rather than proceed to a barbarous, fierce, and unbelieving nation, to whose very language they were strangers. . . . In short, they sent back Augustine, who was to be consecrated bishop in case they were received by the English, that he might persuade the holy Gregory to relieve them from undertaking so dangerous, toilsome and uncertain a journey.*[1]

Gregory responded to their fears and urged them to fulfill their mission:

> ● ● ● *Let not, therefore, the toil of the journey nor the tongues of evil-speaking men deter you; but with all possible earnestness and zeal perform that which, by God's direction, you have undertaken; being assured that much labor is followed by an eternal reward.*[2]

Augustine returned to his mission and led the group to England. There, they established themselves at Canterbury and began their work of converting the Anglo-Saxon people of England to Christianity.

The work of Christian missionaries like Augustine was often dangerous, and many lost their lives. Gradually, however, they achieved success, bringing the outlying parts of Europe into the Christian fold.

---

[1]Venerable Bede, *Ecclesiastical History of the English Nation*, trans. J. A. Giles (1843), I, 23.
[2]*Ibid.*

CONVENTS

In the Middle Ages, women, too, joined religious communities. Benedict's twin sister, Scholastica, was so impressed by her brother's work that she established a convent for women near Monte Cassino. The nuns' duties in prayer and worship as well as in study and labor were the same as those of the monks. In addition, they were encouraged to spin and weave cloth.

In time, many convents were established throughout Europe. Although they usually were less well endowed with land and wealth than monasteries, some convents became very prosperous. Like monks, nuns provided shelter for travelers and cared for the sick. Some convents became famous for their herbs and knowledge of medical matters. Others set up schools, although these schools usually admitted only the children of nobles.

MONASTIC REFORMS

By the 10th century, monasteries had gained great wealth and power. Their material success, however, led to abuses. Many monasteries ignored the austere rules set down by their founders. Abbots sought to amass more wealth and power. Monks and nuns broke their vows. Similar abuses also existed in other parts of the Church. It was possible for people of wealth to buy Church offices, a practice known as **simony**, regardless of their spiritual characters. Moreover, priests were often uneducated, paid little attention to their duties, and ignored their vows of celibacy. In the 10th and 11th centuries, a great religious revival led both lay and Church leaders to recognize the need for reform and to work toward this end.

CLUNIACS

The reform movement that swept across Europe received much of its impetus from a newly-established monastic order of Cluny, in east-central France. In 910, Cluny was set up as a disciplined, spiritual center, divorced from the secular world. Unlike many other monasteries that owed allegiance to lords and rulers, the Cluniac monks were direct subjects of the pope and were thus free from any lay influence. The order adopted the high moral standards that Saint Benedict had advocated almost 400 years earlier, but the Cluniacs spent less energy on physical labor than the Benedictines and devoted more time to religious and intellectual pursuits. Above all, the Cluniacs practiced rigid adherence to their vows.

In time, the abbey at Cluny became a model for reforming other monasteries and for establishing new ones. At its peak, the Cluniac order had 2000 monasteries in France alone. By 1150, there were 314 Cluniac houses, with 110,000 monks, scattered throughout France, Germany, Spain, and Italy. Besides enforcing a strict rule in their own monasteries, the Cluniacs in their reforming zeal called on the Church to abolish simony and to stop other abuses.

CISTERCIANS

Another reform movement that sought to recover the strict monastic discipline of earlier days was directed by the Cistercians, whose order was founded in 1090 at Citeaux in northeastern France. The best known Cistercian was Bernard of Clairvaux (1090-1153). He believed that all Christians should devote their lives to the study and contemplation of God's goodness and should attempt in every way to follow God's guidance. Bernard believed that God's love was so great that even the most miserable sinner could achieve salvation by turning to God with unquestioning faith.

Bernard insisted that the Cistercian monasteries be built in rural areas where the monks could lead simple, austere lives far from the temptations of towns and cities. The only worldly possession that a monk was permitted to own was a small amount of clothing. Bernard also opposed the ornamentation of churches and monasteries, for he wanted to avoid any distractions.

As a symbol of humility, the Benedictines and other monks adopted the tonsure, in which the top of the head was shaved. In Roman times, this haircut had been a mark of slavery.

• • • And in the cloisters, under the eyes of the brethren engaged in reading, what business have those ridiculous monstrosities, that misshapen shapeliness and shapely misshapeness? Those unclean monkeys, those fierce lions, those monstrous centaurs, those semi-human beings. Here we see a quadruped with the tail of a serpent, there a fish with the head of a goat. In short there appears on all sides so rich and amazing a variety of forms that it is more delightful to read the marble than the manuscripts and to spend the whole day in admiring these things, piece by piece, rather than in meditating on the Divine Law.[3]

By the time Bernard died in 1153, there were 353 Cistercian monasteries, tied together by the General Chapter, a governing body made up of the abbots of all the monasteries. By 1300, the number had grown to more than 700 monasteries, plus several convents for women who desired to practice the high ideals of the Cistercian order.

Each monastery included a library and a *scriptorium*, a room in which monks copied and illuminated manuscripts. The scribes vowed to "fight the devil by pen and ink" and hoped that "every letter, line or point is a sin forgiven."[4]

Because of their devotion and hard work, the Cistercians converted swamps and wastelands into productive farms. In England, they were so successful at raising sheep that they controlled a large part of the English wool trade and became very wealthy.

MENDICANT FRIARS After the year 1000, the tempo of life in Europe changed. In the next few centuries, the Church reached its greatest triumphs. In the 13th century, Pope Innocent III (1198-1216) presided over the papacy at its highest level of influence and prestige. During this time, he sanctioned the establishment of two new orders, the Dominicans and the Franciscans. The members of both orders chose to be called *friars* (from the Latin *frater*, meaning "brother"). They dedicated their lives to working among needy people, especially those living in towns and cities, rather than isolating themselves in monasteries. It was said that "the world was their cloister." To finance their good works, they went about begging for alms, which led people to refer to them as *mendicants*, or beggars.

Besides caring for the needy, the Dominicans and Franciscans preached and defended the teachings of the Church and fought heresy wherever they encountered it. Both orders attracted members who became outstanding thinkers and whose writings are studied today. The teachings of the Dominican theologian Thomas Aquinas (c. 1225-1374) are still considered the definitive statement of Roman Catholicism (Chapter 18).

[3]Quoted in Kenneth Clark, *Civilisation* (New York: Harper & Row, 1969), p. 40.

[4]Quoted in Ann Freemantle, *Age of Faith* (New York: Time-Life Books, 1965), p. 48.

DOMINICANS

The Dominican Order was founded in 1216 by Saint Dominic (1170-1221), a well-educated Spaniard. Dominic gained fame by joining the crusade against the Albigensian heresy, which Pope Innocent III was trying to eliminate. The Albigensians were centered in southern France. They believed that the world was a battleground for the forces of good and evil, and they looked on the Church as an evil force because of its wealth and power. Because they challenged Church authority, they at first suffered the full force of its punishment.

Dominic felt that the way to fight heresy was to return to the simple ways of the apostles. Clad in simple clothing, he went among the poor, preaching and teaching. He assembled a group of followers who pledged themselves to preaching, teaching, conducting missionary activities, and combating heresies. In 1216, Pope Honorius III blessed the Order of Friar Preachers, the official name of the Dominicans.

The order won many followers. By 1277, there were 394 Dominican houses throughout Europe and in the Holy Land, where young men prepared for lives of service. Over succeeding centuries, Dominicans established schools and universities around the world, including the United States. Convents for Dominican nuns were also established. Because of their dedication to eliminating heresies, Dominicans were often chosen to staff Church courts. The Dominican order is still one of the largest and most influential in the Roman Catholic Church.

FRANCISCANS

Francis (1182-1226) was the son of a wealthy wool merchant from Assisi, a town in northeastern Italy. Francis dreamed of becoming a knight but was captured during his first military venture in 1202 and spent a year in prison. After returning home, he was ill for a long time. During this illness, he became convinced that he should renounce his

Through preaching and the example of their own lives, Francis and his friars hoped to revitalize Christian faith, especially among the poor. This Church painting shows Francis in an audience with Pope Honorius.

worldly possessions and dedicate the rest of his life to spreading the gospel to the poor.

After recovering his health, Francis wandered throughout Italy and was appalled at what he saw as the hypocrisy of Christians making pilgrimages to Rome. He was struck by the contrast between the living conditions of the rich and the poor. After returning to Assisi, Francis had a dream in which he was directed to repair several ruined churches near the city. Without asking permission, he used some of his father's money to carry out these instructions, but he was flogged and imprisoned for his efforts.

Francis then pledged himself to a life of poverty and to helping the poor and the sick, so that he could demonstrate the teachings of Jesus. Before long, a small group of like-minded people joined him. Pope Innocent III was so impressed with what Francis was doing that he sanctioned the establishment of the Order of Friars Minor (or Little Brothers). Its name derives from the vows of extreme poverty and humility taken by the members and to Francis' teaching that all people are brothers in Christ.

The Franciscan order became immensely popular and influential. In part, this was the result of Francis' personality—his kindliness and sanctity. In part, it was also the result of the simple life of the Franciscans and their fervor, which was said to be as ardent as that of the early apostles. The Franciscans thus became a major outlet for popular piety. By 1282, there were 1583 houses of the order scattered throughout Europe.

In 1212, Francis so impressed a young noblewoman named Clare that she renounced her inheritance and, with help from Francis, founded an order of nuns, known popularly as the Poor Clares. Clare's sister and mother also joined the order. The Poor Clares lived in poverty, cared for the sick and poor, and provided shelter to travelers. In time, they expanded their work into France, England, and Germany.

THE CRUSADES During the early Middle Ages, the Church focused its energies on carrying Christianity to the pagan peoples of western Europe. In the later Middle Ages, its power assured, the Church launched another drive, this time to recapture the Holy Land that had fallen to the Seljuk Turks. For many centuries, Christians from Europe had been making pilgrimages to the Holy Land and to places in Europe that were associated with the lives of various saints. These pilgrimages were acts of penance or manifestations of piety. Of all the pilgrimages, the journey to Jerusalem was the most difficult because of the great distance. But the Moslems who controlled the city that was holy to Moslems, Jews, and Christians alike usually allowed Christian pilgrims to come and go freely.

In the mid-11th century, however, the Seljuk Turks,[5] who came out of central Asia, gained control of much of the Middle East. After moving through present-day Afghanistan and converting to Islam, they migrated westward and sacked Baghdad in 1055. They then pushed further to the west, encroaching on the Byzantine Empire. In 1071, they defeated a Byzantine army at Manzikert, near Lake Van in the eastern part of present-day Turkey.

Gradually, the Turks extended their control over much of Asia Minor, Syria, and Palestine. In 1085, they captured Jerusalem. The Turks were much less tolerant of Christian pilgrims than the Arabs had been. Tales of harassment and persecution of pilgrims filtered into Europe. The Byzantine Empire, which had protected Christians in the East, could no longer do so. Indeed, the Byzantines wanted Western help to recover their lost provinces from the Turks.

FIRST CRUSADE (1096-1099)

In 1091, the Byzantine emperor, Alexius Comnenus I, sent envoys to Pope Urban II requesting military support, both to protect his own domains and to safeguard Christian pilgrims to the Holy Land from attack by the Turks. Four years later, Urban traveled to Clermont (now Clermont-Ferrand), in central France, to address a Church council. Urban II dreamed of reuniting the Eastern Orthodox Church (Chapter 13) with the Roman Catholic Church. To achieve this dream, the pope called on the assembled clergy and nobles to unite and embark on a holy crusade (from the Latin *crux*, meaning "cross"). The purpose of the crusade, he said, was to aid the Christians of the East and to liberate the Holy Land from the infidels—as Christians called all Moslems. Years later, Robert the Monk recalled Urban's words:

● ● ● *Let hatred therefore depart from among you, let your quarrels end, let wars cease,*

---

[5]Seljuk was an early leader of these Turkic people.

and let all dissensions and controversies slumber. Enter upon the road to the Holy Sepulcher; wrest that land from the wicked race, and subject it to yourselves. That land which, as the Scripture says, "floweth with milk and honey" was given by God into the power of the children of Israel. Jerusalem is the center of the earth; the land is fruitful above all others, like another paradise of delights.[6]

To this impassioned plea, his listeners responded with enthusiasm: "God wills it!" As soon as Urban finished speaking, hundreds of people volunteered: the First Crusade had begun; there would be many more. The Crusades were a series of expeditions and wars that continued off and on for 200 years. They involved tens of thousands of European Christians from peasants to monarchs.

From Clermont, the call for a crusade spread throughout Europe, but the people who rallied to this first call were primarily from France, southern Italy, and Sicily. The Normans who had recently conquered England were still consolidating their control of that land; the Christian knights of Spain were fighting their own crusade against the Moslems there; and only a few nobles from Germany responded to this call. Yet thousands of others did respond and sewed crosses to their clothes to announce themselves as Crusaders. Historians estimate that the First Crusade included between 5,000 and 10,000 mounted knights, between 25,000 and 50,000 foot soldiers and an equal number of non-combatants. The response was so great that the pope forbade women to go without their husbands and barred the elderly or the very young from taking up the cross.

Motives. People became crusaders for a variety of reasons. Some looked on the Crusades as a Christian obligation and believed that they were obeying God's will. Some

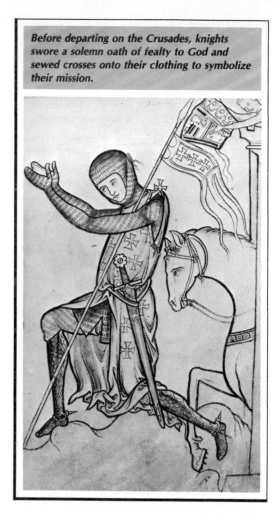

Before departing on the Crusades, knights swore a solemn oath of fealty to God and sewed crosses onto their clothing to symbolize their mission.

hoped to gain wealth or land and improve their status in life. Others dreamed of adventure or an opportunity to escape from the hardship of their lives as peasants. Still others went as penance for their sins or in hopes of achieving salvation.

The pope had his own motives, hoping to extend his influence over the Eastern Orthodox Church, while sending quarrelsome feudal nobles to fight their wars in a distant land. To encourage nobles to go on the Crusades, the pope promised that the Church would protect their property while they were away. He also excused them from some taxes

---

[6]Urban's speech at Clermont, as reported by Robert the Monk, in *Readings in European History*, Vol. 1, ed. J. H. Robinson (New York: Ginn, 1904), p. 314.

and forgave their debts. To many of these nobles, the chance to fight for the glory of God—combined with the lure of winning kingdoms in the Holy Land—was enough to overcome all hesitation.

Peter the Hermit. Since there was far more enthusiasm than organizational planning at the time of the First Crusade, certain unforeseen and tragic events occurred. One of the saddest of these resulted from the religious zeal of Peter the Hermit, a monk from Amiens in France. While the French nobles were still assembling their forces, Peter rode about the countryside recruiting peasants and poor townspeople as Crusaders. After assembling over 30,000 volunteers, Peter refused to wait for the nobles and set forth to the Holy Land by an overland route through eastern Europe to Constantinople.

As these peasant Crusaders passed through the Rhineland, they massacred the Jews whom they encountered and burned their homes. Local rulers promised to protect the Jews living in their lands, but more often than not they ignored their promises. As a result, thousands of Jews were slaughtered.

By the time the straggling peasant mobs reached present-day Bulgaria, they were so desperate for food that they decided that the Christian Bulgars were in fact infidels and their grain could be appropriated. In response, the enraged Bulgars slipped into the Crusader camps at night and murdered many of the peasants. When the remnants of this peasant army reached Constantinople, the emperor Alexius Comnenus I commanded that they be transported across the Bosporus as quickly as possible. Once landed in Asia Minor, they were at the mercy of the Turks who attacked them; those who were not massacred were sold into slavery.

Departure. Several months after this disaster, the second contingent of Crusaders, made up of knights and soldiers under the command of nobles such as Godfrey of Bouillon, his brother Baldwin, and Raymond of Toulouse began to reach Constantinople by the same overland route. Unlike Peter's motley followers, these were organized armies. As each leader arrived in the Byzantine capital, the emperor Alexius exacted a promise that if the Crusaders captured a city the Turks had seized from the Byzantine Empire, the city would be returned to Byzantine control. In exchange for these promises, the emperor agreed to supply the Crusaders with ships, guides, money, and provisions for the march to Jerusalem.

The first city the Crusaders reached was Nicaea, about 50 miles southeast of Constantinople. They began their siege only to awake one morning and find the Byzantine flag flying from the ramparts. Alexius had secretly negotiated with the defenders of Nicaea to surrender the city to the Byzantines. William of Tyre reported the Crusaders' anger at this deception.

● ● ● *To the commanders the monarch [Alexius] sent immense gifts in the hope of gaining their good will. Moreover, he*

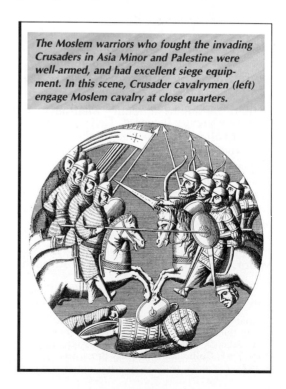

The Moslem warriors who fought the invading Crusaders in Asia Minor and Palestine were well-armed, and had excellent siege equipment. In this scene, Crusader cavalrymen (left) engage Moslem cavalry at close quarters.

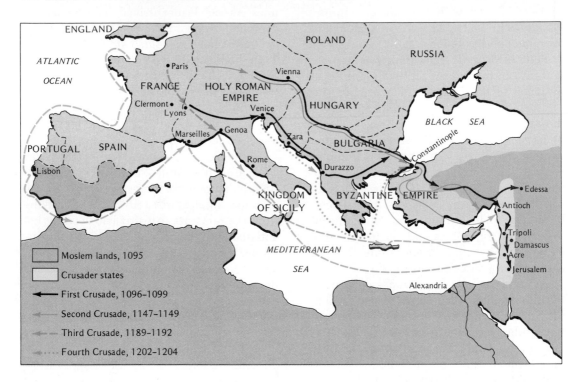

thanked them heartily, both by dispatches and verbal messages, for their honorable service and the great increase that had come to the empire through their efforts.

But the people and the men of second rank were greatly incensed. They too had worked valiantly in the siege of the city and had expected to repair the loss of their own property by the spoils taken from the prisoners and the rich store of goods found in the city itself. They now saw that their labors were not to receive a satisfactory reward.[7]

After a difficult, bloody march through Asia Minor, the Crusaders laid siege to Antioch,

in northern Syria. Betrayed from within, the city fell to the Crusaders, but the Crusaders in turn were soon besieged by a Turkish army. One Crusader, Stephen of Blois, escaped from Antioch and headed for Constantinople. En route, he met Alexius, who was moving southward with an army to attack Antioch. Informed that the Crusaders' cause appeared to be hopeless, Alexius returned to Constantinople. Ever afterward, the Crusaders considered that Alexius had betrayed them.

But the cause was not lost. According to tradition, although exhausted by disease and lack of food, the Crusaders received what they considered to be divine aid. A peasant soldier named Peter Bartholomew had a vision which told him to dig beneath the wall of a church in Antioch. There, Peter found a rusty lance that had supposedly been used by the Roman soldier who stabbed Jesus while he was nailed to the cross. The discovery of

---

[7]William (Guilelmas), archbishop of Tyre, *A History of the Deeds Done Beyond the Sea*, trans. E. A. Babcock and A. C. Krey, ed. A. P. Evans (New York: Columbia University Press, 1943), p. 197.

the lance inspired the Crusaders to return to the battle, and the next day they routed the Turkish army outside the walls of Antioch. From Syria, they moved south and made plans to attack Jerusalem.

Capture of Jerusalem. The Crusaders reached Jerusalem in the spring of 1099 and laid siege to the city. On July 5, 1099, Godfrey of Bouillon and his soldiers broke through the walls and entered the holy city. A terrible massacre ensued. Thousands of Moslems and Jews were killed. So, too, were Christians who lived in the city and were dressed in eastern clothing. Contemporary accounts tell of the Crusaders riding in blood up to their knees. The massacre in Jerusalem was repeated elsewhere as the Crusaders extended their control over Syria and Palestine.

The majority of the Crusaders had left their homes to free the Holy Land. Now, after almost four years of bloody campaigning and with victory in their grasp, most wanted to return home. But their successes had left them with a strip of land stretching over 500 miles along the eastern Mediterranean coast and no means of protecting it from the surrounding Moslems. To strengthen their control over this territory, they divided it into four states: Godfrey of Bouillon was named king of the Latin Kingdom of Jerusalem, which he and his successors ruled until 1187; Baldwin of Lorraine was given charge of the County of Edessa; Bohemond of Italy was made head of the Principality of Antioch; and Raymond of Toulouse was given authority over the County of Tripoli.

The Church of the Holy Sepulcher was first built by Constantine to mark the place where Jesus was crucified, and was one of the holy sites that the Crusaders were fighting to control. After they captured Jerusalem, the Crusaders rebuilt the church.

Since the Church had sponsored the Crusades and had the most effective and far-reaching organization in Europe, the pope assumed responsibility for encouraging nobles and peasants to garrison the Christian strongholds in the Middle East. In each of the Crusader states, they built fortified castles, the remains of which can still be seen at Acre, Sidon, and Tripoli.

In time, the Crusaders who remained in the Holy Land came to respect and develop better relationships with the Moslems of the region. Many adopted local customs in clothing and food, sought help from Moslem physicians, and even married Moslem women. Fulk of Chartres, who took part in the First Crusade and remained in the Holy Land, wrote:

● ● ● We men of the West have become Orientals. He who was a Roman or a Frank is now a Galilean or Palestinian. He who was from Rheims or Chartres is now a Tyrian or Antiochian. We have already forgotten the places of our birth; to most they are either unknown or unheeded. Some possess already their own houses and servants as if they had inherited them from ancestors; others have already married, and not, indeed, a woman of their own country, but a Syrian or an Armenian, sometimes even a baptized Saracen.[8]

RELIGIOUS-MILITARY ORDERS

To help move pilgrims to and from the Holy Land and to maintain Christian troops there, the Crusaders founded three religious-military orders that would later influence events in Europe.

About 1118, a group of knights stationed in Jerusalem organized the *Knights of the Temple.* They chose this name because their headquarters was on the site of the ancient Temple of Solomon. The knights took vows of poverty, chastity, and obedience and took on the responsibility of helping pilgrims. In time, the Templars became so wealthy and powerful that they ignored their original purpose. By the 13th century, for example, the Templars served as a large-scale banking organization.

A second order, the *Knights of Saint John,* or Hospitalers, had been founded about 1083 in the Benedictine abbey at Amalfi in Italy. The original purpose of this order was to provide shelter and food (hospitality) for pilgrims to the Holy Land. In 1201, the Hospitalers expanded their activities to include fighting the Moslems in the Holy Land. After the last Crusader stronghold at Acre fell to the Moslems in 1291, the Hospitalers moved their headquarters from Palestine to Cyprus, Rhodes, and then Malta. Like the Templars, they also became wealthy and entered into power struggles with secular rulers.

A third order, the *Order of Saint Mary of the Teutons,* or Teutonic Knights, was organized in 1127 in Jerusalem by Crusaders from Germany. It later moved to Acre after Jerusalem fell to the Moslems in 1187. Although originally founded as a charitable order, it became involved in military and

[8]Quoted in D. C. Munro, "Christian and Infidel in the Holy Land," in *Readings in Medieval History,* ed. Hutton Webster (New York: Crofts, 1946), p. 284.

The Crusaders built fortified castles in sites throughout the Middle East. This is the Castle of the Knights in Syria, which the Hospitalers occupied until 1271.

political ventures. In the 13th century, the Teutonic Knights embarked on crusades against the pagan peoples in the Baltic region. They conquered the eastern Baltic coast as far north as the Gulf of Finland.

SECOND CRUSADE (1147-1149)

The Crusader states were plagued by rivalry and disunity. They were never more than Christian outposts in an overwhelmingly Moslem Middle East. Once the initial shock of the invasion from the West wore off, the Moslems set out to drive the Crusaders into the sea. Their first victory was the recapture of Edessa in 1144. In response, Pope Eugenius III (1145-1153) ordered Bernard of Clairvaux to call a Second Crusade aimed at the reconquest of Edessa. Bernard spoke to a large group of knights in 1146 and offered the following benefits to volunteers:

● ● ● [W]e decree that their wives and their sons, their goods also and their possessions, shall remain under protection of Holy Church. . . .

Moreover, all they that are burdened by debt and have, with pure heart, undertaken so holy a journey need not pay the interest past due. . . .

Forgiveness of sins and absolution we grant . . . so that he who has devoutly undertaken so holy a journey and finished it or died there shall obtain absolution for all his sins. . . . [9]

---

[9]Quoted in Otto of Freising, *The Deeds of Frederick Barbarossa*, trans. C. C. Mierow and Richard Emery (New York: Columbia University Press, 1953), pp. 72-73.

King Louis VII of France and the Holy Roman Emperor Conrad III responded to the call for the Second Crusade, and both raised large armies. The two monarchs first considered attacking Constantinople but then settled on attacking Damascus. The siege failed, and both Louis and Conrad returned to Europe without ever visiting Jerusalem. The Second Crusade did not achieve its original goal, and Edessa remained in Moslem hands.

SALADIN

In the next decades, the Moslems found a courageous and gifted leader in Saladin, who embodied the virtues they most admired. Saladin conquered Iraq, Syria, and Egypt, and thus his armies surrounded the Crusader states on three sides. In 1185, he declared his intention to lead a holy war to reclaim Jerusalem from the infidel Christians. Two years later he took advantage of quarrels among the Crusaders to invade the Latin Kingdom of Jerusalem. Saladin defeated the main Crusader army, capturing the king, Guy of Lusignan, and many of his nobles. Many of the Crusader strongholds, including Jerusalem, then fell to the Moslems without a struggle. Saladin's conquest of Jerusalem led a Moslem chronicler to write:

● ● ● THE DAY OF CONQUEST, 17 RAJAB. By a striking coincidence, the date of the conquest of Jerusalem was the anniversary of the Prophet's ascension to heaven. Great joy reigned for the brilliant victory won, and words of prayer and invocation to God were on every tongue.[10]

THIRD CRUSADE (1189-1192)

The loss of Jerusalem to the Moslems left Christians holding only the port of Tyre. However the disaster inspired the three most powerful rulers in Europe—Frederick Barbarossa of the Holy Roman Empire, Philip Augustus of France, and Richard the Lion-Hearted of England—to join together for the Third Crusade. With the encouragement of Pope Innocent III, Richard and Philip Augustus levied new taxes on their subjects to finance the crusade. These taxes came to be called the *Saladin tithe* and set a precedent for the levying of other taxes.

Frederick Barbarossa marched his followers overland, through Hungary and the Byzantine Empire. He drowned in a river in Asia Minor, and most of his army returned home. Philip Augustus and Richard met in Sicily on their way to the Holy Land. There, they quarreled bitterly before embarking. Once in Palestine, they again argued, and Philip Augustus decided to return to France to pursue his own ambitious plans at home.

Richard stayed on to fight Saladin alone. Richard's role on the Third Crusade captured the imagination of many people, and a French admirer described him as follows:

● ● ● He had the courage of Hector, the magnanimity of Achilles, and was equal to Alexander and not inferior to Roland in valor; nay, he outshone many illustrious characters of our own times. The liberality of a Titus was his, and, which is so rarely found in a soldier, he was gifted with the eloquence of Nestor and the prudence of Ulysses; and he showed himself preeminent in the conclusion and transaction of business, as one whose knowledge was not without active goodwill to aid it, nor his goodwill wanting knowledge.[11]

Richard laid siege to Acre, the most important port in Palestine, and took it 21 months later. Yet Richard could not recapture Jerusalem, and in 1192 he and Saladin agreed to a treaty which guaranteed Christian pilgrims free access to the city. The Third Crusade accomplished little and highlighted the rivalries that divided the strongest Chris-

---

[10]Quoted in Francesco Gabrieli, *Arab Historians of the Crusades* (Los Angeles: University of California Press, 1969), p. 160.

[11]Richard de Templo, *Itinerarium Regis Ricardi*, Book 2, ch. 5, in *Readings in Medieval and Modern History*, ed. Webster, pp. 100-101.

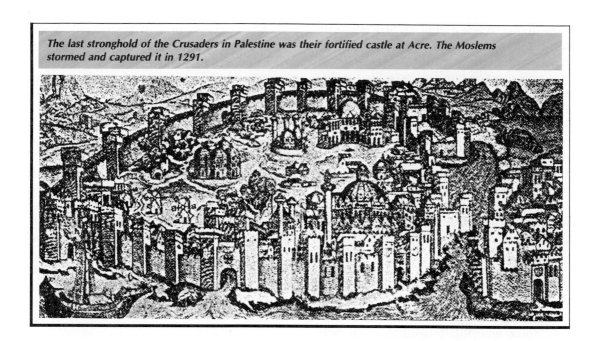

The last stronghold of the Crusaders in Palestine was their fortified castle at Acre. The Moslems stormed and captured it in 1291.

tian rulers in Europe. On his journey back to England, Richard was taken prisoner by Leopold, duke of Austria, whom Richard had insulted during the siege of Acre. Leopold held Richard captive until the English paid a huge ransom for his release.

FOURTH CRUSADE (1202-1204)

The failure of the Third Crusade meant that Jerusalem remained in Moslem hands. Early in the 13th century, Pope Innocent III called for a new crusade to regain the Holy Land. Several thousand French knights and armed men responded to the call and assembled in Venice to embark for the Holy Land. However, the Crusaders did not have money to pay for their passage. The *doge*, or ruler of Venice, told the Crusaders that they could pay for their transportation by capturing the city of Zara, a trade rival of the Venetians located on the eastern Adriatic. The Crusaders took the city but then found themselves in deep trouble with the pope because Zara was a Catholic city.

In a confused series of events, the Crusaders became involved in a power struggle among the various claimants to the Byzantine throne. Urged on by the Venetians, they then attacked Constantinople, which fell after fierce fighting. Constantinople had never fallen before, and the booty was immense. A contemporary described the looting of the Byzantine capital by the Christian crusaders.

● ● ● *That [booty] which was brought to the churches was divided, in equal parts, between the Franks and the Venetians, according to the sworn covenant. And you must know further that the pilgrims, after the division had been made, paid out of their share fifty thousand marks of silver to the Venetians, and then divided at least one hundred thousand marks between themselves, among their own people.*[12]

In spite of these prizes, the attack of Constantinople in 1204 was a major disaster for all concerned. The Latin Kingdom of Constantinople lasted only until 1261, when the

---

[12]Geoffroy de Villehardouin, *La conquette de Constantinople*, chap. 46, in *Readings in Medieval and Modern History*, ed. Webster, pp. 116-117.

Byzantines regained control of Constantinople, but the Byzantine Empire was unable to recover its former wealth and power. Further weakened by internal struggles, the Byzantines later succumbed to the Ottoman Turks in 1453.

The Crusader attack on Constantinople further embittered relations between the Latin and Greek churches. Although the pope condemned the attack, he replaced the Greek orthodox clergy of Constantinople with priests loyal to the Roman Catholic tradition. As long as Latin rule lasted, the orthodox church was persecuted.

LATER CRUSADES

The dream of freeing the Holy Land persisted throughout much of the 13th century, but after the shocking events of the Fourth Crusade, there was little interest in a new crusade. In 1212, a 12-year-old French farm boy, Stephen of Cloyes, had a vision urging him to organize a crusade of children to rescue the Holy Land. Stephen's preaching inspired thousands of French children to leave home and travel to Marseilles. Many believed that the waters of the Mediterranean would part so that they could walk to the Holy Land. Thousands of German children also made their way across the Alps to the ports of Genoa and Pisa in Italy. The Children's Crusade ended in tragedy when the children were taken by unscrupulous traders and sold into slavery in North Africa.

By 1217, several Italian city-states were in bitter competition to dominate the trade routes that were thriving on the commerce generated by the Crusades; therefore, they promoted the Fifth Crusade. This crusade adopted the strategy of invading Egypt, the richest and strongest Moslem state. After landing in Egypt, the Crusaders made little progress and were forced to return to Europe in 1221.

In 1228, Emperor Frederick II undertook the Sixth Crusade. Frederick, who knew and respected Moslem culture, decided to try negotiation instead of war. He visited Egypt and through diplomacy won privileges for Christian pilgrims in Jerusalem, Bethlehem, and Nazareth. He himself controlled these holy cities until 1244, when a new Moslem dynasty retook the cities.

In 1248, the 25-year-old king of France, Louis IX, undertook the leadership of the Seventh Crusade, but his religious fervor was not shared by his fellow monarchs. He gained control of Damietta (now Dumyat) in Egypt, at the mouth of the Nile River, but disease and famine forced him to surrender his army in 1254. The Moslems took Louis captive and held him for ransom. After the ransom was paid, Louis returned to France. In 1270, he again attempted to lead a crusade to Tunis, but he died before reaching his goal.

The Street of the Knights in Rhodes. After losing Jerusalem and Acre, the Knights Hospitalers moved to Rhodes. From their stronghold on this island, they challenged Turkish control of Mediterranean sea routes.

No more crusades were organized to the Holy Land. In 1291, the Moslems captured Acre, the last Christian stronghold. After 200 years of warfare and countless deaths, the Holy Land remained in Moslem control.

RESULTS OF THE CRUSADES

While the Crusades failed in their original purpose of bringing the Holy Land under Christian control, they had far-reaching consequences for western Europe. First, by introducing thousands of Europeans to the larger world beyond their borders, the Crusades shattered the parochialism of medieval Europe.

Second, they greatly increased trade between Europe and the eastern Mediterranean. Crusading knights were awestruck at the more advanced civilizations of the Byzantine and Moslem worlds, and soon developed a desire to enjoy the luxuries of the East. As a result, silks, perfumes, rugs, jewelry, fruits, and spices once again moved from the eastern Mediterranean into Europe, as they had under the Roman Empire. Third, the Crusades increased the pace of economic changes that were already underway. For example, the increase in commerce heightened the need for new systems of money, banking, and credit to replace the barter economy that had emerged in most of western Europe after the fall of Rome.

Fourth, the need to move Crusaders and pilgrims back and forth across the Mediterranean spurred the growth of shipping and enabled several ports in Italy, particularly Venice, Genoa, and Pisa, to become powerful and wealthy city-states. Finally, the taste for luxuries, particularly the spices of the East, and the new knowledge of navigation would eventually lead to the exploration of Africa, Asia, and the New World.

Even before the Crusades, Europeans had begun to acquire the learning of the Byzantine and Islamic worlds. The knowledge continued to filter into Europe in the 200 years of the Crusades, but the process went on largely independent of the Crusades. As a result, not only Moslem learning in mathematics, philosophy, science, and medicine, but also Middle Eastern technologies such as manufacturing and dying cloth were transferred to Europe.

Although the Crusades brought many benefits to the peoples of western Europe, they also resulted in a growing religious intolerance. Relations between Latin and Greek Christians, between Christians and Moslems, and between Christians and Jews all deteriorated in this period. Thousands of Moslems and Christians were massacred in the two centuries of struggle for control of the Holy Land. The greatest tragedy was the persecution of Jews in Europe. When organized mobs of Christians issued ultimatums to Jews to convert or die, whole communities of Jews chose to remain loyal to their faith and were slaughtered. During this period, too, laws were passed forcing Jews to wear yellow patches on their clothes and live apart from Christians. Although some Christians protested, these attacks on Jews persisted.

SUMMARY

During the Middle Ages, the Roman Catholic Church had enormous power and influence. Its power rested not only on its control of religious life but also on its secular role. During this period, thousands of devout Christians came together to live in religious communities called monasteries. The most influential monastic rule was established by Saint Benedict. New monastic orders continued to be founded, especially when abuses in the older orders led to calls for reform. In the 13th century, two non-monastic orders, the Dominicans and the Franciscans, were founded to work and live among the people.

Late in the 11th century, the Church launched the Crusades to rescue the Holy Land from the Turks. The Crusades lasted for two centuries. Although in the end the Moslems regained possession of the Holy Land, the Crusades had far-reaching effects on western Europe.

QUESTIONS

1 Compare the role of the Church in the early Middle Ages to that of the Roman emperor at the time of Augustus. How were they similar? How were they different?

2 Why has the Middle Ages often been called the "age of faith"?

3 What contributions did monasteries make to medieval civilization?

4 Why was the reform movement in the Church so necessary in the 10th and 11th centuries?

5 What motivated people to go on the Crusades? How was the Fourth Crusade different from the earlier Crusades? Describe a cause that might motivate people today to join a crusade.

6 Why are the Crusades often called a "successful failure"?

BIBLIOGRAPHY

Which books might describe the growth of monasteries?

DUBY, GEORGES. *The Knight, the Lady and the Priest.* Translated by Barbara Bray. New York: Pantheon Books, 1983. *A fascinating survey of how the laws created by the Church during the Middle Ages influenced society and still effect our lives today. Contemporary chronicles explain the status of women in medieval times and the appeal of convents and monasteries.*

KNOWLES, DAVID. *Saints and Scholars.* Cambridge University Press, 1962. *A portrayal of monastic life from the 6th to 16th centuries. Examines outstanding spiritual leaders, writers, artists, and politicians; provides insights into the medieval mind.*

OAKLEY, FRANCIS. *The Medieval Experience.* New York: Scribner's, 1974. *A review of the medieval world that shows how much the Church dominated society. Provides insights into the important changes in religion, economy, and politics that occurred during this long period.*

PRAWER, JOSHUA. *The World of the Crusaders.* New York: Quadrangle Books, 1972. *An examination of this period through the eyes of the Crusaders, Byzantines, and Jews. Details the chivalry as well as the barbarism of the age; the military strategies and weapons used; and the culture of the Crusaders' world.*

THEIS, DAN. *The Crescent and the Cross.* New York: Thomas Nelson, 1978. *An account of the struggle for the possession of the Holy Land from the Crusades to today. Examines the careers of medieval heroes such as Bohemond, Raymond of Toulouse, Richard the Lion-Hearted, and Frederick Barbarossa.*

The work of the priest is to pray to God,
And of the knight to do justice.
The farm worker finds bread for them.
One toils in the fields, one prays, and one defends.
In the fields, in the town, in the church,
These three help each other
Through their skills, in a nicely regulated scheme.
ANONYMOUS

Medieval Society

A 13th century poet wrote the lines quoted above to describe the structure of medieval society. In these few lines, he captures an essential element of medieval life: everyone had a well-defined place in society that carried with it certain duties and responsibilities. This social order did not suddenly emerge; rather, it evolved slowly during the early Middle Ages and, once established, supported the flowering of medieval civilization.

The collapse of Rome in the 5th century had profound effects on European life. Without Roman legions to guard the boundaries of the empire, without the Roman legal system to ensure justice, and without the Roman administrative system to maintain the roads and water supplies, life became much more precarious. Trade and the money economy declined. The only food available was what could be grown or hunted locally. Towns and cities decayed as people abandoned them to seek the protection offered by monasteries or large landholders.

For most people, life became much poorer as the economy of trade and commerce gave way in the early Middle Ages to an economy of small, self-sufficient agricultural units.

Perhaps most importantly, the disappearance of the Roman state created a power vacuum which other forces moved to fill. As you read in the last chapter, one of these forces was the Church. In the early Middle Ages, its power and influence grew enormously. So, too, did the power and influence of the large landowners who developed ways to protect their holdings.

FEUDALISM

During the centuries of chaos and invasions that followed the collapse of Rome, a new social, economic, and political system slowly emerged that we know today as **feudalism** (from the latin *feudum*, meaning "estate"). As you will read, feudalism was the way of life that governed medieval Europe for hundreds of years. At the center of feudalism were the ties of loyalty that bound local lords to a king. However, feudalism was not a uniform system, and it did not develop in the same way in all parts of Europe.

ORIGINS OF FEUDALISM

Feudalism grew out of both Roman and German customs. It developed first in France and later emerged in other parts of Europe.

As Rome's power crumbled in the provinces, local nobles acquired vast tracts of land, parts of which they granted to others in exchange for help in defending the land. The granting of land to individuals in exchange for military service would become an essential element in the feudal system.

Feudalism also had its roots in German customs. Among the German tribes, individual warriors swore an oath of loyalty to a chief, and in return, the chief supplied them with food, armor, and weapons. The personal ties between warriors and their chief were another feature of the feudal system.

As the German rulers established their kingdoms in western Europe, these elements of feudalism continued to develop. In the 8th century, the use of the stirrup enabled knights, or mounted warriors, to wear armor while wielding larger weapons. As you read in Chapter 15, the Merovingian mayor of the palace, Charles Martel, saw the need for well-trained and well-armed warriors, so he expanded the practice of granting land in exchange for military service. During the centuries of invasions that followed the collapse of the Carolingian Empire in the 9th century, feudalism emerged as the basic system of government in western Europe.

LORDS AND VASSALS

Feudalism was based on a system of unwritten rules between lords and **vassals** (from the Celtic *vassus*, meaning "servant"). In theory, everyone in medieval society had a lord and owed him something, and the feudal order was like a pyramid. At the highest point stood the king or emperor who was regarded as the vassal of God. Beneath him were the great nobles who controlled extensive holdings. Next came the lesser nobles, vassals of greater nobles, and so on down to the lowest knights, each of whom was a vassal of the noble who granted him land. The grantor of land was known as the *liege lord* of the person to whom he granted land. As feudalism developed, it became a complex interrelationship of privileges and responsibilities. Gradually, too, a hierarchy of titles of nobility evolved. The greatest nobles were called *dukes* (from the Latin *dux*, meaning "leader"). Below dukes were ranks such as *marquis*, *count* (called "earls" in England), *viscount*, and *baron*.

The mutual exchange of promises between a lord and his vassal was sanctified by a solemn ritual known as *investiture*, in which the vassal knelt before his lord and placed both hands between the lord's hands. He then pledged homage and agreed to obey the lord's commands in words such as these:

● ● ● *I will always be a faithful vassal to thee and to thy successors . . . and I will defend thee . . . and all your men and their possessions against all malefactors and invaders . . . and I will give to thee power over all the castles and manors . . . whenever they shall be claimed by thee or by thy successors.*[1]

In return for his vassal's homage, the liege lord agreed to provide his vassal with a **fief**, or estate; help protect him; hear his complaints in open courts; and ensure that he and his dependents received justice. During the investiture ceremony, the lord gave his vassal a charter, or deed, and a blade of grass or a clump of earth as symbol of the fief.

Fiefs could vary in size from a small parcel of land to a vast estate. The vassal had complete control over the land and all the houses, villages, and people on the land. As a feudal lord, he could wage war, coin money, collect tolls, make alliances, or engage in any other activity that he was strong enough to achieve, as long as he supported his liege lord with the required military assistance when called upon to do so. He could pass his fief on to his heirs, but in theory, at least, the liege lord still owned the land.

The system of mutual obligations re-

---

[1]Quoted in Hutton Webster, ed., *Historical Selections* (Boston: Heath, 1969), pp. 468-9.

quired a vassal to perform certain services for his lord in return for his fief, but feudal obligations varied greatly from region to region. In northern France, for example, a vassal was expected to serve for 40 days and nights each year on military campaigns or on garrison duty at the castle of his lord. During this time, he might also help his lord hold court and dispense justice. A vassal could refuse to serve longer than the fixed time unless he was compensated in some way. In the late Middle Ages, when money became more common, knights were permitted to pay "shield money" (scutage) in place of performing military service. Such payments became an important source of revenue to great lords and permitted them to hire mercenaries rather than depending on their vassals.

The vassal was also obliged to contribute to certain expenses of his lord, such as the knighting of the lord's eldest son or the wedding of his eldest daughter. The vassal had to contribute to the ransom that might be demanded by an enemy who captured his lord.

A liege lord could seize a vassal's fief if the latter failed to fulfill his obligations or died without heirs. By the same token, a vassal was absolved of all obligations to his lord if the lord tried to kill him, enslave him, steal his property, or seduce his wife.

FEUDAL WARFARE

Feudalism emerged in western Europe during a time of invasion. It developed in part as a means of providing security and protection. The wealth and power of feudal nobles was derived from the ownership of land, and even after the invasions abated, feudal nobles frequently fought with one another over land, family honor, and other rights. As a result, warfare was the most widespread activity of the feudal nobility.

In the early Middle Ages, knights wore padded leather or linen coats and helmets. Later, small iron rings were sewn to the padding to prevent weapons from cutting through

The flexible chain mail that protected medieval knights could be difficult to remove as well as uncomfortable to wear.

the material. Still later, flexible chain mail was developed to protect the body against blows and cuts. Ultimately, every knight wore armor and frequently used specially designed armor to protect his horse. Armor was made of thin sheets of steel joined in such a way that the knight was covered from head to toe but could still walk, mount a horse, and ride. Since a knight needed to distinguish between friend and foe, he carried a shield inscribed with a symbol or design that came to be called his "coat of arms." A noble family's coat of arms was handed down from generation to generation, and this use of distinctive family symbols became known as "heraldry."

Each knight was armed with a lance, which he used to unhorse an enemy; a two-edged sword, which hung from a belt around his waist; a dagger tucked into his belt; and a heavy club, mace, or battle ax. The armor and weapons carried by a knight could weigh as much as 100 pounds.

In the 11th century, the Church took steps to try to reduce feudal warfare. It issued two pronouncements: the "Peace of God" and the "Truce of God." In the "Peace of God," the Church announced that the sacraments would be withheld from anyone who pillaged churches, monasteries, and other holy places. The sacraments were also denied to those who killed women, children, or elderly people not involved in combat.

The "Truce of God" forbade fighting between sunset of any Wednesday evening and sunrise of the following Monday morning, the period of time that Christians believed Jesus had suffered and died on the cross. The truce was also applied to all holy seasons, such as Advent, the four weeks before Christmas, and Lent, the seven weeks before Easter. While these truces were frequently ignored, any knight found to be violating them faced the threat of excommunication.

In the late Middle Ages, feudal warfare did decline due in part to these efforts of the Church and in part to the rise of powerful medieval monarchs who made great efforts to end the constant fighting among their vassals.

CASTLES

During the early Middle Ages, local lords designed their houses for defense. These fortified houses came to be called "castles" (from the Latin *castellum*, meaning "small military camp"). At first, these fortified houses were made of wood and surrounded by thick wooden walls. Later, feudal lords began to build stone castles on hilltops, in bends of rivers, and at other defensible positions. A castle often was surrounded by a *moat*, or wide, deep ditch that could be filled with water. A bridge that could be raised or lowered gave the only access to the castle.

In time, castles were made quite large; they were designed to house the lord, his household, and, in an emergency, the peasants who lived in the village near the castle walls. Just inside the castle walls was the central court-yard. In peacetime and when the weather was good, the lord held his court in the court-yard. The courtyard also housed the workshops and kitchen necessary to maintain the castle's armaments and feed its defenders. In addition, the castle had stables for horses, storehouses for food and weapons, and dungeons for prisoners. Each castle kept an ample supply of food and water on hand, so that the inhabitants could survive a siege lasting several weeks or even months.

The lord of the castle and his family lived in the innermost defensible structure, a stone tower called the keep or donjon. But the most frequently used room of the castle was the great hall, which was large enough to house all the knights who might be called to defend the castle. There, the lord and his guests drank, sang, played chess or backgammon, and were entertained by wandering minstrels or jesters.

The nobles ate fish, fowl, wild game, and white bread, accompanied by locally produced wines. The peasants ate porridge, cabbage, turnips, and dark bread, which they washed down with home-brewed beer or ale. Meat was a rarity in the peasants' diet, but nobles enjoyed it more regularly since they were free to hunt the game on their preserves. One medieval cookbook describes how to prepare a tasty meat pastry.

• • • *Take a pheasant, a hare, a capon, two partridges, two pigeons and two conies; chop them up, take out as many bones as you can, and add the livers and meats, two kidneys of sheep, force meat into balls with eggs, pickled mushrooms, salt, pepper, spice, vinegar. Boil the bones in a pot to make a good broth; put the meat into a crust of good paste, made craftly into the likeness of a bird's body; pour in the broth, close it up and bake well. Serve it with the head of one of the birds at one end, and the tail at the other, and divers of his long feathers set cunningly all about him.*[2]

---

[2]Quoted in Gertrude Hartman, *Medieval Days and Ways* (New York: Macmillan, 1937), pp. 43-4.

Medieval castles were designed primarily as fortresses, and offered few amenities to their inhabitants.

The great hall had one or more large fireplaces, but the castle was still damp and drafty. Food was prepared in a separate building and often arrived cold or half cooked. By today's standards, a castle was an unpleasant place in which to live. Besides the cold and drafts, it had only primitive sanitation facilities and little light.

EDUCATION

During the early Middle Ages, there was little formal education. Most children learned at home the skills they needed to survive. A few noble children might attend a monastery school where they would learn Christian duties and perhaps be taught to read and write: Charlemagne, you will recall, brought the scholar Alcuin to Aachen to teach his children and those of the nobles at his court. For much of the medieval period, however, education centered not on learning to read and write but on training for warfare.

Training for Knighthood. The sons of nobles were expected to become knights. Usually they were sent, at the age of seven, to another lord's castle for training. There, a young noble served as a page for the lord while the lady of the house taught him Christian values and the manners he must know —respect for women, as well as the arts of singing, dancing, and playing a musical instrument. She might also teach him to read, write, and do arithmetic. At the age of 14, the boy became a squire to the lord, serving him in the castle and on the battlefield, caring for his arms and armor, guarding prisoners, and taking on other noncombatant duties. During this time, the squire learned to handle various weapons and to ride well.

After successfully completing this long training at the age of 21, the squire became a knight. Before being knighted, the young man had to spend a night in a chapel praying for guidance. The next morning, he took the sacrament of Holy Communion, and then after this spiritual preparation, was knighted by his liege lord. In England, this ceremony was accomplished when the lord touched the would-be knight on the back of his neck with the broad side of a sword and declared, "In the name of God, Saint Michael and Saint George, I dub thee knight. Be gallant, be courteous, be loyal." The young knight's parents then provided a great feast to celebrate the occasion.

Young knights trained for real battle at jousts and tournaments. Jousts were mock battles involving two knights in armor riding

In England, a lord performed the ceremony of knighting by touching the candidate on the back with his sword. Sometimes a soldier was knighted on the battlefield in recognition of his valor, as illustrated here.

toward each other at full speed. Each attempted to knock the other from his horse. Tournaments involved teams of knights who engaged in mock fights with blunted lances. In peacetime, a lord and his knights also practiced their skills on horseback as they hunted wild game.

Daughters of Nobles. Like her brothers, the daughter of a noble learned to play the role expected of someone in her position. She learned to supervise the servants in the house, to do needlework, and to see that the household ran smoothly, which meant keeping track of food supplies and other necessities. Often, she knew some simple medicine and tended her own family as well as the people on the estate.

Throughout her life, a woman was legally subject first to her parents and then to the husband that her parents chose for her. Yet once she was married, a noble woman could often achieve a certain measure of responsibility and independence, for she was left in charge of her husband's estate whenever he was absent. As Christine de Pisan, an outstanding scholar and writer of this period, explained:

• • • *Because that knights, esquires and gentlemen go upon journeys and follow the wars, it beseemeth wives to be wise and of great governance and to see clear, in all that they do, for that most often they dwell at home without their husbands who are at court or in divers lands.*[3]

The Code of Chivalry. In the later Middle Ages, the lives of noblewomen improved with the development of the concepts of chivalry and romantic love. These ideas arose first in southern France during the 11th century and by the 14th century had spread throughout Europe. They were based on the code of conduct for knights known as "chivalry."

Chivalry was supposed to govern the behavior of knights; it blended Christian virtues with the conduct required of knights—bravery, loyalty, and courage. The correct behavior toward women was a focal point of chivalry. Under this code, women were idealized and placed on a pedestal. They were praised for their beauty, goodness, and other virtues. In reality, however, women's lives were filled with many hardships, from the dangers of frequent childbirth to those of disease and warfare.

Rules were drawn up describing the proper conduct of knights. Below is a selection of rules taken from a 12th-century work:

• • • *I. Marriage is no real excuse for not loving.*
II. He who is not jealous cannot love.
III. No one can be bound by a double love.
IV. It is well known that love is always increasing or decreasing.
VIII. No one should be deprived of love without the very best reasons.
IX. No one can love unless he is impelled by the persuasion of love.
XIV. The easy attainment of love makes it of little value; difficulty of attainment makes it prized.
XV. Every lover regularly turns pale in the presence of his beloved.
XVI. When a lover suddenly catches sight of his beloved his heart palpitates.
XVII. A new love puts to flight an old one.[4]

The behavior of knights often fell far short of the ideal, and there were customary remedies for such a case. A knight who failed to live by the code of chivalry could be publicly disgraced. His shield would be hung upside down in a public place; his armor stripped from him; his weapons broken; and he himself placed in a coffin and carried to a church, where a priest held a funeral service, declaring him "dead to honor."

---

[3]Christine de Pisan, *Le Livre des Trois Vertus* (ca. 1406), quoted in Eileen Power, *Medieval Women*, ed. M. M. Postan (Cambridge: Cambridge University Press, 1975), p. 43.

[4]Andreas Capellanus, "The Rules of Courtly Love," in J. B. Ross and M. M. McLaughlin, eds., *The Portable Medieval Reader* (New York: Viking Press, 1940), pp. 115-6.

MANORIALISM Feudalism established the relationship between lords and vassals, but at most feudal nobles numbered only 10 percent of the population. Underlying and supporting the feudal order was the remaining 90 percent of the population made up of peasants who worked the land. They were essential to the economic system known as **manorialism** that emerged in the Middle Ages. Manorialism had its origins in the great estates acquired by Roman nobles in Gaul. During the Germanic invasions, smaller landowners often turned over their holdings to these nobles or to monasteries or churches in exchange for protection and a portion of the crops they raised. They thus became tenant farmers. In time, these estates became known as *manors* and developed as the centers of early medieval communities. Under the system of manorialism, the owner of the manor, agreed to protect the people living on the land in exchange for their work in the fields and other services.

During the early Middle Ages, the condition of the peasants who farmed the manor lands changed from what it had been in late Roman times. Instead of being tenant farmers who paid rent in crops and were free to come and go, they became *serfs*. As serfs, they and their descendants were bound to the land and to the service of the lord of the manor. Neither they nor their children could leave the manor. Besides serfs, there were two other kinds of peasants who worked on a manor: slaves who could be bought and sold; and *villeins* (from the Latin *villa*, meaning "farm") who were tenant farmers. Gradually, however, the distinctions among peasants became blurred, and the vast majority of European peasants were serfs.

PLAN OF THE MANOR

A manor consisted of the manor house, the peasant village, and the church plus fields, pastures, forests, and wastelands. The manor house, which belonged to the lord, was by far the largest building on the estate. In the early Middle Ages, it was usually a two-story building made of wood. By the late Middle Ages, many manor houses had been turned into castles. Some were well furnished and decorated with works of art.

A small manor might consist of 350 acres of land and perhaps 10 to 15 peasant families, while a larger manor might have 5000 acres and 50 families. The peasants' houses were irregularly arranged near the manor house, and were known as the village. They were small, one-room cottages built of packed earth with thatched roofs. Smoke from the fires used for heat and cooking escaped through a hole in the roof. The floors were of earth; the windows, if they existed, were unglazed; and the furniture consisted of perhaps a plank table, a few stools, and a bed.

In the early Middle Ages, peasants were granted the use of farmland in return for their labor on the lord's estate. In time, peasants became bound to the land they worked.

The manor lands were used to sustain the lord and his family as well as all the people and animals on the manor. As the source of water, there was a well, a spring, or perhaps a stream dammed to form a pool. Forests provided wild game for the lord's table and trees for firewood. If there was a pond, fish would be stocked for the lord's pleasure. Open land was used as pasture for animals or was cultivated as orchards and vineyards.

All the arable land on a manor was divided into the lord's portion, called the *demesne*, and the peasants' portion. The peasants' land was divided by footpaths into small strips. By the 8th century, peasants were using a system of planting known as the "three-field system" in which each peasant had three strips of land. In the autumn, one strip was planted with wheat or rye; in the spring, the second strip was planted with oats or barley; the third strip was left fallow, or unplanted, each year. Some of the strips were in good soil and some in poor. Besides working their own strips, peasants had to work on the lord's demesne for at least three days a week and sometimes more during harvest time.

The peasants' tools—which included hoes, plows, scythes, and sickles—were primitive. Most were made by hand from pieces of wood, with iron placed along the cutting edge. Serfs did not use fertilizer and had few animals to use to plow or haul heavy loads. Because there was not enough surplus food to feed large animals such as horses or oxen, the manor tended to have only geese, sheep, or goats. The loss of a harvest to drought, insects, flood, or marauders spelled famine, disease, and death for people on the manor.

As you will read in Chapter 23, in the later Middle Ages, improvements in farming techniques and technology greatly increased output. As the heavy plow, the horse collar, horseshoes, and wind and water mills were introduced into western Europe, they helped peasants produce surpluses of food and supported a growing population. New lands were cleared and drained, creating even more agricultural output.

LIFE ON THE MANOR

During the early Middle Ages, the absence of trade meant that most manors had to be self-sufficient. The people on the manor produced not only all the food they consumed but also all the other goods they needed. If the harvest was good, they preserved the food so that they would have enough to eat until the next harvest. Some vegetables and fruits were stored in root cellars; others were pickled. Meat was smoked or salted. Wine and beer were made from the fruits and grains. Bread, the mainstay of the peasant's diet, was baked in the oven of the manor house.

Peasants made all the clothing for themselves, their lord, and his family. They raised sheep for wool and planted flax, which was used to make linen. Linsey-woolsey, a coarse cloth made from linen and wool, was the basic clothing fabric. Women and children were kept busy spinning thread or yarn on small hand bobbins and weaving cloth. Peasants also made leather shoes and harnesses, and fashioned the tools they needed. While some serfs labored on the manor lands, others became skilled workers such as carpenters, leather workers, blacksmiths, or bakers. During the late Middle Ages, as the economic life of Europe was quickening and towns were reviving, manors no longer had to be self-sufficient. Townspeople produced many specialized goods and exchanged them for food grown on the manor.

In the early medieval period, the constant struggle to grow enough food took much of the peasants' time and energy. Still, there were many occasions to celebrate, including births and weddings, saint days, and other holy occasions. On important holy days, pageants and feasts were held at the manor house. Peasants joined in wrestling matches, competed in archery contests, watched dog fights, danced, and gossiped. Wandering poets moved from manor to manor and earned their

The lord of the manor dispensed justice to the peasants who lived under his protection. In this scene, the lord and a village priest look on as a culprit is tortured on a wheel.

lodging and food by entertaining the people and spreading the news of the day. Occasionally, a pedlar passed through with strange wares from distant lands.

For much of the Middle Ages, the peasants' life was one of hardship. Peasants had to serve their lord, fighting at his side if he required. They faced harsh punishments if they were caught poaching his fish or game. They were forced to pay whatever fee he set to grind their grain in his mill and bake their bread in his oven. They could do nothing if the lord's huntsmen rode over their fields, destroying their crops. They faced the constant fear of warfare, disease, and starvation. In the 14th century, the English poet William Langland wrote "The Peasant's Life," in which he described these hardships.

The needy are our neighbours, if we note
  rightly;
As prisoners in cells, or poor folk in hovels,
Charged with children and overcharged by
  landlords.
What they may spare in spinning they spend
  on rental,
On milk, or on meal to make porridge
To still the sobbing of the children at meal
  time.
Also they themselves suffer much hunger.
They have woe in winter time, and wake at
  midnight
To rise and to rock the cradle at the bedside,
To card and to comb, to darn clouts and to
  wash them,
To rub and to reel and to put rushes on paving.
The woe of these women who dwell in hovels
Is too sad to speak of or to say a rhyme.[5]

LORDS OF THE MANOR

For much of the Middle Ages, the lord's word

---

[5]William Langland, "The Peasant's Life," in *The Portable Medieval Reader*, ed. Ross and McLaughlin, p. 137.

was the law of the manor. He owned the water, forests, the mill, and the baking ovens, and he could charge his serfs what he pleased in the way of labor or crops for the use of these assets. When the lord's eldest daughter was to be married or his eldest son was to be knighted, he could charge extra levies, called "customary taxes," on the peasants to cover the expense of these ceremonies. The lord could demand payment to permit a peasant to marry someone from another village or exact a portion of the meager belongings of a peasant who died.

Although the lord enjoyed great power over his peasants, he also had responsibilities toward them. The lord was responsible for defending the manor and dispensing justice. He gave out punishments according to custom, and in theory all punishments had to be approved by the parish priest. A person accused of a crime could admit guilt or face a form of trial—"trial by fire" or "trial by water." In trial by fire, the accused person was required to grasp a red-hot piece of metal, to walk across a bed of hot coals, or face some other physical test. If the burned flesh healed, the accused was assumed to be innocent because God had protected him or her. In trial by water, the accused was thrown into a pool of water. A person who sank was judged innocent because the water "accepted" him or her, but a person who floated was judged guilty because the water rejected him or her. Those who were found guilty of lesser crimes were subjected to public humiliation such as flogging, dunking in a pond, or being put in the stocks or a pillory.

If the manor was very large, or if the lord owned several manors, he might appoint a steward to supervise his lands. The steward carried out the functions of the lord, collecting the fees due to him and judging disputes among peasants.

GROWTH OF TOWNS As you have read, the towns and cities of the Roman Empire declined during the early Middle Ages. Although cities continued to flourish in the Byzantine Empire and in the Islamic world, they virtually disappeared in western Europe. After the great invasions of the 9th and 10th centuries ended, towns and cities began to revive. The pace of the revival picked up during and after the Crusades.

By the later Middle Ages, conditions in Europe had changed from the uncertainties of earlier centuries. As feudal warfare declined, trade increased. In northern Italy, cities such as Venice, Genoa, and Pisa took the

The fortification system of the medieval town of Carcassone in France. The outer walls of the town are lined with ditches, which are crossed by means of drawbridges. The round structure at bottom allows soldiers to obtain water from the town's river without exposing themselves to enemy fire.

The houses, shops, and streets of a medieval town were crowded together within the boundaries of its defensive walls.

and bridges were repaired, allowing merchants to move their goods more easily. Towns grew up along the trade routes: Basel, Mainz, and Strasbourg were important trading centers along the Rhine River; Antwerp, Hamburg, Calais, and London developed as major port cities.

By the 11th century, towns began to form around some strongly fortified castles, or "burgs" (from the Latin *burgus*, meaning "fortified place"). The people who lived in these towns were called "burgers" in Germany, "the bourgeoisie" in France, and "burgesses" in England. Since the towns offered opportunities for advancement, many serfs escaped to them in search of jobs and freedom. According to custom, serfs who lived for a year and a day in a town became free, thus giving rise to the medieval saying, "Town air makes a man free." Other townspeople were former serfs who had bought their freedom, or resident merchants and artisans.

PLAN OF THE TOWN

Most villages that grew up around a manor or castle were a collection of cottages. As some of these villages evolved into towns, homes were crowded into a small area because a lord usually limited the amount of land devoted to housing. As the population of a village increased, two changes took place: the village was enclosed by a wall for protection; and new houses, often two or three stories high, were built. While the walls provided protection, they also limited the size of the town and further increased the crowding. In time, the narrow paths between the houses of the village became the streets of the town. As multistory houses were built, it was common practice to project each new story out over the streets. In some towns, people living on opposite sides of a street could reach out their windows and touch one another.

The largest single building in the town was the church, and the largest open space was the marketplace, usually adjacent to the

lead in carrying goods from the eastern Mediterranean to western Europe. Other cities such as Antwerp, Bruges, Milan, and Florence prospered from the wool trade.

The renewed interest in travel and trade led to improvements in transportation; roads

church. Merchants and artisans built their shops close to the marketplace. The town's water supply usually came from a well, which was often located in the marketplace. Here, merchants, artisans, visitors, and others gathered to exchange news and gossip.

The fastest growing towns were those that were strategically located—perhaps at a river crossing, or at a site associated with a holy person—or boasted a school that could attract students from a wide area. Because of the overcrowding, newcomers were often forced to settle outside the town walls. When they eventually demanded protection, a new wall would be built to enclose the town, and a wide street would take the place of the old wall. Much later, in the 18th and 19th centuries, town walls were torn down and wide boulevards were built in their place.

LIFE IN THE TOWNS

In the towns, the living space for each family was not much larger than the cottage of a peasant. Sanitary conditions were poor, and people simply threw their wastes into the streets. Disease spread rapidly in the overcrowded towns. So, too, did fire, which often destroyed many houses. Despite these disadvantages, more and more people settled in the towns. While some townspeople were merchants and artisans, many others were peasants who worked in the fields outside the town by day but lived inside the town walls at night.

Town life centered on the marketplace, where farmers exchanged their produce and traveling merchants set up booths to display their wares. Like the peasants, townspeople worked from dawn to dusk and usually went to bed at sunset. Only the rich could afford to buy candles to light their homes at night. On Sundays and holy days, people attended church services and enjoyed watching contests or other diversions.

Since few people could read, the life of a town was governed by symbols and sounds. Monks and priests kept track of time by means of marked candles, waterclocks, or sundials. They informed the people of the hour by tolling the church bell. The bell was also used to sound an alarm, mark deaths, and announce happy occasions. Merchants and artisans announced their wares by hanging signs with symbols of their goods over their shops. For example, a gilded boot signaled a shoemaker; a twisted pretzel symbolized a baker; an anvil marked a blacksmith. Street names came from the activities pursued there: the Shambles was the street where animals were slaughtered; the Spicery was the place where spices were sold; Goldsmiths Lane was the location of jewelers.

As towns grew in importance, town leaders gained power and could negotiate with the feudal lords who owned the towns. During the 12th century, nobles who went on the Crusades sometimes tried to raise money by levying extra taxes on the towns under their control. The merchants and artisans of these towns responded by demanding new charters guaranteeing them certain rights and privileges. In 1279, the earl of Chester granted a charter to the city of Chester, in England. Like other feudal lords, he had to promise certain rights to the townspeople:

● ● ● *Let it be known to all of you that I have given and conceded, and by this my present charter confirmed to all my citizens of Chester, their guild merchant, with all liberties and free customs which they have had in the aforesaid guild, best, most freely and most peacefully in the times of my predecessors.*[6]

With the growth of towns, the medieval landscape underwent a change. No longer were people scattered in isolated, self-sufficient communities. Instead, the commerce engendered by the towns greatly expanded their opportunities and supported the emerging late medieval culture (Chapter 23).

---

[6]Quoted in J. H. Robinson, ed., *Readings in European History*, vol. 1 (New York: Ginn, 1904), pp. 408-9.

SUMMARY

After the fall of Rome, urban and economic life decayed. After the centuries of chaos and disorder, a new political, social, and economic system emerged in which wealth, power, and social standing were derived from the ownership of land. Under feudalism, a lord gave his vassals land in return for specific duties. The main occupation of the medieval nobles was warfare. In the later Middle Ages, feudal warfare declined, and knights were supposed to conduct their lives according to the code of chivalry.

During the Middle Ages, the vast majority of people were peasants who lived on self-sufficient estates called manors. In return for protection, the lord of the manor exacted labor and a share of the crops from those who lived on the manor. Gradually, most of these peasants became serfs, and neither they nor their descendants could legally leave the manor.

After the year 1000, economic life in Europe quickened, and towns again became important. Medieval towns were crowded, dirty places surrounded by walls to protect them from attack, but in time they became important centers of medieval culture.

QUESTIONS

1 Describe how warfare and preparing for warfare dominated the lives of feudal nobles. How did the Church seek to curb feudal warfare in the later Middle Ages?
2 What role was a noble woman expected to play in the Middle Ages?
3 Why did manors have to be self sufficient in the early Middle Ages? How did peasants on the manor provide for their basic needs?
4 Describe the structure of medieval society. Explain how each person had his or her place in that society. What is one major difference between medieval society and our society today?
5 Compare life on the manor to life in the towns.
6 How did developments in the later Middle Ages affect the lives of both nobles and peasants?

BIBLIOGRAPHY

Which books might describe how peasants farmed the land in 1250?

BARRACLOUGH, GEOFFREY. *The Crucible of Europe.* Berkeley: University of California Press, 1976. *A portrayal of medieval Europe, from the collapse of Charlemagne's empire to the rise of the early nation-states. Describes how people in various parts of Europe defended themselves against invasions and recounts the recovery between 955-1051 that culminated in the "12th century Renaissance."*

DAVIS, WILLIAM STEARNS. *Life on a Medieval Barony.* New York: Harper & Row, 1951. *A detailed description drawn from primary sources of a typical feudal community in the 13th century. It portrays every walk of medieval life, from peasants and villeins to merchants, artisans, knights, and lords.*

SETTON, KENNETH M. *The Age of Chivalry.* Washington, D.C.: National Geographic Society, 1969. *A well-illustrated survey of the period from 500 to 1350 which captures the spirit of the medieval world.*

WILLIAMS, JAY. *Life in the Middle Ages.* New York: Random House, 1966. *A fascinating recreation of the life of this period with explanations of how the people worked, played, fought, and worshiped. Through colorful contemporary drawings, it shows life on the manor and in castles, the role of the Church, and the importance of pilgrimages.*

The light of faith that is freely infused into us does not destroy the light of natural knowledge [reason] implanted in us naturally. For although the natural light of the human mind is insufficient to show us these things made manifest by faith, it is nevertheless impossible that these things which the divine principle gives us by faith are contrary to those implanted in us by nature [reason]. Indeed, were that the case, one or the other would have to be false, and, since both are given to us by God, God would have to be the author of untruth, which is impossible. . . . it is impossible that those things which are of philosophy can be contrary to those things which are of faith.

THOMAS AQUINAS

The Flowering of Medieval Civilization

During the early Middle Ages, education and learning fell to such a low point that barely literate monks noted in the margins of ancient manuscripts "Greek! It can't be read." This situation so shocked Charlemagne that he took strong measures to ensure a revival in education. Slowly, the seeds planted by Charlemagne took root, and during the 11th century the renaissance in learning began to flower.

In the later Middle Ages, medieval civilization burst forth in a productive outpouring of energy. A central issue in the medieval intellectual revival was the debate over the roles of faith and reason. Saint Thomas Aquinas, quoted above, declared that there was no conflict between faith and reason, and his arguments on the issue have shaped Christian thought to the present. The intellectual debate among scholars was only one of the many signs that marked the vitality of medieval civilization.

LEARNING AND EDUCATION During much of the Middle Ages, education was associated with the Church. Monastic schools educated young boys to work in the monastery, although not every student joined the order. Cathedral schools were established to prepare young men to serve as priests. There were few other opportunities for education. Some parish priests taught boys to read; some churches, and especially the cathedrals, conducted "song schools" to train singers for religious services.

Orders of nuns often provided instruction in reading, writing, account keeping, needlework, surgery, and first aid to prepare noble girls to be ladies on a manor. Most other children remained illiterate. As you have read, sons of nobles were trained as pages and squires in preparation for knighthood. Many boys in towns became apprenticed to artisans in various trades. Peasants taught their children how to farm or perform other work on the manor. But very few learned to read and write before the late 13th century, when literacy became more common among the nobility and the wealthier inhabitants of the towns.

SCHOOLS IN THE EARLY MIDDLE AGES
The curriculum of every cathedral and monastery school consisted of the study of the Bible, the writings of the Church fathers, and

the decrees of Church councils. In the 11th century, this curriculum was gradually broadened to include the "liberal arts" (from the Latin ars, meaning "knowledge of a subject," and liber, meaning "befitting a freeman"). The subject matter was divided into the trivium and the quadrivium. The trivium comprised grammar, the ability to read and write Latin; rhetoric, the ability to express ideas clearly; and logic, the ability to think and reason accurately. The quadrivium was composed of arithmetic, geometry, astronomy, and music. Latin was the language of instruction because it was the language of the Church.

In the early Middle Ages, books were rare and expensive, for each was copied by hand on vellum or parchment. Many original works were written in poor Latin and contained numerous errors, but there were a few notable exceptions. Among them was the work of the Venerable Bede, an 8th century Benedictine monk, who wrote the Ecclesiastical History of the English People. This famous book is considered by some scholars to be the best history of the early Middle Ages.

One of the most widely read books in the Middle Ages was a textbook on Latin grammar, Ars Minor, written by Donatus, who lived in Rome in the 4th century. It was used for 1000 years, wherever Latin was taught. The following is an excerpt from this popular book:

● ● ● Concerning the Parts of Speech
How many parts of speech are there? Eight. What? Noun, pronoun, verb, adverb, participle, conjunction, preposition, interjection.

Concerning the Noun
What is a noun? A part of speech which signifies with the case a person or a thing specifically or generally. How many attributes has a noun? Six. What? Quality, comparison, gender, number, form, case. In what does the quality of a noun consist? It is two-fold, for either it is the name of one and is called proper, or it is the name of many and is called common. How many degrees of comparison are there? Three. What? Positive, as learned; comparative, as more learned; superlative, as most learned. What nouns are compared? Only common nouns signifying quality or quantity.[1]

Other texts commonly used for instruction were: A Handbook of Sacred and Secular Learning by Cassiodorus, a 6th-century interpretation of the Bible; The Consolation of Philosophy by Boethius, a 6th-century view of the misfortunes of man and the love of God; and Etymologies by Isadore of Seville, a 7th-century discussion of the real and imagined roots of words.

After the year 1000, religious schools expanded. The sons of nobles began to apply for admission to these schools, even though they did not intend to join the clergy. Occasionally, even the intelligent son of a serf might be admitted. One serf's son, Gerbert, became an outstanding scholar and teacher. Gerbert originally enrolled in a monastery school to become a monk. His brilliant academic record prompted the abbot to send him to Spain for further education. There, he studied under Moslem and Jewish scholars whose learning far surpassed that of teachers in Christian Europe. Gerbert's knowledge of science and mathematics led people to regard him as a magician.

After completing his education, Gerbert was made master of the cathedral school at Aurillac, in south-central France. In this capacity, he revolutionized the curriculum of the school by declaring that henceforth, he would not accept the works of the Church fathers as the only source of enlightenment. His students also had to read the classical authors and were encouraged to use an abacus to solve problems in arithmetic. In 999, Gerbert was elected pope under the name Sylvester II and ruled until his death in 1003.

---

[1]The Ars Minor of Donatus, trans. W. J. Chase, in Readings in Medieval History, ed. Scott, Hyma, and Noyes (New York: Crofts, 1946), p. 334.

Beginning in the 12th century, students from Italy and throughout northern Europe traveled to Bologna to study at the city's famous university. The university first specialized in rhetoric, a branch of the trivium, and later became a center for law studies.

GROWTH OF UNIVERSITIES

During the 12th century, the cathedral schools of France and Italy developed into universities. In part, this was the result of the increased economic activity and the need for people trained in law, medicine, and other subjects not directly associated with religion. Since few people were qualified to teach such subjects, students who wanted to continue their education had to move to the places where the teachers lived. Thus, students of different backgrounds began to meet one another and to exchange ideas, which in turn encouraged intellectual growth and the demand for learning. As students and scholars came together in increasing numbers, the schools that they formed gradually became separated from the existing religious schools.

Unfortunately, some people who called themselves scholars were poorly educated, and sometimes the towns where schools were established were inhospitable to the influx of students from elsewhere. To counter these problems, early in the 12th century, students in Bologna, Italy, organized themselves into a *universitas*, an association to protect their interests. In time, the *universitas* of students at Bologna came to manage the living arrangements of its members, establish the course of study, and force teachers to follow strict regulations such as the ones described below.

● ● ● *We decree also that no Doctor [teacher] shall hereafter exceed one section [part of a book] in one lecture. And if the contrary be done by any one he shall be charged with perjury and punished to the extent of three pounds. . . . [w]e have decreed that no Doctor shall omit from his sections any chapter, decretal, law, or paragraph. If he does this he shall be obliged to read it within the following section. We have also decreed that no decretal or decree or law or difficult paragraph shall be reserved to be read at the end of the lecture if, through such*

At the university of Paris, professors were organized into a guild, or professional society, and maintained firm control over classroom proceedings.

out Europe for its instruction in the Latin authors, logic, and theology.

When enrollment exceeded the capacity of the cathedral school, the bishop of Paris may have granted the teachers permission to hold classes at other locations in the city, but he retained the power to hire teachers and supervise examinations. The university became so large, however, that it became impossible for the bishop to control it. In 1200, King Philip Augustus of France recognized the University of Paris as a separate institution, independent of the bishop and his cathedral school. When the university moved to the south bank of the Seine, the neighborhood around it came to be known as the "Latin Quarter" because Latin was the language of scholarship.

As universities developed, some became known for the study of a certain subject. Bologna, for example, began as a center of study of law, and Paris was famed as a center of theological study. In the 12th and 13th centuries, other universities were established at Oxford, Montpellier, and Naples, and their number soon multiplied. When the university at Oxford was closed because of student riots in 1209, many students moved to Cambridge, forming the nucleus of a new university.

STUDENT LIFE

To outsiders and even to the townspeople, the university was often seen as a dangerous place where unruly young men gathered and scholars taught about worldly subjects. Women were not permitted to attend the universities, although a few women were able to study with scholars who tutored them in advanced subjects. Townspeople resented the fact that the university operated as a separate and independent organization within the community. The separation was made more visible in the academic robes, or gowns, worn by the students and faculty. These robes, which were worn partly for warmth and partly to disguise differences of wealth among stu-

reservation, promptness of exit at the sound of the appointed bell is likely to be prevented.[2]

The arrangements created by the students at Bologna provided a model for universities in southern Europe. In northern Europe, however, the University of Paris took the lead. It developed in the late 12th century, although little is known about its origins. It probably evolved from the cathedral school of Notre Dame, which was famous through-

---

[2]A. O. Norton, ed., "Readings in the History of Education: Medieval Universities," in *Readings in Medieval History*, ed. Scott, Hyma, and Noyes, pp. 353–4.

dents and teachers, set members of the university apart from townspeople. Throughout the Middle Ages and even today, the tension between members of universities and townspeople have been called "town and gown" disputes.

Some disputes arose from the behavior of students who often spent more time playing dice and pursuing other amusements than studying. In letters like the one below, students wrote home to their parents asking for money.

● ● ● *Well-beloved father, I have not a penny, nor can I get any save through you, for all things at the University are so dear: nor can I study my Code or my Digest, for they are all tattered. . . . Moreover, I owe ten crowns. . . . I send you word of greetings and money.*[3]

Students did have a regular course of study. Although textbooks were few and expensive as they had been in the early Middle Ages, students attended lectures and were expected to memorize the words of the teachers. A typical day might include these activities.

● ● ● *At five or six o'clock each morning the great cathedral bell would ring out the summons to work. From the neighboring houses of the canons, from the cottages of the townsfolk, from the taverns, and hospices, and boarding houses, the streams of the industrious would pour into the enclosure beside the cathedral. The master's beadle, who levied a precarious tax on the mob, would strew the floor of the lecture hall with hay or straw, according to the season, bring the master's text-book, with the notes of the lecture between lines or on the margin, to the solitary desk, and then retire to secure silence in the adjoining street. Sitting on their haunches in the hay, the right knee raised to serve as a desk for the waxed tablets, the scholars would take notes during the long hours of lecture (about six or seven),*
then hurry home—if they were industrious— to commit them to parchment while the light lasted.[4]

DEGREES

The courses of study led to the granting of degrees. After completing from three to five years of study, a student was eligible to take a comprehensive examination. If he successfully completed this examination, he was given the designation *baccalaureatus*, or bachelor, indicating that he had completed the requirements for this first degree. But the bachelor's degree carried little status, and a bachelor could only teach under the guidance of a master teacher.

If a bachelor continued to study for several more years, he became eligible to submit a "masterpiece" on his studies. If he defended this "masterpiece" successfully in an oral examination, he was named a "master." With this title he could become a teacher himself. Today, a student's "masterpiece" is known as a master's thesis.

Masters who continued their studies could earn the degree of *doctus*, or learned. The scholar who took his degree in a specialized field such as law, medicine, or theology was known as a doctor of philosophy (Ph.D.).

SCHOLASTICISM

The growth in education in the late 11th and 12th centuries fostered an interest in applying logic to Christian faith. During the early Middle Ages, the Church fathers had provided official answers (called *dogma*) for all important questions, but the new scholars, or *scholastics*, challenged these teachings. Increasingly, they sought to prove that Christian principles could be known by reason and logic as well as divine revelation. They based their approach on Latin translations of ancient Greek philosophers, whose texts had entered Europe from Moslem Spain. The most

---

[3]Hutton Webster, *Historical Selections* (Boston: Heath, 1929), pp. 586–7.

[4]Joseph McCabe, *Peter Abelard* (New York: Putnam, 1901), p. 79.

The discovery of Plato's accounts of Socrates' teaching method had a great impact on medieval scholars. This 13th-century drawing misinterprets the relationship between the two, for Socrates is shown transcribing Plato's words.

plato. Socrates.

important philosopher for the scholastics was Aristotle, who had taught that theory must be based on facts and that to know a thing one had to know its causes. The scholastics also adopted the teaching methods of Socrates: instead of making statements, teachers would pose a series of questions intended to reveal their students' ignorance and resolve contradictory beliefs. The Socratic method came to be central to scholasticism.

Anselm (1034-1109), a teacher in the monastic school at Bec, in France, was one of the first theologians to attempt to prove his faith by logic. His guiding principle was "I must believe in order that I might understand" (*credo ut intelligam*). Although Anselm put faith above reason, he still emphasized the importance of studying "to understand what we believe." Anselm later became archbishop of Canterbury, the highest Church position in England, and was declared a saint by the Church after his death.

Peter Abelard. Anselm's concept was challenged by the French scholastic, Peter Abelard (1079-1142), who reversed Anselm's principle, saying "I must understand in order that I may believe" (*intelligo ut credam*). In doing so, he put reason before faith. Although Abelard never directly challenged the authority or teachings of the Church, he enjoyed raising philosophical and logical questions about Church doctrine to stimulate discussion among his students. In his best known work *Sic et Non* (*Yes and No*), he examined over 150 statements on theology and ethics and included the opinions of Church authorities for and against each statement. He then urged his students to use reason to reconcile the apparent contradictions.

Many Church officials disapproved of Abelard's approach, believing that it was dangerous to apply the principles of logic to matters that should be accepted on faith. In 1112, one of Abelard's books aroused the hostility of these officials, and he was ordered to stay in a monastery for a year. When he was finally permitted to leave the monastery, Abelard moved to a cottage in a forest outside Paris. In his autobiography, he said of this time:

● ● ● *No sooner had scholars learned of my retreat than they began to flock thither from all sides, leaving their towns and castles to dwell in the wilderness. In place of their spacious houses they built themselves huts; instead of dainty fare they lived on the herbs of the field and coarse bread; their soft beds they exchanged for heaps of straw and rushes, and their tables were piles of turf.*[5]

When Abelard persisted in raising questions about Church doctrine, he was forced to stand trial for heresy. Condemned by a Church court, Abelard took refuge in the

[5]Peter Abelard, *The Story of My Misfortunes*, trans. H. A. Bellows (Glencoe, Ill.: Free Press, 1958), p. 52.

monastery at Cluny, where he spent his last years. Although his own voice was silenced, Abelard's students continued his work.

Thomas Aquinas. The greatest of the medieval scholastics was Thomas Aquinas (1222-1274). Born into a noble family near Naples, he became a Dominican friar and later taught in the universities of Naples, Rome, and Paris. Aquinas was convinced that both human learning, which is gained through the process of reasoning, and supernatural truth, which is achieved only through faith, are gifts from God. Because of his conviction, he decided that there could be no conflict between reasoning and faith.

Aquinas used Abelard's technique of posing questions, but unlike Abelard, he attempted to arrive at an answer that accorded with Church teaching for each question he raised. Aquinas' most influential work was the *Summa Theologica*, an encyclopedia of Christian theology that is still regarded as the highest expression of Roman Catholic theology. In addition to the teaching of Christian scholars, Aquinas drew on the ideas of Greek, Jewish, and Moslem thinkers. To Aquinas, Aristotle was the greatest thinker of all time, but he was also familiar with the writings of Averroes (Chapter 14), who had struggled with the problem of reconciling faith and reason.

MEDIEVAL SCIENCE In the early Middle Ages, science was based on the few surviving works of classical thinkers, but these often contained many errors, mixing superstition and observed facts. As in other areas of learning, the Church and its teachings had the final authority. In the 12th century, European scholars became familiar with the scientific writings of Moslem thinkers, who themselves owed much to the Greeks. The works of Moslem scholars reached Europe in the form of Latin translations, mostly from Spain and Sicily. Moslem learning about the natural world, especially in optics, mathematics, and medicine, was far more advanced than anything known to Christian thinkers, and this "new learning" came as a great revelation to them. Because Moslem and Greek scholarship seldom clashed with Christian principles, Western scholars were able to use it as a foundation for their own scientific work.

NEW APPROACHES

Among the most influential medieval scientists was Robert Grosseteste (1168-1253), who served as bishop of Lincoln and chancellor of Oxford University. Grosseteste has been called the "founder of modern science" because he urged the objective study of natural phenomena and emphasized the importance of mathematics in scientific study. Through his reading of Aristotle and others, he developed a concern for observation and experimentation to verify all findings. Like all medieval scholars, however, Grosseteste sought to reconcile his scientific discoveries with Christian theology. In his most important work, *De Luce* ("Concerning Light"), he argued that since God is the source of all

Roger Bacon, English philosopher and scientist, did experimental work in optics, astronomy, and other subjects. Many of his writings contradicted accepted beliefs and were banned by the Church.

light, knowledge of the properties of light will help a person to know God.

Grosseteste's most famous pupil was Roger Bacon (1214-1292), a Franciscan monk who studied at Paris and Oxford. Bacon is often credited with establishing the foundations for modern scientific inquiry. He believed that all aspects of knowledge are interrelated; therefore, the study of natural sciences is as important as the study of religion and philosophy. Bacon urged scholars to put their beliefs to the test of experimentation:

● ● ● *What others strive to see dimly and blindly, like bats blinking at the sun in the twilight, he gazes at in the full light of day, because he is a master of experiment. Through experiment he gains knowledge of natural things, medical, chemical, indeed of everything in the heavens and on earth.*[6]

After studying Arabic treatises on optics and light, Bacon experimented with various phenomena of light and concluded like Grosseteste that the person who understands the principles of light and optics will understand the divine plan of the universe. Bacon's work led to the development of eyeglasses, and this great medieval thinker also predicted the invention of flying machines and horseless carriages.

MEDICINE

The field of medicine in medieval Europe was greatly affected by the discovery of Greek and Arabic texts. Medicine was not considered a science, as we understand that term today, but rather a branch of philosophy. Medieval physicians did not experiment, and they only rarely performed surgical operations. Surgery was the domain of barbers, who were organized into guilds of barbersurgeons. The role of physicians was to prescribe for patients on the basis of their knowledge of ancient medical texts.

Medieval medicine was thus based on the medical writings of the ancient Greeks and Romans. The most important of these was the ancient Greek medical writer, Galen (130-200 A.D.). A Latin translation of his medical encyclopedia reached western Europe from the Moslems in the 12th century. For the rest of the Middle Ages and beyond, Galen became the definitive medical authority.

In particular, medieval physicians accepted Galen's theory that health depended on a balance among four bodily fluids: blood, mucus, black bile, and yellow bile. Illness resulted if a person had too much or too little of one of these fluids. The art of medicine lay in diagnosing which fluid was out of proportion and then acting to correct the balance. Treatment could take the form of drugs, diet, rest, or, very commonly, bleeding the patient. Medieval physicians believed that diminishing a person's blood supply would bring all the humors into balance.

According to the type of illness, a physician would determine how much blood was to be taken from the patient. It could be as little as an ounce, or as much as a pint for serious illness. A barber-surgeon would then make an incision, draw out the prescribed amount of blood, and bind up the wound. Based as it was on a totally mistaken theory of human physiology, bleeding was useless as a remedy for illness. In fact, it weakened patients and exposed them to infection because medieval surgeons did not sterilize their razors. The practice of bleeding continued for centuries, until medicine ceased to rely on the authority of ancient texts and became an experimental science.

[6]Roger Bacon, "Eulogy of One Who Devoted Himself to Experimental Science," in J. H. Robinson, ed., *Readings in European History*, vol. 1 (New York: Ginn, 1904), p. 460.

Medieval physicians treated many illnesses by letting blood, a practice which often worsened the patient's condition.

Despite the reliance on inaccurate theories, medicine did make some progress in the later Middle Ages. At the universities of Salerno and Montpellier, medicine was studied as a science, and students learned to dissect animals and human cadavers. Such studies gradually led to better skills in surgery.

Epidemics that swept through Europe taking huge death tolls resulted in efforts to control diseases. Some towns appointed doctors to oversee public health. To combat epidemics, Venice set up a system of quarantines for newcomers. A physician examined people arriving by ship and required that ill passengers remain on board for 40 days to prevent their carrying the illness into the city. Some towns and cities did have hospitals set up by monasteries outside the city walls, but these were often little more than places where the sick could die.

In the Middle Ages, most people who lived in rural areas never saw a doctor. They relied on folk medicine that combined magic charms and chants to prevent illness with traditional remedies such as herbs and roots. Because illness was connected to beliefs in devils and evil spirits, people also used prayer and pilgrimages to seek cures.

LITERATURE When the Romans conquered western Europe, they brought the Latin language with them. Latin thus became the language of educated people throughout the West, and kept that position even when Rome collapsed as a political power. Thus, the Church used Latin in its religious services and for its business affairs. Gradually, however, the regions of western Europe that had been influenced by Rome developed their own languages that interwove Latin with the language of the local common people. In each region, the language of the common people became known as the *vernacular*.

The literature of the early Middle Ages was of two varieties. One included the written works in Latin such as poetry and essays on theology. The other consisted of the many traditions and legends that were passed orally from generation to generation until they were eventually written down in Latin or, by the 11th century, in the vernacular.

Before this early vernacular literature was written down, it was carried from town to castle to monastery by wandering minstrels. The stories they told or sang provided entertainment, spread news of events such as battles or plagues, and perpetuated the legends of a particular region. In France, these minstrels were called *jongleurs*, and their songs (*chansons*) evolved into long narrative poems relating the deeds of heroes, both past and present. While based on historic events, these minstrels' accounts were frequently embellished for the greater enjoyment of the audience. Many stories concerned the reign of Charlemagne, which the medieval French regarded as the "golden age" of their nation's history.

Four languages in western Europe —Spanish, Portuguese, French, and Italian—and one in eastern Europe— Romanian—were strongly influenced by Latin and are known as Romance languages. Although the languages of northern Europe included some Latin words, they were most strongly influenced by German and are called Germanic languages. The languages of eastern Europe are known as Slavic languages.

During the Middle Ages, wandering minstrels created and embroidered the legends that were later turned into such epics as the Song of Roland and the Poem of El Cid.

The oldest and most famous of these tales is the *Song of Roland.* Roland was the nephew of Charlemagne and an officer in the army that Charlemagne led into Spain in an unsuccessful effort to drive out the Moslems. While withdrawing to France, the expedition was attacked by fierce Basque tribes in the Pyrenees Mountains. Roland, the commander of Charlemagne's rear guard, led a delaying action in which he and all his soldiers were killed. According to legend, Charlemagne was so moved by this bravery that he marched back into Spain and captured the city of Saragossa from the Moslems. The victory is described in these words:

• • • *The pagans are dead. Many of them . . . . And Charles has won his battle. He has beaten down the gate of Saragossa and he knows beyond any doubt that it will not be defended. He occupies the city. His army enters its walls. His men lodge there that night by right of conquest. The white-bearded King is filled with pride. For Barmimunde [the queen of the city] has surrendered her towers to him—the ten enormous ones and the fifty smaller ones.*

He whom the Lord God helps will triumph.[7]

The *Song of Roland* was probably told at monasteries along the pilgrimage route to the shrine of Saint James at Compostela, in northwestern Spain, because the events had taken place near there. The long epic became very popular because it glorified the role of Christian knights in conflict with the infidels, thereby symbolizing the victory of good over evil. Pope Urban II referred to the "golden age" of France when he preached his call for the First Crusade at Clermont (Chapter 16): "Let the deeds of your ancestors encourage you and incite your minds to manly achievements—the glory and greatness of King Charlemagne."[8]

[7]*Song of Roland,* in *Medieval Epics,* trans. Helen M. Mustard and W. S. Merwin (New York: Modern Library, 1963), p. 193.

[8]Urban's speech at Clermont, as reported by Robert the Monk, in *Readings in European History,* ed. Robinson, p. 313.

Aquitaine, and his daughter Eleanor introduced troubadours to the royal courts of France and England. From there, they spread across Europe. The troubadours and their love songs were closely associated with the knightly code of chivalry.

DANTE ALIGHIERI

One of the most significant works of medieval vernacular literature is the *Divine Comedy* of Dante Alighieri (1265-1321). Dante was born into a wealthy family in Florence and received an excellent education in theology, philosophy, and rhetoric. Around 1300, he was appointed one of the six magistrates in Florence. Two years later, he became involved in a dispute between two political factions and was sentenced to exile. Only the influence of friends saved him from execution, and he never returned to Florence.

The great Spanish epic, *Poem of the Cid* (*Poema del Cid*), was written down between 1150 and 1250. It recounted the adventures of the Cid ("lord") Rodrigo Díaz de Bivar, who led crusades against the Moslems in Spain (Chapter 22). The German epic, *Song of the Nibelungs* (*Nibelungenlied*), is a composite of several legends relating to the slaughter of a Burgundian tribe by the Huns during the 5th century. In the 19th century, the German composer Richard Wagner used this story as the basis for his cycle of four operas, *The Ring of the Nibelungs*. The earliest epic in English is *Beowulf*, dating from the 8th century, which recounts the heroic deeds of the warrior Beowulf.

In addition to the epics, songs of love and romance became extremely popular during the 11th century. These songs originated in southern France, where those who sang them were called troubadours. William, duke of

Like Roland, the legendary Spanish hero El Cid won fame in fighting the Moslems. In this illustration, he kneels before his king.

Dante was familiar with the writings of Aristotle and Saint Thomas Aquinas. His experience in politics made him sensitive to human nature and the ways of the world. Although he became interested in mysticism, he remained a devout member of the Church.

While in exile, Dante wrote his most famous work, *Divine Comedy*, in the vernacular of his home region, Tuscany, completing it just before his death. It is the story of Dante's journey through hell, purgatory, and heaven, the three levels to which souls could be assigned by God after death. Dante peopled each level with the souls of his contemporaries and of people from history, according to his opinion of whether the person was wicked or virtuous. In vivid images, Dante describes the endless torments and sufferings of hell or the blessed joys of heaven.

GEOFFREY CHAUCER

Another outstanding work is *Canterbury Tales*, written by Geoffrey Chaucer (1340-1400). Chaucer was born into a family of prosperous wine merchants in London. He received a good education and entered into the service of King Edward III. Chaucer was later an envoy to the Italian states, where he came into contact with the writings of Dante. Although Chaucer was fluent in both Latin—the language of the Church—and French—

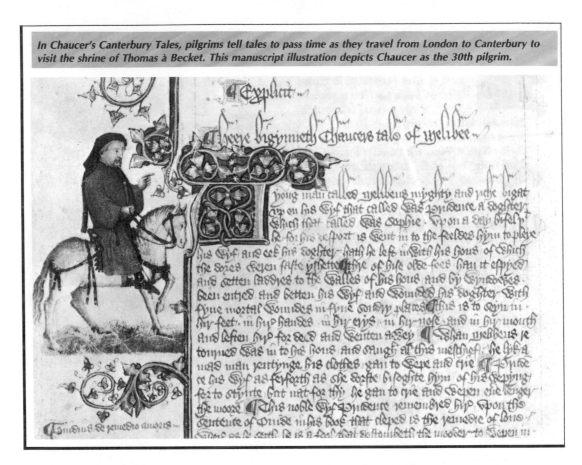

the language of the English court—he decided to write in English.

Chaucer worked on his *Canterbury Tales* from 1385 until his death 15 years later. While the individual tales probably came from a variety of sources, Chaucer presented them as the stories of 29 pilgrims traveling from London to Canterbury, to pray at the tomb of Saint Thomas à Becket. To pass the time along the road, each pilgrim was to tell two stories on the way to Canterbury and two on the return. Of the 120 projected stories, Chaucer completed only 24 before his death.

Chaucer's descriptions of the pilgrims and the stories each pilgrim tells present a vivid picture of life in medieval England.

DRAMA

In the Middle Ages, drama grew out of plays performed in the churches. Late in the 10th century, the clergy began to dramatize sacred stories from the Bible to instruct their parishioners, most of whom could not read. At first, members of the clergy acted out the stories on holy days. The presentations were given in Latin within the church buildings.

These dramatizations became very popular, and the performances were moved to the marketplace to accommodate a larger audience. The casts were also expanded to include laypeople, and the local language was used in place of Latin, so that more people could understand the play. These performances came to be called *mystery plays* because they dealt with unusual events in the Bible and in the life of Jesus.

Later, dramatizations of events in the lives of some saints were presented. These came

Medieval drama evolved from morality plays that were created to teach the lessons of the Church.

the new buildings, new styles of architecture were developed.

ROMANESQUE

In the early Middle Ages, large churches were built as modifications of the style of the Roman basilicas, or courts of law. This style of architecture was later called *Romanesque*. The basic plan of a Romanesque church was a large rectangle surrounded by thick walls of brick or stone. A wooden roof was supported by the outside walls and two rows of columns running the length of the building. Between the rows of columns was a wide central space, called the nave, and a narrower space, or aisle, lay between each column and the outside wall. The columns were taller than the walls. As a result, the central part of the roof, supported by the columns, was higher than the sides. This allowed win-

to be called *miracle plays* after the miracles associated with each saint. Finally, the programs were expanded to include *morality plays*, in which the plot presented a particular moral instruction that the audience could easily understand.

MEDIEVAL ARCHITECTURE

In the early Middle Ages, very little construction was done in western Europe aside from fortified manors for defense and religious buildings such as churches and monasteries. By the 12th century, however, there was a resurgence of construction because of improved economic conditions. The Crusaders, who had seen the beautiful palaces of the Byzantine Empire, returned home with dreams of transforming their own drafty castles into comfortable homes. But the Church with its vast wealth was the greatest builder of the time, spending huge sums on new cathedrals and abbeys. Along with the outpouring of money and faith that went into

A few of the specialized trades involved in building a Gothic cathedral are shown here: a master stonecutter (bottom left) creates delicate ornaments for the columns; masons (top) test the level of each row of stone blocks; and other workmen (bottom center) operate the winch that raises the blocks to the work site.

401

dows to be placed between the two levels of the roof, and light from the windows to illuminate the interior of the building.

Bishops and abbots vied with one another to build the most impressive and grand churches. Thus, further modifications were made in the basic plan. The columns were arranged so that the floor resembled the shape of a cross. A *transept*, or aisle, perpendicular to the nave and longer than the width of the church, was added on each side, to make the cross. When the churches became so wide that wooden beams could no longer support the roofs, barrel vaulting was used. Also the central part of the church was made higher, forcing builders to use buttresses, or brick structures outside the walls, to carry the weight of the roof.

Church leaders also sought to have the most beautiful and elaborate ornamentation on their buildings. The church was decorated both inside and out with sculpture, mosaic, and paintings that showed scenes from the Bible or recounted events in the lives of the saints. A standard stylized form was adopted for each holy person, so that a worshiper entering any church would immediately recognize the person or event shown. For example;

> God, angels, and the apostles go barefoot; other saints are shod. St. Paul must be bald and long-bearded. St. Peter always wears [shaved head], curly hair, and a short beard. The Christ child must lie on the altar. The three Magi represent youth, maturity and old age. In the Crucifixion Mary appears to the right of the cross, St. John to the left. A scene depicting the Resurrection always shows Jesus emerging from an open tomb, cross in hand. Jews invariably wear cone-shaped hats.[9]

GOTHIC

The abbey of Saint Denis near Paris was an important church in the Middle Ages because it not only housed the remains of Charles Martel but also boasted a relic of Saint Denis, who had brought Christianity to northern France in the 3rd century. In the 12th century, Suger, the powerful abbot of Saint Denis, set out to make the abbey the most beautiful building in Europe. For the rebuilding of the abbey, Suger adopted principles of design that had been used in the Middle East. The new style of architecture soon became popular and was at first called the French style. During the Renaissance, however, when everything medieval was disdained, this style of architecture was called *Gothic*, meaning barbaric.

The Gothic style differed from the Romanesque in several ways. The main differ-

[9]Merle Severy, *The Age of Chivalry* (Washington, D.C.: National Geographic, 1969), p. 170.

In addition to religious scenes, cathedral sculpture sometimes included gargoyles and scenes from everyday life. This sculpture of a peasant sharpening his scythe is part of a sequence illustrating the seasons of the year.

ence was height—Gothic churches were hundreds of feet higher. This great height was achieved through the use of ribbed, criss-crossed vaulting and "flying" buttresses, which projected outside the building and helped support the high walls. Because of these supports, the walls did not have to hold all the weight of the building. Thus, the walls

In Gothic architecture, the immense weight of high, vaulted ceilings is carried by flying buttresses on the outside of the structure.

same width, by means of geometrical and arithmetical instruments, as the central nave of the old [Carolingian] church; and, likewise, that the dimensions of the old side aisles, except for that elegant and praiseworthy extension . . . a circular string of chapels, by virtue of which the whole [church] would shine with the wonderful uninterrupted light of the most luminous windows, pervading the interior beauty.[10]

Suger's achievement inspired the building of hundreds of Gothic churches and cathedrals throughout Europe: Notre Dame in Paris (begun in 1163), Chartres (begun in 1194), and Amiens (begun in 1220) in France; Canterbury (begun in 1174) and Salisbury (begun in 1220) in England; Cologne (begun in 1322) in Germany and Milan (begun in 1386) in Italy are just a few examples. Workers toiled for several generations to complete each great cathedral. Each remains as a tribute to the ingenuity of the artisans who designed and built them. The master stonemason, who was usually also the architect, was exempted from taxation, given the right to wear fur-trimmed robes (a right usually reserved for the nobles), and provided with a lifetime pension. Wealthy nobles and merchants gave large sums of money for buildings and decorations such as stained-glass windows. Poorer Christians contributed their labor.

The great cathedrals built during the Middle Ages symbolized the solid security offered by the Church. These monuments, which Christians saw as a tribute to "the greater glory of God," dominated the medieval landscape much as the Church ruled their lives. Yet the building of churches and cathedrals was also good business for the towns and cities where they were located because they attracted pilgrims from far and wide even as they do today.

could be hollowed out to make room for huge stained-glass windows that allowed light into the church.

While only the choir of the abbey was completed in his lifetime, Suger described it as follows:

● ● ● *Moreover, it was cunningly provided that—through the upper columns and central arches which were to be placed upon the lower ones built in the crypt—the central nave of the new addition should be made the*

[10]Erwin Panofsky, trans., *Abbot Suger on the Abbey Church of St. Denis and Its Art Treasures* (Princeton, N.J.: Princeton University Press, 1951), p. 101.

SUMMARY

In the early Middle Ages, the only schools were in monasteries and cathedrals. In the 12th century, the expanding European economy and increased contact with the Byzantine and the Moslem worlds created a climate in which more people were interested in education and the exchange of ideas. As a result, some cathedral schools in France and Italy evolved into universities that taught a variety of subjects to students from all over Europe.

Through contact with the Moslems, European scholars acquired Latin translations of ancient Greek and Moslem works of philosophy, science, and medicine. These texts had an enormous influence on European thought. In theology, the scholastics used the methods of Greek philosophy to reconcile reason with the Christian faith. Moslem writings in science became the foundation of European scientific speculation. Greek medical theory dominated medieval medicine.

During the Middle Ages, Latin was blended into the local languages to produce vernacular languages such as French, Italian, and Spanish. Eventually, a written vernacular literature began to appear. The two most significant works of medieval literature are Dante's Divine Comedy *and Chaucer's* Canterbury Tales. *Throughout the Middle Ages, the building of churches and cathedrals confirmed the strength and importance of the Church.*

QUESTIONS

1 How did universities develop in the Middle Ages? What brought about disputes between "town" and "gown" factions in the Middle Ages? Why do these disputes occur even today?

2 What questions were the scholastics trying to answer? How were they influenced by Greek thinkers like Aristotle?

3 Describe how the work of Robert Grosseteste and Roger Bacon prepared the way for later scientific advances.

4 Why was the development of vernacular literature significant? Read one of the Canterbury Tales and describe what it reveals about medieval life.

5 Compare Romanesque and Gothic styles of building. Why do you think the new Gothic style was appropriate to the Church at the height of its power?

6 What conditions in the later Middle Ages made possible the flowering of medieval civilization?

BIBLIOGRAPHY

Which book might describe a variety of medieval heroes?

HOFSTATTER, HANS H. *Art of the Late Middle Ages.* New York: Harry N. Abrams, 1968. *A beautifully illustrated volume that shows the stained glass, mosaics, illuminated manuscripts, and reliquaries that adorned the majestic cathedrals of the late Middle Ages.*

MCLANATHAN, RICHARD. *The Pageant of Medieval Art and Life.* Philadelphia: The Westminster Press, 1966. *An illustrated survey of the creative arts from medieval Europe, the Byzantine Empire, and the Islamic world. Examines the relationship of faith and artistic expression in cathedrals, paintings, and sculpture.*

HELEN M. MUSTARD and W. S. MERWIN, translators. *Medieval Epics.* New York: The Modern Library, 1963. *A collection of the major medieval epics, including* Beowulf, The Song of Roland, The Nibelungenlied, *and* The Poem of the Cid.

THE MAYAS

300–900

Deep in the dense jungle of Central America, buried under plants, vines, and trees, lie massive stone temples and huge carvings that are evidence of an ancient civilization. These huge stone monuments and *stelae*, or stone pillars carved with pictures, tell the story of the Mayas, a people who lived in Central America as long ago as 2000 B.C. At the height of their civilization, the Mayas produced books and traded across a wide area, using cacao beans (from which chocolate is made) as money. They invented a sophisticated calendar that even today matches our own in accuracy. In terms of our calendar, the starting date for the Maya calendar is August 14, 3114 B.C.—a date that makes it over 5,000 years old.

HISTORICAL OVERVIEW

The Mayas were a farming people who cleared the land and built their villages across a large part of Central America. The area settled by the Mayas includes the present-day regions of southern Mexico, Guatemala, Belize, Honduras, and El Salvador. At different times and at different places within this region, the Mayas developed flourishing cities and strong trading networks.

Maya history can be divided into three periods: the pre-classic, 1500 B.C.–300 A.D.; the classic, 300 A.D.–900 A.D.; and the post-classic, 900 A.D.–1517. During the pre-classic period, the first farming villages were built in the tropical highlands of present-day Guatemala. Maya farmers learned to domesticate a variety of plants, including maize, tomatoes, sweet potatoes, and avocados. They devised farm tools and made pottery. They built large stone buildings, the precursors of the vast religious ceremonial centers that would be so important in the classic period.

By the 1st century B.C., when Rome was expanding its control over the Mediterranean world, the Mayas were constructing irrigation systems to drain the swampy rainforests and were laying the foundations for the major cities that would control the busy trade of the highlands.

Maya civilization reached its peak during the 4th to the 10th centuries when western Europe was experiencing the turmoil and upheavals of the early Middle Ages. At a time when cities in Europe virtually disappeared, those in Central America thrived. For the Mayas, this 600-year period was an age of creativity in architecture and carving, and great advances in mathematics and astronomy. The spectacular achievements in building were made with stone tools and without

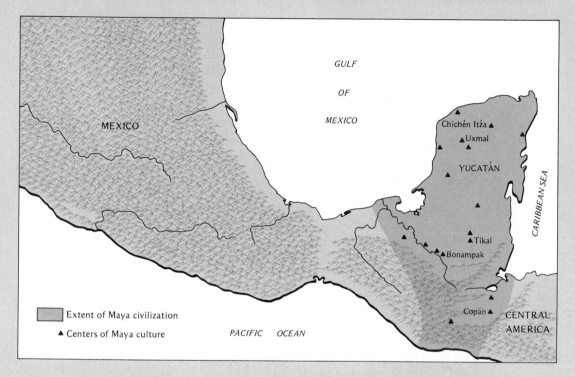

GULF
OF
MEXICO

MEXICO

Chichén Itźa ▲
▲Uxmal

YUCATÁN

CARIBBEAN SEA

▲Tikal
▲Bonampak

Copán ▲   CENTRAL
AMERICA

☐ Extent of Maya civilization

▲ Centers of Maya culture

PACIFIC   OCEAN

the use of the wheel. For despite their many advances, neither the Mayas nor the other peoples of the Americas used the wheel until it was introduced by the Spanish at the time of the conquest.

About 900, Maya civilization declined. The populations of the great cities decreased; trade continued but on a reduced scale; and no new monuments were built. Scholars have yet to discover the reasons for the decline. Various theories have been proposed, including the disruption of trade by invasions, disease, or a major ecological disaster. When the Spanish reached Central America in the early 16th century, they came into contact with the descendants of the ancient Mayas. But by then, the cities and monuments were in ruins.

CITIES

Settling the land, the Mayas developed an agricultural system based upon the domestication of maize, beans, and other plants. They utilized terracing and irrigation canals, and in addition constructed platforms of raised soil that enabled them to grow crops in lowland areas affected by seasonal flooding. As with other civilizations, the settled agricultural system of the Mayas produced a surplus that allowed some individuals to specialize in work and intellectual activity other than agriculture. As elsewhere, settled agricultural life produced villages, towns, and cities.

Maya cities were primarily religious centers, but the recent work of archaeologists and anthropologists has revealed that they were also centers of trade and other activities. Dominating each city and its surrounding land was a towering pyramid temple in the central plaza. The pyramid was built on top of a large stone platform. Nearby were other smaller temples and palaces. Like the great pyramids of Egypt, these monumental buildings were constructed by people who had only stone tools.

The temple at Chichen Itza is one of the best examples of Maya pyramid architecture.

At Maya sites, archaeologists have also uncovered "house mounds"—low dirt platforms that are surrounded by stone retaining walls. On these mounds, the poorer people built their houses of poles and thatched roofs. The earth platforms under the houses insured protection against flooding from summer rains. Even the towering temple buildings were built on platform bases, however, and these platforms served as gravesites for the wealthier people of the community.

With regard to the class structure, Maya society was divided into a number of layers. At the top were the rulers, probably divine kings. Next came a powerful noble class made up of priests and warriors. Only the priests and warriors were educated and knew the art of writing. Priests presided over the elaborate rituals that were part of daily Maya life. Warriors defended the cities, but, like the Vikings of northern Europe, they also apparently launched fierce raids on neighboring people. Supporting the ruling class were the artisans and merchants, as well as peasants and slaves who farmed the lands, built the huge stone structures, and carried the trade goods across great distances.

Because the Mayas had no draft animals, human porters transported all goods from cities in the highlands to those on the coastal lowlands. Burial objects in tombs and carvings on stelae in Tikal, an important Maya site in Guatemala, indicate that the Maya trading ventures reached as far away as Teotihuacán more than 600 miles to the west. The Tikal carvings show non-Maya people carrying weapons and ornaments that are associated with the people of central Mexico. Trade with Mexico was active and included salt from the Yucatan, honey, cotton, cacao beans, quetzal feathers, and slaves. Often, trade goods were carried by large canoes specially built by the coastal Mayas.

RELIGION, SCIENCE, AND MATHEMATICS

The Mayas worshiped a variety of deities, most related to the forces of nature. Many were seen to have a two-sided nature—both good and evil. The rain god, for example, was highly regarded, for without rain the crops would wither. However, this same god could also send disastrous hailstorms and heavy floods. Besides the rain god, there were gods for the sun, moon, wind, sky, and death. Also, each social class and profession had its own god.

Maya life involved a continuous series of ceremonies in which the priests sought to please the gods and determine the will of the gods. The ceremonies conducted by priests were preceded by fasting and ritual purification. Sometimes, the ceremonies included animal and human sacrifices, although archaeologists believe that large-scale human sacrifice was a development of postclassic times. During times of emergency such as drought or famine, priests were likely to demand a greater number of sacrifices.

The Maya achievements in science and mathematics were closely tied to religion. Priests studied astronomy in order to learn the best time for certain religious rituals. To record events, the Mayas developed a form of writing that consisted of hieroglyphics with animals, faces, and abstract designs. To date, scientists have only a limited understanding of these "glyphs" despite the large number that have been found on sculptures, buildings, and other artifacts.

What scientists do know is that priests carefully recorded astronomical occurrences such as eclipses in books and used these records for their calculations. Maya priests developed a sophisticated form of mathematics that includes the number zero. Their method of computing in mathematics was based on 20—a "dot" equaled 1, a "bar" equaled 5, and a stylized shell equaled 0. Taken together, Maya astronomy and mathematics allowed the priests to produce a highly accurate calendar that used 18 months for a year of 365 days. With this calendar, they regulated the all-important events of the year, choosing the appropriate times for planting, harvesting, and processing crops.

Astronomical and historical records allowed the Mayas to predict lunar and solar eclipses, and with an error of only 14 seconds per year, they were able to calculate and plot the path of the planet Venus. These achievements, it should be noted, were made at a time when Europe was mired in the warfare of the early Middle Ages. In fact, Europeans did not have as accurate a calendar as the Mayas until the 18th century.

The dating of the decline of Maya civilization is well known because the Mayas included dates on many stelae. Fewer of these monuments were built in the 9th century than in earlier times. Also, new building platforms in some cities were left unfinished as were temples and palaces. Although the decline can be identified, scholars as yet have been unable to agree on why it occurred. According to one noted expert, the decline of Maya civilization may be linked to problems elsewhere in Mesoamerica.

One may imagine a network of causes. The earlier decline of Teotihuacán and Monte Albán weakened the total fiber of Mesoamerica, but the Maya area took longer to die. Surely one of the factors was the rising of restless, aggressive people in central Mexico who came into the Southern and Northern areas and probably disrupted trade and the complex structure of Central Maya society. This Mexican influence may also have affected the Maya religion, as is suggested by the Mexican motifs in the art of the religious centers. At this time the Maya population was large and dependent for its support on trade and a well-organized social structure, and when its peripheral areas were affected by outside peoples and events the Central area probably collapsed slowly, like a be-

sieged fortress, its gods no longer effective, its economy destroyed. It has also been suggested that trade routes were changed, cutting off the Central areas, and possibly disease or crop disaster or some other ecological problems worsened the situation. Disasters rarely come singly.

INTRODUCTION TO THE DOCUMENTS

Archaeologists, anthropologists, linguists, and historians have searched through the jungles and coastlands of Central America to dig up the remains of the ancient Mayas, and they have found that the secrets are well guarded. Using aerial and satellite photographs of Central America, they have traced ancient irrigation canals, dikes, and man-made earth mounds that show the patterns of settlement. Meantime, others have used computers to help decode the books and writing of the Mayas.

Elizabeth P. Benson, *The Maya World* (New York: T. Y. Crowell, 1967), p. 131.

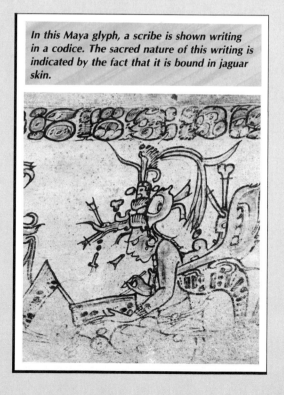

In this Maya glyph, a scribe is shown writing in a codice. The sacred nature of this writing is indicated by the fact that it is bound in jaguar skin.

The Maya religion was characterized by nature worship and human sacrifice. In this scene, a jaguar and a deer—each encircled by a serpent—look on as the man at center performs a ritual suicide.

While they had no apparent alphabet, the ancient Mayas coded their records by combining pictures, ideas, numbers, and sounds in a written language. These records are coded in "signs," called hieroglyphic script or glyphs. Hieroglyphic writing has been found on stelae, on the walls of temples, and on ceramic pottery buried in tombs. Many, but not all of these glyphs have been translated.

Many other Maya documents, however, were destroyed by the Spanish when they conquered the region. The Mayas recorded their history and learning in a number of books, or codices. Only three codices are known to have survived the Spanish conquest: the *Codex Paris*, *Codex Madrid*, and *Codex Dresden*. They are named for the cities in Europe where they are located. Most of the codices were burned in the 16th and 17th centuries by Spanish priests who wanted to eradicate the pagan practices that the Mayan insisted on clinging to. Many others may have perished in the rainforests.

DOCUMENT 1   THE OLD GODS

In Maya mythology, a serpent represents the sky, a deer represents the earth, and the jaguar represents the underworld. The deer and the jaguar may be a coded image for the Hero Twins—twin brothers who were sacrificed to the gods but revived themselves at the wish of the gods of the underworld.

And they marveled,
   The lords.
   "And now sacrifice yourselves in turn.
   So we can see it.
   Truly our hearts are delighted with this dance of yours,"
     the lords repeated.
   "Very well, oh Lord," they said then.
   And so they sacrificed themselves. . . .

SOURCE: "Codex Fragment 1: The Codex of the Old Gods: Vessel 40," quoted in Francis Robicsek and Donald M. Hales, *The Maya Book of The Dead: The Ceramic Code* (Yale University Press, 1981), p. 118.

DOCUMENT 2   PROPHECY OF THE SPANISH CONQUEST

Foretelling the future was the function of a special branch of the priesthood called the chilans. Since many prophecies could be interpreted to have foretold the coming of the Spanish and the conversion of the Mayas to Christianity, the Spanish made extensive use of them to legitimize their rule.

This reading is taken from the Books of Chilam Balam, which were written down in Latin script in the 17th and 18th centuries. Because these books come from such a late date, they are not pure examples of ancient Maya literature. In this selection, Chilam Balam prophesizes the coming of strangers from the East, who will bring a new religion. Since he made this prophecy shortly before the Spanish arrived, it is thought that he foretold the "future" based on rumors that were reaching Central America from the West Indies, where the Spanish first landed.

Then there shall be present the forceful one. . . . Like a jaguar is his head, long is his tooth, withered is his body, [like] a dog is his body. His heart is pierced with sorrow. Sweet is his food, sweet is his drink. Perchance he does not speak, perchance he will not hear. They say his speech is false and mad. No where do the younger sisters, native to the land, surrender themselves. They shall be taken away from the land here. So it shall always be with the maidens, the daughters whom they shall bear tomorrow and day after tomorrow. Give yourselves up, my younger brothers, my older brothers, submit to the unhappy destiny of the katun [a division of time] which is to come. If you do not submit, you shall be moved from where your feet are rooted. If you do not submit, you shall gnaw the trunks of trees and herbs. If you do not submit, it shall be as when the deer die, so that they go forth from your settlement. . . .

Then the judge . . . shall come, when he [who bears] the gold staff shall judge, when white wax [candles] shall be exchanged. It is to be white wax, when justice shall descend from Heaven, for Christian men to come up before the eye of justice. Then it shall shake heaven and earth. In sorrow shall end the katun of the Plumeria flower. No one shall fulfill his promises. The prop-roots of the trees shall be bent over. There shall be an earthquake all over the land. . . . If you surrender yourselves, you shall follow Christ, when he shall come. Then shall come to pass the shaking of the Plumeria flower. Then you shall understand.   ¡all Then it shall thunder from a dry sky. Then shall be spoken that which is written on the wall. . . . I hardly know what wise man among you will understand. He who understands will go into the forest to serve Christianity. Who will understand it?

SOURCE: Ralph L. Roys, ed., The Book of Chilam Balam of Chumayel (University of Oklahoma Press, 1967), pp. 120-23.

How does the prophet believe Maya religion will be affected by the coming of the Spanish?

DOCUMENT 3   THE CREATION

In the 16th century, not long after the Spanish conquered Mexico, a Quiché Maya from the highlands in Guatemala recorded the ancient history and legends of his people. The manuscript, known as the Popul Vah, *included many oral traditions and relates some Maya ideas about the origin of the universe.*

This is the account of how all are in suspense, all calm, in silence: all motionless, still, and the expanse of the sky was empty.

This is the first account, the first narrative. There was neither man, nor animal, birds, fishes, crabs, trees, stones, caves, ravines, grasses, nor forests: there was only the sky. . . .

There was only immobility and silence in the darkness, in the night. Only the Creator, the Maker, Tepeu, Gucumatz, the Forefathers, were in the water surrounded with light. They were hidden under green and blue feathers, and were therefore called Gucumatz. By nature they were great sages and great thinkers. In this manner the sky existed and also the Heart of Heaven, which is the name of God and thus He is called.

Then came the word. Tepeu and Gucumatz came together in the darkness, in the night, and Tepeu and Gucumatz talked together. . . .

Then while they meditated, it became clear to them that when dawn would break, man must appear. Then they planned the creation, and the growth of trees and the thickets and the birth of life and the creation of man. Thus it was arranged in the darkness and in the night by the Heart of Heaven who is called Huracan. . . .

Thus let it be done! Let the emptiness be filled! Let the water recede and make a void, let the earth appear and become solid: let it be done. Thus they spoke. Let there be light, let there be dawn in the sky and on the earth! There shall be neither glory nor grandeur in our creation and formation until the human being is made, man is formed. So they spoke. . . .

SOURCE: Delia Goetz and Sylvanus G. Morley, eds., *Popol Vuh: The Sacred Book of the Ancient Quiche Maya* (University of Oklahoma Press, 1950), pp. 81-4.

How does this Maya narrative compare with other Creation stories that you are familiar with?

TIME LINE FOR THE MAYAS AND WESTERN EUROPE

THE MAYAS

1500 B.C. Pre-classic period: Mayas begin to domesticate maize, build towns and temples

300 A.D. Classic period begins: Maya cities thrive, carry on extensive trade with neighboring cultures; advances in science and mathematics

900 A.D. Post-classic period: Maya civilization declines; cities disappear, temples fall into ruins

964 A.D. New Mayan empire in Yucatan centered in Chichen Itza

1200 A.D. Beginning of Cocom dynasty in Mayapan

1450 A.D. Destruction of Mayapan

1517 A.D. Cortés begins conquest of Mexico

WESTERN EUROPE

1570 B.C. Beginning of New Kingdom period in Egypt

330 B.C. Alexander the Great conquers the Persian Empire

146 B.C. Punic Wars end; Rome rules Carthaginian empire

330 A.D. Constantine I selects Constantinople as capital of Byzantine Empire

476 A.D. Collapse of Roman Empire; Germanic tribes divide up western Europe

632 A.D. Death of Mohammed. Islam is accepted by most people of Arabia and spreads to North Africa and western Europe

840 A.D. Viking, Magyar, and Moslem invasions of western Europe begin; Carolingian empire declines

1066 A.D. Norman conquest of England

1096– 1099 A.D. First Crusade

1215 A.D. Magna Carta signed

1492 A.D. Columbus sets sail from Spain; reaches the "New World"

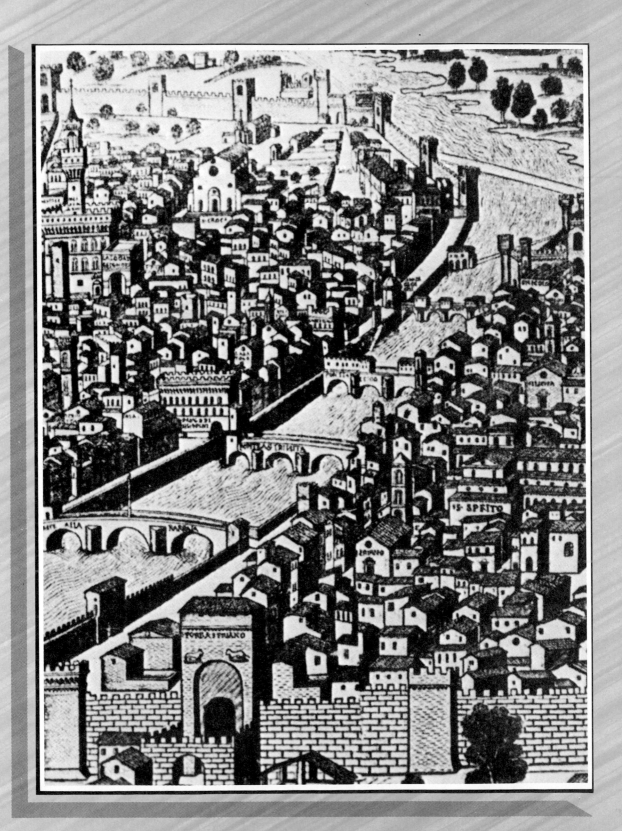

Emergence of
Nation States

● *During all these shocks, there have been formed since the time of Charlemagne only two absolutely independent republics—that of Switzerland and that of Holland.*

What then have been the fruits of the blood of so many millions of men shed in battle, and the sacking of so many cities? Nothing great or considerable. The Christian powers have lost a great deal to the Turks, within these five centuries, and have gained scarcely anything from each other.

VOLTAIRE

● *An emperor is subject to no one but to God and justice.*

FREDERICK BARBAROSSA

● *The pope is the only person whose feet are kissed by all princes. His title is unique in the world. He may depose emperors.*

POPE GREGORY VII

19

● *This agglomeration which was called and which still calls itself
the Holy Roman Empire is neither holy, nor Roman, nor an
empire.*

VOLTAIRE

The Holy Roman Empire

In the 18th century, the French philosopher Voltaire made the famous judgment cited above on the Holy Roman Empire. By then, the empire had existed, in name at least, for more than 800 years, but it was far different from the political unit put together by Charlemagne's successor in the lands east of the Rhine River, the region that we know as Germany.

The Holy Roman Empire developed in the eastern kingdom that Charlemagne's grandson, Louis, had been granted by the Treaty of Verdun (Chapter 15). Although the area had been conquered by Charlemagne, the Germanic tribes who lived there were less influenced by Roman customs than the other peoples of Charlemagne's empire.

Louis and his descendants were generally ineffective rulers. By the time the last of them, Louis the Child, died in 911, the area had become fragmented into five large duchies, each ruled by a duke who was descended from Germanic chiefs. The dukes depended on the ties of tribal loyalty and their own skill to administer their territories. Besides these dukes, the bishops and archbishops of several larger cities exercised considerable power.

From the 10th century on, however, the European political scene slowly changed. Although feudalism remained strong and feudal nobles were carving out great estates for themselves and their heirs, feudal monarchs began to assert their power. Over centuries of struggle, they gradually combated the forces of decentralization by dominating or subduing rebellious nobles; seeking to control the power of the Church; establishing law and order; and inspiring loyalty first to a ruling house and much later to the still emerging concept of a nation. In Germany, England, and France, rulers pursued these goals with varying measures of success. In this chapter, you will study aims and achievements of the Holy Roman emperors.

THE SAXONS The five chief duchies of the area were Saxony, Franconia, Swabia, Bavaria, and Lorraine. On the death of the last Carolingian in 911, the dukes of these regions elected Conrad of Franconia, the weakest of the rulers, to be the king. Conrad held the title for eight years but did little more than rule Franconia. Like the Carolingians before him, Conrad was unable either to control the other dukes or defeat the Magyar invaders who threatened from the east. As he was dying, Conrad recommended that his rival, Henry, duke of Saxony, be elected as his successor.

HENRY THE FOWLER (919-936)

Henry I, who became known as "the Fowler" because his favorite sport was hunting wild-fowl, established the Saxon Dynasty. At first, his leadership was acknowledged only by Franconia and Saxony, but he soon forced Swabia and Bavaria to support him and assumed control of Lorraine, a duchy bordering Saxony in the west.

Besides gaining recognition of his authority, Henry moved firmly against the Vikings in the north and the Magyars and Slavs in the east. He built a line of forts along the eastern frontier to defend against attacks by the Slavs and Magyars. In several battles, he defeated these persistent invaders. As a result of these successes, Henry earned the respect of many people, who then turned to him, rather than to their feudal lords, for protection and leadership. When Henry named his son Otto as his successor, the nobles did not dispute the appointment.

OTTO THE GREAT (936-973)

After Henry died in 936, Otto was crowned at Aachen, the capital of Charlemagne's empire. He strengthened his position by making an alliance with the Church, giving bishops control over vast holdings. In return, the bishops contributed money and soldiers to the king's army. Under the feudal system, the king appointed the bishops to their offices, and the bishops were bound to obey their feudal lord—the king. With the support of the Church, Otto was able to increase his power over the nobles. He seized the land of those who opposed him and either gave it to the Church or to a loyal relative.

Otto scored an impressive victory when he threw back a determined Magyar invasion. In 955, he thoroughly defeated the Magyars at the battle of Lechfeld. Otto followed

With the help of the Church, Otto the Great created a unified Germanic kingdom in the eastern part of Charlemagne's empire. This statue of Otto stood in a cathedral that he built at Magdeburg.

up his success by encouraging missionaries to go into Hungary to convert the Magyars to Christianity. At the same time, he pressed for German expansion to the east, persuading colonists to move into the lands of the Slavs and thereby control them.[1]

Like Charlemagne before him and like his own successors, Otto was drawn into the political battles of Italy. The Lombards who had controlled the north were divided among

---

[1]The idea of the "drive to the east" (*Drang nach Osten*) remained an important factor in German political decisions into the 20th century.

themselves, and their quarrels offered the pretext for interference. Also, the pope often faced difficulty controlling the Papal States in central Italy. In invading Italy, Otto followed the precedent that had been set by Charlemagne and sought to revive the glories of the old Roman empire.

In 951, Otto led his army across the Alps into Italy on the pretext of freeing Queen Adelaide, the widow of a Lombard king, who had been imprisoned by her enemies. He defeated her enemies, rescued her from prison, married her, and claimed the crown of Italy for himself. In 960, Pope John XII, whose lands were under attack, appealed to Otto for help. When Otto marched into Italy again, the grateful pope crowned him emperor in 962. To Otto, the pope's action placed him in the line of succession after the Roman emperors and Charlemagne. Not only was he the king of the German lands but also he was the supreme ruler of Christendom. Otto's coronation formally launched the Holy Roman Empire, as it was later called. It also bound up the fate of Germany with that of Italy for centuries to come.

THE FRANCONIANS

Otto's successors neglected their lands in Germany while they attempted to strengthen their hold over Italy. The Slavs in the east and the Danes in the north exploited this neglect and attacked German strongholds, inflicting much damage. Despite their failings, the Saxon kings were the most powerful in Europe at the time, and the policies they laid down were followed by later German rulers. When the last Saxon king died in 1024, the German nobles elected Conrad II of Franconia (1024-1039) as king. The Franconian Dynasty ruled for only a century, but Conrad and his son Henry III (1039-1056) increased royal authority by centralizing power.

The Franconian rulers reduced the powers of the nobles by replacing as many of them as possible with *ministeriales* (from the Latin *minister* or servant), officials whose authority came directly from the king and whose children could not inherit their offices. The king did this to prevent any family from achieving enough power to challenge him. Conrad and Henry strengthened the royal treasury by collecting long-neglected taxes, making the nobles pay their feudal dues, and developing silver mines from which coins could be minted. The Franconian rulers appointed capable people who were loyal to them to positions of leadership in the Church and worked for much-needed reforms in the Church.

Henry III helped Leo IX become pope in 1049 and supported the new pope's efforts to correct the worst abuses of the clergy, including simony and the failure of priests to obey their vows of celibacy. When Henry III died in 1056, his six-year-old son, Henry IV, ascended the throne. During the boy's long minority, the nobles seized royal property and assumed many royal powers. As a result, when Henry began to rule in his own name, he was constantly struggling to assert royal authority over his unruly nobles.

THE INVESTITURE CONTROVERSY

While Henry was busy recovering royal power, an ambitious new pope was chosen, and these two strong-minded men were destined to clash. In 1073, a monk named Hildebrand, who had been in the forefront of the Cluniac reform movement (Chapter 16), was elected to the papacy as Pope Gregory VII. Under him, the papacy reached new heights of power and prestige. Gregory was determined not only to end abuses among the clergy but also to free the Church from secular control by putting all members of the clergy under papal—not royal—control. Thus, he set out to end the practice of **lay investiture**, whereby monarchs invested, or installed ceremonially, bishops in office. To achieve this goal, Gregory issued a decree in 1075, forbidding lay investiture and threatening to excommunicate anyone who disobeyed it. The famous decree read in part:

• • • [W]e decree that no one of the clergy shall receive investiture with a bishopric or abbey, or church, from the hand of an emperor, or king, or of any lay person, male or female. If he shall presume to do so, let him know that such investiture is void by apostolic authority, and that he himself shall lie under excommunication until fitting satisfaction shall be made.[2]

Although the pope's decree extended to all rulers, he did not enter into the battle with the kings of England or France. Instead, his action brought him into a decisive struggle with the emperor Henry IV, the most powerful ruler in Europe at the time.

With the nobles of the empire restless and resistant to his authority, Henry needed to be able to appoint bishops and archbishops who were loyal to him. His response to Gregory was immediate, forceful, and insulting. Addressing the pope as "Hildebrand, now no longer pope but false monk," Henry accused him of simony and other abuses. "By craft abhorrent to the profession of monk, thou hast acquired wealth; by wealth, influence; by influence, arms; by arms, a throne of peace; thou has turned subjects against their governors."[3]

Gregory then sent papal envoys to warn Henry that his insolence would not be tolerated. Henry, in turn, summoned a synod of German bishops loyal to him, and had them depose the pope. Gregory responded by excommunicating and deposing the em-

The humiliation of Henry IV at the hands of the pope became a celebrated episode in the struggle between church and state. In this illustration, the king begs an abbot and a countess to intercede with the pope on his behalf.

peror and releasing Henry's subjects from their oaths of allegiance to him.

The German nobles were delighted and invited the pope to Augsburg to preside over the election of a new emperor. Recognizing that he was threatened with the loss of his kingdom, Henry decided to seek forgiveness. In the winter of 1077, dressed as a humble pilgrim, he crossed the Alps to Canossa, in northern Italy, where he sought a meeting with the pope who had stopped there en route to Augsburg.

Under Church law, the pope had to pardon a penitent sinner, but he did not do so before Henry had suffered the humiliation of pleading for forgiveness:

• • • Laying aside all the trappings of royalty, he stood in wretchedness, barefooted and clad in wool, for three days before the gate of

[2]"Decree of November 19, 1075," Gregorius Registrium, Book VI, in J. H. Robinson, ed., Readings in European History, vol. 1 (New York: Ginn, 1904), p. 275.

[3]"Henry IV's violent reply to Gregory," Monumenta Germaniae Historica Selecta, edited by Doebel, in Readings in European History, ed. Robinson, p. 280.

the castle, and implored with profuse weeping the aid and consolation of apostolic mercy, until he had moved all who saw or heard of it to such pity and depth of compassion that they interceded for him with many prayers and tears.[4]

After keeping Henry waiting in the snow for three days, the pope readmitted him to the Church. However, the events at Canossa did not end the struggle between the emperor and the pope. Henry at once began plotting his revenge. His chance came in 1083 when he captured Rome and set his own candidate on the papal throne. Supporters of Gregory appealed for help to the Normans, who controlled southern Italy. The Normans and their Moslem allies then marched on Rome, attacking and pillaging the city. When they withdrew, Gregory accompanied them because the Romans held him responsible for the looting of their city. He died in exile in 1085, worn out by his struggle to establish papal power. Henry, too, died alone after failing to regain his throne from his son who had rebelled against him.

CONCORDAT OF WORMS

The conflict between emperors and popes continued until 1122, when the German nobles, weary of endless conflicts, forced the emperor Henry V to agree to a compromise with the pope. This compromise became known as the *Concordat of Worms* because it was signed in the German city of that name.

By the terms of that treaty, the emperor gave up his claim to invest the bishops with the symbols of their religious office (ring and staff), but he was still allowed to invest them with the sceptre that represented their temporal power. Also, the clergy's right to elect their bishops was recognized, but the election had to take place in the presence of the emperor so that the emperor had at least some influence over the choice. While the pope agreed to give up his demand to govern religious estates in Germany, he got full control over the appointment of bishops in northern Italy. The Concordat was a compromise, but it weakened the Holy Roman Empire in both its German and Italian lands. The emperors would never again exert as much control over the Church in Germany as they had in the days of Otto.

THE HOHENSTAUFENS

After the Franconian dynasty died out in 1125, Germany was torn by civil strife. The two most powerful noble families, the Welfs and Hohenstaufens, struggled for the title of emperor. When the German nobles chose a Hohenstaufen prince as Emperor Conrad III (1138-1152), warfare broke out between the families. After Conrad gained the throne, he set off on the Second Crusade but on his return to Germany found the nobles fighting each other and him. When Conrad III died without an heir, the nobles chose as emperor his nephew Frederick of Hohenstaufen, a compromise candidate because his mother had been a Welf.

RULERS OF THE HOLY ROMAN EMPIRE	
911-918	Conrad, duke of Franconia
919-1024	Saxon Dynasty
919-936	Henry I, the Fowler
936-973	Otto I, the Great
1024-1125	Franconian Dynasty
1024-1039	Conrad II
1039-1056	Henry III
1056-1106	Henry IV
1125-1268	Hohenstaufen Dynasty
1138-1152	Conrad III
1152-1190	Frederick Barbarossa
1212-1250	Frederick II

[4]"Gregory's account of Henry's penance at Canossa," in *Readings in European History*, ed. Robinson, p. 283.

FREDERICK I (1152-1190)

Frederick I—called "Barbarossa" because of his red beard—was determined to centralize royal authority. To this end, he forced the nobles to reaffirm their feudal obligations, and attempted to assert control over appointments to Church offices. He suppressed a revolt led by a Welf cousin, and took steps to protect the northern and eastern boundaries of his empire from the Vikings.

As soon as Germany was under control, Frederick turned his attention to Italy where he looked on the cities of Venice, Genoa, Pisa, and Milan as sources of revenue for his empire. These great cities were profiting from the revival of trade that took place in the 12th century and were becoming the most powerful political forces within Italy. In each city, opposing groups struggled for leadership, and the weaker group frequently sought outside help, especially from the emperor.

Pope Adrian IV also sought Frederick's help to prevent the Norman king of Sicily, Roger II, from attacking Italy. At first, the pope was grateful for the emperor's assistance. But the cooperation did not last long, and war erupted between pope and emperor. The former was supported by the *Lombard League*, an association of northern Italian cities that resented the emperor's efforts to rule them. In 1168, Frederick defeated the pope and captured Rome, but he was forced to withdraw from the city when a disastrous epidemic broke out.

In 1176, the combined forces of the pope and the Lombard League defeated Frederick's army at Legnano and forced him to run for his life. However, Frederick recouped his fortunes quickly. The following year, he reconciled himself with the pope. In 1183, he signed the *Peace of Constance* with the Lombard League, in which he granted the cities the right of self-government in exchange for certain taxes. Although Frederick was forced to make some compromises, the terms of the treaty defended his claim as a feudal lord over the north of Italy and extended his direct rule over central Italy.

After asserting the power of the Holy Roman Emperor with some success, Frederick Barbarossa embarked on the Third Crusade. He is shown here in the act of assaulting a Moslem fortress.

According to popular superstition, Frederick Barbarossa did not die during the Crusade, but fell asleep in a secret cave.

Frederick strengthened his position further by marrying his son and heir, the future Henry VI, to Constance, the daughter of the Norman king of Sicily. By this marriage, Frederick posed a new threat to the papacy, whose lands were now enclosed by Hohenstaufen territories both in the north and in the south. When the news reached Europe that Saladin had captured Jerusalem, Frederick set out on the Third Crusade (Chapter 16), but he drowned while crossing a river in Asia Minor.

By sheer ambition and force of personality, Frederick had increased the power of the Holy Roman Empire. So great was his success that he became a German folk hero. For centuries, people believed that he was not really dead but merely asleep in a cave and that he would return to rescue them in a time of need.

Frederick had worked to establish strong feudal ties to himself, so that all feudal power derived from the emperor. However, several important duchies, such as Saxony and Bavaria, remained independent, and in time, German feudalism strengthened these rulers rather than the central government. In Italy, the growing wealth and prestige of the city-states made it possible for their leaders to challenge the control of the emperor.

FREDERICK II (1220-1250)

Frederick Barbarossa's son, Henry VI, continued in his father's tradition, consolidating his power over Sicily and planning further conquests. But he died after a brief reign, leaving only an infant son, the future Frederick II. As a result, the Holy Roman Empire was torn by civil war as various nobles supported their own candidates to the imperial throne. During this period, the nobles became increasingly independent of the authority of the emperor. The pope, Innocent III, also took part in the struggle, supporting first one candidate for emperor and then the youthful Frederick from whom he extracted a promise to give up his claim to Sicily. Having no other choice, Frederick agreed to these terms and was proclaimed the Holy Roman emperor by Innocent.

Frederick turned at once to winning control of his German lands and gradually defeated the powerful forces in the field against him. Soon after Innocent died in 1216, Frederick retreated from his earlier agreement with the papacy and returned to Italy, where he was determined to expand his power over the Kingdom of the Two Sicilies (Sicily and Naples) to include all of the peninsula south of the Papal States.

Because Frederick II spent most of his life in Sicily, he had little interest in the northern part of his empire. To curry favor with the German princes and clergy, he transferred control of many royal estates in Germany to the local princes, bishops, and abbots, and

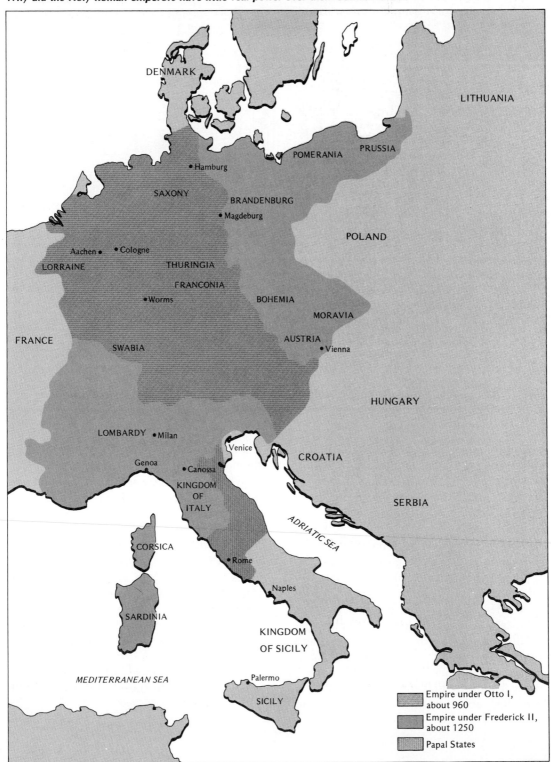

DENMARK

LITHUANIA

POMERANIA

PRUSSIA

•Hamburg

SAXONY

BRANDENBURG

•Magdeburg

POLAND

Aachen• •Cologne

LORRAINE

THURINGIA

FRANCONIA

•Worms

BOHEMIA

MORAVIA

FRANCE

SWABIA

AUSTRIA

•Vienna

HUNGARY

LOMBARDY •Milan

Venice

CROATIA

Genoa•

•Canossa

KINGDOM
OF
ITALY

SERBIA

ADRIATIC SEA

CORSICA

•Rome

Naples

SARDINIA

KINGDOM

OF SICILY

MEDITERRANEAN SEA

Palermo

SICILY

Empire under Otto I,
about 960

Empire under Frederick II,
about 1250

Papal States

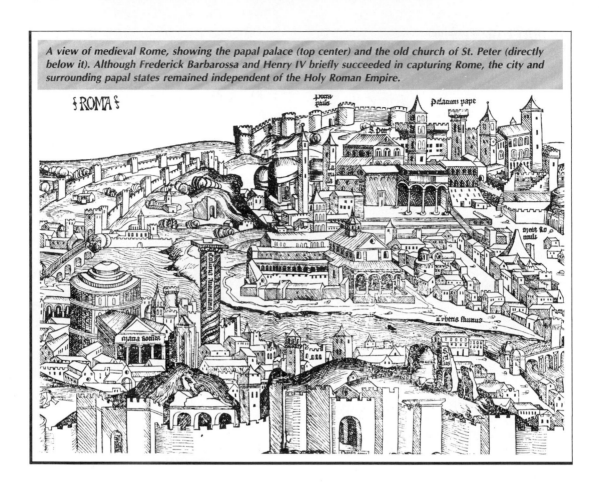

A view of medieval Rome, showing the papal palace (top center) and the old church of St. Peter (directly below it). Although Frederick Barbarossa and Henry IV briefly succeeded in capturing Rome, the city and surrounding papal states remained independent of the Holy Roman Empire.

exempted the churches from imperial jurisdiction. By allowing the clergy and nobles these privileges, Frederick gave up royal rights and set the stage for Germany to become a region of small independent states instead of a unified nation.

In Italy, Frederick first consolidated his power in Sicily, assuming direct control of the government. He then reorganized the army and navy as paid forces rather than feudal levies. He set up a more efficient treasury and established a university at Naples that would train students in Roman law. By these policies, Frederick set up a national monarchy more advanced than those of contemporary rulers in England and France. Yet Frederick's achievement was short-lived and was overshadowed by his titanic conflict with the papacy.

When Gregory IX was elected pope in 1227, he became alarmed at Frederick's plans to unite Italy. In order to thwart such an undertaking, Gregory ordered Frederick to fulfill his earlier promise to lead a Crusade to the Holy Land. When Frederick failed to make plans for the Crusade, Gregory excommunicated him. To redeem himself, Frederick organized and departed on the Sixth Crusade in 1228. Through negotiation with the sultan of Egypt, Frederick gained control of Jerusalem, Bethlehem, and Nazareth—the three cities which were most holy to Christians—and won access to these cities through the port at Sidon.

Despite Frederick's success, his relations with the papacy worsened. Frederick returned from the Crusade to find his lands in southern Italy under attack by papal forces. From then on until his death in 1250, Frederick was at war with the papacy. To Pope Gregory IX and his successor, the emperor's attempt to extend his power over all of Italy was a deadly threat, while the emperor accused the pope of hypocrisy and attacked the clergy for their corruption and greed. Repeatedly deposed and excommunicated by the pope, Frederick fought on, and the bitter struggle raged not only in Italy but also in Germany. It would continue even after Frederick's death in 1250.

While Frederick did not have the political or military skills of his grandfather, he was better educated and more scholarly. Committed to intellectual pursuits, he became a patron of the arts and sciences and made his court in Sicily the cultural center of Europe. He composed one of the first poems ever written in Italian and wrote a treatise on falconry that is still regarded as an authoritative work on the subject. Not without good reason did Frederick's admirers call him *Stupor Mundi* ("the wonder of the world"), although his critics called him a "baptized sultan" because of his interest in and admiration for Islamic civilization. However, his constant conflict with the papacy and his neglect of his German possessions set the stage for the disintegration of the Holy Roman Empire.

DECLINE OF THE HOLY ROMAN EMPIRE

After Frederick's death, the papacy renewed its offensive against his heirs. With the help of Charles of Anjou, brother of the French king Louis IX, the pope succeeded in overthrowing the Hohenstaufens in Sicily, and the last Hohenstaufen was captured and executed in 1268. A few years later in 1273, Rudolf of Hapsburg became emperor, establishing a new ruling dynasty that held power until 1806, when the Holy Roman Empire was finally swept away by the conquests of Napoleon Bonaparte.

In the century that followed Frederick's death, the princes and bishops of Germany gained more and more power at the expense of the emperor. In 1356, an effort was made to restore the prestige of the Holy Roman Empire by urging the stronger German princes to elect one of their number as emperor. The plan was described in a document known as the "Golden Bull." It established a council of seven electors, which was made up of the large archbishoprics of Germany—Mainz, Trier, and Cologne—and the secular rulers of four of the largest regions—the Palatine, Saxony, Brandenburg, and Bohemia. However, the system of electors prevented effective imperial rule. When a new emperor was to be chosen, the electors were able to demand concessions in exchange for their votes.

Without a strong central government, individual princely families came to the forefront of politics in Germany. Each controlled vast lands, and they were more interested in promoting their own interests than in the welfare of the empire as a whole—a situation known as particularism. In the late Middle Ages, several German cities declared their independence from the empire. Some of them, including Lübeck and Ulm, became major centers of industry, commerce, culture, and learning. The absence of a strong emperor also allowed regions on the border of the empire to develop into independent states, giving rise to the medieval states of Poland and Hungary (Chapter 22).

Despite the weakness of the Holy Roman Empire and the failure to centralize royal power, the emperor commanded a dominant position in European politics. The Hapsburg emperors rose to great prominence in the 16th century, ruling vast lands of their own in Austria, the Netherlands, and even Spain, as well as exercising at least nominal control over the states of the Holy Roman Empire.

SUMMARY

The Holy Roman Empire was put together in the eastern lands that were once part of Charlemagne's empire. In 962, Otto I, with papal support, assumed the imperial title and began to extend control over the empire. Otto's successors slowly strengthened their position against powerful dukes. However, the alliance that Otto had formed with the Church did not last as emperors and popes became embroiled in bitter power struggles. In the 11th century, the Holy Roman emperor Henry IV and Pope Gregory VII clashed in the investiture controversy. The struggle was not settled until 1122 with the Concordat of Worms, which gave the Church control over the selection of bishops.

The Hohenstaufen emperors became deeply involved in Italy, and their efforts to extend their control over the peninsula dragged them into wars with the cities of the north and with the papacy. Although Frederick II consolidated his power in southern Italy, he did so at the expense of his German lands. After his death, Germany was fragmented and remained so until the 19th century.

QUESTIONS

1 Describe the growth of the Holy Roman Empire from the 10th to the 13th centuries. Using a map of medieval Europe and a modern political map of Europe, name the present-day countries that were once part of the Holy Roman Empire.

2 How did the personalities of Henry IV and Gregory VII influence the investiture struggle? What were the central issues of this struggle? How was the struggle eventually resolved?

3 Why did Frederick Barbarossa and Frederick II each fail to develop a strong German state?

4 What reasons account for the decline of the Holy Roman Empire after 1250? Despite the decline, why do you think the empire continued to exist until the early 19th century?

5 Do you think that Voltaire's 18th century judgment of the Holy Roman Empire as "neither holy, Roman, nor an empire" was true in the 13th century? Explain.

BIBLIOGRAPHY

Which books might analyze Frederick II's conflict with the papacy?

BARRACLOUGH, GEOFFREY. *The Origins of Modern Germany.* New York: W. W. Norton, 1984. *A revised edition of a useful survey tracing the political, social, and economic forces that shaped Germany.*

BRYCE, JAMES. *The Holy Roman Empire.* New York: Schocken Books, 1961. *A 19th century history of the Holy Roman Empire that is still considered a classic.*

KANTOROWICZ, ERNST. *Frederick the Second, 1194-1250.* New York: Frederick Ungar, 1957. *A detailed, scholarly biography of this unorthodox and ambitious ruler. Explores the bitter rivalry between the papacy and the emperor.*

20

England in the Middle Ages

In the Middle Ages, Europe was a patchwork of many feudal territories that created a confusion of overlapping loyalties. A medieval monarch was not the supreme ruler of the land, but was rather one lord among many, and frequently ruled over nobles who had more land and even exercised more power than he. In legal matters, too, royal authority was limited since both the Church and the feudal lords had their own courts.

During the later Middle Ages, this situation changed dramatically as strong monarchs in different parts of Europe consolidated power. They gained control over the feudal lords and struggled for influence over the Church. In the process, they laid the foundations for the nation-states of today.

These early nation-states sometimes, but not always, welded together groups of people who shared a common language and common traditions, and lived in a clearly defined geographic area. To ensure royal power, strong monarchs established a central authority that kept order within the community; they resisted the efforts of decentralizing forces such as the Church and the feudal nobles; they expanded royal justice, making royal courts preferable to other courts; they set up a stable financial system; organized a royal bureaucracy to carry out royal commands; developed a standing army to replace uncertain feudal levies; and formed an alliance with the emerging middle class. In short, monarchs tried to establish the kind of ideal kingdom described in the English poem cited above. By doing so, they created the notion that the well-being of the state depended upon the ruler.

The establishment of a strong, centralized government did not follow the same pattern in all parts of Europe. As you have read, the struggles between emperors and popes distracted the rulers of the Holy Roman Empire and kept the area of present-day Germany from being united. On the western edge of Europe, however, England became one of the first countries to coalesce into a nation. Over the centuries, England was conquered by a succession of invaders, each of whom left their mark on the country's culture and institutions.

THE BRITISH ISLES The earliest inhabitants of England of whom we have substantial knowledge were the Celts, a group of Indo-European tribes

427

that the Greeks called *Keltoi*, and the Romans called *Gauls*. About 700 B.C., the Celts began to leave their original home, which is believed to have been the region between the upper Rhine and the Danube rivers. Some moved southward into the Italian peninsula, where they destroyed Etruscan cities and sacked Rome in 390 B.C. Others moved eastward into the Balkans, crossed the Hellespont into Asia Minor, and settled in an area that came to be called *Galatia*. Still others moved westward into present-day France and England. There, they defeated the native inhabitants and established their own culture.

The next invaders were the Romans. After conquering Gaul, Julius Caesar landed his legions in Britain and established relations with the inhabitants. Nearly a century later, in 43 A.D., the emperor Claudius conquered Britain and established Roman rule there. The Romans remained in Britain until shortly after 400 A.D. when their legions were withdrawn. But they left their mark on the islands, having brought Christianity to the Celts and built an excellent system of roads across the land. The Celts were left to maintain Roman ways and Christian beliefs against other invaders—the Angles, Saxons, and Jutes from northern Europe. Before long, the Latin language and Christianity disappeared almost completely from England.

Little is known about the 5th century invasions of the Angles, Saxons, and Jutes. These Germanic tribes ravaged the land, destroying the remains of Romano-British culture. According to legend, a Celtic leader named Artorius (or Arthur), who lived in the 6th century, fought heroically against the invaders and is credited with defending western England and Wales against the Saxons. For centuries, oral tales of Arthur's prowess circulated around Britain, and these tales gave rise to the Arthurian legends that were written down in the later Middle Ages. Recent archaeological explorations at Glastonbury in western England have provided scholars with intriguing evidence that there really was

According to legend, King Arthur and his men defended 6th-century Celtic settlements in western Britain against Saxon invaders. Later, other episodes—such as the search for the Holy Grail, and the romance of Lancelot and Guinevere—were added to the story.

a King Arthur, although many of the tales of knights and chivalry were inventions of later medieval minds.

DEVELOPMENT OF CHRISTIANITY

Even while the Roman legions were leaving Britain in the early 5th century, the Church kept up its efforts to bring Christianity to the British Isles. Among the best-known missionaries was Saint Patrick, who carried Christianity to Ireland. As a result of his efforts, Ireland was a Christian stronghold in the early Middle Ages, and many Irish monks traveled to England and other parts of Europe to pursue their missionary activities. Irish monks preserved the scholarly traditions, learning Greek and Latin and producing splendid illuminated manuscripts such as the *Book of Kells*.

During the 6th and 7th centuries. Irish monks traveled to Scotland and northern England to spread Christianity. They built monasteries at Iona, off the coast of Scotland, and at Lindisfarne ("Holy Island") in Northumbria, the ruins of which are shown here.

In the 6th century, an Irish monk named Columba carried Christianity to the Picts, the people who inhabited Scotland. He traveled as far north as Inverness, preaching and baptizing the people. He also set up several monasteries, including one on the small island of Iona off the western coast of Scotland. During the invasions of the next few centuries, the monks of Iona preserved Christian traditions, and Iona eventually became the center of monasticism in Scotland.

As you have read, Pope Gregory the Great sent Augustine to England in 597 (Chapter 16). Augustine landed in Kent and walked to Canterbury, the site of a church dating back to Roman times. There, he established his "chair" and became the first archbishop of Canterbury. Through the work of Augustine and his successors, the Angles, Saxons, and Jutes were converted to Christianity.

ANGLO-SAXON KINGDOMS

During the chaotic centuries of invasion, various tribal leaders set up a number of small kingdoms such as Sussex (kingdom of the South Saxons), Wessex (kingdom of the West Saxons), and Essex (kingdom of the East Saxons). Gradually, distinctions between Angles, Saxons, and Jutes became blurred, and the entire area became known as England, or Land of the Angles. By the 9th century, the kingdom of Wessex in south-central England emerged as the dominant power, and its ruler became the first English king.

Alfred the Great. Anglo-Saxon civilization reached its height under Alfred, king of Wessex (871-899). He was a man of great intelligence and ability, and he needed these qualities to meet the threat to his kingdom posed by the Danes, as the English called the Vikings who raided their shores. By the mid-9th century, the Danes had conquered all of England except Wessex and were readying an all-out assault on that stronghold. Early in his reign, Alfred purchased a truce from the Danes to give himself time to strengthen the defenses of his kingdom. He reorganized his army, had large fortifications constructed at strategic places, and ordered new ships built to defend the coast. These measures

Beginning in 835, Danish Vikings carried out a full-scale invasion of England. In contrast to their earlier behavior, they did not merely raid the coastal areas, but conquered and settled the interior of the country.

writing of the *Anglo-Saxon Chronicle,* an account of English history from Roman times to his own reign. Alfred decreed that a copy of the chronicle be placed in every cathedral and monastery so that events could be added as they occurred. The chronicle serves as our principal source of information about this period.

Alfred journeyed throughout his kingdom to see that local courts were dealing justly with the people, and he called on his officials to inform him of miscarriages of justice. For his many achievements, he earned the title *Alfred the Great.* After his death, the *Anglo-Saxon Chronicle* eulogized him.

• • • *[H]e exalted God's praise far and wide and loved God's law; and he improved the peace of the people more than the kings who were before him in the memory of man. . . . He came to be honored widely throughout the countries, because he zealously honoured God's name, and time and again meditated on God's law, and exalted God's praise far and wide, and continually and frequently directed all his people wisely in matters of Church and State.*[1]

Government. Alfred's successors continued to expand Anglo-Saxon power and unified the kingdom. By the mid-10th century, they had brought all of England under royal control. The Anglo-Saxon kings then developed new means of ruling the land. They divided the kingdom into areas called shires, or counties. Each shire was ruled by an *earl,* appointed by the king. In turn, each shire was subdivided into areas called *hundreds;* a *thegn* was appointed to rule each hundred. In every shire and hundred, a royal official, called a *reeve,* presided over the court system. At first, the shire-reeve (who later became known as the *sheriff*) only collected revenues for the king, but later he was given the duty of administering justice.

succeeded. In 878, Alfred defeated the Danes and set up a treaty under which the Danes were limited to settling in the *Danelaw,* a large area in northeastern England.

In addition to his military successes, Alfred proved his leadership in civil affairs. He collected all the written laws in England and fashioned them into a law code to be used throughout his kingdom. He invited scholars from all over Europe to his kingdom and asked them to recommend ways of reviving culture and learning, which had suffered during the long years of war. He supported education, encouraged the translation of Latin works into the vernacular, and was responsible for the

[1]D. Whitelock, ed., *The Anglo-Saxon Chronicle,* revised translation (New Brunswick: Rutgers University Press, 1961), pp. 74-75.

As the representative of the king, the shire-reeve brought wrongdoers before the local courts to answer for their misdeeds. A court was made up of the thegn who ruled the hundred where the accused lived, and a group of common people, called *doomsmen*. The accused could attempt to prove his or her innocence before the court by one of several methods: *compurgation*, persuading other people to swear to his or her good character; *wager of battle*, fighting the person bringing the complaint with fists or clubs to determine the winner; or *trial by ordeal*, undergoing a test, such as picking up hot metal (Chapter 17). While this system of justice may seem very harsh by today's standards, it formed the basis of the legal system that evolved in much of the Western world. The position of thegn ultimately developed into that of judge, the doomsmen eventually became the jury, and compurgation evolved into the use of character witnesses.

Anglo-Saxon kings also sought the advice of a council known as the *Witan*, or *Witenagemot* (meaning "Council of Wise Men") made up of earls and thegns. The most important function of the Witan was electing a new monarch when the reigning one died.

VIKING INVASIONS

In the late 10th century, the kingdom of Wessex faced a new threat when Vikings from Denmark again raided England. The king, Ethelred, was unable to curtail the growing power of his nobles or rally the people against the invaders. He then levied a heavy tax, called the *Danegeld*, on his subjects, and hoped to use the proceeds to bribe the Danes to stop their attacks. The money failed to accomplish its purpose, but Ethelred and his successors continued to use the Danegeld as a means of raising money. By 1013, Ethelred could no longer restrain the invaders, so he fled to Normandy, leaving his son Edmund to defend England. After Edmund died in 1016, the *Witan* named the Danish leader Canute to be the king of England.

Canute proved to be a wise choice. He eased the strife between the English and the Danes, married Ethelred's widow, Emma, and treated the Church generously. When he died in 1035, however, violence again broke out and lasted until the Witan chose another of Ethelred's sons, Edward, to be king of England.

Edward was devoutly religious and earned the nickname Edward the Confessor. He failed to unite the country, and the nobles steadily increased their powers at the expense of the king. When Edward died in 1066, there were three candidates for the throne of England: William, duke of Normandy; Harold Godwine, son of a prominent Anglo-Saxon noble; and Harold Hadrada, king of Norway. The Witan chose Harold Godwine to be king, but soon after he was crowned, the new ruler faced attacks from both his rivals.

Soon after Harold was crowned as the successor of Edward the Confessor, a luminous sphere—now known as Halley's comet—appeared in the sky. As this scene indicates, both the king and his subjects feared that the comet was an omen of disaster.

William of Normandy was one of the most powerful feudal lords in western Europe and an able administrator. In 1064, William had taken Harold Godwine captive and forced him to recognize William's claim to the English throne. So when Harold accepted the crown in 1066, William accused him of rejecting his oath and prepared to invade England. He convinced the pope to support the invasion by accusing Harold of the sin of perjury in breaking his oath.

NORMAN CONQUEST While William was organizing his expedition, Harold Hadrada of Norway landed in the north of England. Harold Godwine marched his army north to meet this threat. The armies of the two Harolds clashed at Stamford Bridge, near York, on September 28, 1066. Harold of Norway was killed, and his invasion was repulsed. But the king had barely left the battlefield when he heard that William of Normandy had set sail for England. Harold rushed south, giving his few

supporters no time to rest. On the way, he recruited whatever additional forces he could.

The two armies met at Hastings on the morning of October 14, 1066. In the ensuing battle, the Normans routed the Anglo-Saxons, and King Harold was killed. The battle of Hastings assured the Norman conquest of England. It stands as a major turning point in English history because it meant that the Normans rather than the Anglo-Saxons would rule England and shape its language and culture in the centuries ahead.

WILLIAM I (1066-1087)
William of Normandy was crowned king of England on Christmas Day, 1066. He then set about subduing the country and consolidating his power. William was determined to keep the Norman knights who had crossed the English Channel and fought with him at Hastings from becoming powerful enough to challenge his authority. To protect his power, he gave them small, scattered fiefs and demanded their promise to recognize his su-

premacy. He limited the number and size of castles and forbade his Norman barons to build castles without his consent.

In 1086, William traveled to Salisbury where he demanded an oath of fealty, called the *Salisbury Oath*, from every vassal.

• • • *[A]nd there his councillors came to him, and all the people occupying land who were of any account over all England whosoever's vassals they might be; and they all submitted to him, and swore oaths of allegiance to him that they would be faithful to him against all other men.*[2]

Under the Salisbury Oath, vassals owed their primary allegiance to William rather than to the lord from whom they had received their fiefs. This gave William and his successors an advantage over feudal monarchs on the continent who would spend centuries bringing the vassals of the great lords under their direct rule.

In government, William blended the political and social institutions of Anglo-Saxon England with Norman traditions. In the process, he laid the foundations for a strong, centralized government. William changed the Anglo-Saxon Witan into a Great Council that included the great lords of the kingdom. He also established a permanent council of royal advisers called the King's Council, or *Curia Regis.* These institutions would gradually evolve into the English Parliament. William kept the Anglo-Saxon system of local government with the shires, hundreds, and local courts, but he sent out royal commissioners to oversee the courts and sheriffs.

After ensuring his power, William began reforming the Church. He replaced Anglo-Saxon abbots and bishops with Norman clergy, allowed separate ecclesiastical courts to hear cases involving religious matters, enforced the rule of clerical celibacy, and decreed that no papal letter could be read in England without his consent. When Pope Gregory VII attempted to get William to swear allegiance to him and ordered the English bishops to appear in Rome, William rejected both demands. At the time, Gregory was deeply involved in his struggle with the Holy Roman emperor, Henry IV, so he did not contest William's action.

---

[2]Quoted in D. C. Douglas, *William the Conqueror* (Berkeley: University of California Press, 1964), p. 355.

William, duke of Normandy, invaded England with an army of well-trained cavalry troops.

In 1086, William ordered a survey of land ownership to be made throughout England. This survey became known as the *Doomsday Book* because information from it was used as the final *doom*, or judgment, in all disputes over land ownership. The Doomsday Book served an important function: it gave William a detailed record of the economic resources of his kingdom, so that he knew just how much financial and military support he could expect from his subjects. It included a record of all plows, forest land, cows, pigs, and other property in the land. As the *Anglo-Saxon Chronicle* noted, the survey was so complete "that there was not

In the decades following the conquest, Norman barons defended their holdings by building strongly fortified castles like this one.

As king, William the Conquerer deposed the Anglo-Saxon barons of England and gave their lands and possessions to Normans. Here, he gives one of his followers the deed to Northumbria.

one hide of land in England that he did not know who owned it, and what it was worth, and then set it down in his record."[3]

The Norman conquest brought many changes to England. Before 1066, England had been influenced by the culture of Scandinavia and northern Germany. After the Norman conquest, contact with Scandinavia decreased while contacts with other parts of western Europe increased. The new Norman lords of England encouraged artisans and traders from France to establish their businesses in England, and new cathedrals were built in the Norman style. William also introduced to England a centralized and efficient form of feudalism. As a result of the conquest, three languages were used in England: French was the language of the court

[3]*The Anglo-Saxon Chronicle*, ed. D. Whitelock, p. 164.

and the ruling class; Latin was the language of the Church; and Anglo-Saxon, or Old English, was the language of the common people. For some time, the distinction between Anglo-Saxon and Norman remained strong, but eventually, through intermarriage and assimilation, the two cultures were blended.

WILLIAM'S SUCCESSORS

William's successors continued his policies of centralizing royal power. They developed a bureaucracy of paid royal officials who were responsible for administering the kingdom. Unlike the feudal lords, these men owed their positions to the king and could not hand them on to their sons. William's immediate successor was his son, William II (1087-1100), who was also called William Rufus. A harsh

and unpopular ruler, William was killed in a hunting accident and was not much mourned.

Another of William's sons, Henry I, then inherited the throne. Under his leadership, the administration of royal justice was strengthened. Henry sent itinerant judges to outlying areas to hear law cases, thereby diverting cases from the courts of feudal barons and the Church courts. During Henry's reign, vassals were encouraged to pay scutage, or "shield money," instead of performing military service. The royal officials who collected these and other taxes tallied their records on a checkered table resembling a chessboard. In time, the office where this work was done became known as the Exchequer. The Exchequer developed into an account-

Westminster Abbey in London has been the scene of all royal coronations since the time of William the Conquerer. At right is the coronation chair.

ing office and a court: the former collected rents, fees, fines, and taxes while the latter decided cases involving these payments.

HENRY II

When Henry I died in 1135, controversy arose over a successor to the throne. Henry's only son, William, had drowned in a shipwreck, and his daughter, Mathilda, was married to the count of Anjou, the ruler of vast estates in France. The counts of Anjou were traditional enemies of the Normans. In 1154, after a long civil war, Mathilda's son became King Henry II and established a long line of rulers known as the *Plantagenet dynasty.*

By the time Henry II came to the throne of England, he had already inherited the French domains of Anjou and Maine. Through his marriage in 1152 to Eleanor of Aquitaine, he acquired control of Poitou, Gascony, and Aquitaine; thus Henry had authority over more than half of present-day France. He later made himself overlord of Scotland, Ireland, Wales, and Brittany as well.

Henry was a well-educated, intelligent, and able ruler. Soon after gaining the English throne, he set about reestablishing royal authority that had been eroded during the years of civil war. He ordered the destruction of all unlicensed castles and strengthened the royal treasury, dispatching officials to collect the taxes due to the crown. Most important, he broadened the scope of royal justice and extended the jurisdiction of royal courts. He did this through the use of itinerant judges who based their decisions on the common customs and traditions of the people. In doing so, he laid the foundations for the development of *common law*—law that is common to the entire land because it was carried out by royal courts. Gradually, common law came to refer to the body of legal principles based on the decisions of the royal courts. As people came to rely more and more on the royal courts, the importance of the competing Church and baronial courts declined.

Under Henry II, the early forms of a jury

Henry II, the first Plantagenet king, ruled much of modern France as well as England. His efforts to impose secular justice upon the clergy led to conflict with his friend Thomas à Becket.

system began to appear. There were two kinds of juries. One was assembled after a plaintiff purchased a royal *writ*, or order for a hearing before a royal official. At the hearing, the official asked a group of 12 people who were familiar with the case to present their information under oath. These 12 comprised a jury (from the French *juré*, meaning "sworn under oath"). This early kind of jury would eventually evolve into the trial jury of today.

A second kind of jury was established by the *Assize (Edict) of Clarendon* in 1166. It called for the sheriffs to assemble a group of 12 sworn men from each hundred to appear before the royal justices. They were "to reply truthfully to this question: whether anyone, within their hundred . . . has been accused, or publicly suspected of robbery, murder, or theft, or of harboring men guilty of such crimes, since the lord King's accession."[4] This jury became known as a jury of presentment because it presented the names of people suspected of crimes and was the forerunner of today's *grand jury*, which hears testimony concerning an alleged crime and hands down an indictment, or formal charge.

STRUGGLE BETWEEN CHURCH AND STATE Henry II's efforts to extend the activities of the royal courts led him into a bitter struggle with the Church courts. As you have read, Church courts had jurisdiction over many areas including cases that concerned the clergy (Chapter 16). Henry felt that Church courts dealt too leniently with members of the clergy when they were found guilty of serious crimes. Therefore, he issued the Constitution of Clarendon in 1164, which included a provision allowing a member of the clergy to be indicted by a royal court. The person could be tried in a Church court, but if convicted, could be returned to a royal court for punishment. Another provision forbade the clergy from appealing a sentence to the pope without the king's permission.

Henry's action was vigorously opposed by Thomas à Becket, a friend and adviser to the king, whom Henry had recently made archbishop of Canterbury. By this appointment, Henry had hoped to avoid conflict with the Church while he made the changes he wanted. To Henry's surprise, Becket did not acquiesce to the king's assertion of power but instead insisted that no cleric should be subject to the secular laws of England. When a dispute arose over whether royal authorities had the right to punish members of the clergy convicted in a bishop's court, Becket vowed to oppose the Constitution of Clarendon as long as he had breath in his body.

NORMAN AND PLANTAGENET KINGS OF ENGLAND	
The Normans	
1066–1087	William I, the Conqueror
1087–1100	William II
1100–1135	Henry I
The Plantagenets	
1154–1189	Henry II
1189–1199	Richard I
1199–1216	John
1216–1272	Henry III
1272–1307	Edward I
1307–1327	Edward II
1327–1377	Edward III
1377–1399	Richard II

In a fit of anger at his former friend's behavior, Henry is said to have asked, "Is there no one to rid me of this troublesome clerk?" Four of Henry's knights took these words as a command and murdered Becket as he was praying. Whether Henry was responsible for Becket's murder is still uncertain, but at the time people blamed him for it. As penance, Henry walked barefoot through the streets of Canterbury and submitted to flogging by the monks. Henry also agreed to recognize the authority of the pope in Church law and to exempt the clergy from punishment in civil courts. The martyred Becket was soon made a saint, and for centuries, pilgrims journeyed to Canterbury to visit his tomb.

Despite this tragedy, Henry's struggle to establish royal power won him the support of many people. Townspeople and peasants believed that they had a greater chance of obtaining justice in the king's courts than in those of their feudal lords. By setting up a royal bureaucracy of appointed officials who were loyal to the king, Henry II helped to build foundations of a stable government that would function even in the king's absence.

[4]"Assize of Clarendon," in J. J. Bagley and P. B. Rowley, *Documentary History of England*, vol. 1 (Baltimore: Penguin Books, 1966), pp. 54-55.

RICHARD I

Richard I succeeded his father in 1189, but he was almost unknown to the people of England because he lived in his mother's lands of Aquitaine. During his 10-year reign, Richard spent fewer than 6 months in England.

Soon after he became king, Richard decided to take part in the Third Crusade (Chapter 16). Always short of money, he pressed his subjects to support his foreign adventures. Before leaving on the Crusade, he named Hubert Walter to be archbishop of Canterbury and justiciar, the highest positions in the Church and state. Hubert Walter governed England well during Richard's absence and even put down a rebellion fostered by Richard's younger brother, John.

On his way back from the Third Crusade, Richard was captured and held for ransom. The king's mother, Eleanor of Aquitaine, worked tirelessly to raise the ransom money and convinced the English people that their king was a great hero worthy of being called "the Lion-Hearted." The ransom cost workers in England almost a quarter of their annual wages, but it freed their king, who returned to England in 1194. After a few weeks, Richard left again to fight King Philip Augustus, who had seized several of his castles in France. He died in France in 1199.

Richard's wars nearly bankrupted England, and he failed either to defeat the Moslems in the Holy Land or protect his lands in France. Despite these setbacks, he later became a folk hero to the English people and was associated with Robin Hood, a legendary figure who defended the poor against the rich and powerful.

KING JOHN AND THE MAGNA CARTA

Richard's successor was his younger brother, John, a clever but tyrannical ruler who fought and lost battles with the kings of France, the Church, and his nobles. He earned such a bad reputation that no future English monarch ever chose to take the name John. John

Although Richard I, "the Lion-Hearted," spent most of his time in France and imposed heavy taxes on his subjects, he was one of the most popular monarchs in English history. This statue stands in front of the Parliament buildings in London.

The Magna Carta defined the powers and responsibilities of the king in accordance with feudal tradition. Below are the opening lines of the charter; at bottom, the seal of King John, which was affixed to each copy.

fought bitterly with Philip Augustus of France, who not only encouraged John's French vassals to revolt but also drove the English out of Normandy. John led a campaign to recover these lands, but when his allies were decisively beaten at Bouvines in 1214, John was forced to return to England with an empty treasury and shattered prestige.

John's position was further weakened by his struggle with Pope Innocent III. When the archbishop of Canterbury died in 1205,

John named a successor. So, too, did the monks of Christ Church, who had the traditional right to elect the archbishop. The pope, who was determined to make the papacy supreme, rejected both choices and appointed the able and learned Stephen Langton to the office. When John refused to recognize Langton, Innocent retaliated by threatening John with excommunication and placing England under the interdict. The pope further threatened to depose John and encouraged

Philip Augustus to invade England. Realizing that he had no popular support, John submitted. In 1213, he accepted Langton as archbishop, agreed to recognize England and Ireland as fiefs of the pope, and paid homage to the pope as his vassal.

John's defeat at the hands of France and the papacy only worsened his standing with his English barons. Their quarrel with the king grew out of John's constant efforts to raise more money for the fighting in France. The king imposed illegal dues on his barons, and this practice ignored their traditional feudal rights. By 1215, their anger had caused them to join forces, and they drew up a list of demands, stating that they would make war on the king if he refused to accept their charter. On June 15, they confronted John at Runnymede and forced him to sign the *Magna Carta*, or Great Charter.

At the time, the Magna Carta was seen as an agreement between the king and his barons. It defined the rights and responsibilities of both in accordance with feudal traditions. For example, it protected the barons against the arbitrary exaction of feudal dues. Among its most important provisions was one stating that no unusual tax be levied without the consent of the king's Great Council. It also guaranteed the clergy the right to elect their own bishops and make appeals to Rome, and confirmed the charters of liberties for towns.

Although the provisions of the Magna Carta extended to freemen, the Charter did nothing for the serfs who made up the vast majority of the population. Yet eventually, the Magna Carta came to be seen as a vital step in the development of representative government. At its center was the principle that the monarch was subject to the law and must obey it just as everyone else. It provided for justice through the courts and protected some rights of free citizens. For example, if a freeman were arrested, the charter required that he be sent for trial before a court of his peers as quickly as possible. No freeman could be fined, imprisoned, or deprived of his property beyond the measure of the offense; no official could seize his property without immediate compensation; and no one could be tried more than once for the same offense.

Over time, the provisions of the Magna Carta were extended and interpreted to protect the rights of all citizens—not just the barons and Church leaders. And its influence spread. In the 17th century, the provision that the king could not raise taxes without the consent of the barons was interpreted to mean that no taxes could be levied without the consent of Parliament. In the 18th century, the personal liberties guaranteed by the Magna Carta were included in the Bill of Rights of the Constitution of the United States.

ORIGINS OF THE PARLIAMENT

By the time King John died in 1216, two basic elements of English government were gaining acceptance: the use of common law in the system of justice and the concept that the king was subject to the law. By 1300, a third element was added: the practice of consulting Parliament.

Controversies over taxation had not ended with the signing of the Magna Carta. During the long reign of John's son, Henry III (1216-1272), the English were again called on to finance wars to regain royal holdings in France. Henry's frequent appeals for funds met the stubborn resistance of his barons. In 1263, civil war erupted with Simon de Montfort, earl of Leicester, leading the rebellious barons. Simon de Montfort succeeded in capturing the king and ruled in his name for 15 months. In 1265, he summoned an assembly of barons and clergy, and he also invited two knights from each shire and two burgesses (representatives) from each chartered town. Thus, for the first time, representatives of the middle-class were consulted. This assembly and its successors became known as Parliament (from the French *parler*, meaning "to speak"). Although Simon de Montfort was soon killed in battle and Henry III was restored to power, the king continued to con-

In an effort to gather support for their rebellion against Henry III, Simon de Montfort and other barons invited knights and burgesses to attend sessions of the king's Great Council. The new assembly came to be known as Parliament. This is a meeting of the higher and lesser clergy under Edward I.

sult with these representatives whenever he needed more money.

EDWARD I AND THE MODEL PARLIAMENT

Henry's son and successor, Edward I (1272-1307), continued to centralize royal power and consult with Parliament. Edward I fought to extend royal control over Wales, annexing that land in 1284 and later naming his son and heir the Prince of Wales, a title still used today. His efforts to conquer Scotland were less successful, and he died leading an army into that land.

Edward found that by summoning meetings of Parliament, he could raise taxes and deal with popular grievances more easily. In 1295, he summoned the "Model Parliament," so-called because it followed Simon de Montfort's model of including two representatives of the knights from each shire and two burgesses from each chartered town. The barons and knights met in one group; the higher and lesser clergy in another; and the burgesses in a third. In time, the knights and burgesses found they had much in common, and during the 14th century, they joined together so that Parliament became divided into two houses: the House of Lords, consisting of bishops and nobles;[5] and the House of Commons, consisting of knights and burgesses representing the shires and towns, respectively. Although Parliament originated in the king's need to raise money, it would gradually gain additional responsibilities in the governing of the nation.

HUNDRED YEARS' WAR (1337-1453) By the 14th century, the rulers of both England and France had established the foundations for strong national monarchies. However, the goals of English and French rulers were in fundamental conflict: while the English monarchs wanted to regain the vast lands that they had held in France under Henry II, the kings of France were determined to prevent this and to expand their power over other regions such as Flanders in the Lowlands. These conflicting goals resulted in a prolonged conflict known as the *Hundred Years' War.* In fact, the Hundred Years' War was a series of conflicts interrupted by periods of unstable peace.

Besides the clash over territory, the conflict grew out of economic rivalry. The English exported much raw wool to Flanders, the center of textile-making in northern Europe. This mutually beneficial relationship pleased the English and Flemish but not the French. Flanders was nominally under the control of French overlords, and efforts by the French king to assert his control over the region led

---

[5]Gradually, the representatives of the lesser clergy stopped attending Parliament so that the clergy as a whole played a lesser role in political decisions in England than they did in the developing assemblies in France or Spain.

To symbolize his claim to the throne of France, Edward III adopted a coat of arms which combined a French symbol, the fleur de lis, with English lions. His determination to rule France led to the outbreak of the 100 Years' War.

to uprisings that the English were quick to encourage. Another issue underlying the conflict was the aid the French had provided to Scotland when England had tried to conquer that land. The immediate cause of the war, however, was a dispute over the succession to the French throne.

In 1328, the king of France died without a male heir (Chapter 21). King Edward III of England (1327-1377) laid claim to the throne through his mother, a sister of the last Capetian king. However, the French rejected Edward's claim because of the ancient Frankish tradition, known as the Salic Law, that said a woman could not inherit land. Instead, they chose Philip VI, a cousin of the last king. When Philip crushed a revolt of townspeople in Flanders, Edward pressed his claims to the French throne and prepared for war.

THE FIRST PHASE (1337-1380)

When the war began, the English had several advantages over the French. The English army was well trained and regularly paid and had acquired battle experience in its recent wars against the Scots. The English knights were accustomed to dismounting during battle and fighting alongside the infantry, who were equipped with a relatively new weapon—the longbow. This bow proved to be a valuable asset because it could discharge steel-tipped arrows rapidly and accurately for distances up to 250 yards. Finally, the English had a secret ally in the duke of Burgundy, who wanted to expand his territory to control all of France.

By contrast, France was rather poorly prepared, although it was the wealthiest nation in Europe. Philip VI had only recently been crowned king of France, and his leadership ability was unknown. French knights wore heavy armor and generally remained mounted in combat. When they dismounted, they had trouble moving about in their armor, and they refused to fight alongside ordinary foot soldiers. French soldiers were equipped with heavy crossbows, which were far less efficient or effective than the English longbows.

As a result, the English won most of the

At the battle of Crécy, English longbowmen won a decisive victory over French knights armed with crossbows. Crossbowmen (shown at left) had to reload their weapons with a crank mechanism, while longbowmen simply inserted a new arrow.

The "Black Prince," son of Edward III, won a notable victory over the French and even captured the French king. However, the prince fell ill soon afterwards, and Edward III eventually lost most of his French territories.

early battles of the war. In the first battle, Edward III won a great naval victory at Sluys (1340), which gave the English control of the Channel. Edward's next success came at the battle of Crécy in 1346 when some 10,000 English longbowmen defeated a force of 20,000 French knights. The battle was significant because it showed that the heavily armed knight could be routed by foot soldiers, and it forecast the eventual end of the mounted feudal warrior. Edward followed up this victory by besieging Calais until the inhabitants were starved into submission in 1347. Calais would remain in English hands for the next 200 years.

The next year, the Black Death, a terrifying epidemic, swept through Europe, taking the lives of at least a third of the population (Chapter 23). Despite its catastrophic effects, the fighting resumed in 1356. At Poitiers, Edward's oldest son, known as the Black Prince because of the color of his armor, overwhelmed the French and captured their king, John II. Since the French failed to pay his ransom, John remained a prisoner in England until his death in 1364.

John's son, Charles V, took up the fighting again, but suffered several defeats that left France in ruins. Before his death in 1380, however, he had managed to regain control of much of France.

CHANGES IN ENGLAND

During the war, Edward III had to ask Parliament repeatedly for funds to pursue his goals. As a result, Parliament was able to demand concessions from the king and to strengthen its role. During this period, the two houses began to meet separately.

The Black Death, official corruption, and heavy taxes to pay for the war caused peasant discontent to surface in England. In 1381, the peasants found two leaders in Wat Tyler and John Ball. An estimated 100,000 peasants marched on London where they demanded to speak to the king, Richard II. A 14th century chronicler, Jean Froissart described the events that followed:

● ● ● *They shouted much and said, that if the King would not come out to them, they would attack the Tower, storm it, and slay all who were within. The King, alarmed at these menaces, resolved to speak with the rabble; he therefore sent orders for them to retire to a handsome meadow at Mile-end, where in the summer time, people go to amuse themselves, at the same time signifying that he would meet them there and grant their demands. Proclamation to this effect was made in the King's name, and thither, accordingly, the commonalty of the different villages began to march; many, however, did not care to go, but stayed*

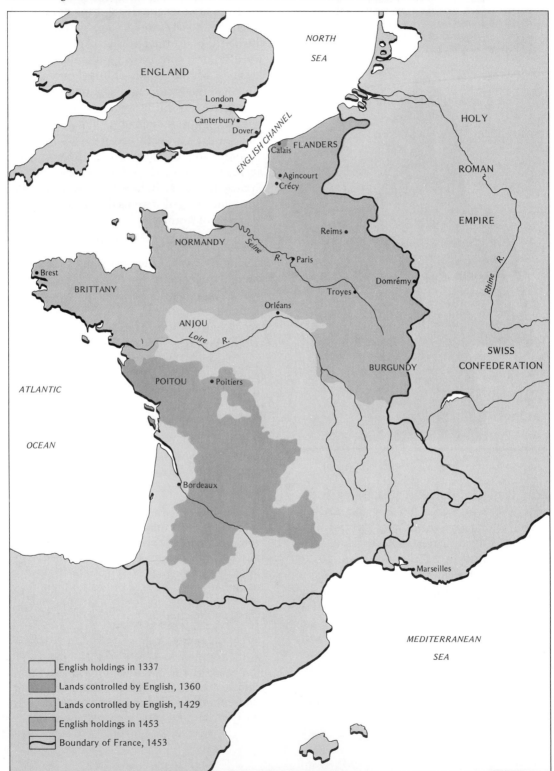

THE HUNDRED YEARS' WAR
How did England win control of so much of France in 1429? What did it control in 1453?

ENGLAND

NORTH SEA

London

Canterbury

Dover

ENGLISH CHANNEL

Calais

FLANDERS

HOLY

ROMAN

EMPIRE

Agincourt

Crécy

NORMANDY

Seine R.

Reims

Paris

Rhine R.

Brest

BRITTANY

Domrémy

Troyes

ANJOU

Orléans

Loire R.

SWISS CONFEDERATION

BURGUNDY

ATLANTIC

POITOU

Poitiers

OCEAN

Bordeaux

Marseilles

MEDITERRANEAN SEA

English holdings in 1337

Lands controlled by English, 1360

Lands controlled by English, 1429

English holdings in 1453

Boundary of France, 1453

The Peasants' Revolt. The ravages of the Black Death and the tax burdens of the 100 Years' War inspired the common people of England to desperate acts. In 1381, a large army of peasants entered London, murdered several officials, and demanded to speak to the king.

behind in London, being more desirous of the riches of the nobles and the plunder of the city. . . . When the gates of the Tower were thrown open, and the King, attended by his two brothers and other nobles, had passed through, Wat Tyler, Jack Straw, and John Ball, with upward of 400 others, rushed in by force, and running from chamber to chamber, found the Archbishop of Canterbury, by name Simon, a valiant and wise man, whom the rascals seized and beheaded.[6]

---

[6]Jean Froissart, *Chronicles of England*, vol. 1, trans. Thomas Johnes (New York: Colonial Press, 1901), pp. 220-1.

In the end, the king tricked the peasants into disbanding and captured and executed Tyler and the other leaders. The *Peasant's Revolt* was then crushed with great brutality.

England changed in other ways during this period. By the late 1300s, the English language replaced French as the official language of the court, and English was being used by writers such as Geoffrey Chaucer in the *Canterbury Tales* (Chapter 18).

Dynastic upheavals also took place. Richard II was a harsh king whose unpopular rule ended in an uprising led by Henry Bolingbroke, the duke of Lancaster. Bolingbroke took power as Henry IV and established the House of Lancaster (1399-1461). During his reign, Henry was forced to give in to the demands of Parliament, allowing it to hold discussions about important matters and accepting the right of the House of Commons to initiate new taxes. Henry V, who succeeded his father in 1413, was a more forceful personality, and he renewed the war with France.

FINAL PHASE (1415-1453)

In 1415, Henry V landed in France and met a strong French army at Agincourt. The English were aided in the battle by the powerful duke of Burgundy. As had happened at Crécy and Poitiers many years before, the English longbowmen took deadly aim at the French knights and won a stunning victory. Henry V then reconquered Normandy and forced King Charles VI of France to accept the Treaty of Troyes (1420). Under it, the French king recognized Henry's conquests, made Henry his heir, and allowed Henry to marry Catherine, Charles' daughter.

The king of England might well have ruled both England and France, but Henry V died of dysentery in 1422, leaving an infant son, the future Henry VI. When Charles VI died soon after, John, duke of Bedford, who ruled in Henry's name, claimed the crown of France for the child. The fighting erupted again as Charles VII, son of the late French king, attempted to win the throne. Charles and his

Henry V won a great victory over France at Agincourt in 1415, and reasserted English claims to the French throne. Here, he is shown wooing Catherine, daughter of Charles VI.

forces had little hope of victory until they were inspired by the visions of a young peasant woman, Joan of Arc (Chapter 21). In 1429, a French army led by Joan of Arc defeated the English at Orléans. Although Joan was later captured by the Burgundians, then tried and executed by the English, her martyrdom revitalized the French. The war dragged on, but the Burgundians later withdrew their support, after signing a separate peace treaty with Charles VII.

The French king reorganized his forces and gradually drove the English out of Normandy and Aquitaine. By 1453, when the Hundred Years' War finally ended, only Calais remained under English control. Although England's loss of its continental holdings ended a tradition dating back to the conquest, it allowed the English people and their rulers to concentrate on developing their resources at home.

By the end of the Hundred Years' War, the authority of the kings of England and France was much greater—each in his own land—than it had been at the beginning. Many feudal nobles who had opposed the centralization of royal powers had been killed in the fighting. During the long conflict, both England and France had begun to establish permanent, paid armies so that the kings no longer had to depend on their vassals for feudal levies. During this period, too, cities expanded and the money economy grew (Chapter 23), giving monarchs another source of taxable wealth besides the feudal dues levied on nobles. The importance of the feudal nobility declined for other reasons. For example, new technologies such as the longbow and the introduction of gunpowder led to new methods of fighting that would make mounted knights obsolete.

WARS OF THE ROSES (1455-1485)

Even before the Hundred Years' War ended, England was torn by dynastic disputes that led to a 30-year struggle known as the *Wars of the Roses*. The dispute pitted two families, the House of Lancaster and the House of York, against each other. Both were descended from the Plantagenet king, Edward III. During their struggle, the Lancastrians used a red rose as their symbol while the Yorkists chose a white rose.

As you have read, Henry Bolingbroke seized power from Richard II in 1399 and established the House of Lancaster. Although he and his successor, Henry V, faced social and religious discontent, they managed to retain power. During the reign of Henry VI, however, troubles arose. Not only were the English defeated in France but also the king began to show signs of mental instability. With a weak king on the throne, corruption grew. Quarrels developed among the various factions vying for control of the government, and royal officials were appointed to office in exchange for their support of one noble faction or another. The crisis broke into the open when Richard, duke of York, gained the backing of Parliament against Henry and his supporters. Although Richard died before he could be crowned king, the ambitious earl of Warwick helped Richard's son take the throne as Edward IV.

Edward established the House of York, but his reign was marked by warfare as his supporters battled the nobles who backed the House of Lancaster. During these battles, many nobles were killed.

Edward IV died in 1483, leaving two young sons. One was briefly named Edward V, but his uncle, Richard of Gloucester, persuaded Parliament to declare the boys illegitimate. The boys were imprisoned in the Tower of London and secretly murdered. Although Richard was suspected of the murder of the "little princes in the Tower," there is much controversy over his guilt or innocence. Richard was then crowned king, and as Richard III, he tried to restore order but with little success because the death of the princes and factional disputes led to new fighting.

The forces opposed to Richard found a leader in Henry Tudor, a Lancastrian who later married Elizabeth of York. In 1485, Henry returned from exile in France and raised an army that defeated Richard III on Bosworth Field. Richard was killed in the fighting, and Henry was named king. As Henry VII, he set out to assure the future of the new dynasty, the House of Tudor.

Although Henry had a vague hereditary claim to the throne, he owed his crown in large part to the acceptance of Parliament.

Henry VII, the first Tudor king, defeated Richard III at Bosworth field. He restored the prestige and power of the monarchy, and won the support of the increasingly powerful middle classes.

KINGS OF ENGLAND IN THE LATE MIDDLE AGES	
House of Lancaster	
1399–1413	Henry IV
1413–1422	Henry V
1422–1461	Henry VI
House of York	
1461–1483	Edward IV
1483	Edward V
1483–1485	Richard III

With the death on the battlefield of large numbers of nobles, Henry had an opportunity to increase royal power. An able and determined ruler, he worked tirelessly to increase royal revenues, end abuses of justice, and reestablish law and order. Henry also restored the prestige of the monarchy and thereby enhanced royal power. However, although Henry VII and his successors were forceful rulers, they did not have absolute power. During the Wars of the Roses, Parliament had strengthened its hand, and both Henry and his Tudor successors carefully avoided confrontations with Parliament that might lead to further limits on royal power.

SUMMARY

After the Romans withdrew their legions from England, the land was invaded by Germanic tribes, including the Angles, Saxons, and Jutes. The Anglo-Saxon kingdoms that emerged were later overwhelmed by the Viking invasions. In 1066, William of Normandy conquered England. William and his successors asserted their authority over rival feudal lords and created a system of royal justice.

The increase of royal power did not go unchallenged. When Henry II pressed his claim of jurisdiction over the clergy, his friend, Thomas à Becket, archbishop of Canterbury, refused to submit. King John's failure on the battlefield and violation of feudal rights of his nobles led to the signing of the Magna Carta. In the 13th century, Parliament began to take shape as an assembly with representatives from the clergy, nobility, and middle class. In time, Parliament would gain greater power, especially when it won the "power of the purse."

During the Hundred Years' War, England lost its holdings in France, and Parliament increased its power. The power of the feudal nobles was greatly reduced during the Wars of the Roses when many nobles were killed. In 1485, with the accession of the Tudor king, Henry VII, England regained stability and entered on a period of development as a strong nation-state.

QUESTIONS

1 How did Anglo-Saxon traditions influence later developments in England?
2 What advantages did William's conquest of England give him over feudal monarchs elsewhere in Europe? How did William ensure royal supremacy?
3 Compare the quarrel between Henry II and Thomas à Becket in England to the struggle between the Holy Roman emperor, Henry IV, and Pope Gregory VII.
4 Study the origins and content of the Magna Carta in England and the Bill of Rights in the Constitution of the United States. How were they similar and how different?
5 What were the causes of the Hundred Years' War? Why were the English victorious in the first phase of the war? What changes took place in England during the war?

BIBLIOGRAPHY

Which books might describe the Norman conquest of 1066?

DAHMUS, JOSEPH. *Seven Medieval Queens.* New York: Doubleday, 1972. *A useful book that discusses the lives of seven medieval women who played decisive roles in history.*
DOBSON, R. B., ed. *The Peasants' Revolt of 1381.* New York: St. Martin's Press, 1970. *A valuable exploration of the various, and often contradictory, accounts of the peasant uprising in England. Uses such documents as trial records, contemporary poems, chronicles, and archives.*
GILES, ST. AUBYN. *The Year of the Three Kings, 1483.* New York: Athenaeum, 1983. *A balanced narrative of the power struggles among the noble families who were determined to control the English throne. Author presents the crimes with which Richard III is usually charged—conspiracy, child-murder and tyranny—and stimulates readers to form their own conclusions.*
KNOWLES, DAVID. *Thomas Becket.* Stanford University Press, 1971. *An excellent biography that traces Becket's complicated career from his friendship with Henry II to his murder in the cathedral in 1170.*
TETLOW, EDWIN. *The Enigma of Hastings.* New York: St. Martin's Press, 1974. *A careful examination of the events leading up to the Battle of Hastings and the battle itself.*

The value placed upon literacy and learning in the Middle Ages may be seen in such manuscript illustrations as this one, from the monastery of Lindisfarne in England.

An idyllic view of medieval peasants as they sow and reap a harvest. The economy of the early Middle Ages was based on the labor of peasants, for there were few other sources of income.

The dispute between Henry II and the Church led to the murder of Thomas à Becket, who had strongly upheld the independence of the Church.

An Anglo-Saxon king and his witan, or council, are shown in the act of dispensing justice to a subject.

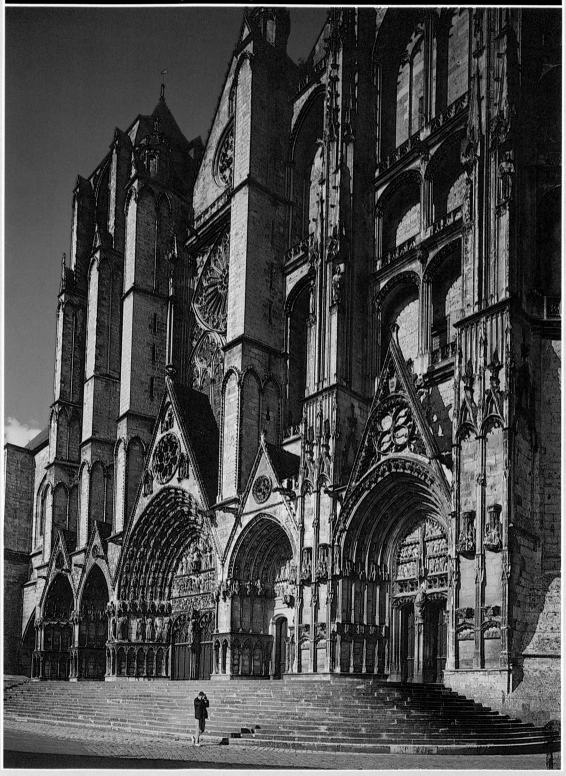

The art of master stonecutters is displayed on the west facade of Bourges Cathedral in France. In some of the decorations, stone has been cut in patterns usually used for lace.

Ghiberti's bronze doors —or "gates of Paradise"—illustrate ten stories from the Old Testament. Within each panel, the different incidents of the story are set apart by varying depths of relief.

The Mona Lisa demonstrates Leonardo's unsurpassed oil-painting technique in its delicate modeling of light and shade. The subject's enigmatic expression and the fantastic landscape in the background are also typical of Leonardo's style.

The Russians joined the Byzantine Church in the 10th century, and enthusiastically adopted its art as well as its religious doctrines. Shown is a richly decorated Russian icon from the 16th century.

A detail from the ceiling of the Sistine Chapel— the creation of the sun and the moon. The massive and powerful figure of God, his flight momentarily checked, creates the two heavenly bodies.

Raphael's School of Athens. *The composition of this fresco embodies the ideals of the High Renaissance—symmetry, individualized figures, and spatial magnificence.*

In contrast to Raphael's method, Titian places his allegorical scene in the natural world rather than in an historical setting. He conveys the idea of an ancient world by idealizing his figures.

21

> This is that house, the glory of the Franks, whose
> Praises the eternal centuries will sing.
> This is that house which holds in its power
> Gaul might in war, Flanders magnificent in wealth.
> This is that house whose sceptre the Burgundian,
> Whose mandate the Norman, and whose arms the
> Britons fear.
>
> GUY OF BAZOCHES (12TH CENTURY)

France in the Middle Ages

In the glowing description above of the palace of King Louis IX of France, the chronicler captures the sense of royal power that was emerging in France in the late 12th century. During the period from about 1100 to 1500, the rulers of France, like their counterparts in England, consolidated their power. Unlike William the Conqueror, however, who took control of England within his lifetime, the kings of France faced an array of competing feudal principalities and had to pursue a painstaking policy of expanding the royal domain.

Like Henry II and Edward I of England, a number of capable rulers helped to weld the fiefs and duchies of medieval France into a nation-state with an efficient royal bureaucracy and a strong standing army. As in England, too, the Church represented a challenge to royal authority and became the center of controversy. But in France, there was no document like the Magna Carta to support evolving ideas about representation. Although the French kings convened an assembly of representatives from the clergy, nobility, and townspeople, this assembly never gained the power that the English Parliament did.

FRANCE AFTER CHARLEMAGNE

In 843, you will recall, Charlemagne's grandsons agreed to the Treaty of Verdun that divided up his empire. Charles the Bald received the western portion, which he and his successors ruled until 987.

The weakness of the Carolingian rulers led to political fragmentation. When it became clear that the king could not defend the land against attack, strong independent nobles organized the defense of their own territories. In 887, after Odo, count of Paris, valiantly defended his city against the Vikings, the French nobles chose him king. Following his death, however, they restored the Carolingians to the throne. But by the 10th century, the descendants of Charlemagne held the title of king in little more than name. They could not control the powerful nobles who ruled a patchwork of counties and duchies as separate, independent kingdoms. When the last Carolingian died in 987 without a direct heir, the French nobles had to choose between two leading candidates: Charles, duke of Lorraine, and Hugh Capet, duke of Franconia and count of Paris. The archbishop of Rheims addressed the assembled feudal lords and clearly stated his preference:

● ● ● *Make a choice, therefore, that shall insure the welfare of the state instead of being its ruin. If you wish ill to your country, choose Charles; if you wish to see it prosperous, make Hugh, the glorious Duke, king. . . . Choose the duke, therefore; he is the most illustrious among us by reason of his exploits, his nobility and his military following. Not only the state, but every individual interest, will find in him a protector.*[1]

The nobles took the bishop's advice and chose Hugh Capet, a descendant of the famous Count Odo. Hugh established the Capetian dynasty that ruled France for 300 years.

THE EARLY CAPETIANS

Some scholars believe that the French nobles chose Hugh Capet because he was not a strong ruler and therefore posed little threat to their power. And in fact, he controlled only a small territory that stretched for about 25 miles around Paris and was known as the Ile de France. Although Hugh's domain was strategically located near the center of France, it was surrounded by the large territories of Flanders, Brittany, Normany, Burgundy, Anjou, and Poitou, whose powerful lords could command larger armies than the king.

Despite this situation, Hugh Capet and his successors slowly increased royal power and influence. First, Hugh was crowned by the Church, a ceremony which legitimized his rule. Then, with the support of the Church, he arranged for the coronation of his eldest son, thus eliminating the nobles' role in electing the new king and firmly establishing the right of primogeniture—the exclusive claim to inheritance of the eldest son. This practice ended quarrels over succession and

ensured a peaceful succession. Fortunately for the Capetians, they continued to have sons who lived to maturity and inherited the throne from 987 to 1328.

Hugh's successors used their base of the Ile de France, their alliance with the Church, and their own wits to extend their holdings. They also enjoyed long reigns that helped to ensure stability. By the 11th century, while William of Normandy was conquering all of England, Philip I (1060-1108) of France still ruled a relatively small domain extending from Paris to Orléans, an area about 150 miles north-south by 50 miles east-west, or about the size of the state of Vermont. Like other medieval rulers, Philip had no permanent capital but moved his court from one fortified stronghold to another while he fought an unending series of wars against his more powerful neighbors.

In the 12th century, French monarchs gradually increased the royal domain and consolidated royal power. Louis VI, who succeeded Philip I, came to be known as Louis the Fat because of an illness that caused him to become overweight in his later years. A more fitting name for him was Louis the Wide Awake because he traveled continually throughout his kingdom, seeking to control his feudal lords. He made Abbot Suger of St. Denis his chief minister, and with his assistance, moved against unruly nobles. He established several new towns and encouraged his subjects to seek protection from him rather than from the local feudal lords. In doing so, he built up a good relationship with the small but growing middle class of townspeople.

Louis VI increased the royal revenues substantially by imposing tolls on those who traveled on the Seine River, an important trade artery. He also tried to make travel safer by severely punishing anyone who attacked travelers. Even more important, he enhanced the prestige of the monarchy to such an extent that he was able to arrange an advantageous marriage between his son, the future

[1]"Adalbero's Plea to Elect Hugh Capet, 987," in Milton Viorst, ed., *The Great Documents of Western Civilization* (Philadelphia: Chilton Books, 1965), p. 66.

Louis VII, and Eleanor, the heiress to Aquitaine, a large, powerful duchy in southern France.

LOUIS VII

In 1137, Louis VII succeeded to the throne and married Eleanor. Raised in the wealthy court of Aquitaine, which placed great emphasis on elegant dress, gracious manner, and stimulating conversation, Eleanor became one of the most influential women in the Middle Ages. During her long life, she negotiated with popes, kings, and emperors, and was a patron of troubadours, the wandering poet-musicians who composed and sang songs extolling chivalry and courtly love.

As queen of France, Eleanor accompanied Louis to the Holy Land on the Second Crusade. She bore Louis two daughters but no son, so in 1152 he secured from the pope an annulment of the marriage. Through this unwise action, he lost much of the territory that his father had won for him. Soon afterward, Eleanor married Henry, duke of Normandy, count of Anjou, and heir to the English throne. Eleanor's vast possessions were joined with those of her new husband so that when Henry II became king of England in 1154, he ruled more of France than Louis did. In addition to Aquitaine, Poitou, and Gascony, which he acquired through his marriage to Eleanor, Henry held Normandy, Anjou, Brittany, and Maine.

English control of extensive lands in France fueled a bitter rivalry between the French and English monarchs that lasted for 300 years (see Chapter 20). Louis and his successors struggled at length against the English threat. Through plotting, marriage, and warfare, French kings slowly ousted the English and cemented a strong nation.

GROWTH OF ROYAL POWER

Between 1180 and 1314, the later Capetians expanded their control over more and more of France so that by the early 14th century the king of France was the most powerful ruler in Europe. The three shrewd monarchs who were largely responsible for this success were Philip II (1180-1223), Louis IX (1226-1270), and Philip IV (1285-1314).

Philip II. The wily ruler Philip II, who became known as Philip Augustus, pursued the two major goals of medieval monarchs —the expansion of the royal domain and the consolidation of royal power—with marked success. Through his marriage to Isabella of Haiment, Philip acquired control of Artois, which gave him access to the English Channel. During his reign, he plotted tirelessly

With her husband, Henry II of England, Eleanor of Aquitaine ruled more than half of France. Her inheritance of these vast territories limited the growth of the French monarchy during her lifetime.

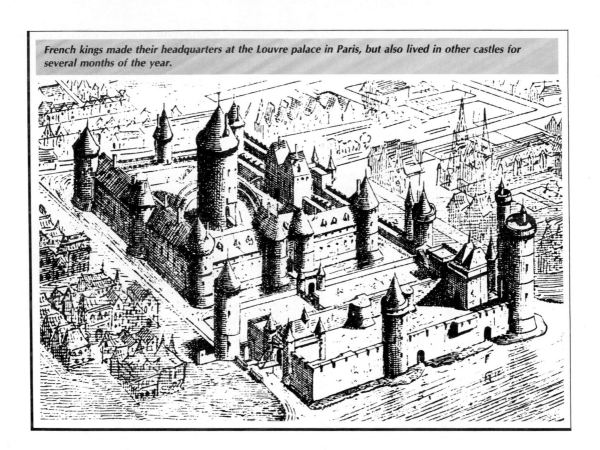

French kings made their headquarters at the Louvre palace in Paris, but also lived in other castles for several months of the year.

against the Plantagenet rulers of England. He tricked Henry II's sons, Richard and John, into rebelling against their father. Then, after Henry's death, he encouraged John to plot against Richard. As you have read, Philip joined the ill-fated Third Crusade in 1190 along with Frederick Barbarossa, the Holy Roman emperor, and Richard the Lion-Hearted, heir to the English throne (Chapter 16). The rivalry between Philip and Richard, however, led to bitter quarrels, so that the French king left his army in Palestine and returned home. After Richard died and his brother John became king of England, Philip continued his fight against John. When Philip seized Normandy and Anjou, John made an alliance with the feudal rulers of Flanders and Toulouse and with the Holy Roman emperor, Otto IV. Philip defeated this powerful alliance at the battle of Bouvines in 1214,

RULERS OF MEDIEVAL FRANCE

	Capetian Dynasty
987–996	Hugh Capet
996–1031	Robert II
1031–1060	Henry I
1060–1108	Philip I
1108–1137	Louis VI (the Fat)
1137–1180	Louis VII
1180–1223	Philip II (Augustus)
1223–1226	Louis VIII
1226–1270	Louis IX (Saint Louis)
1270–1285	Philip III
1285–1314	Philip IV (the Fair)
1314–1316	Louis X
1316	John I
1317–1322	Philip V
1322–1328	Charles IV

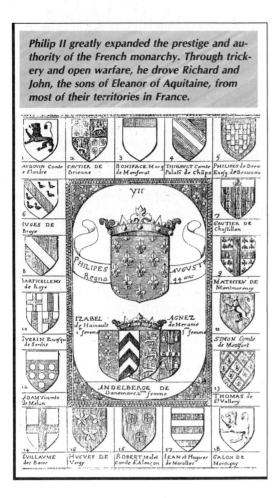

officials, Philip laid the groundwork for a bureaucracy of capable professional civil servants.

Philip amassed a sizable treasury, which he used to pave the muddy streets of Paris and to begin construction on the cathedral of Notre Dame. In 1200, he offered students immunity from certain laws if they would remain in Paris to study, a move that led to the establishment of the University of Paris.

Philip maintained fairly good relations with the Church. When Pope Innocent III called for a crusade against the Albigensians in 1208, Philip was not enthusiastic but he did allow his vassals to participate. When Philip's successor, Louis VIII (1223–1226), personally led an attack against the Albigensians, he acquired control of Languedoc, in southern France, thereby gaining access to the Mediterranean Sea.

Philip Augustus died in 1223, leaving a kingdom much larger and stronger than the one he had inherited. He had reduced the power of the feudal lords, broken the English hold on much of France, and set up an efficient administrative system. He had extended royal justice by making the *curia regis* (king's court) the highest court in the land. In time, this court became known as Parlement. By having nobles convert their feudal services into money payments and by levying a new tax, Philip had also acquired the resources to keep his own standing army.

Louis IX. Although Louis IX was only 12 years old when he inherited the throne, he later continued Philip's policies of strengthening royal power. Louis was raised by his mother, Blanche of Castile, a devout Christian who is reported to have said of her son, "I would rather see him dead at my feet, than guilty of one mortal sin." As an adult, Louis' piety and humility earned him the name Saint Louis, and less than 30 years after his death, he was canonized by the Roman Catholic Church. Louis established hospitals, asylums, orphanages, and homes for reformed prostitutes; he fed the poor at public expense

thereby gaining control of Normandy, Flanders, and Anjou, and becoming more powerful than any of his vassals.

Philip did far more than increase the size of his kingdom, for he also greatly improved its administration. He appointed new officials, many of them from the middle class, and made them directly responsible to him. Unlike the feudal nobles, the new officials owed their paid positions to him and thus formed a corps of loyal and professional administrators. They were charged with collecting revenues, administering justice in the royal courts, and keeping watch on the local nobles. In northern France, these officials were called *baillis* (bailiffs); in southern France, *seneschals*. In setting up this system of royal

Louis IX, later known as Saint Louis, participated in the Sixth and Seventh Crusades. He became famous for the fairness and impartiality of his royal courts, and was even called upon to arbitrate disputes in other countries.

● ● ● *Many a time it happened that in summer time he would go and sit down in the wood at Vincennes, with his back to an oak, and make us take our seats around him. And all those who had complaints to make came to him without hinderance from ushers or other folk. Then he asked them with his own lips: "Is there any one here who has a cause?" Those who had a cause stood up, then he would say to them: "Silence all, and you shall be dispatched one after the other."[2]*

Louis became so renowned for his fairness that he was often called on to mediate disputes between the monarchs of Europe. Within his own lands, he forbade feudal warfare, and even though he defeated the English in battle, he signed a generous treaty with Henry III in 1259 that permitted the English king to retain control of Guienne and Aquitaine. In return for these lands, the English king renounced his claims to Normandy, Anjou, and Poitou. In 1270, Louis IX died of the plague while he was on a Crusade in North Africa.

Philip IV. The third monarch to increase royal power was Philip IV, a grandson of Saint Louis, who was nicknamed "the Fair" because he was so handsome. Unlike his grandfather who was renowned for his devotion to justice and saintliness, Philip was a crafty and cruel ruler who was ruthless in his push for power. His wars with England were so costly that Philip was constantly looking for ways to raise money. When his attempts to gain control of Flanders and Aquitaine severely strained his resources, he borrowed vast sums of money from Jewish and Italian moneylenders as well as from the Templars, who had become leading international bankers. He later arrested the moneylenders and cancelled his own indebtedness. When he found himself unable to pay his debts to the Templars, he abol-

and often waited on them in person. In Paris, he built a beautiful little chapel, called Sainte Chapelle, near the cathedral of Notre Dame to house the religious relics he had acquired on his Crusade against the Moslems in 1248.

Louis IX expanded the administration of royal justice, requiring certain cases, such as treason, to be tried in royal courts. He established a supreme court of justice (*Parlement*), which was composed of trained lawyers, nobles, and members of the clergy. Common people were encouraged to bring complaints before the king's courts, and royal officials were given a maximum of 40 days to render judgment on each complaint. In the more difficult cases, Louis often sat as a judge himself. A contemporary chronicler described Louis' interest in dispensing justice.

[2]Joinville, "Memoirs of St. Louis," in J. F. Scott, A. Hyma, and A. H. Noyes, eds. *Readings in Medieval History* (New York: Crofts, 1946), p.464.

GROWTH OF THE FRENCH ROYAL DOMAIN, 1180–1337
How did the expansion of the royal domain increase the king's prestige and power?

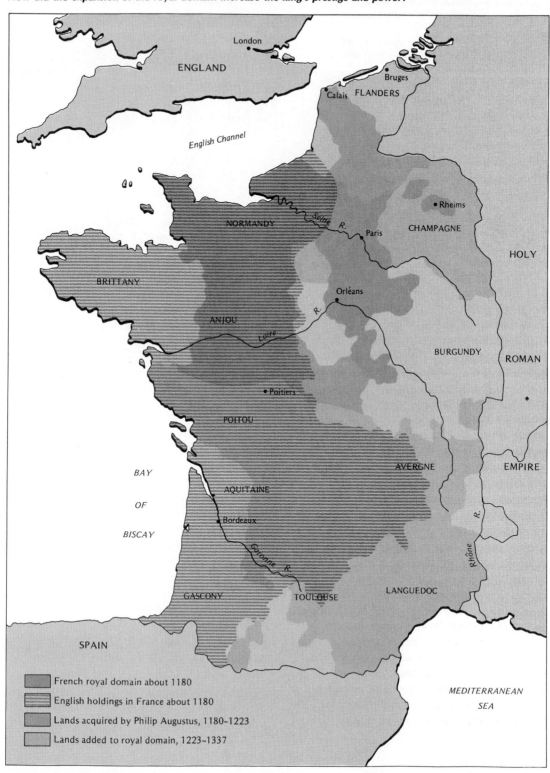

London

ENGLAND

Bruges

Calais   FLANDERS

English Channel

Rheims

NORMANDY

Seine R.

Paris   CHAMPAGNE

HOLY

BRITTANY

Orléans

ANJOU

Loire R.

R.

BURGUNDY   ROMAN

Poitiers

POITOU

AVERGNE   EMPIRE

BAY

OF

AQUITAINE

BISCAY

Bordeaux

Rhône R.

Garonne R.

GASCONY   TOULOUSE   LANGUEDOC

SPAIN

MEDITERRANEAN
SEA

French royal domain about 1180

English holdings in France about 1180

Lands acquired by Philip Augustus, 1180–1223

Lands added to royal domain, 1223–1337

The Estates General of France was first assembled by Philip IV in 1302. He was seeking its consent to additional taxes and also wanted to explain his reasons for quarreling with the pope.

ished the order, had its leaders tortured and murdered, and seized its funds.

During his reign, Philip made several improvements in government organization. He expanded the royal bureaucracy, setting up a treasury department to supervise the collection of taxes and keep accurate records of royal income and expenditure. Like his predecessors, he came to rely on middle-class professionals, many of them trained lawyers, to staff the burgeoning civil service. Increasingly, Paris became the center of the French monarchy, and the Parlement of Paris emerged as the chief court of justice.

To gain support in his efforts to increase royal revenues, Philip called for an assembly made up of representatives from the clergy, nobility, and townspeople. The assembly became known as the *Estates General*. (In France, an estate was a social class, with so-

ciety made up of three estates: the first, the clergy; the second, the nobility; and the third, the common people.) Although Philip and later rulers consulted with the Estates General and sought its backing for their efforts to raise taxes, this representative body never acquired the same power as the Parliament in England. A major reason was that it failed to get the right to approve all taxes, as the Parliament eventually did. As a result, the Estates General remained a tool in the hands of the increasingly powerful monarchy rather than an independent institution with the power to challenge royal authority.

Clash with the Papacy. Philip's need for money led him into a long-running controversy with Pope Boniface VIII. In 1296, in an effort to help finance his wars with England, Philip levied a tax on the French clergy. The pope insisted that the clergy could not be taxed without his permission and forbade the French clergy from paying. In response, Philip placed an embargo on the shipment of all gold, silver and jewels, which greatly reduced the papal revenues received from France. The pope was then forced to back down, and in 1297 he recognized the right of the French king to tax the clergy in an emergency.

The conflict between Philip and Boniface erupted anew in 1301 when Philip imprisoned a French bishop and defied the pope's order to release the man at once. In 1302, Philip assembled the Estates General to gain its support in his quarrel with the pope.

At the same time, the pope was declaring that all monarchs owed allegiance and homage to the pope in both spiritual and temporal matters. In a famous document, the *Unam Sanctam*, he claimed papal supremacy over all secular rulers.

• • • *Both swords, therefore, the spiritual and the temporal, are in the power of the church. The former is to be used by the Church, the latter for the Church; the one by the hand of the priest, the other by the hand of kings and knights, but at the command and permission of the priest. Moreover, it is necessary for one sword to be under the other, and the temporal authority to be subjected to the spiritual; for the apostle says, "For there is no power but of God; and the powers that are ordained of God; but they would not be ordained unless one were subjected to the other, and, as it were, the lower made higher by the other."*[3]

The controversy heated up when Philip charged Boniface with immorality, and the pope excommunicated the French king. In 1303, Philip sent soldiers to arrest Boniface and bring him to France for trial. When the soldiers arrived at Anagni, the pope's summer palace in northern Italy, they found him

resting from the summer heat with a crucifix on his chest. The French troops seized Boniface, but a contingent of Italian soldiers rescued him. Weakened by these struggles and ill health, the pope died soon after.

"Babylonian Captivity." Philip's effort to control the papacy did not end with the pope's death. Benedict XI, successor to Boniface VIII, chose not to continue the quarrel with Philip. When Benedict died in 1305, Philip maneuvered to have a French cardinal elected pope. Philip then insisted that the new pope, Clement V, move the papal headquarters to Avignon in southern France, giving the French king great influence over Church policies.

From 1305 to 1378, the papacy remained in Avignon, a period that became known as the second "Babylonian Captivity"—the first being the time that the Jews were in captivity in Babylon, almost 2000 years earlier. During this time, the popes appeared to be under the direct control of the French kings, and, therefore, the Avignon papacy became an object of contempt outside of France. Although Philip's victory over the papacy increased the prestige of the French king at home, it greatly reduced the influence of the pope in England and the rest of Europe.

The "Babylonian Captivity" was followed by an even greater disaster for the Church. In 1377, Pope Gregory XI returned the papacy to Rome. When he died the next year, the people of Rome forced the cardinals to choose an Italian to be pope. However, most of the cardinals were French, and once they left Rome and returned to Avignon, they met again to declare their earlier election invalid and choose a French pope. Since the Italian pope refused to resign, there were then two popes: one in Rome and one in Avignon.

During the *Great Schism* (1377-1417), as this split in the papacy was called, each pope tried to depose the other, selected his own bishops and cardinals, and claimed that he alone was the rightful head of the Church. European monarchs lined up in support of

---

[3]"The Unam Sanctam of Pope Boniface VIII, 1302," in Viorst, *The Great Documents of Western Civilization*, p. 72.

one pope or the other, depending on their individual interests. The schism caused great dismay to many devout Christians. The Great Schism only furthered the trend toward corruption in the Church since neither pope had the authority to command all of Christendom. Calls for reform multiplied, and heretical movements spread.

This chaotic situation was made worse when a Church council met in 1409 and tried to get the two popes to step down. It chose a new pope, but when the other two refused to abdicate, Christians faced the disgraceful scene of three contending pontiffs. This Great Schism finally was ended in 1417 by the Council of Constance. This council deposed all three popes and elected Martin V, who reestablished the papal court in Rome.

The new pope and his successors could not undo all of the damage to Church power and prestige that had been brought on by the Babylonian Captivity and the Great Schism. Moreover, by the early 15th century, the emergence of strong monarchies in England, France, Spain, and elsewhere had effectively limited the secular power once wielded by the Church. Although some rulers continued to work in alliance with the papacy, no pope would ever again claim supremacy over secular rulers as Innocent III and Boniface VIII had done.

14th- AND 15th-CENTURY FRENCH KINGS

House of Valois	
1328–1350	Philip VI
1350–1364	John II
1364–1380	Charles V (the Wise)
1380–1422	Charles VI
1422–1461	Charles VII
1461–1483	Louis XI (the Spider king)
1483–1498	Charles VIII

HUNDRED YEARS' WAR

The consolidation of royal power in France suffered a severe setback not long after the reign of Philip IV. On Philip's death in 1314, the throne passed in turn to each of his three sons, but none of them had a legitimate male heir. In 1328, the Capetian dynasty ended. The French nobles, you will recall, rejected the claim of King Edward III of England (Chapter 20) and chose Philip VI, head of the House of Valois and a cousin of the last Capetian king. Edward's rejected claim gave him an added incentive to challenge the new French monarch on the battlefield.

For the French, the opening phase of the Hundred Years' War brought devastation to the country, huge losses of territory, and severe social unrest. As you have read, the English won stunning victories at Crécy (1346) and Poitiers (1356) and captured the French king, John II (1350-1364). While the king was held captive, his son, the future Charles V, ruled France.

Early in the war, the French king imposed a salt tax on the people, which not only caused hardship but also led to increased discontent. The pillaging of much of France by bands of English and even French soldiers and the miseries caused by the Black Death also contributed to a peasant uprising in 1358. This revolt became known as the *Jacquerie* after Jacques Bonhomme (Jack Goodfellow), the French nickname for all peasants. During the uprising, peasants burned the manor houses of the nobles, attacked tax collectors, and roamed the countryside in mobs. A popular uprising in Paris led by a merchant named Etienne Marcel also threatened the monarchy. However, Charles V (1364-1380) managed to rally his forces, crush the peasant rebellion, and suppress the uprising in Paris. The struggle led to brutal reprisals in which an estimated 20,000 peasants were killed.

Despite his harshness, Charles V earned a reputation as an effective ruler and was known as Charles the Wise. He called meetings of the Estates General, and although this

Charles VII had little success in claiming the French throne until Joan of Arc came to his aid. Under her leadership, French armies defeated the English and brought the 100 Years' War to an end.

of Agincourt (1415). In the next few years, France suffered more setbacks, culminating in the Treaty of Troyes (1420), in which Charles VI was forced to disinherit the dauphin, as his son was called, and make King Henry V of England his heir. When both kings died suddenly in 1422, the dauphin—the future Charles VII—tried to go to Rheims to claim the throne, but he was unable to rally his demoralized forces against the English, who were besieging the city.

JOAN OF ARC

Within a few years, however, the tide began to turn when France found a savior in a young peasant woman named Joan of Arc (1412-1431). Joan lived in the small town of Domrémy, about 175 miles east of Paris. As a young girl, she began to hear "voices," which she believed to be those of saints and angels. The voices ordered her to help the dauphin claim his crown and lead the French army against the English forces in Orléans.

Because the French situation was so desperate, when Joan sought an audience with the dauphin, she was admitted and eventually convinced him of the validity of her vision. Her leadership so inspired the French soldiers that they recaptured Orléans and ended the English siege of Rheims so that the dauphin could be crowned Charles VII of France in 1429. Soon afterward, Joan was captured by the Burgundians, who sold her to their English allies.

In 1431, Joan was tried on charges of witchcraft and heresy before an ecclesiastical court and was sentenced to death by burning. During the trial, the examiners questioned her closely about her visions.

● ● ● *Asked if God ordered her to wear a man's dress, she answered that the dress is a small, nay, the least thing. Nor did she put on a man's dress by the advice of any man whatsoever; she did not put it on, nor did she do aught but by the command of God and the angels. . . .*

assembly might have taken advantage of the war emergencies to expand its power at the expense of the king, it did not. Instead, Charles managed to play on the distrust among the three estates to gain his own ends.

The Jacquerie led Charles V to accept the Treaty of Bretigny in 1360 in which the French recognized Edward's control over Calais and Aquitaine in exchange for his renunciation of his claim to the French throne. In 1369, however, the fighting was renewed, and before his death in 1380, Charles had forced the English to retreat from many regions that they had won earlier.

Charles' successor, Charles VI (1380-1422), was a weak ruler subject to periods of insanity. During his reign, the powerful dukes of Burgundy and Armagnac carried out a violent and destructive quarrel. The Burgundians finally allied themselves with the English and helped them to win the battle

In these portraits, the two aspects of Joan of Arc's life are commemorated. Left: Joan as a pious country maid from the town of Domremy. Right: As the soldier who inspired French armies to victory during the darkest years of the 100 Years' War.

Asked whether, when she saw the voice coming to her, there was light, she answered that there was a great deal of light on all sides, as was most fitting. She added to the examiner that not all the light came to him alone!

Asked whether there was an angel over her king's head, when she saw him for the first time, she answered: "By Our Lady! if there was, I do not know and did not see it."[4]

Charles VII, who owed his crown to the *Maid of Orleans*, as Joan was later called,

remained indifferent to her plight and made no attempt to help her. But Joan of Arc became a symbol of French pride and patriotism, and her martyrdom proved to be a turning point in the struggle against the English. (Later, the Church overturned Joan of Arc's conviction of heresy, and she was declared a saint in 1920.)

CHARLES VII

When Charles VII was crowned at Rheims in 1429, he was faced with overwhelming problems. The English still controlled Flanders, Brittany, Anjou, and Aquitaine; many villages had been destroyed or deserted; arable land lay uncultivated; and wolves prowled

[4]Quichert, "The Trial of Jeanne D'Arc," in *Readings in Medieval History*, ed. Scott, Hyma, and Noyes, p. 508.

the streets of Paris. Commerce had come to a standstill because the roads and canals had fallen into disrepair. Bands of robbers called "flayers" roamed the countryside. Impoverished nobles attempted to ease their financial difficulties by charging tolls for the right to cross their estates.

With the advice and support of able counselors, Charles VII turned the tide. He enlisted the aid of Jacques Coeur, an astute French banker, to improve the methods of handling the royal finances. In harmony with the spirit of unity generated by Joan of Arc, the Estates General allowed the king to levy taxes to hire soldiers whenever he needed an army, without seeking its approval. The king thus could establish a permanent standing army without relying on his nobles. With this new force, he was able to push the English out of Normandy and Aquitaine so that by 1453, when the Hundred Years' War ended, they held only the port of Calais.

By 1453, Charles had gained great popularity among the French people because of his victory over the English, and he took advantage of this success to reassert royal power. He resisted attempts by the nobles to regain their influence over the government, and he sought advice from merchants and manufacturers. He used his army to seek out and destroy the lawless bands of brigands. Roads and harbors were repaired, and wastelands were brought under cultivation. He enforced laws prohibiting the maintenance of private armies and the collection of tolls by individuals. By the end of the Hundred Years' War, therefore, the king was in a strong position. The Estates General had given him important powers of taxation, and he had limited the power of the Church and the nobles.

THE FRENCH NATION-STATE Louis XI (1461-1483) continued the process of centralizing royal power and expanding the areas under royal control. By the end of his reign, the process of welding a patchwork of rival feudal territories into a nation-state was virtually complete, and France was ready for new adventures.

Louis earned the nickname of the Spider because he wove a web of intrigue throughout Europe. Well educated, with a shrewd mind and a ruthless lust for power, Louis schemed and plotted to achieve his unscrupulous ends. While Louis XI was personally objectionable, the list of his accomplishments is impressive. He destroyed the power of the dukes of Burgundy and built a professional army that was considered the best in Europe. He chose ambitious and talented men to serve as advisers and he imposed more controls on the feudal nobility. He strengthened royal finances and kept the Church in line. He encouraged industry and commerce, further improved the roads and harbors, established a postal system, and invited foreign artisans to settle in France.

The chief rival of Louis XI was Charles the Bold, duke of Burgundy (1467-1477), who ruled the rich agricultural region of southeastern France. Charles also controlled Flan-

Charles the Bold, the powerful duke of Burgundy, continued his predecessors' quarrel with France and tried to conquer enough territory to build a new nation.

Louis XI, the Spider King, prevented Charles the Bold from seizing Alsace and Lorraine. As a result, Burgundy was incorporated into France rather than becoming the center of a separate kingdom.

ders and the Lowlands, and he was eager to gain control of Alsace and Lorraine, the regions extending along the eastern border of France.

To foil Charles' ambitions, Louis incited the leaders of the Swiss Confederation and the princes of the various states of the Holy Roman Empire located along the Rhine River to resist Charles when he marched into Lorraine in 1473. Charles died in battle a few years later, and Louis eventually gained control of Burgundy, Artois, and Picardy. At this point, all of present-day France except Brittany was united under one ruler.

In 1483, Charles VIII succeeded Louis XI as king of France, and eight years later he married Anne, the heiress to the duchy of Brittany, thereby uniting this province to France. Political unity encouraged economic development, but the growing prosperity of France led Charles VIII into ventures beyond his own borders. Like other ambitious monarchs, Charles dreamed of uniting Europe into one nation and even of liberating Constantinople from the Ottoman Turks. His dreams embroiled him and his successors in a series of struggles known as the *Italian Wars*, which lasted from 1494 to 1559.

SUMMARY

In France, as in England, the period from about 1100 to 1500 was one in which monarchs set out to centralize their authority. From a small domain centered on the Ile de France, French rulers gradually gained control over a vast kingdom. They achieved this expansion of territory through war, diplomacy, and marriage. The major figures in the emergence of the French state were Philip II, who organized the early government bureaucracy that would become a mainstay of royal power; Louis IX, who brought dignity and honor to the monarchy; and Philip IV, who built on the successes of his predecessors and triumphed over the papacy.

During the Hundred Years' War, many of these gains were lost, and for a time, France was torn apart by warfare and the rival ambitions of powerful feudal nobles. The appearance on the scene of Joan of Arc, who inspired the French to renew their struggle against the English, helped set Charles VII and his successors on the road to restoring royal authority.

During the reign of Louis XI, the Spider king, France became a unified nation with the machinery of a centralized government in place. Unlike the Parliament in England, which won the right to approve taxes, the Estates General in France did not win similar authority and instead became subject to royal power.

QUESTIONS

1 Describe the domain of the early Capetian kings. Compare it to the Carolingian Empire in 800 and to France in 1483.
2 Why were the rulers of France and England rivals throughout the Middle Ages? How did Philip Augustus use this rivalry for his own ends?
3 What was the cause of the struggle between Philip IV and the Church? How did Philip strengthen royal power in this struggle?
4 In what ways did the Babylonian Captivity and the Great Schism hurt the Church? How do you think it opened the way for the Protestant Reformation that began in the 16th century?
5 What role did Joan of Arc play in the Hundred Years' War? Why is she credited with helping to build the French nation-state?

BIBLIOGRAPHY

Which books might describe the growth of the French nation-state?

DENEUIL-CORMIER, ANNE. *The Wise and Foolish Kings.* New York: Doubleday, 1980. *An interesting account of the Valois kings who ruled France from 1328 to 1498 and helped transform France from a fragmented medieval kingdom into a modern nation-state.*

FOWLER, KENNETH. *The Age of the Plantagenets and the Valois.* New York: Putnam, 1967. *A survey of the origin of the Hundred Years' War and the structure of the late medieval society. It discusses the social and economic impact of the war on the civilian population and on the intellectual climate.*

PERNOUD, REGINE. *Blanche of Castile.* New York: Coward, McCann, & Geoghegan, 1975. *A sympathetic biography of the wise and capable ruler who dominated Europe during the first half of the 13th century. Blanche, the granddaughter of Eleanor of Aquitaine and wife of Louis VIII, was determined to unify the dissident factions in France during her successful regency for her son, the future Louis IX.*

22

> The fame of him resounds in every direction;
> more flock to My Cid, you may know, than go from him
> and his wealth increases. . . .
> My Cid Don Rodrigo did not wish to delay;
> he set out for Valencia and will attack them.
> My Cid besieges it closely; there was no escape.
> He permits no one to enter or depart. . . .
> Great is the rejoicing in that place
> When My Cid took Valencia and entered the city. . . .
> My Cid rejoiced, and all who were with him
> when his flag flew from the top of the Moorish palace.
>
> POEM OF EL CID

Nation-Building on the Periphery

By the late Middle Ages, changes were taking place all over Europe. Trade was reviving, and cities were expanding. Monarchs in England and France were extending their power over feudal nobles. The process of nation-building was affecting other parts of Europe, too. In Spain, feudal monarchs faced a unique situation because their chief rivals were the Moslems, who had conquered the land in the 8th century. The development of royal power, therefore, was often cloaked in the language of a holy crusade against the Moslems. Among the heroes of this Crusade was the Cid, a Christian knight whose capture of the Moslem stronghold of Valencia is described above. The Cid became a symbol of the emerging sense of national pride in Spain.

Other nations on the fringes of Europe emerged in the late Middle Ages, including Portugal, the Swiss Confederation, and the powerful states of Poland and Hungary in eastern Europe. Still further to the east, Russia was a latecomer to the nation-making process. After being conquered by the Mongols in 1223, Russia was isolated from the West and evolved a separate culture based on Byzantine and other ancient traditions.

SPAIN   In the early Middle Ages, Spain, like other parts of western Europe, suffered from the Germanic invasions. Early in the 5th century, the Vandals and later the Visigoths conquered the Iberian peninsula. The Visigoths established a unified kingdom with codified laws and a system of tax collection. But since the Visigoths practiced the Arian form of Christianity and most of the people they ruled were Roman Catholic, civil wars often broke out. In 589, however, the Visigoth king Reccared accepted baptism into the Roman Catholic faith, and Spain came under the protection of the Roman Catholic Church.

Despite the support that the Church gave to the Visigothic monarchy, Christianity was almost destroyed in Spain in the 8th century. As you have read (Chapter 14), Tarik, an energetic Moslem leader, crossed from North Africa to Spain in 711 and swept north at the head of a Moslem army. He easily defeated the Visigoths, whose land had become divided into several rival kingdoms. By 721, the Moslems had conquered all of the Iberian peninsula except the mountainous regions of the northwest.

MOSLEM SPAIN

In the next decades, the Moslems consolidated their control over Spain, and in 756, Abd-al-Rahman established an independent caliphate with its capital at Cordoba (Chapter 14). During the Cordoba caliphate, which lasted until 1031, Spain enjoyed a "golden age": the government was ably administered, the economy thrived, and culture flourished. The Moslems were, in general, tolerant of both the Christian and Jewish communities under their rule. Jewish communities benefited from these tolerant policies and had one of the most prosperous and culturally creative periods in their history.

Cordoba itself was a bustling, wealthy city. At a time when the population of Paris numbered barely 15,000 people and London was even smaller, Cordoba had a population of 500,000. In Cordoba, Granada, and other Spanish cities, merchants sold products from all over the world, including such delicacies as dates, olives, lemons, and peaches. Christian travelers were amazed at the goods they saw in the marketplaces, the beautiful gardens, and the splendid palaces of Cordoba.

Moslem Spain, you will recall, was also a thriving center of culture and scholarship. Arabic civilization was cosmopolitan, and Spanish cities were united to other major Islamic centers in North Africa and the Middle East. Fortunately for western Europe, peaceful contacts took place in Spain between Moslem, Jewish, and Christian scholars. Moslem scholars preserved Greek and Roman texts and translated many of them into Arabic. Later, when Christian scholars translated these works into Latin, Europe was able to recover at least some of the learning of the ancient world.

THE RECONQUEST

In the 8th century, Moslems ruled all of Spain except some tiny Christian kingdoms in the north. In time, these kingdoms became the focus of Christian efforts to conquer Spain. The first campaigns against the Moors, as Christians called the Moslems in Spain, were

SPAIN AND PORTUGAL
In what ways can the reconquest of Spain be compared to the Crusades to win the Holy Land?

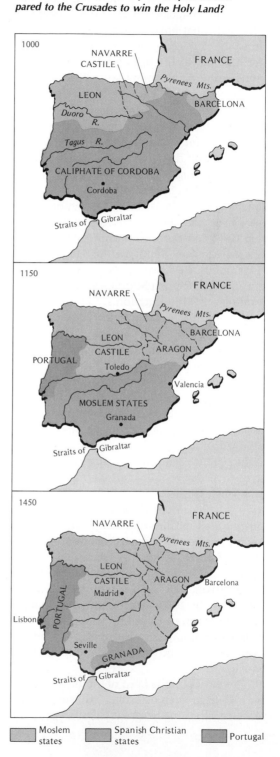

Moslem states | Spanish Christian states | Portugal

465

led by Charlemagne (Chapter 15). As you read, he crossed the Pyrenees Mountains and advanced on Saragossa (present-day Zaragoza). Although Charlemagne was forced to withdraw, he did conquer a small area in the north known as the *Spanish March*. This region became a Christian border kingdom that served as a buffer between the Franks and the Moslems. Unlike the rest of Spain, the Spanish March was influenced by the Christian and Frankish traditions.

The heroic deeds of the Frankish knight Roland during Charlemagne's campaign against Moslem Spain were immortalized in the *Song of Roland*, and this famous epic may have shaped the antagonistic attitude that Christian Europeans continued to hold toward Moslem Spain in the later Middle Ages. After the breakup of the Carolingian Empire, the Spanish March was divided into a number of tiny kingdoms: Catalonia, Galicia, the Asturias, Leon, and Navarre.

Slowly, these small Christian states in the north pushed south. The struggle by Christians to regain Spain became known as the *Reconquista* and went on for more than 500 years. By the late 10th century, the kingdom of Castile, which had grown out of the Asturias and Leon, was beginning to emerge as a powerful force in the reconquest.

In 1031, quarrels among the Moslems led to the overthrow of the caliphate of Cordoba, and Moslem Spain was broken up into more than 20 rival Moorish kingdoms. This disunity gave the Christian kingdoms in Spain an opportunity to make new conquests. Sancho the Great (1000-1035), who ruled Castile, united the local governments north of the Tagus River and led his army against the Moslems. In 1063, the pope proclaimed a crusade for the reconquest of Spain. Many knights from northern Europe answered the pope's call and traveled to Spain to fight the Moslems.

The most famous hero of the *Reconquista* was Rodrigo Díaz de Bivar, whose exploits were recalled in the great Spanish epic, *El Cid*. Although the poem romanticizes the Cid as the perfect Christian knight, in reality Díaz was an adventurer who fought for hire and battled both Christians and Moslems. He led the siege against the Moslem stronghold at Valencia and was made the ruler of that city after it was taken.

The Crusading Spirit. Like the Crusades to the Holy Land, the *Reconquista* was seen as a holy war. It continued for many centuries with periods of fierce struggle and times of relative peace between Christian and Moslem states. Like the earlier Moslem rulers, Christian rulers were generally tolerant of their non-Christian subjects. They allowed Moslem artisans and traders to conduct their businesses, which contributed to the prosperity of their kingdoms.

In Spain, the rallying point for the crusading fervor was the great cathedral of Santiago de Compostela, in northwestern Spain. According to tradition, Saint James, one of the 12 apostles, went to Spain after the death of Jesus. Although he later returned to Palestine and was possibly martyred, the Spanish Christians believed that his body had been miraculously transported back to Spain. According to legend, his burial place was revealed to a shepherd boy in about 900. When the boy reported his vision to the priests, they built a cathedral at Santiago de Compostela, where they enshrined the remains of the saint. During the Middle Ages, thousands of Christians from all over Europe made pilgrimages to this shrine, and the slogan "Santiago!" became the rallying cry for the crusade to drive the Moslems out of Spain.

Early Governments. Gradually, the Christian kingdoms of Spain pushed the Moslems further south. Within each kingdom, feudal monarchs faced problems similar to those of their contemporaries elsewhere in Europe as they tried to establish their authority. Moreover, each kingdom had assemblies known as *Cortés* made up of representatives of the clergy, nobility, and townspeople. The Cortés had the power to vote taxes, monitor finances, and petition the ruler to make new laws or reform existing ones. A ruler had to assemble the Cortés at least once a year and cooperate with it in order to win approval for any new taxes.

The rulers of these Christian kingdoms were unable to establish strong, central governments for several reasons. First, local nobles had assumed many political and military powers during the long struggle with the Moslems. Second, crusading knights from other lands had formed powerful, independent organizations, similar to the Templars and Hospitalers, that defied the local authorities. Third, the Church had been given vast estates and many privileges in exchange for its help in the reconquest, so that it was even more influential in Spain than elsewhere in Europe.

In 1212, three Christian kingdoms—Castile, Aragon, and Navarre—joined in a new drive against the Moslems and defeated them at the battle of Las Navas de Tolosa. Not long afterward, they captured Cordoba and Seville, leaving only the Argave (the southern part of present-day Portugal) and the kingdom of Granada in Moslem control.

During the next 200 years, the momentum of the *Reconquista* slowed, until it was revitalized by the forceful personalities of Ferdinand of Aragon and Isabella of Castile.

FERDINAND AND ISABELLA

By the mid-15th century, the Iberian peninsula was divided among three Christian kingdoms: Aragon in the northeast, Castile in the center, and Portugal along the Atlantic coast. In 1469, Ferdinand, heir to the throne of Aragon, married Queen Isabella of Castile. Through this marriage, they united most of Spain. At the time, royal power was weak in both kingdoms, but Ferdinand and Isabella moved forcefully to centralize and consolidate their authority—each in his or her own kingdom.

To centralize power, they allied themselves with the towns against the nobles. They

Queen Isabella of Castile. Her marriage to Ferdinand of Aragon united the two largest provinces in Spain.

gained the support of townspeople by granting them charters that spelled out the privileges and responsibilities of each town, and appeased lesser nobles by giving them honorary positions in the royal court and exempting them from certain taxes. They destroyed the castles of uncooperative nobles, seized vast amounts of treasures, and appointed royal officials loyal to the crown to positions of responsibility. They seized the property of the powerful crusading orders and established a strong standing army. They seldom consulted with the Cortés of either Aragon or Castile.

Ferdinand and Isabella strengthened the economy by establishing a uniform system of weights and measures for their united kingdoms and replacing the many kinds of money then in use with newly minted coins stamped with their likenesses. They im-

Ferdinand and Isabella receive a delegation of Jews, as a zealous monk gestures at right. During their reign, Ferdinand and Isabella expelled thousands of Jews and Moslems from Spain.

proved roads and harbors, built bridges, and organized trade fairs that attracted merchants from all over the Mediterranean world. They encouraged learning by exempting printers from certain taxes, establishing a new university, and sponsoring translations of classical Greek and Roman writings into Spanish.

Queen Isabella decided that if Spain were to become a strong nation it must enforce religious as well as political unity. To achieve this, the two monarchs made the Church a staunch ally. They thereby avoided the confrontation between Church and state that took place in other emerging nation-states. The Spanish rulers persuaded the pope to give them the authority to appoint bishops and abbots, and they introduced to Spain the In-quisition, a Church court responsible for locating and suppressing heresy.

The Inquisition had been established by the pope in the early 13th century. People accused of heresy were assumed to be guilty by the Inquisition and had to prove their innocence. They were not allowed to question their accusers and were often tortured into making confessions. In Spain, the Inquisition was organized and led by Father Tomás de Torquemada. Anyone found guilty of heresy by the tribunal of the Inquisition was burned at the stake.

By using the Inquisition to enforce religious unity, Ferdinand and Isabella increased royal power. Fear of the Inquisition made the Spanish profess their loyalty to the crown and the Church. The Inquisition di-

In the hope of finding a sea route to India, Ferdinand and Isabella subsidized the westward voyage of Columbus in 1492. His discoveries enabled Spanish monarchs to claim a large portion of the New World.

rected many of its activities against the two religious minorities of Spain: the Moslems and Jews. Although both groups had enjoyed tolerance under many earlier rulers, Christian townspeople had often attacked them, forcing some to convert to Christianity. The Inquisition ruthlessly persecuted those Moslems and Jews who had converted to Christianity but were suspected of clinging to their former beliefs.

In 1492, Spanish Jews were given a choice: convert to Christianity or leave the country at once without taking any of their property. Tens of thousands went into exile. These Jews, called *Sephardim*, settled mostly in North Africa and the Middle East. Ten years later, the Moslems were given no choice: they had to accept baptism and became known as

Moriscoes. Historians estimate that between 120,000 and 250,000 people fled from Spain to escape from the Inquisition and its persecution—most of them Moslems or Jews. Spain never recovered from this loss of its most skilled and learned citizens.

By 1492, Ferdinand and Isabella had achieved another victory in their drive toward centralizing royal power. That year, Christian knights conquered Granada, the last Moslem stronghold in Spain. Territorial unity was at last achieved. At the same time, Queen Isabella sponsored the voyage of Christopher Columbus across the Atlantic Ocean in the hope of finding a sea route to India. The voyages of Columbus and later explorers would enable Spain to acquire a vast empire in Central and South America.

Ferdinand and Isabella achieved national unity, established the basis for absolute royal power, and paved the way for Spain to become the most powerful nation in Europe. However, their successes were achieved at great cost. Many of the most talented people in Spain were forced to leave the country because of their policy of intolerance.

PORTUGAL The unified kingdom of Ferdinand and Isabella included all of the Iberian peninsula except Navarre, in the far north, and Portugal, lying along the western coast. During the early Middle Ages, Portugal was not a separate state and had the same political experience as the rest of the peninsula. For centuries, it was part of the Cordoba caliphate. Then, during the *reconquista*, it was incorporated into the Christian kingdom of Castile.

Portugal remained a province of Castile until 1095, when Alfonso VI, king of Castile, gratefully gave his daughter, Theresa, in marriage to Henry of Burgundy, a Crusader who had helped Alfonso turn back a Moslem assault. For her dowry, Theresa received Portucali and Coimbra, two counties located on the Atlantic coast between the Douro and Minho rivers. This dowry became the foundations of a new kingdom—Portugal.

Henry and Theresa were determined to convert their fiefs into an independent kingdom. After the death of her husband, Theresa continued to struggle for independence from Castile. She fortified the important towns and personally led troops on campaigns to consolidate her control. Her son, Alfonso Henriques, extracted a promise from the king of Castile to let him rule any territory south of the Douro River that he seized from the Moors.

Alfonso Henriques defeated the Moors at Ourique in 1139, but the king of Castile refused to honor his promise. Four years later, Pope Innocent III was asked to mediate the dispute between the two rulers. Although Innocent decided in favor of the king of Castile, Alfonso Henriques continued the struggle.

He offered his kingdom as a fief to Pope Alexander III, successor to Innocent III, if the pope would recognize him as the king of Portugal. In 1143, Alexander III declared Portugal to be a sovereign kingdom under the rule of Alfonso I.

EXPANSION

Since the kingdom of Portugal was bounded to the west by the Atlantic Ocean and to the north and east by the powerful kingdom of Castile, the only route toward expansion lay to the south. During the Second Crusade (1146-1149), a group of knights from northern Europe helped Alfonso free the cities of Lisbon and Santarem from the Moors. The capital of Portugal eventually was moved from Coimbra to Lisbon.[1]

Sancho I (1185-1211), son of Alfonso I, earned the nickname "the Colonizer" (*O Povoador*) because he encouraged Christians to settle in the areas that his father had seized from the Moors. Like other medieval monarchs, he and his immediate successors worked to consolidate royal power by controlling the decentralizing forces of the Church and the nobles. They set up royal commissions charged with recovering lands that they believed the Church had gained illegally. They also expanded royal territory, and in 1249, Alfonso III (1248-1279) captured the last Moslem stronghold in the Algarve region of Portugal.

DINIS

The most important ruler of medieval Portugal was Dinis (1279-1325), known as "the Farmer King" (*O Lavrador*) because he both encouraged his nobles to cultivate their lands and distributed uncultivated tracts to the

---

[1]According to tradition, Lisbon had been founded by the legendary Greek hero, Ulysses, during his wanderings after the fall of Troy. On several medieval maps, the city that is now called Lisbon appears as *Ollissibona* (meaning "Ulysses the Good").

peasants. Dinis founded a school of agriculture to teach farmers better methods of growing crops, raising animals, and controlling soil erosion. As a result of these efforts, the farmers were able to satisfy local needs and developed a surplus that could be sold abroad. To transport this surplus to foreign countries, Dinis organized a merchant marine and encouraged mariners from other lands to settle in Portugal and teach the Portuguese the most modern techniques of navigation.

Dinis required that all official documents be written in the vernacular rather than in Latin, thereby stimulating the use of Portuguese. In 1278, he limited the Church to its existing holdings. He supported poets and scholars and founded a university in Lisbon. During his reign, Portugal achieved political and territorial unity, and its borders have remained unchanged since then.

As in Spain, the Cortés in Portugal at times tried to assume an important role. But the makeup of the Cortés in Portugal was even less representative than the ones in Spain because only the clergy and nobles—and not townspeople—could send official representatives. The Cortés did not develop into a powerful institution, however, since it met only when called into session by the monarch and did not have the right to enact laws.

IMPORTANT MONARCHS OF PORTUGAL

1139–1185	Alfonso Henriques
1185–1211	Sancho I
1245–1279	Alfonso III
1279–1325	Dinis
	House of Aviz
1385–1433	John I
1438–1481	Alfonso V
1481–1495	John II
1495–1521	Manuel

HOUSE OF AVIZ

In 1385, Portugal faced a serious threat when the king of Castile launched an all-out offensive to regain this former province. Portugal preserved its independence under the successful leadership of John I, who established the Aviz dynasty. The House of Aviz set Portugal on a course of expansion that would bring it to the height of its power in the 15th and 16th centuries.

In 1386, John concluded the Treaty of Windsor with England, gaining its support against Moslem and Spanish threats. This treaty is still in effect, making it the oldest political alliance in Europe. John also continued the offensive against the Moors, attacking Moslem strongholds in North Africa.

John's youngest son, Henry (1394-1460), known as Prince Henry the Navigator, followed his example. Prince Henry was driven

Prince Henry the Navigator, although not a sailor himself, encouraged and subsidized voyages to unknown lands. His ventures marked the beginning of the Age of Exploration.

In 1498, Vasco de Gama reached India with the help of Arab pilots from Africa. The valuable cargo of spices he brought back demonstrated the profitability of such expeditions.

In the 15th century, the Portuguese planted trading outposts on the coast of Africa, paving the way for their future empire. Under King John II (1481-1495), the Portuguese sailor, Bartholomeu Dias, rounded the tip of southern Africa (1488), which he named the Cape of Storms. The king renamed it the Cape of Good Hope because it offered the chance of fulfilling a dream: the discovery of an all-water route to the riches of the East. Such a route would break the trade monopoly long held by the northern Italian city-states and give Portugal access to the spices and other trade goods of the East.

When Vasco da Gama reached India in 1498, he opened a sea route to the East. Other navigators followed, and within a few years Portugal controlled a rich commercial empire in India and the Far East.

THE SWISS CONFEDERATION

While Spain and Portugal were cementing their respective frameworks for strong, unified nation-states, other states were emerging elsewhere in Europe. In the Holy Roman Empire, you will recall, the pattern of political development had fallen away from centralization with the emergence of numerous small, virtually independent duchies, counties, and baronies (Chapter 19). Although these states and even some "free cities" such as Lübeck and Ulm owed nominal allegiance to the Holy Roman emperor, most went their own ways. The disunity of the empire enabled several small *cantons*, or states, to emerge on the western frontier. These cantons formed the nucleus of the Swiss Confederation.

EARLY HISTORY

Around 500, the Franks made Helvetica part of the Frankish kingdom. Three centuries later, Charlemagne introduced Christianity into the region now called Switzerland. Several monasteries were established, the most important of which was Saint Galen, which still exists. After the division of Charle-

by religious and economic motives to encourage Portugal to look outside its borders for new opportunities. A devout man, he pursued the Crusade against the infidels by seizing Arab towns along the coast of North Africa, where he dreamed of establishing a Christian kingdom. Because Portugal was poor in land and resources, expansion overseas offered the promise of wealth and power.

Early in the 15th century, Henry set up a center for the study of navigation that would enable Portugal to push its explorations out into the Atlantic and cautiously move south along the coast of West Africa. In 1419, Portuguese sailors reached the Madeira Islands; in 1427, the Azores; and in 1445, the Cape Verde Islands.

magne's empire, most of the area came under the rule of the Holy Roman Empire.

Although feudalism developed in this mountainous region, it did not take hold as firmly as elsewhere, and the peasants enjoyed more freedom than their counterparts in other parts of Europe. Free peasants began to govern themselves through local assemblies. In time, some of the towns that were located on important trade routes—such as Basel, Lucerne, and Zurich—developed into major cities.

In 1231, the Holy Roman emperor, Frederick II, granted the canton of Uri, on Lake Lucerne, a charter guaranteeing it certain freedoms from local feudal lords in exchange for its pledge of loyalty. Soon after, the canton of Schwyz (from which the name Switzerland is derived) received a similar charter.

In 1291, the cantons of Uri, Schwyz, and Unterwalden took the first step toward breaking away from the Holy Roman Empire. That year, they drew up a treaty in which they agreed to defy their feudal obligations to the Holy Roman emperor, render mutual assistance if any one of them was attacked, and settle their internal disputes by arbitration. This union was first known as the *League of Upper Germany*, then as the Swiss Confederation, and in the 19th century as Switzerland.

STRUGGLE FOR FREEDOM

The succeeding centuries saw the Swiss Confederation meet numerous challenges to its independence. Many stories emerged of heroic defenders repulsing powerful invaders. In 1315, Duke Leopold I of Austria invaded Schwyz. As his army marched through the narrow pass at Morgarten, the Swiss peasants, who had assembled on the mountainside above the pass, rolled huge boulders and logs down onto the invaders. They then attacked and defeated the trapped Austrians. Between 1332 and 1335, five more cantons, including Zurich and Lucerne, joined the confederation.

In 1386, Duke Leopold III attempted to invade Switzerland, but the Swiss again defeated the Hapsburgs of Austria and won recognition of their independence. In the 15th century, a dispute that arose between the townspeople of Zurich and the peasants of Schwyz led to another invasion and a Hapsburg alliance with the citizens of Zurich. However, the armed forces of the other cantons inflicted a decisive defeat on the combined armies of Zurich and Austria. Zurich renounced its alliance with Austria and rejoined the confederation. Louis XI of France, who had provided mercenary troops to help Austria, was so impressed with the fighting abilities of the Swiss that he attempted to recruit them to fight for him. The pope, too, recruited Swiss fighting men, an arrangement that still exists in the Swiss Guards who protect the Vatican City.

Although the Swiss Confederation represented a small and not very powerful force, it did influence events in Europe. For example, in 1476, it decisively defeated the ambitious duke of Burgundy, Charles the Bold, greatly reducing the forces of this once powerful ruler. Unfortunately, the victory produced a rift among the cantons when they attempted to divide the spoils. Since the confederation did not have a strong central government to enforce its decisions, there were often disputes between the larger urbanized cantons and the smaller rural ones. Early in the 16th century, the Swiss entered into their only expansionist enterprise. France, you will recall, had become involved in the Italian Wars under Charles VIII and seized parts of northern Italy. The Swiss, who were determined to control the Alpine passes leading into Italy, successfully attacked the French in 1512 and 1513 but were later defeated by them. The Swiss Confederation then retreated from its policy of expansion.

The Swiss Confederation differed markedly from the other emergent nation-states of western Europe. Although its borders were gradually defined and it won independence from the Holy Roman Empire, it did not have a strong centralized government. Instead, it was a union of many states with a weak federal government. Each canton preserved its own character and culture, choosing its own language and religion. The remarkable feature of this small landlocked nation is that it preserved its independence and unique government system even while revolutionary upheavals transformed the powerful states on its borders.

EASTERN EUROPE During the Middle Ages, eastern Europe was culturally very different from western Europe. Most of it had not been ruled by Rome or influenced by Roman civilization. Christianity was not brought to the peoples of eastern Europe until much later than the West, and even then, two churches—Roman Catholic and Eastern Orthodox—competed for victory in converting the Slavs, Magyars, and other peoples of the area. Feudalism did develop in eastern Europe, but it evolved later than in the West and differed in significant ways. The process of nation-building was also different in eastern Europe and was interrupted in the 13th and 16th centuries by Mongol and Turkish invasions.

During the Middle Ages, various groups of migrating people settled along the eastern shores of the Baltic, were conquered, uprooted, and forced to move again. Among those who would leave their mark on the region were Germans, Prussians, Poles, and Lithuanians. In the 10th century, Otto the Great encouraged Germans to colonize the Slavic lands to the east, initiating a policy of expansion that would continue for 1000 years. In the 13th century, the Teutonic Knights, whose crusading order had been founded a century earlier, descended on the pagan Slavs in Prussia to force them to convert. In time, the Teutonic Knights carved out their own states that later were absorbed into the kingdom of Prussia.

POLAND

To the south of Prussia lay the exposed, flat plains of north-central Europe inhabited by the West Slavs. In the late 10th century, the West Slavs, who lived between the Oder and Vistula rivers, were united under a powerful tribe known as the Polanians, or dwellers of the plains. Their chieftain, Miesko, signed a treaty with Otto I, in which the Holy Roman emperor promised not to invade Poland in his "drive to the east."

In 965, Miesko married Dubravka, a Roman Catholic princess of Bohemia, and was baptized a Christian. Within a short time, the Catholic Church became one of the most important institutions in Poland, and so it remains. In 1000, Miesko's son and successor, Bolesaw I, became the first Polish ruler to bear the title king.

From the 11th to 13th centuries, dynastic struggles left Poland weak and divided into many small, independent duchies. Invasions by the Prussians from the north and the Mongols from the east created further chaos. In 1241, the Mongols swept into Poland from the steppes of southern Russia. They burned towns, looted churches, and massacred people. They invaded again in 1259 and 1287. The Teutonic Knights also defeated the Poles and expanded their power in the Baltic region.

In the 14th century, Poland had several rulers who strengthened royal power. Wladislaw I (1320-1333) arranged alliances with Hungary and Lithuania that ensured peace with these neighbors. His son and successor, Casimir III, moved to establish a strong central government. He reorganized the administration of the royal courts, and ordered a comprehensive code of laws to be compiled so that a uniform system of law could be set up for the entire kingdom. Casimir also enacted many measures to improve the economy of his kingdom. He pursued a program of draining marshes and clearing forests to create new farmland, and stimulated trade by improving roads, building bridges, and

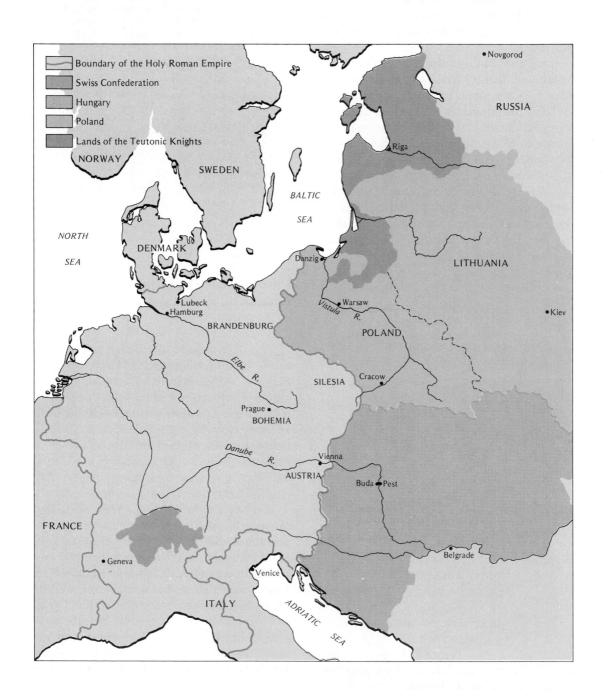

Boundary of the Holy Roman Empire
Swiss Confederation
Hungary
Poland
Lands of the Teutonic Knights

NORWAY

SWEDEN

BALTIC

SEA

NORTH

SEA

DENMARK

Novgorod

RUSSIA

Riga

LITHUANIA

Danzig

Lubeck
Hamburg

BRANDENBURG

Warsaw

Vistula

R.

Kiev

POLAND

Elbe

R.

SILESIA

Cracow

Prague

BOHEMIA

Danube

R.

Vienna

AUSTRIA

Buda Pest

FRANCE

Geneva

Venice

ITALY

ADRIATIC

SEA

Belgrade

strengthening the monetary system. He supported the development of new towns and of cultural centers such as the University of Cracow. He invited Jews, victims of religious persecution in other parts of Europe, to settle in Poland.

Later in the 14th century, the Polish throne went to Casimir's daughter, who became Queen Jadwiga and married Jagello, grandduke of Lithuania in 1384. The marriage merged Poland and Lithuania into the largest kingdom in Europe. In 1410, the kingdom was further expanded when Jagello crushed the Teutonic Knights in the battle of Tannenberg. Under the terms of the treaty that ended the fighting, Poland gained western Prussia; east Prussia (Pomerania), although ruled by the Teutonic Knights, became a vassal state of Poland.

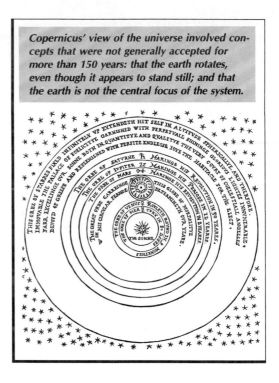

Copernicus' view of the universe involved concepts that were not generally accepted for more than 150 years: that the earth rotates, even though it appears to stand still; and that the earth is not the central focus of the system.

Nicolaus Copernicus was one of Poland's most famous native sons. His theory that the sun, not the earth, was the center of the universe contradicted Ptolemy's geocentric theory and was rejected by the Church.

The descendants of Jadwiga and Jagello ruled the united kingdom of Poland–Lithuania for 200 years until 1572. Although the kingdom was large and had great potential, it faced constant threats from Russia as well as from powerful nobles within. As a result, the Jagellonian dynasty was not able to continue the progress that Casimir had made in developing towns and strengthening the power of the central government.

In 1493, the first national Diet, or parliament, was established, consisting of an upper house that included clergy, nobles, and royal officials, and a lower house that included townspeople. The lower house had little power and had to defer to the nobles. The nobles also controlled the army and held the top positions in the royal bureaucracy. They jealously guarded their powers and enacted laws that reduced the free peasants to serfdom. Although their purpose was to exploit peasant labor on their lands, another effect of their policy was to cripple the economy of the towns so that a middle class could not develop.

Despite the political problems, the two centuries of rule by the Jagellonian dynasty has been called the "Golden Age of Poland." Printing was introduced at an early date, and an almanac was published in Latin in 1473. During this time, Poland produced its most famous scientist—Nicolaus Copernicus (1473-1543). He proclaimed a revolutionary theory in astronomy that shattered beliefs held throughout the Middle Ages. In this theory, he held that the earth and other planets revolved around the sun. In the 16th century, too, the Polish court flourished as a center of Renaissance culture.

HUNGARY

Another state that emerged in eastern Europe during the Middle Ages was the kingdom of Hungary. It was settled by the Magyars after their defeat at the hands of Otto the Great (Chapter 19). Late in the 10th century, the Magyars converted to Christianity. According to tradition, on Christmas Day of the year 1000, Stephen was crowned the first king of Hungary by Pope Sylvester II. Stephen is considered one of the greatest rulers of Hungary, for he set up a system of royal administration, protected the boundaries, and made the Roman Catholic faith the official religion of the kingdom.

Although Stephen laid the foundations for a strong monarchy, his successors were ineffective rulers. Because Hungary had no recognized rule of succession, dynastic struggles frequently erupted, weakening royal power. Without a strong monarchy, feudal nobles competed for control, and the lesser nobles suffered under the tyranny of the higher ones. In the 13th century, a group of nobles forced King Andrew II (1205-1235) to grant the *Golden Bull*, which provided remedies for many of the abuses that had occurred. It prohibited any noble from holding more than one important position in the government, and guaranteed that nobles could not be brought to trial, except before the king. Military obligations were defined, and a noble was allowed to dispose of his fief as he pleased unless he died without an heir, in which case the land would revert to the king. Finally, the Golden Bull granted nobles the right to resist actions of the king that violated any of its provisions. Although there were no provisions for enforcing the bull, feudal nobles asserted their rights and remained strong in Hungary.

In the 13th century, Hungary, too, felt the impact of the Mongol invasions. In 1241, the Mongols devastated the countryside and slaughtered half the population, then withdrew the next year when their leader died. Bela IV, the king of Hungary, tried to ensure against another assault by reorganizing the army and building a chain of fortresses along the borders. The king also encouraged economic growth by inviting colonists to settle in Hungary and granting liberal charters to the towns. However, Bela and his successors struggled unsuccessfully to dominate the powerful feudal nobles.

In the 14th century, Hungary reached its greatest territorial extent. A new ruling house established by Charles Robert of Anjou ushered in a new age. Charles was unable to suppress the feudal nobles, but he did impose some regulations on them. His son and successor Louis (the Great) established his capital at Buda, on the Danube River, and became a great patron of learning. During his long reign (1342-1382), he expanded Hungarian power into the Balkans. In 1370, Louis became the king of Poland as well as of Hungary, but he spent little time or effort on ruling that land, concentrating instead on bringing the feudal nobles of Hungary under royal control.

After the death of Louis, royal power suffered a decline. Sigismund (1387-1447) not only was king of Hungary but also Holy Roman emperor and king of Bohemia. Because he spent much of his time in his Germanic lands, he was unable to supervise the great lords of Hungary.

In the 15th century, the Hungarians launched several crusades against the Turks who were steadily advancing into Europe. Under Osman (1290-1326), the founder of the Ottoman dynasty, the Turks had begun a series of conquests that would eventually lead them to the gates of Vienna. In 1437, John Hunyadi, a Hungarian noble, defeated the Turks and temporarily halted their advance. In the next few years, he repeatedly fought the Turks and ended the Turkish siege of Belgrade. After Hunyadi's death in 1456, his son Mathias (1458-1490) was elected king of Hungary.

Mathias was one of Hungary's greatest kings. He reestablished royal power, codified the laws, and won the title "Mathias the Just," for his efforts to end corruption and ensure justice. He was a distinguished patron of the arts and learning, and founded a university and a library.

Mathias was not only an able administrator but also a brilliant military tactician. He formed a standing army, called the Magyar Hussars, that was the best disciplined army in Europe at the time. With it, he won victories over the Czechs, whom he expelled from northern Hungary, and over the Hapsburgs, whom he forced out of western Hungary. He annexed Moravia, Lusitia, and Silesia. In 1485, he laid siege to Vienna and forced the Holy Roman emperor to cede to him Austria, Styria, and Carunthia.

When Mathias died in 1490, Hungary was the dominant power in central Europe. However, his successors were ineffectual rulers who were forced to give up the lands Mathias had conquered and were unable to control the nobles. During this time, serfdom became more deeply entrenched in Hungary even while it was declining in western Europe. Mathias' successors also faced new threats from the Turks, who seized Belgrade in 1521

and advanced into Hungary. In 1540, the Turks conquered central Hungary, captured Buda, and set up their own government. Large parts of Hungary remained under Turkish rule until the late 17th century.

RUSSIA To the east of Hungary and Poland lay the lands of European Russia. In the early Middle Ages, from about the 5th to 8th centuries, these lands were settled by the eastern Slavs. In the next two centuries, Vikings from Sweden, called Varangians, pushed south, raiding and trading along the river routes that lead from the Baltic to the Black Sea. They extended their control over the Slavic communities and set up their own rulers in two major centers, Novgorod in the north and Kiev in the south. According to legend, a Varangian leader named Rurik became prince of Novgorod about 863, and his successors expanded their power to Kiev, which became the center of the early Russian state.

KIEVAN RUSSIA

Kiev was at the center of a loose association of city-states that thrived on trade. In the 10th century, aggressive Varangians launched raids on the Byzantine Empire, including Constantinople, and forced the Byzantines to grant them trading privileges. In the end, the Byzantine emperors not only granted them such privileges, but also began hiring Varangian mercenaries to defend their empire.

The busy trade that developed between the Byzantine Empire and the Russian city-states led to increasing cultural contacts. In 989, Vladimir, prince of Kiev, converted to the Eastern Orthodox faith and married the daughter of the Byzantine emperor. This event tied the emerging Kievan state closer to the Byzantine Empire. Orthodox priests went to Kiev and presided over the mass conversion of the Russian people. They also set up the Russian Church under the guidance of the patriarch of Constantinople.

THE GROWTH OF MEDIEVAL RUSSIA
In which directions was Russia likely to expand in the 16th and 17th centuries?

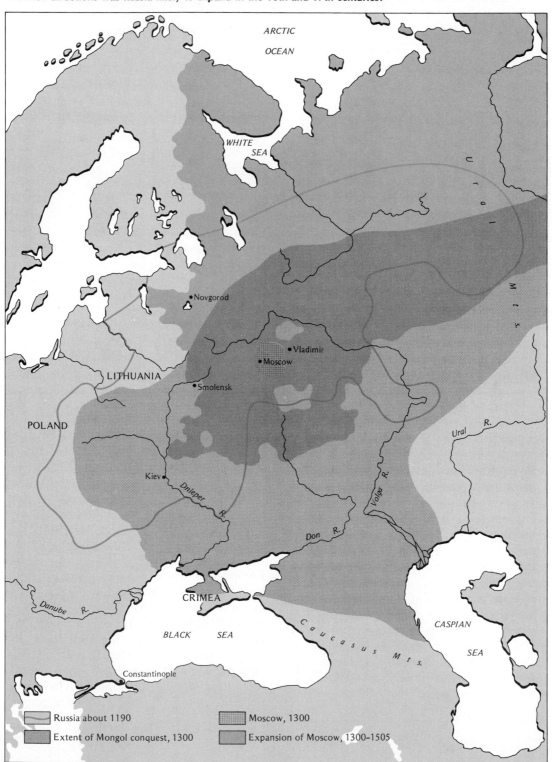

Russia about 1190

Extent of Mongol conquest, 1300

Moscow, 1300

Expansion of Moscow, 1300-1505

In early medieval Russian cities, log buildings mingled with European-style structures.

Vladimir weighed his options carefully before choosing the Eastern Orthodox Church. He looked at Islam but rejected it because Moslems were forbidden pork and wine. He turned down Judaism because he felt that the God of the Jews had failed to protect them. Roman Catholicism, he said, required too much fasting, and he was suspicious of papal claims to supremacy in secular matters. So he was left with the Byzantine Church. The fact that the Byzantine Church was ruled by the emperor probably added to its appeal.

Kievan Russia reached its height under Yaroslav the Wise (1019-1054). A scholarly and able ruler, he promoted education, codified the law, and protected his lands from invaders. During his reign, many beautiful churches were built in Kiev, including the cathedral of Saint Sophia. About this time, Russia was probably in advance of western Europe, but while the West emerged from the chaos of the early Middle Ages and revived after 1000, Russia suffered setbacks in its development. After Yaroslav's death, Kiev slowly declined under pressure from nomadic invaders and internal power struggles. In the next 200 years, other centers including the towns of Vladimir and its nearby neighbor, Moscow, began to gain prominence.

During the 14th century, Moscow became the leading city of Russia, succeeding Kiev and Novgorod. Shown are the government buildings of the Kremlin.

MONGOL INVASION

In the 13th century, Russia was overrun by the Mongols. Under their leader Genghis Khan (1155-1227), these central Asian people had embarked on a course of conquest that would give them an empire stretching from Korea in the East to Poland and Hungary in the West. The Mongols swept into the lands that they conquered with huge numbers of well-mounted horsemen. The Mongol conquest of Russia was achieved in stages, but in 1240, they captured and totally destroyed Kiev. For the next 250 years, they dominated Russia.

The "Golden Horde," or Tartars, as the Mongols in Russia were called, ruthlessly annihilated resistance, leaving terror in their wake. Once they had brought Russia under their control, however, they were relatively tolerant rulers. They let the Russians govern themselves but required them to pay a huge annual tribute in money and men to serve in the khan's army.

The Mongol conquest had profound effects on Russia. It largely cut Russia off from contacts with the rest of Europe. At a time when the intellectual and commercial life of the West was quickening, Russia was forced to submit to its overlords from the East. Although the Mongols established excellent trade routes across their Asian empire, the Russians did not benefit greatly from this commerce. Russian trade and industry declined. The Russian peasants were heavily taxed for the tribute payments to the Mongols. The Russian Church, which was not taxed, urged the peasants to submit to the

481

The Church of the Holy Trinity in Moscow. The distinctive architecture draws upon both Byzantine and Moslem traditions.

"Tartar yoke." Many Mongols intermarried with the Russians, and some of their traditions, including the low status in which they held women, were absorbed by the Russians. Politically, Russia remained a feudal state, and individual Russian princes battled one another to preserve control over their own territories.

One such prince was the Russian hero Alexander Nevski (1236-1263), prince of Novgorod. He accepted Mongol domination, seeing a greater threat in the encroaching forces from the West. He fought and won several decisive battles against invaders from the West. In 1240, he crushed the Swedes; two years later, he destroyed an army of Teutonic Knights. In 1252, he extended his rule over Vladimir, near Moscow, and after his death, his son, Daniel, founded the grand duchy of Moscow that would become the focal point of the future Russian state.

RISE OF MOSCOW

Daniel's descendants in Moscow slowly rose to prominence. Ivan I (1325-1341) earned the nickname "Moneybags" both for his miserly habits and his role as collector of the Mongol tribute from the other Russian princes. He used his carefully acquired wealth to increase his influence with the Mongols, and later princes of Moscow continued this policy. They gained the title grand prince, putting them above their rivals. The position of Moscow was further enhanced when it replaced Kiev as the headquarters of the Russian Church.

In the mid-14th century, Prince Dmitri Dinski (1359-1389) embarked on the long struggle to overthrow the Mongols. Although Mongol power was already declining, the conflict would drag on for the next century. The final defeat of the Mongols was achieved by Ivan III (1462-1505).

Ivan the Great, as he was later called, is often regarded as the founder of the modern Russian nation. A patient but shrewd ruler, he expanded the territory controlled by Moscow. In 1480, he refused to acknowledge Mongol overlordship any longer and gradually drove the Mongols out of Russia. He also renewed contacts with Europe by establishing diplomatic relations with various countries.

In 1472, Ivan married Sophia Paleologus, the niece of the last Byzantine emperor. (Constantinople, you will recall, had fallen to the Turks in 1453.) He thereby claimed to be the successor to the Byzantine and Roman emperors. Ivan proclaimed Moscow the Third Rome and adopted the Byzantine title "autocrat." Many other Byzantine practices, especially court ceremonies, as well as the concept of royal supremacy over Church and state held sway in Russia.

SUMMARY

During the Middle Ages, the process of nation-building influenced events on the periphery of Europe. As elsewhere in Europe, strong rulers tried to consolidate royal power, but the pattern of development varied greatly. In Spain, the Reconquista occupied the attention of Christian rulers for many centuries. Once the land was united under Ferdinand and Isabella, Spain was on its way to becoming the dominant power in Europe.

Portugal, Spain's neighbor to the west, developed its own distinctive government and found its greatness through the conquest of a vast overseas empire. On the western frontier of the Holy Roman Empire, the Swiss cantons offered still another pattern of nation-building. Unlike the nations of western Europe that were united under the strong centralized authority of a monarch, the Swiss Confederation was based on a loosely organized group of states.

The plains of central and eastern Europe were the setting for power struggles first among various migrating people and later among medieval monarchs eager to expand their territories. Poland and Hungary each emerged as powerful states that competed for dominance with the Holy Roman Empire. Further east, the Russian state developed, first centered on Kiev and later on Moscow. Unlike the civilization of western Europe, which was shaped by Roman traditions and the Roman Catholic faith, Russia was influenced by Byzantine traditions and the Eastern Orthodox Church. For more than 200 years after the Mongol conquest, Russia was virtually cut off from the West. During the reign of Ivan the Great, however, Russia inherited the mantle of the fallen Byzantine Empire and renewed its contacts with the West.

QUESTIONS

1 Describe the major steps in the Reconquista. How did Ferdinand and Isabella ensure unity in Spain?
2 Explain how geography and the policies of Prince Henry the Navigator helped set Portugal on a course toward winning an overseas empire.
3 In what ways was the Swiss Confederation different from other states of medieval Europe?
4 Why was eastern Europe a battleground for much of the Middle Ages? How did problems over royal succession hurt the development of both Poland and Hungary?
5 How was medieval Russia influenced by Byzantine civilization? By the Mongol invasions?

BIBLIOGRAPHY

Which book might discuss Switzerland's unique form of government?

HALECKI, O. *History of Poland.* New York: McKay, 1976. *A comprehensive history of Poland from its emergence as a Christian state in the 10th century to modern times.*

JACKSON, GABRIEL. *The Making of Medieval Spain.* New York: Harcourt Brace Jovanovich, 1972. *An excellent account of Spain from the 8th to the 16th century.*

PARES, BERNARD. *A History of Russia.* New York: Knopf, 1968. *The classic survey of the rise of the Russian people from the prehistoric Slavs to the present.*

SINOR, DENIS. *History of Hungary.* New York: Praeger, 1959. *A narrative history of Hungary that examines the impact of outstanding figures on its history and sets them in the cultural, political, social, and economic perspective of their times.*

THURER, GEORGE. *Free and Swiss.* University of Florida Press, 1971. *A fast-moving account of the development of Switzerland from earliest times through the 20th century.*

WEST AFRICA

750–1600

Africa is the second largest continent. Within its boundaries, one can fit both the United States and China. This great landmass contains a variety of climates, ranging from the desert environments of the Sahara in the north and the smaller Kalahari in the south to the belts of steppe and savanna climates that stretch across much of the continent. Only ten percent or less of the continent is rainforest, and a small fringe of land on the northern and southern coasts of Africa has a balmy Mediterranean climate.

GEOGRAPHICAL SETTING

Africa is so large that it is often divided into geographical regions. Of the two main parts—North Africa and sub-Sahara Africa—the latter has been further divided into West Africa, East Africa, and Southern Africa. North Africa is often included in discussions as part of the Middle East because it was conquered by the armies of Islam in the 7th and 8th centuries and its subsequent history and culture were closely tied to developments in the Islamic world. As a result, North Africa has generally been portrayed by Western scholars as Arabic (semitic), Islamic, and "civilized," whereas sub-Sahara Africa has been portrayed as Black (Negro), "tribal,"

and separate from the Judeo-Christian and Islamic heritage of North Africa. In the past, this division has encouraged the mistaken notion that North Africa was culturally distinct and historically separate from sub-Sahara Africa. Recent scholarship has revealed the long and continuous commercial relationship between sub-Sahara Africa—in particular the regions surrounding the Niger River—and the Mediterranean coast of Africa as well as Asia and Europe. These commercial contacts dated back to the ancient Egyptians and Phoenicians. Furthermore, as you will read, from the 8th through the 16th centuries A.D., West Africa was an important and vital link in international trade.

The first great civilizations of Africa, Egypt and Kush, were located along the Nile River—a region that provided an ample supply of fertile soil and water. The ancient Egyptians and Kushites created unique African cultures, and their achievements also had a significant impact on later European and Asian history. You are familiar with the outlines of Egyptian civilization and with the later civilizations—Phoenician, Roman, and Islamic—that flourished in North Africa. What we will focus on here are three major trading empires that emerged in West Africa.

The Arabs called the area south of the

The nomadic "people of the veil" of the western Sudan still ply some of the ancient caravan routes established by their ancestors. These nomads are watering their camels with the use of a leather bag and a trough made from a log.

Trade in Africa using camels dates to the era of Roman rule, and Carthage carried on a large trade using chariots before that. Between 750 A.D. and 1500 A.D., three major trading kingdoms emerged in West Africa: Ghana, Mali, and Songhai. Each owed its power and success to its control over trade. Well before the 8th century, when the first of these kingdoms was emerging, the basic lines of the long and extremely hazardous trans-Saharan trade had been established. After the conquest of North Africa by Islamic armies, Arab and Berber traders set up outposts in the north from which they sent their caravans south, putting themselves into this trading system. For a thousand years until the late 1800s, camel caravans traveled this dangerous two-month desert crossing. Although the risks were great, the profits were equally high.

From the north, merchants sent steel, copper, glass beads, horses, and slaves. On their way south, the caravans stopped at Taghaza, an oasis that stood above a vast salt mine. The salt that was so plentiful at Taghaza was worth its weight in gold just 500 miles to the south in the Sudan. Loading up on huge blocks of salt, the caravans plodded on to busy trading centers that grew up at the southern terminus of the desert. For the return journey, caravans carried back leather goods, cotton cloth, malaquetta pepper, acacia gum, kola nuts, and slaves. Most important, however, they stocked up on gold.

Gold and salt were the two essential commodities of the trans-Saharan trade. Whereas plentiful supplies of gold were found in West Africa, salt was rare and highly prized. The gold-salt exchange not only affected merchants in West Africa and North Africa but also had an impact on the trade of three continents: Africa, Europe, and Asia.

Before Europeans gained access to the gold of the Americas, they had no substantial gold supplies of their own. Instead, it was the gold mined in West Africa that eventually became the basis of international currencies. By the late Middle Ages, the emerging nation-states of Europe were desperate for gold. Monarchs needed money to pay their armies and civil servants as well as to finance the growing expenses of their courts. Also, as trade with the East expanded,

Sahara *Bilad el-Sudan*, or land of the blacks. In the western Sudan, the area immediately south of the Sahara and west of Lake Chad, the Niger, Senegal, and other rivers slice through the open savanna. Since ancient times, small settled populations had farmed the land, raising cereals, millet, and sorghum as well as a variety of fruits and vegetables. Because of limited rainfall and infertile soils, farming was hazardous, and villages faced frequent famines. Yet farmers did produce regular surpluses in most years until the twentieth century that were used to trade at local and regional markets. In fact, these small local exchanges formed part of a more complex trading network that linked up all parts of West Africa and carried goods to the edge of the Sahara.

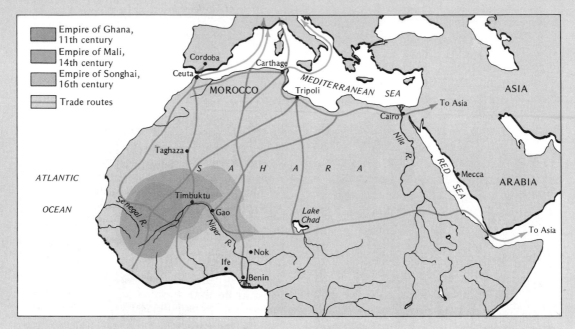

much gold was being sent overseas to buy the goods of India and China. The gold shortage was, therefore, a major concern of medieval monarchs. The influence of West African gold was evident in the English coin called a "guinea," as direct reference to its West African source. The need for gold and the desire to tap West African sources of this precious metal motivated Prince Henry the Navigator's support for voyages of exploration along the coast of West Africa.

EMPIRE OF GHANA

Gold was the foundation of the kingdom of Ghana that emerged in the 8th century and controlled the area between the Senegal and Niger rivers. Originally called Wagadu by its rulers, the name Ghana came into use because one of the king's titles was *ghana*, or "war chief." The rise of Ghana to political and economic domination over neighboring regions was achieved through its control of gold and other valuable resources. Beginning as a trading center, Ghana served as a go-between between the merchants of North Africa and the gold- and ivory-pro-

ducing land to the south. The rulers of Ghana accumulated wealth by taxing all merchants who passed through their lands. Further, the kings of Ghana established a monopoly in gold, allowing only limited quantities to leave the kingdom. In this way, they maintained a high market value for gold.

In the 9th century, Ghana reached the peak of its power, exerting influence over a large region and enjoying the outward trappings of its prosperity. The ruler of Ghana held public audiences dressed in the finest cloth and adorned with spectacular gold ornaments. With riches from gold, the ruler maintained a strong army, which he used to collect taxes and preserve order. While the king and most of his subjects were not Moslem, many of his advisers and officials were. Islam had been brought to West Africa by the trade caravans, and Moslem communities were set up in all the major trading centers.

In the 11th century, Ghana suffered a series of reversals from which it never recovered. The Almoravids, Moslems from North Africa, were inspired to fight a holy war that extended from southern Spain to West Africa. One group marched across the desert and attacked Ghana. In 1055, the Almoravids captured the important trading city of Awdaghost, and Ghana's economy was seriously weakened as a result. Smaller states controlled by Ghana took advantage of the war to revolt, further weakening the empire. Although the Almoravid movement soon collapsed, Ghana was unable to recover its former power. Slowly, it lost control of the gold trade when the states it had dominated broke away and set up their own empires. By the early 13th century, the merchants of Kumbi, capital of the old empire, abandoned the city in favor of other trading centers.

EMPIRE OF MALI

Out of the ruins of Ghana, the small subject state of Kangaba on the upper reaches of the Niger River put together the foundations of a new empire. The Malinke people lived in this region, where they practiced farming. According to tradition, a ruler named Sundiata defeated rival rulers around 1235 and expanded his base of power to include the regions formerly ruled by ancient Ghana. Sundiata took control of the rich gold bearing region of Wangara and within a few years greatly increased his power. The new empire became known as *Mali*.

By the 13th century, the kings of Mali were Moslem, and they were supported in power by Moslem officials and merchants. The majority of the people were pagan, but the rulers of Mali permitted them to practice their ancient traditions with toleration. Like its predecessor, the empire of Mali was built on farming villages but gained wealth and power from its control of the gold-salt trade. During this time, Timbuktu became a great trading center and developed into a city renowned for its learning.

The best known ruler of Mali was Mansa Musa (1312–1337), who achieved fame for his fabulous pilgrimage to Mecca in 1324. At the head of the vast caravan, he led an estimated 60,000 people on the journey across Africa. In Cairo, Moslem chroniclers counted some 500 slaves, each carrying a staff of gold. They commented on the camels laden with gold and other riches and applauded the ruler's decision to

Islam was introduced into West Africa by Arab traders during the 7th century. Shown is a group of Moslems in front of a mosque in present-day Mali—all traffic has ceased during the time of prayer.

carry home Moslem scholars, poets, and architects to improve his empire. During this pilgrimage, Mansa Musa was said to have given away so much gold that the general value of gold was depreciated for the next 12 years.

The empire of Mali flourished until the late 14th century. But then struggles over succession weakened royal power, and in the 15th century attacks by desert nomads and revolts from within further undermined its foundations.

EMPIRE OF SONGHAI

Among the subject states that broke away from Mali was the trading city of Gao. About 1464, Gao and the surrounding Songhai lands were ruled by an especially able king, Sunni Ali, also known as Ali Ber or Shi. He spent much of his reign in battle and conquered a large empire across West Africa. He recaptured Timbuktu from desert nomads and annexed other trading centers that had once been part of the empire of Mali. In addition to battling his enemies, he also built the framework for an imperial government. Sunni Ali died in 1492, the year Christopher Columbus set sail from Spain.

Songhai reached its greatest extent under the reign of Muhammad Toure, better known as Askia Muhammed (1493–1528). A devout Moslem, Askia won the support of the leading merchants and Islamic religious leaders. During his reign, Islam became the official religion of Songhai, and he made all state laws conform to Islamic law. In addition, he established a government bureaucracy in which promotions were based upon merit to run the day-to-day operations of the empire. Further, he continued to expand the borders of the empire, making Songhai the largest empire ever seen in West Africa.

Although Askia put together this vast empire, neither he nor the rulers that followed him were able to ensure a peaceful line of succession. By the late 16th century, the pattern of decline again developed as disunity within and attacks from without weakened the great trading empire. In 1591, the ruler of Morocco launched an attack on Songhai from across the desert, hoping to gain access to the gold country of West Africa. The Moroccans were far outnumbered by the forces of Songhai, but they had the advantage of weapons, being armed with muskets that sent terror through the ranks of the Songhai soldiers. After its defeat at the hands of these invaders, Songhai quickly collapsed. No large successor state emerged as in the past; instead small kingdoms struggled to survive the constant attacks of desert raiders. Despite the uncertainties and dangers, camel caravans continued the ancient gold-salt exchange across the desert and into West Africa.

The age of the great West African trading kingdoms ended in the late 16th century at a time when the newly emergent nation-states of Europe were taking to the seas, ushering in an era of overseas exploration. The urgent need for gold had been somewhat allayed by the discovery of vast gold and silver resources in the Americas. To many Europeans, however, West Africa still meant gold, and it was to the "Gold Coast" that they continued to look for new riches. For the next several centuries, West African rulers held the newcomers in check and determined the terms of the trade. Only in the late 19th century did both internal and external forces create the conditions that would lead for the first time to the conquest of West Africa by European powers.

INTRODUCTION TO THE DOCUMENTS

Until relatively recently, Western scholars knew little about African history except in the regions occupied by the Nile River valley civilizations and Ethiopia. Slowly, however, they have pieced together a knowledge of the people who developed their own distinct cultures in other parts of Africa. In West Africa, for example, the art and artifacts of the Nok culture have provided useful information about the early Iron Age in this region.

In addition to archaeology, much information about West Africa was provided by the oral traditions of the people. In West Africa, as elsewhere on this vast continent, oral history was preserved and passed along from one generation to the next. Such oral histories might record events that took place hundreds of years earlier. The most important written sources for West African history after about 1000 A.D. are writings of Africans. The Tarikh al Sudan and Tarikh al Fattash, chronicles written in Timbuktu, are the most important sources for Mali and Songhai. Yet another source of information, especially after 1000 A.D., are the written works of Moslem scholars, who based their accounts on the reports of Arab travelers to West Africa. With the growth of the trans-Saharan trade came an influx of Moslem scholars and religious leaders into West Africa, and they also added to the record of the great West African kingdoms.

DOCUMENT 1   WEST AFRICAN PROVERBS

Every group of people that has a long history also has a set of proverbs and moral tales associated with its experiences. Many of the communities of Africa have rich oral histories and tales which present religious as well as moral lessons. The selections that follow include proverbs from a variety of West African people, including the Asante of Central Ghana.

Rain beats a leopard's skin, but it does not wash out the spots. [Asante]

Wood already touched by fire is not hard to set alight. [Asante]

One falsehood spoils a thousand truths. [Asante]

When a man is wealthy, he may wear an old cloth. [Asante]

Hunger is felt by a slave and hunger is felt by a king. [Asante]

The ruin of a nation begins in the homes of its people. [Asante]

When a king has good counselors, his reign is peaceful. [Asante]

By the time a fool has learned the game, the players have dispersed. [Asante]

When you are rich, you are hated; when you are poor, you are despised.
    [Asante]

A crab does not beget a bird. [Ghana]

If you find no fish, you have to eat bread. [Ghana]

One camel does not make fun of the other camel's hump. [Guinea]

To make preparations does not spoil the trip. [Guinea]

Knowledge is like a garden: if it is not cultivated, it cannot be harvested.
    [Guinea]

A wise man who knows his proverbs can reconcile difficulties. [Niger]

Ashes fly back into the face of him who throws them. [Niger]

Familiarity breeds contempt; distance breeds respect. [Niger]

Proverbs are the daughters of experience. [Sierra Leone]

SOURCE: Charlotte and Wolf Leslau, eds., *African Proverbs* (Mt. Vernon, N. Y.: Peter Pauper Press, 1962), pp. 7-42.

Compare one of these proverbs to a proverb of a Western civilization.

DOCUMENT 2   TIMBUKTU

Timbuktu was founded in about the 12th century and became one of the richest and most distinguished centers of learning in West Africa during the empire of Mali. In the early 16th century, a Moroccan traveler named Leo Africanus visited Timbuktu and left this description.

Here are many shops of artificers and merchants, and especially of such as weave linen and cotton cloth. And hither do the Barbary [North African] merchants bring the cloth of Europe. All the women of this region except the maidservants go with their faces covered, and sell all necessary victuals. The inhabitants, and especially strangers . . . are exceedingly rich. . . . Here are many wells containing most sweet water; and so often as the river Niger overflows they convey the water thereof by certain sluices into the town. Corn, cattle, milk, and butter this region yields in great abundance. . . . The inhabitants are people of a gentle and cheerful disposition, and spend a great part of the night singing and dancing through all the streets of the city. Here [in Timbuktu] are great store of doctors, judges, priests, and other learned men, that are bountifully maintained at the king's cost and charges. And hither are brought diverse manuscripts or written books out of Barbary, which are sold for more than any other merchandise.

SOURCE: Richard W. Hull, *African Cities and Towns Before the European Conquest* (New York: Norton, 1976), pp. 13-14.

How did geography contribute to the importance of Timbuktu?

The legendary city of Timbuktu prospered from the trade across the Sahara Desert.

TIME LINE FOR WEST AFRICA AND EUROPE

WEST AFRICA		EUROPE	
640	Islamic armies capture Egypt; Moslem traders begin to visit West Africa		
750	Empire of Ghana controls gold trade of West Africa	750	Islamic armies under Omayyad Dynasty conquer all of North Africa and Spain
1055	Decline of Ghana; Almoravids (Moslems from North Africa) capture Awdaghost	1066	Norman conquest of England
1235	Sundiata creates empire of Mali	1180–1223	Philip Augustus strengthens French monarchy
1324	Mansa Musa's pilgrimage to Mecca; empire of Mali at its height	1337–1453	Hundred Years' War
1400	Decline of Mali		
1464	Sunni Ali unites empire of Songhai, largest kingdom in West Africa	1453	Fall of Constantinople to the Turks
1493–1528	Askia Mohammed strengthens empire of Songhai; adapts Islamic law	1492	Columbus sets sail from Spain; reaches "New World"
1591	Moroccans invade Songhai; empire collapses		

Europe in Transition

- All things that are exchanged must be somehow
  comparable. It is for this end that money has been
  introduced, and it becomes in a sense an
  intermediate; for it measures all things.

  ARISTOTLE

- Of couse the Renaissance culture was an aristocratic superstructure raised upon the backs of
  the laboring poor; but, alas, what culture has not been?...We shall not defend the despots...
  but neither shall we apologize for Cosimo and his grandson Lorenzo, whom the Florentines
  obviously preferred to a chaotic plutocracy. As for the moral laxity, it was the price of
  intellectual liberation; and heavy as the price was, that liberation is a valuable birthright of
  the modern world, the very breath of our spirits today.

  WILL DURANT

- There are two ways of contesting, the one by the law,
  the other by force; the first method is proper to men,
  the second to beasts; but because the first is frequently
  not sufficient, it is necessary to have recourse to the
  second.

  MACHIEVELLI

- The arts of painting, sculpture, modeling and architecture had degenerated for so long and so
  greatly that they almost died with letters themselves, but in this age they have been aroused
  and come to life again.

  LORENZO VALLA

A merchant wishing that his worth be great
Must always act according as is right;
And let him be a man of long foresight,
And never fail his promise to keep. . . .
He will be worthier if he goes to church,
Gives for the love of God, clinches his deals
Without haggle, and wholly repeals
Usury taking. Further, he must write
Accounts well-kept and free from oversight.

DINO COMPAGNI

Economic Development in the Late Middle Ages

Between about 1050 and 1300, western Europe made enormous economic progress. This progress was so striking that historians consider it one of the most impressive achievements in European history. For three centuries before the year 1000, Europe had been ravaged by Viking, Moslem, and Magyar invasions. Most of the people had lived and died on the manors where they were born, their energies consumed by the struggle to survive. Diets were poor; trade was negligible; money had virtually disappeared; the few towns of any size that had survived the fall of Rome were stagnant.

By 1300, this bleak picture had been completely transformed. More and better food was being produced. Trade was booming, both within Europe and between Europe and the East. Under the impetus of trade, old cities were expanding, and new towns were springing up. Luxury goods were being imported from the East. Money had become an important medium of exchange, facilitating the exchange of goods and services. This chapter will explore the reasons for this remarkable economic development and the far-reaching changes that accompanied it.

AGRICULTURAL REVOLUTION

The major force behind the economic progress of the later Middle Ages was an agricultural revolution that began in the 11th century. The revolution almost completely transformed the way Europeans grew their food. As a result, peasants produced more to eat. More food meant that the European population could expand: by 1300, there were three times as many people living in western Europe as there had been in the year 1000. In turn, the production of surplus food and the growing population allowed people to become involved in activities outside the manor and thereby encouraged the growth of trade and cities.

The agricultural revolution was the result of several factors, including the political stability that developed after the mid-11th century and changes in the climate of western Europe, which became somewhat warmer and drier from the 8th to 13th centuries. With the decline in feudal warfare and the emergence of national monarchies came an atmosphere of political security that encouraged new ventures such as the clearing of land for farming. The more favorable climate also fa-

The heavy plow included a deep blade and a curved iron to turn over the sod. Because the plow was difficult to turn, fields were made as long as possible.

vored farming, and peasants began to cultivate land in northern France, England, the Low Countries, and Germany.

Political stability also enabled Europeans to take advantage of important inventions in agricultural technology that were made about this time. Among the most useful of these was the development of the heavy plow. With it, peasants could till the heavy soils of northern Europe. New harnesses were invented, including a tandem harness which allowed farmers to use more than one team of animals. As a result, peasants could yoke horses and oxen together to pull heavier loads. The use of iron horseshoes gave horses better footing on rough terrain.

By the 8th century, European peasants had discovered the value of the three-field system of crop rotation (Chapter 17). Before modern fertilizers, part of a farmer's land had to lie fallow each year to avoid exhausting the soil. The Romans had left half of their arable land uncultivated each year. Medieval farmers reduced this to one-third by dividing their plots of land into three parts. Each year, one part would lie fallow, and one part would be sown with grain in the fall that was harvested in the early summer. The third part would be sown in the spring with a different crop, usually beans or oats, that was harvested in the late summer. Thus, while Roman farmers had only been able to have one harvest a year, medieval farmers had two.

Moreover, the widespread growing and eating of beans made for a much healthier diet, since in combination with bread, the mainstay of the peasant diet, beans make up a complete protein.

With the increased grain supply that these methods provided, peasants could increase their livestock. More pigs, cattle, sheep, goats, and poultry meant more meat, milk, cheese, butter, and eggs for Europeans to eat or sell to townspeople.

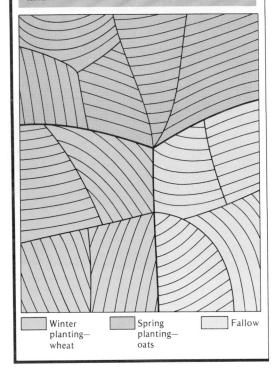

In the three-field system of agriculture, one field was left uncultivated each year, while the others were planted with different crops in the fall and spring. Peasants were allotted strips of land in each of the three fields.

Winter planting— wheat
Spring planting— oats
Fallow

a water wheel into up-and-down motion, or into the faster motion of a smaller wheel. Water-powered mills soon dotted the landscape and allowed people to perform a multitude of tasks—such as grinding grain, tanning leather, forging iron, or even brewing beer—much more efficiently than before. Windmills, invented in Holland around 1170, enabled regions without rivers to utilize wind power for these tasks.

The 13th century saw both the invention of the spinning wheel, which would revolutionize the making of cloth, and the start of commercial coal mining. We do not know when Europeans discovered that coal would burn, but by the 13th century it was being extensively mined near Liege, in what is now Belgium. The use of coal as fuel in the later Middle Ages was made necessary by the deforestation of large parts of northern Europe. As more and more land was cleared for agriculture to feed the growing population, peasants and townspeople could no longer rely on the forests for fuel.

In the late 15th century, new mining tech-

TECHNOLOGY There were important technological advances made at this time that would influence European life profoundly. Soap, for example, was invented in the late 12th century. The Greeks and Romans had cleaned themselves with oil, usually olive oil, that had to be laboriously scraped off afterward. Soap was much easier to use and store. Like many new products, soap at first was a luxury available only to the rich, but it gradually fell in price and became accessible to the poorer classes.

During the Middle Ages, a variety of mechanical devices were invented to convert running water into a source of power. With the use of gears, cams, and pulleys, engineers were able to convert the circular motion of

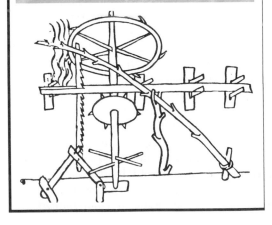

Medieval engineers harnessed water and wind power for many tasks. Shown is a water-powered saw: circular movement is converted to the up-and-down motion of the saw by means of the cams on the wheel shaft. The diagonal twig serves as an automatic feed device, keeping the saw pressed against the wood.

A medieval mining operation. Water and wind power were used to extract ores, to operate the bellows that heated blast furnaces, and to drive the hammers used in forging.

The design of the three-masted carrack, with triangular sails, made navigation of open seas much more feasible. Older ships had just one mast and a square sail.

niques made it possible to extract ores more effectively than before. Horizontal and vertical shafts were braced with timbers, and water-powered or horse-powered devices were developed to pump water from mines. Large power-operated bellows were devised to increase the temperature of fires used for smelting ores and producing cast iron. In turn, the increased availability of cast iron meant more iron tools for farmers and artisans.

Technological advances also made ocean travel more safe and efficient. The magnetic compass and astrolabe, which reached Europe from China during the 13th century, and charts of shorelines and harbors made navigation safer. Also in the 13th century, shipbuilders developed a caravel, a three-masted ship with a rounded bottom that could be operated in shallow water and could be steered in a cross wind. Larger three-masted ships, called *carracks* or *galleons*, were built to carry heavier cargoes. As cargoes became more valuable, many merchant ships carried soldiers and, increasingly after 1400, cannons, for defense against pirates.

TRADE AND COMMERCE On the foundation of the agricultural revolution, trade expanded. As manors produced more food than they needed, the lords began to trade some of it for luxuries or other goods that the manor did not produce. This trade expanded swiftly within Europe and was also directed toward the East after the Crusades increased the growing taste among nobles for luxuries such as silks and spices.

During the Crusades, merchants from Venice, Genoa, and Pisa set up a highly profitable trading enterprise. They purchased luxury goods in the Levant[1] and carried them by ship to ports in Italy and southern France. (These luxury goods had been brought to the Levant by caravans from Persia, India, and China as well as from Moslem lands in North Africa.)

The main French port for the eastern trade was Marseilles. From there, merchants transported the goods up the Rhône valley to the interior of France. At the same time, merchants from cities in Germany and other countries of northern Europe bought goods at Venice or Genoa and carried them across the Alps and along the Rhine valley. Goods that were taken by land into northern Europe were then shipped by water to Britain and Scandinavia. The merchants from the south traded their wares for grain, leather, and especially wool, the principal products of northern Europe.

As trade expanded, the region along the North Sea—known as the *Lowlands* (or Netherlands) because it was low, flat, marshy terrain—came to prominence. In the western part of the Lowlands, called *Flanders*, the Flemish found raising sheep was more profitable than growing grain because sheep thrived on the abundant marsh grasses of the region. As early as Charlemagne's day, the Flemish were renowned for the fine woolen cloth that they produced, and Flemish cloth became a medium of exchange in the commerce between Europe and the East. Since the finest wool available was that produced by English sheepherders, merchants began

A woolweaver and his tools. The textile industry was central to the economies of both England and Flanders.

to import wool from England. As a result, sheepraising expanded in England, and the English and Flemish wool industries became interdependent.

Early in the 14th century, Venetian merchants created what came to be known as the "Flanders Fleet"—ships that traveled 2500 miles along the coast of western Europe from Flanders to Venice. The sea route was easier and less expensive than the 400-mile overland route because ships did not have to pay tolls, climb mountains, ford rivers, or pass through hostile countries. Since Venetian merchants also controlled many trade routes to the East, Venice became a thriving marketplace for goods from every part of the world. It was the most cosmopolitan European city, and also profited from its own distinctive industries such as glass-making and printing.

As trade expanded in the 12th and 13th centuries, towns along the major European trade routes began to set up trade fairs. There, the merchants from various regions met to

---

[1]The eastern coastline of the Mediterranean Sea—present-day Syria, Lebanon, and Israel—was long known as the *Levant*.

498

International trade fairs enabled merchants to expand their businesses and to exchange ideas and opinions with people from other countries.

settle accounts for past shipments and arrange for future trade.

Fairs came to be held annually at such places as Champagne, Ghent, Leipzig, and Winchester. The nobles on whose lands the fairs were held found it profitable to provide services such as special courts to settle disputes, guards to protect the merchants and their goods, clerks to keep track of transactions, and even sheds in which people could meet.

Fairs served as useful centers not only for the exchange of goods but also for the diffusion of ideas. Unlike the markets in towns and villages, which were local affairs, these trade fairs were international. In time, these fairs helped to break down the isolated world of the manor and introduced peasants and nobles to a wider world.

GROWTH OF GUILDS As towns grew, merchants and artisans began to unite in mutual-aid associations known as *guilds*. In time, guilds acquired considerable power: they regulated the quantity and quality of the goods that were produced; set the price for goods; and protected the interests of guild members.

During the Middle Ages, two kinds of guilds emerged: merchant and craft guilds. The merchant guilds were the first to appear, and their goal was to control trade within a certain area. All the merchants in a town would join together to supervise trade, see that foreign merchants paid certain taxes, and regulate weights and measures. If disputes arose, they were settled at the guild courts. Guilds helped to protect merchants on their travels and negotiated with guilds in other towns on issues such as the payment of debts.

Guilds also served religious, social, and charitable functions. They held festivals to honor the patron saint of the guild. At guild meetings, members enjoyed fine dinners with the best food and entertainment in the town. The guild paid the burial expenses of a member who died and contributed to the family of a member who became incapacitated. One guild, for example, made this provision for its members:

• • • [I]f by chance any of the said trade shall fall into poverty, whether through old age or because he cannot labor or work, and shall have nothing with which to keep himself, he shall have every week from the said [offering] box seven pence for his support, if he be a man of good repute. And after he decease, if he have a wife, a woman of good repute, she shall have weekly for her support seven pence from the said box, so long as she shall behave herself well and keep single.[2]

CRAFT GUILDS

In the 11th century, the growth of trade and the specialization of labor within the towns led to the emergence of craft guilds that eventually superseded the merchant guilds. Workers in each trade such as weaving, leatherworking, goldworking, baking, and so on organized themselves into guilds and allowed only people practicing the same craft to join. Like merchant guilds, the craft guilds supervised the production of goods, and each guild had a monopoly over its own product. By controlling the quality of articles they produced, the guilds protected consumers against shoddy goods. The use of poor ma-

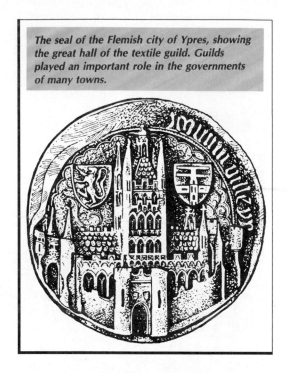

The seal of the Flemish city of Ypres, showing the great hall of the textile guild. Guilds played an important role in the governments of many towns.

terials or the sale of badly made goods could lead to a fine or expulsion from the guild.

Each craft guild limited its membership by establishing a system for admitting newcomers. To become a guild member, a worker had to pass through three stages from apprentice to journeyman to master craftsman. Boys who were accepted for training as apprentices received no pay but were given food and shelter. After anywhere from 3 to 12 years, an apprentice was examined on the skills he had learned. If he passed the examination, he was admitted to the guild as a *journeyman* (from the French *journée*, meaning "a day's work") and could be paid for his work. When he reached the age of 23 years, a journeyman was eligible to submit a *masterpiece*, a complete work to prove his skill in his craft. If his masterpiece were accepted by the guild, he became a master craftsman, was admitted to the guild, and could open his own shop.

As guilds grew in power, they assumed leading roles in the government of the towns. In Florence, for example, the Wool Guild,

[2]"Rules of the Guild of White-Tawyers," quoted in J. H. Robinson, ed., *Readings in European History*, vol. 1 (New York: Ginn, 1904), p. 411.

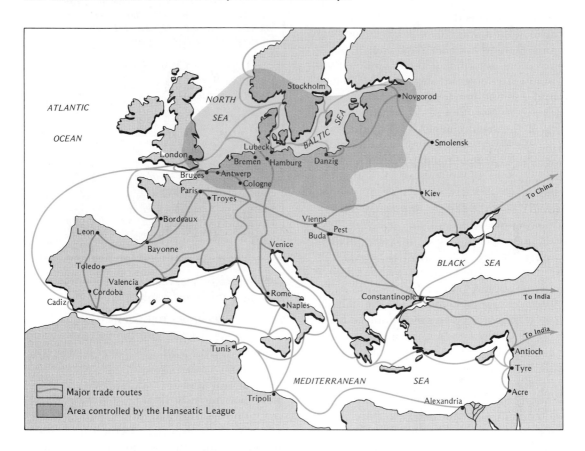

Major trade routes

Area controlled by the Hanseatic League

Silk Guild, and Guild of Bankers and Moneylenders dominated the government. Guilds hired watchmen to patrol the streets, contributed to the building of churches and cathedrals, and set up schools and hospitals.

By the end of the Middle Ages, the guild system had become rigid and restrictive. Often, membership was limited to sons of members. As a result, many young men were forced to remain journeymen, or day-wage laborers, without the hope of being admitted to the guild. The earlier ties of loyalty and trust between journeyman and master craftsman were replaced by frustration and bitterness. In some cities, the discontent of journeymen led to riots, especially during times of economic depression.

THE HANSEATIC LEAGUE

Early in the 14th century, the merchants from several major coastal towns on the Baltic and North seas formed a guild to secure trading privileges for its members in foreign ports. As the guild succeeded in this objective, it attracted the attention of merchants in other ports, and it grew to include members from almost 200 cities. This guild grew into the powerful *Hanseatic League* that dominated the trade of northern Europe for almost 300 years.

In time, the league achieved a virtual monopoly on trade in northern Europe. It gained control of many business operations from England to Russia. It established its own navy to protect the ships and ports of member cities and developed its own system of weights and measures to standardize transactions among the members.

The league was governed by merchant representatives from each of the member cities, but the governing body seldom met unless an emergency threatened. Nevertheless, the league had great political influence because of its wealth and economic domination of the region. When that control was broken in the 16th century, the power of the league rapidly declined.

MONEY ECONOMY In the early Middle Ages, as you have read, most people lived on self-contained manors. The few goods that they needed from the world outside the manor were acquired by barter. In the 11th century, however, the economic climate began to change. Slowly, money transactions began to replace barter as trade revived, and for the first time since the fall of Rome in the 5th century, coins were used as a medium of exchange.

By the 13th century, the use of coins was widespread in Europe. Medieval monarchs and the city-states of northern Italy issued their own coins and established their own monetary systems. As the demand for coins grew, nobles mortgaged or sold their lands to raise the cash they needed. Townspeople also began to use cash, and money came into use at the trade fairs. Of all the coins in use during the late Middle Ages, the ducats of Venice and the florins of Florence were the most widely accepted.

To prevent the counterfeiting of money, individual rulers ordered that gold and silver coins in their lands be minted, or stamped, to a standard size, weight, and design. By this means, they tried to ensure its value by preventing the substitution of less valuable metals, such as tin or copper, for the gold or silver in the coin. Certain Italian merchants began to specialize in the evaluation of coins. Because they weighed and analyzed coins on

As coins became a common medium of exchange, certain merchants began to specialize in moneychanging and lending. They usually worked on a banc, or bench.

benches, or *bancs*, their business operations became known as "banks."

CHANGING ATTITUDES TOWARD WEALTH

The revival of trade and the increased economic activity meant that some people had a surplus of cash, while other people wanted to borrow: monarchs needed money to wage war, merchants to finance trade, nobles to buy luxuries. However, the Church prohibited Christians from practicing usury—that is, charging interest on money.

In the 4th century, Augustine had condemned usury in these words:

● ● ● *I will not have you be money lenders, and for this reason, that God would not have you so. . . . If you have lent your money, that is to say, advanced a loan to someone from whom you expect to receive interest, and not only in money, but in whatever you gave, whether wheat or wine or oil or anything else; if, as I said you expect to receive back more than you gave, you are a usurer, and in this respect you deserve blame and not praise.*[3]

---

[3]*St. Augustine on the Psalms*, vol. 2, trans. Scholastica Hebgen and Felicitas Corrigan (London: Longman, 1961), p. 110.

Therefore, during much of the Middle Ages, some Christians chose to lend their money through Jewish middlemen, who were not restricted by the prohibitions of the Church. Moreover, money lending was one of the few occupations permitted to Jews in medieval society. Most states and cities forbade Jews to own land, practice a profession, or join a guild.

In the later Middle Ages, however, the Jews were overshadowed as money lenders by the Italian merchant-bankers. As commerce and manufacturing expanded, entrepreneurs found it necessary not only to borrow money occasionally, but also to have standardized coins, and to secure places to store money and a safe way of transporting money over long distances. The Italians specialized in these activities. When the importance of such transactions became apparent, the Church removed some of its restrictions on making loans by approving of "reasonable" rates of interest. After this, usury came to mean "the charging of excessive rates of interest."

The quickening economic pace of the late medieval period affected other ideas about acquiring wealth. When the guilds first appeared, they established what was called a "just price" for the goods they produced. In accordance with Church teachings, which condemned making large profits at the expense of others, the just price for an article would include the cost of the material plus a justifiable (small) profit. After setting a just price, the guild was not supposed to change it. As the money economy expanded, however, the attitude of merchants and entrepreneurs changed so that it became possible to charge high prices—or whatever customers would pay—and the making of large profits was no longer condemned as severely.

Enterprising people studied the best ways to do business, and in the 15th century, books began appearing that offered advice on how to operate a successful business. The advice given in the excerpt below might well appear in a business textbook today:

• • • Do not exercise any trade or business in which you have no experience. Do what you are able to do and beware of everything else, for [otherwise] you would be cheated. And if you want to become experienced in anything, practise it as a child, be in shops . . . and in banks with others, go abroad, frequent merchants and merchandise, see with [your own] eyes the places and countries where you have in mind to do business. Try a friend—or rather the man whom you believe to be a friend—a hundred times before you rely upon him a single time, and never rely on anyone so deeply that he may ruin you.[4]

RISE OF BANKING

In the late Middle Ages, merchants and other people handling large sums of money developed a form of banking. They learned that the safest way to move money was by accounting entries: that is, coins were deposited at one point—in Milan, for example—and other coins of the same value were picked up at a distant point such as London. The receipt for a deposit made in 1248 demonstrates how this system operated.

• • • March twenty-eighth, in the year of the Incarnation of the Lord, 1248. I, Giraud Alaman, money-changer, citizen of Marseilles, confess and admit to you, Peter Mazele of Baza, that I have had and received from you by way of deposit ten pounds of mixed money now current in Marseilles . . . I have promised to give and pay to you these ten pounds or to a known messenger of yours or to any one whom you command to receive it, whenever it shall please you. Pledging my goods, etc.; renouncing all delays of the law, etc.[5]

Because the city-states of northern Italy were at the center of the growing money

---

[4]Written in Florence in 1393, quoted in R. S. Lopez and I. W. Raymond, *Medieval Trade in the Mediterranean World* (New York: Norton, 1955), pp. 422 and 375.

[5]Roy C. Cave and Herbert H. Coulson, eds., *Medieval Economic History* (Milwaukee: Bruce Publ. Co., 1936), p. 144.

economy, it was in this region that several families set up the first banking businesses. The Peruzzi family, for example, made a business arrangement with the pope to collect taxes in England for the Church. With profits from this activity, the Peruzzis developed a network of banks in 16 cities across Europe and loaned money to the kings of Naples and England. Their enterprise, however, collapsed when the king of Naples repudiated his debt, and warfare bankrupted the English treasury.

The Medici family of Florence established many independent banks throughout Europe and set up a system to ensure against collapse. The manager of each branch was made responsible for any loans he made and could not expect the debts that he incurred to be assumed by other branches or by the parent bank in Florence. If one Medici bank failed, there would thus be no serious effect on the others. The Medici family became so wealthy that they not only dominated the government of Florence (Chapter 24) but also won control of the papacy and married into the ruling dynasties of Europe.

In France, the most prominent banker was Jacques Coeur (1395–1456), the son of a fur merchant of Bourges. When his father died, Coeur inherited the business, which he and his associates developed into a company that dealt "in every class of merchandise . . . in which they could make a profit."[6] The company established warehouses in several cities, developed mines, and carried on trade with the Middle East.

In 1437, the king of France chose Coeur to organize the mint, and two years later, appointed him treasurer-steward of the royal household. Coeur lent money to rulers, nobles, popes, and in exchange arranged prosperous marriages and high ecclesiastical positions for his children. When jealous no-

bles spread accusations against Coeur, the wealthy banker was imprisoned and tortured, and his property was confiscated. Fortunately for Coeur, the pope intervened to prevent his execution. Coeur escaped from prison in 1454 and fled to an island in the Aegean Sea, where he died two years later.

A leading German bank was established by Jacob Fugger (1459-1525), who was born in Augsburg. Fugger studied to become a monk but later left the monastery to work in the textile industry. He accumulated wealth and became an important moneylender. He loaned vast sums to popes and to the Holy Roman emperor, Maximilian I. His son, Jacob "the Rich," loaned 500,000 gulden to bribe the electors of the Holy Roman Empire to choose Maximilian's grandson as Emperor

Jacob Fugger was one of the most prosperous medieval bankers. He had branch offices in Nuremberg, Venice, Lisbon, Rome, and many other cities.

[6]Kenneth Setton and National Geographic Society staff, Age of Chivalry (Washington, D. C.: National Geographic Society, 1969), p. 303.

Charles V. In return for these loans, the Fuggers gained the right to exploit gold and silver mines in Hungary and Spain. The Fuggers had branches in all the chief cities of Europe. Before the family abandoned banking in the 17th century, they had been granted the title of prince by the emperor.

BUBONIC PLAGUE In the mid-14th century, economic progress came to a temporary halt. The chief cause was an epidemic of bubonic plague, which had originated in Asia and struck Europe in 1348.[7] It is estimated that by the time the plague, which became known as the Black Death, had run its course, it had killed from a third to a half of the population of Europe. Giovanni Boccaccio, a prominent writer of the 14th century, described attempts to thwart the disease:

• • • *[In] spite of all means that art and human foresight could suggest, such as keeping the city clear from filth, the exclusion of all suspected persons, and the publication of copious instructions for the preservation of health; and notwithstanding manifold humble supplications offered to God in processions and otherwise; it began to show itself in the spring of the aforesaid year [1348], in a sad and wonderful manner. Unlike what had been seen in the east, where bleeding from the nose is the fatal prognostic, here there appeared certain tumours in the groin or under the armpits, some as big as a small apple, others as an egg; and afterwards purple spots in most parts of the body; in some cases large and but few in number, in others smaller and more numerous, both sorts the usual messengers of death. To cure this malady,*

The bubonic plague, or Black Death, swept through 14th-century Europe with devastating force, killing one-third of the population and permanently altering the basic values and beliefs of the survivors.

neither medical knowledge nor the power of drugs was of any effect.[8]

ECONOMIC AND SOCIAL DECLINE
The plague killed so many people that there was a critical shortage of labor in agriculture and industry; fields lay fallow, and sheep roamed untended over the pastures. Survivors were stunned by the devastations caused in the three years from 1348 to 1351. Many people wandered homeless through the countryside. Others turned to robbery. Because of the labor shortage, able-bodied workers could charge high wages. In England, King Edward III issued the Statute of Laborers in 1351 to regulate wages and prices and stop the growth of vagrancy.

---

[7]Outbreaks of the bubonic plague had occurred before. In the 5th century B.C., the plague had struck Athens during the Peloponnesian War. An outbreak occurred in the 3rd century A.D. in the Roman Empire. The plague swept through Europe twice in the 14th century, appeared in England in the 17th century, and took huge tolls in India in the late 19th century.

[8]Giovanni Boccaccio, *The Decameron*, in J. F. Scott, A. Hyma, and A. H. Noyes, eds., *Readings in Medieval History* (New York: Crofts, 1946), p. 495.

Medieval physicians did not know how the plague was spread, but took various precautions to avoid contagion. In this satiric portrait, a doctor's protective clothing includes a bird mask.

... And because many strong beggars as they may live by begging, do refuse to labor, giving themselves to idleness and vice, and sometimes to theft and other abominations; none upon the said pain of imprisonment, shall, under the color of pity or alms, give anything to such, who are able to labor, or presume to favor them in their idleness, so that thereby they may be compelled to labor for their necessary living.[9]

The effects of the plague were felt everywhere. In government, experienced officials who died from the plague were replaced with men who were often incompetent and sometimes unscrupulous. Economic activity declined everywhere. Goods became scarce,

causing prices to rise rapidly. Sharp price increases in turn led to further social unrest.

For the rest of the 14th century and well beyond, Europe suffered from the damage of the plague. A second outbreak in the same century caused new panic but took a smaller toll, and the populations of nations such as England or France did not reach their pre-plague levels for 100 years. The economic dislocations were matched by a sense of demoralization. People had seen their families, friends, and neighbors die in a matter of days; they had suffered from the looting, burning, and lawlessness that the breakdown in order had brought.

The plague was not the only factor in the economic decline of the 14th century. The economies of France and England were greatly disrupted by the Hundred Years' War (1337-1453) that wasted enormous resources in both countries and produced widespread social unrest. Thus, the peasants of France rose up in the Jacquerie Rebellion of 1358, and the English peasants revolted in 1381. The uprisings were crushed with brutal measures, but they further contributed to the economic depression of the century.

LASTING CHANGES The 14th century was a time when unsettling currents were undermining the fabric of medieval society. As you have read, the power of the Church declined in the later Middle Ages. In the 14th century, monarchs in England and France consolidated their power and clashed with the Church in disputes over taxes and jurisdiction in legal matters.

The rise of national monarchies and the shift to a money economy changed the way of life of feudal nobles. Monarchs tried to limit the feudal warfare that had marked the medieval world. As a result, nobles no longer had to defend their domains against invaders, and they raised money by requiring payments of feudal obligations in cash instead of military services. With money, they transformed their cold and drafty manors and cas-

---

[9]"The Ordinance of Laborers of Edward III," in David Herlihy, ed., *Medieval Culture and Society* (New York: Walker, 1968), p. 361.

As a result of the bubonic plague, the rise of mercantilism, and other factors, the underlying assumptions of medieval society came to be questioned. In the Dance of Death, one scene of which is illustrated here, Death mocks an emperor, an archbishop, a rich merchant, and other symbols of power and vanity, but shows compassion for the poor laborer in the field.

tles into luxurious palaces and bought splendid clothes and jewelry in which to attend the king at court.

Life changed for the peasants, too, as serfdom declined in western Europe. Many serfs sold the surplus food they produced and used the money to buy their freedom. Some lords began to rent out their land to serfs for money instead of payment through labor so that in time these serfs became tenant farmers—or even earned enough to buy their own farms.

By the mid-15th century, the economy of Europe regained the momentum that it had lost in the 14th century. In the wake of the plague, populations increased again. Commerce revived, and the growing populations of cities provided markets for an increasing volume of agricultural produce and manufactured goods. When the demand for manufactured goods exceeded the supply that the guilds could produce, enterprising businessmen began to finance independent manufacturing facilities. They developed two ways of creating more, high-quality products. A few set up primitive factories, or large buildings in which hired workers with various skills produced goods in one place. Others sent materials out to workers who produced goods in their own homes. This "putting out" system, or cottage industry, gradually began to replace the craft guilds in the 15th and 16th centuries.

SUMMARY

Between 1050 and 1300, Europe made enormous economic progress based on political stability and technological advances. An agricultural revolution transformed the way crops were grown and greatly increased the amount and quality of food that was grown. As a result, the population of Europe tripled between the years 1000 and 1300. Important technological advances were also made during these centuries.

Commerce, both within Europe and between Europe and the East, also revived. Skilled artisans organized themselves into guilds that controlled the quality and price of the goods of their members. The guilds also acted as social welfare organizations for their members.

For the first time since the fall of Rome, Europe returned to a money economy. Gold and silver coins that were minted by cities and states became the medium of exchange, replacing the barter economy of the early Middle Ages. The money economy gave rise to money lending and banks.

In the mid-14th century, the Black Death and the Hundred Years' War caused widespread misery and social upheavals. But the resulting economic decline was only temporary, and Europe recovered its prosperity and self-confidence during the 15th century.

QUESTIONS

1 Explain how the agricultural revolution and other technological developments led to the expansion of the European economy in the late Middle Ages.
2 Describe how a person became a master craftsman. How did the merchant and craft guilds control the economy of medieval towns? Compare medieval guilds to today's labor unions.
3 How did the Hanseatic League become so powerful?
4 Why was banking necessary for increased commerce? How were banking methods of the late Middle Ages similar to or different from those of today?
5 What were the causes of the economic decline in the 14th century?
6 Why did feudalism decline in western Europe during the late Middle Ages?

BIBLIOGRAPHY

Which books might discuss agriculture in the late Middle Ages?

GIES, JOSEPH and FRANCES C. *Life in a Medieval City.* New York: Crowell, 1969. *A very human account of life in Troyes, France, from Roman times to 1250, when it became the capital of Champagne and the site of annual fairs.*

GOTTFRIED, ROBERT S. *The Black Death: Natural and Human Disaster in Medieval Europe.* New York: Free Press, 1983. *A detailed study of the immediate and long-term impact of the Black Death on Europe. Uses Church and tax records as well as the writings of medieval poets, historians, and physicians to describe the epidemic.*

WHITE, JR., LYNN. *Medieval Technology and Social Change.* London: Oxford University Press, 1962. *A brief look at the impact of new technologies on land use, food production, and other aspects of medieval life.*

24

● *In order to represent in some degree the adored image of Our Lord, it is not enough that a master should be great and able. I maintain that he must also be a man of good conduct and morals, if possible a saint, in order that the holy ghost may rain down inspiration on his understanding.*

MICHELANGELO

The Renaissance

The word "renaissance" ("rinascenza" in Italian) is French for rebirth. It was first used by 16th-century Italians, who believed that the civilizations of ancient Greece and Rome had been reborn in Italy after the long, dark night of the Middle Ages. In the 19th century, this view was strongly supported by the famous Swiss historian Jacob Burckhardt. In a famous study, *Civilization of the Renaissance in Italy*, published in 1867, Burckhardt argued that the Renaissance marked the birth of the modern world. According to Burckhardt, the revival of ancient learning allowed Renaissance Italians to replace the medieval outlook, which had been based on religion, with a rational, realistic view of the world.

Burckhardt overstated his case. Many of the changes that he believed had started in the Renaissance had in fact begun in the late Middle Ages. Today, most historians consider the Renaissance to be an era of transition between medieval and modern times. Thus, religion remained extremely important in the Renaissance just as it had been in the Middle Ages, but the difference was that secular values also became important. Whereas in the Middle Ages salvation in the next world was stressed, in the Renaissance the emphasis was on "humanism," or the need for each person to realize his or her potential as an individual in this world. The combination of religious and secular values is evident in the words and works of Renaissance artists such as Michelangelo, who is quoted above.

Changes also took place in the political and economic structure of Europe during the Renaissance. Medieval Europe had been a feudal society with weak central governments and an economy based on agriculture. Renaissance Europe was marked by political centralization and an increasingly urban economy based on large-scale commerce and capitalism. Centralization took different forms: in Italy, powerful city-states presided over political and economic affairs; in France and England, national monarchies triumphed over the decentralizing forces of feudalism.

In this chapter, we will concentrate on the Renaissance in Italy between the 14th and 16th centuries. The Renaissance began in northern Italy, which saw its most distinctive and striking achievements, but it soon spread north of the Alps to France, England, and Germany and other parts of Europe.

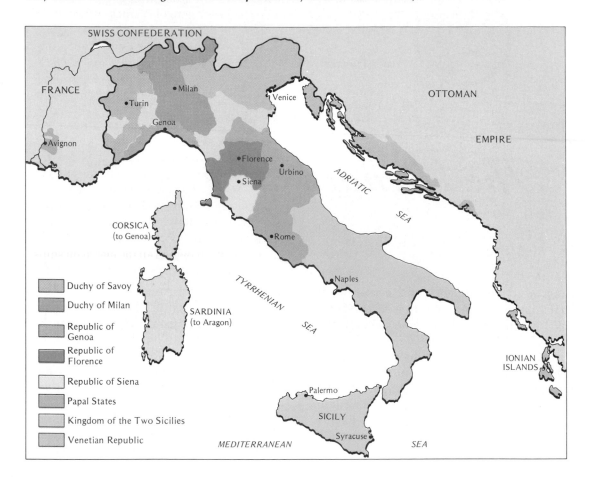

SWISS CONFEDERATION

FRANCE

•Turin
•Milan

Genoa

Venice

OTTOMAN

EMPIRE

•Avignon

•Florence

•Siena

Urbino

ADRIATIC

SEA

CORSICA
(to Genoa)

•Rome

TYRRHENIAN

SARDINIA
(to Aragon)

Naples

SEA

IONIAN
ISLANDS

Duchy of Savoy

Duchy of Milan

Republic of
Genoa

Republic of
Florence

Republic of Siena

Papal States

Kingdom of the Two Sicilies

Venetian Republic

Palermo

SICILY

Syracuse•

MEDITERRANEAN

SEA

ITALY IN 1350 Geography gave Italy a certain advantage over northern Europe because it jutted into the Mediterranean, a natural artery along which both trade goods and ideas flowed between Europe and the East. Throughout the Middle Ages, the cities of northern Italy prospered from trade, bringing luxury goods from the Byzantine Empire and the Moslem world to the rest of Europe. In the 14th century, the greatest of these cities—Venice, Florence, and Milan—became powerful states ruling large areas of the countryside around them.

During the Middle Ages, feudalism did not achieve the importance in northern Italy

that it attained elsewhere in Europe. This was due in part to the survival of trade and a money economy there. And Italy did not develop a centralized monarchy along the lines of those in France and England. By the mid-14th century, the attempts of the Holy Roman emperors to impose their rule on Italy had failed, and Italy was divided into a number of states. Later, another obstacle to unity was the competition between the city-states in the north and the papacy, which ruled a large territory in the center of Italy known as the Papal States. Yet these rival centers of power and wealth became the cradle of the Renaissance.

510

The magnificent cathedrals and private palaces of Venice reflected the city's prosperity and international importance. Shown is the Plaza of Saint Mark.

ships, giving it domination over the commerce of the Mediterranean.

The government of Venice reflected its commercial interests. In 1297, the leading merchants of the city took charge of its affairs. They prepared the *Golden Book*, listing the names of the most influential families of the city. Thereafter, only people listed in this book were eligible to serve on the Great Council, the body that appointed all public officials and enacted all laws. Each year, the Great Council elected from its members the Council of Ten to serve as administrators of the city. The Great Council also selected one of its members to be doge (duke) of Venice, the ceremonial head of the city. The doge served for life but had little power.

The city itself owned all the merchant ships and leased them to individual merchants for particular voyages. It also collected duties, or taxes, on all merchandise brought into the harbor. Venice built warships to protect the valuable cargoes of its merchant ships from pirate raids. The city also controlled the passes through the Alps and collected tolls from merchants of northern Europe who came to Venice to trade. With the vast wealth from trade, the leading families of Venice vied with one another to build the finest palaces or support the work of the greatest artists.

VENICE

The city of Venice was founded by people fleeing from Attila's invasions during the 5th century. It was located on a group of islands at the northern end of the Adriatic Sea, close to the foothills of the Alps. From the start, its economy was tied to the sea, and it traded with the Byzantine Empire and the Moslem world. During the Crusades, its power and influence grew, especially because it provided transportation to people bound for the Holy Land. By the late 13th century, it was the most prosperous city in Europe. During the 14th century, Venetian ships carried goods to ports all over Europe from England and Flanders to the Black Sea. At the peak of its power, it had 36,000 sailors operating 3300

FLORENCE

Florence, the "city of flowers," was located in the hill country of north-central Italy. It became an independent city in 1250. During the Middle Ages, Florence had a much more turbulent history than Venice, for it was the center of the struggle between popes and emperors. In Florence, a deep division arose between the Guelfs (those who favored the pope) and the Ghibellines (those who favored the emperor). Other struggles disrupted the city as workers fought the wealthy, and nobles fought the bourgeoisie. Street fighting was so common that the expression "going to the public square" came to mean "going to a riot." Despite the turmoil, the city

Rivalries between noble families as well as conflicts between the Guelfs and the Ghibellines led to constant street violence in Florence and other Renaissance city-states. Assassinations such as the one depicted here were a common occurrence, and most people surrounded their houses with defensive walls.

The people of Renaissance Florence were divided into four social levels. The nobles owned much of the land, lived in splendid castles on large estates outside the city walls, behaved according to the rules of chivalry, and disdained the newly rich merchants. The wealthy merchants, who formed the class called the "fat people," sought to protect their wealth by controlling the government and tried to enhance their social status by marrying into the nobility. To curry public favor and gain recognition, they became great patrons of the arts. The middle class was made up of shopkeepers and professionals, who were called the "little people."

At the lowest level were almost 30,000 workers, most of whom lived under the domination of the wool merchants. Working long hours for low wages, they were dependent on their employers for most aspects of life. Workers who violated rules could have their wages withheld or be discharged from their

prospered because it had set up a profitable wool industry. Sheep were raised in the rocky hill country of central Italy, and Florence was a center of wool processing.

During most of the Renaissance, the political power of Florence was concentrated in the hands of a few wealthy merchants, who dominated the wool industry. Like the rich families of Venice, these merchants competed with one another in building the grandest palaces for themselves in the city and villas in the country. They contributed in many ways to the beautification of the entire city. They believed that people who prospered should show their appreciation for their success by financing the construction of churches in which God could be glorified. To carry out these ambitions, they hired the most talented artists and artisans and encouraged them to produce their best work.

Although the government of Florence was nominally a democracy, Cosimo de Medici was recognized as its real governor. His liberal endowment of public monuments won him the title "father of his city."

Lorenzo "the Magnificent" was a central figure of the Florentine Renaissance. Due to his generous patronage, many of the most talented artists in Italy made their homes in Florence.

works of Plato and appointed Marsilio Ficino (1433-1499), a priest, as its first director. The scholars who were invited to join this elite group lived in gracious villas near the city, and the only requirement placed on them, besides pursuing their studies, was to dine with Cosimo once a week.

When Cosimo died in 1464, his son, Piero (1464-1469), and grandson, Lorenzo (1469-1492), continued his policies. The Medici maintained the stability of the city by exiling people who disagreed with them and encouraging other cities in Italy to join with Florence in shifting alliances to maintain the balance of power.

Under the leadership of Lorenzo, the economy of the city expanded greatly, and the workers, although still poorly paid, were protected from fluctuations in the economy. During this period, Florence became the most important city-state in Italy and the most beautiful in Europe. Because of his extensive

Savonarola, a fanatical priest, was opposed to everything the Medici stood for. His sermons won him enough popular support to seize control of the government of Florence.

jobs. As difficult as their lives were, however, these urban workers were better off than the rural peasants.

The Medici. In the 15th century when neighboring city-states posed growing threats to Florence, the influential people of the city came to the realization that they needed a strong leader. They chose Cosimo de Medici, a wealthy banker, to head the government and by 1434 he had consolidated power in his own hands. He maintained the appearance of the republican form of government that Florence had had but appointed his relatives and people he could control to important positions.

Cosimo commissioned works of art to beautify the city and encouraged architects to construct new churches. In 1438, he established an academy for the study of the

Within a few years, the Florentines tired of Savonarola's apocalyptic teachings, and he and his supporters were executed in a public square.

patronage of the arts, Lorenzo became known as "the Magnificent."

Savonarola. In 1494, two years after Lorenzo's death, a popular uprising forced the Medici to flee Florence. The uprising was inspired by a fiery Dominican priest, Girolamo Savonarola (1452-1495). Since 1491, when he had been elected prior of the Convent of San Marco in Florence, Savonarola's passionate sermons, condemning the worldliness of the papacy and the paganism of the Renaissance, had attracted enthusiastic crowds. He called for a return to the simple faith of the early Christians and warned of the spiritual corruption caused by wealth and power.

● ● ● *These wicked princes are sent as punishment for the sins of their subjects; they are truly a great snare for souls; their palaces and halls are the refuge of all the beasts and monsters of the earth, and are a shelter . . . for every kind of wickedness. Such men resort to their courts because there they find the means and the excitements to give vent to all their evil passions. There we find the wicked counsellors who devise new burdens and new imposts for sucking the blood of the people. There we find the flat-*

tering philosophers and poets, who, by a thousand stories and lies, trace the genealogy of those wicked princes from the Gods; and, what is still worse, there we find priests who adopt the same language. That, my brethren, is the city of Babylon, the city of the foolish and the impious, the city which the Lord will destroy.[1]

When Savonarola assumed the leadership of Florence after the Medici had been expelled, he drafted a constitution, based on that of Venice, reorganized the collection of taxes, and reformed the system of justice. He was determined to convert the pleasure-loving city of Florence into an example of medieval piety for all Christendom. He exiled many scholars and patrons of the arts. He encouraged people to gather up what he considered immoral books, frivolous objects, and pagan artwork and burn these symbols of corruption in huge bonfires. In this manner, many valuable works of art were destroyed.

In 1495, Pope Alexander VI ordered Savonarola to stop preaching and threatened to put Florence under the interdict. In reply, Savonarola issued a call for a general council to depose the pope. By this time, however, the Florentines had turned against the fiery reformer. In the political intrigues that followed, Savonarola was proclaimed a heretic, tortured, and burned at the stake.

After the death of Savonarola, the Medici returned to Florence and resumed their leadership of the city, but Florence never again regained its position of preeminence in Italy. In 1494, you will recall, Charles VIII of France invaded Italy, and during the next 50 years, the monarchs of France and Spain would struggle for control of Italy. Despite this turmoil and political disorder, however, the Renaissance spirit continued to flourish in Florence.

---

[1]Quoted in Pasquale Villari, *The History of Girolamo Savonarola and His Times*, trans. Leonard Horner (London: Longman, Green, 1863), p. 171.

MILAN

Milan, near the center of the broad, fertile plain of Lombardy, came to dominate much of the Po River valley. Although it was situated on a major trade route connecting Genoa to northern Europe, Milan developed greater military than economic importance. Because of its strategic location and the need for a strong military leader, Milan became a monarchy under a succession of dukes, rather than a republic like Venice or Florence.

The Visconti family ruled Milan as dukes almost continuously from 1317 to 1447. At the height of their power, they controlled much of northern Italy. After the last Visconti died in 1447, the Milanese tried to replace the monarchy with a republic, but this form of government failed to provide the military discipline needed to protect the city's vulnerable position. In 1450, Francesco Sforza, a mercenary soldier who had been hired by the Visconti to defend Milan, seized control of the government. He and his successors ruled Milan until France and Spain gained control of northern Italy in the late 15th century.

Francesco Sforza, a professional solider, seized control of Milan in 1450. Leonardo da Vinci sketched this plan for an equestrian statue in his honor.

The fortified palace of the Sforza family in Milan. The Sforzas were renowned for their cruelty and ruthlessness, and their wealth rivaled that of the pope. Like the Medici, they displayed their wealth in lavish public pageants and commissioned many great works of art.

HUMANISM During the Renaissance, the attitudes of the people in western Europe changed, especially among the better educated middle class. People wanted to understand the nature of how things worked. They became interested in individual achievement and emphasized life in this world rather than looking to that of the next world. The interest in learning and the importance of the individual were reflected in education as well as in the arts. Renaissance scholars rejected much of medieval civilization, which they considered backward and unenlightened. Instead, they looked further back in history to the ancient Greeks and Romans. In the works of the ancients, they found a spirit similar to theirs that valued the individual in the world.

In the 15th century, many Greek scholars left Constantinople, which was coming under increasing pressure from the Ottoman Turks, and took refuge in the Italian city-states. When Constantinople fell in 1453, the exodus turned into a flight, and the newcomers brought to the West not only the treasures of the Byzantine Empire but also their knowledge of ancient Greek civilization. The arrival of so many Greeks in the West caused some people to remark that "Athens has migrated to Florence." In Florence and elsewhere, the Greeks contributed to the growing interest in the learning of the ancient world.

Renaissance scholars stressed the *studia humanitatis*, or the study of the humanities, that included such subjects as grammar, rhetoric, poetry, and history. People who studied these subjects became known as **humanists**. Renaissance humanists believed strongly in the potential for achievement of human beings whether in the arts, literature, politics, or simply in one's personal life. The word "humanism," meaning a stress on human dignity as the most valuable of God's creatures, sums up the Renaissance intellectual ideal.

PETRARCH

One of the first writers to express the humanist spirit of the Renaissance was Francesco Petrarch (1304-1374), often called the "founder of humanism." Petrarch believed that the only true models of eloquence and ethical wisdom were to be found in the works of the ancient Roman authors, especially Virgil and Cicero. He traveled throughout France, Germany, and Italy, searching the libraries of monasteries and cathedrals for ancient manuscripts to copy for his own study. It is said that by the time of his death, Petrarch had one of the finest libraries in Europe.

Petrarch's major writings expressed his deep religious conviction and admiration of Latin literature. He was best known, however, for his love sonnets to Laura, which were written in Italian.

Petrarch's enthusiasm and reverence for classical literature led him to imitate its style, content, and form. He wrote epic poems, biographies of historical figures, and letters in polished and eloquent Ciceronian Latin. One of his most popular letters, "The Ascent of Mount Vertoux," was written to explain his feelings as he climbed Mount Vertoux. The story it tells represents more than a desire to see the view from the top of a mountain. Rather, it is an allegory in which Petrarch compares the hardships involved in climbing a mountain to the struggles that are necessary to achieve Christian virtue:

● ● ● *The life that we call blessed is situated on a high place; and narrow, we are told, is the way that leads to it; and many hills stand in the way, and we must advance from virtue to virtue up shining steps. The summit is the ultimate goal, the terminus of the road on which we journey. Everyone wishes to arrive there, but, as Ovid says, "To wish is not enough; to gain your end you must ardently yearn." . . . What then holds you back? Surely nothing but the level road that seems at first sight easier, amid base earthly pleasures. But after much wandering you will either have to climb upward eventually, with labors long shirked, to the heights of the blessed life, or lie sluggishly in the valley of your sins. And if—I shudder at the thought! —the darkness and shade of death find you there, you will spend an eternal night in perpetual torture.*[2]

Like many Renaissance intellectuals, Petrarch had two sides to his personality. While he felt comfortable in the seclusion of a monastery, he loved to travel; while he believed in the medieval ideal of self-denial, he enjoyed the pleasures of the world; while he loved learning, he feared that worldly knowledge might prevent him from achieving salvation.

Although Petrarch aspired to equal the

[2]*Letters from Petrarch*, trans. Morris Bishop (Bloomington: Indiana University Press, 1966), p. 47.

achievements of the great authors of ancient Rome, he won fame during his lifetime mainly for the love poems that he wrote in vernacular Italian to honor Laura, a beautiful woman whom he admired. These poems consist of 14 lines, rhymed according to a certain pattern, that became known as the *Petrarchan sonnet*. The pattern was later adopted by the great poet of the English Renaissance, William Shakespeare.

THE EARLY RENAISSANCE The humanists who followed Petrarch agreed with the need for eloquence and the study of classical literature, but they also stressed the need for an active life. To fulfill their natures, they believed, people had to achieve in as many fields as possible—in politics, in the quest for material possessions, in art and literature, and in the appreciation of beauty.

This concept eventually developed into the ideal of the "Renaissance man," a polished, well-rounded individual who was comfortable with every expression of human activity. The Renaissance ideal was best expressed by Baldassare Castiglione (1478-1529) in his work, *The Book of the Courtier*, published in 1518. The book depicts the ideal courtier as intelligent, charming, chivalrous, honorable, and skillful in sports; all these talents were expressed with seemingly little effort. The ideal courtier should also be knowledgeable about the classics, appreciative of the arts, and a connoisseur of beauty.

Castiglione's ideal was reflected in the goals of Renaissance education, at least for the upper classes. While the universities retained much of their medieval structure and curriculum, particularly in theology, medicine, and law, it became fashionable in the Renaissance for the sons of nobles to attend a university, as their medieval counterparts had not. At the university, young nobles were expected to learn the accomplishments that they needed to display in polite society. They learned to read and write Latin (and perhaps even Greek), speak well, and know something of the classical authors.

PAINTING

The arts—particularly painting, sculpture, and architecture—changed significantly during the 15th century. In keeping with the spirit of humanism, artists created lifelike people dressed in contemporary clothes set against backgrounds of Italian scenery. They experimented with new techniques and materials, developed formulas to guide them in showing the human body in correct proportion, and set standards for judging the merits of works of art. They developed techniques of shading and perspective in paintings that gave scenes and objects a three-dimensional appearance, very different from the flat and stiff works of medieval artists. They observed flora and fauna and studied the anatomy of animals and humans to achieve more perfect representations of natural objects.

While medieval artists usually belonged to a guild and remained largely anonymous, Renaissance artists tended to work in schools, signed their works, and enjoyed the fame and glory of their success. When a master artist received a commission for a major work of art, he usually painted or carved the most prominent features of the work and assigned his students to complete the rest. In this way, aspiring artists learned the techniques from their masters and then went on to produce works on their own. The competition among wealthy individuals for the services of the best artists led some artists to feel that their talents entitled them to special privileges and consideration.

Giotto. The first important painter of the early Italian Renaissance was Giotto di Bondone (1266-1337), who broke away from the rigid forms of medieval Gothic and Byzantine art and inspired his successors to study nature so that they could depict the real world. As a youth, Giotto studied with a prominent Florentine painter named Cimabue. On one occasion, Cimabue tried to brush a fly from a

Giotto's paintings had a great influence upon Renaissance artists. This is his Adoration of the Magi.

canvas that Giotto was painting only to discover that his target was a picture of the insect. Giotto set the stage for later artists, who refined and developed many of his techniques. As one art historian has explained, "Giotto . . . discovered, to a certain extent, the necessity of foreshortening the figure, and began to give some intimation of the passions and affections, so that fear, hope, anger, and love were in some sort, expressed by his faces."[3]

In 1334, Giotto was appointed chief ar-

[3]Giorgio Vasari, *The Lives of the Most Eminent Painters, Sculptors, and Architects,* trans. Mrs. Jonathan Foster, in J. F. Scott, A. Hyma, and A. H. Noyes, eds. *Readings in Medieval History* (New York: Crofts, 1946), pp. 604-605.

519

chitect in Florence and was placed in charge of civic and military construction. During this period, he designed the bell tower (*campanile*) for the cathedral of that city. As his reputation grew, rulers of other Italian cities tried to lure him away to beautify their palaces and churches.

Masaccio. Giotto's foreshortening of figures was the first step in the development of the techniques of perspective that gave paintings a three-dimensional look. A later painter, Tommaso Guidi (1401-1428), developed rules of perspective. He was given the nickname Masaccio (Messy Tom) because of his disheveled appearance, and in time this nickname replaced his real name. He is credited with mastering the techniques of perspective and is believed to have been the first Renaissance artist to paint human figures in the nude and to model figures through the use of light and shadow (*chiaroscuro*) rather than by means of sharp lines.

Masaccio's best known work is *The Tribute Money*, an excellent example of the use of the principle of "continuous narration" because three separate episodes are united into one harmonious composition. Like many Renaissance paintings, it portrays scenes from the Bible. In another work, *Expulsion From Paradise*, he shows Adam and Eve as they leave the Garden of Eden, covering their faces to hide their shame and grief. Masaccio died in 1428 at the age of 27.

Botticelli. Among the outstanding artists of the late 15th century was Sandro Botticelli (1444-1510). Botticelli became a member of the circle of artists and scholars sponsored by the Medici in Florence, and he was greatly influenced by the mysticism of *Neoplatonism*, a philosophy that sought to blend the teachings of Christianity with the ideas of Plato. Botticelli's most famous work, the *Birth of Venus*, shows the goddess of love rising from the sea on a conch shell, and clearly expresses the spirit of Neoplatonism. As one art historian has commented, "a modern scholar sees, beyond the simple depiction of a myth of the birth of Venus, an allegory of the innocence and truth of the human soul naked to the winds of passion and about to be clothed in the robe of reason."[4]

As a resident of Florence in the late 1490s, Botticelli was inspired by the teachings of Savonarola and burned many of his paintings with pagan themes. Thereafter, he devoted himself exclusively to the painting of religious themes.

SCULPTURE AND ARCHITECTURE

Renaissance artists turned their talents to many fields. Often, they were painters, sculptors, and architects, and applied the rules of perspective that they developed in one endeavor to their work in another. In architecture, Renaissance artists attempted to achieve the symmetry and harmony of Greek and Roman buildings, the remains of which they studied in great detail. They were encouraged in their pursuit of perfection by wealthy patrons who commissioned them to design palaces that were more beautiful in grace and proportion than those of their neighbors.

As city officials, these same wealthy patrons planned the finest possible public buildings and churches. They invited architects and sculptors to compete for commissions by submitting innovative plans and designs. In the early 15th century, the most prominent architects and sculptors were Lorenzo Ghiberti, Filippo Brunelleschi, and Donato di Niccolo di Betto Bardi—better known as Donatello. For a time, one of these three won almost every major commission.

Ghiberti. In 1401, a competition was announced in Florence to choose the artist to design and sculpt a pair of bronze doors for the north side of the Baptistry, a church dedicated to Saint John the Baptist. Each contestant was required to submit a sample panel,

[4]Helen Gardner, *Art Through the Ages*, 7th ed., rev. Horst de la Croix and R. G. Tansey (New York: Harcourt Brace Jovanovich, 1980), p. 518.

One of the greatest treasures of Florence is the pair of bronze doors sculpted by Ghiberti. This panel from one of the doors illustrates the Biblical story of the sacrifice of Isaac.

the subject of which was the sacrifice of Isaac, to be set within a *quatrefoil* (a Gothic framework with four foils, or lobes). Lorenzo Ghiberti (1378-1455) and Filippo Brunelleschi (1377-1446), the two most respected artists in Florence, entered the contest. Ghiberti was declared the winner, but even with the help of his assistants, it took him 28 years to complete the panels.

In the panels, Ghiberti developed the techniques of three-dimensional sculpture, with the figures closest to the viewer in high relief and the figures in the background in low relief. Later, he designed other panels for the east doors. Many years later when Michelangelo saw these doors, he reportedly exclaimed, "These doors are worthy to decorate the gates of Paradise." The Florentine authorities were so impressed with Ghiberti's work that they made him a city magistrate.

Brunelleschi. After losing to Ghiberti, Brunelleschi traveled to Rome. There, he studied the ancient Roman statues scattered about the city and sketched the remains of Roman buildings. Brunelleschi took measurements of many ruins, and became convinced that the beauty of an impressive building is based on certain mathematical relationships among its various dimensions.

In 1417, he again competed for a commission with Ghiberti; this time, to design the dome for the still unfinished cathedral of Florence. Brunelleschi was awarded the commission for his design of a great octagonal dome, which was inspired by the domes seen in late Roman architecture. The dome, constructed of two separate shells that rein-

Donatello's portrait of a famous condottiere (mercenary soldier) was the first equestrian statue to be created since classical times.

Brunelleschi's great dome for the cathedral of Florence was inspired by the architecture of the Romans and Byzantines, but its design was more daring than those of earlier domes.

force each other, rises 133 feet above the supporting walls of the cathedral. It still dominates the skyline of Florence.

Donatello. Donatello (1386-1466), the greatest sculptor of the early Renaissance, was born in Florence and worked in the studio of Ghiberti. He accompanied Brunelleschi to Rome, and like him, was inspired by the classical sculpture and architecture he saw there. Donatello created several masterpieces for his patron, Cosimo de Medici, the most important of which is the statue of *David*. This work was unique at the time because Donatello portrayed the ancient Hebrew hero, King David, in the classical tradition as a Greek god. More importantly, Donatello's *David* was the first free-standing nude figure sculpted since the Roman era.

In 1443, Donatello cast the first bronze statue of the Renaissance. It shows a soldier on horseback, and the figure is so realistic that it appears ready to move.

In his portraits and caricatures, as in his other activities, Leonardo Da Vinci demonstrated his versatility. Shown are a self-portrait, the head of a young woman, and caricatures or "grotesques" of elderly subjects.

THE HIGH RENAISSANCE

Artists of the early Renaissance (1350-1450) broke away from the rigidity of Byzantine and Gothic conventions by using the laws of perspective and representing humans and animals in a naturalistic manner. Artists of the High Renaissance (1450-1550) went beyond these advances to create works of beauty that would evoke emotional responses in their viewers. Florence produced more great artists in the early period than in the later period, but the works of Florentine artists of the High Renaissance are more widely known. The best known of these artists are Leonardo da Vinci, Michelangelo, Raphael, and Titian. Each was considered to have been divinely inspired, and wealthy patrons were anxious to secure their services.

LEONARDO DA VINCI

Leonardo da Vinci (1452-1519) epitomized the Renaissance ideal: he was a talented painter and sculptor; he was fascinated by technology, and his interests and curiosity were limitless. Born in a small town near Florence, Leonardo exhibited his artistic talent at a young age and was apprenticed to a leading Florentine painter and craftsman.

In 1482, Lorenzo de Medici learned that Leonardo had created a silver lyre in the shape of a horse's head. Lorenzo purchased this masterpiece to present to Lodovico Sforza, the duke of Milan, in the hopes of winning his favor. Leonardo begged permission to deliver the lyre in person, and when Lodovico saw it, he asked Leonardo to stay in Milan. While there, Leonardo painted the *Last Supper* on the wall of a monastery.

When the French captured Milan in 1499, Leonardo returned to Florence. There, he took on the position of chief military engineer, designing fortifications and weapons for the city. In 1513, Leonardo went to Rome, hoping to secure a commission from Pope Leo X, a son of Lorenzo de Medici, but the pope preferred the work of Raphael, a younger artist. When he left Rome two years later, Leonardo was reported to have said, "The Medici made me and broke me." In 1516, he was appointed court painter and chief engineer to King Francis I of France, and he remained in that position until his death in 1519.

Leonardo felt impelled to explore the mysteries of the universe. He always carried notebooks, which he filled with sketches, notes, and excerpts from books. Perhaps to make his notes harder for others to read, he wrote from right to left, which meant that the notes could be read easily only if held up to a mirror. This unusual style of writing caused his enemies to accuse him of witchcraft. His notebooks that have recently been published include ideas for such varied devices as a scaling ladder, rotating bridge, machine to mint coins, breach-loading cannon, submarine, armored vehicle, and flying machine.

Leonardo was a keen observer of nature because he felt that he could draw more accurately if he understood how things worked. He analyzed the anatomy, behavior, and flight of birds and predicted that humans would someday fly. He studied the structures and sexual characteristics of plants, noted the arrangements of leaves on stems, and concluded that the rings in a cross-section of a tree indicate its age. He examined fossils and developed a theory of the origin of the earth; he watched the flow of streams around rocks and deduced the cause of whirlpools. He expanded his knowledge of human anatomy by dissecting cadavers, sketched the chambers of a human heart, and detected the problem known as double curvature of the spine. He was, in sum, the first medical illustrator.

While painting the *Last Supper* as a fresco in Milan, Leonardo experimented with an oil-tempera medium on the plaster wall; unfortunately, the mural began to disintegrate a few years after completion. (It is currently being restored.) In showing the moment when Jesus announced to his apostles, "One of you will betray me," Leonardo interpreted each apostle's reactions so vividly that the viewer

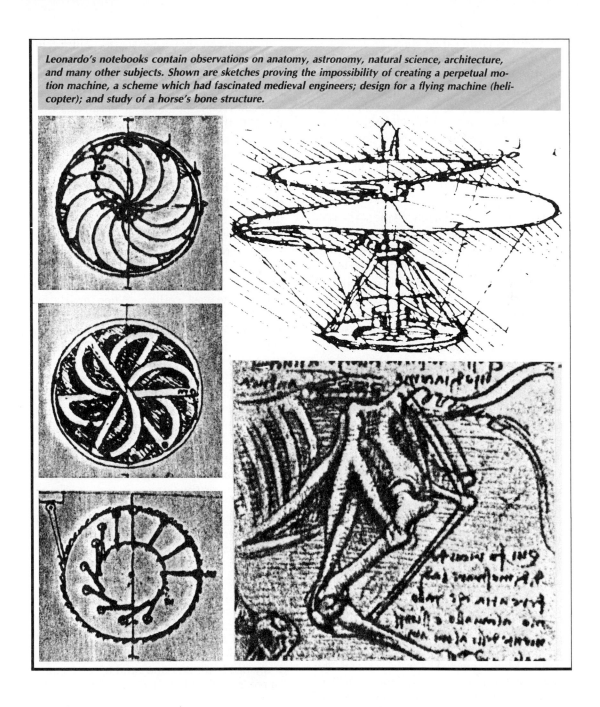

Leonardo's notebooks contain observations on anatomy, astronomy, natural science, architecture, and many other subjects. Shown are sketches proving the impossibility of creating a perpetual motion machine, a scheme which had fascinated medieval engineers; design for a flying machine (helicopter); and study of a horse's bone structure.

can speculate what each is thinking. When King Louis XII of France saw this painting in 1499, he wanted to have it moved to Paris.

In addition to the *Last Supper*, his best known painting is the *Mona Lisa*, a portrait of Lisa della Giaconda, the wife of a Florentine merchant. Her enigmatic smile has fascinated viewers from the time it was painted. The remote, dream-like quality of the portrait results from a technique developed by Leonardo called *sfumato*, in which very delicate gradations of light and shade are used in modeling the figure. In his later years, Leonardo painted less frequently and devoted his time almost exclusively to scientific studies. While his notebooks reveal that he planned many projects, he completed very few of them, perhaps because he did not have the necessary tools or resources.

MICHELANGELO

Michelangelo Buonarroti (1475-1564)— sculptor, painter, architect, and poet—has come to represent the genius of the High Renaissance. At the age of 13, Michelangelo enrolled in the school for sculptors established by Lorenzo de Medici, and before long, his work attracted the personal attention of Lorenzo. For several years he lived in the Medici palace in Florence as a member of the family, and he was strongly influenced by the concepts of humanism and Neoplatonism that flourished under the Medici's patronage. While seemingly preoccupied with the classical Greek and Roman concepts of beauty, Michelangelo never wavered from his deep Christian faith or sense of divine mission as expressed in the quotation cited at the beginning of this chapter.

When the Medici were driven from Florence in 1494, Michelangelo fled to Bologna. Later, he traveled to Rome, where, at the age of 23, he carved the *Pietà* on commission from a French cardinal. The idealized beauty of the Madonna and the sensitivity of her expression brought him instant recognition as an important sculptor. When he returned to Florence in 1501, he was commissioned to carve a statue of the Hebrew hero-king David. Michelangelo's *David* shows the muscular body of a youthful hero who appears to be filled with a sense of purpose and power. To many, *David* came to symbolize the city of Florence itself, and it can still be admired there.

Michelangelo was summoned to Rome in 1505 by Pope Julius II and commissioned to build a monumental tomb for the pontiff. This assignment was never completed, because Michelangelo interrupted his work on the tomb to decorate the Sistine Chapel in the Vatican. When Michelangelo began this work in 1508, the chapel was a long, unadorned, rectangular room—44 feet wide and 132 feet long. Its vaulted ceiling reaches 68 feet above the floor. Michelangelo decorated the walls and ceiling with scenes from Genesis illustrating Biblical events from the Creation of the world through the Flood. The scenes were peopled with over 300 human figures.

The project was enormously difficult. Working alone, Michelangelo had to lie on his back atop high scaffolding while he painted the vast ceiling. When finally exposed to view, the huge frescoes met with both praise and criticism. Seeing the many figures that the artist had drawn, Cardinal Biagio do Cesena noted that such a crowd would be more appropriate in a wineshop than in the papal chapel. In response to this criticism, Michelangelo added a portrait of Biagio among the figures of the damned in the scene of the Last Judgment.

While painting the Sistine Chapel, Michelangelo composed these verses to express his agony and frustration:

I've got myself a goiter from this strain,
As water gives the cats in Lombardy
Or maybe it is some other country;
My belly's pushed by force beneath my chin.
My beard toward Heaven, I feel the back of
*   my brain*
Upon my neck, I grow the breast of a Harpy;
My brush, above my face continually,
Makes it a splendid floor by dripping down. . . .
John, come to the rescue
Of my dead painting now, and of my honor;
I'm not in a good place, and I'm not a painter.[5]

---

[5]Michelangelo, *Sonnet to John Pistolo on the Sistine Ceiling*, in *Complete Poems and Selected Letters of Michelangelo*, 3rd. ed., trans. with Foreword and notes by Creighton Gilbert (Princeton University Press, 1980), pp. 5-6.

Michelangelo preferred to work as a sculptor or architect, but was persuaded to paint the ceiling of the Sistine Chapel. Shown is his rendering of the moment of man's creation.

During the last years of his life, Michelangelo worked almost exclusively as an architect. He was chosen to complete the basilica of St. Peter's that had originally been designed by another artist. The immense dome designed by Michelangelo is 138 feet in diameter and rises 400 feet above the floor of the sanctuary. While Michelangelo was inspired by Byzantine architecture, his work would later inspire both Christopher Wren, architect of Saint Paul's Cathedral in London, and Charles Bulfinch, architect of the Capitol in Washington, D.C., in designing domes for these famous buildings.

RAPHAEL

Raphael (1483-1520), the leading painter of the High Renaissance, was born Raffaello Santi in Urbino. In 1504, Raphael moved to Florence to study the principles of anatomy, drawing, and perspective under Leonardo. He was so talented that in 1508, at the age of 25, he was summoned to Rome by Pope Julius II to decorate the papal apartments in the Vatican. On the walls of the pope's private library, he painted four frescoes depicting what he considered to be the four most important fields of study: philosophy, theology, the arts, and law. The most widely

The Venetian artist Titian became court painter to the Holy Roman emperor Charles V. This is Titian's portrait of his patron.

ziana Vecellio in the Italian Alps, he later moved to Venice to study painting. Prior to 1518, Titian painted frescoes and murals, including the famous *Sacred and Profane Love*, an allegorical work showing the two aspects of Christian love, love of God and of neighbor. Between 1518 and 1532, he served as a court painter in the city-states of Ferrara, Mantua, and Urbino, before becoming official painter to the Holy Roman emperor, Charles V. During this period, he specialized in portraiture, and his clients included Francis I of France and Philip II of Spain as well as the emperor.

Titian ignored the traditional rules of painting by using bright colors, bold brush strokes, and the technique of *impasto*, by which repeated layers of opaque pigment are used to give colors greater subtlety and depth.

CELLINI

Benvenuto Cellini (1500-1571) was an outstanding Florentine sculptor and goldsmith whose services were sought by princes and popes. His autobiography, the *Life of Benvenuto Cellini*, gives us a picture of the adventures, determination, and talents of this

known of these paintings, the *School of Athens*, is an imaginary assembly of famous philosophers, including Plato and Aristotle, discussing their ideas in a huge basilica. Not one to be modest, Raphael painted himself as an observer among these scholars.

Raphael held many other commissions from the pope. Although he died at the early age of 37, he was so renowned that he was buried in the Pantheon in Rome.

TITIAN

The greatest Venetian artist of the High Renaissance was Titian (1485-1576). Born Ti-

Cellini's gold-plated saltcellar symbolized the meeting of sea and land.

gifted Renaissance figure. In 1540, Cellini was invited by King Francis I of France to set up his workshop in Paris. There, he served as consultant on royal fortifications and fashioned exquisite works for the king. Among them was a silver and gold saltcellar with Neptune, god of the sea, holding table salt, while the goddess of earth rests beside a small Greek temple holding pepper. This saltcellar is Cellini's only work in a precious metal to have survived. In 1545, he returned to Florence where he remained until his death in 1571.

INVENTION OF PRINTING

During the Renaissance, a large number of scholars and writers produced a rich array of works on subjects ranging from history

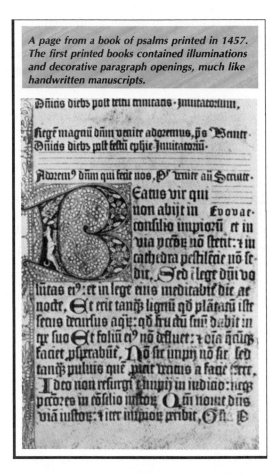

A page from a book of psalms printed in 1457. The first printed books contained illuminations and decorative paragraph openings, much like handwritten manuscripts.

The first printed book, a Bible, was produced in the shop of Johann Gutenberg in 1454.

and science to technology and religion. Their writings reached larger audiences than ever before, not only because more people were learning to read and write but also because books were becoming cheaper and easier to obtain. This latter development was due to the invention of printing in Europe in the mid-15th century.

The invention of printing was based on earlier techniques, including printing from wood blocks. The Chinese were the first people to invent movable type that allowed the printer to use and reuse pieces of metal engraved with letters and words. Whether Europeans knew of the Chinese printing processes that had been developed in the 11th century is subject to debate, although by the 15th century a number of Europeans had visited China and written about other Chinese inventions. From the Moslems, Europeans had learned to make paper, an important ingredient for producing printed books.

The first European to use movable type to produce a printed book was Johann Gutenberg of Mainz, Germany. In 1454, he published the famous *Gutenberg Bible*, and this event ushered in the age of printed books. Before long, printing presses had spread all over Europe and were pouring out a wealth of new works. The new technology brought the price of books tumbling so that many more authors could be published and read.

LITERATURE

Boccaccio. In literature as in painting and sculpture, writers explored both secular and religious themes. Among the outstanding figures of the early Renaissance was Giovanni

Giovanni Boccaccio is best known for his series of stories called the Decameron in which medieval fables, morality tales, and romances were updated for a Renaissance audience.

Boccaccio (1313-1375), a Florentine writer whose most famous work is the *Decameron* (meaning "ten days"). The *Decameron* is a collection of 100 stories written in the Italian vernacular and set in Florence during the Black Death that struck the city in 1348. In the story, three men and seven women seek refuge from the plague in a country villa and pass the time telling stories. The tales are based on humor, folklore, fables, moral examples, and romance. They reflect the traditions and values of various social classes, including the urban middle class, the clergy, and the peasantry.

Pico. Other Renaissance writers dealt with themes reminiscent of the scholastics. Their conclusions, however, differed from those of medieval writers, who had emphasized faith above all things. Among the Renaissance writers who studied the works of Aristotle and the ancient Greeks was Giovanni Pico della Mirandola (1431-1494). In 1484, Pico became a member of the Platonic academy in Florence, the literary and intellectual circle sponsored by the Medici. While living in Florence, Pico learned Hebrew and Aramaic. He studied the Talmud under Jewish scholars and struggled to reconcile the teachings of Judaism, Christianity, and Islam. In 1486, he published a collection of 900 philosophical treatises dealing with all aspects of human knowledge. Like the scholastics, he tried to reconcile his ideas with doctrines of the Roman Catholic Church, but his conclusions often differed from theirs.

In his best known work, the "Oration on the Dignity of Man," Pico explained that God created people "to know the laws of the universe, to love its beauty, to admire its greatness. He bound him to no fixed place, to no prescribed form of work, and by no iron necessity, but gave him freedom to will and to move."[6] Pico's oration pointed to a major dif-

---

[6]Quoted in Jacob Burckhardt, *Civilization and the Renaissance* (New York: Harper & Row, 1958), p. 352.

ference between the teachings of the Church and the ideals of the Italian humanists. Contrary to Church dogma, Pico believed that people possessed free will, enabling them to make decisions, and that the study of philosophy prepared people to recognize the truth. He further believed that any individual could commune directly with God, an idea that would become central to Protestant thought during the Reformation. Not surprisingly, the Church condemned Pico's writings and declared him a heretic. Forced to flee, Pico was saved by Lorenzo de Medici, who intervened on Pico's behalf so that he could return to Florence.

Machiavelli. One of the most influential writers of the Renaissance was Niccolo Machiavelli (1469-1527), who was born in Florence to an impoverished noble family. When the French invaded northern Italy in 1494, the ruling council of Florence appointed Machiavelli to be an ambassador. On a mission to France, Machiavelli realized that the relatively small Italian city-states would be no match for French military strength. He decided that Italy could be saved only if it were united under a respected and powerful ruler.

After 10 years' involvement in the endless wars and intrigues of the various city-states of Italy, Machiavelli retired to a small farm to write *The Prince* (1513), which may have been intended as a guidebook for the leader whom he hoped would unite Italy. Machiavelli was convinced that Christianity was an inadequate basis for government and that a ruthless patriotic citizen-soldier was the best kind of ruler to defend the state.

A political realist, Machiavelli believed that a ruler's job was to succeed by any means necessary. In *The Prince*, he advised rulers to be benevolent only if it suited their purposes. Otherwise, he warned, it was better to be feared than loved. This handbook for rulers had a great impact on European political life as rulers attempted to follow Machiavelli's recommendations and came to accept views such as this:

Macchiavelli's work The Prince *set forth a program of action for creating a unified Italian state, based upon the methods that the Medicis, Sforzas and others had used to achieve power.*

● ● ● *You must know, then, that there are two methods of fighting, the one by law, the other by force; the first method is of men, the second of beasts; but as the first method is often insufficient, one must have recourse to the second. It is therefore necessary for a prince to know well how to use both the beast and the man. . . .*

A prince being thus obliged to know well how to act as a beast must imitate the fox and the lion, for the lion cannot protect himself from traps, and the fox cannot defend himself from wolves. One must therefore be a fox to recognize traps, and a lion to frighten wolves. Those that wish to be only lions do not understand this. Therefore, a prudent ruler ought not to keep faith when by so doing it would be against his interests, and when the reasons which made him bind himself no longer exist.[7]

[7]Niccolo Machiavelli, *The Prince*, with analysis by J. P. Barricelli (Woodbury, N.Y.: Barron's, 1975), pp. 105-106.

531

During the Renaissance, scholars developed new methods of analyzing the past and examined historical documents in the light of their new learning. Two high-ranking clergymen, Lorenzo Valla (1407-1457), a secretary to the pope, and Nicholas of Cusa (1400-1464), a cardinal, introduced a research technique that became known as "textual criticism." In this type of study, a written document is analyzed to determine both internal and external consistency. Are the words, spellings, and references, for example, consistent with the time that the document was written?

The use of this technique led to astonishing results. For example, the Roman Catholic Church had long claimed that the emperor Constantine had bestowed control of Italy on Pope Sylvester I when he had moved the capital of the Byzantine Empire to Constantinople. The Church's claim was based on a document called "The Donation of Constantine." Valla and Nicholas of Cusa proved that the document was a forgery that had been written about 400 years after the death of Constantine. By examining the document, they found that it used words such as "fief" that were unknown in Constantine's time. This spirit of inquiry inspired later thinkers who were willing to put aside accepted notions and discover new ideas. The Church, however, frowned on Valla's work since it led people to question long-accepted truths.

WOMEN IN THE RENAISSANCE

For most women, life in the Renaissance remained much as it had been during the Middle Ages. They were expected to be wives and mothers; subject to their parents before marriage, to their husbands after it. Peasant women worked in the fields alongside their husbands. In the cities, women ran households and helped with their husbands' work. Women who did not marry either lived in the households of their male relatives or entered convents.

Lucretia Borgia (top), once portrayed as a monster of cruelty and deceit, is now considered to have been merely the pawn of her ambitious father, Pope Alexander VI (below).

A few wealthy women from the aristocracy, however, were able to break out of this mold. Two of the most famous and accomplished of these women were Lucrezia Borgia (1480-1519) and her sister-in-law Isabella d'Este (1474-1539).

Lucrezia Borgia was the daughter of Rodrigo Borgia, who became Pope Alexander VI (1492-1503). As pope, he decided to further his political ambitions by arranging an advantageous marriage for Lucrezia. Accordingly, she was married at the age of 13 to a member of the Sforza family, which ruled Milan. Four years later, when Alexander no longer needed support from that city, he annulled the marriage. He then arranged for Lucrezia to marry an illegitimate son of the king of Naples, by whom she bore a son. According to tradition, this husband was murdered by Lucrezia's brother Cesare. In 1502, when Lucrezia was 22, Alexander married her to the duke of Ferrara, Alfonso d'Este. The trousseau for this third marriage was so vast that 150 mules were required to carry it. Until her death in 1519, Lucrezia remained in Ferrara, a devoted wife and mother and a noted patron of the arts.

Isabella d'Este, Lucrezia's sister-in-law, was a brilliant woman who mastered Greek and Latin and memorized the writings of Virgil and Terence. She frequently gave performances in which she displayed her talents in singing, dancing, and playing musical instruments. In 1490, she was married to the duke of Mantua, Francesco Gonzaga, who approached Castiglione's version of the ideal courtier. Under the guidance of Isabella d'Este, the court of Mantua became renowned as a center of wit, elegance, and artistic genius. She promoted the textile and clothing industries so that the manufacture of velvet, satin, and damask became the chief source of income for the inhabitants of the city.

When her husband was captured in battle, Isabella ruled Mantua and the small duchy of Romagna. Her successful reign in Romagna gained her the respect of the people.

Isabella D'Este was noted for her patronage of the arts and capable management of Mantua. This portrait was sketched by Leonardo da Vinci.

As a generous patron of the arts, she assembled an outstanding collection of paintings, sculpture, manuscripts, and musical instruments.

INFLUENCE OF THE RENAISSANCE

By 1500, the independence of the Italian city-states was diminishing as they became prizes sought by ambitious rulers of the emerging nation-states of northern Europe. After 1500, the culture of the Renaissance began to move northward to France, Germany, England, and other parts of Europe as scholars, students, and soldiers from these lands carried the achievements of the Italians to their homes. As a result, the Renaissance became less Italian and more European in scope.

SUMMARY

The Renaissance continued the political, economic, and social changes that were already underway in the late Middle Ages. It began in Italy, which had a long tradition of commercial and cultural ties to the East and a vigorous urban society. By the mid-13th century, Venice, Florence, and Milan had become rich and powerful city-states. Their wealthy upper classes vied with one another in support of the arts and humanities.

Early Renaissance artists developed new techniques that paved the way for the masterpieces of the High Renaissance. The invention of printing and the increase in education spread the ideas of Renaissance humanists, who believed in human dignity and individual potential for achievement. Renaissance humanism fostered a creative outburst in literature and the arts that was best expressed in the works of writers such as Petrarch and Boccaccio and the artists Leonardo, Michelangelo, and Raphael.

QUESTIONS

1 What are some possible explanations why the city of Florence presided over so many achievements of the Renaissance?

2 Compare the attitudes of Renaissance humanists to those of medieval scholastics. Why do you think these attitudes developed first in the city-states of northern Italy?

3 What contributions did painters and sculptors of the early Renaissance make? Who were the outstanding artists of the High Renaissance? Describe one achievement of each.

4 Why was Leonardo da Vinci regarded as the ideal Renaissance person? Would it be possible for someone today to match his achievements? Explain your answer.

5 Explain how the art and literature of the Renaissance reflected society in the 14th and 15th centuries. What do modern art and literature tell us about our own society?

6 What impact did the invention of printing have on Europe?

BIBLIOGRAPHY

Which books might tell you about life in Renaissance Florence?

COUGHLIN, ROBERT. *The World of Machiavelli, 1475-1564.* New York: Time-Life, 1966. *An examination of the works of Machiavelli and of the outstanding artists of the Renaissance from Giotto to Raphael.*

KETCHUM, RICHARD M., ed. *The Horizon Book of the Renaissance.* New York: American Heritage Publishing, 1961. *A finely illustrated review of the ideas and institutions of the Renaissance that shows how the Renaissance developed gradually and was nurtured by the circumstances of the 14th century.*

LUCAS-DUBRETON, J. *Daily Life in Florence in the Time of the Medici.* New York: Macmillan, 1961. *A reconstruction of the habits and customs of the Florentine people during the years of Medici rule. Based on contemporary diaries and historical accounts, the book describes fashions, food, and the ceremonies of daily life.*

STRAGE, MARK. *Women of Power.* New York: Harcourt Brace Jovanovich, 1976. *A careful study of the lives of three powerful Renaissance women: Catherine de Medici, who dominated France for three decades; Diane de Poitiers, who exerted great political influence on Henry II; and Marguerite, queen of Navarre, who presided over a brilliant court.*

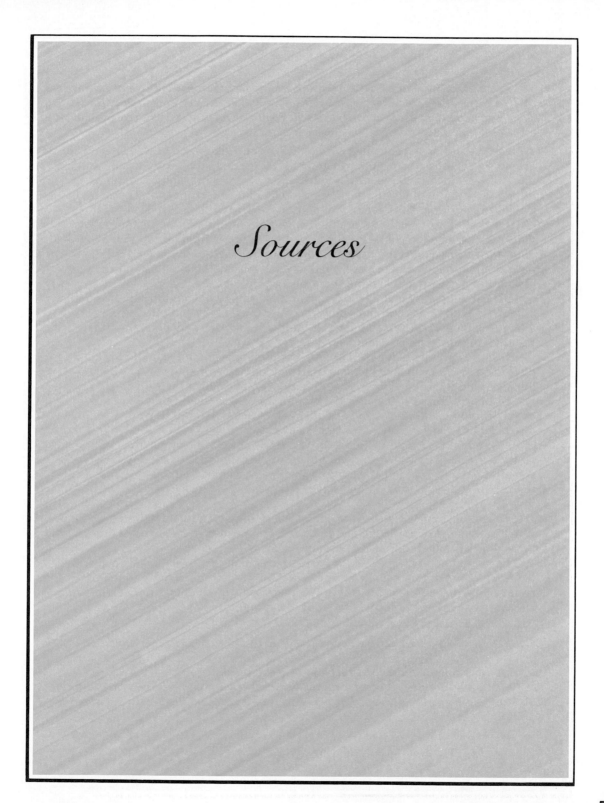

Sources

WHEN DOES HISTORY HAPPEN?

Barbara Tuchman's Practicing History, *from which the following excerpt was taken, is a compilation of essays on the difficulties a scholar faces when trying to write a history book. Select an important current event, and prepare two written explanations of it, first subjectively and then objectively.*

Who are [historians]: contemporaries of the event or those who come after? The answer is obviously both. Among contemporaries, first and indispensable are the more-or-less unconscious sources: letters, diaries, memoirs, autobiographies, newspapers and periodicals, business and government documents. These are historical raw material, . . . but that does not make [the writers] historians. . . .

At a slightly different level are the I-was-there recorders, usually journalists, whose accounts often contain golden nuggets of information buried in a mass of daily travelogue which the passage of time has reduced to trivia. . . . Daily journalism, however, even when collected in book form, is, like letters and the rest, essentially source material rather than history.

Still contemporary but dispensable are the Compilers who hurriedly assemble a book from clippings and interviews in order to capitalize on public interest when it is high. . . . The Compilers, in their treatment, supply no extra understanding and as historians are negligible.

All these varieties being disposed of, there remains a pure vein of conscious historians of whom among contemporaries, there are two kinds. First, the Onlookers, who deliberately set out to chronicle an episode of their own age—a war or depression or strike or social revolution or whatever it may be—and shape it into a historical narrative with character and validity of its own. Thucydides' *Peloponnesian War* . . . [is an] . . . example.

Second are the Active Participants or Axe-Grinders, who attempt a genuine history of events they have known, but whose accounts are inevitably weighted, sometimes subtly and imperceptibly, sometimes crudely, by the requirements of the role in which they wish themselves to appear. Josephus' *The Jewish War,* . . . [is in] this category.

The contemporary has no perspective; everything is in the foreground and appears the same size. Little matters loom big, and great matters are sometimes missed because their outlines cannot be seen. . . .

The contemporary, especially if he is a participant, is inside his events, which is not an entirely unmixed advantage. What he gains in intimacy through personal acquaintance—which we can never achieve—he sacrifices in detachment. He cannot see or judge fairly both sides of a quarrel. . . .

SOURCE: Barbara W. Tuchman, *Practicing History* (New York: Knopf, 1981), pp. 27-8.

1. *Into what categories does Ms. Tuchman divide historians?*
2. *What is Ms. Tuchman's concept of the relationship between "current events" and history?*
3. *How can the political and/or religious beliefs of a historian affect what is written as "history"?*

THE LITTER OF THE PAST

Richard Leakey is the son of Mary and the late Louis Leakey, who uncovered the fossil remains of "Zinjanthropus" at Olduvai Gorge in Kenya in 1959. Like his parents, Richard is interested in studying human beginnings and behavior. During the late 1960s, Richard excavated at Lake Rudolph, in northern Kenya, where he found an almost complete skull, which he named "1470."

People have always dropped litter. We see evidence of this all around us, in our city streets and rubbish dumps. Our museums display objects salvaged from the litter of past eras: Roman coins, Egyptian pottery, Ming china, Inca textiles. The list is endless, and each item tells us the same general story: that humans make things, use them, and then dispose of them, either casually as rubbish or occasionally as part of a ceremony such as the burial of an important person.

Litter of the past is the basis of archeology. The coins, the pottery, the textiles and the buildings of bygone eras offer us clues as to how our predecessors behaved, how they ran their economy, what they believed in and what was important to them. What archeologists retrieve from their excavations are images of past lives, but these images are not ready made from the ground: they are pieced together slowly and painstakingly from the information contained in the objects found. Archeology is a detective story in which the principal characters are absent and only a few broken fragments of their possessions remain. Nevertheless it has been possible, in many cases, to fill out the details of the story. We know, for instance, how the Incas operated their highly structured welfare/feudal economy and how the Romans organized their sprawling empire.

Although the detective work involved in reconstructing such civilizations can be difficult, those of us who are concerned with the very early stages of human evolution look with envy at the abundant evidence about these recent periods. One of the outstanding features of human history is the steady increase in the production of objects, such as tools, clothing and artificial shelters. As we search back through time, towards our origins, we find an ever-thinning archeological record. Somewhere between two and three million years ago, human artifacts disappear from the fossil record entirely. The task of discovering what our ancestors did in their daily lives therefore becomes more and more difficult the farther we search into the past.

SOURCE: Richard L. Leakey, *The Making of Mankind* (New York: E. P. Dutton, 1981), p. 76.

1. What characteristics must discarded items have in order to be useful to an archaeologist 100 years from now?

2. What is meant by the statement: "As we search back through time ... we find an everthinning archaeological record"?

THE ROYAL GRAVES OF UR

In 1922, Sir Leonard Woolley excavated the Royal Graves at Ur. His discoveries revealed much about the Sumerian way of life, including the fact that they practiced human sacrifice. From the remains he uncovered, Woolley reconstructed the course of events that led to one such sacrifice.

In [the royal grave pit] lay the bodies of 6 men-servants and 68 women; the men lay along the side by the door, the bodies of the women were disposed in regular rows across the floor, every one lying on her side with legs slightly bent and hands brought up near the face, so close together that the heads of those in one row rested on the legs of those in the row above. . . .

That [the victims] were dead, or at least unconscious, when the earth was flung in and trampled down on top of them is an equally safe assumption, for in any other case there must have been some struggle which would have left its traces in the attitude of the bodies, but these are always decently composed; indeed, they are in such good order and alignment that we are driven to suppose that after they were lying unconscious someone entered the pit and gave the final touches in their arrangement. . . . It is most probable that the victims walked to their places, took some kind of drug—opium or hashish would serve—and lay down in order; after the drug had worked, whether it produced sleep or death, the last touches were given to their bodies and the pit was filled in. There does not seem to have been anything brutal in the manner of their deaths.

Of the 68 women in the pit, 28 wore hair-ribbons of gold. At first sight it looked as if the others had nothing of the kind, but closer examination showed that many, if not all, had originally worn exactly similar ribbons of silver. Unfortunately silver is a metal which ill resists the action of the acids in the soil, and where it was but a thin strip and, being worn on the head, was directly affected by the corruption of the flesh, it generally disappears altogether, and at most there may be detected on the bone of the skull slight traces of a purplish color which is silver chloride in a minutely powdered state; we could be certain that the ribbons were worn, but we could not produce material evidence of them.

But in one case . . . as the body was cleared, there was found against it, about on the level of the waist, a flat disk a little more than 3 inches across of a grey substance which was certainly silver; it might have been a small circular box. Only when I was cleaning it in the house that evening, hoping to find something that would enable me to catalogue it more in detail, did its real nature come to light; it was the silver hair-ribbon, but it had never been worn—carried apparently in the woman's pocket, it was just as if she had taken it from her room, done up in a tight coil with ends brought over to prevent its coming undone . . . Why the owner had not put it on one could not say; perhaps she was late for the ceremony and had not had time to dress properly, but her haste has in any case afforded us the only example of a silver hair-ribbon which we are likely ever to find.

SOURCE: Leonard Woolley, *Ur of the Chaldees* (New York: Scribner's, 1930), pp. 58-60, 62-3.

1. *What clues helped Woolley deduce how the people in the Royal Grave met their deaths?*
2. *How did the manner of death help him deduce the cause of their death?*
3. *Cite an example of how an archaeologist must "interpret" what is found.*

THE STORY OF THE FLOOD

Several cultures in various parts of the world have legends about a time when there was a great flood that covered the entire region. This flood story from an ancient book of Sumer, The Epic of Gilgamesh, involves several Sumerian gods, including Enlil, the most powerful deity, and Ea, a lesser deity who warned Utnapishtun that Enlil was planning to destroy the world by means of a great flood.

I loaded into [the boat] all that I had of gold and of living things, my family, my kin, the beast of the field both wild and tame, and all the craftsmen. I sent them on board, for the time that Shamash had ordained was already fulfilled . . . the evening came, the rider of the storm sent down the rain. I looked out at the weather and it was terrible so I too boarded the boat and battened her down. . . .

A stupor of despair went up to heaven when the god of the storm turned daylight to darkness, when he smashed the land like a cup. One whole day the tempest raged, gathering fury as it went, it poured over the people like the tides of battle; a man could not see his brother nor the people be seen from heaven. Even the gods were terrified at the flood, they fled to the highest heaven. . . . The great gods of heaven and hell wept, they covered their mouths.

For six days and six nights the winds blew, torrent and tempest and flood overwhelmed the world, tempest and flood raged together like warring hosts. When the seventh day dawned the storm from the south subsided, the sea grew calm, the flood was stilled; I looked at the face of the world and there was silence, all mankind was turned to clay. The surface of the sea stretched as flat as a roof-top; I opened a hatch and the light fell on my face. Then I bowed low, I sat down and I wept, the tears streamed down my face, for on every side was the waste of water. I looked for land in vain, but fourteen leagues distant there appeared a mountain, and there was a boat grounded; on the mountain of Nisir the boat held fast, she held fast and did not budge. . . . A sixth day she held fast on the mountain. When the seventh day dawned I loosed a dove and let her go. She flew away, but finding no resting-place she returned. Then I loosed a swallow, and she flew away, but finding no resting-place she returned. I loosed a raven, she saw that the waters had retreated, she ate, she flew around, she cawed, and she did not come back. Then I threw everything open to the four winds. I made a sacrifice and poured a libation on the mountain top. . . .

SOURCE: *The Epic of Gilgamesh*, ed. N. K. Sandars (New York: Penguin Books, 1972), pp. 108-13.

1. Read the Biblical story of Noah and the Flood (Genesis 7:7 to 8:13) and compare it to the Sumerian version cited above. What might explain why the stories are so similar?
2. What differences are there between the two stories?

THE BUILDING OF THE PYRAMID

Herodotus was born at Halicarnassus, a Greek colony in Asia Minor, early in the 5th century B.C. He had an inquiring mind and the ability to write, and set out to record as much as he could about the world in which he lived. Herodotus traveled to Egypt to learn about the marvels of that land, and reported on the pyramids— particularly the one built by Cheops about 2600 B.C.

The pyramid was built in steps, battlement-wise, as it is called, or, according to others, altar-wise. After laying the stones for the base, they raised the remaining stones to their places by means of machines formed of short wooden planks. The first machine raised them from the ground to the top of the first step. On this there was another machine, which received the stone on its arrival, and conveyed it to the second step, whence a third machine advanced it still higher. Either they had as many machines as there were steps in the pyramid, or possibly they had but a single machine, which, being easily moved, was transferred from tier to tier as the stone rose—both accounts are given, and, therefore, I mention both. The upper portion of the pyramid was finished first, then the middle, and finally the part which was lowest and nearest the ground. There is an inscription in Egyptian characters on the pyramid which records the quantity of radishes, onions, and garlic consumed by the labourers who constructed it; and I perfectly well remember that the interpreter who read the writing to me said that the money expended in this way was 1600 talents of silver. If this then is a true record, what a vast sum must have been spent on the iron tools used in the work, and on the feeding and clothing of the labourers, considering the length of time the work lasted, which has already been stated, and the additional time— no small space, I imagine—which must have been occupied by quarrying of the stones, their conveyance, and the cutting of the underground canal.

SOURCE: Herodotus II, 125. In *The Greek Historians*, ed. M. I. Finley (New York: Viking Press, 1960), p. 80.

1. *What do we call the "machines formed of short wooden planks"?*
2. *What technique does Herodotus use to describe the achievement of the pyramid builders? Are his deductions reasonable, given the evidence he cites?*

SONG OF ATON

Akhenaton, a pharaoh of Egypt during the 14th century B.C., instituted a new religion based on worship of the sun, Aton-Re, as the only god. The masses of Egyptian people were opposed to the concept of monotheism. But the Hebrews—who were captives in Egypt at this time—were apparently more receptive to Akhenaton's ideas.

Thou appearest beautifully on the horizon of heaven,
Thou living Aton, the beginning of life!
When thou art risen on the eastern horizon,
Thou hast filled every land with thy beauty.
Thou art gracious, great, glistening, and high over every land;
Thy rays encompass the lands to the limit of all that thou hast made:
As thou art Re, thou reachest to the end of them;
(Thou) subduest them (for) thy beloved son.
Though thou art far away, thy rays are on earth;
Though thou art in their faces, no one knows thy going.

When thou settest in the western horizon,
The land is in darkness, in the manner of death.
They sleep in a room, with heads wrapped up,
Nor sees one eye the other.
All their goods which are under their heads might be stolen,
(But) they would not perceive (it).
Every lion is come forth from his den;
All creeping things, they sting.
Darkness is a *shroud*, and the earth is in stillness,
For he who made them rests in his horizon.

At daybreak, when thou arisest on the horizon,
When thou shinest as the Aton by day,
Thou drivest away the darkness and givest thy rays.
The Two Lands are in festivity every day,
Awake and standing upon (their) feet,
For thou hast raised them up.
Washing their bodies, taking (their) clothing
Their arms are *raised* in praise of thy appearance.
All the world, they do their work. . . .

SOURCE: James B. Pritchard, *Ancient Near Eastern Texts Relating to the Old Testament* (Princeton University Press, 1969), p. 70.

1. *Why has the sun been an object of worship in so many cultures?*
2. *What can you deduce from the line, "All their goods which are under their heads might be stolen"?*
3. *Compare the* Song of Aton *to Psalm 104 in the Bible.*

SOLON ON HAPPINESS

During his travels abroad, the Athenian philosopher Solon was reportedly enter-tained by Croesus, the king of Lydia in Asia Minor. After showing off his vast treasures, Croesus asked Solon to name the happiest man in the world. In reply, Solon cited the names of several Athenians who had lived modestly and died glorious deaths. Angered by this answer, Croesus asked Solon to explain his reasoning.

Later, Croesus lost his kingdom to the Persians and was taken prisoner by Cyrus. In light of these circumstances, Solon's answer to Croesus acquired new meaning and was widely cited as an example of his wisdom.

"O Croesus," cried [Solon], "you asked a question concerning the condition of man, of one who knows that the god is full of jealousy, and fond of troubling our lot. A long life gives one to witness much, and experience much oneself, that one would not choose. Seventy years I regard as the limit of the life of man. . . . The whole number of days contained in the seventy years will . . . be 26,250, whereof not one but will produce events unlike the rest. Hence man is wholly accident. For yourself, O Croesus, I see that you are wonderfully rich, and are king over many men; but with respect to that on which you questioned me, I have no answer to give, until I hear that you have closed your life happily. For assuredly he who possesses great stores of riches is no nearer happiness than he who has what suffices for his daily needs, unless it so hap that luck attend upon him, and so he continue in the enjoyment of all his good things to the end of life. For many of the wealthiest men have been unfavored of fortune, and many whose means were moderate have had excellent luck. Men of the former class excel those of the latter but in two respects; those last excel in many. The wealthy man is better able to content his desires, and to bear up against a sud-den buffet of calamity. The other has less ability to withstand these evils (from which, however, his good luck keeps him clear), but he enjoys all the following blessings: he is whole of limb, a stranger to disease, free from misfortune, happy in his children, and comely to look upon. If, in addition to all this, he ends his life well, he is of a truth the man of whom you are in search, the man who may rightly be termed happy. Call him, however, until he die, not happy but fortu-nate. Scarcely, indeed, can any man unite all these advantages; as there is no country which contains within it all that it needs, but each, while it posesses some things, lacks others, and the best country is that which contains the most; so no single human being is complete in every respect—something is always lacking. He who unites the greatest number of advantages, and, retaining them to the day of his death, then dies peaceably, that man alone, sire, is, in my judg-ment, entitled to bear the name of 'happy.' But in every matter it behooves us to mark well the end; for oftentimes the god gives men a gleam of happiness, and then plunges them into ruin."

SOURCE: Herodotus I, 32. In *The Greek Historians*, ed. M. I. Finley (New York: Viking Press, 1960), pp. 42-4.

1. Why does Solon withhold his judgment of Croesus' life?
2. According to Solon, what role does wealth play in determining the quality of a person's life?

THE WOLVES AND THE SHEEP

The identity of the ancient writer known as Aesop is still a mystery. Herodotus, writing in the 5th century B.C., thought that Aesop had been a slave and had lived in the 6th century B.C. In the 1st century, Petrarch identified the poet as an adviser to Croesus. Most likely, the collection of animal fables known as "Aesop's Tales" were composed by a variety of anonymous authors. "The Wolves and the Sheep" may have been written in the 5th century B.C. as a commentary on the wars that had devastated the Greek world.

After a thousand years of war declared,
The sheep and wolves on peace agreed,
Of which it seems both parties stood in need;
For if the wolves no fleecy wanderer spared,
The angry shepherds hunted them the more,
And skins of wolves for coats in triumph wore.
No freedom either knew,
The harmless sheep or bloody crew;
Trembling they ate, or from their food were driven,
Till peace was made, and hostages were given.
The sheep gave up their dogs, the wolves their young.
Exchange was made, and signed and sealed
By commissaries on the field.
Our little wolves soon after getting strong,
Nay, wolves complete, and longing now to kill,
The shepherd's absence watched with care.
One day, when all within the fold was still,
They worried half the lambs, the fattest there,
And in their teeth into the forest bore.
Their tribes they slyly had informed before.
The dogs, who thought the treaty sure,
Were worried as they slept secure;
So quick that none had time to wail,
For none escaped to tell the tale.

From hence we may conclude—
That war with villains never ought to end.
Peace in itself, I grant, is good,
But what is peace with savages so rude,
Who scoff at faith and stab a peaceful friend?

SOURCE: Aesop, "The Wolves and the Sheep." In *Five Centuries of Illustrated Fables*, selected by J.J. McKendry (Greenwich, Conn.: New York Graphic Society), p. 58.

1. A common element of all "Aesop's fables" is the use of animal characters. What reasons might the author(s) have had to tell their stories through animals?

FUNERAL ORATION OF PERICLES

In 431-430 B.C., Pericles was invited to give a eulogy for the Athenians who had died during the first year of the Peloponnesian War. In his speech, Pericles outlined the unique institutions and character of Athenian democracy, and presented his view of the city's role in the Greek world.

Our constitution does not copy the laws of neighbouring states; we are rather a pattern to others than imitators ourselves. Its administration favours the many instead of the few; this is why it is called a democracy. If we look to the laws, they afford equal justice to all in their private differences; if to social standing, advancement in public life falls to reputation for capacity, class considerations not being allowed to interfere with merit; nor again does poverty bar the way, if a man is able to serve the state, he is not hindered by the obscurity of his condition. . . .

If we turn to our military policy, there also we differ from our antagonists. We throw open our city to the world, and never by alien acts exclude foreigners from any opportunity of learning or observing, although the eyes of an enemy may occasionally profit from our liberality . . . while in education, where our rivals from their very cradles by a painful discipline seek after manliness, at Athens we live exactly as we please, and yet are just as ready to encounter every legitimate danger. . . .

We cultivate refinement without extravagance and knowledge without effeminacy; wealth we employ more for use than for show, and place the real disgrace of poverty not in owning to the fact but in declining the struggle against it. Our public men have, besides politics, their private affairs to attend to, and our ordinary citizens, though occupied with the pursuits of industry, are still fair judges of public matters; for, unlike any other nation, regarding him who takes no part in these duties not as unambitious but as useless.

In short, I say that as a city we are the school of Hellas; while I doubt that the world can produce a man, who where he has only himself to depend upon, is equal to so many emergencies, and graced by so happy a versatility as the Athenian. . . . For Athens alone of her contemporaries is found when tested to be greater than her reputation, and alone gives no occasion for her assailants to blush at the antagonist by whom they have been worsted, or to her subjects to question her title by merit to rule.

SOURCE: Thucydides II, 37-41. In *The Complete Writings of Thucydides*, the unabridged Crawley translation, with introduction by John H. Finley, Jr. (New York: Modern Library), pp. 104-6.

1. *How does Pericles describe the difference between "public" and "private" men in Athenian society?*
2. *How does the Athenian democracy of Pericles' time compare to present-day democratic governments?*
3. *How does Pericles characterize Athens' role in the Greek world?*

During the Peloponnesian War (431-404 B.C.), Athens' hegemony over its allies in the Delian League became critical to its war strategy, and the measures that should be taken to control reluctant allies were a subject of much debate.

In 416 B.C., the 16th year of the war, the Athenians decided that they could not allow any of the Greek island states to remain neutral in the war—especially Melos, which had been founded as a Spartan colony. The dialog excerpted below took place as the Melians struggled to maintain their neutrality.

Melians: Your military preparations are too far advanced to agree with what you say, as we see you are come to be judges in your own cause, and that all we can reasonably expect from this negotiation is war, if we prove to have right on our side and refuse to submit, and in the contrary case, slavery. . . .

Athenians: For ourselves, we shall not trouble you with specious pretenses— either of how we have a right to our empire because we overthrew the Mede, or are now attacking you because of wrong you have done us—and make a long speech which would not be believed; in return we hope that you . . . will aim at what is feasible, holding in view the real sentiments of us both; since you know as well as we do that right, as the world goes, is only in question between equals in power, while the strong do what they can and the weak suffer what they must. . . .

Melians: So that you would not consent to our being neutral, friends instead of enemies, but allies of neither side.

Athenians: No; for your hostility cannot so much hurt us as your friendship will be an argument to our subjects of our weakness, and your enmity of our power. . . . As far as right goes, they [our subjects] think one has as much of it as the other, and that if any maintain their independence it is because they are strong, and that if we do not molest them it is because we are afraid . . . the fact that you are islanders and weaker than others rendering it all the more important that you should not succeed in baffling the masters of the sea. . . .

Melians: You may be sure that we are as well aware as you of the difficulty of contending against your power and fortune, unless the terms be equal. But we trust that the gods may grant us fortune as good as yours, since we are just men fighting against unjust. . . .

Athenians: When you speak of the favor of the gods, we may as fairly hope for that as yourselves; neither our pretensions nor our conduct being in any way contrary to what men believe of the gods, or practice among themselves. Of the gods we believe, and of men we know, that by a necessary law of their nature they rule wherever they can. . . .

SOURCE: Thucydides XVII, 86-105. In *The Complete Writings of Thucydides*, the unabridged Crawley edition, with introduction by John H. Finley, Jr. (New York: Modern Library), pp. 330-7.

1. Do the Athenians cite moral or religious principles to support their demands? On what principle is their argument based?
2. What do the Athenians say about the behavior of the gods? How do they characterize the nature of man in comparison?

THE CAVE

Plato wrote The Republic *to present his concepts of an ideal state. The work is written in the form of a dialog between Socrates, who makes the long comments, and a person named Glaucon, who makes brief responses. In the extract given below, Socrates uses the image of a cave to describe the state of ignorance or partial knowledge in which most people live.*

And now, I said, let me show you in a figure how far our nature is enlightened or unenlightened:—Behold! human beings living in an underground den, which has a mouth open towards the light and reaching all along the den; here they have been from their childhood, and have their legs and necks chained so that they cannot move, and can only see before them, being prevented by the chains from turning round their heads. Above and behind them a fire is blazing at a distance, and between the fire and the prisoners there is a raised way; and you will see, if you look, a low wall built along the way, like the screen which marionette players have in front of them over which they show the puppets.

I see.

And do you see, I said, men passing along the wall carrying all sorts of vessels, and statues and figures of animals made of wood and stone and various materials, which appear over the wall? Some of them are talking, others silent. . . .

Yes, he said.

And if they were able to converse with one another, would they not suppose that they were naming what was actually before them?

Very true.

And suppose further that the prison had an echo which came from the other side, would they not be sure to fancy when one of the passersby spoke that the voice which they heard came from the passing shadow?

No question, he replied.

To them, I said, the truth would be literally nothing but the shadows of the images.

That is certain.

And now look again, and see what will naturally follow if the prisoners are released and disabused of their error. At first, when any of them is liberated and compelled suddenly to stand up and turn his neck around and walk and look towards the light, he will suffer sharp pains; the glare will distress him, and he will be unable to see the realities of which in his former state he had seen the shadows; and then conceive some one saying to him, that what he saw before was an illusion, but that now, when he is approaching nearer to being and his eye is turned toward more real existence, he has a clearer vision,—what will be his reply? And you may further imagine that his instructor is pointing to the objects as they pass and requiring him to name them,—will he not be perplexed? Will he not fancy that the shadows which he formerly saw are truer than the objects as which are shown to him?

Far truer.

And if he is compelled to look straight at the light, will he not have a pain in his eyes which will make him turn away to take refuge in the objects of vision which he can see, and which he will conceive to be in reality clearer than the things which are now being shown to him?

True, he said.

And suppose once more, that he is reluctantly dragged up a steep and rugged ascent, and held fast until he is forced into the presence of the sun himself, is he not likely to be pained and irritated? When he approaches the light his eyes will be dazzled, and he will not be able to see anything at all of what are now called realities.

Not all in a moment, he said.

He will require to grow accustomed to the sight of the upper world. And first he will see the shadows best, next the reflections of men and other objects in the water, and then the objects themselves; then he will gaze upon the light of the moon and the stars and the spangled heaven; and he will see the sky by night better than the sun or the light of the sun by day?

Certainly.

Last of all he will be able to see the sun, and not mere reflections of him in the water, but he will see him in his own proper place, and not in another; and he will contemplate him as he is.

Certainly.

> Socrates and Glaucon then speculate about a meeting between the cave-dwellers and a person from the outside world: the cave-dwellers would likely despise the newcomer, for his sunblindness would render him unable to see the shadows in the cave. The "newcomer," of course, is comparable to a philosopher, who has a superior vision of reality and truth. Socrates then goes on to describe the role of the philosopher in an ideal state.

Observe, Glaucon, that there will be no injustice in compelling our philosophers to have a care and providence of others; we shall explain to them that in other States, men of their class are not obliged to share in the toils of politics; and this is reasonable, for they grow up at their own sweet will, and the government would rather not have them. Being self-taught, they cannot be expected to show any gratitude for a culture which they have never received. But we have brought you into the world to be rulers of the hive, kings of yourselves and of the other citizens, and have educated you far better and more perfectly than they have been educated, and you are better able to share in the double duty. Wherefore, each of you, when his turn comes, must go down to the general underground abode, and get the habit of seeing in the dark. When you have acquired the habit, you will see ten thousand times better than the inhabitants of the den, and you will know what the several images are, and what they represent, because you have seen the beautiful and just and good in their truth. And thus our State, which is also yours, will be a reality, and not a dream only, and will be administered in a spirit unlike that of other States, in which men fight with one another about shadows only and are distracted in the struggle for power, which in their eyes is a great good. Whereas the truth is that the State in which the rulers are most reluctant to govern is always the best and most quietly governed, and the State in which they are most eager, the worst.

SOURCE: Plato, *The Republic* (trans. Benjamin Jowett), VII, 514-20. In *Greek Literature in Translation*, ed. George Howe and Gustave Harrer (New York: Harper & Row, 1924), pp. 608-11.

1. Why do people within the cave look away from the sun and from the objects outside? How do they perceive the real world when they are led outdoors?
2. In Plato's ideal state, what role do philosophers play? How does Plato characterize their attitude toward their responsibilities?

THE THIRD PHILIPPIC

Demosthenes (384-322 B.C.) delivered his first oration against Philip in 351 B.C., just five years after Philip had become king of Macedonia. By the time he delivered his third "Philippic," in 341 B.C., Philip had gained control of much of northern Greece, and was preparing to seize Byzantium, the gateway to the Black Sea area.

Heavens! is there any man in his right mind who would judge of peace or war by words, and not by actions? Surely, no man. To examine then the actions of Philip. . . . The peace he had ratified by the most solemn oaths. And let it not be asked, of what moment is all this? . . .

But farther: when he sends his forces into the Chersonesus, which the king, which every state of Greece acknowledged to be ours; when he confessedly assists our enemies, and braves us with such letters, what are his intentions? for they say that he is not at war with us. For my own part, so far am I from acknowledging such conduct to be consistent with his treaty, that I declare that . . . by his constant recourse to the power of arms, in all his transactions, he has violated the treaty, and is at war with you; unless you will affirm that he who prepares to invest a city is still at peace until the walls be actually assaulted. You cannot, surely, affirm it! He whose designs, whose whole conduct, tends to reduce me to subjection, that man is at war with me, though not a blow hath yet been given, not one weapon drawn. . . .

That Philip, from a mean and inconsiderable origin, hath advanced to greatness; that suspicion and faction divide all the Greeks; that it is more to be admired that he should become so powerful from what he was, than that now, after such accessions of strength, he should accomplish all his ambitious schemes; these and other like points which might be dwelt upon, I choose to pass over. But there is one concession, which, by the influence of your example, all men have made to him, which hath heretofore been the cause of all the Grecian wars. And what is this? an absolute power to act as he pleases, thus to harass and plunder every state of Greece successively. . . .

All Greece, all the barbarian world, is too narrow for this man's ambition. And though we Greeks see and hear all of this, we send no embassies to each other, we express no resentment: but into such wretchedness are we sunk (blocked up within our several cities) that even to this day we have not been able to perform the least part of that which our interest or our duty demanded; to engage in any associations, or to form any confederacies; but look with unconcern upon this man's growing power, each fondly imagining (as far as I can judge) that the time in which another is destroyed is gained to him, without ever consulting or acting for the cause of Greece; although no man can be ignorant, that, like the regular periodic return of a fever, or other disorder, he is coming upon those who think themselves most remote from danger.

SOURCE: Demosthenes, *The Third Philippic*, trans. Thomas Leland (New York: Colonial Press, 1900), pp. 134-7.

1. *In your own words, summarize Demosthenes' opinion of Philip.*
2. *What did Demosthenes think the Greeks should do about the threat of Philip?*

FIRST ORATION AGAINST CATILINE

During the 1st century B.C., *the Roman Republic was beset by a series of political crises. One of these crises occurred in 63* B.C., *when Catiline, a young Roman nobleman, ran for the office of consul. His campaign promise to cancel all private debts made him popular with poor Romans and also with nobles who, like himself, had squandered their fortunes. After losing the election to Cicero, Catiline plotted to seize the government by force.*

In the speech below, Cicero urged Roman senators (the "Conscript Fathers") to take action against Catiline.

And now . . . Conscript Fathers, . . . listen carefully, I pray you, to what I shall say and store it deep in your hearts and minds. For if our country, which is much dearer to me than my life, if all Italy, if all the state should speak to me thus: "Marcus Tullius, what are you doing? This man is a public enemy as you have discovered; he will be the leader of the war, as you see; men are waiting for him to take command in the enemies' camp, as you know: author of crime, head of a conspiracy, recruiter of slaves and criminals—and you will let him go, in such a way that he will seem to be not cast out of the city by you but let loose against the city! Will you not command him to be cast into chains, to be hauled to death, to be punished with the greatest severity? What, pray, hinders you? The custom of our ancestors? But often even private citizens in this state have punished with death dangerous men. Is it the laws which have been enacted regarding the punishment of Roman citizens? But never in this city have those who revolted against the state enjoyed the rights of citizens. Or do you fear the odium of posterity? A fine return you must be making to the Roman people who have raised you, a man distinguished only by your own deeds, and by no achievements of your ancestors . . . if because of the fear of unpopularity or any danger whatever you neglect the safety of your fellow-citizens!

But if that did seriously threaten me, still I have always believed that unpopularity won by uprightness was glory and not unpopularity. And yet there are some in this body who either do not see the disasters which threaten us or pretend that they do not see them; these have fostered the hopes of Catiline by mild measures and they have strengthened the growing conspiracy by not believing in its existence; under their influence many ignorant men as well as villains would be saying that I acted cruelly and tyrannically if I punished Catiline. Now I know that if he arrives in Manlius' camp whither he is now making his way, no one will be so stupid as not to see that a conspiracy has been formed, no one will be so depraved as to deny it. But if this man alone is executed, I know that this disease in the state can be checked for a little time, but it cannot be completely crushed. But if he shall take himself off, if he shall lead out his friends with him and gather together in the same place other derelicts now collected from all sources, not only this plague rampant in the state but even the roots and seeds of all evil will be obliterated and destroyed.

SOURCE: Cicero, *First Oration Against Catiline*, trans. L.E. Lord. In *Portable Roman Reader*, ed. Basil Davenport (New York: Viking Press, 1951), pp. 239-41.

1. *Explain Cicero's ideas about "unpopularity."*
2. *What plan does Cicero suggest to the "Conscript Fathers" for dealing with Catiline?*
3. *Compare Cicero's oration against Catiline to Demosthenes' oration against Philip.*

The Roman poet Virgil (70-19 B.C.) wrote the epic poem The Aeneid *to describe the adventures of the legendary hero Aeneas, who escaped from the destruction of Troy, traveled to North Africa, and eventually established a colony on the western coast of Italy.*

In this excerpt, Aeneas is speaking to Dido, the queen of Carthage, who has protested his decision to go to Italy. (He addresses her as "Elissa.")

"For me, O Queen, I never will deny
But that I owe you more than you can say,
Nor shall I stick to bear in memory
Elissa's name, whilst breath these limbs doth sway.
But to the point. I never did intend,
Pray charge me not with that, to steal away:
And much less did I wedlock-bands pretend,
Neither to such a treaty ever condescend.

"Would Fates permit me mine own way to take,
And please myself in choosing of a land,
Ilium out of her ashes I would rake,
And glean my earth's sweet relics; Troy should stand,
The vanquish'd troops replanted by my hand,
And Priam's towers again to Heav'n aspire.
But now I have the oracles' command
To seek great Italy; the same require
The Destinies. My country's this; this my desire.

"If you of Tyre with Carthage towers are took,
Why should our seeking Latin fields offend?
May not the Trojans to new mansions look?
As oft as night moist shadows doth extend
Over the earth, and golden stars ascend,
My father's chiding ghost affrights my sleep:
My son on whom that realm is to descend,
And those dear eyes do freshly seem to weep,
Complaining that from him his destin'd crown I keep.

"And now Jove's son, by both their heads I swear,
Was sent to me, myself the god did see
In open day, and with these ears did hear:
Then vex not with complaints yourself and me,
I go against my will to Italy."

SOURCE: Virgil, *Aeneid* (trans. Sir Richard Fanshave), IV. In *Portable Roman Reader*, ed. Basil Davenport (New York: Viking Press, 1951), pp. 376-7.

1. *What can you deduce about the relationship between Aeneas and Dido?*
2. *Explain the relationship of Tyre to Carthage.*

Dionysius, a native of Halicarnassus in Ionia, came to Italy in 29 B.C., the year that Octavian celebrated the end of his civil war with Mark Antony. He spent the next 22 years researching and writing his work Roman Antiquities, a comprehensive account of the rise of Roman civilization. In the excerpt below, he describes the climate and natural resources of Italy.

Italy is, in my opinion, the best country, not only of Europe, but even of all the rest of the world. . . .

For Italy does not, while possessing a great deal of good arable land, lack trees, as does a grain-bearing country; nor, on the other hand, while suitable for growing all manner of trees, does it, when sown to grain, produce scanty crops, as does a timbered country; nor yet, while yielding both grain and trees in abundance, is it unsuitable for the grazing of cattle; nor can anyone say that, while it bears rich produce of crops and timber and herds, it is nevertheless disagreeable for men to live in. Nay, on the contrary, it abounds in practically everything that affords either pleasure or profit. To what grain-bearing country, indeed . . . do the plans of Campania yield, in which I have seen fields that produce even three crops in a year, summer's harvest following upon that of winter and autumn's upon that of summer? . . . But most wonderful of all are the forests growing upon the rocky heights, in the glens and on the uncultivated hills, from which the inhabitants are abundantly supplied with fine timber suitable for the building of ships as well as for all other purposes. Nor are any of these materials hard to come at or at a distance from human need, but they are easy to handle and readily available, owing to the multitude of rivers that flow through the whole peninsula and make the transportation and exchange of everything the land produces inexpensive. . . . There are also mines of all sorts, plenty of wild beasts for hunting, and a great variety of sea fish, besides innumerable other things. . . . But the finest thing of all is the climate, admirably tempered by the seasons, so that less than elsewhere is harm done by excessive cold or inordinate heat either to the growing fruits and grains or to the bodies of animals.

SOURCE: Dionysius, *Roman Antiquities* I, 36-7. Loeb Classical Library ed., trans. Earnest Cary (Cambridge, Mass. and London: Harvard University Press and William Heinemann Ltd., 1937), pp. 119, 121.

1. *How do the natural advantages of Italy, as described above, compare to those of ancient Greece and Egypt?*
2. *How does Dionysius contribute to the idea that the rise of a great civilization in Italy was preordained?*

CICERO'S LETTERS TO ATTICUS

Cicero's letters to his friend Atticus provide much insight into the social and political life of Rome during the last years of the Republic. The letters excerpted below were written during the political crisis of 50-49 B.C., as it appeared increasingly likely that Caesar and Pompey would dissolve their alliance. Like other prominent Romans, Cicero had to decide which man he would support in the event of a civil war.

The final break between Caesar and Pompey came when Caesar led his army across the Rubicon on January 11, 49 B.C. Cicero chose to follow Pompey to the East, but later returned to Rome and received Caesar's pardon.

Formiae, December 17, 50 B.C.

My fears as to the political situation are great. And so far I have found hardly a man who would not yield to Caesar's demand [that both he and Pompey simultaneously give up command of their armies] sooner than fight. That demand is shameless, it is true, but stronger in its appeal than we thought. But why should we choose this occasion to begin resisting? . . . You will say, "What then will your view be?" My view will be not what I shall say; for my view will be that every step should be taken to avoid a conflict, but I shall say the same as Pompey.

Formiae, December 25 or 26, 50 B.C.

Your guess that I should meet Pompey before coming to Rome has come true. On the 25th he overtook me near the Lavernium. We reached Formiae together, and were closeted together from two o'clock until evening. As to your query whether there is any hope of a peaceful settlement, so far as I could tell from Pompey's full and detailed discourse, he does not even wish it. He thinks that the constitution will be subverted if Caesar is elected consul even after disbanding his army; and he reckons that when Caesar hears of the energetic preparations against him, he will give up the idea of the consulship this year and prefer to keep his army and his province. Still, if Caesar should play the fool, Pompey has an utter contempt for him and firm confidence in his own and the state's resources. Well, although the "uncertainty of war" came constantly to my mind, I was relieved of anxiety as I listened to a soldier, a strategist, and a man of the greatest influence discoursing in a statesmanlike manner on the risks of a hollow peace. We had before us a speech of Antony made on December 21, which attacked Pompey's entire life, complained about the condemnation of certain people, and threatened war. Pompey's comment was, "What do you suppose Caesar will do, if he becomes master of the state, when a wretched, insignificant subordinate dares to talk like that?" In a word, Pompey appeared not only not to seek peace, but even to fear it. But I fancy the idea of leaving the city shakes his resolution. What annoys me most is that I have to pay up to Caesar. . . . It is bad form to owe money to a political opponent.

Menturnae, January 22, 49 B.C.

It is a civil war, though it has not sprung from division among our citizens but from the daring of one abandoned citizen. He is strong in military forces, he attracts adherents by hopes and promises, he covets the whole universe. Rome is delivered to him stripped of defenders, stocked with supplies: one may fear anything from one who regards her temples and her homes not as his native land but as his loot. What he will do, and how he will do it, in the absence of senate and magistrates, I do not know. He will be unable even to pretend constitutional methods. But where can our party raise its head, or when? . . . We depend entirely upon two legions that were kept here by a trick and are practically disloyal. For so far the levy has found unwilling recruits, disinclined to fight. But the time of compromise is past. The future is obscure. We, or our leaders, have brought things to such a pass that, having put to sea without a rudder, we must trust to the mercy of the storm.

Formiae, February 8 or 9, 49 B.C.

I see there is not a foot of ground in Italy which is not in Caesar's power. I have no news of Pompey, and I imagine he will be captured unless he has taken to the sea. . . . What can I do? In what land or on what sea can I follow a man when I don't know where he is? In fact, on land, how can I follow, and by sea whither? Shall I then surrender to Caesar? Suppose I could surrender with safety, as many advise, could I do so with honor? By no means. I will ask your advice as usual. The problem is insoluble.

Formiae, March 1, 49 B.C.

I depend entirely on news from Brundisium. If Caesar has caught up with our friend Pompey, there is some slight hope of peace: but if Pompey has crossed the sea, we must look for war and massacre. Do you see the kind of man into whose hands the state has fallen? What foresight, what energy, what readiness! Upon my word, if he refrain from murder and rapine he will be the darling of those who dreaded him most. The people of the country towns and the farmers talk to me a great deal. They care for nothing at all but their lands, their little homesteads, and their tiny fortunes. And see how public opinion has changed: they fear the man they once trusted and adore the man they once dreaded. It pains me to think of the mistakes and wrongs of ours that are responsible for this reaction.

SOURCE: Cicero, *Letters to Atticus* VII, 6, 8, 13, 22; VIII, 13. Loeb Classical Library ed., trans. E.O. Winstedt (Cambridge, Mass. and London: Harvard University Press and William Heinemann Ltd., 1913), Vol. 2, pp. 37, 45-6, 62-3, 89, 161-2.

1. *What is Cicero's attitude toward Caesar? Does his attitude change as Caesar's success appears more certain?*
2. *In Cicero's opinion, who is to be blamed for the crisis?*

Caesar's work De Bello Gallico (On the Gallic War) *was essentially a political pamphlet, written for the purpose of advancing Caesar's reputation and political career in Rome. Nevertheless, it provides much valuable information about the early societies of the Gauls and the Germans as well as about the military tactics of the Roman army. Moreover, the book earned Caesar a reputation as one of the greatest writers of the Latin language. In an essay entitled* Brutus, *Cicero described Caesar's language as "pure and uncorrupted," and praised his style in these words: "His aim was to furnish others with material for writing history . . . but men of sound judgment he has deterred from writing, since in history there is nothing more pleasing than brevity clear and correct."*

On the Gauls

Throughout Gaul only two classes of men are of any real consequence—the Druids and the baronage. The common people are treated as little better than slaves: they never venture to act on their own initiative, and have no voice in public affairs. Most of them, burdened with debt, crushed by heavy taxation, or groaning under the hand of more powerful men, enter the service of the privileged classes, who exercise over them the rights enjoyed by a master over his slaves.

The Druids are a priestly caste. They regulate public and private sacrifices and decide religious questions. The people hold them in great respect, for they are the judges of practically all inter-tribal as well as personal disputes. They decide all criminal cases, including murder, and all disputes relating to boundaries or inheritance, awarding damages and passing sentence. Any individual or tribe refusing to abide by their decision is banned from taking part in public sacrifices— the heaviest of all their punishments. . . .

The druidical doctrine is commonly supposed to have reached Gaul from its original home in Britain, and it is a fact that to this day men going on for higher studies usually cross to Britain for the purpose. The Druids are exempt from military service and do not pay the same taxes as the rest of the people. Such privileges attract a crowd of students. . . . It is said that these young men have to memorize endless verses, and that some of them spend as long as 20 years at their books; for although the Druids employ Greek characters for most of their secular business . . . they consider it irreverent to commit their lore to writing. I suspect, however, that a double motive underlies this practice—unwillingness to publicize their teaching, and a desire to prevent students relying upon the written word at the expense of memory training; for recourse to text-books almost invariably tends to discourage learning by heart and to dull the powers of memory.

Their central dogma is the immortality and transmigration of the soul, a doctrine which they regard as the finest incentive to courage since it inspires contempt of death. But they also hold frequent discussions on astronomy, physics, and theology, in all which subjects their pupils receive instruction.

The whole baronage takes the field in the event of war—and indeed before my time these outbreaks (aggressive or defensive) might have been described as annual occurrences. Every nobleman is accompanied by his servants and armed retainers, whose greater or less number is an indication of his wealth and rank, and in fact the only recognized criterion of position and authority.

On the Germans

The German institutions are entirely different. They have no Druids to organize religious observances and rarely indulge in sacrifice. They recognize as gods only those visible objects from which they derive obvious benefits—the Sun, for instance, the Moon, and Fire—they have never so much as heard of any others. They spend all their lives in war and the chase, and inure themselves from their earliest years to toil and hardship. Those who retain their chastity longest are held in highest honour by their fellow men; for continence, so they believe, makes a man taller, hardier, more muscular. . . .

The Germans are not agriculturalists: their principal diet is milk, cheese, and meat. They have no landed estates with definite boundaries, but the magistrates and local chiefs make an annual assignment of holdings to clans, groups of kinsmen, and other corporate bodies. . . .

Every German state takes the utmost pride in devastating an area adjacent to its frontier and thereby surrounding itself with the widest possible belt of uninhabited territory. To drive one's neighbor from his land and make it too dangerous for others to settle in the vicinity is considered the essence of greatness as well as a precaution against surprise attack. On the declaration of war a high command is set up and invested with powers of life and death; but in peacetime there is no central government. Justice is administered and disputes settled by various local chiefs. . . .

The Germans have never risen above their ancient standards of poverty and privation; they have never so much as improved their diet and clothing. The Gauls, on the contrary, live close to the Roman Province: they have experience of sea-borne trade, and are plentifully supplied with luxuries in addition to their daily requirements. Yet these same Gauls have become gradually so used to their inferiority, after numerous disasters on the field of battle, that they no longer pretend to rival the martial eminence of Germany.

SOURCE: Caesar, *The Gallic War*, VI. In *Caesar's War Commentaries*, Everyman's Library ed., trans. John Warrington (London: J.M. Dent & Sons Ltd., 1953), pp. 103-7.

1. *Based on Caesar's descriptions, how did the religion and political system of the Germans differ from those of the Gauls?*
2. *In the last paragraph on the Gauls cited above, Caesar makes a reference to himself. How does he describe his impact upon Gaul?*

In the first century A.D., *the historian Tacitus wrote an account of the Germans which, together with Caesar's commentary, is the most important source of information we have concerning the early history of these peoples. Like Caesar, Tacitus noted that the Germans had a relatively democratic political system in which all of the armed men of the tribe participated. He also described the battle tactics that had made the Germans such formidable adversaries.*

They choose their kings by birth, their generals for merit. These kings have not unlimited or arbitrary power, and the generals do more by example than by authority. If they are energetic, if they are conspicuous, if they fight in the front, they lead because they are admired. . . . And what most stimulates their courage is, that their squadrons or battalions, instead of being formed by chance or by a fortuitous gathering, are composed of families and clans. Close by them, too, are those dearest to them, so that they hear the shrieks of women, the cries of infants. *They* are to every man the most sacred witnesses of his bravery—*they* are his most generous applauders. The soldier brings his wounds to mother and wife, who shrink not from counting or even demanding them and who administer both food and encouragement to the combatants. . . .

About minor matters the chiefs deliberate, about the more important the whole tribe. Yet even when the final decision rests with the people, the affair is always thoroughly discussed by the chiefs. They assemble, except in the case of a sudden emergency, on certain fixed days, either at new or at full moon; for this they consider the most auspicious season for the transaction of business. . . . Their freedom has this disadvantage, that they do not meet simultaneously or as they are bidden, but two or three days are wasted in the delays of assembling. When the multitude think proper, they sit down armed. Silence is proclaimed by the priests, who have on these occasions the right of keeping order. Then the king or the chief, according to age, birth, distinction in war, or eloquence, is heard, more because he has influence to persuade than because he has power to command. If his sentiments displease them, they reject them with murmurs; if they are satisfied, they brandish their spears. The most complimentary form of assent is to express approbation with their weapons. . . .

When they go into battle, it is a disgrace for the chief to be surpassed in valour, a disgrace for his followers not to equal the valour of the chief. And it is an infamy and a reproach for life to have survived the chief, and returned from the field. To defend, to protect him, to ascribe one's own brave deeds to his renown, is the height of loyalty. The chief fights for victory: his vassals fight for their chief. . . .

It is well known that the nation tribes of Germany have no cities, and that they do not even tolerate closely contiguous dwellings. They live scattered and apart, just as a spring, a meadow, or a wood has attracted them. Their villages they do not arrange in our fashion, with the buildings connected and joined together, but every person surrounds his dwelling with an open space, either as a precaution against the disasters of fire, or because they do not know how to build.

SOURCE: Tacitus, *Germany and Its Tribes*, 7, 11, 14, 16. In *The Complete Works of Tacitus*, Modern Library ed., trans. Alfred Church and William Brodribb (New York: Random House, 1942), pp. 712, 714, 715-7.

1. *How did the assemblies of the Germanic tribes function?*
2. *In Tacitus' time, the role of hereditary kings in German societies was becoming less important, while military chiefs were gaining authority and prestige. Eventually, the new alignment of loyalties led to the system known as feudalism that predominated in the Middle Ages. How does Tacitus characterize the relationship between chiefs and vassals?*

CARACALLA AND THE GERMANS

The emperor Augustus originally planned to safeguard the northern boundaries of the Roman Empire by conquering and resettling Germanic territories as far east as the Black Sea area. This campaign failed, however, and the presence of hostile Germanic tribes remained a problem for all of Augustus' successors.

The historian Dio Cassius described the behavior of the Germanic tribes that the emperor Caracalla encountered. Like other emperors, Caracalla attempted to bribe the Germans when military tactics failed.

Caracalla waged war also against the Cenni, a Germanic tribe. These warriors are said to have assailed the Romans with the utmost fierceness, even using their teeth to pull from their flesh the missiles with which the Osroëni wounded them, so that they might have their hands free for slaying their foes without interruption. Nevertheless, even they accepted a defeat in name in return for a large sum of money. . . .

Many also of the people living close to the ocean itself near the mouths of the Albis sent envoys to him asking for his friendship, though their real purpose was to get money. This was made clear by the fact that, when he had done as they desired, many attacked him, threatening to make war, and yet he came to terms with all of them. . . . The gold that he gave them was of course genuine, whereas the silver and the gold currency that he furnished to the Romans was debased. . . .

SOURCE: Dio Cassius, *Roman History* LXXVIII, 14. Loeb Classical Library ed., Vol. 9, trans. Earnest Cary (Cambridge, Mass. and London: Harvard University Press and William Heinemann Ltd., 1927), pp. 313, 315.

1. *What disadvantages arose from the Roman policy of bribing Germanic tribes to accept peace settlements?*

Marcus Aurelius, emperor of Rome from 161 to 180 A.D., adopted the principles of Stoicism when he was a young man. Because of his strong convictions, he became known as the "philosopher-king" of Roman emperors, but was forced to spend most of his time in military campaigns. While leading Roman troops along the Danube, he wrote a series of philosophical statements which were later published under the title Meditations: *the quotation below is one of these statements.*

Begin the morning by saying to thyself, I shall meet with the busybody, the ungrateful, arrogant, deceitful, envious, unsocial. These are so by the reason of their ignorance of what is good and evil. But I who have seen the nature of the good, that it is beautiful, and of the bad, that it is ugly, and the nature of him who does wrong, that he is akin to me, not only of the same blood and origin, but that he participates in the same intelligence and the same portion of divinity, I can neither be injured by any of those I meet, for no one can fix on me what is ugly, nor can I be angry with my kinsman, nor hate him. For we are made for cooperation, like feet, like hands, like eyelids, like the rows of the upper and lower teeth. To act against one another then is contrary to nature; and it is acting against one another to be vexed and to turn away. . . .

If thou workest at that which is before thee, following right reason seriously, vigorously, calmly, without allowing anything else to distract thee, but keeping thy divine part pure, as if thou shouldst be bound to give it back immediately; if thou holdest to this, expecting nothing, fearing nothing, but satisfied with the present activity according to nature, and with heroic truth in every word and sound which thou utterest, thou wilt live happy. And there is no man who is able to prevent this.

SOURCE: Marcus Aurelius, *Thoughts.* In *Readings in European History*, vol. 1, ed. J.H. Robinson (New York: Ginn and Co., 1904), p. 17.

1. *What is Aurelius' attitude toward those who "do wrong"?*
2. *Why does he consider himself to be impervious to injury or bad fortune?*

OF GOD'S GOVERNMENT

In the 5th century, as Rome fell prey to Germanic invaders, many Romans debated why their proud and ancient civilization was unable to withstand the onslaught. Some blamed Rome's weakness on Christianity. Others, like Salvian, a Christian priest, believed that God was punishing Romans for their evil ways. In his work Of God's Government, *written about 440, he argued that Roman citizens had become morally inferior to the Germanic peoples who were attacking them.*

In what respects can our customs be preferred to those of the Goths and Vandals, or even compared with them? And first, to speak of affection and mutual charity (which our Lord teaches is the chief, saying, "By this shall all men know that ye are my disciples, if ye have love one for another"), almost all the barbarians, at least those who are of one race and kin, love each other, while the Romans persecute each other. For what citizen does not envy his fellow-citizen? What citizen shows to his neighbor full charity? . . .

Even those in a position to protest against the iniquity which they see about them dare not speak lest they make matters worse than before. So the poor are despoiled, the widows sigh, the orphans are oppressed, until many of them, born of families not obscure, and liberally educated, flee to our enemies that they may no longer suffer the oppression of public persecution. They doubtless seek Roman humanity among the barbarians, because they cannot bear barbarian inhumanity among the Romans. And although they differ from the people to whom they flee in manner and in language; although they are unlike as regards the fetid odor of the barbarians' bodies and garments, yet they would rather endure a foreign civilization among the barbarians than cruel injustice among the Romans.

So they migrate to the Goths, or to the Bagaudes or to some other tribe of the barbarians who are ruling everywhere, and do not regret their exile. For they would rather live *free* under an appearance of slavery than live as captives under an appearance of liberty. The name of Roman citizen, once so highly esteemed and so dearly bought, is now a thing that men repudiate and flee from . . . .

SOURCE: Salvian, *Of God's Government.* In *Readings in European History*, Vol. 1, ed. J.H. Robinson (New York: Ginn, 1904), pp. 28-9.

1. In Salvian's opinion, why were Roman citizens moving to the regions controlled by Germanic tribes?
2. What types of conduct is Salvian referring to in the phrases "Roman humanity" and "barbarian inhumanity"?

IBN KHALDUN ON HISTORIANS

The Moslem scholar ibn Khaldun was born in Tunis, North Africa, in 1332. He pioneered in developing a philosophy of politics and of good government as well as concepts of historical research.

Untruth naturally afflicts historical information. There are various reasons that make this unavoidable. One of them is partisanship for opinions and schools. If the soul is impartial in receiving information, it devotes to that information the share of critical investigation the information deserves, and its truth or untruth thus becomes clear. . . .

Another reason making untruth unavoidable in historical information is reliance upon transmitters. Investigation of this subject belongs to [the theological discipline of] personality criticism.

Another reason is unawareness of the purpose of an event. Many a transmitter does not know the real significance of his observations or of the things he has learned about orally. He transmits the information, attributing to it the significance he assumes or imagines it to have. The result is falsehood.

Another reason is unfounded assumption as to the truth of a thing. This is frequent. It results mostly from reliance upon transmitters.

Another reason is ignorance of how conditions conform to reality. Conditions are affected by ambiguities and artificial distortions. The informant reports the conditions as he saw them, but on account of artificial distortions he himself has no clear picture of them.

Another reason is the fact that people as a rule approach great and high-ranking persons with praise and encomiums [tributes]. They embellish conditions and spread the fame [of great men]. The information made public in such cases is not truthful. . . .

Another reason making untruth unavoidable—and this one is more powerful than all the reasons previously mentioned—is ignorance of the nature of the various conditions arising in civilization. Every event (or phenomenon), whether (it comes into being in connection with some) essence or (as the result of an) action, must inevitably possess a nature peculiar to its essence as well as to the accidental conditions that may attach themselves to it. If the student knows the nature of events and the circumstances and requirements in the world of existence, it will help him to distinguish truth from untruth in investigating the historical information critically. . . .

Students often happen to accept and transmit absurd information that, in turn, is believed on their authority. Al–Mas'udi, for instance, reports such a story about Alexander. Sea monsters prevented Alexander from building Alexandria. He took a wooden container in which a glass box was inserted, and dived in it to the bottom of the sea. There he drew pictures of the devilish monsters he saw. He then had metal effigies of these animals made and set up opposite the place where the building was going on. When the monsters came out and saw the effigies, they fled. Alexander was thus able to complete the building of Alexandria.

It is a long story, made up of nonsensical elements which are absurd for various reasons. Thus, (Alexander is said) to have taken a glass box and braved the sea and its waves in person. Now, rulers would not take such a risk. Any ruler who would attempt such a thing would work his own undoing and provoke an outbreak of revolt against himself, and (he would) be replaced by the people with someone else. That would be his end. People would not (even) wait one moment for him to return from the (dangerous) risk he is taking.

Furthermore the jinn [supernatural spirits] are not known to have specific forms and effigies. They are able to take on various forms. The story of the many heads they have is intended to indicate ugliness and frightfulness. It is not meant to be taken literally.

All this throws suspicion on the story. Yet the element in it that makes the story absurd for reasons based on facts of existence is more convincing than all the other (arguments). Were one to go down deep into the water, even in a box, one would have too little air for natural breathing. Because of that, one's spirit would quickly become hot. Such a man would lack the cold air necessary to maintain a well-balanced humour of the lung and the vital spirit. He would perish on the spot. . . .

There are many similar things. Only knowledge of the nature of civilization makes critical investigation of them possible. . . .

SOURCE: Ibn Khaldun, *The Book of the 'Ibar, the Record of the Origins and Events of the Days of the Arabs, Persians, and Berbers and Those of Their Contemporaries who were Possessors of Great Power*. In *Readings in Medieval Historiography*, ed. Speros Vryonis, Jr. (Boston: Houghton Mifflin, 1968), pp. 371-3.

1. What pitfalls does ibn Khaldun describe in the writing of history? Which did he consider to be most important?
2. How can you evaluate the reliability of news that you read or hear about world events?

THE EMPEROR CHARLES

Einhard was one of the renowned scholars whom Charlemagne invited to his court. He became a close friend of the emperor and served as his ambassador to Rome. Einhard was with Charlemagne when the pope crowned him emperor on Christmas Day of the year 800. Later, Einhard wrote **The Life of the Emperor Charles** *to honor the man who had been his patron.*

He took constant exercise in riding and hunting, which was natural for a Frank, since scarcely any nation can be found to equal them in these pursuits. He also delighted in the natural warm baths, frequently exercising himself by swimming, in which he was very skillful, no one being able to outstrip him. It was on account of the warm baths at Aix-La-Chapelle [Aachen] that he built his palace there and lived there constantly during the last years of his life. . . .

He wore the dress of his native country, that is, the Frankish; next his body a linen shirt and linen drawers; then a tunic with a silken border, and stockings. He bound his legs with garters and wore shoes on his feet. In the winter he protected his shoulders and chest with a vest made of the skins of otters and sable. He wore a blue cloak, and was always girt with his sword, the hilt and belt being of gold and silver. Sometimes he wore a jewelled sword, but he did so only on great festivals or when receiving foreign ambassadors. . . .

In his eating and drinking he was temperate; more particularly so in his drinking, for he had the greatest abhorrence of drunkenness in anybody, but more especially in himself and his companions. He was unable to abstain from food for any length of time, and often complained that fasting was injurious to him. On the other hand, he very rarely feasted, only on great festive occasions, when there were very large gatherings. The daily service of his table consisted of only four dishes in addition to the roast meat, which the hunters used to bring in on spits, and which he partook more freely than any other food.

While he was dining, he listened to music or reading. History and the deeds of men of old were most often read. He derived much pleasure from the works of St. Augustine, especially from his book called *The City of God*. He partook very sparingly of wine and other drinks, rarely taking at meals more than three draughts. In summer, after the midday repast, he would take some fruit and one draught, and then, throwing aside his clothes and shoes as at night, he would repose for two or three hours. He slept at night so lightly that he would break his rest four or five times, not merely by waking, but even getting up.

While he was dressing and binding on his sandals, he would receive his friends; and also, if the count of the palace announced that there was any case which could only be settled by his decision, the suitors were immediately ordered into his presence, and he heard the case and gave judgement as if sitting in court. And this was not the only business that he used to arrange at that time, for he also gave orders for whatever had to be done on that day by any officer or servant.

He was ready and fluent in speaking, and able to express himself with great clearness. He did not confine himself to his native tongue, but took pains to learn foreign languages, acquiring such knowledge of Latin that he could make an address in that language as well as his own. Greek he could better understand than speak. Indeed, he was so polished in speech that he might have passed for a learned man.

SOURCE: Einhard, *Life of the Emperor Charles.* In *Readings in European History*, Vol. 1, ed. J.H. Robinson (New York: Ginn, 1904), pp. 126-8.

1. *What evidence does Einhard provide of Charlemagne's character and contribution to the Carolingian Renaissance?*
2. *Despite Einhard's biases, why is his work valuable to historians?*

BENEDICT'S RULE

*Benedict's **Rule**, written during the 6th century, became the standard code of conduct for most western European monastic orders. The **Rule** contains 73 chapters governing such aspects of daily life as the recitation of prayers, care of the sick, responsibilities of the abbot, and the amount and type of food to be distributed to each monk.*

Chapter 34   WHETHER ALL SHOULD RECEIVE NECESSARIES IN LIKE MEASURE

Let us follow the scripture: *Distribution was made to every man according as he had need.* By this we do not mean that there should be respect of persons (God forbid), but consideration for infirmities. He that needeth less, let him thank God and not be discontented; he that needeth more, let him be humbled for his infirmity and not made proud by the mercy shown to him: so will all the members be at peace. Above all, let not the vice of murmuring show itself in any word or sign, for any reason whatever. But if a brother be found guilty of it, let him undergo strict punishment.

Chapter 57   THE CRAFTSMEN OF THE MONASTERY

If there be craftsmen in the monastery, let them practice their crafts with all humility, provided the abbot give permission. But if one of them be puffed up because of his skill in his craft, supposing that he is conferring a benefit on the monastery, let him be removed from his work and not return to it, unless he have humbled himself and the abbot entrust it to him again. . . . And, as regards the price, let not the sin of avarice creep in; but let the goods always be sold a little cheaper than they are sold by people of the world, *that in all things God may be glorified.*

SOURCE: Benedict, *The Rule of Saint Benedict*, trans. Abbot Justin McCann (London: Broadwater Press Ltd., 1952), pp. 87, 129.

1. *In what ways might the rules cited above help to promote the ideals of obedience and humility?*

WALDO OF LYONS

In 1176, Peter Waldo, a wealthy merchant of Lyons, renounced his possessions and established a religious order called the Poor Men of Lyons. The order that became known as the Waldensians believed that lay people could preach the gospel and condemned the worldliness of the Church. The following passage, written by an unidentified person in 1218, describes Peter Waldo's decision to change his life.

And during the same year, that is the 1173rd since the Lord's Incarnation, there was at Lyons in France a certain citizen, Waldo by name, who had made himself much money by wicked usury. One Sunday, when he had joined a crowd which he saw gathered about a troubadour, he was smitten by his words and, taking him to his house, he took care to hear him at length. The passage he was reciting was how the holy Alexis died a blessed death in his father's house. When morning had come, the prudent citizen hurried to the schools of theology to seek counsel for his soul, and when he was taught many ways of going to God, he asked the master what way was more certain and more perfect than all others. The master answered him with this text: "If thou wilt be perfect, go and sell all that thou hast," etc.

Then Waldo went to his wife and gave her the choice of keeping his personal property or his real estate. . . . She was much displeased at having to make this choice, but she kept the real estate. From his personal property he made retribution to those whom he had treated unjustly.

At the Assumption of the blessed Virgin, casting some money among the village poor, he cried, "No man can serve two masters, God and mammon." Then his fellow-citizens ran up, thinking he had lost his mind. But going on to a higher place, he said: "My fellow-citizens and friends, I am not insane, as you think, but I am avenging myself on my enemies, who made me a slave, so that I was always more careful of money than of God, and served the creature rather than the Creator."

On the next day, coming from the church, he asked a certain citizen, once his comrade, to give him something to eat, for God's sake. His friend, leading him to his house, said, "I will give you whatever you need as long as you live." When this came to the ears of his wife, she was not a little troubled, and as though she had lost her mind, she ran to the archbishop of the city and implored him not to let her husband beg bread from anyone but her. . . .

[Waldo was accordingly conducted into the presence of the archbishop.] And the woman, seizing her husband by the coat, said, "Is it not better, husband, that I should redeem my sins by giving you alms than that strangers should do so?" And from that time he was not allowed to take food from anyone in that city except from his wife.

SOURCE: "Waldo of Lyons, the founder of the Waldensians," by a writer of about 1218. In *Readings in European History*, Vol. 1, ed. J.H. Robinson (New York: Ginn, 1904), pp. 380-1.

1. *Is the author of this passage sympathetic to Waldo?*
2. *What evidence suggests that the Church did not approve of Waldo's actions?*
3. *Find out more about Waldo and his followers. Why did the Church declare his teachings to be heresy?*

As a young man, Francis of Assisi renounced personal comfort and wealth to live a simple life of poverty and service to others. He soon attracted a group of followers, who became known as Franciscans. The Franciscans chose to live and preach among the poor rather than to cloister themselves in monasteries. The excerpt below was written in 1228, two years after the death of Saint Francis at the age of 44.

The father of the blessed Francis, when he learned that his son was ridiculed in the open streets, first strove by abuse to turn him from his chosen way. When he could not thus prevail over him, he desired the servant of God to renounce all his inheritance. That this might be done, he brought the blessed Francis before the bishop of Assisi. At this Francis did greatly rejoice and hastened with a willing heart to fulfill his father's demands.

When he had come before the bishop he did not delay, nor did he suffer others to hinder him. Indeed, he waited not to be told what he should do, but straightway did take off his garments and cast them away and gave them back to his father; and he stood all naked before the people. But the bishop took heed of his spirit and was filled with exceeding great wonder at his zeal and steadfastness; so he gathered him in his arms and covered him with the cloak that he wore. Behold now had he cast aside all things which are of this world.

The holy one, lover of all humility, did then betake himself to the lepers and abode with them most tenderly for the love of God. He washed away all the putrid matter from them, and even cleansed the blood and all that came forth from the ulcers, as he himself spake in his will: "When I was yet in my sins it did seem to me too bitter to look upon the lepers, but the Lord himself did lead me among them and I had compassion upon them."

Now upon a certain day, in the church of Santa Maria Portiuncula the gospel was read—how that the Lord sent forth his disciples to preach. It was while they did celebrate the solemn mystery of the mass, and the blessed one of God stood by and would fain understand the sacred words. So he did humbly ask the priest that the gospel might be expounded unto him. Then the priest set forth plainly to him, and the blessed Francis heard how the disciples were to have neither gold nor silver, nor money, nor purse, nor script, nor bread, not to carry any staff upon the road, not to have shoes nor two coats, but to preach repentance and the spirit of God, rejoicing always in the spirit of God.

Then said the blessed Francis, "This is what I long for, this is what I seek, this is what I desire to do from the bottom of my heart."

SOURCE: Thomas of Celano, *Life of St. Francis.* In *Readings in European History*, Vol. 1, ed. J.H. Robinson (New York: Ginn, 1904), pp. 390-1.

1. *Look up the words* **leper** *and* **leprosy.** *Why was the behavior of Francis toward the lepers courageous?*

2. *What opinion does Thomas of Celano, the author of this excerpt, have of Francis of Assisi?*

3. *Why do you think the Franciscans were accepted by the Church while the Waldensians were declared heretical?*

Among the most important sources of information about the Crusades are the letters written by Crusaders to their families in Europe. Count Stephen, who wrote the following letter while on the First Crusade, later deserted the cause and returned home. He was unable to live down the disgrace of his desertion, however, and eventually lost his life in a later Crusade to the Middle East.

Count Stephen to Adele, his sweetest and most amiable wife, to his dear children, and to all his vassals of all ranks—his greeting and blessing:

You may be very sure, dearest, that the messenger whom I sent to you left me before Antioch safe and unharmed and, through God's grace, in the greatest prosperity. And already at that time, together with all the chosen army of Christ, endowed with great valor by him, we had been continuously advancing for twenty-three weeks toward the home of our Lord Jesus. You may know for certain, my beloved, that of gold, silver, and many other kinds of riches, I now have twice as much as you, my love, supposed me to have when I left you. For all our princes, with the common consent of the whole army, though against my own wishes, have made me, up to the present time, the leader, chief, and director of their whole expedition.

You have assuredly heard that after the capture of the city of Nicaea we fought a great battle with the perfidious Turks and, by God's aid, conquered them. Next we conquered for the Lord all Romania and afterwards Cappadocia.

The bolder of the Turkish soldiers, indeed, entering Syria, hastened by forced marches night and day, in order to be able to occupy the royal city of Antioch before our approach. The whole army of God, learning this, gave due praise and thanks to the omnipotent Lord. Hastening with great joy to the aforesaid chief city of Antioch, we besieged it and had many conflicts there with the Turks. Seven times we fought with the citizens of Antioch and with the innumerable troops coming to their aid; we rushed to meet them and we fought with the fiercest courage under the leadership of Christ; and in all these seven battles, by the aid of the Lord God, we conquered, and most assuredly killed an innumerable host of them. In those battles, indeed, and in very many attacks made upon the city, many of our brethren and followers were killed, and their souls were borne to the joys of paradise. . . .

I can write to you only a few, dearest, of the many things which we have done. Although I am not able to tell you all that is in my mind, I trust that all is going well with you, and urge you to watch over your possessions and to treat as you ought your children and your vassals. You will certainly see me as soon as I can possibly return to you. Farewell.

SOURCE: Letter from Stephen, Count of Blois, to his wife, Adele, March 29, 1098. In *Readings in European History*, Vol. 1, ed. J.H. Robinson (New York: Ginn, 1904), pp. 321-5.

1. **What motives for joining the Crusades does Stephen's letter reveal?**
2. **What view does he hold of the Moslem Turks?**

THE TRUCE OF GOD

During the 9th through 11th centuries, Europeans were victimized by several waves of foreign invaders, and feudal lords fought one another for land and power. In the late 11th century, the Church tried to limit the fighting by issuing orders such as the "Truce of God."

From the first day of the Advent of our Lord through Epiphany, and from the beginning of Septuagesima to the eighth day after Pentecost and through that whole day, and throughout the year on every Sunday, Friday and Saturday, and on the fast days of the four seasons, and on the eve and the day of all the apostles, and on all days canonically set apart—or which shall in the future be set apart—for fasts or feasts, this decree of peace shall be observed; so that both those who travel and those who remain at home may enjoy security and the most entire peace, so that no one may commit murder, arson, robbery or assault, no one may injure another with a sword, club, or any kind of weapon. Let no one, however irritated by wrong, presume to carry arms, shield, sword, or lance, or any kind of armor [during the times specified above]. . . .

And in order that this statute of peace should not be violated by anyone rashly or with impunity, a penalty was fixed by the common consent of all, namely: If a free man or noble violates it, i.e., commits homicide, or wounds any one, or is at fault in any manner whatever, he shall be expelled from his lands, without any indulgence on account of the payment of money or the intercession of friends, and his heirs shall take all his property. If he holds a fief, the lord to whom it belongs shall receive it again. Moreover, if it appears that his heirs after his expulsion have furnished him any support or aid, and if they are convicted of it, the estate shall be taken from them and revert to the king. But if they wish to clear themselves of the charge against them, they shall take oath, with twelve who are equally free or equally noble.

If a slave kills a man, he shall be beheaded; if he wounds a man, he shall lose a hand; if he does any injury in any other way with his fist or a club, or by striking with a stone, he shall be shorn and flogged. If, however, he is accused and wishes to prove his innocence, he shall clear himself by the ordeal of cold water, but he must himself be put into the water and no one else in his place. If, however, fearing the sentence decreed against him, he flees, he shall be under a perpetual excommunication. . . . In the case of boys who have not yet completed their twelfth year, the hand ought not to be cut off; but only in the case of those who are twelve years or more of age. . . .

If any one attempts to defy this pious institution and is unwilling to promise peace to God with the others, or to observe it, no priest in our diocese shall presume to say a mass for him . . . unless he repents. . . .

SOURCE: "The Truce of God," issued by a synod at Cologne, 1083. In *Readings in European History*, Vol. 1, ed. J.H. Robinson (New York: Ginn, 1904), pp. 187-90.

1. *What does this document tell about conditions in medieval Europe?*
2. *By issuing this order, what role did the Church assume?*
3. *Does this document demonstrate that the concept of "equal justice under the law" was practiced? Explain your answer.*

DICTATUS, POPE GREGORY VII

Soon after he became pope in 1073, Gregory VII issued the Dictatus, *in which he stated his views on the Church and the role of the pope. A portion of the document is given below. The Holy Roman emperor Henry IV attempted to challenge Gregory's authority, but was forced to yield to the pope's demands during their meeting at Canossa in 1076.*

The Roman church was founded by God alone.

The Roman bishop alone is properly called universal.

He alone may depose bishops and reinstate them.

His legate, though of inferior grade, takes precedence, in a council, of all bishops and may render a decision of deposition against them.

He alone may use the insignia of empire.

The pope is the only person whose feet are kissed by all princes.

His title is unique in the world.

He may depose emperors.

No council may be regarded as a general one without his consent.

No book or chapter may be regarded as canonical without his authority.

A decree of his may be annulled by no one; he alone may annul the decrees of all.

He may be judged by no one.

No one shall dare to condemn one who appeals to the papal see.

The Roman church has never erred, nor ever, by the witness of the Scripture, shall err to all eternity.

He may not be considered Catholic who does not agree with the Roman church.

The pope may absolve the subjects of the unjust from their allegiance.

SOURCE: Pope Gregory VII, *Dictatus* (1075). In *Readings in European History*, Vol. 1, ed. J.H. Robinson (New York: Ginn, 1904), pp. 274-5.

1. *Make a list of words that have the same root as "dictatus." What connotation do these words have in common?*

2. *Which of the powers claimed by Gregory conflicted with those claimed by the Holy Roman emperor?*

3. *Compare the Church of Gregory's time to the early church described in Chapter 12.*

STATUTE OF LABORERS

Between 1348 and 1351, the Black Death ravaged the population of Europe. In an attempt to alleviate the economic and social disruptions caused by the plague in England, Edward III (reigned 1327–1399) issued the Statute of Laborers. In this document, he forbade laborers to profit from the fact that their services were in much greater demand than they had been before the plague struck.

Because a great part of the people and especially of the workmen and servants has now died in that pestilence, some, seeing the straights of the masters and the scarcity of servants, are not willing to serve unless they receive excessive wages, and others, rather than through labor to gain their living, prefer to beg in idleness: We, considering the grave inconveniences which might come from the lack especially of ploughmen and such laborers, have held deliberation and treaty concerning this with the prelates and nobles and other learned men sitting by us; by whose consentient counsel we have seen fit to ordain: that every man and woman of our kingdom of England, of whatever condition, whether bond or free, who is able bodied and below the age of sixty years, not living from trade nor carrying on a fixed craft, nor having of his own the means of living, or land of his own with regard to the cultivation of which he might occupy himself, and not serving another—if he, considering his station, be sought after to serve in a suitable service, he shall be bound to serve him who has seen fit so to seek after him; and he shall take only the wages, liveries, meed or salary which, in the places where he sought to serve, were accustomed to be paid in the 20th year of our reign of England, or the five or six common years next preceding.

And if a reaper or mower, or other workman or servant, of whatever standing or condition he be, who is retained in the service of any one, do depart from the said service before the end of the term agreed, without permission or reasonable cause, he shall undergo the penalty of imprisonment, and let no one, under the same penalty, presume to receive or retain such a one in his service. Let no one, moreover, pay or permit to be paid to any one more wages, livery, meed or salary than was customary as has been said. . . .

SOURCE: Edward III, *Statute of Laborers*. In *Select Historical Documents of the Middle Ages*, ed. Ernest F. Henderson (New York: Biblo and Tannen, 1965), pp. 165–6.

1. To what category of laborers is Edward's decree directed?
2. How does Edward view the efforts of laborers to profit from increased demand for their services, and the willingness of employers to pay higher wages?

EFFECTS OF THE PLAGUE IN FLORENCE

In 1348, the Bubonic plague swept over Europe. At least one third of the population died within three years, and outbreaks reoccurred several times during the following century. Giovanni Boccaccio, one of the great writers of the early Renaissance, described the effects of the plague on Florence in the stories of the Decameron.

My own eyes, as I said a little while ago, saw one day (and other times besides) this occurrence. The rags of a poor man dead from this disease had been thrown in a public street. Two pigs came to them and they, in their accustomed manner, first rooted among them with their snouts, and then seized them with their teeth and tossed them about with their jaws. A short hour later, after some staggering, as if the poison was taking effect, both of them fell dead to earth upon the rags which they had unhappily dragged.

Such events and many others similar to them or even worse conjured up in those who remained healthy diverse fears and imaginings. Almost all were inclined to a very cruel purpose, that is, to shun and to flee the sick and their belongings. By so behaving each believed that he would gain safety for himself. Some persons advised that a moderate manner of living, and the avoidance of all excesses, greatly strengthened resistance to this danger. Seeking out companions, such persons lived apart from other men. They closed and locked themselves in houses where no sick person was found. To live better they consumed in modest quantities the most delicate foods and the best wines, and avoided all sexual activity. They did not let themselves speak to anyone, nor did they wish to hear any news from the outside, concerning death or the sick. They lived amid music and those pleasures which they were able to obtain.

Others were of a contrary opinion. They affirmed that heavy drinking and enjoyment, making the rounds with singing and good cheer, the satisfaction of the appetite with everything one could, and the laughing and joking which derived from this, were the most effective medicine for this great evil. As they recommended, so they put into practice, according to their ability. Night and day, they went now to that tavern and now to another, drinking without moderation or measure. . . . This they could easily do, since everyone, as if he was destined to live no more, had abandoned all care of his possessions and of himself. Thus most houses had become open to all, and strangers used them as they happened upon them, as their proper owner might have done. With this inhuman intent, they continuously avoided the sick with all their power.

In this great affliction and misery of our city, the revered authority of both divine and human laws was left to fall and decay by those who administered and executed them. They too, just as other men, were all either dead or sick or so destitute of their families, that they were unable to fulfill any office. As a result, everyone could do just as he pleased.

SOURCE: Giovanni Boccaccio, *The Decameron*, trans. David and Patricia Herlihy. In *Medieval Culture and Society* (New York: Walker and Co., 1967), pp. 353-4

1. *In light of today's medical knowledge, explain the merits of the two plans people used to avoid the plague.*
2. *What were the most devastating effects of the plague on the lives of the survivors?*

In the late 14th century, Geoffrey Chaucer produced one of the greatest works in vernacular English. The Canterbury Tales *includes a prologue in which Chaucer introduces the reader to each of the 29 pilgrims traveling to the shrine of Thomas à Becket at Canterbury. Two of these introductions are reproduced below. The language in these excerpts has been updated; it is not the language of Chaucer's time.*

THE WIFE FROM BATH

A Good Wife was there from beside the city
Of Bath—a little deaf—which was a pity.
Such a great skill on making cloth she spent
That she surpassed the folk of Ypres and Ghent.
No parish wife would dream of such a thing
As going before her with an offering,
And if one did, so angry would she be
It put her wholly out of charity. . . .

Bold was her face, and fair and red of hue.
She was a worthy woman all her life;
Five times at church door had she been a wife,
Not counting other company in youth—
But this we need not mention here, in truth.
Thrice at Jerusalem this dame had been,
And many a foreign river she had seen,
And she had gone to Rome and to Boulogne,
To St. James' in Galicia, and Cologne.
Much lore she had from wandering by the way;
Still, she was gap-toothed, I regret to say. . . .
No tongue was readier with a jest than hers.
Perhaps she knew love remedies, for she
Had danced the old game long and cunningly.

THE KNIGHT

A Knight there was, and that a noble man,
Who from the earliest time when he began
To ride forth, loved the way of chivalry,
Honor and faith and generosity.
Nobly he bare himself in his lord's war,
And he had ridden abroad (no man so far),
In many a Christian and a heathen land,
Well honored for his worth on every hand.
He was at Alexandria when that town
Was won, and many times had sat him down
Foremost among the knights at feast in Prussia.
And everywhere he went his fame was high.
And though renowned, he bore him prudently;
Meek was he in his manner as a maid.
In all his life to no man had he said
A word but what was courteous and right:
He was a very perfect noble knight.
But now to tell you what array he had—
His steeds were good, but he himself was clad
Plainly . . .

SOURCE: Geoffrey Chaucer, *The Canterbury Tales*, trans. Frank E. Hill (London: Longman, Green & Co., 1945), pp. 4-5, 18-19.

1. *List the places the woman of Bath had visited. What was the importance of each in medieval Europe?*
2. *Analyze Chaucer's attitude toward each of these two pilgrims.*

THE MAGNA CARTA

In 1215, the barons of England forced King John to sign the Magna Carta, a document which defined the rights of the king and the feudal privileges of the nobility. Although the articles of the charter addressed the specific issues of the time, many of them became the foundation for new freedoms which eventually extended to all British people. For example, paragraph 12 addressed the fact that King John had repeatedly imposed burdensome feudal taxes upon his free subjects. In time, the language of this paragraph led to the concept that no taxes can be levied without the consent of the governed. Another important article of the charter is paragraph 39, which eventually led to the right of all subjects to a trial by a jury of their peers.

2. If any earl, baron, or other person that holds lands directly of the Crown, for military service, shall die, and at his death his heir shall be of full age and owe a "relief," the heir shall have his inheritance on payment of the ancient scale of "relief." That is to say, the heir or heirs of an earl shall pay 100 pounds for the entire earl's barony, the heir or heirs of a knight 100 shillings at most for the entire knight's "fee," and any man that owes less shall pay less, in accordance with the ancient usage of "fees."

8. No widow shall be compelled to marry, so long as she wishes to remain without a husband. But she must give security that she will not marry without royal consent, if she holds her lands of the Crown, or without the consent of whatever other lord she may hold them of.

12. No "scutage" or "aid" may be levied in our kingdom without its general consent, unless it is for the ransom of our person, to make our eldest son a knight, and (once) to marry our eldest daughter. For these purposes only a reasonable "aid" may be levied. "Aids" from the city of London are to be treated similarly.

13. The city of London shall enjoy all its ancient liberties and free customs, both by land and by water. We also will and grant that all other cities, boroughs, towns, and ports shall enjoy all their liberties and free customs.

17. Ordinary lawsuits shall not follow the royal court around, but shall be held in a fixed place.

20. For a trivial offence, a free man shall be fined only in proportion to the degree of his offence, and for a serious offence correspondingly, but not so heavily as to deprive him of his livelihood. In the same way, a merchant shall be spared his merchandise, and a husbandman the implements of his husbandry, if they fall upon the mercy of a royal court. None of these fines shall be imposed except by the assessment on oath of reputable men of the neighborhood.

23. No town or person shall be forced to build bridges over rivers except those with an ancient obligation to do so.

28. No constable or other royal official shall take corn or other movable goods from any man without immediate payment, unless the seller voluntarily offers postponement of this.

35. There shall be standard measures of wine, ale, and corn . . . throughout the kingdom. There shall also be a standard width of dyed cloth, russett, and haberject, a type of cloth, namely two ells within the selvedges. Weights are to be standardised similarly.

39. No free man shall be seized or imprisoned, or stripped of his rights or possessions, or outlawed or exiled, or deprived of his standing in any other way, nor will we proceed with force against him, or send others to do so, except by the lawful judgment of his equals or by the law of the land.

40. To no one will we sell, to no one deny or delay rights or justice.

41. All merchants may enter or leave England unharmed and without fear, and may stay or travel within it, by land or water, for purposes of trade, free from all illegal exactions, in accordance with ancient and lawful customs. This, however, does not apply in time of war to merchants from a country that is at war with us.

45. We will appoint as justices, constables, sheriffs, or other officials, only men that know the law of the realm and are minded to keep it well.

48. All evil customs relating to forests and warrens, foresters, warreners, sheriffs and their servants, or river-banks and their wardens, are at once to be investigated in every county by 12 sworn knights of the county, and within 40 days of their enquiry the evil customs are to be abolished completely and irrevocably. But we, or our chief justice if we are not in England, are first to be informed.

52. To any man whom we have deprived or dispossessed of lands, castles, liberties, or rights, without the lawful judgment of his equals, we will at once restore these. In cases of dispute the matter shall be resolved by the judgment of the 25 barons referred to below in the clause for securing peace (61). In cases, however, where a man was deprived or dispossessed of something without the lawful judgment of his equals by our father King Henry or our brother King Richard, and it remains in our hands or is held by others under our warranty, we shall have respite for the period commonly allowed to Crusaders. . . . On our return from the Crusade, or if we abandon it, we will at once render justice in full.

61. Since we have granted all these things for God, for the better ordering of our kingdom, and to allay the discord that has arisen between us and our barons, and since we desire that they shall be enjoyed in their entirety, with lasting strength, for ever, we give and grant to the barons the following security:

The barons shall elect 25 of their number to keep, and cause to be observed with all their might, the peace and liberties granted and confirmed to them by this charter. . . .

SOURCE: *The Magna Carta*. In *British Documents of Liberty* by Henry Marsh (Rutherford, N.J.: Fairleigh Dickinson University Press, 1971), pp. 41-6.

1. *What were the major concerns of the barons who forced John to sign the Magna Carta?*
2. *Compare the articles cited above to the American Bill of Rights (the first ten amendments to the Constitution of the United States). Which articles in the two documents are comparable? What are the similarities and differences?*

Niccolo Machiavelli presented his book The Prince *as a handbook for a medieval ruler who wanted to stay in power. The methods he advocates seem cynical to modern readers, and some have even suggested that the book is a parody.*

Laying aside, therefore, all imaginary notions of a prince, and discoursing of nothing but what is actually true, I say that all men when they are spoken of, and especially princes, who are in a higher and more eminent station, are remarkable for some quality or other that makes them either honorable or contemptible. Hence it is that some are counted liberal, others miserable . . . some munificent, others rapacious; some cruel, others merciful; some faithless, others precise; one poor-spirited and effeminate, another fierce and ambitious; one sincere, another cunning; one rugged and morose, another accessible and easy; one grave, another giddy; one devout, another an atheist.

No man, I am sure, will deny but that it would be an admirable thing and highly to be commended to have a prince endowed with all the good qualities aforesaid; but because it is impossible to have, much less to exercise, them all by reason of the frailty and grossness of our nature, it is convenient that he be so well instructed as to know how to avoid the scandal of those vices which may deprive him of his state, and be very cautious of the rest, though their consequences be not so pernicious, so that where they are unavoidable he need trouble himself the less.

To come now to the other qualities proposed, I say that every prince should desire to be esteemed merciful rather than cruel, but with great caution that his mercy be not abused. Caesar Borgia was counted cruel, yet that cruelty reduced Romagna, united it, settled it in peace, and rendered it faithful. . . .

And from hence arises a new question, Whether it is better to be beloved than feared, or feared than beloved? It is answered both would be convenient, but because that is hard to attain, it is better and more secure, if one must be wanting, to be feared rather than beloved; for, in general, men are ungrateful, inconstant, hypocritical, fearful of danger, and covetous of gain. Whilst they receive any benefit by you, and the danger is at a distance, they are absolutely yours; their blood, their estates, their lives, and their children, as I said before, are all at your service. But when mischief is at hand, and you have present need of their help, they make no scruple to revolt; and that prince who leaves himself naked of other preparations, and relies wholly upon their professions, is sure to be ruined; for amity contracted by price, and not by greatness and generosity of the mind, may seem a good pennyworth, yet when you have occasion to make use of it, you will find it of no account.

SOURCE: Machiavelli, *The Prince.* In *Readings in European History*, Vol. 1, ed. J.H. Robinson (New York: Ginn, 1904), pp. 518-20.

1. *How does Machiavelli justify his statement that it is better for a ruler to be feared than loved?*

2. *Machiavelli is well known for his stated belief that "the ends justify the means." What are the "means" that he advocates here, and what is the "end" that justifies them?*

A STREET FIGHT IN MILAN

Benvenuto Cellini, a talented Renaissance sculptor and goldsmith, lived an extraordinarily full and adventurous life. His fiery temper led him to engage in many exploits such as the one recounted below.

In the meanwhile my enemies had proceeded slowly toward Chiavica, as the place was called, and had arrived at the crossing of several roads, going in different directions; but the street in which Pompeo's house stood was the one which leads straight to the Campo di Fiore. Some business or other made him enter the apothecary's shop which stood at the corner of Chiavica, and there he stayed a while transacting it. I had just been told that he had boasted of the insult which he fancied he had put upon me; but be that as it may, it was to his misfortune; for precisely when I came up to the corner, he was leaving the shop, and his bravi [guards] had opened their ranks and received him in their midst. I drew a little dagger with a sharpened edge, and breaking the line of his defenders, laid my hands upon his breast so quickly and coolly, that none of them were able to prevent me. Then I aimed to strike him in the face; but fright made him turn his head around; and I stabbed him just beneath the ear. I gave only two blows, for he fell stone dead at the second. I had not meant to kill him; but, as the saying goes, knocks are not dealt by measure. With my left hand I plucked back the dagger and with my right hand drew my sword to defend my life. However, all those bravi ran up to the corpse and took no action against me; so I went back alone through Strada Giulia, considering how best to put myself in safety.

. . . A few days afterwards the Cardinal Farnese was elected Pope.

After he had put affairs of greater consequence in order, the new Pope sent for me, saying that he did not wish anyone else to strike [design and make] his coins. To these words of his Holiness a gentleman very privately acquainted with him, named Messer Latino Juvinale, made answer that I was in hiding for a murder committed on the person of one Pompeo of Milan, and set forth what could be argued for my justification in the most favorable terms. The Pope replied: 'I knew nothing of Pompeo's death, but plenty of Benvenuto's provocation; so let a safe conduct be at once made out for him, in order that he may be placed in perfect security.' A great friend of Pompeo's, who was also intimate with the Pope, happened to be there; he was a Milanese, called Messer Ambrogio. This man said: 'In the first days of your papacy it were not well to grant pardons of this kind.' The Pope turned to him and answered: 'You know less about such matters than I do. Know then that men like Benvenuto, unique in their profession, stand above the law; and how far more he, then, who received the provocation I have heard of?' When my safe conduct had been drawn out, I began at once to serve him, and was treated with the utmost favor.

SOURCE: Benvenuto Cellini, *The Life of Benvenuto Cellini* (Garden City, N.Y.: Phaidon, 1960), pp. 136-8.

1. *What did Cellini mean by the phrase "knocks are not dealt by measure"?*
2. *What does this excerpt reveal about Cellini's character and about the society in which he lived?*
3. *What do you think of the pope's statement that "men like Benvenuto stand above the law"?*

Index

Aachen
  and Charlemagne's court, 344, 346
  and Holy Roman Empire, 417
Abbasid caliphate, 314–15
Abd-al-Rahman, and caliphate at Cordoba, 322–3, 465
Abelard, Peter, 393–4
Abraham (Hebrew prophet), 84–5
Abu Bakr (first caliph), 311
Abu'l Abbas, and Abbasid caliphate, 314
Ab Urbe Condita (Livy), 200
Abu Simbel, temple at, 60
Achaean League, 189, 221. See also Greek federations
Achaeans, 98. See also Mycenaean civilization
Achaemenes, 74
Achaemenid Dynasty, 74, 76
Achilles, 120
Acre, castle of, 371, 373
Acropolis (Athenian), 150–52
Acropolis (term), 118
Ad-Din al-Farisi, Kalam (physicist), 319
Adrian IV (pope), 421
Aedile, 209
Aegean civilization, 91–102
Aegeus, in legend of Theseus, 97
Aeneas, 200, 241
Aeneid (Virgil), 241, 550
Aequi tribe of ancient Italy, 210
Aeschylus, 156–8
Aesop, 543
Aetolian League, 189. See also Greek federations
Africa, in Punic Wars, 218–19, 226–7
Africanus Minor (grandson of Scipio Africanus), 220
Agamemnon, 92, 99, 157
Age of Exploration, 471, 472
Age of Faith, 356
Ager publicus, 223
Agincourt, battle of, 459
Agora (term), 118
Agriculture
  in Byzantine Empire, 300–01
  in Egypt, 53, 190
  in Greece, 117, 162–3
  and Hittites, 73
  in late Middle Ages, 494–5
  in Maya civilization, 406
  in Middle Ages, 382

and Roman Empire, 224–5
  in the Sudan, 485
Agrippina, 245, 246–7
Ahmose I (pharaoh), 52, 54
Ahriman, and Zoroastrianism, 75
Ahuramazda, and Zoroastrianism, 75
Akhenaton, 52, 57–8
Akkad, 30
Alamanni, and division of Gaul, 340
Alaric II (king of Visigoths), 340
Albigensians, 362, 453
Alchemy, 319
Alcibiades, 161, 168–71
Alcuin of York, 346, 349–50
Alexander III (pope), and Portugal, 470
Alexander VI (pope), 515, 532, 533
Alexander the Great, 75, 84, 125, 162, 178–88
Alexandria, Egypt, 182, 188, 191–6
Alexius Comnenus I (Byzantine emperor), 365–6
Alfonso I (king of Portugal), 470, 471
Alfonso III (king of Portugal), 470, 471
Alfonso VI (king of Castile), 470
Alfonso Henriques. See Alfonso I (king of Portugal)
Alfred the Great (Anglo-Saxon king), 350, 429–31
Algebra, 317
Alhambra Palace, 321, 322
Alhazen (Moslem physicist), 319
Ali (fourth caliph), 311
Alighieri, Dante, 398–9
Allah, 304, 306, 310. See also Islam
Alphabet. See also Hieroglyphics; Writing system
  Cyrillic, 302
  Etruscan, 202
  Greek, 122
  Phoenician, 83, 84
Ambrose, Saint, 287, 288
Amenemhet I, 52, 53
Amenhotep III, 52, 56
Amenhotep IV. See Akhenaton
Ammon, oracle of, 182
Amos (Hebrew prophet), 89
Amphipolis, 168
Amun-Re, 52, 57, 58
Anabasis of Alexander (Arrian), 178
Analects (Confucius), 263, 268
Analytic geometry, 318
Anatolia, 67, 68, 93, 94
Anaximander, 147

Anaximenes, 147
Ancus Martius, 205
Andrew II (king of Hungary), 477
Andronikas, Manolis (archaeologist), 178
Angles, and Britain, 428
Anglo-Saxon Chronicle, 430
Anglo-Saxon kingdoms, 429–31
"Anno domini," 277
Anselm, Saint, 393
Anthropomorphism, religious, 26, 47, 73
Antigonus (Macedonian general), 189–90
Antioch, 192, 279
Antiochus III of Syria, 219, 220–21
Antiochus IV of Syria, 221, 275
Antipater, 180
Antoninus Pius (Roman emperor), 251
Antony, Mark, 235, 236–8
Anubis (Egyptian god), 47, 48
Aphrodite (goddess), 96, 101, 119
"Aphrodite of Cnidus" (statue), 154
Apollo, 119, 125, 204. See also Delphi, oracle at
Apollonius of Rhodes, 193
Apostolic succession, 287
Appian Way, 211
Aqueducts, Roman, 211
Aquinas, Saint Thomas, 361, 388, 394, 399
Arabia, before Islam, 304–05. See also Islamic Empire
Arabian Nights, 320
Arabian peninsula, 304–05
Arabic language
  and English word origins, 323
  and Islamic unity, 309
Arabic numerals, 317
Aragon, as Christian Kingdom of Spain, 467
Aramaic language, 84
Arameans, 84
Archaic Age, 102. See also Greece, ancient
Archbishop, 286
Archelaus of Macedonia, 175
Archimedes, 197, 218
Architecture
  of Babylon, 40–41
  in Byzantine Empire, 301–02
  Classical Greek, 150–52, 165
  early Roman, 199

Egyptian, 45–6, 59, 60. *See also of* pyramids.
Gothic, 401, 403
of Hittites, 71
Islamic, 320–22
of the Mayas, 408
medieval, 401–04
Minoan, 94, 95
Mycenaean, 98
of Persians, 78
of pyramids, 50–51, 408
in Renaissance, 520–23, 527
Romanesque, 401–03
Russian, 482
Sumerian, 23
of *tholoi*, 100–01
of ziggurats, 26
Arch of Titus, 282
Archons, 126, 127
Arc of Peace, 240
Argonautica (poem), 193
Argos, 169
Adriadne, in legend of Theseus, 97
Arianism, 286–7
Aristarchus of Samos, 197
Aristocracy (term), 126
Aristogoras of Miletus, 137
Aristophanes, 159, 160, 167
Aristotle, 127, 130, 158, 162, 179, 392–3
Arius, and Arianism, 286–7
Arjuna (in *Bhagavad gita*), 111
Ark of the Covenant, 86
Armor, 377
Arrian (historian), 178, 181, 182, 185, 186, 187
Ars Minor (Donatus), 389
Art
    of Assyrians, 38
    Byzantine, 301–02
    Classical Greek, 153–5
    early Greek, 152
    Egyptian
        Amarna period, 57
        mastabas, 46
    Hellenistic, 193–4
    Islamic, 320–22
    of the Mayas, 408
    Minoan, 96
    of Persians, 78
    and perspective, 520
    Renaissance, 518–29
    Romanesque, 401–03
    Russian, 482
    Semitic, 30
    of Uruk, 22–3
Arthurian legends, 428
Aryans. *See also* India; Vedas
    and castes, 107, 108
    conquest of India by, 106
    oral traditions of, 107
    religious writings of, 106–07
    settling by, 66, 74
    social structure of, 107, 108

Askia Muhammed (ruler of Songhai), 488
Assembly of Athens, 127, 129, 132, 133
Assize of Clarenson, 436–7
Assurbanipal, 36–8, 39
Assurnasirpal, 34, 39
Assyria, 35–6, 38–9, 74
Astrolabe, 318, 497
Astronomy
    Babylonian, 41–2
    and Greek civilization, 196–7
    in Islamic civilization, 318–19
    in Maya civilization, 408–09
    in Poland, 477
Aswan Dam, 44, 60
Athanasius (bishop of Alexandria), and Arianism, 286
Athena (deity), 96, 119, 150–51
Athena Parthenos (statue), 150
Athenian Confederation, 172
Athenian Empire. *See* Greece, Classical
Athens, 126–33, 148–65, 171. *See also* Greece, Classical
Atman, 107
Aton (sun god), 57, 540–41
Attila the Hun, 339
Augustine, Saint (354–430 A.D.), of Hippo, 257, 287–8, 502
Augustine, Saint (d. 604), Archbishop of Canterbury, 359, 429
Augustus, 238–41. *See also* Octavian
Augustus (term), 258
Augustus, Philip. *See* Philip II (king of France)
Aurelius, Marcus, 251–2, *558*
Autocracy, 252–3
Averroes (Moslem philosopher), 323, 394
Avicenna (Moslem physician), 316, 317
Avignon papacy, 457. *See also* Roman Catholic Church (Middle Ages)
Ay (pharaoh), 52, 58

Baal, 83–4, 88
Babylon, 40–41, 75, 187, 189
Babylonia, 31–4, 40–41
Babylonian captivity
    of Jews, 274
    as term for Avignon papacy, 457
Bacon, Roger, 394, 395
Baghdad, in Moslem world, 315
Baillis, 453
Ball, John, and Peasants' Revolt, 443, 445
Banking, rise of, 503–05
Barbarian (term), 123
Barbarossa, Frederick. *See* Frederick I (Holy Roman emperor)
Barca, Hamilcar, 215
Barrel vaulting, in architecture, 402
Barsine (wife of Alexander), 187
Barter, and medieval economy, 502
Basil II (Byzantine emperor), 297

Bavaria, in Holy Roman Empire, 416
Becket, Thomas à, 437
Bede, The Venerable, 359, 389
Bedouins, 304, 305
Beehive tombs, 100, 101
Behistun Rock, 27–8
Beirut, Lebanon, 81
Bela IV (king of Hungary), 477
Belisarius (Byzantine general), 292
Belshazzar, 40
Benedict, Saint, 358–9, *563*
Benedict XI (pope), 457
Benedictines, 358–9
Beowulf, 352, 398
Berbers, 313
Bernard of Clairvaux, 360–61, 369
Bessus, and Alexander the Great, 185
Bezant (coin), 300
Bhagavad Gita (quoted), 111
Bible, 287
Bibulus (Roman consul), 233
Bill of Rights (U.S.), 440
Bishop, in Christian churches, 285–6, 287
Bishop of Rome (pope), 286
Black Death. *See* Bubonic plague
Black Prince, in England, 443
Black Sea area
    colonization of, 122–3
    strategic importance of, 101, 102
Black Stone, of Mecca, 305, 308, 309
Blanche of Castile, 453
Bloodletting, in medieval medicine, 395, 396
Boccaccio, Giovanni, 505, 530, *570*
Boghazköi, Turkey, 71
Bolesaw I (Polish king), 474
Bolingbroke, Henry. *See* Henry IV (king of England)
Bologna, university at, 390–91
Boniface VIII (pope), 456–7
Book of Kells, 428
Book of the Courtier (Castiglione), 518
Book of the Secret of Secrets (Rhazes), 319
Books, in Middle Ages, 389. *See also* Printing
Books of the Dead, Egyptian, 47
Borgia, Lucretia, 532, 533
Bosporus (strait), 122
Botta, Paul Emilie (archaeologist), 38
Botticelli, Sandro, 520
Boule, 132, 133
Bouvines, battle of, 452
Brahma, 106
Brahmans (caste), 108–09
Bronze, in ancient China, 261
Bronze Age, 79, 91, 118
Brunelleschi, Filippo, 522
Brutus, 236, 237
Bubonic plague
    economic effects of, 505–06, 507
    in England, 443
    in Florence, *570*

Buddha, 109
Buddhism, 108–09
  in China, 266–7
  in Japan, 326–7
  sects of, 112, 326–7
Bulgaria, 179. *See also* Thrace
Bull vaulting, 98
Buonarroti, Michelangelo. *See* Michelangelo
Burckhardt, Jacob (historian), 509
Burgundians, and division of Gaul, 340
Burial customs
  and Egyptian tombs, 47, 50
  and Etruscan necropoleis, 202–03
  of Mycenaeans, 100, 101
  in Royal Cemetary of Ur, 29
Buttresses, in architecture, 402, 403
Byzantine Church. *See* Orthodox
  Church
Byzantine Empire, 257, 290–303
  agriculture in, 300–01
  architecture in, 301–02
  art in, 301–02
  citizenship in, 294
  civilization in, 300–02
  commerce in, 300–01
  decline of, 297–8
  and dynasty of Heraclius, 295–6
  education in, 301
  extent of, during Justinian's reign,
    292–3
  and fall of Constantinople, 297–8,
    371–2
  influences of, 301, 302
  invasions of, 295
  under Justinian, 291–5
  and Leo III, 296–7, 298–9, 314
  and Macedonian dynasty, 297
  and Roman legal traditions, 294
  rulers of, 294
  theological controversies in, 298–9
  and spread of Islam, 312
  and Viking raids, 351
  and wars with Persia, 295
Byzantium, 122, 255, 290–91. *See also*
  Constantinople
Byzas, and Byzantium, 290

Caesar (term), 258
Caesar, Julius, 232–6, *552–3*, *554–5*
Caesaropapism, 294–5
Cairo, in Moslem world, 315
Calendar
  in ancient China, 266
  Babylonian, 42
  Egyptian, 63
  Gregorian, 277
  Islamic, 307
  Julian, 235
  of the Mayas, 409
  of Meton, 42
  Roman, 202
  Sumerian, 24

Caligula, 244–5
Caliph, 311
Calligraphy, Moslem, 321
Callimachus (poet), 191, 192–3
Cambyses (Persian king), 76
Canaanites, 80, 96
Cannon of Medicine (Avicenna), 317
Canossa, 419–20
Canterbury, first archbishop of, 429
Canterbury Tales (Chaucer), 399–400,
  445, 571
Cantons, Swiss, 472
Canuleian Law, 210
Canute (Danish king), 350, 431
Canute (king of England), 431. *See also*
  Canute (Danish king)
Cape of Good Hope, 472
Capet, Hugh, 348, 449–50
Capetians, 348, 450–58
Caphtor, as homeland of Philistines,
  86
Capitoline Jupiter, 205
Caracalla, 253, 557
Carolingian Empire, 342–8. *See also*
  Charlemagne; France, medieval
  and Charlemagne, 342–6
  division of, 347–8
  end of, 449
  and Louis the Pious, 347
Carolingians (term), 342
Carta pergama. See Parchment
Carter, Howard, 58
Carthage, 83
  destruction of, 220
  Hannibal's reforms in, 219
  and Punic wars, 214–20
Cartography
  of Hipparchus, 97
  of Moslem astronomers, 318–19
Caryatids, 152
Casimir III (Polish king), 474–6
Cassius, 236, 237
Caste system in India, 107
Castiglione, Baldassare, 518, 533
Castile, as Christian Kingdom of Spain,
  466, 467
Castles, in Middle Ages, 378–9
Cataline, 234–5
Cathedrals. *See also* specific cathedrals
  Byzantine, 293–4
  Gothic, 402–04
  in Middle Ages, 378–9
  Renaissance, 520–23, 527
  Romanesque, 401–02
Cato the Censor, 219
Cave, The (Plato), 546–7
Cedars of Lebanon, 53
Cellini, Benvenuto, 528–9, *575*
Celts, 427–8. *See also* Gauls
Censor, in Roman Republic, 209
Chalcedon, 122
Chalcidice, 122, 176
Chaldea, 40–42

Champollion, Jean François, and Rosetta
  stone, 62–3
Chandragupta, Maurya, 189
Chariot design, and Hittites, 69
Chariot racing
  in Constantinople, 292
  in Etruscan civilization, 203
Charlemagne (Carolingian ruler), 342–7
  campaign in Spain of, 343
  description of (Einhard), *562*
  education under, 346–7
  as "Emperor of the Romans," 343
  government under, 343–6
  and Harun al-Rashid, 315
  and Pope Leo III, 297
  and reconquest of Spain, 465–6
  renaissance under, 346–7
Charles V (Holy Roman emperor), 528
Charles V (king of France), 443, 458–9
Charles VI (king of France), 445, 459
Charles VII (king of France), 445–6, 459,
  460–61
Charles VIII (king of France), 462, 473,
  515
Charles of Anjou, 425, 477
Charles the Bald (Carolingian ruler),
  347, 449
Charles the Bold (duke of Burgundy),
  461–2, 473
Charles the Simple (Frankish king), 351
Charles the Wise. *See* Charles V (king of
  France)
Chaucer, Geoffrey, 399–400, *571*
Chemistry, in Islamic civilization, 319
Cheops, 50, 52
Chephren. *See* Khafre
Chiaroscuro technique in painting, 520
Childeric III (Frankish king), 342
Children's Crusade, 372
China, ancient, 260–71
  and Ch'in dynasty, 264–5
  and Chou dynasty, 260–64
  extent of, in Chou dynasty, 261
  extent of, in Han dynasty, 265
  and Han dynasty, 262, 265–6
  important rivers to, 260
  philosophy in, 262. *See also* Bud-
    dhism; Confucianism; Legalism;
    Taoism
  pictographic writing in, 260
  science in, 266
China's Sorrow, 260
Ch'in dynasty, 264–5
Chivalry, code of, 380–81, 398
Chou dynasty, 260–64
Christ. *See* Jesus of Nazareth
Christianity, 274–89. *See also* Byzantine
  Empire; Christians; Jesus of Nazareth; Orthodox Church; Roman
  Catholic Church (Middle Ages)
  appeal of, 284
  in Britain, 428–9
  and Church fathers, 287–8
  and Constantine, 255

Christianity (*cont.*)
    doctrine in, 286, 287–8, 308, 356
    and East-West split, 294–5, 299–300
    in England, 428–9
    and excommunication, 286
    and Gentile converts, 280, 281
    and heresy, 286, 287, 288
    and Jewish sects, 275–6
    and life of Jesus, 276–9
    organization of early Church in, 285–6
    orthodox belief in, 286–7
    problems of early Church in, 286–7
    and rite of baptism, 277, 285
    setting for growth of, 274–6
    spread of, 279–84, 285
Christians. *See also* Christianity
    Moslem tolerance of, 312–13, 465
    as name, 279
    persecution of, 247, 248, 280–83
Chroeses II (ruler of Persia), 295
Church of the Holy Sepulcher (Jerusa-
    lem), 284, 368
Church of the Nativity (Bethlehem), 284
Cicero, Marcus Tullius, 234–5, 549,
    552–3
Cid, the, 464. *See also* Diaz de Bivar,
    Rodrigo; *Poem of the Cid*
Cincinnatus (Roman legend), 207
Cinna (Roman consul), 230
Cisalpine (term), 211
Cistercians, 360–61
Cities
    and medieval Europe, 384
    in Roman Empire, 224
Citizenship
    in Byzantine Empire, 294
    in Athens, 163. *See also* Assembly of
        Athens
    Roman, 211–12, 226, 228, 229, 245,
        253
    in Sparta, 134
City of David. *See* Jerusalem
City of God (Saint Augustine), 257, 288
City-states
    Greek, 116–43, 171–2, 189, 213. *See*
        also Athenian empire; Delian
        League; Greek federations; *Polis*
    in Philistia, 86
    Phoenician, 81–2
    Roman, 210–12
Civil service system, in ancient China,
    265
Clans. *See* Tribes and Clans
Claudius (Roman emperor), 246–7,
    428
Cleisthenes, 131–3
Clement V (pope), 457
Cleon, 159, 167–8
Cleopatra, 61, 235, 237–8
Clergy, in early Christian Church, 285–6
Clio (muse), 120
Clitus, and Alexander the Great, 185
Cloaca Maxima, 205

Cloisonné process, 302
Clouds (Aristophanes), 159, 160
Clovis (Frankish ruler), 287, 340–41
Cluniacs, 360
Cluny, 360
Clytemnestra, 157
Coat of arms, 377
Coeur, Jacques (French banker), 461,
    504
Coins, 77, 300, 502
Colossus of Rhodes, 192. *See also* Seven
    Wonders of the World
Columbus, Christopher, 469
Comedy, Classical Greek, 159
Comitia Centuriata, 206, 207, 208
Comitia Curiata, 204, 205, 206, 207–08.
    See also Curiae
Comitia Tributa Populi, 208
Commerce. *See* Trade and Commerce
Commodus (Roman emperor), 252
Compass, magnetic, 497
Compurgation, in Anglo-Saxon system
    of justice, 431
Concilium Latinorum, 210
Concilium Plebis, 207, 208, 213
Concordat of Worms, 420
Confessions (Saint Augustine), 287–8
Confucianism, 263–4, 267, 327, 332
Confucius, 263–4, 267, 268
Conrad II (Holy Roman emperor), 418
Conrad III (Holy Roman emperor), 370,
    420
Conrad of Franconia, 416–17
Consolation of Philosophy (Boethius),
    389
Constans (Roman emperor), 256
Constantine (Roman emperor), 255–6
    and Constantinople, 290–91
    toleration of Christians under, 283–4,
        286–7
Constantine II (Roman emperor), 256
Constantine VI (Byzantine emperor),
    296–7, 298
Constantinople, 255–6. *See also* Byzan-
    tine Empire
    attack on by Crusaders, 371–2
    and Byzantine empire, 290–303
    capture of, by Ottoman Turks, 293,
        298
    as center of commerce, 300
    defensibility of, 291, 314
    fall of, 297–8, 516
    founding of, 290–92
    Latin Kingdom of, 371–2
    Moslem attacks on, 314
Constantius (Roman emperor), 256
Consulship, in Roman Republic, 207,
    208
Convents, 360
Copernicus, Nicolaus, 197, 476, 477
Coptic Church, 298
Corcyra, 166
Cordoba, 315, 322–3, 465

Corinth
    at beginning of Peloponnesian War,
        166
    and colonization movement, 123
    destruction of, 221
Corpus Juris Civilis (Justinian), 33, 294
Corruption, and Roman Empire, 225–7
Cortés, 466–7, 471
Council of Constance, 458
Council of Elders (Senate)
    in ancient Rome, 204. *See also* Ro-
        man Empire
    in Sparta, 135
Council of Nicaea, 284, 286–7
Council of the Areopagus, 126–7
Craft guilds, 500–01
Crassus, 231–2, 233, 234
Creation, myths of
    in ancient Sumer, 28, 539
    in India (*Rig Veda*), 110
    in Maya civilization, 412
Crécy, battle of, 443
Crete, 93–4
Croesus (king), 39, 74
Cronus (Greek god), 120
Crop rotation in medieval Europe, 382,
    495, 496
Crusade (term), 297
Crusades, 363–73
    and Crusader states, 368
    and division of the Holy Land, 367
    and Latin Empire, 297, 371–2
    and motives of Crusaders, 364–5
    and Peter the Hermit, 365
    and religious-military orders, 368–9
    results of, 373
    and Saladin tithe, 370
Cuneiform writing, 26–8, 72. *See also*
    Writing systems
Curiae, 204, 206. *See also Comitia Cur-
    iata*
Curia regis, 453
Cursus honorum, 231
Cybele (Greek goddess), 74
Cyclopes, 98
Cynicism, 194–6

Da Gama, Vasco, 472
Damascus, 84
Dance of Death, 507
Danegeld, 431
Danelaw (region), 350, 430
Danes. *See* Vikings
Dante. *See* Alighieri, Dante
Dardanelles, 102
Darics (coins), 77
Darius III, 181, 182–4, 185
Darius the Great, 76–8, 137–8, 139
Dark Ages. *See* Middle Ages
Dauphin, 459. *See also* Charles VII
    (king of France)
David (Hebrew king), 86

"David" (sculpture by Michelangelo), 526
Da Vinci, Leonardo, 523, 524–6
Dead Sea scrolls, 276
Decameron (Boccaccio), 505, 530, *570*
Decius (Roman emperor), 282–3
Degrees, in medieval universities, 392
Delian League, 143, 148–9, 166, 168, 212
Delphi, oracle at, 125–6, 179
Delphic Amphictyony, 125, 126
Demagogue (term), 167
Demes, 131, 132, 164
Demesne, 382
Demeter (Greek goddess), 120
Democracy (term), 126
    in Athens, 127–9, 131–3, 148, 544
    beginnings of, in Greece, 118
    Plato's description of, 161
Democritus, 147
De Montfort, Simon, and origins of Parliament, 440
Demosthenes (general), 168, 169, 170
Demosthenes (orator), 176, 177
Demotic script, 62
d'Este, Isabella, 533
Deus ex machina, 158
Dharma, 107, 111
Dias, Bartholomeu (Portuguese explorer), 472
Diaspora, 89
Diaz de Bivar, Rodrigo, 398, 466. *See also Poem of the Cid*
Di Bondone, Giotto. *See* Giotto
Dictator, in Roman Republic, 207
Diet (Polish parliament), 476–7
Dinis (ruler of Portugal), 470–71
Dinski, Dmitri (Russian prince), 482
Diocese
    in Christian church, 285–6
    in Roman Empire, 254
Diocletian (Roman emperor), 254–5, 257–8
Diogenes, and cynicism, 194–6
Dionysius of Halicarnassus, 200, 202, 551
Dionysus (Greek god), 155–6, 158
"Discus Thrower" (statue), 154
Divine Comedy (Dante), 399
Doge (Venice), 511
Dome of the Rock (Jerusalem mosque), 321
Dominic, Saint, 362
Dominican Order, 361, 362
Domitian (Roman emperor), 248
Donatello, 522
Donation of Pepin, 342
Donativum, 245
Do-nothing kings (Germanic), 341
Doomsday Book, 434
Doomsmen, in Anglo-Saxon system of justice, 431
Dorians, 102, 116

Draco, 128
Drama, Greek, 155–9
Dravidians, 104–06, 108. *See also* Untouchables
Drusus (Son of Tiberius), 244
Dur-Sharrakin, 38

Earl, in Anglo-Saxon government, 430
Eastern Europe, medieval, 474–8
Eastern Orthodox Church. *See* Orthodox Church
Eastern Roman Empire, and Constantinople, 290–91
Ecclesiastical History of the English People (Venerable Bede), 389
Edessa, 369–70
Edict of Milan, 255, 283–4
Education
    in Byzantine Empire, 301
    under Charlemagne, 346–7
    in Middle Ages, 388–92
    in Renaissance, 518
Edward (Anglo-Saxon king of England), 431
Edward I (Plantagenet king of England), 441
Edward III (king of England), 442–3, 505, 569
Edward IV (king of England), 447
Edward the Confessor. *See* Edward (king of England)
Edwin Smith papyrus, 63
Egypt. *See also* Cleopatra
    Amarna period in, 52, 56–8, *541*
    and Coptic Church, 298
    decline of civilization in, 61
    dynasties of, 48–61
    18th dynasty, 54–6
    11th dynasty, 52–3
    Hyksos rule in, 52, 53–4
    and Mediterranean trade, 53
    Middle Kingdom in, 49, 52–4
    New Kingdom in, 52, 54–61
    19th dynasty, 58–60
    Old Kingdom in, 50–52
    predynastic, 46–8
    Ptolemaic dynasty in, 188, 190
    12th dynasty, 53–4
    20th dynasty, 60–61
Einhard (biographer of Charlemagne), 341, 342–3, *562*
Eleanor of Aquitaine, 398, 436, 438, 451
Elements of Geometry (Euclid), 196–7
Elgin, Lord, 152
Elgin Marbles, 152
Elis, 169
"Emperor of the Romans." *See* Charlemagne
Emperor-worship, 189, 282–3. *See also* Augustus; Claudius; Decius; Religion

England, medieval, 427–47
    and Anglo-Saxon kingdoms, 429–31
    Christianity in, 428–9
    and church-state struggle, 437
    government in, 430, 433–5, 440
    and House of Lancaster, 445–6, 447
    and House of Tudor, 447
    and House of York, 446–7
    and Hundred Years' War, 441–6
    invasions of, 427–8
    justice in, 430–31, 436–7
    kings of, 437, 447
    languages in, 434–5, 445
    and Norman conquest, 432–6
    and Parliament, 433, 440–41, 447
    under Plantagenets, 436–45
    taxation in, 431, 435, 438, 440, 441, 443
    and War of the Roses, 446–7
Epaminondas (Theban leader), 171–2
Ephors, 7. *See also* Sparta
Epics
    of Gilgamesh, 28, *539*
    Homeric, 100, 118
    of the Middle Ages, 397–8
Epicureanism, 196
Epicurus, 196
Equites, in Roman army, 206
Eratosthenes (Greek geographer), 197
Erechtheum, 152
Ericson, Leif, 351, 352
Eric the Red, 351, 352
Esarhaddon, 36, 39
Essenes, 275–6. *See also* Dead Sea scrolls
Essex, 429
Estates General, 456, 461
Ethelred (king of England), 431
Ethical monotheism, 85–6, 274. *See also* Judaism; Religion
Ethical religion, 75. *See also* Religion
Etruria, 202
Etruscans, 199, 202–03, 205, 206
Etymologies (Isadore of Seville), 389
Euclid, 196–7, 318
Eugenius III (pope), 369
Eumenides, in Greek drama, 158
Euripides, 158–9, 175
Europe, medieval. *See also* specific countries; Medieval civilization
    and Canon law, 357–8
    invasion by Vikings of, 348–52
    invasion by Magyars of, 354
    Moslem attacks on, 353
    and role of Roman Catholic Church, 356–73
Euterpe (muse), 120
Euximus Pontus, 123
Evans, Sir Arthur, 92, 94, 95
Exchequer, 435–6
Excommunication, 357, 419
Exiguus, Dionysius, 277

Fabius Maximus, Q., 216
Farmer King. *See* Dinis
Fasces, 205, 207
Fate, in Greek drama, 157
Fates, 120
Father of Greek tragedy. *See* Aeschylus
Father of history. *See* Herodotus
Father of optics. *See* Alhazen
Father of scientific geometry. *See* Euclid
Fatima (daughter of Mohammed), 311, 315
Fatimid caliphate, 315
Ferdinand of Aragon, 467–70
Fertile Crescent, 30, 80, 85
Feudal Age. *See* Egypt, Middle Kingdom in
Feudalism in Europe, 354, 375–8. *See also* Medieval civilization
   in China, 261–2
   in Japan, 328–9
Ficino, Marsilio, and the Medicis, 513
Fief, 376
Filial piety, 263, 267
Fine, John V.A., 131
First Crusade, 363–9, 397. *See also* Crusades
First Triumvirate, 233–4
Flamines, 201
Flamininus, Quinctius, 216, 220
Flanders, 498
Flavian emperors, 248
Florence, and the Renaissance, 511–15
Flying buttresses, 403
Folk medicine, in medieval rural Europe, 396
Fortification, in medieval Europe, 384–5, 434
Founder of humanism. *See* Petrarch
Founder of modern science. *See* Grosseteste, Robert
Four Noble Truths, 109, 112, 327
Fourth Crusade, 297, 371–2. *See also* Crusades
France, and division of Charlemagne's empire, 347
France, medieval, 449–62
   under Capetian dynasty, 450–58
   Carolingian beginnings of, 347
   after Charlemagne, 449–58
   early Moslem attacks on, 353
   and Estates General, 456
   extent of, 455
   government in, 453, 456
   and House of Valois, 458–62
   and Hundred Years' War, 441–2, 458–61
   justice in, 453, 454
   nation states of, 461–2
   and papacy, 456–7
   and Parlement of Paris, 453, 454, 456
   popular uprisings in, 458
   rulers of, 452, 458
   taxation in, 453, 458, 461

Francis I (king of France), 529
Franciscan Order, 361, 362–3
Francis of Assisi, Saint, 362–3, 565
Franconia, in Holy Roman Empire, 416
Franconians, 418–20
Franks. *See also* Carolingian Empire; Merovingian dynasty
   and Gaul, 340–48
   and Moslems, 314
Frederick I (Holy Roman emperor), 370, 421–2, 424, 452
Frederick II (Holy Roman emperor), 372, 422–5, 473
Friar (term), 361–3
Fugger, Jacob, 504–05
Furies, 120, 158. *See also* Oresteian Trilogy

Gaius (grandnephew of Tiberius). *See* Caligula
Galen, 395–6
"Gallic Chieftain" (sculpture), 194
Gallipoli, 102
Ganesha (Hindu god), 107
Garden of Eden, 22
Gaugamela, 182, 183, 184
Gauls, 210–11, 212, 428, 429, 554. *See also* Celts
Gaza Strip, 86
Gebel Tarik, 314
Gentes, in ancient Rome, 204, 206
Geocentric theory, 197
Geography. *See also* Eratosthenes, Hecataeus, Hipparchus
   in Islamic civilization, 318–19
Geometry, 45, 196–7, 318. *See also* Archimedes; Euclid
Gerbert. *See* Sylvester II (pope)
Germanic tribes. *See also* Alemanni; Angles; Burgundians; Goths; Jutes; Lombards; Ostrogoths; Saxons; Visigoths
   descriptions of, 555, 556–7
   and fall of Rome, 256–7
   migrations of, 338–40
Germany, and division of Charlemagne's empire, 347
Gezer, 87, 88
Genghis Khan, 481
Ghibellines, 511–12
Ghiberti, Lorenzo (artist), 520–22
Gilbraltar, 314
Giotto (painter), 518–20
Gizeh, royal tombs at, 51
Gladiatorial contests, 203
Glassmaking, in Islamic civilization, 322
Glaucia (Roman tribune), 228–9
Glyphs. *See* Hieroglyphics, or Pictographs
Gnosticism, 286
Godfrey of Bouillon, 365, 367–8

Gods. *See also* Religion; Sun god
   Aryan, 109
   Egyptian, 46–7
   Greek, 119–20
   Hebrew, 85, 86, 88, 89
   Hindu, 106, 107
   Hittite, 73
   of Mayas, 408
   Roman, 201–02
   Sumerian, 26
   of Vikings, 352
Godwinson, Harold (king of England), 431–2
Golden Age, mythical Greek, 118
Golden Book, in Venetian Society, 511
"Golden Bull," 425, 477
Golden Horde, 481
Gonzaga, Francesco (duke of Mantua), 533
Gordian knot, 181
Gospels. *See also* Bible
   and life of Jesus, 277
   and New Testament, 285
   synoptic, 277
Goths. *See* Ostragoths; Visigoths
Government. *See also* Aristocracy; Autocracy; Democracy; Oligarchy; Theocracy; Timocracy; Tyranny
   under Charlemagne, 343–6
   Confucius on, 268
   federal, 189–90
   forms of, 126
   in medieval England, 430, 433–5, 440
   in medieval France, 453, 456
   representative, 127, 440
   roles of guilds in, 500–01
   in Spain, 466–7
Gracchi brothers, 224–6
Gracchus, Gaius, 225–6
Gracchus, Tiberius, 224–5
Great Charter. *See* Magna Carta
Great Council (Venice), 511
Great Schism, 457–8
Great Wall of China, 264
Greece, ancient. *See also* Athens; City-states, Greek; Greece, Classical; Hellenistic era; Sparta
   climate of, 117
   economy in, 120–21, 162–5
   end of independence of, 221
   evolution of government in, 126
   family in, 121, 164
   geography of, 116–17
   during Iron Age, 102, 118–25
   natural resources in, 116–17
   early religion in, 119–20
   and second Punic War, 217
   social structure in, 120–21, 162–5
   trade in, 121–4
Greece, Classical, 140–73
   architecture in, 150–52, 165
   citizenship in, 163

demise of, 165. *See also* Peloponnesian War
drama in, 155–9
economy of, 162–5
education in, 164–5
factories in, 163
family life in, 164
philosophy in, 147–8, 160–62
sculpture of, 152–5
social structure of, 162–5
taxation in, 163–4
Greek Dark Ages (term), 102
Greek federations, 189–90
Greek fire (flamethrower), 295
Gregory the Great (pope), 359, 429
Gregory VII (pope), 418–20, 433, *568*
Gregory IX (pope), 424–5
Gregory XI (pope), 457
Grosseteste, Robert, 394–5
Grotefend, Georg Friedrich (linguist), 27–8
Guelfs, 511, 512
Guidi, Tommasco (Masaccio), 520
Guilds
    in Byzantine Civilization, 300
    in Japan, 329
    in late Middle Ages, 499–502
    at university of Paris, 391
Gutenberg, Johann, 529, 530
Gutenberg Bible, 530
Guthrum (king of the Danes), 350
Gutians, 30

Hades, 120
Hadrada, Harold, 431, 432
Hadrian (Roman emperor), 249–51, 258
Hadrian's Wall, 250
Hagia Sophia (Byzantine cathedral), 293–4
Halley's comet, 432
Hamilton, Edith, 146, 156–7
Hammurabi, 31–4, 49, 68, 81
Hammurabi's Code, 32–4, 73
Handbook of Sacred and Secular Learning (Cassiodorus), 389
Han dynasty, 262, 265–6
Han Fei Tzu, 264
Hanging Garden of Babylon, 41
Hannibal, 215–18, 219
Hanseatic League, 501–02. *See also* Guilds
Hanukkah, 275
Hapsburg dynasty, 425, 473
Harappa, 104, 105
Harun al-Rashid (caliph), 315, 317, 318
Hasdrubal, 215–18
Hastings, battle of, 432
Hatshepsut, 51, 55
Hattusas, 71
Hattusilis III, 69
Hazor, 87, 88
Heavy plow, 495

Hebrew prophets, 89
Hebrew, 84–6, 88–9. *See also* Jews
Hecale (poem), 193
Hecataeus (Greek geographer), 24, 145
Hegemony, 46, 171–2
Hegira, year of, 307
Heian period, in Japan, 328
Heir apparent (term), 39
Helena (Constantine's mother), 284
Helen of Troy, 101
    of Aristarchus, 197
Heliocentric theory
    of Aristarchus, 197
    and Copernicus, 476, 477
Hellas, 123. *See also* Greece, ancient
Hellenes, 123, 124
Hellenistic era, 188–97
    art of, 193–4
    class system in, 190–91
    economy in, 190
    literature of, 192–3
    philosophy of, 194–6
    science in, 196–7
Hellenization, in Macedonia, 175
Helots, 134, 136
Henry I (Holy Roman emperor), 417
Henry I (king of England), 435–6
Henry II (king of England), 436–7, 451
Henry III (Holy Roman emperor), 418
Henry III (king of England), 440–41
Henry IV (Holy Roman emperor), 418–20, 424
Henry IV (king of England), 445, 446
Henry V (Holy Roman emperor), 420
Henry V (king of England), 445, 446
Henry VI (Holy Roman emperor), 422
Henry VI (king of England), 446
Henry VII (king of England), 447
Henry of Burgundy, 470
Henry the Fowler. *See* Henry I (Holy Roman emperor)
Hera (Greek goddess), 119
Heraclitus (Greek philosopher), 147
Heraclius (Byzantine emperor), 295–6
Heraldry, 377
Herculanean, 248
Hermes (Greek god), 120
"Hermes and Dionysius" (statue), 154, 155
Hermits, 358
Herod (king of Palestine), 277
Herodotus, 40–41, 44, 51, 82, 136, 137, 141–2, 145–7, 165, *540*
Heroic Age of Greece, 118
Hesiod, 119, 120–21, 122
Hieratic script, 62
Hieroglyphics, or Pictographs
    Chinese, 264–5
    Egyptian, 61–3
    and the Hittites, 72
    in Maya civilization, 408, 410
    and the Minoans, 93, 97

Hildebrand, 418. *See also* Gregory VII (pope)
Hinduism, 106, 107
Hipparchus (Greek astronomer), 197
Hippias (Athenian tyrant), 131
Hippo, bishop of. *See* Augustine, Saint, of Hippo
Hippocrates, 148
Hippocratic Oath, 148
Hisham (caliph), 321
Hissarlik, Turkey, 91
Historia (term), 145
Hittites, 54, 67–74
    archaeological findings from, 71–2
    economy of, 73
    government of, 72
    language of, 72
    legal system of, 72–3
    and nonaggression treaty, 59
    religion of, 73–4
    technology of, 34
    use of iron by, 73
Hohenstaufens, 420–25
Holistic healing, 148. *See also* Medicine
Holy Land. *See* Crusades
Holy Roman Empire, 416–25
    decline of, 425
    duchies of, 416
    emperor-pope conflicts in, 419–20, 421, 424–25
    and Franconian rulers, 418–20
    and Hohenstaufens, 420–25
    and investiture controversy, 418–20
    rulers of, 420
    and Saxon dynasty, 416–18
    and Swiss Confederation, 472–3
Holy war, Islamic. *See Jihad*
Homer
    as source on Minoan-Mycenaean civilizations, 91, 92, 93, 97–8, 99, 100, 101, 102, 118–19
    as source on Iron-Age Greece, 118–19, 120–21
Honorius III (pope), 362
Hoplites, 127, 205
Horemheb (pharaoh), 52, 58
Hortensian law, 209, 213
Horus (Egyptian god), 46, 47
"Hospitable sea," 123
Hospitalers. *See* Knights of Saint John
Hour, 60-minute, 26
House of Aviz, 471–2
House of Commons, 441
House of Lancaster, 445–6, 447
House of Lords, 441
House of Tudor, 447
House of Two Towers, 71–2
House of Valois, 458
House of Wisdom (Islamic), 316
House of York, 446, 447
Hrozny, Bedrich (linguist), 72
Hsia dynasty, 260
Huang Ho River, 260

Humanism, 516–18
Hunayn ibn Ishaq (Moslem translator),
    316
Hundred Years' War, 441–6, 458–61,
    506
Hungary, 354, 477–8
Huns, 256, 338, 339
Hunyadi, John (Hungarian general), 478
Husayn (Shiite caliph), 313
Hussars, 478
Hyksos, 52, 53–4
"Hymn of Creation," 110

Iadwiga (queen of Poland), 476
Ibn-al-Walid Khalid, (Moslem general),
    311
Ibn Khaldun (historian), 320, *560–61*
Ibn-Rushd. *See* Averroes
Ibn Sina. *See* Avicenna
Icons, 298–9
Ideograms, 61
Idrisi, al- (Moslem geographer), 319, 354
Idylls (of Theocritus), 192
Ile de France, 450
Illiad (Homer), 91, 98, 99, 100, 101
Illumination, in Moslem manuscripts,
    322
Imam, in Islam, 310
Imhotep (Egyptian vizier), 50, 64
"Immortals," in Persian army, 76
Impasto technique in painting, 528
Imperium, 203, 207
India. *See also* Aryans
    and Alexander the Great, 169–70
    ancient, 104–14
    sea route to, 186–7
Indigenous peoples (term), 202
Indo-European invasion, 93–4
Indo-European languages, 66–7, 72
Indo-Europeans, 66
Indo-Gangetic plain, 106
Indra (Aryan god), 109
Indus Valley, 105
Indus Valley civilization, 104–05, 106
Innocent III (pope), 356, 361–3, 370,
    422, 439–40, 453, 470
Inquisition, 468–9
Intellectual revival, in Middle Ages,
    388–94. *See also* Renaissance
Investiture, 376. *See also* Lay investi-
    ture
Ionia, 102, 145–8
Iran, 66, 74
Iranian Plateau, 74
Ireland, and Christianity, 428
Irene (Byzantine emperor), 296–7
Iron Age, and Hittites, 79
Iron Age of Greece, 118–25
Isabella of Castile, 467–70
Isabella of Haiment, 451
Ishtar (Babylonian goddess), 73
Isis (Egyptian goddess), 47, 274

Islam, 304–23. *See also* Islamic Empire;
        Moslems
    Arabia before, 304–05
    and Byzantine empire, 294
    and charity, 308
    divisions within, 313
    five pillars of faith in, 308–09
    and *Hajii*, 309
    and *Kaaba*, 308
    and *Koran*, 309
    and monotheism, 305, 306
    moral code of, 310
    and pilgrimage to Mecca, 308–09
    prayer and, 308
    and priesthood, 310
    social code of, 310
    teachings of, 308–10
Islamic Empire. *See also* Islam; Mos-
        lems
    and Abbasid caliphate, 314
    architecture of, 320–22
    art in, 320–22
    and astronomy, 318–19
    civilization of, 315–22
    commerce in, 315–16
    and conquered peoples, 312–13
    establishment of, 311
    expansion of, 310–14
    first caliphs and, 310–11
    and geography, 318–19
    industry in, 315–16
    literature of, 319–20
    and mathematics, 317–18
    medicine in, 316–17
    and military conquests, 311–14
    and Omayyad dynasty, 313–14
    and political decline, 315
    scholarship in, 316
Israel (person), 86. *See also* Jacob
Israel, Kingdom of, 80, 86–9. *See also*
        Hebrews; Jews
Istanbul, as new name for
        Constantinople, 298
Italian marble, 199
Italian merchant-bankers, 503
Italian Wars, 462, 473
Italy. *See also* Roman Empire; Rome, as
        republic
    ancient tribes in, 210
    climate of, 200
    and California, 199
    geography of, 199–200
    Greek colonization in, 123
    natural resources of, 199–200,
        551
    and the Renaissance, 509–33. *See*
        also Renaissance
    and Papal States, 510
    in *1350*, 510–16
    and trade, 510–11
Ivan I (Russian prince), 482
Ivan III (Russian prince), 482
Ivan the Great. *See* Ivan III

Jabir (Moslem alchemist), 319
Jacob (Israel), 85, 86
Jacquerie, 458, 459, 506
Jagello (grand-duke of Lithuania), 476
James, Saint, 466
Janus (Roman god), 201
Japan (500–1500 A.D.), 325–35
    Buddhism in, 326–7
    Confucianism in, 327–32
    early history of, 325–6
    feudal period in, 328–9
    influence of China on, 326–8
    Shinto religion of, 325
Jehoiachin, 40
Jehoiakim, 39–40
Jehovah. *See* Yahweh
Jemdet Nasr, 23
Jen, 267
Jeremiah (Hebrew prophet), 89
Jeroboam, 88
Jerome, Saint, 287, 339
Jerusalem (city), 36, 86, 89. *See also*
        Crusades; Jews
    conquests of, in Crusades, 367–8,
        370–71
    destruction of, 281
    Dome of the Rock mosque in, 321
Jerusalem, Temple at
    and Hagia Sophia, 293
    and Jesus, 278
    looting of, 282
    return of Jews to, 274, 275
    and Wailing Wall, 283
Jesus, as name, 277
Jesus of Nazareth, 89. *See also* Christi-
        anity
    birth of, 277
    death of, 279
    followers of, 277, 278, 279
    life of, 276–9
    as Messiah, 278, 279
    nature of, and Arian controversy,
        286–7, 298
    teachings of, 278–9
Jews. *See also* Hebrews
    and Antiochus IV, 275
    Babylonian exile of, 40, 75, 274
    dispersion of, 281
    history of, 274–5
    independence of, under Maccabeans,
        275
    in late Middle Ages, 503
    literature of, 89
    as medieval money lenders, 503
    and Messiah, 275, 276, 277, 278
    Moslem tolerance of, 312–13, 465
    persecution of, 248, 365, 372
    in pre-Islamic Arabia, 305
    religion of, 274–5. *See also* Judaism
    revolt of, against Rome 281
    sects among, 275–6
    and Spanish Inquisition, 468–9
Jihad (Moslem holy war), 307

Joan of Arc, 446, 459–60
John (king of England), 438–40
John I (ruler of Portugal), 471
John II (king of France), 443
John II (ruler of Portugal), 471, 472
John XII (pope), 418
John the Baptist, 277–8
Jongleurs, 397
Jordan, 80
Josephus, Flavius (Jewish historian), 275, 276, 281
Journeymen, in medieval guilds, 500
Jousts, 379–80
Judah (kingdom), 86, 88–9
Judaism, 76, 89, 192, 274–6. See also Jews
Jugurtha, 226
Jugurthian War, 226–9
Julian (Roman emperor), 256
Julian calendar, 235
Julio-Claudian emperors, 243–7. See also Augustus
Julius II (pope), 526
Jupiter (Roman god), 201
Jury system, in England, 436–7
Justinian (Byzantine emperor)
    achievements of, 293–5
    and campaign in the West, 292–3
    and Nika Revolt, 292
    and unity of Roman Empire, 291–5, 339
Jutes, and Britain, 428

Kaaba, and Islam, 305, 307–08, 309
Kadesh, battle at, 59, 69, 70
Kamares style pottery, 96
Kamose (pharaoh), 53–4
Karma, 108
Khadija (wife of Mohammed), 306
Khafre (pharaoh), 51, 52
Khatti, 68
Khayyam, Omar, 318, 319
Kheta. See Hittites
Khufu. See Cheops
Khwarizmi (Moslem mathematician), 317
Kiev, 478–80
"King's Peace" treaty, 171
King Tut. See Tutankhamun
Kitto, H.D.F., 121
Knights
    early use of, 354
    in Middle Ages, 377–8, 379–80
Knights (play by Aristophanes), 167
Knights of Saint John, 368, 372
Knights of the Temple. See Templars
Knossos, 92, 93, 94–95, 97
Koine (dialect), 175, 176, 191, 192
Koran, 304, 309–10, 319–20
Koure, 152
Kouros, 151
Krishna, 111

Kshatriyas (caste), 108
Kung Tzu. See Confucius

Labyrinth, 97
Lacedaemon. See Sparta
Laconia, 134
Laertes (king), 120
Laevinus (Roman praetor), 218
Lamachus (Athenian general), 169
Land between the Rivers, 88–9. See also Mesopotamia
Land of the Angles (England), 429
Langton, Stephen (archbishop), 439
Languages. See also Arabic language; Aramaic language; Latin language
    in England, 434–5, 445
    in Europe, 397
"Laocoon" (Hellenistic sculpture), 195
Lao-tse, 262–3, 267, 269
Las Navas de Tolosa, battle of, 467
"Last Supper" (painting by Da Vinci), 524–5
Latin Empire, 297, 371–2
Latin language, in Middle Ages, 389
Latin League, 210–11
Latin Quarter, in Paris, 391
Latins, 199, 210
Latin-Sabine kings, 204–05
Latitude, as concept, 197
Law of Moses, 33
Law of the 12 Tablets, 209–10, 212
Layard, Sir Henry Austen, 38
Lay investiture, 418–20. See also Investiture
League of Corinth, 167–8
League of Upper Germany. See Swiss Confederation
Leakey, Richard, 537
Lebanon, 80
Lebanon Mountains, 80–82
Legalism, 264, 270
Leo III (Byzantine emperor), 296–9, 314
Leo III (pope), 296–7, 339, 343, 344
Leo IX (pope), 418
Leonidas (king) at Thermopylae, 141
Leopold I, Duke of Austria, 473
Leopold III, Duke of Austria, 473
Lepidus (Roman consul), 231, 237
Leuctra, battle at, 172
Library
    at Alexandria, 191, 192, 197, 311
    at Pergamum, 192
Licinius (Roman Augustus), 255
Lictor, 205, 207
Liege lord (term), 376
Linear A (syllabic script), 97
Lion Gate, 99
Lisbon, 470
Literacy, in ancient Egypt, 54
Literature. See also Drama, Greek; Epics; Poetry

Hellenistic, 192–3
    of Islamic Empire, 319–20
    in late Middle Ages, 396–401
    in Renaissance, 530–32
    Sumerian, 28–9
    of Vikings, 352
Lithuania, 476
Liu Pang, 265
Livy
    on early Rome, 200, 241
    on Hannibal, 215
Lombard League, 421
Lombards, 339–40, 343
Longitude, as concept, 197
Lorenzo the Magnificent. See Medici, Lorenzo de
Lorraine, in Carolingian Empire, 347
    in Holy Roman Empire, 416
Lost Tribes of Israel, 35
Lothair (Carolingian ruler), 345, 347, 348
Louis, Saint. See Louis IX (king of France)
Louis VI (king of France), 450–51
Louis VII (king of France), 370, 451
Louis VIII (king of France), 452
Louis IX (king of France), 372, 451, 453–4
Louis XI (king of France), 461–2
Louis XII (king of France), 525
Louis the Fat. See Louis VI (king of France)
Louis the German (Carolingian ruler), 347
Louis the Great (king of Hungary), 477
Louis the Pious (Charlemagne's son), 347
Louvre palace, 453
Lyceum, of Aristotle, 162
Lycurgus, constitution of, 134
Lydia, 74, 202
Lysippus (sculptor), 154, 180

Maccabeans, 275, 276
Maccabeus, Judas, 275
Macedon. See Macedonia
Macedonia, empire of, 171, 172, 173–87, 221
Macedonian dynasty of Byzantine Empire, 297
Macedonian phalanx, 213. See also Oblique phalanx; Phalanx
Machiavelli, Niccolo, 531, 574
Magi, of Persia, 75, 76
Magna Carta, 439, 440, 572–3
Magna Graecia (Great Greece), 123, 200, 202, 213
Magyars, 354, 477–8
Mahabharata, 107
Maid of Orleans. See Joan of Arc
Maimonides, Moses, 323
Mali, empire of, 487

Mamertines, and Punic wars, 214
Mamum, al (caliph), 315, 316
Mandate of Heaven, 261
Manetho, and dynasties of Egypt, 49
Manors, in Middle Ages, 381–4
Mantinea, 169
Marathon, battle of, 139–40
Marcel, Etienne, and *Jacquerie*, 458
Marduk, priests of, 40
Marius, Gaius, 227–9, 230
Mars (Roman god), 201, 202
Martel, Charles (Carolingian ruler), 314, 342, 354, 403
Masaccio. *See* Guidi, Tommasco
Masada (Zealot fortress), 281
Masinissa, and third Punic war, 219
Mastabas, 46, 50
Master craftsmen, 500
Mathematics. *See also* Geometry
    in Hellenistic era, 196–7
    in Islamic civilization, 317–18
    in Maya civilization, 408–09
    and Pythagoras, 147–8
Mathias (king of Hungary), 478
Mauryan dynasty of India, 189
Maximian (Roman *Augustus*), 254
Mayas, civilization of, 406–13
    early history, 406–07
    religion in, 408
    science and mathematics of, 408–09
Mayor of the palace, in Germanic kingdoms, 341
Measures. *See* Weights and Measures
Mecca, 305, 306–09. *See also* Islam;
    Islamic Empire
Medea (play by Euripides), 159
Medes, 74
Medici, Cosimo de, 512, 513, 522
Medici, Lorenzo de, 513, 524, 526, 531
Medici, Piero de, 513
Medici family, 504, 513–15
Medicine
    Egyptians' interest in, 63
    and Hippocrates, 148
    in Islamic Empire, 316–17
    in medieval Europe, 395–6, 506
Medieval civilization, 375–86. *See also*
    Roman Catholic Church (Middle Ages)
    agriculture in, 382, 494–5
    architecture in, 401–04
    and authority of manor lord, 383–4
    and castles, 378–81, 398
    and code of chivalry, 380–81, 398
    drama in, 400–01
    and education, 379–81, 388–94
    economic development in late, 494–507
    economic system in, 381–4
    and feudal warfare, 377–8
    and guilds, 500–01
    justice in, 384
    knights in, 377–8, 379–80

lifestyles in, 381–3, 386, 391–2, 506–07
literature of, 396–400
and lord-vassal relationship, 376–7
medicine in, 395–6
oral traditions of, 396
and scholasticism, 392–4
science in, 394–6
technology in late, 496–7
towns in, 384–6
women in, 380
Medina, 305, 306–07
Megara, 122
Megiddo, 87, 88
Meleager, statue of, 155
Menander (playwright), 193
Menelaus, and Trojan War, 101
Mentohotep II (pharaoh), 52–3
Mercantilism, rise of, in late Middle Ages, 502–05
Merchant guilds, 499–500
Merovingian dynasty, 340–42
Mesopotamia, 22–43
Messenia, 134
Messiah, and Jews, 89, 275, 276, 277, 278
Metalworking
    in ancient China, 261
    and Etruscans, 202
    and Hittites, 73
    in Islamic civilization, 322
    and Minoans, 96
    and Sumerians, 25
Metellus, Q. Caecilius (Roman general), 227
Michelangelo, 509, 526–9
Middle East, modern political boundaries of, 81
Miesko (chieftain of Polanians), 474
Milan, Italy
    as Maximian's capital, 254
    in the Renaissance, 515, 516
Miletus, 122–3, 137
Military technology
    and Archimedes, 197
    of Assyrians, 34, 39
    and chariot design, 69
    and flamethrower, 295
    of Hyksos, 53, 54
    and iron weapons, 69, 86
    longbow vs. crossbow and, 442
    and stirrup, 266, 354
Miltiades, and battle of Marathon, 139, 140
Minerva (Roman goddess), 201
Mining, in late Middle Ages, 496–7
Ministeriales, in government of Holy Roman Empire, 418
Minoan civilization, 93–8
    archaeological findings from, 93–5
    decoration in, 93–4, 96
    destruction of, 97
    economy of, 96

legends in, 97–8
religion in, 95
Minos (king), 91, 94, 95, 97–8
Minotaur, 97
Minstrels, 396–7
Miracle plays, 400–01
Mishnah, 89
Mitanni, 54, 56
Mithras (ancient Persian god), 75
Mithridates of Pontus, 229–30
Mithridatic War, 229–30
"Model Parliament," 441
Mohammed (prophet of Allah), 295, 304, 306–08
Mohammed II (Ottoman Turk ruler), 297–8
Mohenjo-daro, 104, 105, 106
Mole (passageway), 181–2
"Mona Lisa" (painting by Da Vinci), 525–6
Monarchy, in Middle Ages, 427, 506–07
Monasticism, 358–61
Money economy. *See also* Trade and Commerce
    in late Middle Ages, 502–05
Mongol invasions
    and Baghdad, 315
    and Hungary, 477
    and Poland, 474
    and Russia, 481–2
Monks, 358–61
Monophysitism, 294, 298
Monotheism
    and Akhenaton, 57, *540–41*
    and Christianity, 274
    and Judaism, 85–6, 274, *540*
    and Islam, 305, 306
Monte Cassino (monastery), 358–9
Moors, 465–6. *See also* Moslems
Morality plays, 401
Moriscoes, in Catholic Spain, 469
Moscow, 481–2
Moses (Hebrew prophet), 85
Moslems, 304. *See also* Islam; Islamic Empire; Moors
    and Byzantine Empire, 295
    and Spain, 465
    and Spanish Inquisition, 469
    and Southern Europe, 353
Mother Goddess, Minoan, 95, 96
Mount Moriah, 321
Mount Vesuvius, 248
Muawiya (caliph), 313
Muezzin, 307
Muhammed. *See* Mohammed (prophet of Allah)
Mullahs in Islam, 310
Mursilis I, 68
Muses, 119, 120
Muslims. *See* Moslems
Mycenae, 91, 92, 98, 102

Mycenaean civilization, 98–102, 103
   archaeological findings from, 98, 99,
      100
   end of, 102
   government of, 99
   Homer and, 119
Myron (sculptor), 154
Mythology, Greek, 119–20
Mytilene, 168

Nabonidus (Chaldean ruler), 40
Nabopolassar, 21, 23, 37, 39
Napoleon Bonaparte, 425
Naramsin, 28, 39
Narmer (pharaoh), 48–9
Navarre, as Christian Kingdom of Spain,
      467, 470
Navigation
   and Phoenicians, 82
   and Prince Henry of Portugal, 471,
      472
Navy
   Athenian, and Delian League, 149
   established by Minos, 94
   Roman, and Punic wars, 214, 215
Nazarenes, 279
Nearchus, and Alexander the Great,
      186–7
Nebuchadnezzar II, 39–41
Necho (pharaoh), 39
Necropoleis (Estruscan), 203
Nefertiti, 57
Neo-Babylonia. See Chaldea
Neoplatonism, 520, 526
Nero, 245, 246, 247
Nerva (Roman emperor), 248
Netherlands, 498
Nevski, Alexander (prince of Novgorod),
      482
Nibelungenleid, 398
Nicaea, Crusader seige of, 365–6
"Nicene Creed," 286–7, 299
Nicholas V (pope), 298
Nicholas of Cusa, 532
Nicias, and Peloponnesian War, 168,
      169–70
Nicodemia, as Diocletian's capital, 254
Nika Revolt, 292
Nile River Valley, 44–6
Nile Year, 63
Nineveh, palace of, 37, 38
Nirvana, 109
Nobiles, in Roman Empire, 224
Nobility, hierarchy of, in Middle Ages,
      376
Noble Eightfold Path, 109, 112
Nomarch, 46
Nome, 46
Nonaggression treaty, first recorded, 69–
      71
Norman conquest, 432–6
Normandy, Viking beginnings of, 351

Normans, 348. See also Vikings
Northmen, 348. See also Vikings
Notre Dame, Cathedral of, 402
Novitiate, 359
Numa Pompilius, 201, 205
Number systems, 317
Numidia (North Africa), and Rome, 226

Obelisks, 55
Oblique phalanx, 172, 182–3. See also
      Macedonian phalanx; Phalanx
Octavia, 237
Octavian, 236–8. See also Augustus
Octavius (Roman tribune), 225
Odo, Count of Paris, 350–51, 449–50
Odoacer (leader of Goths), 257, 339
Odysseus, 99, 102, 120
Odyssey (Homer), 91, 98, 100, 102, 120
Oedipus Rex (Sophocles), 158
Of God's Government (Salvian), 559
"Old Market Woman" (sculpture), 194,
      195
Oligarchy, 170, 171. See also Sparta
Olympias (wife of Philip of Macedonia),
      175, 178
Olympic Games, 124, 125, 284
Omar (second caliph), 311
Omayyad Dynasty, 313–14
Omayyad Mosque (Damascus), 321
Optimates, in Roman Empire, 224
Oracle bones, in ancient China, 260,
      261
Oracles
   in ancient Greek world, 125–6
   and Alexander the Great, 179, 182
Order of Friars Minor ("Little Broth-
      ers"), 363
Order of Saint Mary of the Teutons. See
      Teutonic Knights
Oresteian Trilogy (Aeschylus), 157–8
Orestes, 157–8
Orthodox Church, 299–300
   doctrine of, 299–300
   language of services in, 300
   and Roman Catholic Church, 298–
      300
   and Russia, 478–80
Osiris, 46–7
Osman (Ottoman ruler), 478
Ostrogoths
   and Christianity, 287
   in Italy, 292
   and Roman Empire, 292, 339
Ostrokon, 132
Othman (Islamic caliph), 311
Ottoman Turks, 293, 297–8, 478
Otto the Great (Holy Roman emperor),
      354, 417–18, 474, 477

Pagan (term), 284
Paleologus, Sophia, 482

Palermo, 353
Palestine, 80
Panathenaic Festival, 151
Panhellenic Games, 125
Panhellenism, 124–25
Pantheon of gods. See also Gods.
   in ancient Greece, 119–20
Pantheon temple, Roman, 250, 251
Papal States, 342, 418, 510
Paper, 266. See also Papyrus
Papyrus, 62, 63
Parchment, development of, 181
Paris, and Trojan War, 101
Parish, in early Christian church, 285
Parlement of Paris, 453, 454, 456
Parliament
   English, 440–41
   of Poland-Lithuania, 476–7
Parmenio (Macedonian general), 178,
      179, 185
Parsis, 76. See also Zoroastrianism
Parthenon, 150–52
Parthians, 189, 258
Patriarchal society, 67
Patricians, Roman, 207
Patrick, Saint, 478
Paullus (Roman consul), 217
Paul of Tarsus (apostle)
   death of, 247, 280
   letters of, and New Testament,
      279–80
   and spread of Christianity, 279–80
Pausanias (assassin), 142, 178
Pausanias (writer), 150–51
Pax Romana period, 238–41
Pax Sinica, 265
Peace of Constance, 421
Peace of God, 378
Peace of Nicias, 168
Peasants, in Middle Ages, 281, 382–3
Peasants' Revolt, in England, 443–5
Pedagogos, 164. See also Slavery
Pediment, 151
Pelagius (British monk), 288
Pelopidas (Theban leader), 171, 172
Peloponnesian League, 136–7, 166, 171,
      172
Peloponnesian War, 165–71
Peloponnesus, 98, 116
Penelope (wife of Odysseus), 120, 121
Pentathlon, 125
Pentecosiomediamni, 129
Pepin (Carolingian ruler), 342
Pergamum, 189, 192
Pericles, 164, 166, 167, 544
Period of Six Dynasties, 266–7
Peripatetic school, 162. See also
      Aristotle
Permanent Edict, 249
Persepolis, palace at, 78
Persians, 74–78, 184–5, 295
Persians (play by Aeschylus), 156, 157
Persian Wars, 137–43

Peruzzi family, and banking, 504
Peter (apostle), 247, 279–80
Peter the Hermit, 365
Petrarch, Francesco, 517–18
Petrarchan sonnet, 518
Phalanx, 127. See also Macedonian
    phalanx; Oblique phalanx
Pharissees, 275, 278. See also Zealots
Pharaoh, origin of, 46
Pharos lighthouse, 191
Phidias (sculptor), 150–51, 154
"Philipics" (orations of Demosthenes),
    176, 177, 548
Philip I (king of France), 450
Philip II (king of France), 370, 391, 438,
    440, 451–3
Philip II of Macedonia, 171, 175–8
Philip IV (king of France), 451, 454–7
Philip V of Macedonia, 218, 220–21
Philip VI (king of France), 442, 458
Philip Augustus. See Philip II (king of
    France)
Philip of Macedonia. See Philip II of
    Macedonia; Philip V of Macedonia
Philistines, 86
Philosopher (term), 147
Philosopher-kings, 162
Philosophers' stone, 319
Philosophy
    in China, 262
    Classical Greek, 160–62
    early Greek, 147–8
    in Hellenistic era, 194–6
    in the Renaissance, 530–31. See also
        Humanism
Philotas, and Alexander the Great, 185
Phoenicians, 80–84
    city-states and, 81–2
    colonies of, 83
    and Greek colonists, 121, 123
    religion of, 83–4
    as seafarers, 81
Phoinix, 82
Phonograms, 61
Phrygians, 71
Physics
    and Hellenistic theorists, 196–7
    and Ionic Greek theorists, 147–8
    in Islamic civilization, 319
"Pi," 197
Pico, Giovanni (philosopher), 530–31
Pictographs. See Hieroglyphics, or Pic-
    tographs
"Pietà" (sculpture by Michelangelo),
    526
Pirates, and Pompey, 232
Pisistratus, 120–21
Pithoi, 95
Plain of Shinar, 21
Plantagenet dynasty, 436, 437
Plato, 161–2, 546–7
Plebecita, 207
Plebeians, in ancient Rome, 204, 207–
    09, 212–13

Plebs, 204
Pliny the Younger, 282
Plutarch, 178–9, 180, 182, 184, 185,
    224–5, 230, 231, 232, 233, 236,
    237, 238
Poem of the Cid, 398, 464
Poetry
    epigrammatic, 176
    lyric, 145
Poland, 474–7
    and Copernicus, 476
    Golden Age of, 477
    and Lithuania, 476
Polaris (North star), 82
Polis, 117–18, 126. See also City-States,
    Greek
Politics (Aristotle), 162
Polybius, 193, 215, 219
Polyclitus, 154
Pompeii (Italian city), 248
Pompey (Roman general), 231–2, 233,
    234, 235, 552–3
Pontius Pilate, 279
Poor Clares (order of nuns), 363
Pope, origin of, 286. See also specific
    popes
Populares, in Roman Empire, 224,
    225–6
Portugal, medieval, 465, 470–72
    and Age of Exploration, 471–2
    agriculture in, 470–71
    expansion of, 470
    founding of, 470
    and House of Aviz, 471–2
    monarchs of, 471
    under rule of Dinis, 470–71
Poseidon (Greek god), 119
Pottery wheel, 93, 96
Praetor, in Roman Republic, 209
Praetorian Guard, 245, 248
Praxiteles (sculptor), 154
Prefectures, 254
Primogeniture, 348
Prince, The (Machiavelli), 531, 574
Prince Henry the Navigator (Portugal),
    471–2
Princeps, as title, 241
Principate, 223, 241
Printing
    and Chinese, 529–30
    invention of, 529–30
    in Poland, 477
Proletarii, 206
Prophets (Hebrew), 86
Propylaea, 131
Proscriptions, in Roman Republic, 230–
    31
Proverbs, West African, 489
Province, in early Christian church, 286
Ptolemaic planetary system, 197
Ptolemy (2nd-century astronomer), 197
Ptolemy (Macedonian general) and Pto-
    lemaic dynasty of Egypt, 188, 190
Punic Wars, 214–20

Punt, expedition to, 55
Purple, and royalty, 82
Pylos, 87, 102
Pyramid Age. See Egypt, Old
    Kingdom in
Pyramids
    construction of Egyptian, 64
    of Khafre (Chephren), 51
    of Khufu (Cheops), 47, 50–51
    in Maya civilization, 407, 408
    of Zoser, 50
Pyrrhic victory, 213, 215
Pyrrhic Wars, 213–14
Pyrrho of Elis, andd skepticism, 194
Pyrrhus (king of Epirus), 213–14
Pythagoras, 147–8, 318

Quadrivium, 389
Quaestor, in Roman Republic, 209
Qumran, Essene monastery at, 276,
    278
Quran. See Koran
Quraysh tribe (Arabia), 305, 306

Ra. See Re
Rabbis, 73
Rajahs, 106
Ramayana, 107, 108
Ramses I, 52, 58
Ramses II, 58–60, 69
Ramses III, 60, 61
Raphael, 527–8
Rassam, Harmuz (explorer), 38
Rawlinson, Sir Henry (linguist), 27–8
Re, 46–8
Re-Atum, 46, 47
Reconquista, 465–7
Red Crescent, 308
Reincarnation, 107
Relics, Christian, 295
Religion. See also Buddhism; China, an-
    cient, philosophy in; Christianity;
    Emperor-worship; Gods; Hindu-
    ism; Judaism; Shinto religion; Sun
    god; Taoism; Zoroastrianism
    and anthropomorphism, 26, 47, 73
    early Greek, 119–20
    in Indian civilization, 106–07,
        109–12
    of the Mayas, 408, 410
    in pre-Islamic Arabia, 305
    and Romans, 201, 240–41
Reliquaries, 302
Remus, and Romulus, 200
Renaissance, 509–33
    and architecture, 520–23, 527
    early, 518–23
    and education, 518
    and humanism, 516–18
    influence of, 533
    and Italy in 1350, 510–16
    and literature, 530–32

and painting techniques, 518–20, 526, 528
and Petrarch, 517–18
and sculpture, 520–23
"Renaissance man," 518
Republic (Plato), 161
Reverence statues in Crete, 95
Rex (term), 207
Rhazes, 316–17, 319
Rheoboam (son of Solomon), 88
Rhetoric, and the sophists, 160
Rhodes
  in Hellenistic era, 192
  as base for Knights Hospitalers, 368, 372
Richard I (king of England), 370–71, 438
Richard II (king of England), 443, 444
Richard III (king of England), 447
Richard of Gloucester. *See* Richard III (king of England)
Richard the Lion-Hearted. *See* Richard I (king of England)
Rig Veda, 106, 110
Roads, Roman, 211
Robert the Monk, 363–4
Robin Hood, 438
Roger (Norman count), 353–4
Roland. *See Song of Roland*
Rollo (Viking leader), 351
Roman Antiquities (Dionysius of Halicarnassus), 200
Roman Catholic Church (early). *See also* Christianity
  and alliance with Franks, 340
  and Byzantine Church, 299
Roman Catholic Church (Middle Ages). *See also* Christianity
  and canon law, 357–8
  civil role of, 356–8
  and Crusades, 362–73
  and Eastern Europe, 474
  and excommunication, 357, 419
  and Great Schism, 457–8
  and interdict, as political weapon, 357
  and mendicant Friars, 361–3
  and monasticism, 358–61
  and Poland, 474, 477
  sacraments of, 356
  and simony, 360
  in Spain, 464
Roman confederation, 211–12
Roman Empire. *See also* Byzantine Empire; Rome; ancient; Rome, as republic
  army reform in, 228–9
  artifacts of, 239
  and consequences of expansion, 223–4
  decline of, 257–8
  development of, 199–222
  eastern portion of, 257
  extent of, under Trajan, 249, 250

fall of, 257–8
and Germanic migrations, 338–40, 341
and "Good" emperors, 248–52
and invasion of Britain, 245, 428
invasions of, 256–7
and Jewish revolt, 248, 281, 282
judicial system in, 244
and massacre by Mithridates, 229–30
military autocracy in, 252–3
and persecution of Christians, 247, 280–83
Roman law, codification of, and Justinian, 293–4
Romanus IV (Byzantine emperor), 297
Rome (city). *See also* Roman Empire; Rome, ancient; Rome, as republic
  burning of, 247, 281
  as center of Christian Church, 287
  dropped as capital of Empire, 254
  and Holy Roman Empire, 424
  Moslem attacks on, 353
Rome, ancient
  and archaeological findings, 200–01
  army reform in, 205–06
  development of republic in, 199, 207–10
  expansion of, 210–12, 213–14
  judicial system in, 209–10
  legendary kings of, 204–06
  oral traditions of, 200
  origin of, 200–01
  religion of, 201
  Senate in, 207
Rome, as republic
  assemblies in, 207–09
  civil wars in, 230–31, 235–6
  conquest of Etruscans by, 210
  economic crisis in, 212–13, 224–5
  end of, 223, 241, 242
  equality in, 209–10
  extent of, at Caesar's death, 238
  government in, 207–10
  and Greek city-states, 213
  and Philip V of Macedonia, 218, 220–21
  policy in East of, 221
  and Punic wars, 214–20
  revision of constitution of, 212–13
  role of Senate in, 207, 208, 224, 226, 227
  southern expansion of, 213–20
Romulus (legendary founder of Rome), 200, 201, 204–05
Romulus Augustulus (Roman emperor), 257
Rosetta stone, 61–2
Roxane (wife of Alexander), 185
Royal Cemetery of Ur, 29
Royal Standard of Ur, 29
Rubaiyat, as form of poetry, 319
Rudolf of Hapsburg (Holy Roman emperor), 425
Rumania, 179. *See also* Thrace

Runic script, 352
Russia, medieval, 478–82
  and Byzantine influence, 297, 302
  and Kiev, 478–80
  and Mongol invasion, 480–82
  Moscow and, 481–2
  and Orthodox Church, 478–80
  and Vikings, 351, 478
Russian Church, 478, 481. *See also* Orthodox Church

Sabines, 205, 210
Sadducees, 275, 278
Sagas, Viking, 352
Saint Chapelle, 454
Saint Denis, abbey of, 403–04
Saite dynasty of Egypt, 39
Saladin (Moslem leader), 370
Salian Franks, 340
Salic Law, 442
Salisbury Oath, 433
Samaria, 88
Samaritans, 35
Sama Veda, 106
Samnites, 212, 229
Samuel (Hebrew judge), 86
Samurai, in feudal Japan, 328–9
Sancho I (king of Portugal), 470
Sancho the Great (ruler of Castile), 466
Sanctuaries, 356
Sanskrit, 106
Santi, Raffaello. *See* Raphael
Santigo de Compostela, cathedral of, 466
Sappho of Lesbos, 145
Saracens, 353
Sardinia, and second Punic War, 217–18
Sargon I, 39, 81
Sargon II, 35, 39
Sassanian Persians, 258
Satrap, 76
Satrapies, 76
Saturninus, 228–9
Satyrs, 155–6
Saul (Hebrew king), 86
Savonarola, Girolamo, 513, 514–15
Saxons, 416–18, 428
Saxony, in Holy Roman Empire, 416
Scandinavians. *See* Vikings
Scheherazade. *See Arabian Nights*
Schliemann, Heinrich, 91, 100
Scholarship
  in Hellenistic World, 191–2
  in Islamic Empire, 316
  in Renaissance Italy, 513, 516–17, 530–31, 532
  in Spain, 465
Scholastica (nun), 360
Scholasticism, medieval, 392–4
Schools, in Middle Ages, 388–9
Schwyz (Swiss canton), 473

Science
    and Classical Greece, 148
    in Egypt, 63–4
    in Hellenistic era, 196–7
    in Islamic Empire, 316–19
    medieval, 394–6
Scipio, Gnaeus, 217
Scipio, Publius (father), 217
Scipio, Publius (son), 217, 218
Scipio Africanus. See Scipio, Publius
    (son)
Scopas (sculptor), 154
Scotland, 429
Scriptorium, 361
Sculpture
    Greek, 150, 154, 155
    Hellenistic, 193–4
    Renaissance, 522, 526
Seafaring. See also Navy
    of Egyptians, 53
    in Greek Iron Age, 121–2, 124
    in late Middle Ages, 497, 498
    and Phoenicians, 81
    and Vikings, 348–9
Sea People, 60–61, 71, 86. See also
    Philistines
Second Crusade, 369–70
Sejanus, and Tiberius, 244
Seleucus (Macedonian general), and
    Seleucid dynasty, 189, 221
Seljuk Turks
    and Byzantine Empire, 297
    capture of Baghdad by, 315
    and Christian pilgrims, 363
Semites, 66
Seneca, 246–7
Seneschals, 453
Sennacherib, 35–6, 39
Sephardim, 469
Septuagint Bible, 193. See also Judaism
Serfs
    in Byzantine civilization, 301
    in early Middle Ages, 381, 385
    in late Middle Ages, 507
Sermon of the Turning of the Wheel of
    the Law, 112
Servilius, 216
Servius Tullius, 205–06
Seth (Egyptian god), 46, 47
Seti I (pharaoh), 60, 69
Seven Wonders of the World, 191, 192
Severi, the, 252–4
Severus, Alexander (Roman emperor),
    253
Severus, Septimus (Roman emperor),
    252–3
Sforza, Francesco, 515, 516
Sfumato technique in painting, 525–6
Shabti, 48
Shadoof, 44, 45
Shaft graves, Mycenaean, 100
Shang dynasty, 260
Sheiks, Bedouin, 305
Shepherd Kings. See Hyksos

Shield money, 377, 435
Shih Huang-ti, 264–5
Shiites, in Islam, 313, 314
Shinto religion, 325
    and Buddhism, 327, 329
Ships. See also Seafaring
    Athenian triremes, 150
    in late Middle Ages, 497
    and Venice, 511
    Viking, 349
Shire, 430
Shire-reeve, 430–31
Shiva (Hindu God), 107
Shotoku, Prince, 327
    and Confucianism, 332
Sic et Non (Abelard), 393
Sicily
    and Greek colonization, 123
    and Holy Roman Empire, 422
    Moslem occupation of, 353
    Norman rule of, 353–4
    in Peloponnesian War, 169–70
    in Punic wars, 214–15
    and Roman Empire, 217–18
Siddhanta (Hindu treatise), 318
Siddhartha Gautama, 109. See also
    Buddha
Sigismund (king of Hungary), 477–8
Silk industry
    in ancient China, 266
    in Byzantine civilization, 300–01
Silver Age, mythical Greek, 118
Si River, 260
Sistine Chapel, 526, 527
Sixth Crusade, 372, 424. See also Cru-
    sades
Skepticism, 194
Slavery
    in Classical Greece, 163, 164
    and decline of Rome, 257
    in Hellenistic era, 191
    and Islamic law, 310
    in Middle Ages, 381
Slayer of the Bulgars. See Basil II
Smerdis (Persian prince), 76
Soap, 496
Social classes, in Renaissance, 512–13
Social War, and Roman Republic, 228–9
Socrates, 120, 160–61, 168–9, 546–7
    and medieval scholastics, 393
Solar cycle, discovery of, 63
Solomon (Hebrew king), 81, 86–8
Solomon's Temple, 87
    destruction of, 248, 281, 282
Solon, 128–30, 542
Song of Roland, 343, 397, 398, 466
Songhai, empire of, 487–8
Sophists, 159, 160
Sophocles, 158
Spain
    early Christian governments of, 466–7
    and the Inquisition, 468–9
    in the Middle Ages, 464–70
    under Moslem rule, 314, 322–3, 465

    in Second Punic War, 215, 217
    reconquest of, 465–7
    and reign of Ferdinand and Isabella,
      467–70
    Roman Catholic Church in, 464
    and voyage of Columbus, 469
Spanish March, 343, 466
Sparta, 134–7, 166. See also Peloponne-
    sian War
Spartacus, 231
Spider King. See Louis XI (king of
    France)
Spinning wheel, 496
Statute of Laborers, and post-plague
    economy in England, 505, 569
Stele of Victory, 30
Stephan (king of Hungary), 477
Stephen of Clayes, and Children's
    Crusade, 372
Steppe lands, 66
Step Pyramid at Sakkara, 50
Stirrup, 266, 354
Stoa Poikile, 196
Stoicism, 196
Strasbourg Oath, 347
Strategos (term), 133
    in Byzantine Empire, 295
Strigil (tool), 155
Studia humanitatis (term), 516
Stupa (burial mound), 109
Succession
    apostolic, 287
    in Assyria, 39
    and Hittites, 68, 72
    of pharaohs, 54–5
    in Roman Empire, 243, 258
      Diocletian and, 254
      "Good" emperors and, 248, 252
Sudras (caste), 108
Suetonius (Roman historian), 244, 245,
    247
Suger (abbot), 403–04
Sui dynasty, 326
Sulla, Cornelius, 227, 230, 231
Sumer, ancient, 23–29
    archaeological findings from, 29
    climate of, 23–5
    government in, 26
    literature of, 28–9
    natural resources of, 23–5
    religion in, 25–6
    writing system of, 26–9
Sumerian temples. See Ziggurat
Summa Theologica (Aquinas), 394
Sun god, Egyptian, 46–8, 73, 540–41
Sunna (Moslem), 305, 309–10, 313
Sunnites, in Islam, 313
Suppululiumas, 68–9
Surgery
    in ancient Egypt, 63–4
    in Islamic civilization, 317
    in medieval Europe, 395
Susa, palace at, 78
Sussex, 429

Swabia, in Holy Roman Empire, 416
Sweden, and Russia, 478, 482
Swiss Confederation, 472–4
Switzerland, 472, 473. *See also* Swiss Confederation
Swiss Guards, 473
Sword of Allah. *See* Ibn-al-Walid Khalid
Sybarite (term), 123
Sylvester I (pope), 532
Sylvester II (pope), 389, 477
Symposium (Alcibiades), 168
Syracuse, Sicily, colonization of, 123. *See also* Sicily
Syria, 80, 84
Syria-Palestine, 80

Tacitus (Roman historian), 243–4, 245–6, 247, 281
Taika reforms, in Japan, 327
Taj Mahal (India), 321–2
Tale of Genji (Lady Murasaki), 332
Talmud, 89
T'ang dynasty, 326, 327, 328
Tannenberg, battle at, 476
Taoism, 262–3, 267
Tao Te Ching, 263
Tarentum, 123, 134, 213
Tarik, and Moslem conquest of Spain, 313–14, 464
Tarquinius Priscus, 205
Tarquinius Superbus, 205, 206
Tartars, 481. *See also* Mongol invasions
Taxation
    in ancient Athens, 149–50, 163–4
    in Islamic Empire, 314
    in medieval England, 431, 435, 438, 440, 441, 443
    in medieval France, 453, 458, 461
    Ptolemies' system of, 190
    and Roman Empire, 257
Technology. *See also* Military technology.
    in the late Middle Ages, 496–7
Telipinus (Hittite King), 68
Tell (term), 87
Tell el-Amarna, 57
Templars, 368, 454–6
Ten Commandments, 85
Terpsichore (muse), 120
Teshub (Hittite god), 73
Teutonic Knights, 368–9, 474, 476, 482
Textual criticism, 532
Thalassocracy, 94
Thales, 147
Thebes, Egypt
    as Egyptian capital, 52, 53
    and Ramses III, 59
Thebes, Greece
    and Alexander the Great, 179
    and Philip of Macedonia, 175, 177. *See also* Oblique phalanx.
    and Sparta, 171–2

Thegn, in Anglo-Saxon system of justice, 430, 431
Themistocles (Athenian leader), 140, 142
Theocracy
    in Egypt, 61
    in Mesopotamia, 26
Theocritus, 192
Theodora (wife of Justinian), 292, 293, 294
Theodoric (leader of Goths), 339
Theodosius (Roman emperor), 284
Theodosius II (Byzantine emperor), 291
Theresa, of Portugal, 470
Thermopylae, 141
Theseus, legend of, 97
Thetes, 127
Third Crusade, 370–71, 422. *See also* Crusades
Tholoi, 100, 101
Thoth (Egyptian god), 47
Thrace, and Macedonian empire, 176, 177–8, 179
Three-field system, 382, 495, 496
Thucydides, 94, 149, 164, 165–7, 168, 170
Thutmose III, 51, 55–6, 58, 81
Tiberius, 243–4
Tiglathpilesar III, 34–5, 39
Timbuktu, 487, 490
Timocracy
    in ancient Greece, 126, 127
    in ancient Rome, 206
Tiryns, 98, 102
Tithe, in Roman Empire, 215
Titian, 528
Titus (Roman emperor), 248, 281
Tomb of Clytemnestra, 100
Tonsure, 361
Torah, 84–5, 89
Tower of Babel, 41
Trade and Commerce
    and alphabet, 83
    in Byzantine Empire, 300–01
    and colonization in Iron-Age Greece, 122–3
    and Egyptians, 53, 55–6
    in Hellenistic era, 190
    and Italy, 510–11
    in late Middle Ages, 385–6, 464, 497–9, 501–2
    in Maya civilization, 408
    in medieval Europe, 385, 464
    in Moslem world, 315–16
    and Phoenicians, 83
    in Renaissance, 502–05
    and Russian city-states, 478
    and Venice, 511
    in West Africa, 485, 486, 487, 488
Trade fairs, in late Middle Ages, 498–9
Traditions of the Elders, 89
Trajan (Roman emperor), 248–9, 258, 282
Tragedoi, 156

Tragedy, in Greek theater, 156–9
Transept, in architecture, 402
Treasure of Priam, 91
Treasury of Atreus, 100, 101
Treaty of Bretigny, 459
Treaty of Troyes, 445, 459
Treaty of Verdun, 416, 449
Treaty of Windsor, 471
Trial by fire, in medieval Europe, 384. *See also* Trial by ordeal
Trial by ordeal, in Anglo-Saxon system of justice, 431
    in medieval Europe, 384
Tribes and Clans
    in ancient Rome, 204, 206. *See also* Gentes; Curiae.
    in ancient Greece, 126, 131–2. *See also* Demes.
    in Japan, 325–6
Tribunes, in Plebeian government, 207–08
Trinity, Christian doctrine of, 308
Triremes, 150
Trivium, 389
Trojan War, 99, 101–07
Trojan Women (play), 158–9
Troubadours, 398
Troy, 91–2, 93, 101, 102
    and Alexander the Great, 180
Truce of God, 378, 567
Tuchman, Barbara, on history, 536
Tudor, Henry. *See* Henry VII (king of England)
Tufa rock, 199
Tullus Hostilius, 205
Turks. *See* Ottoman Turks; Seljuk Turks
Tuscany, 202
Tutankhamun, 51, 58, 69
Tutankhaton. *See* Tutankhamun
Twelve tribes, 86
Tyler, Wat, 443, 445
Tyranny, 129–31
Tyrant, 126
Tyre, 81, 84, 181–2
Tyrrhenians, as term for Etruscans, 202

Ubaidians, 22
Ulfilas (priest), 287
Unam Sanctam, 457
Universities
    Hellenistic, 191
    medieval European, 390–91
    and Taika reforms in Japan, 327
University of Paris, 391
Unterwalden, 473
Untouchables, 108
Upanishads, 106
Ur, Third dynasty of, 20–21
Uranus (Greek god), 120
Urban II (pope), 363–5, 397
Uri (Swiss canton), 473
Ur-Nammu, 20–21, 31, 39
Uruk, 22–3

Usury, 502–03
Utnapishtun epic, 28, *539*

Vaisyas (caste), 108
Valens (Roman emperor), 339
Valhalla, 352
Valkyries, 352
Valla, Lorenzo, and textual criticism, 532
Valley of the Kings and Queens, 52, 55, 58
Vandals
    and Christianity, 287
    in North Africa, 256, 292
    and Roman Empire, 256, 339
Varangians, 351, 478. *See also* Vikings
Varro (Roman consul), 217
Varus, and Augustus, 240
Vassals, 376–7
Vassal states (term), 35
Vecellio, Tiziana. *See* Titian
Vedas, 106, 107
Vedic Age, 106, 109
Venice, 511
"Venus de Milo" (Hellenistic sculpture), 153, 194
Vespasian, Flavian (Roman emperor), 248
Vesta (Roman god), 201
Vestal Virgins, 201
Veto power, in Roman government, 207, 208–09
Vicarius (in Roman Empire), 254
Vikings, 348–52
    and Byzantine Empire, 351, 478
    culture of, 352
    and England, 350, 429–30, 431–2
    and Eric the Red, 351
    gods of, 352
    literature of, 352
    and North America, 351–2
    raids by, 348, 349–52
    and Russia, 351, 478
Villeins, 381
Vinland, 351–2
Virgil, 241, *550*
Visconti family, 517
Visigoths (western Goths)
    and Christianity, 287
    and defeat by Moslems, 314
    and fall of Roman Empire, 256, 257, 288
    in Spain, 292, 464
Vizier, in ancient Egypt, 50
Vladimir (prince of Kiev), 478–80

Volsci tribe of ancient Italy, 210
Voltaire, on Holy Roman Empire, 416

Wager of battle, in Anglo-Saxon system of justice, 431
Wagner, Richard, 398
Wailing Wall, 281, 283
Wales, 441
Walter, Hubert (archbishop of Canterbury), 438
War of the Roses, 446–7
Water-power, as energy source, 323, 496
Water supply system, in ancient Israel, 87–8
Wealth, attitudes toward in late Middle Ages, 503
Weights and Measures
    Aramaic system of, 84
    Athenian system of, 149
    Darius' system of, 77
    Spanish system of, 467
    system of, in Hellenistic era, 190
Welfs (German family), 420
Wessex, 429
West Africa (750-1600 A.D.), 484–91
    agriculture of, 485
    geography of, 484–5
    and gold-salt trade, 485–8
    proverbs of, 489
Westminister Abbey, 435
West Slavs, 474
Wheel, and Sumerians, 29
    and Maya civilization, 407
William (duke of Normandy), 350, 431–2. *See also* William I (king of England)
William I (king of England), 432–5, 450
William II (king of England), 435
William Rufus. *See* William II (king of England)
William the Conqueror. *See* William I (king of England)
Winckler, Hugo (archaeologist), 71
Wind power as energy source, 497
"Winged Victory of Samothrace" (sculpture), 194
Witan, in Anglo-Saxon government, 431
Wladislaw I (Polish king), 474
Women
    and *bushido* code of feudal Japan, 329
    in Byzantine civilization, 301
    in classical Greek society, 164
    in Cretan society, 95
    and early Christianity, 284, 285
    in Etruscan society, 203

    in Hittite government, 71
    in Iron Age Greece, 121
    under Islam, 310
    in medieval Europe, 360, 379, 380, 391
    in medieval Russia, 482
    and the Renaissance, 532–3
    in Viking society, 352
Wool industry, in Florence, 512
Woolley, Leonard, 29
Woolweaving, in Middle Ages, 498
Working class, in Renaissance, 512–13
Writing system. *See also* Alphabet; Hieroglyphics or Pictographs
    Aryan, 106
    Chinese, 264–5
    of Egyptians, 61–3
    Etruscan, 202
    in Greek Iron Age, 122
    Japanese, 327, 330
    of the Mayas, 408, 410
    of Minoans, 93, 97
    Sumerian, 26–8
    Viking, 352
Wrought iron, 73
Wu Ti, 265

Xanthippus, and Punic wars, 214
Xerxes, 77, 78, 140, 141, 142

Yadin, Yigael, 87–8
Yahweh, 85, 86, 88, 89
Yajur Veda, 106
Yamato clan, in Japan, 326
Yang principle, 267
Yangtze (Huai) River, 260
Yaroslav the Wise, 480
Yathrib. *See* Medina
Yellow River, 260
Yemen, 305
Yin principle, 267
Young, Thomas, and Rosetta stone, 62
Ypres, seal of, 500

Zacharias (pope), 342
Zealots, 276, 281
Zedekiah, 40
Zeno, and Stoicism, 196
Zenodotus (librarian at Alexandria), 191
Zeus, 95, 97, 119
Ziggurat, 26, 31
Zoroastrianism, 75–6
Zoser (pharaoh), 50, 52
Zurich, 473